P9-BIH-397

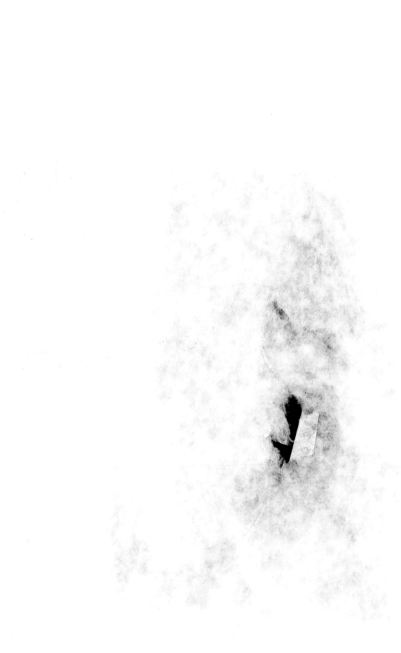

The Country Girls Trilogy

A N D   E P I L O G U E

BY EDNA O'BRIEN

A Fanatic Heart: Selected Stories
Returning
A Rose in the Heart
I Hardly Knew You
Mother Ireland
A Scandalous Woman and Other Stories
Night
Zee & Co
A Pagan Place
The Love Object and Other Stories
Casualties of Peace
August Is a Wicked Month
Girls in Their Married Bliss
The Lonely Girl
The Country Girls

The Country Girls Trilogy

AND EPILOGUE

Edna O'Brien

FARRAR STRAUS GIROUX New York

All rights reserved
Printed in the United States of America
Designed by Jacqueline Schuman
First printing, 1986

This omnibus edition, with a new Epilogue by the
author, first published 1986.
The Lonely Girl, first published in 1962, was republished
in 1964 as *Girl with Green Eyes.*

Library of Congress Cataloging-in-Publication Data

O'Brien, Edna.
  The country girls trilogy and epilogue.
  Contents: The country girls—The lonely girl—
Girls in their married bliss.
  I. Title.
PR6065.B7C68 1986   823'.914   85-32113

Acknowledgment is made to the following
for permission to reprint copyrighted material:

Lewis Music Publishing Co., Inc.: Lyrics from
"I Didn't Know the Gun Was Loaded" by Hank Fort
and Herb Leighton. Copyright 1948 by Lewis Music
Publishing Co., Inc. All rights reserved. Copyright
renewed.

Volta Music Corporation, 43 Welbeck Street, London
W1M 7NF, England: Lyrics from "High Noon" by Dmitri
Tiomkin and Ned Washington.

For Susan Lescher

Contents

The
Country
Girls

1

I wakened quickly and sat up in bed abruptly. It is only when I am anxious that I waken easily and for a minute I did not know why my heart was beating faster than usual. Then I remembered. The old reason. He had not come home.

Getting out, I rested for a moment on the edge of the bed, smoothing the green satin bedspread with my hand. We had forgotten to fold it the previous night, Mama and me. Slowly I slid onto the floor and the linoleum was cold on the soles of my feet. My toes curled up instinctively. I owned slippers but Mama made me save them for when I was visiting my aunts and cousins; and we had rugs, but they were rolled up and kept in drawers until visitors came in the summertime from Dublin.

I put on my ankle socks.

There was a smell of frying bacon from the kitchen, but it didn't cheer me.

Then I went over to let up the blind. It shot up suddenly and the cord got twisted around it. It was lucky that Mama had gone downstairs, as she was always lecturing me on how to let up blinds properly, gently.

The sun was not yet up, and the lawn was speckled with daisies that were fast asleep. There was dew everywhere. The grass below my window, the hedge around it, the rusty paling wire beyond that, and the big outer field were each touched with a delicate, wandering mist. The leaves and the trees were bathed in the mist, and the trees looked unreal, like trees in a dream. Around the forget-me-nots that sprouted out of the side of the hedge were haloes of water. Water that glistened like silver. It was quiet, it was perfectly still. There was smoke rising from the blue mountain in the distance. It would be a hot day.

Seeing me at the window, Bull's-Eye came out from under the hedge, shook himself free of water, and looked up lazily, sadly, at me. He was our sheep dog and I named him Bull's-Eye because his eyes were speckled black and white, like canned sweets. He usually slept in the turf house, but last night he had stayed in the rabbit hole under the hedge. He always slept there to be on the watch-out when Dada was away. I need not ask, my father had not come home.

Just then Hickey called from downstairs. I was lifting my night-gown over my head, so I couldn't hear him at first.

"What? What are you saying?" I asked, coming out onto the landing with the satin bedspread draped around me.

"Good God, I'm hoarse from saying it." He beamed up at me, and asked, "Do you want a white or a brown egg for your breakfast?"

"Ask me nicely, Hickey, and call me dotey."

"Dotey. Ducky. Darling. Honeybunch, do you want a white or a brown egg for your breakfast?"

"A brown one, Hickey."

"I have a gorgeous little pullet's egg here for you," he said as he went back to the kitchen. He banged the door. Mama could never train him to close doors gently. He was our workman and I loved him. To prove it, I said so aloud to the Blessed Virgin, who was looking at me icily from a gilt frame.

"I love Hickey," I said. She said nothing. It surprised me that she didn't talk more often. Once, she had spoken to me, and what she said was very private. It happened when I got out of bed in the middle of the night to say an aspiration. I got out of bed six or seven times every night as an act of penance. I was afraid of hell.

Yes, I love Hickey, I thought; but of course what I really meant was that I was fond of him. When I was seven or eight I used to say that I would marry him. I told everyone, including the catechism examiner, that we were going to live in the chicken run and that we would get free eggs, free milk, and vegetables from Mama. Cabbage was the only vegetable they planted. But now I talked less of marriage. For one thing, he never washed himself, except to splash rainwater on his face when he stooped in over the barrel in the evenings. His teeth were green, and last thing at night he did his water in a peach tin that he kept under his bed. Mama scolded him. She used to lie awake at night waiting for him to come home, waiting to hear him raise the window while he emptied the peach-tin contents onto the flag outside.

"He'll kill those shrubs under that window, sure as God," she used to say, and some nights when she was very angry she came downstairs in her nightgown and knocked on his door and asked him why didn't he do that sort of thing outside. But Hickey never answered her, he was too cunning.

I dressed quickly, and when I bent down to get my shoes I saw fluff and dust and loose feathers under the bed. I was too miserable to mop the room, so I pulled the covers up on my bed and came out quickly.

The landing was dark as usual. An ugly stained-glass window gave it a mournful look as if someone had just died in the house.

"This egg will be like a bullet," Hickey called.

"I'm coming," I said. I had to wash myself. The bathroom was cold, no one ever used it. An abandoned bathroom with a rust stain on the handbasin just under the cold tap, a perfectly new bar of pink soap, and a stiff white facecloth that looked as if it had been hanging in the frost all night.

I decided not to bother, so I just filled a bucket of water for the lavatory. The lavatory did not flush, and for months we had been expecting a man to come and fix it. I was ashamed when Baba, my school friend, went up there and said fatally, "Still out of order?" In our house things were either broken or not used at all. Mama had a new clippers and several new coils of rope in a wardrobe upstairs; she said they'd only get broken or stolen if she brought them down.

My father's room was directly opposite the bathroom. His old clothes were thrown across a chair. He wasn't in there, but I could hear his knees cracking. His knees always cracked when he got in and out of bed. Hickey called me once more.

Mama was sitting by the range, eating a piece of dry bread. Her blue eyes were small and sore. She hadn't slept. She was staring directly ahead at something only she could see, at fate and at the future. Hickey winked at me. He was eating three fried eggs and several slices of home-cured bacon. He dipped his bread into the runny egg yolk and then sucked it.

"Did you sleep?" I asked Mama.

"No. You had a sweet in your mouth and I was afraid you'd choke if you swallowed it whole, so I stayed awake just in case." We always kept sweets and bars of chocolate under the pillow and I had taken a fruit drop just before I fell asleep. Poor Mama, she was always a worrier. I suppose she lay there thinking of him, waiting for the sound of a motorcar to stop down the road, waiting for the sound of his feet coming through the wet grass, and for the noise of the gate hasp—waiting, and coughing. She always coughed when she lay down, so she kept old rags that served as handkerchiefs in a velvet purse that was tied to one of the posts of the brass bed.

Hickey topped my egg. It had gone hard, so he put little knobs of butter in to moisten it. It was a pullet's egg that came just over the rim of the big china egg cup. It looked silly, the little egg in the big cup, but it tasted very good. The tea was cold.

"Can I bring Miss Moriarty lilac?" I asked Mama. I was ashamed of myself for taking advantage of her wretchedness to bring the teacher flowers, but I wanted very much to outdo Baba and become Miss Moriarty's pet.

"Yes, darling, bring anything you want," Mama said absently. I went over and put my arms around her neck and kissed her. She was the best mama in the world. I told her so, and she held me very close for a minute as if she would never let me go. I was everything in the world to her, everything.

"Old mammypalaver," Hickey said. I loosened my fingers, which had been locked on the nape of her soft white neck, and I drew away from her, shyly. Her mind was far away, and the hens were not yet fed. Some of them had come down from the yard and were picking at Bull's-Eye's food plate outside the back door. I could hear Bull's-Eye chasing them and the flap of their wings as they flew off, cackling violently.

"There's a play in the town hall, missus. You ought to go over," Hickey said.

"I ought." Her voice was a little sarcastic. Although she relied on Hickey for everything, she was sharp with him sometimes. She was thinking. Thinking where was he? Would he come home in an ambulance, or a hackney car, hired in Belfast three days ago and not paid for? Would he stumble up the stone steps at the back door waving a bottle of whiskey? Would he shout, struggle, kill her, or apologize? Would he fall in the hall door with some drunken fool and say:

"Mother, meet my best friend, Harry. I've just given him the thirteen-acre meadow for the loveliest greyhound. . . ." All this had happened to us so many times that it was foolish to expect that my father might come home sober. He had gone, three days before, with sixty pounds in his pocket to pay the rates.

"Salt, sweetheart," said Hickey, putting a pinch between his thumb and finger and sprinkling it onto my egg.

"No, Hickey, don't." I was doing without salt at that time. As an affectation. I thought it was very grown-up not to use salt or sugar.

"What will I do, mam?" Hickey asked, and took advantage of her listlessness to butter his bread generously on both sides. Not that Mama was stingy with food, but Hickey was getting so fat that he couldn't do his work.

"Go to the bog, I suppose," she said. "The turf is ready for footing and we mightn't get a fine day again."

"Maybe he shouldn't go so far away," I said. I liked Hickey to be around when Dada came home.

"He mightn't come for a month," she said. Her sighs would break your heart. Hickey took his cap off the window ledge and went off to let out the cows.

"I must feed the hens," Mama said, and she took a pot of meal out of the lower oven, where it had been simmering all night.

She was pounding the hens' food outside in the dairy, and I got my lunch ready for school. I shook my bottle of cod-liver oil and Parrish's food, so that she'd think I had taken it. Then I put it back on the dresser beside the row of Doulton plates. They were a wedding present, but we never used them in case they'd get broken. There were bills stuffed in behind them. Hundreds of bills. Bills never worried Dada, he just put them behind plates and forgot.

I came out to get the lilac. Standing on the stone step to look across the fields, I felt, as I always did, that rush of freedom and pleasure when I looked at all the various trees and the outer stone buildings set far away from the house, and at the fields very green and very peaceful. Outside the paling wire was a walnut tree, and under its shade there were bluebells, tall and intensely blue, a grotto of heaven-blue flowers among the limestone boulders. And my swing was swaying in the wind, and all the leaves on all the treetops were stirring lightly.

"Get yourself a little piece of cake and biscuits for your lunch," Mama said. Mama spoiled me, always giving me little dainties. She was mashing a bucket of meal and potatoes; her head was lowered and she was crying into the hen food.

"Ah, that's life, some work and others spend," she said as she went off toward the yard with the bucket. Some of the hens were perched on the rim of the bucket, picking. Her right shoulder sloped more than her left from carrying buckets. She was dragged down from heavy work, working to keep the place going, and at nighttime making lampshades and fire screens to make the house prettier.

A covey of wild geese flew overhead, screaming as they passed over the house and down past the elm grove. The elm grove was where the cows went to be cool in summertime and where the flies followed them. I often played shop there with pieces of broken china and cardboard boxes. Baba and I sat there and shared secrets, and once we took off our knickers in there and tickled one another. The greatest secret of all. Baba used to say she would tell, and every time she said that, I gave her a silk hankie or a new tartan ribbon or something.

"Stop moping, my dear little honeybunch," Hickey said as he got four buckets of milk ready for the calves.

"What do you think of, Hickey, when you're thinking?"

"Dolls. Nice purty little wife. Thinking is a pure cod," he said. The calves were bawling at the gate, and when he went to them each calf nuzzled its head into the bucket and drank greedily. The white-head with the huge violet eyes drank fastest, so that she could put her nose into the bucket beside her.

"She'll get indigestion," I remarked.

"Poor creature, 'tis a meat supper she ought to get."

"I'm going to be a nun when I grow up; that's what I was thinking."

"A nun you are in my eye. The Kerry Order—two heads on the one pillow." I felt a little disgusted and went around to pick the lilac. The cement flag at the side of the house was green and slippery. It was where the rain barrel sometimes overflowed and it was just under the window where Hickey emptied the contents of his peach tin every night.

My sandals got wet when I went over onto the grass.

"Pick your steps," Mama called, coming down from the yard with the empty bucket in one hand and some eggs in the other. Mama knew things before you told her.

The lilac was wet. Drops of water like overripe currants fell onto the grass as I broke off each branch. I came back carrying a foam of it like lumber in my arms.

"Don't, it's unlucky," she called, so I didn't go into the house.

She brought out a piece of newspaper and wrapped it around the stems to keep my dress from getting wet. She brought out my coat and gloves and hat.

" 'Tis warm, I don't need them," I said. But she insisted gently, reminding me again that I had a bad chest. So I put on my coat and hat, got my school bag, a piece of cake, and a lemonade bottle of milk for my lunch.

In fear and trembling I set off for school. I might meet him on the way or else he might come home and kill Mama.

"Will you come to meet me?" I asked her.

"Yes, darling, soon as I tidy up after Hickey's dinner, I'll go over the road to meet you."

"For sure?" I said. There were tears in my eyes. I was always afraid that my mother would die while I was at school.

"Don't cry, love. Come on now, you better go. You have a nice little piece of cake for your lunch and I'll meet you." She straightened the cap on my head and kissed me three or four times. She stood on the flag to look after me. She was waving. In her brown dress she looked sad; the farther I went, the sadder she looked. Like a sparrow in the snow, brown and anxious and lonesome. It was hard to think that she got married one sunny morning in a lace dress and a floppy buttercup hat, and that her eyes were moist with pleasure when now they were watery with tears.

Hickey was driving the cows over to the far field, and I called out to him. He was walking in front of me, his trouser legs tucked into his thick wool socks, his cap turned around so that the peak was on the back of his head. He walked like a clown. I would know his walk anywhere.

"What bird is that?" I asked. There was a bird on the flowering horse-chestnut tree which seemed to be saying: "Listen here. Listen here."

"A blackbird," he replied.

"It's not a black bird. I can see it's a brown bird."

"All right, smartie. It's a brown bird. I have work to do, I don't go around asking birds their names, ages, hobbies, taste in snails, and so forth. Like these eejits who come over to Burren to look at flowers. Flowers no less. I'm a working man. I carry this place on my shoulders." It was true that Hickey did most of the work, but even at that, the place was going to ruin, the whole four hundred acres of it.

"Be off, you chit, or I'll give you a smack on your bottom."

"How dare you, Hickey." I was fourteen and I didn't think he should make so free with me.

"Givvus a birdie," he said, beaming at me with his soft, gray, very large eyes. I ran off, shrugging my shoulders. A birdie was his private name for a kiss. I hadn't kissed him for two years, not since the day Mama gave me the fudge and dared me to kiss him ten times. Dada was in hospital that day recovering from one of his drinking sprees and it was one of the few times I saw Mama happy. It was only for the few weeks immediately after his drinking that she could relax, before it was time to worry again about the next bout. She was sitting on the step of the back door, and I was holding a skein of yarn while she wound it into a ball. Hickey came home from the fair and told her the price he got for a heifer, and then she dared me to kiss him ten times for the piece of fudge.

I came down the lawn hurriedly, terrified that Dada would appear any minute.

They called it a lawn because it had been a lawn in the old days when the big house was standing, but the Tans burned the big house and my father, unlike his forebears, had no pride in land, and gradually the place went to ruin.

I crossed over the briary part at the lower end of the field. It led toward the wicker gate.

It was crowded with briars and young ferns and stalks of ragwort, and needle-sharp thistles. Under these the ground was speckled with millions of little wildflowers. Little drizzles of blue and white and violet—little white songs spilling out of the earth. How secret and beautiful and precious they were, hidden in there under the thorns and the young ferns.

I changed the lilac from one arm to the other and came out onto the road. Jack Holland was waiting for me. I got a start when I saw him against the wall. At first I thought it was Dada. They were about the same height and they both wore hats instead of caps.

"Ah, Caithleen, my child," he greeted me, and held the gate while I edged out sideways. The gate only opened back a little and one had to squeeze one's way out. He put the wire catch on and crossed over to the towpath with me.

"How are things, Caithleen? Mother well? Your dad is conspicuous by his absence. I see Hickey at the creamery these mornings." I told him things were well, remembering Mama's maxim "Weep and you weep alone."

2 "I shall convey you, Caithleen, over the wet winding roads."

"It's not wet, Jack, and for God's sake, don't talk of rain; it's as fatal as opening umbrellas in the house. It just reminds it to rain."

He smiled and touched my elbow with his hand. "Caithleen, you must know that poem of Colum's—'wet winding roads, brown bogs and black water, and my thoughts on white ships and the King of Spain's daughter.' Except of course," said he, grinning to himself, "my thoughts are nearer home."

We were passing Mr. Gentleman's gate, and the padlock was on it.

"Is Mr. Gentleman away?" I asked.

"Indubitably. Odd fish, Caithleen. Odd fish." I said that I didn't think so. Mr. Gentleman was a beautiful man who lived in the white house on the hill. It had turret windows and an oak door that was like a church door, and Mr. Gentleman played chess in the evenings. He worked as a solicitor in Dublin, but he came home at the weekends, and in the summertime he sailed a boat on the Shannon. Mr. Gentleman was not his real name, of course, but everyone called him that. He was French, and his real name was Mr. de Maurier, but no one could pronounce it properly, and anyhow, he was such a distinguished man with his gray hair and his satin waistcoats that the local people christened him Mr. Gentleman. He seemed to like the name very well, and signed his letters J. W. Gentleman. J.W. were the initials of his Christian names and they stood for Jacques and something else.

I remembered the day I went up to his house. It was only a few weeks before that Dada had sent me with a note—it was to borrow money, I think. Just at the top of the tarmac avenue, two red setters shot around the side of the house and jumped on me. I screamed and Mr. Gentleman came out the conservatory door and smiled. He led the dogs away and locked them in the garage.

He brought me into the front hall and smiled again. He had a sad face, but his smile was beautiful, remote; and very condescending. There was a trout in a glass case that rested on the hall table, and it had a printed sign which read: CAUGHT BY J. W. GENTLEMAN AT LOUGH DERG. WEIGHT 20 LB.

From the kitchen came the smell and sizzle of a roast. Mrs. Gentleman, who was reputed to be a marvelous cook, must have been basting the dinner.

He opened Dada's envelope with a paper knife and frowned while he was reading it.

"Tell him that I will look the matter over," Mr. Gentleman said to me. He spoke as if there were a damson stone in his throat. He had never lost his French accent, but Jack Holland said this was an affectation.

"Have an orange?" he said, taking two out of the cut-glass bowl on the dining-room table. He smiled and saw me to the door. There was a certain slyness about his smile, and as he shook my hand I had an odd sensation, as if someone were tickling my stomach from the inside. I crossed over the smooth lawn, under the cherry trees, and out onto the tarmac path. He stayed in the doorway. When I looked back the sun was shining on him and on the white Snowcemmed house, and the upstairs windows were all on fire. He waved when I was closing the gate and then went inside. To drink elegant glasses of sherry; to play chess, to eat soufflés and roast venison, I thought, and I was just on the point of thinking about tall eccentric Mrs. Gentleman when Jack Holland asked me another question.

"You know something, Caithleen?"

"What, Jack?"

At least he would protect me if we met my father.

"You know many Irish people are royalty and unaware of it. There are kings and queens walking the roads of Ireland, riding bicycles, imbibing tea, plowing the humble earth, totally unaware of their great heredity. Your mother, now, has the ways and the walk of a queen."

I sighed. Jack's infatuation with the English language bored me.

He went on: " 'My thoughts on white ships and the King of Spain's daughter'—except that my thoughts are much nearer home." He smiled happily to himself. He was composing a paragraph for his column in the local paper—"Walking in the crystal-clear morning with a juvenile lady friend, exchanging snatches of Goldsmith and Colum, the thought flashed through my mind that I was moving amid . . ."

The towpath petered out just there and we went onto the road. It was dry and dusty where we walked, and we met the carts going over to the creamery and the milk tanks rattled and the owners beat their donkeys with the reins and said, "Gee-up there." Passing Baba's house I walked faster. Her new Pink-Witch bicycle was gleaming against the side wall of their house. Their house was like a doll's house on the outside, pebble-dashed, with two bow windows downstairs and circular flower beds in the front garden. Baba was the veterinary surgeon's daughter. Coy, pretty, malicious Baba was my friend and the person whom I feared most after my father.

"Your mam at home?" Jack finally asked. He hummed some tune to himself.

He tried to sound casual, but I knew perfectly well that this was why he had waited for me under the ivy wall. He had brought over his cow to the paddock he hired from one of our neighbors and then he had waited for me at the wicker gate. He didn't dare come up. Not since the night Dada had ordered him out of the kitchen. They were playing cards and Jack had his hand on Mama's knee under the table. Mama didn't protest, because Jack was decent to her, with presents of candied peel and chocolate and samples of jam that he got from commercial travelers. Then Dada let a card fall and bent down to get it; and next thing the table was turned over sideways and the china lamp got broken. My father shouted and pulled up his sleeves, and Mama told me to go to bed. The shouting, high and fierce, came up through the ceiling because my room was directly over the kitchen. Such shouting! It was rough and crushing. Like the noise of a steamroller. Mama cried and pleaded, and her cry was hopeless and plaintive.

"There's trouble brewing," said Jack, bringing me from one world of it more abruptly to another. He spoke as if it were the end of the world for me.

We were walking in the middle of the road and from behind came the impudent ring of a bicycle bell. It was Baba, looking glorious on her new puce bicycle. She passed with her head in the air and one hand in her pocket. Her black hair was plaited that day and tied at the tips with blue ribbons that matched her ankle socks exactly. I noticed with envy that her legs were delicately tanned.

She passed us and then slowed down, dragging her left toe along the blue tarred road, and when we caught up with her, she grabbed the lilac out of my arms and said, "I'll carry that for you." She laid it into the basket on the front of her bicycle and rode off singing, "I will and I must get married," out loud to herself. So she would give Miss Moriarty the lilac and get all the praise for bringing it.

"You don't deserve this, Caithleen," he said.

"No, Jack. She shouldn't have taken it. She's a bully." But he meant something quite different, something to do with my father and with our farm.

We passed the Greyhound Hotel, where Mrs. O'Shea was polishing the knocker. She had a hairnet on and pipe cleaners so tight in her head that you could see her scalp. Her bedroom slippers looked as if the greyhounds had chewed them. More than likely they had. The hotel was occupied chiefly by greyhounds. Mr. O'Shea thought he would get rich that way. He went to the dogs in Limerick every night and Mrs. O'Shea drank port wine up at the dressmaker's. The dressmaker was a gossip.

"Good morning, Jack; good morning, Caithleen," she said over-affably. Jack replied coldly; her business interfered with his. He had a grocery and bar up the street, but Mrs. O'Shea got a lot of drinkers at night because she kept good fires. The men drank there after hours and she had bribed the police not to raid her. I almost walked over two hounds that were asleep on the mat outside the shop door. Their noses, black and moist, were jutting out on the pavement.

"Hello," I said. My mother warned me not to be too free with her, as she had given my father so much credit that ten of their cows were grazing on our land for life.

We passed the hotel, the gray, damp ruin that it was, with window frames rotting and doors scratched all over from the claws of young and nervous greyhounds.

"Did I tell you, Caithleen, that her ladyship has never given a commercial traveler anything other than fried egg or tinned salmon for lunch?"

"Yes, Jack, you told me." He had told me fifty times, it was one of his ways of ridiculing her; by lowering her he hoped to lower the name of the hotel. But the locals liked it, because it was friendly drinking in the kitchen late at night.

We stood for a minute to look over the bridge, at the black-green water that flowed by the window of the hotel basement. It was green water and the willows along the bank made it more green. I was looking to see if there were any fish, because Hickey liked to do a bit of fishing in the evenings, while I waited for Jack to stop hedging and finally tell me whatever it was that he wanted to say.

The bus passed and scattered dust on either side. Something had leaped down below; it might have been a fish. I didn't see it, I was waving to the bus. I always waved. Circles of water were running into one another and when the last circle had dissolved he said, "Your place is mortgaged; the bank owns it."

But, like the dark water underneath, his words did not disturb me. They had nothing to do with me, neither the words nor the water; or so I thought as I said goodbye to him and climbed the hill toward the school. Mortgage, I thought, now what does that mean? and puzzling it over, I decided to ask Miss Moriarty, or better still to look it up in the big black dictionary. It was kept in the school press.

The classroom was in a muddle. Miss Moriarty was bent over a book and Baba was arranging the lilac (my lilac) on the little May altar at the top of the classroom. The smaller children were sitting on the floor mixing all the separate colors of plasticine together, and the big girls were chatting in groups of three or four.

Delia Sheehy was taking cobwebs out of the corners of the ceiling. She had a cloth tied to the end of the window pole, and as she moved from one corner to another, she dragged the pole along the whitewashed walls and the dusty, faded, gray maps. Maps of Ireland and Europe and America. Delia was a poor girl who lived in a cottage with her grandmother. She got all the dirty jobs at school. In winter she lit the fire and cleaned the ashes every morning before the rest of us came in, and every Friday she cleaned the closets with a yard brush and a bucket of Jeyes Fluid water. She had two summer dresses and she washed one every second evening, so that she was always clean and neat and scrubbed-looking. She told me that she would be a nun when she grew up.

"You're late, you're going to be killed, murdered, slaughtered," Baba said to me as I came in. So I went over to apologize to Miss Moriarty.

"What? What's this?" she asked impatiently, as she lifted her head from her book. It was an Italian book. She learned Italian by post and went to Rome in the summertime. She had seen the Pope and she was a very clever woman. She told me to go to my seat; she was annoyed that I had found her reading an Italian book. On my way down Delia Sheehy whispered to me, "She never missed you."

So Baba had sent me to apologize for nothing. I could have gone to my desk unnoticed. I took out an English book and read Thoreau's "A Winter Morning"—"Silently we unlatch the door, letting the drift fall in, and step abroad to face the cutting air. Already the stars have lost some of their sparkle, and a dull leaden mist skirts the horizon"—and I was just there when Miss Moriarty called for silence.

"We have great news today," she said, and she was looking at me. Her eyes were small and blue and piercing. You would think she was cross, but it was just that she had bad sight from overreading.

"Our school is honored," she said, and I felt myself beginning to blush.

"You, Caithleen," she said, looking directly at me, "have won a scholarship." I stood up and thanked her, and all the girls clapped. She said that we wouldn't do much work that day as a celebration.

"Where will she be going?" Baba asked. She had put all the lilac in jam jars and placed them in a dreary half circle around the statue of the Blessed Virgin. The teacher said the name of the convent. It was at the other end of the county and there was no bus to it.

Delia Sheehy asked me to write in her autograph album and I wrote something soppy. Then a little fold of paper was thrown up from behind, onto my desk. I opened it. It was from Baba. It read:

---

*I'm going there too in September. My father has it all
fixed. I have my uniform got. Of course we're paying. It's
nicer when you pay. You're a right-looking eejit.*

Baba

My heart sank. I knew at once that I'd be getting a lift in their car
and that Baba would tell everyone in the convent about my father.
I wanted to cry.

The day passed slowly. I was wondering about Mama. She'd be
pleased to hear about the scholarship. My education worried her. At
three o'clock we were let out, and though I didn't know it, that was
my last day at school. I would never again sit at my desk and smell
that smell of chalk and mice and swept dust. I would have cried if I
had known, or written my name with the corner of a set square on my
desk.

I forgot about the word "mortgage."

3 I was wrapping myself up in the cloakroom when Baba came out. She said "Cheerio" to Miss Moriarty. She was Miss Moriarty's pet, even though she was the school dunce. She wore a white cardigan like a cloak over her shoulders so that the sleeves dangled down idly. She was full of herself.

"And what in the hell do you want a bloody coat and hat and scarf for? It's the month of May. You're like a bloody Eskimo."

"What's a bloody Eskimo?"

"Mind your own business." She didn't know.

She stood in front of me, peering at my skin as if it were full of blackheads or spots. I could smell her soap. It was a wonderful smell, half perfume, half disinfectant.

"What soap is that you're using?" I asked.

"Mind your own bloody business and use carbolic. Anyhow, you're a country mope and you don't even wash in the bathroom, for God's sake. Bowls of water in the scullery and a facecloth that your mother made out of an old rag. What do you use the bathroom for, anyhow?" she said.

"We have a guest room," I said, getting hysterical with temper.

"Jesus, ye have, and there's oats in it. The place is like a bloody barn with chickens in a box in the window; did ye fix the lavatory chain yet?"

It was surprising that she could talk so fast, and yet she wasn't able to write a composition but bullied me to do it for her.

"Where is your bicycle?" I asked jealously, as we came out the door. She had cut such a dash with her new bicycle early in the morning that I didn't want to be with her while she cycled slowly and I walked in a half-run alongside her.

"Left it at home at lunchtime. The wireless said there'd be rain. How's your upstairs model?" She was referring to an old-fashioned bicycle of Mama's that I sometimes used.

The two of us went down the towpath toward the village. I could smell her soap. The soap and the neat bands of sticking plaster, and the cute, cute smile; and the face dimpled and soft and just the right plumpness—for these things I could have killed her. The sticking plaster was an affectation. It drew attention to her round, soft knees. She didn't kneel as much as the rest of us, because she was the best singer in the choir and no one seemed to mind if she sat on the piano stool all through Mass and fiddled with the half-moons of her nails: except during the Consecration. She wore narrow bands of sticking plaster across her knees. She got it for nothing from her father's surgery, and people were always asking her if her knees were cut. Grown-ups liked Baba and gave her a lot of attention.

"Any news?" she said suddenly. When she said this I always felt obliged to entertain her, even if I had to tell lies.

"We got a candlewick bedspread from America," I said, and regretted it at once. Baba could boast and when she did everybody listened, but when I boasted everybody laughed and nudged; that was since the day I told them we used our drawing room for drawing. Not a day passed but Baba said, "My mammy saw Big Ben on her honeymoon," and all the girls at school looked at Baba in wonder, as if her mother was the only person ever to have seen Big Ben. Though, indeed, she may have been the only person in our village to have seen it.

Jack Holland rapped his knuckles against the window and beckoned me to come in. Baba followed, and sniffed as soon as we got inside. There was a smell of dust and stale porter and old tobacco smoke. We went in behind the counter. Jack took off his rimless spectacles and laid them on an open sack of sugar. He took both my hands in his.

"Your mam is gone on a little journey," he said.

"Gone where?" I asked, with panic in my voice.

"Now, don't be excited. Jack is in charge, so have no fears."

In charge! Jack had been in charge the night of the concert when the town hall went on fire; Jack was in charge of the lorry that De Valera nearly fell through during an election speech. I began to cry.

"Oh, now, now," Jack said, as he went down to the far end of the shop, where the bottles of wine were. Baba nudged me.

"Go on crying," she said. She knew we'd get something. He took down a dusty bottle of ciderette and filled two glasses. I didn't see why she should benefit from my miseries.

"To your health," he said as he handed us the drinks. My glass was dirty. It had been washed in portery water and dried with a dirty towel.

"Why do you keep the blind drawn?" Baba said, smiling up at him sweetly.

"It's all a matter of judgment," he said seriously, as he put on his glasses.

"These," he said, pointing to the jars of sweets and the two-pound pots of jam, "these would suffer from the sunshine."

The blue blind was faded and was bleached to a dull gray. The cord had come off and the blind was itself torn across the bottom slat, and as he talked to us Jack went over and adjusted it slightly. The shop was cold and sunless and the counter was stained all over with circles of brown.

"Will Mama be long?" I asked, and soon as I mentioned her name he smiled to himself.

"Hickey could tell you that. If he's not snoring in the hay shed, he could enlighten you," Jack said. He was jealous of Hickey because Mama relied on Hickey so utterly.

Baba finished her drink and handed him the glass. He sloshed it in a basin of cold water and put it to drain on a metal tray that had GUINNESS IS GOOD FOR YOU painted on it. Then he dried his hands most carefully on a filthy, worn, frayed towel, and he winked at me.

"I am going to beg for a favor," he said to both of us. I knew what it would be.

"What about a kiss each?" he asked. I looked down at a box that was full of white candles.

"Tra la la la, Mr. Holland," Baba said airily, as she ran out of the shop. I followed her, but unfortunately I tripped over a mousetrap that he had set inside the door. The trap clicked on my shoe and turned upside down. A piece of fatty bacon got stuck to the sole of my shoe.

"These little beastly rodents," he said, as he took the bacon off my shoe and set the trap again. Hickey said that the shop was full of mice. Hickey said that they tumbled around in the sack of sugar at night, and we had bought flour there ourselves that had two dead mice in it. We bought flour in the Protestant shop down the street after that. Mama said that Protestants were cleaner and more honest.

"That little favor," Jack said earnestly to me.

"I'm too young, Jack," I said helplessly, and anyhow, I was too sad.

"Touching, most touching. You have a lyrical trend," he said, as he stroked my pink cheek with his damp hand, and then he held the door as I went out. Just then his mother called him from the kitchen and he ran in to her. I clicked the latch tight, and came out to find Baba waiting.

"Bloody clown, what did you fall over?" She was sitting on an empty porter barrel outside the door, swinging her legs.

"Your dress will get all pink paint from that barrel," I said.

"It's a pink dress, you eejit. I'm going home with you, I might feck a few rings."

"No, you're not," I said firmly. My voice was shaky.

"Yes, I am. I'm going over to get a bunch of flowers. Mammy sent over word at lunchtime to ask your mother could I. Mammy's having tea with the archbishop tomorrow, so we want bluebells for the table."

"Who's the archbishop?" I asked, as we had only a bishop in our diocese.

"Who's the archbishop! Are you a bloody Protestant or what?" she asked.

I was walking very quickly. I hoped she might get tired of me and go into the paper shop for a free read of adventure books. The woman in the paper shop was half blind, and Baba stole a lot of books from there.

I was breathing so nervously that the wings of my nose got wide.

"My nose is getting wider. Will it go back again to normal?" I asked.

"Your nose," she said, "is always wide. You've a nose like a bloody petrol pump."

We passed the fair green and the market house and the rows of tumbling, musty little shops on either side of us. We passed the bank, which was a lovely two-story house and had a polished knocker, and we crossed the bridge. Even on a still day like that, the noise from the river was urgent and rushing, as if it were in full flood.

Soon we were out of the town and climbing the hill that led to the forge. The hill rose between the trees, and it was dark in there because the leaves almost met overhead. And it was quiet except for the clink-clank from the forge where Billy Tuohey was beating a horseshoe into shape. Overhead the birds were singing and fussing and twittering.

"Those bloody birds get on my nerves," she said, making a face up at them.

Billy Tuohey nodded to us through the open window space. It was so smoky in there we could hardly see him. He lived with his mother in a cottage at the back of the forge. They kept bees, and he was the only man around who grew Brussels sprouts. He told lies, but they were nice lies. He told us that he sent his photo to Hollywood and got a cable back to say COME QUICK YOU HAVE THE BIGGEST EYES SINCE GRETA GARBO. He told us that he dined with the Aga Khan at the Galway races and that they played snooker after dinner. He told us that his shoes were stolen when he left them outside the door of the hotel. He told us so many lies and so many stories, his stories filled in the nights, the dark nights, and their colors were exotic like the colors of the turf flames. He danced jigs and reels, too, and he played the accordion very well.

"What's Billy Tuohey?" she asked suddenly as if she wanted to frighten me.

"A blacksmith," I said.

"Jesus, you lumping eejit. What else?"

"What?"

"Billy Tuohey is a fly boy."

"Does he get girls into trouble?" I asked.

"No. He keeps bees," she said, and sighed. I was a dull dog.

We came to her gate and she ran in with her school bag. I didn't wait for her; I didn't want her to come. The wild bees from a nest in the stone wall made a sleepy, murmuring sound, and the fruit trees outside the barber's house were shedding the last of their petals. There was a pool of white and pink petals under the apple tree, and the children stepped over the petals, crushing them under their bare feet. The two youngest were hanging over the wall saying "Good afternoona" to everyone who went by. They were eating slices of bread-and-jam.

"What do Mickey the Barber's eat for breakfast?" she asked as she caught up with me. The barber's children were always known as Mickey the Barber's because their father's name was Mickey and there were too many children for one to remember their separate names.

"Bread and tea, I suppose."

"Hair soup, you fool. What do Mickey the Barber's eat for lunch?"

"Hair soup." I felt very smart now.

"No. Jugged hair, you eejit." She picked a stalk of tough grass off the side of the ditch, chewed it thoughtfully, and spat it out. She was bored and I didn't know why she came at all.

As we came near our gate I ran on ahead of her and almost walked over him. He was sitting on the ground with his back against the bark of an elm tree and there were shadows of leaves on his face. The shadows moved. He was asleep.

"I couldn't mind you," he said finally. "I have to milk cows and feed calves and feed hens. I have to carry this place on my shoulders." He was enjoying his importance.

"I don't need minding," I said. "I just want you to stay in at night with me." But he shook his head. I knew that I would have to go. So I was determined to be difficult. "What about my nightgown?" I asked.

"Go up for it," Baba said calmly. How could they be so calm when my teeth were chattering?

"I can't. I'm afraid."

"Afraid of what?" asked Hickey. "Sure, he's in Limerick by now."

"Are you sure?"

"Sure! Didn't he come down and get a lift on the mail car? You won't see him for ten or eleven days, not till all the money is spent."

"Come on, booby, I'll go with you," Baba said. I wanted to ask Hickey if Mama was all right. I whispered.

"Can't hear you."

I whispered again.

"Can't hear you."

I let it go. He went over across the field whistling, and we went up the avenue. The avenue was full of weeds and there were wheel ruts on either side of it from carts that went up and down every day.

"Have you nits?" she asked, making a face.

"I don't know. Why?"

"If you had nits, you couldn't stay. Couldn't have things crawling over my pillow; creepy-crawly things like that would carry you off."

"Off where?"

"To the Shannon."

"That's daft."

"No. You're daft," she said, lifting up a coil of my hair and looking carefully at the scalp. Then suddenly she dropped the coil of hair as if she had seen some terrible disease. "Have to dose you. You're full of bugs and fleas and nits and flies and all sorts of vermin." I came out in gooseflesh.

Bull's-Eye was eating bread off an enamel plate that someone had put on the flag for him. Poor Bull's-Eye, so someone had remembered.

Inside, the kitchen was untidy and the range was out. Mama's Wellingtons were in the middle of the floor and there were two cans of milk on the kitchen table; so was the stationery box. It was in it she kept her powder and lipstick and things. Her powder puff was gone and her rosary beads were taken from the nail off the dresser. She was gone. Really gone.

"Come upstairs with me," I said to Baba. My knees were shaking uncontrollably.

"Anything a person could eat?" she asked, opening the breakfast-room door. She knew that Mama kept tins of biscuits in there behind one of the curtains. The room was dark and sad and dusty. The whatnot, with its collection of knickknacks and chocolate-box lids and statues and artificial flowers, looked silly now that Mama wasn't there. The crab shells that she used as ashtrays were all over the room. Baba picked up a couple and put them down again.

"Jesus, this place is like a bloody bazaar," said Baba, going over to the whatnot to salute all the statues.

"Hello, St. Anthony. Hello, St. Jude, patron of hopeless cases." She picked up an Infant of Prague and the head came off in her hand. She roared laughing, and when I offered her a biscuit from a tin of assorted ones, she took all the chocolate ones and put them in her pocket.

Then she saw the butter on the tiled curb of the fireplace. Mama kept it there in summertime to keep it cool. She picked up a couple of pounds. "Might as well have this toward your keep. We'll go up and have a look at her jewelry," she said.

Mama had rings that Baba coveted. They were nice rings. Mama got them for presents when she was a young girl. She had been to America. She had a lovely face then. A round, sallow face with the most beautiful, clear, trusting eyes. Turquoise blue. And hair that had two colors. Some strands were red-gold and some were brown, so that it couldn't possibly have been dyed. I had hair like her. But Baba put it out at school that I dyed mine.

"Your hair is like old mattress stuffing," she said when I told her what I was thinking.

Soon as we went into the guest room, where the rings were, the ewer rattled in the basin, and the flowers that were laid into it moved, as if propelled by a gentle wind. They weren't flowers really but ears of corn that Mama had covered with pieces of silver paper and gold paper. They were displayed with stalks of pampas grass that she had dyed pink. They were garish, like colors in a carnival. But Mama liked them. She was house-proud. Always doing something.

"Get out the rings and stop looking into the damn mirror." The mirror was clouded over with green spots, but I looked in it out of habit. I got out the brown and gold box where the jewelry was kept and Baba fitted on everything. The rings and the two pearl brooches and the amber necklace that came down to her stomach.

"You could give me one of these rings," she said, "if you weren't so bloody stingy."

"They're Mama's, I couldn't," I said in a panic.

"They're Mama's, I couldn't," she said, and my voice was high and thin and watery when she mimicked it. She opened the wardrobe and got out the green georgette dance dress and then admired herself in the clouded mirror and danced a little on her toes. She was very pretty when she danced. I was clumsy.

"Sssh, I thought I heard something," I said. I was almost certain that I heard a step downstairs.

"Ah, it's the dog," she said.

"I better go down, he might knock over one of the cans of milk. Did we leave the back door open?" I ran down and stopped dead in the kitchen doorway, because there he was. There was my father, drunk, his hat pushed far back on his head and his white raincoat open. His face was red and fierce and angry. I knew that he would have to strike someone.

"A nice thing to come into an empty house. Where's your mother?"

"I don't know."

"Answer my question." I dreaded looking at those eyes, which were blue and huge and bulging. Like glass eyes.

"I don't know."

He came over and gave me a punch under the chin so that my two rows of teeth clattered together, and with his wild lunatic eyes he stared at me. "Always avoiding me. Always avoiding your father. You little s——. Where's your mother or I'll kick the pants off you."

I shouted for Baba and she came tripping down the stairs with a beaded bag of Mama's hanging from her wrist. He took his hands off me at once. He didn't like people to think that he was brutal. He had the name of being a gentleman, a decent man who wouldn't hurt a fly.

"Good evening, Mr. Brady," she said.

"Well, Baba. Are you a good girl?" I was edging nearer the door that led to the scullery. I'd be safer there where I could run. I could smell the whiskey. He had hiccups, and every time he hicked Baba laughed. I hoped he wouldn't catch her, or he might kill both of us.

"Mrs. Brady is gone away. It's her father, he's not well. Mrs.

Brady got word to go and Caithleen is to stay with us." She was eating a chocolate biscuit while she spoke, and there were crumbs in the corners of her pretty lips.

"She'll stay and look after me. That's what she'll do." He spoke very loud, and he was shaking his fist in my direction.

"Oh." Baba smiled. "Mr. Brady, there is someone coming to look after you—Mrs. Burke from the cottages. As a matter of fact, we have to go down now and let her know that you're here." He said nothing. He let out another hiccup. Bull's-Eye came in and was brushing my leg with his white hairy tail.

"We better hurry," Baba said, and she winked at me. He took a pile of notes out of his pocket and gave Baba one folded, dirty pound note.

"Here," he said, "that's for her keep. I don't take anything for nothing." Baba thanked him and said he shouldn't have bothered, and we left.

"Jesus, he's blotto, let's run," she said, but I couldn't run, I was too weak.

"And we forgot the damn butter," she added. I looked back and saw him coming out the gate after us, with great purposeful strides.

"Baba," he called. She asked me if we should run. He called again. I said we'd better not because I wasn't able.

We stood until he caught up with us.

"Give me back that bit of money. I'll settle up with your father myself. I'll be getting him over here next week to do a few jobs."

He took it and walked off quickly. He was hurrying to the public house or maybe to catch the evening bus to Portumna. He had a friend there who kept racehorses.

"Mean devil, he owes my daddy twenty pounds," Baba said. I saw Hickey coming over the field and I waved to him. He was driving the cows. They straggled across the field, stopping for a minute, as cows will, to stare idly at nothing. Hickey was whistling, and the evening being calm and gentle, his song went out across the field. A stranger going along the road might have thought that ours was a happy farm; it seemed so, happy and rich and solid in the copper light of the warm evening. It was a red cut-stone house set among the trees, and in the evening time, when the sun was going down, it had a luster of its own, with fields rolling out from it in a flat, uninterrupted expanse of green.

"Hickey, you told me a lie. He came back and nearly killed me." Hickey was within a few yards from us, standing between two cows with a hand on each of them.

"Why didn't you hide?"

"I walked straight into him."

"What did he want?"

"To fight, as always."

"Mean devil. He gave me a pound for her keep and took it back again," Baba said.

"If I had a penny for every pound he owes me," Hickey said, shaking his head fondly. We owed Hickey a lot of money and I was worried that he might leave us and get a job with the forestry, where he'd be paid regularly.

"Sure you won't go, Hickey?" I pleaded.

"I'll be off to Birmingham when the summer is out," he said. My two greatest fears in life were that Mama would die of cancer and that Hickey would leave. Four women in the village had died of cancer. Baba said it was something to do with not having enough babies. Baba said that all nuns get cancer. Just then I remembered about my scholarship and I told Hickey. He was pleased.

"Oh, you'll be a toff from now on," he said. The brown cow lifted her tail and wet the grass.

"Anyone want lemonade?" he asked, and we ran off. He slapped the cow on the back and she moved lazily. The cows in front moved, too, and Hickey followed them with a new whistle. The evening was very still.

4

Baba called her mother—"Martha, Martha"—as we went into the hall. It was a tiled hall and it smelled of floor polish.

We went up the carpeted stairs. A door opened slowly and Martha put her head out.

"Sssh, sssh," she said, and beckoned us to come in. We went into the bedroom and she shut the door quietly behind us.

"Hello, horror," Declan said to Baba. He was her younger brother. He was eating a leg of a chicken.

There was a cooked chicken on a plate in the center of the big bed. It was overcooked and was falling apart.

"Take off your coat," Martha said to me. She seemed to be expecting me. Mama must have called. Martha looked pale, but then she was always pale. She had a pale Madonna face with eyelids always lowered, and behind them her eyes were big and dark so that you could not see their color, but they reminded one of purple pansies. Velvety. She was wearing red velvet shoes with little crusts of silver on the front of them, and her room smelled of perfume and wine and grown-upness. She was drinking red wine.

"Where's the aul fella?" Baba asked.

"I don't know." Martha shook her head. Her black hair, which was usually piled high on her head, hung below her shoulders and curled upward a little.

"Whatja bring the chicken in here?" Baba asked.

"Whatja think?" Declan said, throwing her the wishbone.

"So's the aul fella won't get it," she said, addressing the photograph of her father on the mantelpiece. She shot at him with her right hand and said, "Bang, bang."

Martha gave me a wing of chicken. I dipped it in the salt cellar and ate it. It was delicious.

"Your mam's gone away for a few days," she said to me, and once again I felt the lump in my throat. Sympathy was bad for me. Not that Martha was motherly. She was too beautiful and cold for that.

Martha was what the villagers called fast. Most nights she went down to the Greyhound Hotel, dressed in a tight black suit with nothing under the jacket, only a brassiere, and with a chiffon scarf knotted at her throat. Strangers and commercial travelers admired her. Pale face, painted nails, blue-black pile of hair, Madonna face, perched on a high stool in the lounge bar of the Greyhound Hotel; they thought she looked sad. But Martha was not ever sad, unless being bored is a form of sadness. She wanted two things from life and she got them— drink and admiration.

"There's trifle in the pantry. Molly left it there," she said to Baba. Molly was a sixteen-year-old maid, from a small farm up the country. During her first week at Brennans' she wore Wellingtons all the time, and when Martha reproved her for this, she said that she hadn't anything else. Martha often beat Molly, and locked her in a bedroom whenever Molly asked to go to a dance in the town hall. Molly told the dressmaker that "they," meaning the Brennans, ate big roasts every day while she herself got sausages and old potato mash. But this may have been just a story. Martha was not mean. She took pride and vengeance in spending his money, but like all drinkers, she was reluctant to spend on anything other than drink.

Baba came in with a Pyrex dish that was half full of trifle, and she set it down on the bed along with saucers and dessert spoons. Her mother dished it out. The pink trifle with a slice of peach, a glacé cherry, a cut banana, and uneven lumps of sponge cake, all reminded me of the days when we had trifle at home. I could see Mama piling it on our plates, my father's, my own, and Hickey's, and leaving only a spoonful for herself in the bottom of the bowl. I could see her getting angry and wrinkling her nose if I protested, and my father snapping at me to shut up, and Hickey sniggering and saying, "All the more for us." I was thinking of this when I heard Baba say, "She doesn't eat trifle," meaning me. Her mother divided the extra plate among the three of them, and my mouth watered while I watched them eat.

"Martha, hey, old Martha, what will I be when I grow up?" Declan asked his mother. He was smoking a cigarette and was learning to inhale.

"Get out of this dive—be something—somebody. An actor, something exciting," Martha said as she looked in the mirror and squeezed a blackhead out of her chin.

"Were you famous, Mammy?" Baba asked the face in the mirror.

The face raised its eyes and sighed, remembering. Martha had been a ballet dancer. But she gave up her career for marriage, or so she said.

"Why did you chuck in?" Baba asked, knowing the answer well.

"Actually I was too tall," said Martha, doing a little dance away from the mirror and across the room, waving a red georgette scarf in the air.

"Too tall? Jesus, stick to the same story," Baba reminded her mother, and her mother went on dancing on the tips of her toes.

"I could have married a hundred men, a hundred men cried at my wedding," Martha said, and the children began to clap.

"One was an actor, one was a poet, a dozen were in the diplomatic service." Her voice trailed off as she went over to speak to her two pet goldfish on the dressing table.

"Diplomatic service—better than this dump," Baba mourned.

"Christ," Martha replied, and then a car hooted and they all jumped.

"The chicken, the chicken," said Martha, and she put it in the wardrobe with an old bed jacket over it. In the wardrobe there were summer dresses and a white fur evening cape.

"Get out, be doing something in the kitchen—your exercises," Martha said as she got down her toothbrush and began to wash her teeth over the handbasin. Their house was very modern, with handbasins in the two front bedrooms. Later she followed us down to the kitchen.

"All right?" she asked, breathing close to Baba.

"He'll say you give your damn teeth great care." Baba laughed, and then made a straight face when she heard him come in the back door. He was carrying an empty Winchester, an open packet of cotton, and a shoebox full of garden peas.

"Mammy. Declan. Baba." He saluted each of them. I was behind the door and he couldn't see me. His voice was low and hoarse and slightly sarcastic. Martha knelt down and got his dinner out of the lower oven of the Aga cooker. It was a fried chop that had gone dry and some fried onions that looked very sodden. She put the plate on an elaborately laid silver tray. The Brennans, my mother always claimed, would make a meal on cutlery and doilies.

"I thought we had chicken today, Mammy," he said, taking off his glasses and cleaning them with a large white handkerchief.

"That half-wit Molly left the meat safe open and Rover got off with the chicken," Martha said calmly.

"Stupid fool. Where is she?"

"Gallivanting," said Baba.

"Molly will have to be chastised, punished, do you hear me, Mammy?" and Martha said yes, that she wasn't deaf. It was then I coughed, because I wanted him to see me, to know that I was there. He had his back to me, but he turned around quickly.

"Ah, Caithleen, Caithleen, my lovely child." He came over and put his arms on my shoulders and kissed me lightly on either cheek. He had had a few drinks.

"I wish, Caithleen, that others, others," he said, waving his hand in the air, "others would be as clever and gentle as you are." Baba stuck her tongue out, and as if he had eyes in the back of his head he turned around to address her.

"Baba."

"Yes, Daddy?" She was smiling now, a sweet loganberry smile, and the dimples in her cheeks were just the right hollowness.

"Can you cook peas?"

"No."

"Can your mother cook peas?"

"I don't know." Martha had gone into the hall to answer the telephone, and she came back writing a name into an address book.

"They want you to go to Cooriganoir. People by the name of O'Brien. They have a heifer dying. It's urgent," she said, as she wrote directions on how to find the place into the notebook.

"Can you cook peas, Mammy?"

"They want you to go at once. They said you were late the last time and the horse died and a foal was born lame."

"Stupid, stupid, stupid," he said. I didn't know whether he meant his wife or the family at Cooriganoir. He drank milk from a jug that was on the dresser. He drank it noisily, you could hear it going down the tunnel of his throat.

Martha sighed and lit herself a cigarette. His dinner had gone cold on the tray and he hadn't touched it.

"Better look up how to cook peas, Mammy," he said. She began to whistle softly, ignoring him, whistling as if she were walking over a dusty mountain road and whistled to keep herself company, or to recall a dog that had followed a rabbit through a hedge and over a field. He went out and banged the door.

"Is he gone?" Declan called from the pantry, where he had locked himself in. His father often asked Declan to go with him, but Declan preferred to sit around smoking and talking to Martha about his career. He wanted to be a film actor.

"Are we going to the play tonight, Martha?" Baba asked.

"With knobs on! He can cook his own bloody peas. Such arrogance. I was eating peas when his thick lump of a mother was feeding them nettle tops. Jesus." It was the first time I saw Martha flushed.

"*You* better not come to the play. Your aul fella might be getting sick and puking all over the damn floor," Baba said to me.

"She is coming," said Declan. "Isn't she, Martha?"

Martha smiled at me, and said I was, of course.

"Well, if Mr. Gentleman is there, I'm sitting next to him," Baba said, tossing her black plaits with a shake of her head.

"No. You are not. I am," Martha said, smiling. Martha had dimples, too, but they were not so hollow as Baba's and not so pretty, because her skin was very white.

"Anyhow, he has some dame in Dublin. A chorus girl," Baba said, and she lifted up her dress to show her knees, because that was how chorus girls behaved.

"Liar. Liar," Declan called her, and he threw the box of peas at her. They scattered all over the floor and I had to get down on my knees to pick them up. Baba opened several pods and ate the delicious young peas. I put the empty pods in the fire. Martha went upstairs to get ready and Declan went into the drawing room to play the gramophone.

"Who told you about Mr. Gentleman?" I asked timidly.

"You did," she said, giving me one of her brazen, blue-eyed stares. "I did not. How dare you?" I was trembling with anger.

"How dare you say how dare you to me—in my own house?" she said as she went off to bathe her feet before going to the play. She shouted back from the hallway, to ask if my mother still washed hers in a milk bucket at the end of the kitchen table. And for a second I could see Mama in the lamplight bathing her poor corns, to soften them, before she began paring them with a razor blade.

The grandfather clock in the hall struck five, and the sky was very dark outside. A wind began to rise, and an old bucket rattled along the gravel path. The rain came quite suddenly, and Baba shouted down to me to bring in the clothes off the line, for Christ's sake. It was a shower of hailstones and they beat against the window like bullets, so that you expected the glass to break. I ran out for the clothes and got wet to the skin. I thought of Mama and I hoped that she was in out of it. There was very little shelter along the road from our village to the village of Tintrim, and Mama was very shy and wouldn't dare ask for a shelter in a house that she passed by. The rain was over in ten minutes and the sun appeared in a rift between the clouds. The apple blossoms were blown all over the grass, and there was a line of water on the branch of the tree that rose outside the kitchen window. I folded the sheets and smelled them for a minute, because there is no smell so pleasant as that of freshly washed linen. Then I put them to dry on the rack over the Aga cooker because they were still a little damp, and after that I went upstairs to Baba's room.

5 We set out for the town hall just before seven. Mr. Brennan was not home, so we left the table set, and when Martha was upstairs getting ready, I put a damp napkin around his plate of sandwiches. I was sorry for Mr. Brennan. He worked hard and he had an ulcer.

Declan went on ahead. He thought it was sissyish to walk with girls.

The sun was going down and it made a fire in the western part of the sky. Running out from the fire, there were pathways of color, not red like the sun, but a warm, flushed pink. The sky above it was a naked blue, and higher still, over our heads, great eiderdowns of clouds sailed serenely by. Heaven was up there. I knew no one in heaven, except old women in the village who had died, but no one belonging to me.

"My mammy is the best-looking woman around here," Baba said. In fact I thought my mother was—with her round, pale, heartbreaking face and her gray, trusting eyes—but I didn't say so because I was staying in their house. Martha did look lovely. The setting sun, or maybe it was the coral necklace, gave her eyes a mysterious orange glow.

"*Bbbip bbbip*," said Hickey as he cycled past us. I was always sorry for Hickey's bicycle. I expected it to collapse under his weight. The tires looked flat. He was carrying a can of milk on the handlebar and a rush basket with a live hen clucking in it. Probably for Mrs. O'Shea in the Greyhound Hotel. Hickey always treated his friends when Mama was away. I supposed Mama had the chickens counted, but Hickey could say the fox came. The foxes were always coming into the yard in broad daylight and carrying off a hen or a turkey.

In front of us, like specks of brown dust, the hordes of midges were humming to themselves under the trees and my ears were itchy after we had passed through that part of the road near the forge, where there was a grove of beech trees.

"Hurry," said Martha, and I took longer steps. She wanted seats in the front row. Important people sat there. The doctor's wife and Mr. Gentleman and the Connor girls. The Connor girls were Protestants but well-thought-of. They passed us just then in their station wagon and hooted. It was their way of saying hello. We nodded back to them. There were two Alsatians in the back of the car and I was glad they hadn't offered us a lift. I was afraid of Alsatians. The Connor girls had a sign on their gate which said BEWARE OF DOGS. They spoke in haughty accents, they rode horses and followed the Hunt in wintertime. When they went to race meetings they had walking sticks that they could sit on. They never spoke to me, but Martha was invited there for afternoon tea once a year. In the summertime.

We mounted the great flight of concrete steps and went into the porch that led to the town hall. There was a fat woman in the ticket office and we could see only the top half of her. She was wearing a puce dress that had millions of sequins stitched onto it. There were crusts of mascara on her lashes, and her hair was dyed puce to match her dress. It was fascinating to watch the sequins shining as if they were moving on the bodice of her dress.

"Her bubs are dancing," Baba said, and we both sniggered. We were sniggering as we held the double doors for Martha to enter. Martha liked to make an entrance.

"Children, stop laughing," she said, as if we didn't belong to her.

An actor with pancake makeup beamed at us and went on ahead to find our seats. Martha had given him three blue tickets.

The country boys in the back of the hall whistled as we came in. It was their habit to stand there and pass remarks about the girls as they came in, and then laugh or whistle if the girl was pretty. They were in their old clothes, but most of them probably had their Sunday shoes on, and there was a strong smell of hair oil.

"Uncouth," Martha said under her breath. It was her favorite word for most of her husband's customers. There was one nice boy who smiled at me; he had black curly hair and a red, happy face. I knew he was on the hurley team.

We were sitting in the front row. Martha sat next to the oldest Connor girl, Baba next to her, and I was on the outside. Mr. Gentleman was farther in, near the younger Connor girl. I saw the back of his neck and the top of his collar before I sat down. I was glad to know that he was there.

The hall was almost dark. Curtains of black cloth had been put over the windows and pinned to the window frames at the four corners.

The light from the six oil lamps at the front of the stage barely showed people to their seats. Two of the lamps smoked and the globes were black.

I looked back to see if there was any sign of Hickey. I looked through the rows of chairs, then along the rows of stools behind the chairs, and farther back still I searched with my eyes along the planks that were laid on porter barrels. He was at the end of the last row of planks, with Maisie next to him. The cheapest seats. They were laughing. The back of the hall was full of girls laughing. Girls with curly hair, girls with shiny black coils of it, like bunches of elderberries, falling onto their shoulders; girls with moist blackberry eyes, smirking and talking and waiting. Miss Moriarty was two rows behind us and she bowed lightly to acknowledge that she saw me. Jack Holland was writing in a notebook.

A bell gonged and the dusty gray curtain was drawn slowly back. It got stuck halfway. The boys at the back booed. I could see the actor with the pancake makeup pulling a string from the wings of the stage, and finally he came out and pushed the curtain back with his hands. The crowd cheered.

On stage were four girls in cerise blouses, black frilly pants, and black hard hats. They had canes under their arms and they tap-danced. I wished that Mama were there. In all the excitement I hadn't thought of her for over an hour. She would have enjoyed it, especially when she heard about the scholarship.

The girls danced off, two to the right and two to the left, and then a man carrying a banjo came on and sang sad songs. He could turn his two eyes inward, and when he did everyone laughed.

After that came a laughing sketch where two clowns got in and out of boxes, and then the woman in the puce dress sang "Courting in the Kitchen." She waved to the audience to join in with her and toward the end they did. She was awful.

"And now, ladies and gentlemen, there will be a short interval, during which time we will sell tickets that will be raffled immediately before the play. And the play, as you probably know, is the one and only, the heart-warming, tear-making *East Lynne*," said the man with the pancake makeup.

I had no money, but Martha bought me four tickets.

"If you win it's mine," said Baba. Mr. Gentleman passed his package of cigarettes all along the front row. Martha took one and leaned forward to thank him. Baba and I ate Turkish Delight.

When the tickets were sold the actor came down and stood under the oil lamps; he put the duplicate ones into a big hat and looked around for someone to draw the winning numbers. Children were usually picked to do this, as they were supposed to be honest. He looked down the hall, and then he looked at Baba and me and he chose us. We stood up and faced the audience, and she picked the first number and I picked the next one. He called out the winning numbers. He called them three times, but nothing happened. You could hear a pin drop. He said them once more, and he was just on the point of asking us to draw two more tickets when there came a shout from the back of the hall.

"Here, down here," people said.

"Now you must come forward and show your tickets." People liked winning, but they were ashamed to come up and collect the prizes. At last they shuffled out from among the standing crowd and the two winners came hesitantly up the passage. One was an albino and the other was a young boy. They showed their tickets, collected their ten shillings each, and went back in a half-run to the darkness at the end of the hall.

"And how about a little song from our two charming friends here?" he said, putting a hand on each of our shoulders.

"Yes," said Baba, who was always looking for an excuse to show off her clear, light, early-morning voice. She began: "As I was going one morning, 'twas in the month of May, a mother and her daughter I spied along the way," and I opened and closed my mouth to pretend that I was singing, too. But she stopped all of a sudden and nudged me to carry on, and there I was, seen by everyone in the hall with my mouth wide-open as if I had lockjaw. I blushed and faded back to my seat, and Baba went on with her song. "Witch," I said under my breath.

East Lynne began. There was dead silence everywhere, except for voices on the stage.

Then I heard noise in the back of the hall, and shuffling as if someone had fainted. A flashlight traveled up along the passage, and as it came level with us, I saw that it was Mr. Brennan.

"Jesus, it's about the chicken," Baba said to her mother, as Mr. Brennan called Martha out. He crossed over, stooping so as not to be in the way of the stage, and he whispered to Mr. Gentleman. Both of them went out. I heard the door being shut noisily and I was glad that they were gone. The play was so good, I didn't want to miss a line.

But the door was opened again and the beam of the flashlight came up along the hall. A thought struck me that they wanted me and then I put it aside again. But it was me. Mr. Brennan tapped me on the shoulder and whispered, "Caithleen love, I want you a minute." My shoes creaked as I went down the hall on tiptoe. I expected it was something about my father.

Outside in the porch they were all talking—Martha and the parish priest, and Mr. Gentleman and the solicitor and Hickey. Hickey had his back to me and Martha was crying. It was Mr. Gentleman who told me.

"Your mother, Caithleen, she's had a little accident"; he spoke slowly and gravely and his voice was unsteady.

"What kind of an accident?" I asked, staring wildly at all the faces. Martha was suffocating into her handkerchief.

"A little accident," Mr. Gentleman said again, and the parish priest repeated it.

"Where is she?" I asked quickly, wildly. I wanted to get to her at once. At once. But no one answered.

"Tell me," I said. My voice was hysterical and then I realized that I was being rude to the parish priest, and I asked again, only more gently.

"Tell her, 'tis better to tell her," I heard Hickey say behind my back. I turned around to ask him, but Mr. Brennan shook his head and Hickey blushed under the gray stubble of his two-day beard.

"Take me to Mama," I begged as I ran out of the doorway and down the flight of concrete steps. At the last step, someone caught me by the belt of my coat.

"We can't take you yet, not yet, Caithleen," Mr. Gentleman said, and I thought that they were all very cruel, and I couldn't understand why.

"Why? Why? I want to go to her," I said, trying to escape from his grip. I had so much strength that I could have run the whole five-mile journey to Tintrim.

"For God's sake, tell the girl," Hickey said.

"Shut up, Hickey," Mr. Brennan shouted, and moved me over to the edge of the curb, where there were several motorcars. There were people gathering around the motorcars and everyone was talking and mumbling in the dark. Martha helped me into the back of their car, and just before she slammed the door, I heard two voices in the street talking, and one voice said, "He left five children."

"Who left five children?" I said to Martha, clutching her by the wrists. I sobbed and said her name and begged her to tell me.

"Tom O'Brien, Caithleen. He's drowned. In his boat, and, and . . ." She would rather be struck dumb than tell me, but I knew it by her face.

"And Mama?" I asked. She nodded her poor head and put her arms around me. Mr. Brennan got into the front seat just then and started the car.

"She knows," Martha said to him, between her sobs, but after that I heard nothing, because you hear nothing, or no one, when your whole body cries and cries for the thing it has lost. Lost. Lost. And yet I could not believe that my mother was gone; and still I knew it was true, because I had a feeling of doom and every bit of me was frozen stiff.

"Are we going to Mama?" I said.

"In a while, Caithleen; we have to get something first," they told me as they helped me out of the car and led me into the Greyhound Hotel. Mrs. O'Shea kissed me and put me sitting in one of the big leather armchairs that sloped backward. The room was full of people. Hickey came over and sat on the arm of my chair. He sat on a white linen antimacassar, but no one cared.

"She's not dead," I said to him, pleading, beseeching.

"They're missing since five o'clock. They left Tuohey's shop at a quarter to five. Poor Tom O'Brien had two bags of groceries," Hickey said. Once Hickey said it, it was true. Slowly my knees began to sink from me and everything inside of me was gone. Mr. Brennan gave me brandy from a spoon, and then he made me swallow two white pills with a cup of tea.

"She doesn't believe it," I heard one of the Connor girls say, and then Baba came in and ran over to kiss me.

"I'm sorry about the bloody aul song," she said.

"Bring the child home," Jack Holland said, and when I heard him I jumped off the chair and shouted that I wanted to go to my mother. Mrs. O'Shea blessed herself, and someone put me sitting down again.

"Caithleen, we're waiting to get news from the barracks," Mr. Gentleman said. He was the only one that could keep me calm.

"I never want to go home again. Never," I said to him.

"You won't go home, Caithleen," he said, and for a second it seemed that he was going to say, "Come home to us," but he didn't. He went over to where Martha was standing beside the sideboard and spoke to her. Then they beckoned to Mr. Brennan and he crossed the room to them.

"Where is *he*, Hickey? I don't want to see him." I was referring to my father.

"You won't see him. He's in hospital in Galway. Passed out when they told him. He was singing in a pub in Portumna when a guard came in to tell him."

"I'm never going home," I said to Hickey. His eyes were popping out of his head. He wasn't used to whiskey. Someone had put a tumbler of it in his hand. Everyone was drinking to try to get over the shock. Even Jack Holland took a glass of port wine. The room was thick with cigarette smoke, and I wanted to go out of it, to go out and find Mama, even to go out and find her dead body. It was all too unreal in there and my head was swimming. The ashtrays were overflowing and the room was hot and smoky. Mr. Brennan came over to talk to me. He was crying behind his thick lenses. He said my mother was a lady, a true lady, and that everyone loved her.

"Bring me to her," I asked. I was no longer wild. My strength had been drained from me.

"We're waiting, Caithleen. We're waiting for news from the barracks. I'll go up there now and see if anything's happened. They're searching the river." He put out his hands, humbly, in a gesture that seemed to say, "There's nothing any of us can do now."

"You're staying with us," he said as he lifted wild pieces of hair out of my eyes and smoothed them back gently.

"Thank you," I said, and he went off to the barracks, which was a hundred yards up the road. Mr. Gentleman went with him.

"That bloody boat was rotten. I always said it," Hickey said, getting angry with the whole world for not having listened to him.

"Can you come outside, Caithleen? It's confidential," Jack Holland said as he leaned over the back of my chair. I got up slowly, and though I cannot remember it, I must have walked across the room to the white door. Most of the paint had been scraped off it. He held it while I went out to the hall. He led me into the back of the hall, where a candle guttered in a saucer. His face was only a shadow.

He whispered, "So help me God, I couldn't do it."

"Do what, Jack?" I asked. I didn't care. I thought I might get sick or suffocate. The pills and the brandy had gone to my head.

"Give her the money. Jesus, my hands are tied. The old woman owns everything." The old woman was his mother. She sat on a rocking chair beside the fire, and Jack had to feed her bread and milk because her hands were crippled with rheumatism.

"God, I'd have done anything for your mama; you know that," and I said that I did.

Upstairs in a bedroom two greyhounds moaned. It was the moan of death. Suddenly I knew that I had to accept the fact that my mother was dead. And I cried as I have never cried at any other time in my life. Jack cried with me and wiped his nose on the sleeve of his coat.

Then the hall door was pushed and Mr. Brennan came in.

"No news, Caithleen, no news, love. Come on home to bed," he said, and he called Martha and Baba out of the room.

"We'll try later," he said to Mr. Gentleman. It was a clear, starry night as we walked across the road to the car. We were home in a few minutes, and Mr. Brennan made me drink hot whiskey and gave me a yellow capsule. Martha helped me take off my clothes, and when I knelt down to say one prayer, I said, "Oh God, please bring Mama back to life." I said it many times, but I knew that it was hopeless.

I slept with Baba, in one of her nightgowns. Her bed was softer than the one at home. When I turned on my left side she turned, too. She put her arm around my stomach and held my hand.

"You're my best friend," she said in the darkness. And then after a minute she whispered, "Are you asleep?"

"No."

"Are you afraid?"

"Afraid of what?"

"That she'll appear," and when she said it I started to shiver. What is it about death that we cannot bear to have someone who is dead come back to us? I wanted Mama more than anything in the world, and yet if the door had opened and she had entered, I would have screamed for Martha and Mr. Brennan. We heard a noise downstairs, a thud, and we both hid completely under the covers and she said it was death knocks. "Get Declan," I said, under the sheet and the blankets.

"No, you go over for him." But neither of us dared to open the door and go out on the landing. My mother's ghost was waiting for us at the top of the stairs, in a white nightgown.

The pillow slip under me and the white counterpane were wet when I woke up. Molly woke me with a cup of tea and toast. She helped me sit up in the bed and fetched my cardigan off the back of a chair. Molly was only two years older than me, and yet she fussed over me as if she were my mother.

"Are you sick, love?" she asked. I said that I was hot, and she went off to call Mr. Brennan.

"Sir, come here for a second. I want you. I think she has a fever," and he came and put his hand on my forehead and told Molly to phone the doctor.

They gave me pills all that day, and Martha sat in the room and painted her nails and polished them with a little buffer. It was raining, so I couldn't see out the window because it got all fogged up, but Martha said it was a terrible day. The phone rang sometime after lunch and Martha kept saying, "Yes, I'll tell her" and "Too bad" and "Well, I suppose that's that," and then she came up and told me that they had dragged the great Shannon lake but they hadn't found them; she didn't say that they had given up, but I knew they had, and I knew that Mama would never have a grave for me to put flowers on. Somehow she was more dead then than anyone I had ever heard of. I cried again, and Martha gave me a sip of wine from her glass and she made me lie back while she read me a story from a magazine. 'Twas a sad story, so I cried worse. It was the last day of childhood.

6 That summer passed quickly. I stayed in Baba's house and went home in the daytime to get the dinner and wash up. Some days I made the beds. Hickey had moved upstairs since Mama's death (we always referred to it as death, not drowning), and the rooms were very untidy. They were sad, too, with the smell of dust and old socks and a staleness that comes from never opening the windows.

They were over in the fields most days, cutting the corn and binding it into stooks, and I used to go over with bottles of tea at four o'clock. My father ate very little that summer, and every time he drank tea he swallowed two aspirins with it. He was quiet and his eyelids were red and swollen. When they came in, Hickey milked the cows and my father drank more tea, took off his shoes in the kitchen, and went off to bed. I think he must have cried in bed, because it was too bright to sleep, and anyhow, Hickey made a lot of noise downstairs banging milk cans about and no one could sleep through it.

One day I was clearing out Mama's drawers and putting her good clothes in a box to send to her sister, when he came upstairs. I hadn't spoken to him very much since he came home from the hospital. I preferred not to.

"There's a little matter you ought to know," he said. He had just come in from the village and he was loosening the knot of his tie. I thought for one awful minute that he was drunk, because he looked so disheveled.

"The place has to go," he said flatly.

"Go where?" I asked.

He shoved his hat back on his head and began to scratch his forehead. He hesitated. "There was a bit of debt, and with one thing and another it got bigger. I hadn't such luck with the horses. Oh well, we didn't make ends meet."

"And who's buying it?" I remembered Jack Holland's warning to me about our place being endangered.

"What?" my father asked. He heard me quite well but this was a trick of his when he didn't want to answer. He was narrowing his eyes now, giving that shrewd look to make it seem that he was an astute man. I asked again. I wasn't afraid of him when he was sober.

"The bank practically owns it," he said at last.

"And who'll run it?" I couldn't believe that someone else other than Hickey would plow and milk and clip the hedge in the summer evenings.

"Jack Holland will probably buy it."

"Jack Holland!" I was appalled. The rogue. He would get it cheaply. All his palaver about kings and queens and his promising me a new fountain pencil before I went away to the convent. And to think that he got seven Masses said for Mama. He sent money to a special order of priests in Dublin for a bouquet of Masses.

"Where will you go?" I asked. I was thinking of the awful luck if he followed me to the town where the convent was.

"Well, I'm all right. I have a little bit of land for myself and I'll be able to live in the gate lodge." The way he spoke, anyone would think he had done a smart bit of manipulation in securing the old, disused gate lodge behind the rhododendron bushes. It was damp, and the front door and two small windows were choked with briars.

"And Hickey?"

"He'll have to go, I'm afraid. There's no more work for him." It was impossible. Hickey had been with us twenty years, he was there before I was born. He was too fat to go anywhere else and I told my father this. But he shook his head. He didn't like Hickey, and he was ashamed of all that had happened.

"What are you doing?" he asked, looking down at the little neat piles of clothes that were spread around the floor.

"Poor Mama, the poor aul creature," he said, and he went over to the window and cried.

I didn't want a scene, so I said, as if he weren't crying, "I'll have to get a uniform before going away and shoes and six pairs of black stockings."

"And how much will that be?" he asked, turning around. There were tears on his cheeks and he snuffled a bit.

"I don't know. Ten or fifteen pounds." He took out notes from his pocket and gave me three fivers. The bank must have given him some money.

"I never deprived you of anything, or your mother, either. Now did I?"

"No."

"Ye had only to mention a thing and ye got it." I said that was true and went downstairs immediately to fry him a rasher and make a cup of tea. I called him when it was ready and he came down in his old clothes. He wasn't going out anymore; the temptation to drink was over for this time.

"Will you write to me, when you go away?" he asked, dipping a biscuit into the hot tea. He had taken his teeth out and could only eat a softened biscuit.

"I will." I was standing with my back to the range.

"Don't forget your poor father," he said. He put out his arm and tried to draw me over onto his knee, but I pretended not to know what he was doing and ran off to the yard to call Hickey for his tea. He was gone upstairs to bed when I came back, and Hickey and I fried some cold cabbage with the rashers and it was delicious. We ate it with mustard. Hickey was a great one for making mustard. Five of the six egg cups had hardened mustard in them. He blended a fresh lot each day in a clean egg cup.

Baba was having a birthday party that night, so I asked Hickey for a bottle of cream so that she would have it with the jelly we had made. He skimmed the two buckets of milk and with his fingers tipped the cream into a can. He wasn't supposed to. Our milk at the creamery next day would have a very low fat content.

"Goodbye, Hickey."

"Goodbye, sweetheart." Bull's-Eye came with me over across the fields. It was a shortcut to Baba's house. Passing the lower cornfield, I stood for a minute to admire it. It was high and ripe and golden, and here and there where it had lodged the jackdaws were feeding. It had a sunlight of its own. The sun was shining from it and the ears stirred in the light sun-gold wind. I sat down on the ditch for a minute. I remembered the day Hickey plowed that field; we went over with tea and several thick hunks of buttered bread. And later the little green threads came shooting through the red-brown earth and the jackdaws came. Mama loaned one of her beaded hats to put on the scarecrow. I could see her walking over the field with the hat self-consciously laid on her head. Sometimes a sharp and sudden memory of her came to me, and to ease the pain I cried. Bull's-Eye sat on his tail and looked at me while I cried. Then, when I stood up, he came another few yards with me and stopped. He was loyal to Dada, he went back home.

There were five bicycles inside the gate of Baba's house, and the curtains in the front room were drawn. The radio was playing— ". . . where women are women, and French perfume that rocks the room"—and there was a lot of laughing and talking besides. I knew she wouldn't hear me if I knocked, so I went around and tapped at the side window. It was a french window that opened out onto the path. Baba opened it. She was smoking madly, and was dressed in a new blue dress with gorgeous puff sleeves.

"Jesus, I thought you were some yahoo coming for my aul fella," she said suddenly. She had been nice to me for several weeks since Mama died, but when there were other girls around she always made little of me. Declan danced past the window with Gertie Tuohey in his arms. Her black ringlets, like fat sausages, fell down onto her shoulders. Declan had a paper hat on the side of his head, and he winked at me.

"Jesus, we're having a whale of a time. I'm delighted you're not here. Go home to hell and make stirabout," Baba said.

I thought for a minute that she was joking, so I said, very gently, "I brought the cream."

"Gimme," she said, stretching her arm for it. She was wearing a silver bracelet of Martha's. Her arm was grown-up and had a bloom of little golden hairs on it.

"Be off, trash," she said, and she shut the window and drew the white bawneen curtain across. Inside, I could hear her splitting with laughter.

I didn't go around and let myself in the back door because I knew that Martha was gone with her husband to see *For Whom the Bell Tolls* in Limerick, and that Baba would have me helping Molly cut sandwiches and making tea all night, so I came back home for an hour.

Hickey was carving his name with a nail on the chicken house. Dada had told him, so he was leaving traces of himself behind to be remembered by.

"Where will you go, Hickey?"

"I'll go to England. I was going anyhow soon as you went." Even though he sounded cheerful he looked sad.

"Are you lonesome?"

"Lonesome for what? Not at all. I'll have twenty quid a week and a mott in Birmingham"—but he was lonesome all right.

"What brought you back?" he asked. I told him.

"She's a ringing divil, that one," he said, and I was delighted.

He said that he would clip the hedge, and he thanked God that it would be his last time. He made quick snips with the shears and I collected the pieces and put them into a wheelbarrow. He clipped it right down to the brown twigs and it looked very bare and cold. The wind would come through it now. Where it was very thick in one corner he made a figure of an armchair and I sat in it to see if I would fall through it. I didn't. Then we emptied the wheelbarrow in the old cellar, and we shut the hens in. Bull's-Eye had already gone to bed in the turf house. It was unnatural to see Bull's-Eye and Dada going to bed on these lovely, still, golden evenings. Dada's blind was drawn so I didn't go up to see him, though I knew he would have liked a cup of tea. I hated going into his room when he was in bed. I could see Mama on the pillow beside him. Reluctant and frightened as if something terrible were being done to her. She used to sleep with me as often as she could and only went across to his room when he made her. He wore no pajamas in bed, and I was ashamed even to think of it.

The old white beehive was still there, in the corner of the kitchen garden. Two of the legs had come off so that it sagged a little to one side.

"What'll you do with the beehive?" I asked Hickey. A few years before that he had decided to keep bees. He thought he would get very rich by selling the honey to all the local people, and he made the hive himself in the evenings, after work. Then he got a swarm of heather honey bees out in the mountain, and he was very excited about all the money he was going to make. But like everything else, it failed. The bees stung him, and he roared and yelled in the kitchen garden and made Mama get him a hot poultice. For some reason or another he never got any honey, and he got rid of the bees by smothering them.

"What'll you do with it?" I asked again.

"Let it rot," he said. His voice was somewhat weary, and I think he sighed, because he knew what failures we all were. The place was gone, Mama was gone; the flag was white with hen dirt, and there were thistles and ragwort covering every inch of the front lawn.

"I'll convey you," said Hickey, and he linked me as we walked down the field in the dusk. It was chilly and the cows were lying under the trees with their eyes wide open, staring at us. Dogs barked in the distance. The grass was quiet, and two bats flew in front of us.

"Don't grow up to be a snotty-nose now, when you go to that convent," he said.

"I'm afraid of Baba; she makes so little of me, Hickey."

" 'Tis a kick in the backside she wants, the little upstart. I'd give her something to make her afraid." But he didn't say what.

"I'll send you an odd bob from England," he said, to cheer me up. He left me at Baba's gate and went down to the Greyhound Hotel to have a few drinks. It was after hours but he preferred drinking then.

Upstairs in Baba's room I took out the three five-pound notes that I had hidden inside my vest since earlier in the evening. They were warm and I hid them under the pillow. I decided to go to Limerick next day to buy my school uniform. When Baba came up she tried to waken me. She plucked at my eyelashes and tickled my face with the wet stem of a snapdragon. I had brought over a bunch from home and put them in a vase beside the bed.

If I wakened she might find out that I was going to Limerick and she would come with me and spoil my day.

"Declan." She called her brother from the bathroom.

"Isn't she like a pig asleep?" she said, and drew back the covers so that he could see the full length of my body. I felt chilly when she did that and drew my feet up under my nightgown.

"She snores like a bloody sow," she said, and I almost sat up and called her a liar. Next thing, the two of them were boxing and Declan knocked her onto the floor while she yelled for Molly.

"Say that again. Say that again," he said, holding one of my shoes over her. I could see them by peering through my eyelashes. Declan was my friend that night.

After she got into bed, Baba kept saying, "She's coming. She's appearing. She's coming back to tell you to give me all her jewelry." But no matter what she said, I stayed perfectly still and kept my eyes closed.

The moon shone in on us and there was a streak of silver light across the carpeted floor. I slept badly, and when the grandfather clock struck seven I got out of bed and carried my clothes off to the bathroom. I forgot my money and I had to go back for it. Her black hair was spread out on the pillow and she stirred a little when I was coming away. "Cait, Cait," she called me, but I didn't answer her. She must have gone to sleep, because I came down to the kitchen and dressed there in front of the Aga cooker. I was delighted to be going off for the whole day, away from everybody.

7

I was standing outside the gate waiting for the bus when Mr. Gentleman's car passed by and went up the street. It stopped outside the garage on the hill for petrol; then he turned around and came back.

"Are you going somewhere, Caithleen?" he asked, winding down the window. I said that I was going to Limerick and he said to sit in. So I sat on the black leather seat beside him and my heart fluttered. The moment I heard him speak and the moment I looked at his eyes, my heart always fluttered. His eyes were tired or sad or something. He smoked little cigars and threw the butts out the window.

"Are they horrible?" I asked. I had to say something.

"Here, try one," he said, and he took the cigar out of his mouth and handed it to me. I was thinking of his mouth, of the shape of it, and the taste of his tongue, while I had one short, self-conscious puff. I began to cough at once. I said it was worse than horrible, and he laughed. He drove very fast.

We parked the car down a side street, and I thanked him and went off. He was locking the door. I hated leaving him. There was something about him that made me want to be with him. He called me back. "What about lunch, Caithleen?" I intended having tea and cream buns but I didn't tell him that.

"Would you like to meet me?"

I said that I would. His eyes were still sad, but I was singing as I came away.

"You won't forget, will you?"

"No, Mr. Gentleman, I won't forget." I hurried off to the shops.

I went into the biggest shop on the main street. Mama always shopped there. I asked a woman who was down on her knees scrubbing the floor where I'd go for a gym frock.

"Fourth floor, love. Take the lift." She had no teeth when she smiled. I gave her a shilling. I had saved three shillings on my bus fare. I could afford to be extravagant.

I got into the lift. A small boy with a buttoned tunic operated it. "I want a gym frock," I said. He ignored me.

I sat on a stool in the corner, because it was my first time in a lift and I felt dizzy. We passed three floors with a click at each floor; then it clicked, stopped, and he let me out. The gym-frock counter was directly opposite and I went across.

Afterward I weighed myself in the cloakroom and learned that I was seven pounds too light. There was a chart printed on the side of the scales that gave the correct weight for each person's height.

I went down the stairs. The carpet was worn but it was soft under the feet. In the basement I bought presents for everybody. A scarf for Dada, a penknife for Hickey, a boat-shaped bottle of perfume for Baba, and pink hand cream for Martha. Then I came out onto the street and looked in a jewelry window. I saw a lot of watches that I liked. I went into a big church at the corner, to have three wishes. We were told that we had three wishes whenever we went into a new church. The holy water wasn't in a font like at home, but there was a drop at the end of a narrow tap, and I put my finger under it and blessed myself. I wished that Mama was in heaven, that my father would never drink again, and that Mr. Gentleman would not forget to come at one o'clock.

I came to the hotel a half hour before the time so that I wouldn't miss him, and I was afraid to go inside to the hall in case a porter should tell me that I had no right to be there.

He had had a haircut, and as he came up the steps his face looked sharp and I could see the tops of his ears. Before that they were hidden under a soft fall of fine gray hair. He smiled at me. My heart fluttered once again, and I found it hard to speak.

"Men prefer to kiss young girls without lipstick, you know," he said. He was referring to the two thin lines of pink lipstick that I had put on. I bought a tube in Woolworth's and went round to the mirror counter and applied it in front of a mirror that showed all the pores on my face.

"I wasn't thinking of kissing. I never kiss anyone," I said.

"Never?" He was teasing me. I knew by the way he smiled.

"No. Nobody. Only Hickey."

"Nobody else?" I shook my head, and he caught my elbow as we went into the dining room. My arms were thin and white and I was ashamed of them.

It was my first time in a city hotel. I decided to have the cheapest thing on the menu.

"I'll have Irish stew," I said.

"No, you will not," he replied. He was cross, but it wasn't real crossness, only pretending. He ordered little chickens for both of us. Another waiter brought a tall, slender, dark-green bottle of wine. There was a bowl of mixed flowers on the table between us, but they had no smell.

He poured some wine into his own glass, sipped it, and smiled. Then he poured some into mine. I had my confirmation pledge, but I was ashamed to tell him. He was smiling at me all the time. It was a sad smile and I liked it.

"Tell me about your day."

"I bought my school uniform and I walked around. That's all."

The wine was bitter. I would have rather'd lemonade. I had ice cream afterward, and Mr. Gentleman had a white cheese with green threads of mold in it. It smelled like Hickey's socks, not the new socks I bought him, but the old ones under his mattress.

"That was lovely," I said, pushing my plate over to the edge of the table, where it would be handy for the waiter to get it.

"It was," he agreed. I didn't know whether Mr. Gentleman was shy, or whether it was that he was just too lazy to talk. Or bored. He was no good for small talk.

"We must have another lunch someday," he said.

"I'm going away next week," I replied.

"Going away to America? Too bad we'll never meet one another again." I think he thought he was being very funny. He drank some more wine, and his eyes got very large and very, very wistful. They met mine for as long as I wanted.

"So you tell me that you have never kissed anyone?" he said. He had a way of looking at me that made me feel innocent. He was staring now. Sometimes directly into my pupils, other times his eyes would roam all over my face and settle for a minute on my neck. My neck. My neck was snow-white and I was wearing a silk dress with a curved neckline. It was an ice-blue dress with blossoms on it. Sometimes I thought they were tiny apple blossoms, and then again I thought the pattern was one of snow falling; but either way it was a nice dress, and the skirt was composed of millions of little pieces that flowed when I walked.

"The next time we have lunch, don't wear lipstick," he said. "I prefer you without it."

The coffee was bitter. I used four lumps of sugar. We came out and went to the pictures. He bought me a box of chocolates with a ribbon on it.

I cried halfway through the picture because there was a sad bit about a boy having to leave a girl in order to go off to war. He laughed when he saw me crying and whispered that we should go out. He took my hand as we went up the dark passage, and out in the vestibule he wiped my eyes and told me to smile.

We drove home while it was still bright. The hills in the distance were blue and the trees in the folds of the hills were a dusty lilac. Farmers were saving hay in fields along the roadside and children were sitting on haycocks eating apples and throwing cores over the ditch. The smell of hay came through the window, half spice, half perfume.

A woman wearing Wellingtons was driving cows home to be milked. We had to slow down to let them in a side gate, and I caught him looking at me. We smiled at each other, and his hand came off the steering wheel and rested on the lap of my ice-blue dress. My hand was waiting for it. We locked our fingers, and for the rest of the journey we drove like that, except going around sharp bends. His hand was small and white and very smooth. There were no hairs on it.

"You're the sweetest thing that ever happened to me," he said. It was all he said and it was only a whisper. Afterward, lying in bed in the convent, I used to wonder whether he said it or whether I had imagined it.

He squeezed my hand before I got out of the car. I thanked him and reached into the back seat for my packages. He sighed, as if he were going to say something, but Baba ran out to the car and he slipped away from me.

My soul was alive; enchantment; something I had never known before. It was the happiest day of my whole life.

"Goodbye, Mr. Gentleman," I said through the window. There was an odd expression in his smile, which seemed to be saying, "Don't go." But he did go, my new god, with a face carved out of pale marble and eyes that made me sad for every woman who hadn't known him.

"What'n the hell are you mooning about?" Baba asked, and I went into the house laughing.

"I bought you a present," I said, and in my mind I kept singing it, "You're the sweetest thing that ever happened to me." It was like having a precious stone in my pocket, and I had only to say the words in order to feel it, blue, precious, enchanting . . . my deathless, deathless song.

8 The last view I had of home was in the rain. We drove past the gate in Mr. Brennan's car, and there was a white horse galloping over the front field.

"Goodbye, home," I said, wiping the steam from the inside of the window so that I could wave and have a last look at the rusty iron gate and the avenue of dripping trees.

My handkerchief was wet from crying. I had cried all morning. I cried saying goodbye to Hickey and Molly and Maisie at the hotel; and Baba cried, too. Baba and I weren't speaking.

Martha sat between us, and we each looked out the window at our own side, but there wasn't much more to see—the wind-bent hedges, the melancholy mountains, and wet hens huddled in farm-yards.

My father sat in front talking to Mr. Brennan.

"This is a good car now. How many miles do you get to the gallon?" my father asked. He called Mr. Brennan "Doc" and lit two cigarettes at a time. He gave one to Mr. Brennan. "Here, Doc." Mr. Brennan mumbled his thanks. He never addressed my father by name.

Martha lit one of her own, out of spite. My father neglected her. He had no interest in women.

I began to worry if I had forgotten anything, and went over the contents of my case. I wondered had I put in the small things, and if there were name tapes on all my underwear. Baba had printed name tapes from Dublin, but I wrote my name with marking ink on strips of white tape, and stitched the tape onto my clothes. I hate stitching, so Molly did most of it for me, and I gave her two of Mama's dresses in return. The cake and the two jars of honey Mrs. Tuohey gave me were in a travel bag, and I had Jack Holland's fountain pencil clipped to the front of my gym frock. I had the doll's tea set in the travel bag, too. All the little cups and saucers wrapped in separate pieces of tissue paper, and the teapot and sugar bowl were in a nest of chaff. I took the chaff out of the bottom row of Mr. Gentleman's box of chocolates. There were only a few sweets in the bottom row, all the rest was chaff. I thought of writing to the makers to complain, because there was a slip of paper which said that people should write in if they weren't satisfied, but in the end I didn't bother.

The doll's tea service was the only thing I brought from home. I always liked it. I used to sit and look at it in the china cabinet, just sit there admiring it in the sunlight. It was pale-blue china and it looked very tender and breakable. I mean, even more breakable than ordinary china. Mama gave it to me the Christmas I discovered there was no Santa Claus. At least, the Christmas Baba told me that I was a bloody fool to believe in Santa Claus, when every halfwit knew that it was your damn mother or father dressed up. When my mother gave me the tea set I asked if I might put it in the china cabinet. I was very grown-up that way; I never played with toys, or broke them, or dismantled them, like other children. I had five dolls, each without a scratch. Mama often put a lump of sugar into one of the little cups as a surprise for me; and every time I lost a tooth I put it in one of these cups at night, and in the morning the tooth was gone and there was a sixpence in its place. Mama said that the fairies left the money when they were dancing down in the room at night.

Remembering these little things made me cry, and my father looked back and said, "You'd think you were going to America. Sure we'll visit you every few Sundays, won't we, Doc?" I could hardly tell him that I wasn't crying for him. I could hardly say, "I don't care if you never visit me," or "I'll be happier in the convent than at home in the gate lodge, coaxing a fire with damp sticks, and worrying about the whiff of whiskey on your breath." But I said nothing. I was trying to control my tears, and I prayed that I would last the journey without having to root in the case for a clean handkerchief. The case was under Martha's feet.

"Now you two *must* make it up," Martha said. We looked at one another, and Baba drooped her eyelids until the lashes were fluttering on her cheeks. They were long lashes, like daisy petals dyed coal black. "Be off, trash," she said, between her teeth, and she turned away again.

I felt like a crow in my navy serge gym frock and my navy knitted jumper. A woman in the village who owned a knitting machine made it for me as a present. I got a lot of presents after Mama's death. People pitying me, I suppose. My legs were thin and sad in the black cotton stockings, and they were itchy, too, because I had been used to wearing no stockings all the summer. I was thin and much too tall for my fourteen years.

"Jesus, they'll say you have worms," Baba said, the night I fitted on my uniform. She looked pretty in hers, plump and round. Her curly hair was cut short, her face brown from the sun, and she looked like an autumn nut, brown and smooth.

"What is it, anyhow, between you two?" Martha asked. Neither of us spoke.

"You'll just have to talk when you get there. There won't be anyone else to talk to," she said. She was right. In the convent we would only have each other.

"We will never speak again, never," I kept repeating under my breath. Baba had broken my heart, destroyed my life. This was how she had done it.

The night I came home from Limerick, I was gay and happy, thinking of my day with Mr. Gentleman, smiling to myself as I sat on the bed with my feet curled in under the red satin eiderdown.

"You're very happy in yourself," Baba said, as she undressed and laid her clothes on the back of the wicker chair. "Hurry up and get into bed, this candle is nearly burnt out."

She was jealous of my happiness.

"I want to sit here all night and dream." I spoke slowly and, I thought, dramatically.

"Jesus, you're nuts. What's happened to you anyhow?"

"Love," I said, throwing out my arms in a hopeless, lost gesture.

"Who's the fool?"

"You wouldn't know."

"Declan?"

"Nonsense," I replied, as if Declan were some little nonentity whom I couldn't even tolerate.

"Hickey?"

"No," I said. I was enjoying myself.

"Tell me."

"I can't."

"Tell me," she said, tucking the top of her pajamas into the trousers. "Tell me, or I'll tickle it out of you," and she began to tickle me under the arms.

"I will. I will. I will." I'd do anything not to be tickled. So when I got back my breath I told her.

"No sir, not on your bloody life. It's a lie."

"It's not a lie. He gave me chocolates, and took me to the pictures. He told me that I was the sweetest thing that ever happened to him. He said the color of my hair was wonderful, and my eyes were like real pearls and my skin like a peach in the sunlight." He had said none of these things of course, but once I started telling lies, I couldn't stop.

"Go on, tell me more," she said. Her mouth was half open with wonder and astonishment and envy.

"You won't tell anyone," I said, because I was going to tell her the bit about holding my hand. And then all of a sudden I could see that look coming into her eyes. It was a green look, the eyes narrowed like a cat's. I've seen it since a thousand times, in trains, in wedding photographs, and I always say to myself, "Some poor fool is going to be put through it," so once again I said, "You won't tell anyone, Baba?"

"No"—pause—"only—*Mrs.* Gentleman."

"Don't tell a single solitary person," I pleaded.

"No—only Mrs. Gentleman and Mammy and Daddy and your aul fella."

"I was only joking," I lied. "I never met him. I was only pulling your leg. He just gave me a seat from Limerick. That's all."

"Really!" she said, trying to raise one eyebrow. "Well," she added, blowing out the candle, "Mammy, Daddy, and I are having dinner with the Gentlemans tomorrow night and I'll mention it to him."

I undressed in the dark, and when I got into bed she had all the blankets pulled over to her side.

"No, don't, don't tell," I begged, but she was asleep while I was still pleading with her.

Next evening they did have dinner with the Gentlemans, and drove home just before midnight. I was behind the hall door, waiting.

"Not in bed yet, Caithleen?" Mr. Brennan said to me as he looked in the address book beside the telephone, to see if there were any night calls. Martha came in with a big bunch of gladioli in her arms, and her eyes were large and smiling.

"No, Mr. Brennan," I said. I curled my finger and beckoned Baba to follow me into the study.

"Baba, I have a present for you, one of Mama's rings . . . the one you like best. The black one." I gave it to her and she put it on in the dark. There was a diamond in the center of it, and you could see it sparkle in the faint light that wandered in from the hall lamp.

"You didn't tell," I said.

"Oh, tell? Oh no, I didn't tell. Old Mrs. Gentleman would be over here with a hatchet if I told. But J.W." (that was Mr. Gentleman, she meant) "and I were having a stroll in the garden and I mentioned you and he said, 'Oh, that little one, she suffers greatly from her imagination.'"

"Impossible," I said aloud.

"Oh yes. He was linking me around, showing me the various flowers, offering me a bunch of grapes, asking me what I thought of this and that, imploring me to play chess with him, and I mentioned your name and he said, 'Oh, let's not discuss her,' so I dropped the subject. We were out there a hell of a long time; old Ma Gentleman stuck her head out the window finally and said, 'You two,' so we had to come in."

That finished it. I would never be able to look him in the face again. And to think that I had given her Mama's best ring.

Next morning Baba went to confession, and at eleven o'clock the phone rang.

Molly came upstairs for me. I was filling in my diary—doleful pieces about Mr. Gentleman.

"Mr. Gentleman wants you on the phone," she said, and my heart started to race.

To go down and talk to him was all I desired. But now he was

ringing to tell me how vulgar and disgusting I had been, how falsely
I had redescribed our day together, and I could not endure it.

"Tell him I'm out and that I'll ring him," I said to Molly. I had
some idea that I would write him a beautiful letter, a magnificent
letter, most of which I'd copy out of *Wuthering Heights*. I'd wait
around, and dart out from behind a tree to hand it to him as he got
out to open the gate.

Molly went down and said I was gone to confession and that she'd
tell me soon as I got in. They talked for another minute. I was demented, wondering what he'd have to say to Molly, and then she put
down the phone.

"Well?" I was hanging over the banister, deathly white, with
ink shadows under my eyes. I hadn't slept for two nights.

"He's terrible sorry but he's gone to Paris on a trip," she said,
rolling up her sleeves and showing her fat, pink, strong arms to the
daylight.

"To Paris?" I thought of girls and sin at once. How dare he?

"Yeah, he had to go sudden, some relative of his is dying," she
said, and she began to attack the hall floor with a scrubbing brush.

I saw no more of Mr. Gentleman, because we left for the convent
three days later.

It took me only a second to recall all of this in the motorcar, and
then I returned to my wet handkerchief and to Baba offering me a
conversation lozenge.

It had *Let us be friends* written on it, but I was too bitter to smile.

We got into the convent town at dusk; just outside it there was a
lake, a dark sheet of water, and when we drove past it, a bleak wind
blew in through the half-open window. Then we drove through a
narrow street that had electric lights every fifty yards or so along the
pavement and there were poplar trees in between the green metal
lamp posts. The dark sheet of water and the sad poplar trees and the
strange dogs outside the strange shops made me indescribably sad.

"Nice place," my father said, and snuffled. Nice place! A lot he
knew about it. How could he think it was a nice place by just looking
out the window?

"What about a drink, Bob?" he asked; and Martha, who had been dozing in the back seat, brightened up and said, "Yes, let's give the children some lemonade."

We stopped on the main street and went into a hotel. My knees were stiff. There was faded red Turkish carpet in the front hall and on the stairs that rose out of the hall. To the right was a dining room with lots of little tables laid with white cloths. There were two bottles of ketchup on each table. A red bottle and a brown bottle. We went into a room marked LOUNGE.

"Well, Bob, what will it be?" my father asked. I was trembling in case he should take anything strong himself.

"Whiskey," said Mr. Brennan, taking off his glasses. They were mizzled with rain, and he wiped them with a clean white hand-kerchief.

"And you, mam?" my father asked Martha. She hated being called "mam." It was aging.

"Gin," she said in an ungracious whisper. She hoped her husband was not listening, but I saw him grind his teeth as he went over to look at a faded hunting picture on the wall.

"I'll have a lemonade, I suppose," my father said, sighing. He was looking at me. He wanted me to acknowledge him, to give him a glance that told him he was brave and strong and good. But I looked the other way, preoccupied with my own miseries. In my mind I could see Mr. Gentleman's hand on the steering wheel, and his gaze as he turned from the windshield to look at me when the car slowed down for the cows in the gateway.

Baba had grapefruit. To be different, I thought resentfully. We didn't sit down, because we were in a hurry. We had to report at the convent before seven. There was a nice turf fire in the big red-brick fireplace and I hated leaving the hotel. My father paid for the drinks and we left.

The convent was a gray stone building with hundreds of small square curtainless windows, like so many eyes spying out on the wet sinful town. There were green railings around it and high green gates that led to a dark cypress avenue. My father got out of the car to open the gates, and gave the door a godawful bang. Mr. Brennan winced, and I was ashamed that my father didn't know better.

We parked the car under a tree and got out. We went down a flight of stone steps and crossed a concrete yard toward an open door. In the hallway a nun came forward to meet us. She wore a black, loose-fitting habit and a black veil over her head. Framing her face, and covering her forehead, her ears, and her chest, was a stiff white thing which they call a wimple. It almost covered her eyebrows, but you could just barely see the tips of them. They were black and they met in the middle over the bridge of her red nose. Her face was shiny.

My father took off his hat and told her who we were. Mr. Brennan followed with the cases.

"You're welcome," she said to Baba and me. Her hand was cold.

"Well, Baba, try to behave yourself," Mr. Brennan said doubtfully to Baba. Martha kissed me and put two coins into my hand. I said "Oh no," but as I was saying it, my fingers closed over them gratefully. Reluctantly I kissed my father, and I clung for a second to Mr. Brennan and tried to thank him, but I was too embarrassed.

The nun smiled all through her farewells. She had been watching others since early morning.

"They will settle down," she said. Her voice was determined though not harsh; but when she said, "They will settle down," she seemed to be saying, "They must settle down."

Our parents left. I thought of them going off to have tea and mixed grill in the warm hotel, and I could taste the hot pepper tang of Yorkshire relish.

"Well now," said the nun, taking a man's silver watch out of her pocket. "First your tea. Follow me," and we followed her down a long hallway. It had red tiles on the floor and there were shiny white tiles halfway up the walls. On each tiled window ledge there was a castor-oil plant, and at the bottom of the hall there was a row of oak presses. It was like a hospital, but it smelled of wax polish instead of anesthetics. It was scrupulously and frighteningly clean. Dirt can be consoling and friendly in a strange place, I thought.

We hung our coats in the cloakroom, and she helped us find a compartment in the press where our names were already written and where we were to store caps, gloves, shoes, boot polish, prayer books, and small things like that. The press was like a honeycomb, and not all the compartments were filled yet.

We followed her across another concrete yard to the refectory. She walked busily, and the thick black rosary beads hanging from her waist swung outward as she walked. We went into a big room with a high ceiling and long wooden tables stretching lengthwise. There were benches at either side of the tables.

The big girls, or the "senior" girls, sat at one table and they were talking furiously. Talking about the holidays and the times they had. I suppose a lot of them were inventing things that never happened, just to make themselves important. Most of them had their hair freshly washed, and one or two were very pretty. I picked out the pretty ones at once. At the junior table the new girls were strangers to one another. They looked lost and mopey, and cried quietly to themselves.

We were put sitting opposite one another, and Baba smiled across at me, but we still hadn't spoken. A little nun poured us two cups of tea from a big white enamel teapot. She was so small I thought she'd drop the teapot. She wore a white muslin apron over her black habit. The apron meant that she was a lay nun. The lay nuns did the cooking and cleaning and scrubbing, and they were lay nuns because they had no money or no education when they entered the convent. The other nuns were called choir nuns. I didn't know that then, but one of the senior girls explained it to me. Her name was Cynthia and she taught me a lot of things.

The bread was already buttered and a dopey girl next to me kept passing me a plate of dull gray bread.

"It looks awful," I said, and shook my head. I had cake in my case and knew that I would eat some later on. She passed me the plate twice more and Baba sniggered. After tea we trooped up to the convent chapel to say the Rosary aloud.

It was a pretty chapel and there were pale pink roses on the altar. The nuns sang during Benediction. One nun sang like a lark. Her voice was different from all the others, singing, "Mother, Mother, I am coming," and I cried for my own mother. I thought of the day when we sat in the kitchen and saw the lark take the specks of sheep's wool off the barbed wire and carry it off to build her nest.

"Will you be a nun when you're big?" Mama asked me. She would have liked me to be a nun, it was better than marrying. Anything was, she thought.

That first evening in the chapel was strange and emotional. The incense floated down the nave, followed by the articulate voice of the priest, who knelt before the altar in a gold-crusted cloak.

We knelt in the back of the chapel on wooden benches, and there were wooden rails separating us from where the nuns knelt. The nuns were one in front of the other in little oak compartments that were fixed to the walls on either side. They all looked alike from the back except the postulants, who wore lace bonnets and whose hair showed through the lace.

We all filed out of the chapel, making as much noise as twenty horses galloping over a stony road. Some girls had studs in their shoes and you could hear the studs scratching the tile floor of the chapel porch. We went down to the recreation hall, where Sister Margaret was sitting on a rostrum, waiting to speak to us. She welcomed the new girls, rewelcomed the old ones, and gave a quick summary of the convent rules:

> *Silence in the dormitory, and at breakfast.*
> *Shoes to be taken off before going into the dormitory.*
> *No food to be kept in presses in the dormitory.*
> *To bed within twenty minutes after you go upstairs.*

"Now," she said, "will the girls who wish to have milk at night please put up their hands?" I had a bad chest, so I put up my hand and committed myself to a lukewarm cup of dusty milk every night; and committed my father to a bill for two pounds a year. Scholarships did not cater to bad chests.

We went to bed early.

Our dormitory was on the first floor. There was a lavatory on the landing outside it, and twenty or thirty girls were queueing there, hopping from one foot to another as if they couldn't wait. I took off my shoes and carried them into the dormitory. It was a long room with windows on either side, and a door at the far end. Over the door was a large crucifix, and there were holy pictures along the yellow distempered walls. There were two rows of iron beds down the length of the room. They were covered with white cotton counterpanes, and the iron was painted white as well. The beds were numbered and I found mine easily enough. Baba was six beds away from me. At least it was nice to know that she was near, in case we should ever speak. There were three radiators along the wall, but they were cold.

I sat down on the chair beside my bed, took off my garters, and peeled my stockings off slowly. The garters were too tight and they had made marks on my legs. I was looking at the red marks, worrying in case I'd have varicose veins before morning, and I didn't know that Sister Margaret was standing right behind me. She wore rubber-soled shoes and she had a way of stealing up on one. I jumped off the chair when she said, "Now, girls." I turned around to face her. Her eyes were cross and I could see a small cyst on one of her irises. She was that near to me.

"The new girls won't know this, but our convent has always been proud of its modesty. Our girls, above anything else, are good and wholesome and modest. One expression of modesty is the way a girl dresses and undresses. She should do so with decorum and modesty. In an open dormitory like this . . ." She paused, because someone had come in the bottom door and had bashed a ewer against the woodwork. Even my earlobes were blushing. She went on: "Upstairs the senior girls have separate cubicles; but, as I say, in an open dormitory like this, girls are requested to dress and undress under the shelter of their dressing gowns. Girls should face the foot of the bed doing this, as they might surprise each other if they face the side of the bed." She coughed and went off twiddling a bunch of keys in the air. She unlocked the oak door at the end of the room and went out.

The girl allotted to the bed next to mine raised her eyes to heaven. She had squint eyes and I didn't like her. Not because of the squint, but because she looked like someone who would have bad taste about everything. She was wearing a pretty, expensive dressing gown and rich fluffy slippers; but you felt that she bought them to show off, and not because they were pretty. I saw her put two bars of chocolate under her pillow.

Trying to undress under a dressing gown is a talent you must develop. Mine fell off six or seven times, but finally I managed to keep it on by stooping very low.

I was rooting in my travel bag when the lights went out. Small figures in nightgowns hurried up the carpeted passage and disappeared into the cold white beds.

I wanted to get the cake that was in the bottom of my bag. The tea service was on top, so I took it out piece by piece. Baba crept up to the foot of my bed, and for the first time we talked, or, rather, we whispered.

"Jesus, 'tis hell," she said. "I won't stick it for a week."

"Nor me. Are you hungry?"

"I'd eat a young child," she said. I was just getting my nail file out of my toilet bag, to cut a hunk of cake with, when the key was turned in the door at the end of the room. I covered the cake quickly with a towel and we stood there perfectly still, as Sister Margaret came toward us, holding her flashlight.

"What is the meaning of this?" she asked. She knew our names already and addressed us by our full names, not just Bridget (Baba's real name) and Caithleen, but Bridget Brennan and Caithleen Brady.

"We were lonely, Sister," I said.

"You are not alone in your loneliness. Loneliness is no excuse for disobedience." She was speaking in a penetrating whisper. The whole dormitory could hear her.

"Go back to your bed, Bridget Brennan," she said. Baba tripped off quietly. Sister Margaret shone the flashlight to and fro, until the beam caught the little tea service on the bed.

"What is this?" she asked, picking up one of the cups.

"A tea service, Sister. I brought it because my mother died." It was a stupid thing to say and I regretted it at once. I'm always saying stupid things, because I don't think before I say them.

"Sentimental childish conduct," she said. She lifted the outside layer of her black habit and shaped it into a basket. Then she put the tea service in there and carried it off.

I got in between the icy sheets and ate a piece of seed cake. The whole dormitory was crying. You could hear the sobbing and choking under the covers. Smothered crying.

The head of my bed backed onto the head of another girl's bed, and in the dark a hand came through the rungs and put a bun on my pillow. It was an iced bun and there was something on top of the icing. Possibly a cherry. I gave her a piece of cake and we shook hands. I wondered what she looked like, as I hadn't noticed her when the lights were on. She was a nice girl, whoever she was. The bun was nice, too. Two or three beds away I heard some girl munch an apple under the covers. Everyone seemed to be eating and crying for their mothers.

My bed faced a window and I could see a sprinkling of stars in one small corner of the sky. It was nice to lie there watching the stars, waiting for them to fade or to go out, or to flare up into one brilliant firework. Waiting for something to happen in the deathly, unhappy silence.

9 We were wakened at six next morning. The Angelus bell was ringing from the convent tower when Sister Margaret came in chanting the morning offering. She put on the lights and I was up and staggering on my feet before I even knew where I was.

She told us to wash and dress quickly. Mass was in fifteen minutes.

Drawing a comb, limply, through my tangled hair, I saw that Baba was still in bed. Poor Baba, she could never waken in the mornings. I went down and dragged her out. She yawned and rubbed her eyes and asked, "Where are we and what time is it?" I told her. She said, "Jesus wept!" It was her new phrase, instead of just plain "Jesus." Her face was pale and sad and she couldn't open the knots in her shoelaces.

We were the last to leave the dormitory. The prefect had put the lights out. It was rather dark and we had to grope to find our way up the passage and down the steep wooden stairs that led to the recreation hall. There were birds singing in the convent trees as we crossed the tarmac driveway to the chapel. The birds reminded us both of the same thing. Home wasn't such a bad place, after all.

Mass had started when we got in, so we knelt on the kneeler nearest the door, but there was no bench for us to sit on.

"We'll get housemaid's knee from this," Baba whispered.

"What's that?"

"It's a disease. All nuns have it from kneeling." A senior girl turned around and gave us an eye that told us to shut up. My mind wandered all through Mass. The dandruff on girls' gym frocks, the sun coming through the stained-glass window, the shadows where nuns knelt. Nuns with heads bowed humbly, nuns kneeling upright, older nuns kneeling slackly, resting a little on their haunches. I wondered if I would ever get to know them from their backs. A nun served Mass, too. It was funny to hear her thin voice answering the priest in Latin.

Her name was Sister Mary and the priest's name was Father Thomas, Cynthia told me on the way out.

"You're new. Do you like it?" she asked, as she overtook us going down the steps. She ignored Baba.

"It's awful," I said.

"You'll get used to it. It's not so bad."

"I'm lonesome."

"For whom? Your mammy?"

"No. She's dead."

"Oh, poor you," she said, putting her arm around my waist. She promised to take care of me. The big girls always took care of the new ones, and Cynthia was going to take care of me. I liked her. She was a tall girl with yellow hair and small alert brown eyes. She had a bust, too, a thing no other girl in the convent dared have. But Cynthia was different, because she was half Swedish and her mother was a convert.

First we had drill in the open yard that looked out on the street. There were school walls on three sides of it, and there were railings at the fourth side dividing us from the street. Near the railings was an open shed where the day girls kept their bicycles. The day girls were those whose parents lived in the town, and they came in and out of school every day. Cynthia told me that they were all very obliging. She meant that they would post letters on the sly for me, or bring sweets from the shops.

"Arms forward. Arms to toes. Don't bend knees," Sister Margaret said. You could hear knees crack and breaths gasping. Seventy bottoms were humped up in the air and I could see the white thighs of girls in front of me. That space where their black stocking tops ended which the legs of their knickers did not cover.

"Jesus, it's worse than the army," Baba said to me. Her voice came from upside down, because our heads were near the ground.

"Winter and summer," a girl next to us said.

"Silence, please," said Sister Margaret. She was standing on her toes, counting ten. And while we waited, a boy with milk cans went by whistling. His whistle was sweeter than the notes of a flute. Sweeter, because he didn't know how happy he had made us. All of us. He reminded us of our lives at home. We went in to breakfast.

_____

We had tea and buttered bread, and there was a spoon of marmalade on each girl's plate. We began to talk furiously.

"Thanks for the cake," said a girl across the table. She had black hair, a fringe, and pale, freckled skin.

"Oh, it's you?" I said. She was nice. Not pretty or flashy or anything, but nice. Sisterly.

"Where are you from?" she asked, and I told her.

"I have a scholarship," I said. It was better to tell it myself than have Baba tell it.

"God, you must be a genius," she said, frowning.

"Not at all," I said. But I liked the praise. It warmed me inside.

"I'm having visitors Sunday week. I'll get more cakes and things," she said. I was just going to say something very friendly to her, because after all she was next to me in the dormitory and she was likely to get lots of cakes, but Sister Margaret came in, clapping her hands.

"Silence," she said. Her words seemed to remain in the room, hanging over our heads. She began to read from her spiritual book. She read a story about St. Teresa and how Teresa worked in a laundry and let the soap spatter into her eyes as an act of mortification.

"Don't let the soap get in your eyes," Baba hummed quietly to herself, and I was terrified lest she should be heard.

"I'll drink Lysol or any damn thing to get out of here," she said to me on the way out. A man at home had poisoned himself that way. Sister Margaret walked past us and gave us a bitter and suspicious eye. But she hardly overheard us, or we would have been expelled.

"I'd rather be a Protestant," Baba said.

"They have convents, too," I said, sighing.

"Not like this jail," she replied. She was almost crying. We went up to the dormitory, and Cynthia was waiting for me on the first landing.

"That's for you," she said, handing me a holy picture for my prayer book. She ran off quickly. In purple ink was written: *To my new lovely friend, from her loving Cynthia.*

"That sort of mush gives me acidosis," Baba said, sneering. She went in ahead of me with her shoes on.

A lay nun came along to examine our hair, after we had made our beds.

"I have dandruff. I have dandruff," I said excitedly, in case she'd mistake it for anything else.

She gave me a tap on the cheek with the comb and told me to be quiet. She looked through my hair. "I don't know what this great weight of hair is for. Our Lady would hardly approve it," she said as she passed on to the next girl. My honor was saved. The girl next to me, with the squint and the expensive dressing gown, had nits. "Disgraceful," the nun said as she looked through the thin, mousy hair. I was afraid that bugs might crawl from her pillow to mine at nighttime.

Just before nine we went to our classrooms. Baba sat in the desk with me. We sat in the back row. Baba said it was safer back there, and while we were waiting for the nun to come, Baba wrote out a little rhyme in her copybook. It was:

The boys sit on the back bench
The girls in front quite still.
The boys are not supposed to pinch
But there are boys who will.

A girl is asked to tell
If a boy pinches from behind.
Some girls yell
But some girls don't mind.

The first nun who came to the classroom was young and very pretty. Her skin was pink-white and almost moist. Like rose petals in the early morning. She taught Latin and began by teaching us the Latin for table and its various cases. Nominative, vocative, and so on. The lesson lasted forty minutes, and then another nun came, who taught us English. There were two new sticks of chalk and a clean suede eraser on the table beside her hands. Her hands were very white and she wore a narrow silver ring on one finger. She was twisting the ring around her finger all the time. She was delicate-looking and she read us an essay by G. K. Chesterton.

Then a third nun came to teach us algebra. She began to write on the blackboard, and she talked through her nose.

"Nawh, gals," she said. I wasn't listening. The autumn sun came through the big window and I was looking to see if there were any cobwebs in the corners of the ceilings, as there had been at the National School, when she threw down the chalk and called for every girl's attention. I trembled a little and looked at the x's and y's she had written on the blackboard. The morning dragged on until lunchtime. Lunch was terrible.

First there was soup. Thin gray-green soup. And sections of dry gray bread on our side plates.

"It's cabbage water," Baba said to me. She had changed places with the girl next to me and I was glad of her company. She wasn't supposed to change, and we hoped that it would go unnoticed. After the soup came the plates of dinner. On each plate there was a boiled, peeled potato, some stringy meat, and a mound of roughly chopped cabbage.

"Didn't I tell you it was cabbage water?" Baba said, nudging me. I wasn't interested. My meat was brutal-looking and it had a faint smell as if gone off. I sniffed it again and knew that I couldn't eat it.

"This meat is bad," I said to Baba.

"We'll dump it," she said sensibly.

"How?" I asked.

"Bring it out and toss it into that damn lake when we're out walking." She rooted in her pocket and found an old envelope.

I had the meat on my fork and was just going to put it in the envelope when another girl said, "Don't. She'll ask you where it's gone to so quickly," so I put just one slice in the envelope and Baba put a slice of hers.

"Sister Margaret searches pockets," the girl said to us.

"Talk of an angel," said Baba under her breath, because Sister Margaret had just come into the refectory and was standing at the head of the table surveying the plates. I was cutting my cabbage, and seeing something black in it, I lifted some out onto my bread plate.

"Caithleen Brady, why don't you eat your cabbage?" she asked.

"There's a fly in it, Sister," I said. It was a slug really, but I didn't like to hurt her feelings.

"Eat your cabbage, please." She stood there while I put forkfuls into my mouth and swallowed it whole. I thought I might be sick. Afterward she went away and I put the remainder of my meat into Baba's envelope, which she put inside her jumper.

"Do I look sexy?" she asked, because she bulged terribly at one side.

When our plates were empty we passed them up along to the head of the table.

The lay nun carried in a metal tray, which she rested on the corner of the table. She handed round dessert dishes of tapioca.

"Jesus, it's like snot," Baba said in my ear.

"Oh, Baba, don't," I begged. I felt terrible after that cabbage.

"Did I ever tell you the rhyme Declan knows?"

"No."

" 'Which would you rather: run a mile, suck a boil, or eat a bowl of snot?' Well, which would you?" she asked impatiently. She was vexed because I hadn't laughed.

"I'd rather die, that's all," I said. I drank two glasses of water and we came out.

Classes continued until four o'clock. Then we all crowded into the cloakroom, got our coats, and prepared for our walk. It was nice to go out on the street. But we bypassed the main street and went out a side road, in the direction of the lake. As we passed the water's edge, several parcels of meat were pitched it.

"I have done the deed; didst thou not hear the noise?" said one of the senior girls, and the lake was full of little ripples as the small parcels sank underneath. The walk was short, and we were hungry and lonely as we passed the shops. It was impossible to go into the shops because there was a prefect in charge of us. We walked in twos, and once or twice the girl behind me walked on my heel.

"Sorry," she kept saying. She was that mopey girl who kept passing me the bread the first evening. Her gym frock dipped down under her navy gabardine coat and she had steel-rimmed spectacles.

"A penny for your thoughts," Baba said to me, but they were worth more. I was thinking of Mr. Gentleman.

After the walk we did our home lessons; then we had tea and then Rosary. Rosary over, we went around the convent walks. Cynthia came with us and the three of us linked. We walked past the gardens, and smelled damp clay and the spicy perfume of the late-autumn flowers; then we climbed the hill that led to the playing fields. It was almost dusk.

"The evenings are getting shorter," I said fatally. I said it the way Mama would have said it, and the resemblance frightened me, because I did not want to be as doleful as Mama was.

"Tell us everything," Cynthia said. Cynthia was gay and secretive and full of spirit. "Have you boyfriends?" she asked.

An old man, I thought. But it was absurd to think of him as a boyfriend; after all, I was not much more than fourteen. Already our day in Limerick seemed far away, like a dream.

"Have *you*?" Baba asked her.

"Oh yeh. He's terrific. He's nineteen and he works in a garage. He has his own motorbike. We go to dances and everything on it," she said. Her voice was flushed. She liked remembering it.

"Are you fast?" Baba asked bluntly.

"What's fast?" I interrupted. The word puzzled me.

"It's a woman who has a baby quicker than another woman," Baba said quickly, impatiently.

"Is it, Cynthia?" I asked.

"In a way." She smiled. Her smile was for the motorbike, riding with a red kerchief around her hair, over a country road with fuchsia hedges on either side, her arms clasped around his waist, her earrings dangling like the fuchsia flowers.

"Tighter, tighter," he was saying. She obeyed him. Cynthia was not an angel, but very very grown-up.

We sat in a summerhouse up on the hill and watched the other girls as they trooped past in groups of three or four. There were garden seats piled on top of one another in one corner of the summerhouse, and there were a lot of garden tools thrown on the floor.

"Who uses these?" I asked.

"The nuns," Cynthia said. "They have no gardener now." She laughed slyly to herself.

"Why?" I was curious.

"A nun ran away with the gardener last year. She used to be out here helping him, arranging flower beds and all that, and didn't they get friendly! So she ran off." This was excitement, the kind of thing we liked to hear. Baba sat forward and brightened considerably at the prospect of hearing something lively.

"How'd she manage it?" she asked Cynthia.

"At night, over the wall."

Baba began to hum. "And when the moon shines over the cowshed, I'll be waiting at the ki-i-tchen door."

"Did he marry her?" I asked. I found myself trembling again, trembling with anxiety until I had heard the end of the story, trembling because I wanted it to have a happy ending.

"No. We heard he left her after a few months," Cynthia said casually.

"Oh, God!" I exclaimed.

"Oh, God, my eye! She was no beauty when she climbed over the wall to meet him. Bald and everything. 'Twas all right when she was a nun, she had the white wimple around her face and she looked mysterious. And I imagined that dress she wore was hickish."

"Whose dress?" Baba asked. Baba was always practical.

"Marie Duffy's. She's the prefect this year. The nun was in charge of the Christmas concert, and Marie Duffy got a dress from home to play Portia in. After the concert the dress was hanging up in the cloakroom, and then one day it disappeared. I suppose the nun took it."

The convent bells rang out, summoning us away from the summerhouse and the smell of clay and the joy of shared secrets. We ran all the way back to the school and Cynthia warned us not to tell.

That night, when I was going to bed, Cynthia kissed me on the landing. She kissed me every night after that. We would have been killed if we were caught.

Baba saw us and she was hurt. She hurried into the dormitory, and when I went to whisper her good night, she looked at me with a sort of despondent look.

"All that talk about old Mr. Gentleman was a joke," she said.

She was begging me to exclude Cynthia from our walks and our little chats together. I think I stopped being afraid of Baba that night, and I went to bed quite happily.

The girl whose bed backed onto mine was munching under the covers. I could hear her. For a long time I expected something from her, because I'd brought my seed cake over to the refectory and divided it out among the whole table. I didn't do this to be generous; I did it because I was afraid. Afraid of being caught and afraid of drawing mice into my press. Hickey said that girls who were afraid of mice were afraid of men, too.

She was eating for hours. In the end I got desperate. I was going to ask her for a bit, but finally I remembered the Vicks Vapo-rub in my toilet bag. I often tasted it at home and I knew it had a sickening taste. So I reached out, got it from under my washstand, and put a small blob on the back of my tongue. It killed the hunger at once.

I went to sleep wondering if I should write to him, and wondering if Mrs. Gentleman read his letters.

10 The days passed. Days made different only by the fact that it was raining outside, or the leaves were falling, or our algebra nun got a new crocheted shawl. Her old black one was gone green and had frayed at the edges. She was proud of the new one, and whenever she took it off she shook the rain out of it and spread it carefully over the radiator. The central heating was on, but the radiators were only faintly warm. In between classes we warmed our hands on the one that was close to our desk. Baba said we'd get chilblains, and we did.

Baba had got very quiet and she was not a favorite with the nuns. She was put standing for three hours in the chapel, because Sister Margaret overheard her saying the Holy Name. She was stupid at lessons, although she was so smart in her conversation otherwise. I came first in the weekly tests and the strain of this nearly killed me. Always worrying in case I shouldn't come first the following week. So I used to study at night in bed with a flashlight.

"Jesus, you'll get cross-eyed, and it serves you right," Baba said when she saw me reading a book under the covers, but I told her that I liked studying. It kept my mind off other things.

One Saturday a few weeks later Sister Margaret gave us our letters. She had already opened them.

"Who are these gentlemen?" she asked as she handed me two envelopes: one from Hickey and the other from Jack Holland. There was a third letter, from my father. It was like a letter to a stranger. He said that he had moved to the gate lodge and was happy there. He added that the big house was too much anyhow, now that Mama had gone. I made a tour in my mind of all the rooms; I saw the patchwork quilts, the homemade crinoline fire screens edged with red piping, and the damp walls painted with flat green oil paint. I could even open drawers and see the things Mama had laid into them—old Christmas decorations, empty perfume bottles, silk underwear in case she ever had to go to hospital, spare sets of curtains, and everywhere white balls of camphor.

Bull's-Eye misses you, and so do I. With these words he concluded the short letter, and I crumpled it up in my hand because I didn't want to read it again.

Jack Holland's note was as flowery as I had expected. His handwriting was spidery and he wrote on ruled copybook pages. He talked of the clemency of the weather, and two lines later he said he was taking precautions against the downpours. Which meant that he was putting basins in the upstairs rooms to catch the water, and if there were not enough basins he would put old dishcloths there to soak up the drips from the ceilings. One paragraph of his letter puzzled me. It read:

> And, my dear Caithleen, who is the image and continuation of her mother, I see no reason why you shall not return and inherit your mother's home and carry on her admirable domestic tradition.

I wondered if he was going to give the place back to me; but another thought flitted across my mind and I laughed to myself. He said that he and his invalid mother were not living in our house but that he had an attractive offer from an order of nuns who wished to rent it as a novitiate. French nuns, he said. Nice for Mr. Gentleman, I thought acidly. He hadn't written and I was disappointed.

A photograph fell out of Hickey's letter, a passport photograph of himself that he had got taken for his journey to England. There he was, beaming and happy and very self-conscious; exactly like himself, except that he had a collar and tie on in the picture, whereas at home he wore his shirt open and you could see the short black hairs on his chest. His spelling was all wrong. He said Birmingham was sooty, with *droves of people everywhere and porter twice the price.* He had a job as a night watchman in a factory, so he was able to sleep all day. He sent me a postal order for five shillings and I thanked him several times over, hoping that if I said it often enough he would divine it over there in black Birmingham. I kept it for the Halloween party.

October dragged on. The leaves fell and there were piles of leaves under the trees, piles of brown, withered leaves that had curled up at the edges. Then one day a man came and gathered them into a heap and made a bonfire in the corner of the front garden. That night when we were going up to the Rosary, the fire was still smoking and the grounds had the wistful smell of leaf smoke. After the Rosary we talked about the Halloween party.

"Get the one with the nits," Baba said to me. She meant the girl in the bed next to mine.

"Why?" I knew Baba hated her.

"Because her damn mother has a shop and the reception room is bursting with parcels for her." The parcels for the Halloween party were coming every day. I couldn't ask my father for one because a man is not able to do these things, so I wrote to him for money instead and a day girl bought me a barmbrack, apples, and monkey-nuts.

When the day came for the party, we carried small tables from the convent down to the recreation hall; we sat in groups of five or six and shared the contents of our parcels. Cynthia and Baba and the girl with the nits, whose name was Una, and I shared the same table. Una got four boxes of chocolates and three shop cakes and heaps of sweets and nuts.

"Have a sweet, Cynthia?" Baba said, opening Una's chocolates, but Una didn't mind. No one liked her and she was always bribing people to be her friend. Cynthia got lovely homemade oatcakes; when you ate them, the coarse grains of oats stuck in your teeth.

"Have one, Sister," Cynthia said to Sister Margaret, who was walking in and out among the tables. She was smiling that day. She even smiled at Baba. She took two oatcakes but she didn't eat them. She put them into her side pocket, and when she moved away, Baba said, "They starve themselves." I think she was right.

"You got a hell of a stingy parcel," Baba noted, leaning over to look into the cardboard box of mine that had the barmbrack and the few things in it. I blushed and Cynthia squeezed my hand under the table. Baba had mixed her own things with Una's, so that I wasn't sure what she had got. But I know that Martha told her to share with me. We ate until we were full, and afterward we cleared off the tables and the floor was littered with nutshells, apple cores, and toffee papers. Nearly every girl was wearing a barmbrack ring. Then we went up to the chapel to pray for the Holy Souls, and Cynthia had her arm around my waist.

"Don't mind Baba," she said to me tenderly. But I had minded. Baba walked behind with Una. Una gave her an unopened box of chocolates and some tangerines. The tangerine skin had an exotic smell and I brought some in my pocket so that I could smell it in the chapel.

"See you tonight," Cynthia said. We put on our berets and went in. The chapel was almost dark, except for the light from the sanctuary lamp up near the altar. We prayed for the souls in Purgatory. I thought of Mama and cried for a while. I put my face in my hands so that the girls next to me would think I was praying or meditating or something. I was trying to recall how many sins she had committed from the time she was at confession to the time she died. I knew that we had been given too much change in one of the shops and I said I'd bring it back.

"You will not, they have more than that out of us," she said, and she put the change into the cracked jug on the pantry shelf. And she told a lie, too. Mrs. Stevens from the cottages came up to borrow the donkey and Mama said the donkey was in the bog with Hickey, when all the time the donkey was above in the kitchen garden, asleep under the pear tree with his knees bent. I saw him there because Mama had sent me to look for the black hen who was laying out. Every year the black hen laid out and hatched her chickens in the ditch. It was a miracle to see her wander back to the hen house with a clutch of lovely little furry yellow chickens behind her. When I stopped crying my face was red and my eyelids hot.

"What are you dripping about?" Baba asked me when we came out.

"Purgatory," I said.

"Purgatory. What about hell, burning forever and ever?" I could see flames and I could smell clothes scorching.

"You'd never guess who wrote to me," she said. Her voice was perky and she had a mint in her mouth.

"Who?" I asked.

"Old Mr. Gentleman." She turned toward me as she said it.

"Show it to me," I said anxiously.

"What in the hell do you take me for?" she said, and she went on ahead, skipping lightly in her black patent-leather shoes.

"I'll ask him at Christmas," I called after her, but Christmas seemed years away.

And yet it came.

One day in the middle of December we prepared for the holidays. Cynthia gave me a hanky sachet for a present, and I was awarded a statue of St. Jude for coming in first place in the Christmas examination. We looked out through the window all evening, expecting Mr. Brennan's car. He came just after six o'clock, and we put on our coats and followed him out to the car. The three of us sat in front and Mr. Brennan lit himself a cigarette before we set off. The cigarette smelled lovely, and it was nice to sit there while he started the car and turned on lights and then drove slowly down the avenue. Soon we were out of the town and driving between the stone walls that skirted the road on both sides. The darkness was delicious. We could almost smell it. We talked all the time, and I talked more than Baba. There were milk tanks on wooden stands outside the farm gates that we drove past.

A rabbit ran out from the wall and darted across the road in the glare of the headlights.

"Got 'im," Mr. Brennen said as he slowed down. He got out and walked back forty or fifty yards. He left the door open and the cold air came into the car. It was nice to feel the cold air. The convent was prison. He flung the rabbit in the back. It was stretched out along the length of the black leather seat. I couldn't see it in the dark, but I knew how it looked and I knew there was blood everywhere on its soft dun-colored fur.

When we stepped out of the car outside Brennans', there were lights in all the front windows and there was excitement behind the lights. We ran in ahead of Mr. Brennan and Martha kissed us in the hall. Molly and Declan kissed us, too, and we went into the drawing room. My father sat in front of the big blazing fire with his feet inside the oak curb.

"Welcome home," he said, and he stood up and kissed us both. The room was warm and happy. The curtains were different. They were red hand-woven ones and there were cushions to match on the leather armchairs. The table was set for tea, and I could smell the delicious odor of hot mince pies. A spark flew out onto the sheepskin rug and Martha rushed across to step on it. She wore a black dress, and I hated to admit to myself that she had got older. Somehow in the few months she had passed over into middle age and her face was not quite so defiantly beautiful.

"Marvelous fire," I said, warming my hands and enjoying the smell of the turf.

"I provide that," my father said proudly. At once, I felt the old antagonism which I had toward him.

"I keep them supplied in turf and timber," he said a second time. I thought of saying, How in God's name can you do that, when you don't own a cabbage garden? but it was my first night home and I said nothing. Anyhow, I supposed that he had kept some turf banks and perhaps a wood or two at the very far boundary where the farm degenerated in wild birch woods.

"You got tall," he said to me ominously, as if it were abnormal for a girl of fourteen to grow.

"Tomorrow's dinner, Mammy," Mr. Brennan said as he carried in the slaughter. He had it held by the two hind legs and it was a very long rabbit.

"Oh no," Martha said wearily, and she put her hands across her eyes.

"That man has never gone out but he's brought something back for tomorrow's dinner," she said to my father, when Mr. Brennan went down to the scullery to wash his hands and to hang the rabbit in the meat safe.

"A good complaint," my father replied. He had no insight into the small irritations that could drive people mad.

Before supper we went upstairs to change our clothes. Molly carried the brass candlestick and Martha called after her not to spill grease all over the stair carpet. The thought of getting into a colored dress and silk stockings after months of black clothes lifted my heart.

I felt sorry for the poor nuns, who never changed at all. Molly had our clothes airing in the hot press and she carried them into the bedroom.

"That's yours," she said, pointing to a parcel on the bed. I opened it and found a pair of brown, high-heeled, suede shoes. I put them on and walked unsteadily across the floor, for Molly's approval.

"They're massive," she said. They were. Nothing I had ever got before gave me such immense pleasure. I looked in the wardrobe mirror at myself and admired my legs a thousand times. My calves had got fatter and my legs were nicely shaped. I was grown-up.

"Where did they come from?" I said at last. In the excitement I had forgotten to ask.

"Your dad got them for you, for Christmas," she said. She liked my father and gave him a cup of tea every time he called at the house. A twinge of guilt overtook me and lowered my spirits for a second. I found it difficult to come downstairs and thank him. And even when I did thank him, he had no idea that the shoes gave me such secret pleasure. All through supper I was lifting up the big white tablecloth to look at my feet under the table. Finally I sat sideways, so that I could look at them constantly and admire my legs in the golden nylon stockings. The stockings were a present from Martha.

We had ham and pickles for supper, and homemade fruit cake that Martha had made specially for us.

" 'Tis reeking with nutmeg," Baba said. Cooking was her best subject at school. She looked pretty in her white overall, rolling pastry, and her face was always coyly flushed as she stood near the oven waiting to take out an apple pie or to test a Madeira cake with a knitting needle.

"How much nutmeg d'you use?" Baba asked her mother.

"Just a ball," said Martha innocently, and Baba laughed so much that the crumbs went down her windpipe and we had to thump her on the back. Declan ran off for a glass of water. She drank some and finally she was calm again. Declan was wearing long gray-flannel trousers, and Baba said that his bottom looked like two eggs tied in a handkerchief. He was trying to catch my eye all the time through supper, and he was winking at me furiously.

The doorbell rang, and after a second Molly tapped on the drawing-room door and said, "Mr. Gentleman, mam. He's come to see the girls."

When he walked into the room I knew that I loved him more than life itself.

"Good night, Mr. Gentleman," we all said. Baba was nearest the door, and he kissed the top of her head and patted her hair for a minute. Then he came around the side of the table, and my knees began to quake at the prospect of his kissing me.

"Caithleen," he said. He kissed me on the lips. A quick dry kiss, and he shook hands with me. He was shy and strangely nervous. But when I looked into his eyes they were saying the sweet things which they had said before.

"No kiss for me?" Martha said, as she stood behind him with a tumbler of whiskey in her hand. He gave her a kiss on the cheek and took the whiskey. Mr. Brennan said that as it was Christmastime he'd have a drink himself, and we all sat around the fire. I wanted to clear off the table but Martha said to leave it. My father filled himself several cups of cold tea from the teapot and Baba went off with Martha to put hot-water bottles in our bed. Mr. Gentleman and Mr. Brennan were talking about foot-and-mouth disease. My father coughed a little to let them know that he was there, and he passed them cigarettes two or three times, but they did not include him in the conversation because he was in the habit of saying stupid things. Finally, he played Ludo with Declan, and I was sorry for him.

I just sat there on the high-backed chair, admiring the colors in the turf flames. Every few seconds Mr. Gentleman gave me a look that was at once sly and loving and full of promises. When at last he noticed my new shoes and my legs flattered in the new nylons, his eyes dwelt on them for a while as if he were planning something in his mind, and he took a long drink of whiskey and said it was time to go.

"See you tomorrow," he said directly to me.

"Are you going my way, sir?" my father asked him, knowing that of course he was. He offered my father a seat in the car and they both left.

"Well, it's lovely to see you here again," Mr. Brennan said, as he put his arms around me. He was always a little maudlin after a few drinks. He was sleepy, too, and his eyes kept closing.

"You should go to bed," Martha said to him. He opened the buttons of his waistcoat and said good night to all of us and went off to bed.

"Go to bed, Declan," Martha said.

"Ah, Mammy," he pleaded. But Martha insisted. When they were gone she filled three glasses of sherry and gave us a glass each. We sat, huddled over the fire, and talked, the way women who like each other can talk once the men are out of sight.

"How's life?" Baba said.

"Lousy," Martha said, and she told us all that had happened since we went away. The fire had died into a bed of gray ashes before we climbed the stairs. Martha carried the lamp and its light was very dim, because the oil was nearly burned out. She put it in the hallway between our room and hers, and when we had undressed she came out and quenched it. Mr. Brennan was snoring, and she went to her own room, sighing.

11

Next day was cold. Mr. Gentleman called for me after lunch. Baba had gone up the street to show off her new mohair coat, and Martha was lying down. Baba told me in great secrecy that Martha was going through the change of life, and I sympathized with her. I didn't know what it meant, except that it had something to do with not having babies.

Molly was brushing the collar of my coat in the hall when the doorbell rang.

"You wanted a seat to Limerick," Mr. Gentleman said. He was wearing a black nap coat, and his face looked petrified.

"I do," I said, and kicked Molly's toe with my shoe. Earlier I had told her that I was going out to visit my mother's sister, and that he was giving me a lift.

We said nothing for a long time after I got into the car. It was a new car with red-leather seats, and the ashtray was stuffed with cigarette butts. I wondered whose they were.

"You got plump," he said finally. I hated the sound of the word. It reminded me of young chickens when they were being weighed for the market.

"You got pretty, too—terribly pretty," he said, frowning. I thanked him and asked him how his wife was. Such a stupid question! I could have killed myself.

"She's well, and how are you? Have you changed?" There were all sorts of meanings behind his words and behind the yellow-gray luster of his eyes. Even though his face was weary, life-weary, and dead in a peculiar way, his eyes were young and large and fiercely expectant.

"Yes, I have changed. I know Latin and algebra. And I can do square roots." He laughed and told me that I was funny; and we drove away from the gate, because Molly was looking out the sitting-room window at us. She had a corner of the lace curtain lifted, and her nose flat against the windowpane.

I closed my eyes as we passed our own gate. I had no wish to see it.

"Can I hold your hand?" he asked gently. His hand was freezing and his nails were almost purple with the cold. We drove along the Limerick road, and while we were driving it began to snow. Softly the flakes fell. Softly and obliquely against the windshield. It fell on the hedges and on the trees behind the hedges, and on the treeless fields in the distance, and slowly and quietly it changed the color and the shape of things, until evening outside the motorcar had a mantle of soft white down.

"There's a rug in the back of the car," he said. It was a tartan wool rug and I would have liked to wrap it around us, but I was too shy. I watched the snowflakes tumble through the air. The car was slowing down and I knew that before the flakes began to show on the front hood Mr. Gentleman was going to say that he loved me.

True enough, he drove down a side track and stopped the car. He cupped my face between his cold hands and very solemnly and very sadly he said what I had expected him to say. And that moment was wholly and totally perfect for me; and everything that I had suffered up to then was comforted in the softness of his soft, lisping voice, whispering, whispering, like the snowflakes. A hawthorn tree in front of us was coated white as sugar, and the snow got worse and was blowing so hard that we could barely see. He kissed me. It was a real kiss. It affected my entire body. My toes, though they were numb and pinched in the new shoes, responded to that kiss, and for a few minutes my soul was lost. Then I felt a drip on the end of my nose and it bothered me.

"Blue Noses," I said, looking for my handkerchief.

"What are blue noses?" he asked.

"The name for winter noses," I said. I had no handkerchief so he loaned me his.

On the way back he had to get out a few times because the windshield wipers got choked up. Even for the second he was away I was lonesome for him.

I was home in time for tea. We had boiled eggs. Mine was fresh and boiled to the right hardness; I had forgotten its lovely country flavor. Eating it, I thought of Hickey, and I decided to post him a dozen fresh eggs to Birmingham.

"Can you post eggs to England?" I asked Baba. There was egg yolk all over her lips and she was licking it.

"Can you post eggs to England? Of course you can post eggs to England if you want the postman to deliver a box of sop and mush with egg white running up his sleeve. If you want to be a moron you can post eggs to England, but they'll turn into chickens on the way."

"I only asked," I said peevishly.

"You're a right-looking eejit," she said. She was making faces at me. There were only the two of us at the table.

"What are you sending Cynthia for Christmas?" I asked.

"I won't tell you. Mind your own bloody business."

"I won't tell *you*," I said.

"As a matter of fact, I have given her mine. A valuable piece of jewelry," Baba told me.

"Not the ring I gave you?" I asked. It was the only piece of jewelry she had brought with her to the convent. We weren't allowed to wear trinkets there, so she kept the ring in her rosary-bead purse. I finished my tea quickly and went out to the hall and searched her pocket for the purse. The ring was gone out of it. Mama's favorite ring. Once Baba had got something, she no longer valued it.

I put on my coat and went upstairs for my flashlight. There was a light showing under Martha's door so I knocked and stuck my head in. She was sitting up in bed with a cardigan over her shoulders.

"I'm going up the street. I won't be long," I said.

"Don't. We're playing cards tonight, all of us. Your dad is coming over." She smiled faintly. She was suffering. She was paying back for all the gay nights that she'd spent down at the hotel, her legs crossed, her tongue tasting a thick, expensive liqueur. She and Mr. Brennan slept in separate beds.

The snow had turned to slush in the few hours and the footpath was slippery. The battery of my flashlight was almost gone and the light kept fading. It was hard to see and I wasn't used to the darkness. Still, I remembered where the steps were, just before the hotel, and two more steps before I crossed the bridge. The water had the same urgent sound and I thought of the day Jack Holland and I leaned over the stone bridge and looked for fish down underneath. I was on my way to see him, just then.

Water ran down the street, too, in the gutters where the snow had melted. It was bitterly cold.

There had been a turkey market that day and there were a lot of horses and carts outside the shops. The horses were neighing and jerking their heads to keep themselves warm and you could almost see their breaths turning into plumes of frost. The windows of the drapery shops were dressed for Christmas with holly and Christmas stockings and shreds of tinsel. I couldn't see them very well with my flashlight but inside in the shops there were countrywomen buying boots and vests and calico. I looked in the doorway of O'Brien's drapery and saw Mrs. O'Brien, under the lamplight, measuring curtain material. There was a country man sitting on a chair fitting on a pair of boots, and his wife was feeling the leather with her hands and searching to see if his toe came to the very tip of the boot. Jack's shop was next door. I went in, hoping there would be lots of people drinking in the bar. Alas, it was empty. Jack sat like a ghost behind the counter, writing in a ledger by the light of a very dim hand lamp.

"Dearest," he said, when he looked up and saw me. He took off his steel-rimmed glasses and came outside to greet me. He brought me in behind the counter and sat me on a tea chest. There was an oil stove at my feet and it was smoking. The shop smelled of paraffin oil.

"An Irish colleen," he said, and sneezed fiercely. He took out an old flannel rag, and while he was blowing his nose I looked at the ledger that he had been writing in. There was a dead moth on the opened page and a brown stain just below it. When he saw that I was looking at it, he closed the book, being very secretive about his customers.

"Who's there? Who is it, Jack?" a voice called from the kitchen.

It was exactly the voice one would expect from an old, dead woman. It was high and hoarse and croaking.

"Jack, I'm dying," the voice moaned. I jumped off the tea chest, but Jack put a hand on my shoulder and made me sit down again.

"She's just curious to know who's here," he said. He didn't bother to whisper.

"It's thrilling to see you," he said, beaming at me. The beam divided his lips and I saw his last three teeth. They were like brown, crooked nails and I imagined that they were loose.

"Thrilling," I said to myself, and wondered if he thought Goldsmith thrilling.

"Jack, I'm dying," the voice said again, and Jack swore bad-temperedly and ran into the kitchen. I followed him.

"Good God Almighty, you're on fire," he shouted. There was a smell of something burning.

"On fire," she said, looking at him like a baby.

"Goddamn it, take your shoe out of the ashes," he said. She had the toe of her black canvas shoe in the bed of ashes under the grate.

She was an old bent woman dressed in black, a little black shadow doubled up in a rocking chair. The fire had died into gray clinkers that were still red in the center and the ashes hadn't been cleaned out for a week. The kitchen was big and drafty.

"A sup o' milk," she said. I was sure she was dying. Her eyes had that desperate, dying look. I looked in the jugs along the table for milk. There was some in the bottom of two jugs, but it had gone sour.

"Over there," Jack said, pointing to a fresh can of milk on the form along the wall. He was holding her by the shoulders because she had taken a fit of coughing. There were hens on the form picking out of a colander of cold cabbage, and when I went near them they flew down and crossed over to the bottom step of the stairs. The milk was fresh and yellow and there were specks of dust floating on the top of it.

"It's dusty," I said.

"There's a cheesecloth on the dresser." He pointed. I strained some of the milk through the yellowed, smelly strip of dried muslin, and he put the cup to her lips.

"I don't want it," she said, and I could have shaken her. After all that commotion she said she wanted a sweet.

"A sweet for the cough," she said, gasping for breath between the words. He took some sugar-coated pastilles out of the salt hole in the wall and wiped the dust off them. He put two between her lips and she sucked them like a child. Then she looked at me and beckoned for me to come over.

A candle stood on the mantelpiece beside her, and though it had nearly burned out, the wick had sprung into a final, tall flame and I could see her face very clearly. The yellow skin stretched like parchment over her old bones, and her hands and her wrists were thin and brown like boiled chicken bones. Her knuckles were bent with rheumatism, her eyes almost dead, and I hated to look at her. I was looking at death.

"I must go, Jack," I said suddenly. I was suffocating.

"Not yet, Caithleen," he said, and he eased her back in the chair. He put a cushion at the back of her head so that the hard chair did not hurt her scalp. Her hair was white and thin like an infant's. She smiled as I walked away.

Out in the shop Jack filled me a glass of raspberry cordial and I wished him a happy Christmas.

"Thank you for your letters," I said.

"You have caught their full implication?" he said, raising his eyes so that his forehead broke into worried lines.

"What implications?" I asked foolishly. So very foolishly.

"Caithleen," he said, as he breathed deeply and caught hold of my hands. "Caithleen, in time to come I hope to marry you," and the red cordial in my throat froze to ice.

I got away somehow. There was a threat that the chapped colorless lips would endeavor to kiss mine, so I put the glass on the counter and said, "My father is waiting outside, Jack, I'll have to run." I ran and the little latch that clicked as I closed the door clicked on Jack's face, which was transformed by a vague, happy smile. I suppose he thought that he had made a success of it.

I fell over a damn dog in the outside porch. He yelped and turned around as if he was going to bite me, but in the end he didn't.

"Happy Christmas," I said to him in gratitude, and went down the street. A motorcar drove up the hill toward me. The headlights were blinding. It slowed down as it came to the top of the hill. It was Mr. Gentleman's.

"Are you going somewhere?" I asked.

"Yes, I came over for petrol," he said. It was a lie. I sat in beside him and he warmed my fingers. I put my gloves in my coat pocket.

"Will we go into Limerick for dinner?" he asked. His voice was very tentative, as if he expected to be refused.

"I can't. I'm going home to play cards. I promised them, and my father is coming over." He sighed, but otherwise he was quite resigned. It was then that he noticed that I was shivering.

"Caithleen, what's wrong?" he asked. I tried to tell him about Jack and the old woman's shoe smoldering away, and the sour milk, and the candle dying in the dirty saucer, and the smell of must on everything. And I told him also about Jack's proposal and how idiotic it was.

"Curious," he said, as he smiled.

Please have more feeling, Mr. Gentleman, I begged of him in my mind.

"Have to go now," he said, and he turned the car in the alley of the bakery shop. I was lonely with him then, because he had not understood what I had been telling him.

He dropped me at the gate and said that he was going home to bed.

"So early?" I asked.

"Yes, I didn't sleep last night, only on and off."

"Why not?"

"You know why." His voice caressed me and his eyes were almost crying when I got out and shut the door gently. He had to open it again and give it a proper bang.

When I went into the hall I knew there was something wrong. Molly and Martha had decorated the Christmas tree and it was standing in a red wooden bucket at the side of the hall stand. It was pretty, with icicles trembling on it and orange sugar-barleyed candles rising out of the green needles. But something *was* wrong.

"Caithleen." Martha called me into the room.

"Caithleen," she said fatally, "your daddy hasn't come."

"Why?" I asked, not thinking of the old reason.

"He's gone, Caithleen—off on a batter. He was giving away fivers in a hotel in Limerick half an hour ago." I sat down on the arm of her chair and played with the button of my coat and felt the happiness drain out of me.

Molly stopped blowing balloons for a second to tell me something.

"He came here looking for you in the evening, and he said 'twas a wonder you didn't go over to see your father instead of off driving with big shots," Molly said calmly. Mr. Gentleman was a big shot because he never drank in the local pubs, and because he had visitors from Dublin and foreign places. They came to stay with him in the summer. Once a Chief Justice from New York had come and it was mentioned in the local paper.

Baba had the pack of cards in her hands and she was juggling them idly. We played, as we had arranged, and they were all very nice to me and Baba let me win, even though I was a fool at cards. Afterward Molly carried the tree in and put it beside the piano. Some of the icicles fell off and she had to pick them up again.

That Christmas, then, like all the others, was one of waiting, waiting for the worst, except that I was safe in the Brennans' house. But of course I was never safe in my thoughts, because when I thought of things I was afraid. So I visited people every day, and not once did I go over the road to look at our own house. Declan told me that there were shutters on the windows, and I wondered what the foxes thought when they went into the empty hen houses. Bull's-Eye came most days for food, and he cried and moaned the first day when he saw me and smelled my clothes.

Late on Christmas Eve Mr. Gentleman came when all the others were out. Molly had gone to get a seat in the chapel, two hours before the midnight Mass, and the Brennans went to Limerick to get wine and last-minute things for the Christmas dinner. The turkey was stuffed, and there were several boxes wrapped in fancy paper laid under the tree. A lot of the pine needles had dropped onto the fawn carpet and I was picking them up when he rang. I guessed that it was him. He came in and kissed me in the hall and gave me a little package. It was a small gold watch with a bracelet of gold lace.

"It ticks," I said, putting it to my ear. It was so small that I had expected it to be a toy. He was going to kiss me again, but we heard a car and he drew back from me, guiltily.

"Oh, Caithleen, we'll have to be very careful," he said. The car went past the gate.

"It's not them," I said, and went closer to thank him for the beautiful present.

"I love you," he whispered.

"I love you," I said. I wished that there was some other way of saying it, some more original way.

My neck was hurting the way he had me held, but it was nice, despite that. I knew the smell of his skin by then and the strength of his arms, shielding me.

"We'll have to be very careful," he said a second time.

"We are," I replied. I hadn't seen him for two days and thought it a lifetime.

"I can't see you too often. It's difficult," he said. He stammered over the last word. He hated to say it. I shook my head. I, too, was sorry for that tall, dark woman who lived so entirely to herself behind the trees and the white stone house. No one ever saw her except to get a glimpse of her when she knelt in the back seat of the chapel on Sundays. She always hurried away before the last gospel and drove off in Mr. Gentleman's car. I admired her strength, and it puzzled me why she never bothered to make herself handsome. Always in tweed things and flat laced shoes and mannish hats with a wide brim on them.

"Can I write to you?" I asked. He had kissed me behind the ear, in a place that made me shudder.

"No," he said firmly.

"And will I ever see you?" I asked. My voice was more tragic than I meant it to be.

"Of course," he said impatiently. It was the first time he had looked irritated and I winced. He was sorry at once.

"Of course, of course, my little darling; later, when you go to Dublin." He was stroking my hair, and his eyes looked far ahead and longingly toward the future.

Then he pushed up my sleeve and put the watch on my wrist, and we went in and sat at the fire until we heard the car coming. I sat on his lap and he opened his overcoat and let the sides of it drop onto the floor.

"Where will I say I got the watch?" I asked as I jumped up. The car was coming in the front drive.

"You won't say. You'll put it away," he said.

"But I can't, that's cruel."

"Caithleen, go up and put it somewhere," he told me. He lit a cigar and tried to look casual as he heard the front door being opened. Baba rushed in with her arms full of parcels.

"Hello, Baba, I came to wish you happy Christmas," he said, lying, as he took some of the parcels out of her arms and laid them on the hall table.

I put the watch into a china soap dish. It curled up very nicely in the bottom of the soap dish, and it looked as if it were going to sleep. It was a pale gold, the color of moth dust.

When I came down to the room, Mr. Gentleman was talking to Mr. Brennan, and for the rest of the night he ignored me. Baba held a sprig of mistletoe over his head and he kissed her, and then Martha put the gramophone on and played "Silent Night," and I thought of the evening when the snow fell on the windshield and when he parked the car under the hawthorn tree. I tried to catch his eye, but he did not look at me until he was leaving, and then it was a sad look.

And so, of course, the time came for us to go back, and once more we got out our gym frocks and our black cotton stockings.

"I should have cleaned my gym frock," I said to Baba. "It's all stained."

She was looking out at the vegetable garden and she was crying. It was that time of year when the garden was lifeless. The sad, upturned damp clay looked desolate, and there was nothing to suggest that things would grow there ever again. Over in the corner there was a hydrangea bush, and the withered flowers looked like old floor mops. Near it was the rubbish heap, where Molly had just thrown empty bottles and the Christmas tree. It was raining and blowing outside and the sky was dark.

"We'll run away," she said.

"When? Now?"

"Now! No. From the damn convent."

"They'll kill us."

"They won't find us. We'll go with a traveling show company and be actors. I can sing and act, and you can take the tickets."

"I want to act, too," I said defensively.

"All right. We'll put in an advertisement. 'Two female amateurs, one can sing; both have secondary education.'"

"But we're not females, we're girls."

"We could pass as females."

"I doubt it."

"Oh, Christ, don't damp my spirits. I'll kill myself if I have to stay five years in that jail."

"It's not so bad." I was trying to cheer her.

"It's not so bad for you, winning statues and playing up to nuns. You give me the sick anyhow, jumping up to open and close the damn door for nuns as if they had cerebral palsy and couldn't do it themselves." It was true, I did play up to the nuns, and I hated her for noticing it.

"All right, then, *you* run away," I said.

"Oh no," she said desperately, catching my wrist, "we'll go together." I nodded. It was nice to know that she needed me.

She remembered then that she had to get something downstairs and she bolted off.

"Where are you going?"

"To feck a few samples from the surgery."

I got into my gym frock. It was creased all over and the box pleats had come out at the edges. She came back with a new roll of cotton and several little sample tubes of ointments. I picked one tube up off the bed, where she threw them. Its name was printed on a white label and a note underneath which read FOR UDDER INFUSION.

"What's this for?" I asked. I was thinking of Hickey milking the fawn cow and holding the teat so that the milk zigzagged all over the cobbled floor. He did this to be funny, whenever I went up to the cow house to call him to his tea.

"What's this for?" I asked again.

"Make us look females," she said. "We'll rub it into our bubs and they'll swell out; it says it's for udders."

"We might get all hairy or something," I said. I meant it. I distrusted ointments with big names on the label, and anyhow it *was* for cows.

"You're a right-looking eejit," she said. She yelled with laughter.

"Supposing we told your father?" I suggested. I didn't really want to run away.

"Tell my father! He has no bloody feelings. He'd tell us to exercise control. Martha told him the other day that she had an ulcer on her foot and he told her to will it away with the power of the mind. He's a lunatic," she said. Her eyes were flashing with anger.

"There's no other way then," I said flatly.

"We can always get expelled," she said, carefully measuring each word. And she began to consider the various ways we could achieve that.

12

On and off, for three years, she thought about it. But I discouraged her by reminding her that we were too young to go to the city. During those three years nothing special happened to us, so I can pass quickly over them.

We did examinations and Baba failed hers. Cynthia left the convent; we cried saying goodbye, and swore lifelong friendship. But after a few months we stopped writing letters. I forget who stopped first.

The holidays were always enjoyable. In the summer Mr. Gentleman took me out in his boat. We rowed to an island far out from the shore, and boiled a kettle on his primus stove to make tea. It was a happy time, and he often kissed my hand and said I was his freckle-faced daughter.

"Are you my father?" I asked wistfully, because it was nice playing make-believe with Mr. Gentleman.

"Yes, I'm your father," he said as he kissed the length of my arm, and he promised that when I went to Dublin later on he would be a very attentive father. Martha and Baba and everyone thought he was bringing me to see my Aunt Molly. One day, we actually did call. Aunt Molly got very excited at having Mr. Gentleman as a guest, and she fussed about and brought down the good cups from the parlor. The cups were dusty and she insisted on putting cream in Mr. Gentleman's tea, though he told her that he used no milk. The cream was a great luxury and she thought she was doing us a favor.

But, all the time, Baba was thinking of how we might escape from the convent. She read film magazines in bed and said we could get into pictures, if we knew anyone in America.

The chance came in March. I mean the chance to escape. We had a retreat in the convent and the priest, who came from Dublin to lecture us, enjoined us to keep silent in order to think of God and of our souls.

On the second morning of the retreat he told us that the afternoon lecture would be devoted to the Sixth Commandment. This was the most important lecture of all and it was also very private. Sister Margaret did not want the nuns to come into the chapel while it was going on, as the priest spoke very frankly about boys and sex and things. It was not likely that the nuns would come into the chapel by the main door, but some nun might go into the choir gallery upstairs. To prevent this, Sister Margaret wrote out a warning notice which read DO NOT ENTER—LECTURE ON HERE, and she asked me to pin it on the door upstairs. She chose me because I had rubber-soled shoes and was not likely to go pounding up the convent stairs. I felt nervous and excited as I climbed the oak stairs. It was my first time to go in there, to the nuns' quarters, and I had no idea which door I was to pin the notice on. The stairs were highly polished and the white wall on one side was covered with large paintings. Paintings of the Resurrection, and the Last Supper, and a circular, colored painting of the Madonna and Child. I hoped that at least I'd see a nun's cell, so that I could tell Baba and the others. We were dying to know what the cells were like, because some senior girl said that the nuns slept on planks, and another girl said that they slept in coffins. On the first landing I paused for breath and dipped my hand in the white marble Holy Water font that curved out from under the windowsill. There was a maidenhair fern trailing out of a Chinese vase and the strands were so long that they dipped onto the pale Indian rug that covered the landing floor.

Slowly I climbed the next flight of steps and saw a wooden door on my right. I decided that this must be it. With four new drawing pins I secured the notice to the center panel of the door, and then stood back from it to read it. It was written very clearly and all the letters were even. To the left there was a long, narrow corridor with doors on either side, and though I guessed that these were the cells, I did not dare go down and peep through a keyhole. I hurried back to the chapel and was just in time for the beginning of the lecture.

When it was almost over, I nipped out and hurried up the convent stairs to remove the notice. I found Sister Margaret waiting for me. She was fuming with temper.

"Is this your idea of a joke?" she asked. She opened the door and pointed inward. It was a lavatory. I had to smile.

"I'm sorry, Sister," I said.

"You're an evil girl," she said. Her eyes were piercing me, and she was so angry that when she spoke little spits flew out of her mouth and spattered my face.

"I'm sorry, Sister," I said again. I wondered to myself if the nuns were deprived of the lavatory for the whole evening, and the more I thought of it, the funnier it seemed. But I was afraid, too, and shaking like a leaf.

"You have insulted my sisters in religion and you have vulgarized the name of your school," she said.

"It was an accident," I said meekly.

"You will remain standing in front of the Blessed Sacrament for three hours, and you will then apologize to the Reverend Mother."

After I had stood for three hours and had apologized to the Reverend Mother, I was coming down the convent steps, wiping my eyes with the back of my hand, when Baba accosted me. She held up a sheet of paper and written on it was this: *I have a plan at last that will expel us.*

We were supposed to be on silence so we had to go somewhere to talk. I followed her down to the school and up the back stairs to one of the lavatories.

She began at once—knowing that we couldn't stay in there very long—"We'll leave a dirty note in the chapel as if it fell out of our prayer books." She was shaking all over.

"Oh, God, we can't," I said. I was shaking, too—after the Reverend Mother. The scene was in my mind vividly. How I knocked on the door and went into the big, cold parlor. She was sitting on a rostrum, reading her office. She pushed her spectacles farther down her nose, and fixed me with a pair of cold, blue, penetrating eyes.

"So you are the rotten apple," she said. Her voice was quiet but enormously accusing.

"I'm sorry, Sister," I said. I should have called her "Mother," but I was so frightened that I got mixed up.

"I'm sorry, Mother," I repeated.

"Are you?" she asked. The question echoed through the length of the cold room, so that the high, ornamented ceiling seemed to ask "Are you?" and the gilt clock on the mantelpiece ticked "Are you?" and everything in that room accused me until I was petrified. It was a comfortless room and I doubted that anyone had ever drunk tea at the great oval table with its thick, strong legs. I was waiting for her to really begin, but she said nothing more, and then I realized that the interview was over. I withdrew shamefully, closing the door as quietly as possible behind me, and saw that she was looking after me.

"We can't," I said to Baba. "Think of all the trouble." All I wanted was peace.

"What is it anyhow?" I asked.

"It's this." She whispered in my ear. Even *she* was a little shy about saying it aloud.

"Oh, God." I put my hand across my mouth, in case I should repeat it.

"There's no 'Oh, God.' There will be hell for three or four days and then we're off. Free."

"We'll get killed."

"We won't. Martha won't mind and your aul fella will probably be on a batter, and my aul fella can have a run-an'-jump for himself."

She took her pen out of her pocket and a lovely sky-blue holy picture. It was a picture of the Blessed Virgin coming out of the clouds with a blue cloak opening out behind her.

"You write it," I said.

"Our two names are going on it," she said as she knelt down. There on the lavatory seat she wrote it in block capitals. I was ashamed of it then, and I am ashamed of it now. I think it's something you'd rather not hear. Anyhow, we both signed our names to it.

Though I closed my eyes and tried not to repeat it, the wicked sentence kept saying itself in my ears, and I was ashamed for Sister Mary, my favorite nun. Because what we wrote concerned her and Father Tom.

Father Thomas was the chaplain and Sister Mary was the nun who dressed the altar and served Mass. She was a pretty, pink-cheeked nun, and she was always smiling as if she had some secret in life that no one else had. Not a smug smile but ecstatic. As Baba wrote it, the doorknob was turned from the outside. Two or three times, impatiently each time.

"Suppose it's her," I said in a gasping whisper. Baba unlocked the door and went out blushing. Standing there was one of the junior girls. She blessed herself when she saw us and went in hurriedly. God knows what she thought, but the following day when we were disgraced she told everyone that we came out of the lavatory together.

For the remainder of the evening, whenever I saw Sister Margaret come into the study, my legs and knees began to tremble, and I could feel her cruel eyes on me.

So, to avoid her, I went to bed early, because during the retreat we were free to go to bed at any hour before ten o'clock. There was no one in the dormitory when I went up, and it was deathly quiet. I was folding the counterpane when I heard footsteps rushing up the stairs.

"Jesus, Cait, where are you?" Baba called.

"Ssh, ssh," I said, as Sister Margaret was likely to be snooping about.

"She's gone off to the nuthouse," said Baba. Baba's eyes were flashing and she was so excited she could hardly talk.

"Is it found?" I asked.

"Found! The whole school knows about it. That mope Peggy Darcy handed it to Sister Margaret below in the recreation hall, and didn't old Margaret think 'twas a prayer and she began to read it, out loud." I could feel the color travel up my neck, and my hands were perspiring.

"Imagine," said Baba, "she read out, 'Father Tom stuck his long thing,' and when she realized what it was, she went purple at the mouth and began to fume around the recreation hall. She beat several girls with her strap, and she was yelling, 'Where are they, where are they, those children of Satan!'" Baba was enjoying every moment of this.

"Go on," I begged her.

"She had the holy picture in her hand, and she was beating all before her, so Christ, I made a beeline for the cloakroom and hid in one of the presses. All the girls were yelling by then, though half the young ones didn't know what the thing meant; so in the end she got so delirious that the prefect had to call another nun, and they carried her off."

"And what'll we do?" I asked. If only we could run quickly, get out of the place.

"They're looking for us. So for Chrissake, don't tremble or break down or anything. Say 'twas a joke we heard somewhere," Baba warned me, and just then the prefect came into the dormitory and called us out.

As we walked past her she withdrew close to the wall, because now we were filthy and loathsome and no one could speak to us. In the hallway girls looked at us as if we had some terrible disease, and even girls who had stolen watches and things gave us a hateful, superior look.

The Reverend Mother was waiting for us in the reception room. She had a shawl over her shoulders, and her face was deathly pale.

"I wish to say that you must leave at once," she said. I tried to apologize, and she addressed me individually.

"Your mind is so despicable that I cannot conceive how you have gone unnoticed all these years. Poor Sister Margaret, she has suffered the greatest shock of her religious life. This afternoon you did a disgusting thing, and now you have done something outrageous," she said. Her voice was trembling and her poise was gone. She was really upset. I began to cry and Baba gave me a dig in the ribs to shut up.

"We can explain," I said to the Reverend Mother.

"I have already informed your parents; you shall leave tomorrow," she told us.

That night we were put in the infirmary, in two separate wards. It was the longest night I have ever lived, and the thought of going home the next day was terrifying. All night, a mouse scraped the wainscoting, and I lay awake with my feet curled up under me, thinking of some way that I could put an end to my life.

We left next afternoon and no one said goodbye to us.

"Say the Rosary," Baba said to me, in the back of the hired car. The driver was a stranger but he must have had a great old ride, listening to us, as we prayed and alternated our prayers with surmisal. He was from the convent town and Reverend Mother had hired him. News of our disgrace had gone home ahead of us.

There was a man mowing the Brennans' front lawn when we got out of the car. His name was Charlie and he nodded to us, but he didn't stop the mower. It looked as if it was running away from him. It was a cold, sunny day and under the rhododendron shrub there were crocuses in bloom. Yellow ocher crocuses. The wind had got inside some of them and the petals had fallen down on the grass. They looked like pieces of crepe paper, just thrown there. There were primroses, too. A cluster of them around the roots of the sycamore tree. They had cut down the tree because they were afraid it would fall on the house in a big wind. Mr. Brennan had grown ivy around the roots and had trailed it across the ugly brown stump, and now there were primroses, merry little primroses, shooting up through the ivy. I had been looking at primrose leaves for seventeen years, and I had never noticed before that their leaves were hairy and old and wrinkled. I kept looking at them. Always on the brink of trouble I look at something, like a tree or a flower or an old shoe, to keep me from palpitating.

"Chrissake, go in," Baba said. She was walking behind me, dragging the big suitcase across the concrete. She hit the back of my leg with the case and I knocked on the door. Molly let us in. She was a little cold. They must have told her not to be friendly.

Mr. Brennan and Martha and my father were in the breakfast room. I didn't look at any of them directly but I saw that Martha was uneasy. She had a handkerchief in her hand and it was shaking.

"A nice thing. You filthy little—" my father said, coming forward. He was trying to think of a word bad enough to describe me. He had his hand raised, as if he was going to strike me.

"I hate you," I said suddenly and vehemently.

"You stinking little foul-mouth," and he struck me a terrific blow. I fell and hit my head on the edge of the china cabinet, and cups rattled inside in it. My cheek was smarting from the blow.

Mr. Brennan rushed across the room and drew up his sleeves.

"Leave her alone," he said, but my father was about to strike me again.

"Take your hands off her," Mr. Brennan shouted, as he tried to pull my father away. I stood up, and edged over toward Martha.

"I'll do what I like to her," my father threatened. He was in a raging temper, and I could see him grind his false teeth. He tried to pursue me, but Mr. Brennan caught him by the shoulders and led him to the door.

"Get to hell out of here," he said.

"You can't do this to me," my father protested.

"Can't I!" said Mr. Brennan, as he reached for my father's brown hat and placed it sideways on his head.

"I tell you, you won't get away with this," my father said, but Mr. Brennan chucked him out and banged the door in his face. Out in the hall, we could hear him cursing and swearing, and he beat the door with his fists, because Mr. Brennan had turned the key from the inside.

"Go home, Brady," Mr. Brennan said, and within a few seconds we heard him go out the hall door. I was crying, of course, and Martha and Baba were pale and shocked.

The homecoming we had dreaded was over. Instead of it being about us, and the dreadful thing we wrote, it was a scene between Mr. Brennan and my father. I knew then that Mr. Brennan hated my father, and had always hated him.

"Sit down," Mr. Brennan said to Baba and me. We sat on the couch and looked imploringly at Martha.

"Mammy, what about some tea?" Mr. Brennan said to her, and she smiled vaguely. At least he was reasonable.

"Hello, I didn't say hello to you," she said to me as she passed by my chair. She touched the top of Baba's hair tenderly.

"Well, now," said Mr. Brennan, when she had gone out.

"We hated it, we hated it; we love home," I said to him. Baba had said nothing since we came into the room. She had her head lowered and her hands clasped, as if she were praying. She was determined not to help.

"We're sorry, we hated it," I said again, and I repeated, "We love it here." He smiled faintly to himself and shook his head. He was touched. Somehow the possibility that we had done this because we were lonely seemed fair and reasonable to him.

"But why didn't you tell me?" he asked, and I was thinking of an answer when the phone rang. He had to go off urgently to the mountains, because there was a sow dying, and we were left to drink the tea and talk to Martha.

Later that evening, I was sitting on the couch in the front room when Mr. Brennan came back. He came in to talk to me. It was dusk. We could see the silver gleaming on the sideboard, and there was a smell of hyacinths in the room.

"Declan is doing well at school," he said. I knew exactly what he was thinking.

"I'm sorry, Mr. Brennan. I really am."

"You know, Caithleen, 'tis a great pity. You were clever at school. You would have gone far. Why did you undermine your whole future?" He held my hand while he was asking me.

"Don't ask me," I said.

"I know why," he said. His voice was calm, and his hand was soft and warm. He was a good and gentle man.

"Poor Caithleen, you've always been Baba's tool."

"I like Baba, Mr. Brennan. She's great fun and she doesn't mean any harm." It was true.

"Ah, if one could only choose one's children," he said sadly. A lump came in my throat, and I knew all the things that he was trying to tell me. And it seemed to me that life was a disappointment to him. The years of driving over bad roads at night, crossing fields with the light of a lantern to reach some sick beast in a drafty outhouse, had been a waste. Mr. Brennan had not found happiness, neither in his wife nor in his children. And the thought came to me that he would have liked Mama as his wife and me as his daughter. I felt that he was thinking so himself.

There was a light knock on the door. He said, "Come in." It was my father. Martha must have told him that we were in the sitting room.

"Good evening." He spoke cheerfully, as if nothing awkward had happened. "Grand evening." Mr. Brennan clicked on the light. The electricity had come since we were home last time. The friendly lamplight made a shadow on the mantelpiece. It was a white china lamp with a china shade on it. Pure and enchanting, like a child's First Communion veil. It was an old-fashioned oil lamp that Mr. Brennan had adapted for electricity.

"You wouldn't want to mind me. I might shout or anything, but 'tis all over in three minutes," my father said to both of us, and Mr. Brennan said, "Oh, let's forget it." I said nothing. Father sat down and took two pounds out of his coat pocket.

"Here," he said, throwing them over onto my lap. I thanked him and sat there glumly while they talked. But the talk was strained, and neither one liked the other anymore.

Behind the china lamp there was a postcard. It was of a dancing girl. A Spanish dancer, in a big red hooped skirt and a white blouse with puffed sleeves. I went over and picked it up to look at it. Mr. Gentleman's handwriting was on the back, and it said, *Best wishes to all of you.* It had a foreign stamp. I ran out of the room.

"Molly, Molly," I called. She was upstairs getting ready to go out. She had a boyfriend now.

"Come up," she answered. I went up and stuck my head in her door. She was bathing her feet in a basin of steaming water.

"I'm crippled with corns," she said. Her room was small and there was linoleum on the floor.

"Molly, where's Mr. Gentleman?" I asked. I couldn't wait and lead up to it casually, though I meant to.

"Off sunning himself," she said. My heart stopped.

"Why?"

"Mrs. Gentleman's nerves are at her, and they're gone off on a cruise to the Mediterranean." I was vexed and jealous and guilty all at once. But at least it was lucky that he wasn't there to hear of our disgrace. Because he was very polite in his own way and he would have been shocked by our behavior.

13   I was free to go to another convent because my scholarship was still valid, but Mr. Brennan was sending Baba
to Dublin to take a commercial course and I said that
I would go, too. I promised my father that I would do
examinations to get into the civil service, but meanwhile
I was going to work in a grocery shop.

I answered an advertisement in the paper and got a job as shop
assistant with a man named Thomas Burns. Jack Holland gave me a
glowing reference, which said that I had served my apprenticeship
with him. The reference was full of adjectives and flowery talk, and
he signed it *Jack Holland, Author and Spirit Merchant.*

"Of course, Caithleen, if ever you change your mind . . . It's a
lady's privilege," he said as he licked the brown business envelope and
sealed it by pressing it with his fist.

"Thank you, Jack," I said. "I'll think about it." It was a lie, but
it kept him happy. His mother was still dying, and the jubilee nurse
came two days a week now to wash her. He went over and opened
the wooden drawer of the till. It was stiff and only opened halfway.
He stuck his hand far in, to where the notes were kept, and took out
a pound, folding it into a small square.

"For your perusal," he said, stuffing it down inside my blouse.
One of the sharp edges of the square pricked my skin, but I was
thankful and I let him shake my hand three or four times in return,
and stroke my hair. His stroke was clumsy.

When I came out, I went to O'Brien's drapery and bought some
materials for a blouse and a pinafore dress, and went down the street
to the dressmaker's. She came to the door with a bunch of plain pins
between her teeth and loose white threads all over her dress. "Come
in," she said. She was about to eat her lunch. The three geraniums
on the windowsill were just beginning to flower. Two were vivid
red and the other was white. The leaves gave the kitchen a nice greenhouse smell.

"Makes them grow," she said, putting the tea leaves from the
breakfast on the geranium plant. She rinsed the teapot and made
some fresh tea.

"And how do you come to be free, this time of year?" she asked in her buttering-up voice. She lived alone and was the town gossip. She knew when unmarried girls were in trouble, even before they knew it themselves. The priest's housekeeper and she discussed everything, and everyone, under the sun.

"There's an epidemic in the convent," I said. Baba and I had agreed on the same story. Not even our parents wanted it known that we were expelled.

"How terrible. Is it a bad one now? And 'tis a wonder that the young Jones one from up the mountain isn't home."

"No. Mountainy girls don't get this particular epidemic," I said. She gave me a wicked eye. She was from the mountains herself and cycled there every second Sunday to see her father. She used to bring tins of fruit and a jar of calf's-foot jelly in the canvas bag on the back of her bicycle.

"Have this," she said, handing me a cup of tea and a slice of shop sponge cake. Afterward she measured me.

"You have a bit of a pot belly," she noted. She wanted to get some dig at me. I showed her the postcard, so that she could copy the blouse exactly. She looked at the writing on the back.

"Didn't the Gentlemans go off real sudden," she said.

"Did they?" I asked. She wrote my measurements in a notebook, and I left soon after. She didn't see me out, which meant that she was vexed with me. She expected me to talk about the Gentlemans. I hoped she wouldn't ruin my two pieces of material out of spite.

It was one of those clear, windy days which we get around that part of the country, with a fine strong wind blowing and clouds sailing happily by. It was clear and windy and airy, and I was happy to be alive. The wind was blowing in my face, so I pushed my bicycle up the hill. I left it inside the Brennans' gate and walked over the road to see my own home. There were French nuns there now. Only five or six of them, with a mistress of novices in charge of them. Young nuns came from the mother house in Limerick to spend their spiritual year in our large, secluded farmhouse.

The old gateway was abandoned, with nettles growing around it. The nuns had made a new gateway, with concrete piers on either side and concrete walls curving out from the piers. The avenue, which

THE COUNTRY GIRLS TRILOGY

had been one of weeds and loose stones and cart tracks, was now tarmacked and steamrolled, and easy to walk on. Some of the trees around the house were cut, and the white, weather-beaten hall door was painted a soft kindly green. The curtains of course were different, and Hickey's beehive was gone.

"Our Mother is expecting you," said the little nun who answered the door.

She went off noiselessly down the carpeted hall. The room that was once our breakfast room seemed utterly strange. I felt that I had never been there before. There was a writing desk in the corner where the whatnot had been, and they had added a mahogany mantelpiece.

"You are welcome," the Mother said. She was French, and she didn't look half as severe as the nuns in the convent. She rang a bell to summon the little nun and asked her to bring some refreshments. I got a glass of milk and a slice of homemade cake that was decorated with blanched almonds. It was difficult chewing the food while she watched me, and I hoped that I didn't make a noise while I ate.

"And what are you planning to be?" she asked.

Grocer's apprentice, I thought of saying, but instead I said, "My father hasn't decided yet." It sounded pretty impertinent, because Molly had told me that Mother Superior helped my father get over his drinking bouts. She brought down flasks of beef tea when he was in bed, and gave him little books to read prayers from. She took a tiny blue medal out of her pocket and handed it to me. That night I pinned it to my vest and always wore it there after that. Mr. Gentleman laughed when he came to see it, months later.

"You might care to see the kitchen?" she asked, and I followed her out to the kitchen. There were white presses built in along the walls, and the wood range had been replaced by an anthracite cooker. In the kitchen garden outside, there were six or seven young nuns walking singly, with heads lowered as if they were meditating. I was waiting to hear Bull's-Eye chase the hens off the flag, but of course there were no hens to chase. The visit upset me more than I had expected, and things that I thought I had forgotten kept floating to the surface of my mind. The skill with which Hickey set the mousetraps and put them under the stairs. The smell of apple jelly in the autumn, and the flypaper hanging from the ceiling with black flies all over it. Flitches of bacon hung up to smoke. The cookery book on the window ledge stained with egg yolk. These small things crowded in on me, so I felt very sad going down the drive.

On the way down I thought I ought to go into the gate lodge and see my father. I lifted the latch, but the door was locked. And I was just going out the gate, feeling very relieved, when I heard him call, "Who's there?"

He opened the door and was lifting his braces up onto his shoulders. He was in his bare feet.

"Oh, I was lying down for an hour. I had a bad aul headache."

"Go on back to bed," I said. I was praying that he would.

"Not at all. Come on in." He shut the door behind me. The kitchen was small and smoky, and the little white lace half-curtain on the window was the color of cigarette ash. There were three enamel mugs on the table with tea leaves in each of them.

"Have a cup o' tea," he said.

"All right." I filled the kettle from the bucket on the floor, and spilled some water of course. I'm always clumsy when people are watching me do something. He sat down and put on his socks. His toenails needed to be cut.

"Where were you?" he asked.

"Up home." It would always be home.

"Whojusee?"

I told him.

"Was she asking for me?"

"No."

"Her and I are the best of friends."

"They have the house lovely," I said, hoping that it would make him feel guilty.

"The grandest house in the country," he said. "I don't miss it at all," he said then. And I thought of my mother at the bottom of the lake, and how enraged she'd be if she could only hear him.

"Anyhow, I was robbed of it," he said, scratching his forehead.

So that's the story, I thought.

"How were you robbed?" I asked impertinently.

"Well, I was, you know. They all said when I inherited it from my grand-uncle that I wouldn't have it long. And they did their best to get me out of it."

So that was the story now. And to strangers and people going the road in summertime, he'd scratch his forehead, point to the big house, and tell them that he was robbed of it. I thought of Mama, and I could see her shaking her head woefully. Always when I was with him, I thought of Mama.

The kettle boiled and water bubbled from the spout. I looked around for the teapot.

"Where's the teapot?"

"Oh, a cup will do the finest. It makes lovely tea," and he instructed me to empty the tea leaves out of the enamel mugs. He told me how much tea to put into each mug, and then I poured the boiling water into them and put them on a hot coal to draw. I added milk and sugar to his, but couldn't stir it, for fear of disturbing all the tea leaves at the bottom. Mine looked like boiled turf.

"Isn't that a marvelous cup o' tea I made," he said. I made, I thought.

" 'Tis all right," I answered. Why was I so halting? I couldn't bring myself to be friendly.

"Finest tea in the country. The Connor girls were down here gathering mushrooms last year and they came in out of a shower, so I gave them a cup of that tea. They said they never drank anything like it." I smiled and tried to look agreeable.

"Where's Bull's-Eye?"

"He's gone. He got poisoned." Soon there would be nothing good left from the old life.

"How did he get poisoned?"

"There was strychnine down for foxes and he took it."

"You should have complained about that," I said. I was angry.

"Complain! Is it me to complain? Sure I never bothered anyone in my life." I searched desperately for something to say. Quickly.

"Any news of Hickey?" I asked. I hadn't heard from him for two

Christmases. Maisie said that he was engaged to someone, but we never heard whether he got married or not.

"Is it that fella? I never trusted him. Too good a time he had, wiping my eye like everyone else." I looked into the cluster of tea leaves in the bottom of my mug and tried to foresee my future. I was looking for romance, thinking that next week I would be in Dublin, free from it all. He coughed nervously. He was going to say something important. I trembled.

"There's something I want to say to you now, my lady, and I don't want you to get up on your high horses either." He took his teeth off the dresser and put them in. Felt better, more important, perhaps?

"You're to behave yourself in Dublin. Live decent. Mind your faith, and write to your father. I don't like the way you've turned out at all. Not one bit."

'Tis mutual, most mutual, I thought, but did not say so. I was afraid of getting struck, and all I wanted was to get quickly out of the smoky kitchen. Even my eyes were hurting, and the damn smoke made me cough.

"I'll be careful," I said. I looked around for the clock; it was ticking but I couldn't see it. It was on the mantelpiece, face downward. I lifted it up and said I was very sorry but I had to go, as tea was at half past five.

"I'll convey you over the road," he said, and he put on his boots. It was all right once we got out in the air; there were lots of other people around and I was not so afraid.

Molly was waxing the hall when I got in. The house was quiet.

"Where's Martha?"

"In the chapel, I suppose," said Molly.

"The chapel?" Martha always sneered at religion and praying and craw thumpers.

"Oh yes, she's off every day now. Mass and everything," Molly said.

"Since when?"

"Since the children's First Communion. She went up to see the dresses and got a fit o' crying in the chapel. Then she began to go to devotions after that, and in no time she was going to Mass."

"That's funny," I said, remembering Martha's remark once—that religion was dope for fools.

"Age changes people," said Molly, shaking her head like an old woman.

"How does it?"

"Ah, it softens them. They'll stick up for things when they're young. But when they get on, they get soft."

"Will you marry your boy, Molly?" I asked. She seemed a little strange. Not like herself. Wise instead of cheerful.

"I suppose so."

"Do you love him?"

"I'll tell you that when I'm married ten years."

"Molly! How have you so much sense?" Molly could teach me things about life. I was ashamed of myself when I saw how sensible she was. She had a hard life and she never pitied herself, never felt sorry for herself like me.

"I had to have it. My mother died when I was nine and I had to rear two younger ones."

"Wasn't she killed?" I said. I had heard some terrible story about her being burned.

"Yeh. Burned to death," she said.

"How?" I asked, though of course I shouldn't have.

"It was near six, the potatoes weren't boiled for dinner, and the men were nearly home. We heard the cart coming in at the bottom of the lane. 'Oh, God,' says she, 'blow up the fire,' and she threw paraffin on it and the fire flared up into her face and she was a mass o' flames in two seconds. I threw a can o' milk on her but 'twas no use." Molly told me this without crying, without breaking down, and I envied her for being so brave.

"We'll make a cup o' tea," she said, getting up off her knees.

"If I drink any oftener this day, I'll overflow," I said, but we went down to the kitchen and made a pot of tea, and in a little while Martha came in. Afterward, when Mr. Brennan got home, Martha went upstairs with him to wash his hair. They were laughing and talking in the bathroom, and when I was passing I saw her rubbing the short black hairs briskly, between two halves of a towel. He was sitting on the bath and he had his arms around her bottom, with his head buried in her stomach. I was delighted to see them friendly.

Maybe they'll be happy, I thought, and I hoped they would. Though in a way I was ashamed to see married people embrace each other. Because Mama and Dada never did.

When I went into the room I let a shout out of me. Baba was prostrate on the bed, with a mass of white mud all over her face.

"Oh!" I yelled, and Molly ran up to know what was wrong.

"Christ, you're a bloody aul eejit," Baba said. "I have my French mud pack on, preparing for Dublin. Did you never hear of it?" she asked. Her voice was stiff; because of the stuff around her lips, she couldn't move them properly.

"No," I said sullenly. I hated being such a fool.

"You're a right-looking eejit," she said, as she sat up and reached to the dressing table for a wet sponge and a bowl of water.

"Your mam and dad are great friends," I whispered.

"Yeh. Before she knows where she is, she'll have a damn child or something."

"Would you mind?" I asked.

"Like hell. Bloody sure I'd mind. I'd be the laughingstock of the whole country. What would Norman Spalding say?" Norman Spalding was the bank manager's son, and Baba was doing a line with him. Just for the few days before we left for Dublin. She said that the boys around home were little squirts anyhow, and no use. Sometimes during the holidays I made dates with some of them, but when I was out with them I was bored, and when they held my hand I felt disgusted. I always wanted to rush back to Mr. Gentleman, he was so much nicer than young boys.

All that week we prepared for Dublin.

On the last day I went up the village to say goodbye to a few people and to buy a packet of labels.

There was a pig fair around the market house. There were carts and red turf creels outside the shops and pink baby pigs in nests of straw, squeaking in the back of the creels. The pigs grunted and stuck their noses through the holes in the creels, trying to get out.

It was another wild, windy day, with dust blowing up the street and wisps of straw and torn paper. On the wind came the smell that prevails at every country fair. The pleasant smell of fresh dung, the warm smell of animals, and old clothes, and tobacco smoke.

The wind got inside the heavy topcoats of the farmers and flapped them out so that they looked like men in a storm; they looked fierce as they argued about prices and spat on their palms and argued more.

Two men came out of Jack Holland's. The commotion and tobacco smoke came out with them, when they held the door open for a second, and more men smelled the noise and the porter and went in hurriedly. Mountainy children stood around minding donkeys and waiting for their fathers. Their clothes were too big for them, and they looked foolish. Their large eyes noticed everything, their gaze followed the women who came out of the houses and crossed over to fill a bucket of water from the green pump. The mountainy children looked at the untidy village women with surprise, and the village women looked back with that certain disdain which villagers have for poor mountainy people.

Billy Tuohey was weighing pigs on the big scales outside the little market house, and the pigs were screaming to get away. It was dark and there were black storm clouds racing across the sky. Everyone said it would rain.

I bought the labels and said goodbye to Jack. The shop was full and there was no time to call me aside and whisper things to me. Fortunately.

I was not sorry to be leaving the old village. It was dead and tired and old and crumbling and falling down. The shops needed paint and there seemed to be fewer geraniums in the upstairs windows than there had been when I was a child.

The next hour flew. Once again we were saying goodbye. Martha cried. I suppose she felt that *we* were always going, and that life stood still for her. Life had passed her by, cheated her. She was just forty.

We were in a third-class carriage that said NO SMOKING, and the train chugged along toward Dublin.

"Chrissake, where's there a smoking carriage?" Baba asked. Her father had put us on the train, but we didn't let on that we each had a package of cigarettes in our handbags.

"We'll look for one," I said, and we went down the corridor, giggling and giving strangers the "So what" look. I suppose it was then we began that phase of our lives as the giddy country girls brazening the big city. People looked at us and then looked away again, as though they had just discovered that we were naked or something. But we didn't care. We were young and, we thought, pretty.

Baba was small and thin, with her hair cut short like a boy's, and little tempting curls falling onto her forehead. She was neat-looking, and any man could lift her up in his arms and carry her off. But I was tall and gawky, with a bewildered look, and a mass of bewildered auburn hair.

"We'll have sherry or cider or some damn thing," she said, turning around to face me. Her skin was dark, and when she smiled I thought of autumn things, like nuts and russet-colored apples.

"You're lovely-looking," I said.

"You're gorgeous," she said in return.

"You're a picture," I said.

"You're like Rita Hayworth," she said. "Do you know what I often think?"

"What?"

"How the poor bloody nuns managed the day you kept them out of the lavatory."

At the mention of the convent, I got a faint smell of cabbage; that smell that lingered in every corner of the school.

" 'Twas tough on them, holding it," she said, and she let out one of her mad, donkey laughs.

The train turned a sharp bend and we fell onto the nearest seat. Baba was laughing, so I smiled at a man opposite. He was half asleep and didn't notice me. We got up and went down the aisle of the carriages, between the dusty velvet-covered seats. In a while we came to the bar.

"Two glasses of sherry," Baba said, blowing smoke directly into the barman's face.

"What kind?" he asked. He was friendly and didn't mind the smoke.

"Any kind." He filled two glasses and put them on the counter. After we had drunk the sherry I bought cider for us, and we were a little tipsy as we swayed on the high stools and looked out at the rain as it fell on the fields that shot past the train. But being tipsy we did not see very much and the rain did not touch us.

14

We got in to Dublin just before six. It was still bright, and we carried our bags across the platform, stopping for a minute to let others pass by. We had never seen so many people in our lives.

Baba hailed a taxi and told the driver our new address. It was written on the label of her suitcase. We had got lodgings through an advertisement in the paper and our future landlady was a foreigner.

"Jesus, Cait, this is life," Baba said, relaxing in the back seat, as she took out a hand mirror to look at herself. She brought a lock of hair down onto her forehead, and it looked well there, falling over one eyebrow.

I remember nothing of the streets we drove through. They were all too strange. At six the bells rang out from some church, which were followed by other bells, with other chimes, ringing from churches all over the city. The peals of the bells mingled together and were in keeping with the fresh spring evening, and there was a special comfort in their toll. I liked them already.

We passed a cathedral, whose dark stone was still wet from the afternoon rain, though the streets were dry. We were dizzy trying to see the clothes in the shop windows.

"Christ, there's a gorgeous frock in that window. Hey, sir," she yelled, leaning forward in the seat.

The driver, without looking back, pushed a sliding window that separated the front of the car from the back.

"D'ju say something?" He had the singsong accent that is spoken in County Cork.

"Are you from Cork?" Baba said, sniggering. He pretended not to hear and closed the sliding window. Then, soon after, he turned to the left, drove down an avenue, and we were there. We got out and split the fare between us. We knew nothing about tipping. He left the cases on the footpath outside the gate. There was a motorbike against the railings, and inside, a narrow concrete path ran between two small squares of cut grass. Between the grass and the path was an oblong flower bed, at either side, and a few sallow snowdrops wilted in the damp clay. The house itself was red-brick, two-story, with a bay window downstairs.

Baba gave a cheeky knock on the chromium knocker and rang the bell at the same time.

"Oh, God, Baba, don't be impatient like that."

"None o' your cowardy-custard nonsense," she said, winking at me. The lock of hair was very rakish. There were milk bottles beside the foot scraper and I heard someone come up the hallway.

The door was opened and we were greeted by a woman in thick-lensed glasses, who wore a brown knitted dress and knitted, hairy, gray stockings.

"Ah, you are the welcome," she said, and called upstairs, "Gustav, they're here."

There were white mackintoshes on the hall stand and a colored umbrella that reminded me of a postcard Miss Moriarty sent me from Rome. We took off our coats.

She was a low-sized woman, and was almost the width of the dining-room doorway. Her bottom was like the bottom of a woman in a funny postcard. It was a mountain in itself. We followed her into the dining room.

It was a small room crowded with walnut furniture. There was a piano in one corner, and next to it was a sideboard that had framed photographs on top of it, and opposite that was a china cabinet. It was stuffed with glasses, cups, mugs, and all sorts of souvenirs. Sitting at the table was a bald, middle-aged man eating a boiled egg. He held it in one hand and spooned the contents out with the other hand. He looked very funny holding the egg on his lap as if he wasn't supposed to be eating it. He greeted us in some foreign accent and went on with his tea. He was not handsome. His eyes were too close together and he looked somehow treacherous.

We sat down. The circular table was covered with a green velvet cloth that was tasseled at the edges, and there was a vase of multi-colored everlasting anemones in the middle of the table.

Something about the room, perhaps the velvet cloth or the cluttered china cabinet, or perhaps the period of the furniture, reminded me of my mother and of our house as it had once been.

Our landlady brought in two small plates of cooked ham, some buttered bread, and a small dish of jam.

"Gustav," she called again, as she came in the dining room. I was a little afraid of her. Her voice was brutal and commandeering.

"Very good, my own make, homemade," she said, putting a fancy spoon into the jam.

We ate quickly and ravenously, and when we had cleared the bread plate, we looked at one another and at the bald man opposite us. He had finished eating and was reading a foreign paper.

"Joanna," he called, and she came in, drying her hands on her flowered apron. He said something in a foreign language to her. I supposed it was to ask for more bread.

"*Mein Gott* Almighty, save us! Country girls have big huge appetite," she said, raising her hands in the air. They were fat hands and roughened from years of work. She had a marriage ring and an eternity ring. Poor Gustav.

She went out and the man continued reading.

Baba and I were certain that he didn't understand English. So while we were waiting for the bread, Baba did a little mime act. Bowing to me, she begged in a trembling voice, "Oh, lady divine, will you pass me the wine?" I passed her the bottle of vinegar.

"Put on the tea cozy," she said, and christened me "lady supreme." Then, in another voice, she pleaded, "Oh, lady supreme, will you pass me the cream?" and I passed her the milk jug. Then she turned toward him, though he was hidden behind the paper, and said, "You bald-headed scutter, will you pass me the butter?" and while we were grinning, his hand came out from behind the newspaper and slowly he pushed the empty butter dish in her direction. We laughed more and saw that his hands were shaking. He was laughing, too. It was a nice beginning.

Joanna brought back two more slices of bread and some small pieces of cake. It was cake with two colors. Half yellow, half chocolate. Mama called it marble cake, but Joanna had some other name for it. The pieces were cunningly cut. Each piece only a mouthful. The man opposite took two pieces, and Baba kicked me under the table as if to warn me to eat quickly. She stuffed her own mouth full.

Gustav came in and we stood up to shake hands with him. He was a small, pale-faced man with cunning eyes and an apologetic smile. His hands were white and refined-looking.

"No, ladies, stay be sitting," he said humbly, too humbly. I preferred Joanna. Baba was delighted that he called us ladies, and she gave him one of her loganberry smiles.

"Up there shaving all the night. What you got your new shirt on for?" Joanna said, looking carefully at his shirt and the top of his waistcoat. He said that he was going down to the local.

"Just for a small time, Joanna," he said.

"*Mein Gott!* I have two chickens to pluck and you not help me." The smile never left his face.

"Nice, nice ladies," he said, pointing to us, and Baba was fluttering her eyelashes at a furious rate.

"Oh yes, yes; eat, eat up," Joanna said suddenly, remembering us. But there was nothing else to eat, as we had cleared the table.

I began to tidy up the things, and pile the plates on top of one another, but Baba said in my ear, "Chrissake, we'll be doing it day and night if we begin once. Skivvies, that's what we'll be." So I took her advice and followed her upstairs to the bedroom, where Gustav had put our cases.

It was a small room that looked out on the street. There was dark brown linoleum on the floor and a beaded lampshade over the electric bulb that hung from the ceiling.

I went over to the open window to smell the city air and see what it looked like. There were children down below, playing hopscotch, and picky beds. One boy had a mouth organ and he put it to his lips and played whenever he felt like it. Seeing me, they all stared up, and one, the biggest one, asked, "What time is it?" I was smoking a cigarette and pretended not to hear him. "Eh, miss, what time is it? Thirty-two degrees is freezing point, what's squeezing point?"

You could hear Baba laughing at the dressing table, and she told me for Chrissake to come in or we'd be thrown out. She said he was great gas, and we must get to know him.

The wardrobe was empty but we couldn't hang our clothes because we had forgotten to bring hangers. So we laid them across the big armchair in the corner of the room.

At the gate below a motorbike started up and went roaring down the avenue. Gustav was gone.

In the next room a man began to play a fiddle.

"Jesus," Baba said, simply, and put her hands to her ears. She was walking around the room with her hands to her ears, swearing, when Joanna knocked and came in.

"Herman, he does to practice," she said, smiling, when Baba pointed with her thumb toward the other room. "Very talent. A musician. You like music?" And Baba said we adored music, and that we had come all the way to Dublin to hear a man playing a fiddle.

"Oh, nice. Good. Very nice," and Baba made a gesture which told me that she thought Joanna was nuts. I was still unpacking, so Joanna came over and looked at my clothes. She asked me if my father was rich, and Baba chimed in and said he was a millionaire.

"A millionaire?" You could see her pupils get large behind her thick lenses.

"My charge too cheap then, hah?" she said, grinning at us. Her way of grinning was unfortunate. It was thick and stupid and made you hate her. But perhaps it was the glasses.

"No. Too dear," Baba said.

"Dear? Darling? *Klein*? I not understand."

"No. Too costly," I said, catching my hair up with a ribbon and hoping before I consulted the mirror that it would make my face beautiful.

"You happy?" she asked, suddenly anxious, suddenly worried in case we should leave.

"We happy," I said, for both of us, and she grinned. I liked her.

"I give you a present," she said. We looked at one another in astonishment as she went out of the room.

She came back with a bottle of something yellow and two thimble-sized glasses. They were glasses such as the chemist had at home. They were for measuring medicines. She poured some of the thick yellow liquid into each glass.

"Your health here. Hah!" she said. We put the glasses to our lips.

"Good?" she asked, before we had tasted it at all.

"Good," I said, lying. It was eggy and had a sharp spirit taste besides.

"Mine." She put her hand across her stout chest. Her breasts were not defined; she was one solid front of outstanding chest.

"On the Continent we make our own. Parties, everything, we make our own."

"God protect us from the Continent," Baba said to me in Irish, and was smiling so that her two dimples showed.

I had put a jar of face cream and a small bottle of Evening in Paris perfume on the table, to make the room habitable, and Joanna went over to admire them. She took the lid off the cream jar and smelled it. Then she smelled the perfume.

"Nice," she said, still smelling the contents of the dusky-blue perfume bottle.

"Have some," I said, because we were under a compliment to her for the little drink.

"Expensive? Is it expensive?"

"Costs pounds," Baba said, smirking into her glass. Baba was going to make a fool of Joanna, I could see that.

"Pounds. *Mein Gott!*" She screwed the metal cork back on the bottle and laid it down quickly. In case it should break.

"Tomorrow perhaps I have some. Tomorrow Sunday. You Catholics?"

"Yes. Are you?" Baba asked.

"Yes, but we on the Continent are not so rigid as you Irish." She shrugged her shoulders to show a certain indifference. Her knitted dress was uneven at the tail and sagged at both sides. She went out and we heard her go downstairs.

"What will we do, Cait?" Baba asked as she lay full-length on the single bed.

"I don't know. Will we go to confession?" It was what we usually did on Saturday evenings.

"Confession. Christ, don't be such a drip, we'll go downtown. Oh, God, isn't it heaven?" She kicked her feet up in the air and hugged the pillow that was under the chenille bedspread.

"Put on everything you've got," she said. "We'll go to a dance."

"So soon?"

"Christ, so soon! Soon, and we cooped up in that jail for three thousand years."

"We don't know the way." I wasn't really interested in dancing. At home I walked on the boys' toes and couldn't turn corners so well. Baba danced like a dream, spinning round and round until her cheeks were flushed and her hair blown every way.

"Go down and use your elegant English on Frau Buxomburger."

"That's not nice," I said, putting on my wistful face. The face Mr. Gentleman liked best.

"Christ, she's gas, isn't she? I keep expecting that her old arse will drop off. Looks like one that's stuck on."

"Ssh, ssh," I said. I was afraid the fiddler would hear us, as he had stopped sawing.

"Go down and ask, and stop this ssh-ing business."

Joanna was pouring a kettle of scalding water over a dead Rhode Island Red chicken. When the bird was completely wet she began to tear the feathers away. I was in the kitchen watching her, but she hadn't heard me because there was ceilidh music being played on the wireless.

The dead chicken reminded me of all our Sunday dinners at home. Hickey would wring a chicken's neck on Saturday morning, leave it outside the back door, and it would stir and make an effort to move itself for a long time after it was killed. Bull's-Eye, thinking it was alive, would bark at it and try to chase it away.

"*Mein Gott!* you give me a fright," she said, turning around, as she held the chicken in one hand. I said I was very sorry and asked her the way downtown. She told me, but her instructions were very confusing and I knew that we would have to ask somebody else on the street.

When I came upstairs Baba had gone out to the bathroom, and without her the room was cheerless and empty. Outside in the avenue it was evening. The children were gone. The street was lonesome. A child's handkerchief blew on one of the spears of our railing. There were houses stretching across the plain of city, houses separated by church spires, or blocks of flats, ten and twenty stories high. In the distance the mountains were a brown blur with clouds resting on them. They were not mountains really but hills. Gentle, memorable hills.

As I looked toward them, I thought of lambs being born in the cold and in the dark, of sheep farmers trudging down across the hills, and afterward I thought of the shepherds and their dogs stretching out in front of the fire, to doze for an hour until it was time to go out again and face the sharp wind. Our farm was not on the mountain, but four or five miles away there were mountains, where Hickey brought me once on the crossbar of his bicycle. He put a cushion on the bar, in case my bottom got sore. We went for a sheep dog. It was early spring, with lambs being born, and you could hear them bleating pitifully against the wind. We got the sheep dog. A handful of black and white fur, asleep in a box of hay. He grew up to be Bull's-Eye.

"Will you come a-waltzing, Matilda, with me; waltzing, Matilda," Baba sang behind my back, and drew me into a waltz.

"What in the hell are you thinking about?" she asked. But she did not wait to hear.

"I've a smashing idea. I'll change my name. I'll be Barbara, pronounced 'Baubra.' Sounds terrific, doesn't it? Pity you're going to work in that damn shop. 'Twill cramp our style," she said thoughtfully.

"Why?"

"Oh, every little country mohawk is in a bloody grocer's. We'll say you're at college if anyone asks."

"But who's to ask?"

"Fellows; we'll have them swarming around us. And, mind you, Christ, if you take any fellow of mine, I'll give you something to cry about."

"I won't," I said, smiling, admiring the big wide sleeves of my blouse and wondering if he would notice it and wondering, too, when he and Mrs. Gentleman would return home.

"Your cigarette, your cigarette," I said to Baba. She had left it on the bedside table and it had burned a mark in from the edge. You could smell the burnt wood.

"*Mein Gott!* what you mean?" Joanna said, bursting in without knocking.

"My best table, my table," she said, rushing over to examine the burn mark. I was crimson with fear.

"Smoking, young girls, it is forbid," she said; there were tears in her eyes as she threw the cigarette into the fireplace.

"We must have an ashtray," Baba said, and then she looked at the little bamboo table and got down on her knees to look under it.

"It's useless anyhow, it's reeking with worms," she said to Joanna.

"What you mean?" Joanna was breathing terribly hard, as if she were going to erupt.

"Woodworm," Baba said, and Joanna jumped and said it was impossible. But in the end Baba won and Joanna took the table away and brought it out to a shed in the yard.

"Please, ladies, not to lie on the good bedspreads, they are from the Continent, pure chenille," she said imploringly, and I promised that we would be more careful.

"Now we have no table," I said to Baba, when Joanna went out.

"So what?" she asked, as she took off her dress.

"Was it wormy?" I asked.

"How the hell would I know?" She began to spray deodorant under her arms. Her neck was not as white as mine. I was pleased.

We got ready quickly and went down into the neon fairyland of Dublin. I loved it more than I had ever loved a summer's day in a hayfield. Lights, faces, traffic, the enormous vitality of people hurrying to somewhere. A dark-faced woman in an orange silk thing went by.

"Christ, they're in their underwear here," Baba said. The woman had enormous dark eyes, with dark shadows under them. She seemed to be searching the night and the crowd for something poignant. Something to equal the beauty of the shadows and her carved, cat-like face.

"Isn't she beautiful?" I said to Baba.

"She's like something dug up," Baba said as she crossed over to look in the glass door of an ice-cream parlor.

A doorman opened it, and held it open. So there was nothing for us to do but to go in.

We had two large dishes of ice cream. It was served with peaches and cream, and the whole lot was decorated with flaked chocolate. There were songs pouring out of a metal box near our table. Baba tapped her feet and swayed her shoulders, keeping time with the melody. Afterward she put money in the slot herself and played the same songs over again.

"Jesus, we're living at last," she said. She was looking around to see if there were any nice boys at the other tables.

"It's nice," I said. I meant it. I knew now that this was the place I wanted to be. Forevermore I would be restless for crowds and lights and noise. I had gone from the sad noises, the lonely rain pelting on the galvanized roof of the chicken house; the moans of a cow in the night, when her calf was being born under a tree.

"Are we going dancing?" Baba asked. My feet were tired and I told her so. We went home and bought a bag of chips in a shop quite near our avenue. We ate them going along the pavement. The lights overhead were a ghastly green.

"Jesus, you look like someone with consumption," Baba said as she handed me a chip.

"So do you," I said. And together we thought of a poem that we had learned long ago. We recited it out loud:

> *From a Munster Vale they brought her*
> *From the pure and balmy air,*
> *An Ormond Ullin's daughter*
> *With blue eyes and golden hair.*
> *They brought her to the city*
> *And she faded slowly there,*
> *For consumption has no pity*
> *For blue eyes and golden hair.*

There were people looking at us, but we were too young to care. Baba blew into the empty chip bag until it was puffed out. Then she bashed it with her fist, and it burst, making a tremendous noise.

"I'm going to blow up this town," she said, and she meant it, that first night in Dublin.

15

It was a clear spring day when I drew back the dusty cretonne curtains to let the sun into our bedroom on Monday morning. The room seemed shabby, now that I knew it better. The linoleum was worn thin, and Joanna had brought up an orange box and stood it on end between our two beds. She had covered it with a strip of cretonne that matched the curtains, but no matter how it was covered, it was still only an orange box.

"Breakfast," she called as she knocked loudly on the bedroom door. Baba was asleep. She said she was going to miss college the first day because we had been dancing the night before and went to bed late. The room was untidy, there were clothes strewn all over the floor, and already the dressing table had a film of powder on it. It was nice to see the room so untidy. We were grown-up and independent.

I came downstairs and found Herman, the bald-headed lodger, eating some raw minced steak.

"Good for a man," he said, smiling and tapping his chest to show how healthy he was. He did physical exercises morning and night, and Baba and I listened outside his door while he counted and thrust his arms and legs into the atmosphere.

"No egg, thank you," I said to Joanna when she brought it in to me. Baba said that all the eggs in the city were rotten, and more than likely we'd find a dead chicken inside soon as we topped one. I took her advice and developed a disgust against all eggs, even against the little brown pullets' eggs that Hickey coddled for me, long ago.

I ate quickly and set out, just before nine. Gustav wished me luck and saw me to the door.

"Gustav, come watch your toast," Joanna called, so he waved and shut the door very quietly.

The grocery shop was only a five-minute walk. There were trees along the footpath, and it was a soft day. The buds had thrust their way to the very tips of the thin, black, graceful birch branches. The buds were lime-green and the branches black, slender branches stirring in the wind. There were pigeons on the chimney tops, and pigeons walking assuredly over the gray, sloping roofs. They were cheeky pigeons who didn't mind the traffic. It was funny to watch them do their droppings, it squirted out easily and happily. I had never been so close to pigeons before.

My shop was in a shopping center, between a drapery and a chemist's.

TOM BURNS—GROCERY was written over the door, and painted crookedly on the window was a sign which read HOME-COOKED HAM A SPECIALTY. There were fancy biscuit tins in the window and posters of girls eating crunchies. Nice girls with healthy teeth.

I went in nervously. Behind the counter stood a stout man with a brown mustache. He was weighing bags of sugar, which he scooped out of a big sack.

"I'm the new girl," I said.

"Oh, you're welcome," he said as he shook hands with me. I followed him into the back of the shop. It was very untidy, with cardboard boxes littered all over the floor. Sitting on a high stool, copying bills from a large ledger, was a woman whom he introduced as his wife. She was wearing a white shop coat.

"Ah, darling, you're welcome," she said, as she swiveled around on the stool and faced me.

"Isn't she lovely?" she said to him. "Oh, darling, you're as welcome as the flowers in May. Gorgeous hair and everything." She stroked my hair and I thanked her. Outside in the shop someone tapped the glass counter impatiently with a coin and Mr. Burns went out.

"Any empty boxes?" I heard a child's voice ask, and he must have shaken his head, because light footsteps went out the door.

Mrs. Burns was smiling at me. She had a pale, round face and sleepy, tobacco eyes. She was fat (though not as comically fat as Joanna) and lazy-looking.

"Darling, did you bring your shop coat?" I said that I hadn't heard about one and she said, "Oh, darling, how terrible, he should have told you. He's so forgetful, he forgets to charge people for things."

I said that was a pity and tried to look sympathetic.

"Darling, there's a drapery two doors away. Maybe you'd like to nip out and get one. Tell Mrs. Doyle I sent you."

"I have no money," I said. I had spent ten shillings at the dance the previous night. (It cost me five shillings to go in, another shilling to put my coat in the cloakroom, and I drank three minerals because nobody asked me to dance after I fell. I fell dancing a barn dance. I must have tripped over my partner's shoes; anyhow, I fell, and my flared skirt blew up around me, so that people saw my garters and things. Baba looked away as if she didn't know me, and my partner slunk off toward the bandstand. It was an awful moment. Then I got up, smoothed my skirt, and went upstairs. I sat on the balcony and drank minerals for the rest of the night. I tried to look casual as hell, to show that I wasn't interested in dancing anyhow. Down below, Baba was drifting under the soft pink lights, and hundreds of boys and girls were dancing cheek to cheek up and down the ballroom under the twists of colored papers that hung from the ceiling and moved to a music of their own. Waltzing was forgetfulness and I wished that Mr. Gentleman would suddenly appear out of nowhere and steer me through the strange, long, sweet night, and say things in my ear and keep his arms around me, even when the music stopped and the girls went back to their seats until the music struck up and they were asked for the next dance.)

"Well, darling, you better wait then, until you get paid on Saturday," Mrs. Burns said churlishly. She folded her thin lips inward so that you thought she had none. She was displeased.

Mr. Burns told me to weigh bags of tea and sugar, and after that he said I could weigh half pounds of streaky rashers.

"Tom, I think I'll make the bed now and get a few hams on," his wife said, and disappeared for the rest of the morning. He filled the shelves with tins of peas and bottles of relish, and all the time he talked to me. He told me he was a country man and how much he loved the country, and the Sundays long ago in Galway when he played hurley. Very long ago, I thought to myself.

"I go back there every year. Last year I helped them cut the turf," he said. And in that instant I saw Hickey's boot on a slane, cutting a sod from the black-brown turf bank. When he dug the slane into the bank, water squelched out and flowed down into the pool of black bog water. I saw the bog water and the bog lilies and the blackened patches of ground where we had made fires to boil a kettle, and the heather which brushed my ankles and the great limestone ridges that rose out of the brown and purple earth. Often, while Hickey was cutting or footing the turf, I used to wander away over to the bog lake, picking my steps from one limestone rock to the next. The edge of the bog lake was fringed with bulrushes, and at certain times of the year their heads were a soft brown plush. And at other times of the year, flowers came on the water-lily leaves. Wax flowers, swaying, on the flat green saucer leaves. Pretty flowers that no one ever saw because the men cutting turf were too busy. The rushes were lonesome; when the wind cried through them the cry was like the curlew, and the curlew was the Uileann pipe that Billy Tuohey played in the evenings. At the far edge of the lake there was a belt of poplar trees, shutting out the world. The world I wanted to escape into. And now that I had come into the world, that scene of bogs and those country faces were uppermost in my thoughts.

"Oh, God, I'm sorry," I said. In my daydreaming I had let the sack of sugar fall sideways and the sugar was flowing onto the floor. The wood floor was dusty, so I couldn't recover the sugar. He sent me into the kitchen for the brush and the dustpan.

Mrs. Burns was drinking tea and she had an open tin of fancy biscuits on the table. The hams were simmering in big black pots on top of the coal range. She had put apples and cloves in the water and the smell was delicious.

"I came in for the dustpan," I said.

"It's over there beside the range. Are you doing a little cleaning, darling?" Her eyes brightened.

"No. I spilled sugar." I wouldn't have told her but I was afraid that Mr. Burns might mention it when she asked him in bed that night what he thought of me.

"Oh, darling angel, how much sugar?" Her face changed its expression and once again her lips disappeared.

"Just a little," I said placatingly.

"Now you must learn to be careful. Mr. Burns and I never waste a thing. Now, darling, you will be careful?" Never waste a thing and she stuffing herself with biscuits.

"I will," I said. I wasn't looking at her suet-pale face but at the top button of her yellow jersey dress. It was an expensive dress but stained all over. She had a pencil over her ear and the point of it showed through her gray-black hair. She was about fifty.

Later on in the morning the daily help came. Mr. Burns introduced me to her. Her name was Joe. A withered little woman in a black coat and a black hat that was going green. She disappeared into the hallway and I heard her coughing. She had a bad cough. A cigarette cough, she told me afterward.

The messenger boy came at eleven.

"Willie, you're late again," Mr. Burns said, looking up at the railway clock that was fixed to the wall.

"My mother is sick, sir," Willie said, saying mudder for mother.

He had a comb and a mouth organ in his breast pocket, and he got the sweeping brush and began to brush the floor languidly. That was the entire household, except for the sleek black cat, which I dreaded. Mr. Burns told me that he locked her into the shop at night as there were a lot of mice around. At half past eleven he went inside for a cup of tea.

"Hello," Willie said, winking lightly at me. We were friends.

"Is she up?" he asked.

"Who?"

"Mrs. Burns."

"Oh yes, hours ago."

"She's a right old hag. She wouldn't give you a fright." ("Froight" was the way Willie pronounced it.)

"Do we get tea?" I whispered. I was thinking of the biscuits and the one I would choose first, and if she was likely to pass me the tin twice.

"Tea, my eye." (Moy oy.) A customer came in for a large packet of corn flakes and Willie got them down for me. They were high up on a shelf and he had to mount the stepladder. It was a shaky-looking ladder and I got dizzy just watching him climb.

Then he showed me where things were kept, cloves and Vicks and currants and packet soups and all the little things that I might miss. On a postcard I wrote down the prices of obvious things like tea and sugar and butter, and the morning dragged on slowly until the Angelus rang. Willie laughed while he was praying. Then he took a pinup girl out of his pocket and said, "She's like you, Miss Brady." I was four or five years older than Willie, so I didn't mind what he said.

"Peckish, darling?" Mrs. Burns asked as she came out. I said yes, but in fact Willie and I had eaten two doughnuts and sugar barley while Mr. Burns was having his tea. I put the money for them in the till. It was an elaborate metal till, and every time you opened the drawer it gave a sharp ring, so that you couldn't open the drawer secretly. Across the front of it were little buttons with numbers on them, and you had to press the numbers, depending on how much money you put in.

My fingers were sticky from weighing sugar, so I asked if I might go upstairs to wash my hands. I was dying to see upstairs. Their bedroom door was half open. I could see part of the carpeted floor, and the unmade bed with the pile of fluffy, soft, pink blankets on it. There was a box of chocolates beside the bed, on a wicker table, and copies of a magazine called *Field and Stream*.

The bathroom was untidy, with towels thrown on the floor and two open tins of talcum powder on the washbasin ledge. I washed myself and had a free sprinkle of lavender talc.

Downstairs in the hall, while I was putting on my coat, I could see Mrs. Burns examining two plates of dinner which Joe, the cleaning woman, had got ready. There was chicken and potato salad on both plates. Mrs. Burns took the breast of chicken off one plate and put it on the other plate. Then she put a leg on the plate which she had raided. She sat down to table and began to eat from the plate that had the white delicate meat. I coughed to let her know that I was there.

"Tell Mr. Burns to lock up and come in for dinner. The creature, he must be starved," she said. The creature, I thought, and wondered if he ever caught her fiddling with the dinner plates.

"All right, Mrs. Burns. 'Bye, 'bye now."

"Goodbye, darling." Her mouth was full.

I went over to my new home, wondering about the Burnses and their life together. I bet that she ate chocolates in bed and had three hot-water bottles, and while she was eating, Mr. Burns was turned on his side reading *Field and Stream*, and the sleek cat downstairs was devouring frightened mice in the dark.

16

Easter was a month later. There were lilies in the window of the flower shop at the corner and there were purple sheets covering the statues in the chapel. On Good Friday the shops were closed and every place was sad. Purple-sad. Death-sad. Baba said we might as well be dead, so we cleaned our bedroom and went to bed early. I liked reading but Baba couldn't bear to see me reading. She'd pace about the room and ask me questions and read a passage over my shoulders and finally say it was "bloody rubbish."

Easter Saturday night, after I got paid, I went to confession and then came down to Miss Doyle's drapery and bought a pair of nylons, a brassiere, and a white lace handkerchief. The handkerchief was one I'd never use, never dare to; it was a spider's web in the sunlight, frail and exquisite. I looked forward to the summer when I would wear it stuck into Mama's silver bracelet, with the lace frill hanging down, temptingly, over the wrist. While I was out boating with Mr. Gentleman, it would blow away, moving like a white lace bird across the surface of the blue water, and Mr. Gentleman would pat my arm and say, "We'll get another." There was still no news of him, though Martha said in a letter that he had come home and was as brown as a berry from all the sun.

The brassiere I bought was cheap. Baba said that once brassieres were washed they lost their elasticity, so we might as well buy cheap ones and wear them until they got dirty. We threw the dirty ones in the dustbin, but later we found that Joanna brought them back in and washed them.

"Christ, she'll resell them to us," Baba said, and bet me sixpence; but Joanna didn't. She put them in the linen press and said that they would be useful. We thought she'd put pieces in at the side and make them bigger, so that they fitted her. But she didn't. Next time, when the woman came to scrub, Joanna gave her the brassieres instead of money. She was thrift itself. Mending. Patching. She ripped an old faded cardigan that had shrunk and used the wool to knit bedsocks for Gustav. Her knitting was under the cushion of the armchair, and one day when Herman was drunk he disturbed the knitting. The stitches fell off the needle, crawled off the needle like little brown beetles, and settled on the cushion.

"*Mein Gott!*" Joanna flew into a temper, her blood pressure soared, and her head began to spin. We carried her (oh, the weight and the indecency of it) onto the sofa in the drawing room. The drawing room was never used. There were preserved eggs in a bucket on the floor and along the window seat there were apples. Some of them were bad, and the room had a pleasant cider smell. Herman gave her a spoonful of brandy, and she recovered and flew into a fresh rage.

"This room is sumptuous," Baba said to Joanna. Baba went across to speak to the porcelain nymph in the fireplace. Joanna had rouged the nymph's cheeks and put nail polish on her fingernails. She was a lollipop nymph.

"Will you fit on the brassiere, Miss Brady?" the shopgirl asked. Pale, First Communion voice; pale, pure, rosary-bead hands held the flimsy, black, sinful garment between her fingers, and her fingers were ashamed.

"No. Just measure me," I said. She took a measuring tape out of her overall pocket, and I raised my arms while she measured me.

The black underwear was Baba's idea. She said that we wouldn't have to wash it so often, and that it was useful if we ever had a street accident, or if men were trying to strip us in the backs of cars. Baba thought of all these things. I got black nylons, too. I read somewhere that they were "literary" and I had written one or two poems since I came to Dublin. I read them to Baba and she said they were nothing to the ones on mortuary cards.

"Good night, Miss Brady, happy Easter," the First Communion voice said to me, and I wished her the same.

When I came in they were all having tea. Even Joanna was sitting at the dining-room table, with tan makeup on her arms and a charm bracelet jingling on her wrist. Every time she lifted the cup, the charms tinkled against the china, like ice in a cocktail glass. Cool, ice-cool, sugared cocktails. I liked them. Baba knew a rich man who bought us cocktails one evening.

There were stuffed tomatoes, sausage rolls, and simnel cake for tea.

"Good?" Joanna asked before I had swallowed the first mouthful of crumbly pastry. I nodded. She was a genius at cooking, surprising us with things we had never seen, little yellow dumplings in soup, apple strudel, and sour cabbage, but how I wished that she didn't stand over us with imploring looks, asking "Good?"

"Tell jokes, my tell jokes?" Herman asked Gustav. He had taken a glass of wine, and always after a glass of wine he wanted to tell jokes.

Gustav shook his head. Gustav was pale and delicate. He looked unemployed, which of course was proper, because he did not go to work. He suffered from a skin disease or something. I was never sure whether I liked Gustav or not. I don't think I liked the cunning behind his small blue eyes, and I often thought that he was too good to be true.

"Let him tell jokes," Joanna said; she liked to be made to laugh.

"No, we go to pictures. We have good time at pictures," Gustav said, and Baba roared laughing and lifted her chair so that it was resting on its two back legs.

"There no juice at pictures," Joanna said, and Baba's chair almost fell backward, because she had got a fit of coughing on top of the laughing. She coughed a lot lately, and I told her she ought to see about it.

"No juice" was Joanna's way of saying that the pictures were a waste of money.

"We go, Joanna," Gustav said, gently nudging her bare, tanned arm with his elbow. His shirt-sleeves were rolled up and his jacket was hanging on the back of his chair. It was a warm evening and the sun shone through the window and lit up the apricot jam on the table.

"Yes, Gustav," Joanna said. She smiled at him as she must have smiled when they were sweethearts in Vienna. She began to clear off the table and warned us about the good, best, china.

"Ladies come nightclub with me?" Herman asked jokingly.

"Ladies have date," Baba said. She lowered her chin onto her chest, to let me know that it was true. Her hair was newly set, so that it curved in soft black waves that lay like feathers on the crown of her head. I was raging. Mine was long and loose and streelish.

"More cake?" Joanna asked. But she had put the simnel cake into a marshmallow tin.

"Yes, please." I was still hungry.

"*Mein Gott,* you got too fat." She made a movement with her hand, to outline big fat woman. She came back with a slice of sad sponge cake that was probably put aside for trifle. I ate it.

Upstairs, I took off all my clothes and had a full view of myself in the wardrobe mirror. I was getting fat all right. I turned sideways, and looked around so that I could see the reflection of my hip. It was nicely curved and white like the geranium petals on the dressmaker's window ledge.

"What's Rubenesque?" I asked Baba. She turned around to face me. She had been painting her nails at the dressing table.

"Chrissake, draw the damn curtains or they'll think you're a sex maniac." I ducked down on the floor, and Baba went over and drew the curtains. She caught the edges nervously between her thumb and her first finger, so that her nail polish would not get smudged. Her nails were salmon pink, like the sky which she had just shut out by drawing the curtain.

I was holding my breasts in my hands, trying to gauge their weight, when I asked her again, "Baba, what's Rubenesque?"

"I don't know. Sexy, I suppose. Why?"

"A customer said I was that."

"Oh, you better be *it* all right, for this date," she said.

"With whom?"

"Two rich men. Mine owns a sweets factory and yours has a stocking factory. Free nylons. Yippee. How much do your thighs measure?" She made piano movements with her fingers, so that the nail polish would dry quickly.

"Are they nice?" I asked tentatively. We had already had two disastrous nights with friends that she had found. In the evenings, after her class, some other girls and she went into a hotel and drank coffee in the main lounge. Dublin being a small, friendly city, one or the other of them was always bound to meet someone, and in that way Baba made a lot of acquaintances.

"Gorgeous. They're aged about eighty, and my fellow has every bit of himself initialed. Tiepin, cuff links, handkerchief, car cushions. The lot. He has leopards in his car as mascots."

"I can't go, then," I said nervously.

"In Christ's name, why not?"

"I'm afraid of cats."

"Look, Caithleen, will you give up the nonsense? We're eighteen and we're bored to death." She lit a cigarette and puffed vigorously. She went on: "We want to live. Drink gin. Squeeze into the front of big cars and drive up outside big hotels. We want to go places. Not to sit in this damp dump." She pointed to the damp patch in the wall-paper, over the chimneypiece, and I was just going to interrupt her, but she got in before me. "We're here at night, killing moths for Joanna, jumping up like maniacs every time a moth flies out from behind the wardrobe, puffing DDT into crevices, listening to that lunatic next door playing the fiddle." She sawed off her left wrist with her right hand. She sat on the bed exhausted. It was the longest speech Baba had ever made.

"Hear! Hear!" I said, and I clapped. She blew smoke straight into my face.

"But we want young men. Romance. Love and things," I said despondently. I thought of standing under a streetlight in the rain with my hair falling crazily about, my lips poised for the miracle of a kiss. A kiss. Nothing more. My imagination did not go beyond that. It was afraid to. Mama had protested too agonizingly all through the windy years. But kisses were beautiful. His kisses. On the mouth, and on the eyelids, and on the neck when he lifted up the mane of hair.

"Young men have no bloody money. At least the gawks we meet. Smell o' hair oil. Up the Dublin mountains for air, a cup of damp tea in a damp hostel. Then out in the woods after tea and a damp hand fumbling under your skirt. No, sir. We've had all the bloody air we'll ever need. We want life." She threw her arms out in the air. It was a wild and reckless gesture. She began to get ready.

We washed and sprinkled talcum powder all over ourselves.

"Have some of mine," Baba said, but I insisted, "No, Baba, you have some of mine." When we were happy we shared things, but when life was quiet and we weren't going anywhere, we hid our things like misers, and she'd say to me, "Don't you dare touch my powder," and I'd say, "There must be a ghost in this room, my perfume was interfered with," and she'd pretend not to hear me. We never loaned each other clothes then, and one worried if the other got anything new.

One morning Baba rang me at work and said, "Jesus, I'll brain you when I see you."

"Why?" The phone was in the shop and Mrs. Burns was standing beside me, looking agitated.

"Have you my brassiere on?"

"No, I haven't," I said.

"You must have; it didn't walk. I searched the whole damn room and it isn't there."

"Where are you now?"

"I'm in a phone booth outside the college and I can't come out."

"Why not?"

"Because I'm flopping all over the damn place," and I laughed straight into Mrs. Burns's face and put down the phone.

"Oh, darling, I know how popular you must be. But tell your friends not to phone in the mornings. There might be orders coming through," Mrs. Burns said.

That night Baba found the brassiere mixed up in the bedclothes. She never made her bed until evening.

We got ready quickly. I put on the black nylons very carefully so that none of the threads would get caught in my ring and then looked back to see if the seams were straight. They were bewitching. The stockings, not the seams. Baba hummed "Galway Bay" and tied a new gold chain around the waist of her blue tweed dress.

I was still wearing my green pinafore dress and the white dancing blouse. They smelled of stale perfume, all the perfume I had poured on before going to dances. I wished I had something new.

"I'm sick o' this," I said, pointing to my dress. "I think I won't go."

So she got worried and loaned me a long necklace. I wound it round and round, until it almost choked me. The color was nice next to my skin. It was turquoise and the beads were made of glass.

"My eyes are green tonight," I said, looking into the mirror. They were a curious green, a bright, luminous green, like wet lichen.

"Now mind—Baubra; and none of your Baba slop," she warned me. She ignored the bit about my eyes. She was jealous. Mine were bigger than hers and the whites were a delicate blue, like the whites of a baby's eyes.

There was nobody in the house when we were leaving, so we put out the hall light and made sure that the door was locked. A gas meter two doors down had been raided and Joanna warned us about locking up.

We linked and kept step with one another. There was a bus stop at the top of the avenue, but we walked on to the next stop. It was a penny cheaper from the next stop, to Nelson's Pillar. We had plenty of money that night, but we walked out of habit.

"What'll I drink?" I asked, and distantly somewhere in my head I heard my mother's voice accusing me, and I saw her shake her finger at me. There were tears in her eyes. Tears of reproach.

"Gin," Baba said. She talked very loudly. I could never get her to whisper, and people were always looking at us in the streets, as if we were wantons.

"My earrings hurt," I said.

"Take them off and give your ears a rest," she said. Still aloud.

"But will there be a mirror?" I asked. I wanted to have them on when I got there. They were long giddy earrings, and I loved shaking my head so that they dangled and their little blue-glass stones caught the light.

"Yeh, we'll go into the cloaks first," Baba said. I took them off and the pain in the lobes of my ears was worse. It was agony for a few minutes.

We passed the shop where I worked; the blind was drawn, but there was a light inside. The blind wasn't exactly the width of the window; there was an inch to spare at either side and you could see the light through that narrow space.

"Guess what they're doing in there," Baba said. She knew all about them and was always plying me with questions—what they ate and what kind of nightgowns were on the clothesline and what he said to her when she said, "Darling, I'll go up and make the bed now."

"They're eating chocolates and counting the day's money," I said. I could taste the liqueur chocolates Mr. Gentleman had given me long ago.

"No, they're not. They're taking a rasher off every half pound you've weighed before going up to confession," she said, going over and trying to see through the slit at the corner. I saw a bus coming and we ran to the stop thirty or forty yards away.

"You're all dolled up," the conductor said. He didn't take our fares that night. We knew him from going in and out of town every other evening. We wished him a happy Easter.

17

The foyer of the hotel was brightly lit and there were palm plants in a huge vase over in one corner.

We went into the cloakroom first and I put on my earrings. We washed our hands and dried them on a hot-air dryer and found this so funny that we washed them again and dried them a second time. We came out and I followed Baba through the foyer into the lounge. There were a lot of people sitting at the tables, people drinking and talking and flirting with one another. Under the pink, soothing lights, all of these people looked smooth and composed, and their faces were not at all like the faces of men who drank in Jack Holland's public house. It would have been nice if we were coming in to drink by ourselves and to look at people and admire the jewelry that some of the women wore.

Baba stood on her toes and I saw her wave airily over toward a corner table. I followed her across, a little unsteady on my high heels.

Two middle-aged men stood up and she introduced me. I wasn't sure which was which, but even under such kind lights both were obviously unattractive. They had already had a few drinks, and the empty glasses were on the table between them.

"You're at college, too, I hear," the man with the gray hair said to me. The man with the black hair was complimenting Baba on how well she looked, so I took it that he was Reginald, and this was Harry who had just spoken to me.

"Yes," I said. I was sitting on the edge of my chair as if I were waiting for the chandelier over my head to fall on me. It was a nice chandelier, much nicer than the big one over in the center of the room.

"What's your subject?"

"English," I said quickly.

"Oh, how interesting. I have more than a flair for English myself. As a matter of fact, I have a theory about Shakespeare's sonnets."

Just then a boy came over to take our order.

"Pink gin," Baba said, imitating a little girl's voice for Reginald.

"I'll have the same," I said to the boy. He wiped the glass-topped table clean, and took the empty glasses away. When he came back with the drinks, neither of them offered to pay at first, and then they both offered the money at the same moment, and finally Harry paid and left a two-shilling tip. The pink gin sounded better than it tasted, and I asked if I could have a bottle of orange. The orange drowned the bitter taste of the gin.

I didn't want to talk about Shakespeare's sonnets because I only knew one of them by heart, so I said to Reginald, "Do you work hard?"

"Work! No, I'm a confectioner . . . I sweeten life. Ha, ha, ha."

They laughed. I was wondering how many times he had told it before, how worn out it must be by now.

"Laugh, Caithleen, Chrissake, laugh," Baba said, and I tried a little laugh, but it didn't work.

Then she said that she wanted to speak to me for a minute and we went out onto the carpeted landing that led to the residents' bathroom.

"Will you do me a favor?" she asked. She was looking up earnestly into my face. I was much taller than she.

"Yes," I said, and though I was no longer afraid of her, I had that sick feeling which I always have before someone says an unpleasant thing to me.

"Will you, for Chrissake, stop asking fellas if they've read James Joyce's *Dubliners*? They're not interested. They're out for a night. Eat and drink all you can and leave James Joyce to blow his own trumpet."

"He's dead."

"Well, for God's sake, then, what are you worrying about?"

"I'm not worrying. I just like him."

"Oh, Caithleen! Why don't you get sense?"

"I hate it. I'll scream if that lump Harry touches me."

"He won't, Caithleen. We'll all stick together. Think of the dinner. We'll have lamb and mint sauce. Mint sauce, Caithleen, you like it." She could be very sweet when she wanted to coax me into a good humor. I sent her back to them, and I went upstairs and sat in front of a mirror for a while. Just to be away from them.

And I thought of all the people downstairs enjoying themselves, and I thought especially of the women, cool and rich and mysterious. It is easy for a woman to be mysterious when she is rich. And for no reason that I could understand, I remembered back to the time when I was four or five and I got a clean nightgown and a clean handkerchief on Saturday nights.

When I came down, they were ready to leave. We were going out to a country hotel for dinner.

Baba sat in the back seat with Reginald. They were giggling and whispering all the time, and I was ashamed to look back in case they were embracing or anything like that.

"Well, to go back to this business of Shakespeare's sonnets," Harry said. He was still droning away when we drove up to the hotel, at the foot of the Sugarloaf mountain. It was a white Georgian house with pine trees all around it. There were masses of daffodils on the front lawn. They were far nicer and far happier than any other daffodils that I had ever seen anywhere else.

"Must get a flower, boys," Baba said, walking precariously on her icicle heels over the marbled chips. "Boys!" How could she be so false? She was a little drunk. I made an attempt to follow her, because I didn't want to be alone with them, but halfway across I felt that they were measuring me from behind and I couldn't walk another step. My legs failed me.

"My dish is a lovely dish," I heard Harry say, and when Baba came back with her button nose in the daffodil cup, there were tears in my eyes.

"Jesus, I'll never bring you out again," she muttered.

"I'll never come," I said under my breath.

Before dinner we had sherry. The men played darts in the public bar and Harry stood a round of drinks to the local boys. You could see him swell with importance when they raised the glasses of stout and wished, "Happy Easter, sir."

We had lamb and mint sauce, as Baba promised, and there was a dish of boiled potatoes and some tinned peas. Reginald took three potatoes at once and asked the girl to bring him a double whiskey.

"Eat up, Reg," Harry said, with sarcasm in his voice. Harry ordered red wine for us. It was bitter but I forgave its bitterness because of its color. It was nice just to hold the glass up to the evening light and look through it at the brick fireplace and the copper pans along the wall.

"You're a grand girl," Harry said.

"I hate you," I said to myself, but aloud I said, "It's a grand dinner."

"You're artistic," he said, touching my glass with his. "You know a thing about me? I'm artistic, too. I had a little hobby once and you know what it was?"

"No." How the hell could I?

"I made chairs, beautiful Hepplewhite chairs out of matchboxes. Artistic chairs. You'd like them. You're artistic. Let's drink to that," and they all drank and Reg said, "Bravo."

"Happy?" Baba asked me, and I cut her with a look.

"You know, I understand you," Harry said, moving his chair closer to mine. I was uneasy with him. Apart from despising him, I felt he was the kind of man who would get in a huff if you neglected to pass him the peas. I decided to drink, and drink, and drink, until I was very drunk.

"More potatoes, miss?" Reginald asked, as the girl came up the room with a tray of desserts. He had his elbows on the table and was resting his head on his hands. He was asleep when the potatoes came, so she took them away again, and she took his dinner plate and the bread plate, which was piled high with potato skins.

"Come on now, eat your trifle." Baba shook him, and his round, small, pig eyes focused on the plate of trifle underneath.

"Sure. Sure." He ate it quickly, as if he couldn't get enough of it. Harry ate with great precision. We had an Irish coffee, which was so rich and creamy that I felt sick after it. Then Reginald paid the bill and stuffed a note into the girl's apron pocket.

We drove back just after ten o'clock, and there was a stream of cars coming from the opposite direction.

"Sit close to me, will you?" Harry said in an exasperated way. As if I ought to know the price of a good dinner. Obediently I sat near him. I thought that the worst was over now and that we were going home to our little room.

"Closer," he said. The way he spoke, you'd think I was a dog.

"Isn't the traffic terrible?" I said. "You're a great driver," I added. All I wanted was to get home safely. We were within inches of death three or four times. Reginald began to snore, and Baba put her elbows on the back of my seat and began to talk. She was talking foolishly, about being a virgin, and she was very drunk.

"What's this?" I asked. The car had slowed down outside a large, detached, Tudor-style residence.

"This is home," Harry said. The double gates were open and he drove the car in within an inch or two of the white garage door. We got out.

There was a cherry tree flowering over near the railings, and the lawn was smooth and cared-for.

"Don't leave me," I whispered to Baba as we went up the steps.

"Chrissake, shut up," she said. She took off her shoes and climbed in her stockinged feet. Reginald picked her up in his arms and carried her into the hallway. Harry switched on the lights and we followed him into the drawing room. It was a big room with a high ceiling, and it was full of expensive furniture. You could smell the money.

We took off our coats and laid them on the sofa. Harry clicked a button and the front of a mahogany cabinet opened out, displaying all sorts of bottles.

"What will it be?" he asked.

"Let's all have Scotch on the rocks," Reginald said, and Baba cooed with furry delight. I said nothing. I had my back to them and was looking at a portrait over the fireplace. It was a woman petting a horse's forehead. His wife, I supposed.

"That's my wife," Harry said as he handed me a huge drink.

"How *is* Betty?" Reginald said. Determined to be bluff about her.

"Fine. She's gone down to the West for a golf championship," he said, taking off his jacket. He had a fawn buttoned cardigan underneath, and he pulled it down over his hips and swaggered in front of me. His body was fat and vain and idiotic.

"Come back, Betty," I begged the plain, horse-faced woman in the oak frame. He drew the curtains. They were the most sumptuous curtains I had ever seen. They were plum velvet and they hung to the floor in soft rich folds. A pelmet of the same material came down in waves over the curtains, and they were fringed with red and white tassels. Mama would have loved them.

"Sit down," he said, and I sank into the high-cushioned sofa. He sat beside me and began to stroke my hair.

"Happy?" he asked. Reginald and Baba were playing a duet on the piano. The piano stool was long enough for them to sit side by side.

"I'd love some tea," I said. Anything to keep us moving.

"Tea?" he repeated, as if it were something that only savages drank.

"Come on, Cait, we'll make tea," Baba said, getting up off the piano stool and patting her hair with her hands to keep the waves in place. Harry showed us the kitchen and went back sulkily to drink.

"Christ, can we feck anything?" she said, opening the door of the big white refrigerator. A light came on inside when the door was opened and we looked in eagerly, expecting to see a few cold chickens. The metal racks were perfectly empty: there was nothing but a tray of ice cubes in a metal box.

"Help yourself," Baba said, standing back so that I could have a full view.

We made the tea and carried the tray back to the drawing room. There was no milk, but the black tea was better than nothing.

"Harry, can I show Barbara your oils?" Reginald said, and Harry said, "Certainly." Reginald took Baba's hand and they went out of the room. I yawned and called after her not to be long.

"At last," Harry said, laying his drink on the brass table and approaching me with a look of determination. I had my legs crossed and my hands folded demurely on my lap. I looked up at him with a look of nonchalance, but underneath I was trembling. He sat on the couch and kissed me fiercely on the lips.

"Come on," he said, and he tried to lift one knee off the other. The light from behind was shining on his face and his smile was strange.

"No. Let's talk," I said, trying to be casual.

"I'll tell you a fairy story," he said.

"Do. Do that. That's nice." I smiled and accepted another drink. Talk, that was what I must do. Talk. Talk. Talk. And all would be well and I would get home somehow, and make a novena in thanksgiving.

"Ready?" he asked, and I nodded and crossed my legs again. He held my hand and I endured it for peace's sake.

He began: "Once upon a time there was a cock and a fox and a pussy cat, and they lived on an island far away . . ."

It wasn't a long story, and though I didn't understand it fully, I knew that it was dirty and double-meaning and that he was a dirty, horrible, stupid man.

I stood up and said hysterically, "I want to go home."

"Cold little bitch. Cold bitch," he said, swigging a long drink.

"You're vile and horrible," I said. I had lost control of my temper.

"Why in God's name did you come, then?" he asked as I went to the door and called Baba. She came downstairs fastening the gold chain around her waist.

"I want to go home," I said frantically. "Where's Reginald?"

"He's asleep," she said. She took her shoes off the hall table and went into the room for our coats.

She asked Harry if he would take us home, and he put on his jacket and came out waving a bunch of keys venomously.

It was nice to come out in the air and find the lawn white with moonlight. The lawn and the moonlight had dignity. Life was beautiful if one only met the beautiful people. Life was beautiful and full of promise. The promise one felt when one looked at a summer garden of hazy blue flowers at the foot of an incredibly beautiful fountain. And in the air were the sprays of hazy silver water that would descend to drench the blue parched flowers.

I sat in the back. He drove quickly and I expected him to kill us.

At the top of our avenue Baba said we'd get out because he might never turn the big car once he came into the narrow avenue.

"Good night, Barbara. You're a nice girl, and if I can ever be of help, don't forget to give me a ring," he said to her, and to me he said good night.

We walked quickly up the street. It was chilly and the gardens seemed to be frozen over. It was bright from the moon and the stars and the streetlights, and all the curtains were drawn in all the windows. There was a light behind one window and a baby's cry came from that direction.

THE COUNTRY GIRLS TRILOGY

"Here, Jesus, we might as well have this much," she said, pulling a guest towel, two tomatoes, and a jar of chicken and ham paste from somewhere inside her dress.

"How in the hell did you get them?"

"When I went out with Reg. He fell asleep, so I went rooting around the house; these condiments were in a press in the kitchen." She handed me a tomato. I wiped it on the sleeve of my coat and bit it. It was sweet and juicy and I was glad of it, because I was thirsty after all that drink.

"What happened to you?" she asked.

"What happened to me! That fellow should be shot," I said.

"Carrying on like a bloody lunatic; why didn't you slap his face?"

"Did *you* slap Reginald?"

"No, I didn't. We're going steady. I like him."

"Is he married?" I asked.

"Could we be going steady if he was married?" she said sharply.

"He looks married," I said, but I didn't care. I was happy. It was all over and here we were walking up the pavement under the trees at one o'clock. Tomorrow was Sunday, so I could sleep late. I danced a little, because I was so happy and the tomato was nice and life was just beginning.

There was a small black car parked farther up. It seemed to be outside our gate or the gate next to ours. As we came nearer I saw the window being lowered, and when we got up to it I saw that it was him. He smiled, moved over to the window near the curb, and opened the door. I came forward to meet him.

"Oh, Mr. Gentleman," Baba said, surprised.

"Hello," I said. He looked very tired, but he was pleased to see us. You could see by his eyes that he was pleased. They were excited-looking.

"This is a shocking hour of the night to be coming home," he said. He was looking at me.

"Shocking," said Baba as she went in the gate. She didn't bother to close it, and it gave a clank.

"Leave the key in the door," I called. I got into the car and we

156

sat near one another. The gear lever was in the way of our knees, so we got out and sat in the back. His face was cold when he kissed me.

"You've been drinking," he said.

"Yes, I have. I was lonely," I said.

"Me too. Not drinking but lonely," and he kissed me again. His lips were cold, beautifully cold like the ice in the cocktail glasses.

"Tell me everything," he said, but before I could talk or before he could listen we had to embrace each other for a long time. Once during a kiss I opened my eyes to steal a look at his face. The street-light was shining directly on the car. His eyes were closed tight, his lashes trembling on his cheeks, and his carved, pale face was the face of an old, old man. I closed my own eyes and thought only of his lips and his cold hands and the warm heart that was beating beneath the waistcoat and the starched white shirt. It was then I remembered to take off my coat and show him my blouse. He pushed up the dancing sleeves and kissed my arms from the wrist to the elbow, in a row of light, consecutive kisses.

"Will we go somewhere?" he asked.

"Where?"

"Let's drive out and look at the sea."

We got into the front seat and drove off.

"Were you long there, waiting?" I asked.

"Since midnight. I asked your landlady when you'd be back."

"You sent me no postcard from Spain," I said.

"No," he said matter-of-factly. "But I thought of you most of the time."

He caught my hand. His clasp was at once delicate and savage. Then when he kissed me, my body became like rain. Soft. Flowing. Amenable.

And though it was nice to sit there facing the sea, I thought of us as being somewhere else. In the woods, close together, beside a little stream. A secret place. A green place with ferns all about.

"And you got expelled?" he remarked.

"Yes, we wrote a bad thing," I said. I blushed, wondering if Martha had told him exactly.

"You funny little girl," he said, and smiled. At first I was indignant at his calling me a funny little girl, and then I found his words sweet. Everything after that was touched with sweetness and enchantment.

That was how I came to see dawn rising over Dublin Bay. It was a cold dawn and the sea desolately gray underneath. We had been sitting there for hours, talking and smoking and embracing. We had admired the green lights across the harbor; we had gazed at each other in the partial darkness, and we had said lovely things to one another. Then dawn came; the green lights went out quite suddenly as one white seagull rose into the sky.

"Would you like it if it was moonlight all day long?" I said.

"No. I like the mornings and the daylight." His voice was dull and sleepy and remote. He was gone from me again.

He backed the car toward the sand dunes, which were half covered with grass, and turned it around, quickly and skillfully. We drove over the smooth sand. The tide was coming in, and I knew that it would wash away the marks of the wheels and I would never be able to come back and find them. We were quiet and strange. It was always like that with Mr. Gentleman. He slipped away, just when things were perfect, as if he couldn't endure perfection.

He left me at my own gate. I wished that I could ask him in for breakfast. But I was afraid of Joanna.

"Are we friends?" I said anxiously.

"We are," he said, and he smiled at me. We made a date for Wednesday.

"Are you going off home now?" I asked.

"Yes." He looked sad and cold, and I wanted to tell him so.

"Think of me," he said as he drove off.

Joanna was cooking sausages when I went in, and she blessed herself when she saw me. I ate my breakfast and went straight to bed. That was the first Sunday I missed Mass.

18 Gradually, in the weeks that followed, Baba and I became strangers. I went out with Mr. Gentleman as often as he was free, and she met Reginald every night. She didn't even come home from class in the evenings, and she wore her best coat going out in the morning.

"Go to rot," Joanna said at the breakfast table when she saw our faces pale for want of sleep and our fingers brown from nicotine.

"Go to hell," Baba said. Her cough was getting worse and she had got thinner.

Three days later she told me that she had to go to a sanatorium for six months. Reginald had made her have an X-ray and it was found that she had tuberculosis.

"Oh, Baba," I said, going around to her side of the table to put my arms around her. Why had we become strangers? Why had we been sharp and secretive in the last few weeks? I put my cheek close to hers.

"Christ, don't, there's probably germs floating everywhere around me," she said, and I laughed. Her face was pale now, and the boyish bloom was going off it. She looked older and wiser in the last few weeks. Was it Reginald? Or was it her sickness? She got her belongings ready.

"I'm leaving some clothes here and don't you be sporting them every damn day," she said as she put two summer dresses back on a hanger.

Later on, Reginald's car hooted outside the gate and I called up to ask her if she was ready.

I helped her into her tweed coat in the hallway. The lining of one sleeve was all ripped, but finally we got her arm in. She stood for a minute, very small and thin, with a deep flush in both cheeks. Her blue eyes were misted over with the beginnings of tears and she bit at her bottom lip to try and stop herself from crying. Then she put on some pinkish lipstick and smiled at herself bravely in the hall mirror.

Joanna took off her apron in case Reginald should come in.

"I'll visit you as often as I can," I said to Baba. She was going to a sanatorium in Wicklow and I knew that I couldn't afford the bus fare more than once a week. Mr. Brennan was to pay £3 a week for her there.

"Smoke like hell when you come, so's you won't get any god-damn bugs around the place," she said. She was still smiling.

Gustav and Joanna said goodbye to her, and Reginald brought out the case and put a rug around her when she got into the car. He was very attentive to her and I was beginning to like him.

I waved to the car and she waved back. Her thin white fingers behind the glass waved to the end of our friendship. She was gone. It would never be the same again, not even if we tried.

Joanna went upstairs to spray disinfectant all over the room, and she grumbled about having to wash the blankets again, when they had been washed only a few months before. The way she grumbled, you'd think Baba went and got the tuberculosis on purpose.

The bedroom was tidy but deserted. Baba's makeup and the huge flagon of perfume Reginald gave her, these were gone, and the dressing table was bare. She left the blue necklace on my bed with a note. It said: *To Caithleen in remembrance of all the good times we had together. You're a right-looking eejit.* It was then I cried for her, and thought of all the evenings we walked home from school and how she used to set dogs after me and write dirty words on my arm with indelible pencil.

I was fidgety and bit my nails because I had to ask Joanna a favor.

"Joanna, can I have a friend in the drawing room tonight?"

"*Mein Gott*, you give the house a bad name. The ladies next door, they say, 'What kind of girls you got, keeping disgrace hours?'"

"He's rich," I said. I knew this would impress her. Joanna had some notion that if a rich man came into the house, he'd leave five-pound notes under the tablecloth, or forget his overcoat on purpose and leave it behind for Gustav. She was simple that way. I could see the look of hope that came into her stupid blue eyes when I said that he was rich. Finally she said yes, and I began to get ready for my date.

It is the only time that I am thankful for being a woman, that time of evening when I draw the curtains, take off my old clothes, and prepare to go out. Minute by minute the excitement grows. I brush my hair under the light and the colors are autumn leaves in the sun. I shadow my eyelids with black stuff and am astonished by the look of mystery it gives to my eyes. I hate being a woman. Vain and shallow and superficial. Tell a woman that you love her and she'll ask you to write it down so that she can show it to her friends. But I am happy at that time of night. I feel tender toward the world, I pet the wall-paper as if it were white rose petals flushed pink at the edges; I pick up my old, tired shoes and they are silver flowers that some man has laid outside my door. I kissed myself in the mirror and ran out of the room, happy and hurried and suitably mad.

I was late and Mr. Gentleman was annoyed. He handed me an orchid that was two shades of purple—pale purple and dark. I pinned it to my cardigan.

We went to a restaurant off Grafton Street, and climbed the narrow stairs to a dark, almost dingy, little room. It had red-and-white-striped wallpaper, and there was a black-brown portrait over the fire-place. It was in a thick gilt frame, and I wasn't sure whether it was a portrait of a man or a woman, because the hair was covered with a black mop cap. We sat over near the window. It was half open; the nylon curtains blew inward and brushed the tablecloth lightly and fanned our faces. As usual we were very shy. The curtains were white and foamy like summer clouds, and he was wearing a new paisley tie.

"Your tie is nice," I said stiffly.

"You like it?" he asked. It was agony until the first drink came, and then he melted a little and smiled at me. Then the room seemed charming, with its lighted red candle in a wine bottle, on the table. I shall never forget the pallor of his high cheekbones when he bent down to pick up his napkin. He patted my knee for a second and then looked at me with one of his slow, intense, tormented looks.

"I feel hungry," he said.

"I feel hungry," I said. Little did he know that I had eaten two shop buns on my way to meet him. I loved shop buns, especially iced ones.

"For all sorts of things," he said, as he scooped some melon with a spoon. He reminded me of the melon. Cool and cold and bloodless and refreshing. He twined his ankles around mine under the big linen tablecloth and the evening began to be perfect. Candle wax dripped onto the cloth.

We drove home after eleven and he was pleased when I asked him in. I was ashamed of the hallway and the cheap carpet on the stairs. There was a stale, musty smell in the drawing room when we first went in. He sat down on the sofa and I sat on a high-backed chair across the table from him. I was happy from the wine and I told him about my life and how I fell in the dance hall and went upstairs to drink minerals for the rest of the night. He was amused, but he didn't laugh outright. Always the remote, enchanting smile. I had drunk a lot and I was giddy. But the tiny remaining sober part of me watched the rest of me being happy and listened to the happy, foolish things that I said.

"Come over near me," he asked, and I came and sat very quietly beside him. I could feel him trembling.

"You're happy?" he said, tracing the outline of my face with his finger.

"Yes."

"You're going to be happier."

"How?"

"We're going to be together. I'm going to make love to you." He spoke in a half whisper and kept looking uneasily toward the window, as if there might be someone watching us from the back garden. I went over and drew the blind, as there were no curtains in that room. I was blushing when I came back to sit down.

"Do you mind?" he asked.

"When? Now?" I clutched the front of my cardigan and looked at him earnestly. He said that I looked appalled. I wasn't appalled really. Just nervous, and sad in some way, because the end of my inno-cence was near.

"Sweetling," he said. He put an arm around me and brought my head down on his shoulder, so that my cheek touched his neck. Some tears of mine must have trickled down inside his collar. He patted my knees with his other hand. I was excited, and warm, and violent.

"Do you know French?" he asked.

"No. I did Latin at school," I said. Imagine talking about school at a time like that. I could have killed myself for being so juvenile.

"Well, there's a French word for it. It means . . . an . . . atmosphere. We'll go away to the right atmosphere for a few weeks."

"Where?" I thought with horror of the bacon-and-egg hotels across the central towns of Ireland with ketchup dribbles on the relish bottles and gravy stains on the checkered cloth. And rain outside. But I might have known that he would be more careful. He always was. Even to the extent of parking his car right outside the restaurants where we ate, so that no one would see us walking up the street to the car park.

"To Vienna," he said, and my heart did a few somersaults.

"Is it nice there?"

"It's very nice there."

"And what will we do?"

"We'll eat and go for walks. And in the evenings we'll go up to eating places in the mountains and sit there drinking wine and looking down at the town. And then we'll go to bed." He said it quite simply, and I loved him more than I would ever love a man again.

"Is it good to go?" I asked. I just wanted him to reassure me.

"Yes. It's good. We have to get this out of our systems." He frowned a little, and I had a vision of coming back to the same room and the same life and being without him.

"But I want you for always," I said imploringly. He smiled and kissed me lightly on the cheeks. Kisses like the first drops of rain. "You'll always love me?" I asked.

"You know I don't like you to talk like that," he said, playing with the top button of my cardigan.

"I know," I said.

"Then why do you?" he asked tenderly.

"Because I can't help it. Because I'd go mad if I hadn't you."

He looked at me for a long time. That look of his which was half sexual, half mystic; and then he said my name very gently. ("Caithleen.") I could hear the bulrushes sighing when he said my name that way, and I could hear the curlew, too, and all the lonesome sounds of Ireland.

"Caithleen. I want to whisper you something."

"Whisper," I said. I put my hair behind my ear and he held it there because it had a habit of falling back into its old place. He leaned over and put his mouth close to my ear and kissed it first and said, "Show me your body. I've never seen your legs or breasts or anything. I'd like to see you."

"And if I'm not nice, then will you change your mind?" I had inherited my mother's suspiciousness.

"Don't be silly," he said, and he helped me take off my cardigan. I was trying to decide whether to take off my blouse or my skirt first.

"Don't look," I said. It was difficult. I didn't like him to see suspenders and things. I peeled off my skirt and everything under it, and then my blouse and my cotton vest, and finally I unclasped my brassiere, the black one, and I stood there shivering a little, not knowing what to do with my arms. So I put my hand up to my throat, a gesture that I often do when I am at a loss. The only place I felt warm was where my hair covered my neck and the top part of my back. I came over and sat beside him and nestled in near him for a little warmth.

"You can look now," I said, and he took his hand down from his eyes and looked shyly at my stomach and my thighs.

"Your skin is whiter than your face. I thought it would be pink," he said, and he kissed me all over.

"Now we won't be shy when we get there. We've seen one another," he said.

"I haven't seen you."

"Do you want to?" and I nodded. He opened his braces and let his trousers slip down around his ankles. He took off his other things and sat down quickly. He was not half so distinguished out of his coal-black suit and stiff white shirt. Something stirred in the garden, or was it in the hall? I thought what horror if Joanna should burst in in her nightgown and find us like two naked fools on the green velveteen couch. And she would shout for Gustav, and the ladies next door would hear her, and the police would come. I looked down slyly at his body and laughed a little. It was so ridiculous.

"What's so funny?" He was piqued that I should laugh.

"It's the color of the pale part of my orchid," I said, and I looked over at my orchid, which was still pinned to my cardigan. I touched it. Not my orchid. His. It was soft and incredibly tender, like the inside of a flower, and it stirred. It reminded me when it stirred of a little black man on top of a penny bank that shook his head every time you put a coin in the box. I told him this, and he kissed me fiercely and for a long time.

"You're a bad girl," he said.

"I like being a bad girl," I replied, wide-eyed.

"No, not really, darling. You're sweet. The sweetest girl I ever met. My country girl with country-colored hair," and he buried his face in it and smelled it for a minute.

"Darling, I'm not made of iron," he said, and he stood and drew his trousers up from around his ankles. When I got up to fetch my clothes, he fondled my bottom and I knew that our week together would be beautiful.

"I'll make you a cup of tea," I said after we had dressed ourselves and he had combed his hair with my comb.

We went out to the kitchen on tiptoe. I lit the gas and filled the kettle noiselessly by letting the water from the tap pour down the side of the kettle. The refrigerator was locked because of Herman's fits of night hunger, but I found a few old biscuits in a forgotten tin. They were soft but he ate them. After the tea he left. It was Friday so he was making the long journey down the country. On week nights he stayed in a men's club in Stephen's Green.

I stood at the door and he let down the window of the car and waved good night. He drove away without making any noise at all. I came in, put my orchid in a cup of water, and carried it upstairs to the orange box beside my bed. I was too happy to go to sleep.

19

Some men came and lopped the trees that skirted the pavement. They left nothing but the short fat branches, which somehow looked obscene. The feathery branches were gone and the buds, too. It was the wrong time of year to lop trees and I could never understand why they did it then, unless it was because people had complained about the light being shut out from their sitting rooms.

But I was so happy I hardly noticed the trees. We were going away together. He was going on one airplane to London and I was following on the next one. He said it was better that way, in case we should be seen at the airport.

I was so happy and he was happy, too. Sitting in the drawing room for hours, I used to look at his face, his bony ascetic face, with his fine nose and his eyes that were always saying things, eyes that flashed amber because of the yellow lampshade on the table lamp. Some nights I put on the electric heater and I was afraid Joanna would smell it upstairs.

"You know what worries me?" he said, catching my hands and stroking them.

"Your low blood pressure, or maybe your age?" I said, smiling.

"No," and he gave me a gentle slap on the face.

"What then?"

"The coming back. Being separated."

But I didn't think about that. I only thought of going.

"Did you ever go before?" I asked nervously.

"Don't ask me that." He was frowning a little. His forehead was yellow-white, as if he had lemon juice instead of blood under his skin.

"Why not?"

"It's pointless, really. If I say yes, it will only make you sad."

And already I was sad. No one would ever really belong to him. He was too detached.

"I'll watch you as you come down the airplane runway," he said. Then he got out his diary and we tried to fix a date. I had to go out of the room to think; not every week suited me, and I couldn't think when his arms were around me. Finally we settled on a week, and he made a note of it in pencil.

In the days that followed I thought only of it. When I was washing my neck, I made a soap lather for him, and when I was weighing sugar in the shop, I was singing to myself. I gave children free sugar barleys and I bought Willie a dickey bow for his Sunday shirt. Going along the street I talked to myself all the time. Arranging conversations between us, smiling at everyone; helping old women to cross the road and flirting with bus conductors.

A few little things worried me. I had to ask for the week off. Mr. Burns was easy to handle, but sleepy-eyed Mrs. Burns could read your mind.

Also, I had stopped going to Mass and confession and things. But most of all, I hadn't enough underwear. I wanted a blue flowing transparent nightgown. So that we could waltz before we got into bed. To tell you the truth, I always shirked a little at the actual getting into bed.

Mama had nice nightgowns, but I had left them in the drawers, and I didn't know if my father got them before the furniture was auctioned. I could have written to ask him, but at the thought of him my heart started to race. I hadn't written for six weeks and I didn't want to write anymore. Mr. Gentleman mentioned that my father had flu, and that the nuns were looking after him.

Then I thought of asking Joanna. Joanna and I had got very friendly since Baba went away. I helped with the washing up, and we went to the pictures one night after tea. Joanna laughed so much that she was snorting in the back of her nose and the couple near us were horrified.

"I'm going to Vienna," I said as we walked home through the fresh spring night. There was a smell of night-scented stock. She linked me and I was uncomfortable about this. I hate women linking me.

"*Mein Gott!* For what?"

"With a friend," I said carelessly.

"A man?" she asked, opening her eyes very wide and looking with astonishment, as if men were monsters.

"Yes," I said. It was easy talking to Joanna.

"The rich man?" she asked.

"The rich man," I added; and a sudden anxiety came to me about paying my fare and my hotel bill. Did he expect me to pay my own?

"Good. It is beautiful there. The opera, lovely. I remember my brothers spending me a night at the opera for my twenty-one birthday. They gave me a wristwatch. Fifteen-carat gold." It was the nearest Joanna ever got to being nostalgic. I was still worrying about the money for the airplane ticket.

"Will you loan me a nightgown?" I asked.

She said nothing for a moment and then she said, "Yes. But you must be very careful. It is from my own honeymoon. Thirty years old." I blanched a little and held the gate open for her. Gustav was at the door with his hands stretched out, like a man begging for alms. There was something wrong.

"Herman. He do it again, Joanna," he said. Joanna shot in the door and rushed up the stairs. She took two steps at a time and you could see the legs of her knickers. A torrent of German ascended ahead of her. I heard her rattle the doorknob of Herman's room, and then knock on the door and pound it and call, "Herman, Herman, you leave this night," and Herman said nothing. But when I went up, there seemed to be crying from behind his door. He had been in bed all day with flu.

"What's wrong?" I thought they were all mad.

"His kidneys. He has kidney trouble. The best hair mattress and my good pure linen sheets," Joanna said. We stood in the narrow landing waiting for him to open his door and Joanna began to cry.

"Leave him, Joanna, until morning." Gustav came up and stood on the step where the stairs turned left. She cried more and talked about the mattress and the sheets, and you could see that Gustav was embarrassed because of her. She took off her white knitted coat and picked loose hairs off the collar.

I went into my own room and in a few minutes she came in after me. She had the nightgown in her hand. It was folded in tissue paper, and as she opened the paper camphor balls kept falling out and rolling onto the floor. It was lilac color and it was the biggest night-gown I'd ever seen. I put it on and looked like a girl playing Lady

Macbeth for the Sacred Heart Players. I was shapeless in it. I tied the purple sash tight around the waist, but it was still hickish.

"Lovely. Pure silk," she said, fingering the deep frill that fell over my hand and almost covered it.

"Lovely," I agreed. He would smell the camphor and sneeze for the entire week and go home trying to remember which of his grand-aunts I resembled. Still, it was better than nothing.

"Show Gustav," she said, arranging it so that it fell in loose pleats from around the waist. She held it up while I went down the stairs, as if I were wearing a wedding dress.

Gustav got red and said, "Very smart."

"You remember, Gustav?" she said. She was grinning at him.

"No, Joanna." He was reading the advertisements in the evening paper. He said that Herman would have to go and they would get a nice proper gentleman.

"You remember, Gustav?" she said, going over to him. But Gustav said no as if he wanted to forget. Joanna was hurt.

"They are all the same," she said, as we prepared the tray for supper. "All men, they are all the same. No soft in them," and I thought of something very soft about my Mr. Gentleman. Not his face. Not his nature. But a part of his soft, beseeching body.

"Mind you not fill up with baby," she said. I laughed. It was impossible. I had an idea that couples had to be married for a long time before a woman got a baby.

I kept the nightgown on during supper because I had my other clothes under it. We sat very late looking through all the advertisements, and finally Gustav found one that was suitable.

"Italian musician requires full board in foreign household," and he got the ink off the sideboard and Joanna spread a newspaper over the velvet cloth, then unlocked the china cabinet and took out a sheet of headed stationery. It was locked because Herman was in the habit of stealing sheets of it to write to his mother and his sisters.

There was a skin on my cocoa and I lifted it off with my spoon. The cocoa was cold.

Gustav put on his glasses and Joanna got him the old fountain pen that had no top on it. One they found out on the road. It wrote like a post-office pen.

"What date is it, Joanna?" he asked. She went over to the calendar on the wall and looked at it, screwing up her eyes.

"May 15," she said, and I felt myself go cold. The morning paper was on the tea trolley and I reached over the back of my armchair and picked it up. There on the very first page under the anniversaries was a memorium for my mother. Four years. Four short years and I had forgotten the date of her death; at least I had overlooked it! I felt that wherever she was she had stopped loving me, and I went out of the room crying. It was worse to think that he had remembered. I recalled it in my head, the short, simple insertion, signed with my father's name.

"Caithleen." Joanna followed me out to the hall.

"It's nothing," I said over the banisters. "It's nothing, Joanna."

But all that night I slept badly. I tucked my legs up under my nightgown and was shivering. I was waiting for someone to come and warm me. I think I was waiting for Mama. And all the things I am afraid of kept coming into my mind. Drunk men. Shouting. Blood. Cats. Razor blades. Galloping horses. The night was terrifying and the bathroom door kept slamming. I got up to close it around three and filled myself a hot-water bottle from the hot tap. It wasn't my own, and I knew that if Baba were there now she'd warn me that it would give me some damn disease like athlete's foot or eczema or something. I missed Baba. She kept me sane. She kept me from brooding about things.

I went back to bed, and Joanna woke me with a cup of tea just after eight o'clock. When I opened my eyes she was drawing back the curtains to let the sun in. I looked up at the cracked gray ceiling and wasn't afraid anymore. We were going away the following Saturday.

I drank the tea, fondled my stomach for a while, and as soon as I heard Herman move next door, I jumped out, so as to have the first of the bathroom.

20 The next week flew. I plucked my eyebrows, packed my case, and bought postcards, so that I could send some to Joanna. I was afraid that I mightn't get to buy any there. I washed my hairbrush and put it out on the windowsill to dry and borrowed two of Baba's dresses. Writing to Baba, I told her I had flu, but said nothing about borrowing the dresses or about going away. You couldn't trust Baba.

On Thursday morning there was a letter from Hickey which had been readdressed from the Brennans'. He said that he was arriving in Dublin on the mail boat the following Tuesday and asked me to meet him. He didn't say whether he was married or not and I was curious to know. His spelling had improved. Of course I had to send him a telegram to say I couldn't manage it. The thought came to me that I was foolish and disloyal, not only to Hickey, who had been my best friend, but to Jack Holland and Martha and Mr. Brennan. To all the real people in my life. Mr. Gentleman was but a shadow, and yet it was this shadow I craved. I sent the telegram, instantly made myself forget about Hickey, and thought of our holiday in Vienna.

I could see myself sitting up in bed with a big breakfast tray across my lap. I could see the tray and the cups and a brown earthenware dish that was warmed. I would lift the lid off the dish and find fingers of golden toast that the butter had soaked right into. Sometimes in my fantasy he was asleep and I was wakening him by tickling his forehead; and then at other times he was awake and drinking a glass of orange juice. I thought Saturday would never come.

It came and it was raining. The rain upset my plans. I was to wear a white feather hat and I could not possibly let it get wet. It was a lovely hat that fitted tight to the head, and the feathers curved down over my ears and gave my face a soft, feathered look.

When I was leaving the shop at four, Mr. Burns gave me my wages and a pound extra for the journey home. I had told them there was an aunt dying.

"Good God, you can't go out in that rain," he said.

"I'll miss my train if I don't." So he went into the hallway and found me an old umbrella. A godsend. I could wear my hat now. I almost kissed him. I think he expected me to, because he smoothed the brown hairs of his mustache.

"Bye, miss," Willie said, as he held the door for me. It was lashing rain outside. It pelted against my legs and my stockings got drenched. Joanna had tea ready, and she loaned me a little phrase book that had English and German words in it.

"Mind you not lose," she warned me. I put it in my handbag.

"I not charge while you're away," she said, beaming at me. Everything was working out marvelously. The new lodger was coming that evening so Joanna was happy.

"*Mein Gott*, you are so lovely," she said when I came downstairs in my black coat and my white feather hat.

I had made my face pale with pancake makeup and darkened my eyelids with green mascara.

The long coils of auburn hair fell loosely around my shoulders, and though I was tall and well developed around the bust, I had the innocent look of a very young girl. No one would have suspected that I was going off with a man.

I had put my gloves in my bag, so that they wouldn't get wet. They were white kid gloves of Mama's. There were stains of iron mold where they buttoned at the wrist but otherwise they were lovely.

It was still raining when I came out. It was awkward trying to manage the suitcase and the umbrella as well as carry my handbag. A telegram boy went by on a motorcycle and spattered my stockings, so I swore after him. I got a bus immediately and was there twenty minutes too early.

We were meeting outside an amusement palace on the quays. It was convenient for him to pick me up there, as he came from his office, but neither of us had thought of the rain when we fixed the place.

I stood in the porchway that led to the sweetshop and put my case down. My hands were wet, so I wiped them on the lining of my coat. In at the back of the shop there were slot machines and a room where boys played snooker. They were all dressed alike, in colored jerseys and tight-fitting tartan trousers. They all needed haircuts.

The rain had got less. It was only spotting now. I looked at my watch, his little moth-gold watch; he was ten minutes late. The church bells from the opposite side of the Liffey chimed seven. I looked at all the cars as they came up the quays.

At half past seven I began to get anxious, because I knew that his plane went at half past eight and mine left shortly before nine o'clock. I sat on the edge of my suitcase and tried to look absorbed as the long-haired boys went in and out to play snooker. They were passing remarks about me. I began to count the flagstones on the lane nearby. I thought, He'll come now, while I'm counting, and I won't see the car drive up to the curb and he'll have to blow the hooter to call me. I knew the sound of the hooter. But I counted the flagstones three times and he hadn't come. It was nearing eight and there were pigeons and seagulls walking along the limestone wall that skirted the river Liffey.

"Are you waiting for someone?" the woman from the sweetshop called out to me. She was fat and her hair was dyed blond.

"I'm waiting for my father," I said. "We're going away somewhere."

"Come in and sit down," she said. I went in and sat on a wicker chair. It squeaked when you sat on it. I bought a bottle of orange, just to pass the time, and drank it through a straw. Every few minutes I came out to look. I was getting anxious now, and when he came I'd tell him how anxious and frightened I'd been. I went across the road to look at a Guinness barge that was going up the river. The river was brown and filthy, and the top of the wall was spattered white from all the bird droppings. His small black car came buzzing up the quay, and I ran to the edge of the footpath and waved. But the car went by. It was exactly like his, except that the registration number was not the same. I went back to finish my orange.

"Kill you, wouldn't it," the blond woman said to me. Her name was Dolly. The boys playing snooker called her that and were fresh with her.

My whole body was impatient now. I couldn't sit still. My body was wild from waiting. The streetlights came on outside, the wet bulbs gave out a blurred yellow light, and the street took on that look of night mystery that I always love. The raindrops hung to the iron bars that held up the gray awning; they clung to it for a while and then they dropped onto a man's hat as he went by. I think it was then that I admitted to myself for the first time that he just might not be coming. But only for the shadow of a second did I allow myself to think it. I bought a woman's magazine and looked for my horoscope. The magazine was a week old so my horoscope was of no help.

"Afraid, love, we're closing up now," Dolly said. "Wouldju like to come in and sit in the kitchen for a while?"

I thanked her but said I'd rather not. He might come unknown to me. She took the money out of the cash register, counted it, and put it into a big black purse.

"Good night, love," she said as she closed the door after me. I sat in the porch. People passed by, with heads lowered. Gray, sad, indiscriminate people, going nowhere. Two sailors passed and winked at me. They kept looking back, but when they saw that I wasn't interested, they walked on.

It rained on and off.

I knew now that he wasn't coming; but still I sat there. An hour or two later I got up, picked up my things, and walked despondently toward the bus stop in O'Connell Street.

Joanna rushed out when she heard the gate squeak. Her hands were raised; her fat, greasy face was beaming. The lodger had arrived.

"A real gentleman. Rich. Expensive. You like him, he is so nice. Real pigskin gloves. *Gut* suit, everything," she said.

"Come, you meet him." She caught hold of my wet wrist and tried to coax me. Then she saw that I was crying.

"Oh, a telegram. One came. You had just gone, but I could not follow now because my new man was coming and I could not go out of the house, for fear of he arriving and find nobody." She was hoping that I wasn't cross. I took off my hat and threw it on the hall stand. It was a wet, gray hen by now.

"I am sad for you. It is all for best," Joanna said, as she nodded toward the room.

I opened the telegram. It said:

EVERYTHING GONE WRONG. THREATS FROM YOUR
FATHER. MY WIFE HAS ANOTHER NERVOUS BREAKDOWN.
REGRET ENFORCED SILENCE. MUST NOT SEE YOU.

It was not signed and it had been handed in at a Limerick post office
early that morning.

"Come, meet my nice new friend," Joanna pleaded, but I shook
my head and went upstairs to cry.

I cried on the bed for a long time, until I began to feel very cold.
Somehow one feels colder after hours of crying. Eventually I got up
and put on the light. I came downstairs to make a cup of tea. The
telegram was still in my hand, crumpled into a ball. I read it again. It
said exactly the same thing.

After I'd put the kettle on the gas, I went automatically to get
my cup off the dining-room table, as Joanna always laid the breakfast
things before going to bed. As I came to the door, I heard a sound
from within. I peeped around the side of the door and looked straight
into the face of a strange young man who was holding a brass instrument in one hand and a polishing rag in the other.

"I'm sorry," I said, picked up my cup off the table, and ran
straight out of the room. My face must have been a nice sight.
Blotchy from crying.

When I had made the tea, I recollected that he must think it a
very odd house, so I went down the hall and called in, "Would you
like a cup of tea?" I didn't want him to see my face again.

"No English speak," he said.

God, I thought, as if it makes any difference to whether you'd
like tea or not.

I poured him a cup and brought it in.

"No English speak," he said, and he shrugged his shoulders.

I came out to the kitchen and took two aspirins with my tea. It
was almost certain that I wouldn't sleep that night.

The
Lonely
Girl

1

It was a wet afternoon in October, as I copied out the September accounts from the big gray ledger. I worked in a grocery shop in the north of Dublin and had been there for two years.

My employer and his wife were country people like myself. They were kind, but they liked me to work hard and promised me a raise in the new year. Little did I know that I would be gone by then, to a different life.

Because of the rain, not many customers came in and out, so I wrote the bills quickly and then got on with my reading. I had a book hidden in the ledger, so that I could read without fear of being caught.

It was a beautiful book, but sad. It was called *Tender Is the Night*. I skipped half the words in my anxiety to read it quickly, because I wanted to know whether the man would leave the woman or not. All the nicest men were in books—the strange, complex, romantic men; the ones I admired most.

I knew no one like that except Mr. Gentleman, and I had not seen him for two years. He was only a shadow now, and I remembered him the way one remembers a nice dress that one has grown out of.

At half past four I put on the lights. The shop looked shabbier in artificial light, too; the shelves were dusty and the ceiling hadn't been painted since I went there. It was full of cracks. I looked in the mirror to see how my hair was. We were going somewhere that night, my friend Baba and me. My face in the mirror looked round and smooth. I sucked my cheeks in, to make them thinner. I longed to be thin, like Baba.

"You look like you were going to have a child," Baba said to me the night before, when I was in my nightgown.

"You're raving," I said to her. Even the thought of such a thing worried me. Baba was always teasing me, although she knew I'd never done more than kiss Mr. Gentleman.

"It happens to country mopes like you, soon as you dance with a fellow," Baba said, as she held an imaginary man in her arms and waltzed between the two iron beds. Then she burst into one of her mad laughs and poured gin into the transparent plastic tooth mugs on the bedside table.

Lately Baba had taken to carrying a baby gin in her handbag. We didn't like the taste of gin and tonic so much, but we loved the look of it; we loved its cool blue complexion as we sprawled on our hard beds, drinking and pretending to be fast.

Baba had come back to Joanna's boardinghouse from the sanatorium, and it was like the old days, except that neither of us had men. We had dates of course—no steady men—but dates are risky.

Only the Sunday before, Baba had had a date with a man who sold cosmetics. He came to collect her in a car painted all over with slogans: GIVE HER PINK SATIN, LOVELY PINK SATIN FOR THAT SCHOOLGIRL BLOOM. It was a blue, flashy car and the slogans were in silver. Baba heard him honk and she looked out to see what kind of car he had.

"Oh, Holy God! I'm not going out in *that* circus wagon. Go down and tell him I'm having a hemmoridge."

I hated the word "hemmoridge," it was one of her new words to sound tough. I went down and told him that she had a headache.

"Would you like to come instead?"

I said no.

On the back seat there were advertisement cards and little sample bottles of "pink satin face lotion," packed in boxes. I thought he might offer me a sample, but he didn't.

"Sure you wouldn't like to see a show?"

I said that I couldn't.

Without another word he started up the car and backed out of the cul-de-sac.

"He was very disappointed," I said when I got back upstairs.

"That'll shake him. Feck any samples? I could do with a bit of suntan stuff for my legs."

"How could I take samples with him sitting there in the car?"

"Distract him. Get him interested in your bust or the sunset or something."

Baba is unreasonable. She thinks people are more stupid than they are. Those flashy fellows who sell things and own shops, they can probably count and add up.

"He hardly spoke two words," I said.

"Oh, the silent type!" Baba said, making a long face. "You can imagine what an evening with him would be like! Get your mink on, we're going to a hop," and I put on a light dress and we went downtown to a Sunday-night dance.

"Don't take cigarettes from those Indian fellows with turbans, they might be doped," Baba said.

There was a rumor that two girls were doped and brought up the Dublin mountains the week before.

Doped cigarettes! We didn't even get asked for one dance; there weren't enough men. We could have danced with each other, but Baba said that was the end. So we just sat there, rubbing the gooseflesh off our arms and passing remarks about the men who stood at one end of the hall sizing up the various girls who sat, waiting, on long benches. They never asked a girl to dance until the music started up, and then they seemed to pick girls who were near. We moved down to that end of the hall, but had no luck there either.

Baba said that we ought never go to a hop again; she said that we'd have to meet new people, diplomats and people like that.

It was my constant wish. Some mornings I used to get up convinced that I would meet a new, wonderful man. I used to make my face up specially and take short breaths to prepare myself for the excitement of it. But I never met anyone except customers, or students that Baba knew.

I thought of all this in the shop as I gummed red stickers on any bills which were due for over three months and addressed them hurriedly. We never posted bills, because Mrs. Burns said it was cheaper to have Willie, the messenger boy, deliver them. Just then he came in, shaking rain from his sou'wester.

"Where were you?"

"Nowhere."

As usual at that time of evening, he and I had a snack, before the shop got busy. We ate broken biscuits, raisins, dried prunes, and some cherries. His hands were blue and red with cold.

"Do you like them, Will?" I said as he made a face at my new white shoes. The toes were so long that I had to walk sideways going upstairs. I had put them on because Baba and I were going to a wine-tasting reception that night. We read about it in the papers and Baba said that we'd crash it. We had crashed two other functions—a fashion show and a private showing of a travel film of Ireland. (All lies, about dark-haired girls roaming around Connemara in red petticoats. No wonder they had to show it in private.)

At half past five, customers began to flock in on their way from work, and around six Mrs. Burns came out, to let me go off.

"Very stuffy here," she said to Willie. A hint to mean that we shouldn't have the oil heater on. Stuffy! There were drafts every-where, and a great division between the floor and the wainscoting.

I made my face up in the hall and put on rouge, eye shadow, and lashings of Ashes-of-Roses perfume. The very name Ashes-of-Roses made me feel alluring. Willie sneaked me a good sugar bag, so that I could bring my shoes in the bag and wear my Wellingtons. The gutters were overflowing outside, and rain beat against the skylight in the upstairs hall.

"Don't do anything I wouldn't do," he said as he let me out by the hall door, and whistled as I ran to the bus shelter a few yards down the road. It was raining madly.

The bus was empty, as there were very few people going down to the center of the city at that hour of evening. It was too early for the pictures. There were toffee papers and cigarette packages on the floor, and the bus had a sweaty smell. It was a poor neighborhood.

I read a paper which I found on the seat beside me. There was a long article by a priest, telling how he'd been tortured in China. I knew a lot about that sort of thing, because in the convent where I went to school the nun used to read those stories to us on Saturday nights. As a treat she used to read a paper called *The Standard*. It was full of stories about priests' toenails being pulled off and nuns shut up in dark rooms with rats.

I almost missed my stop, because I had been engrossed in this long article by the Irish priest.

Baba was waiting for me outside the hotel. She looked like something off a Christmas tree. She had a new fur muff and her hairdo was held in place with lacquer.

"Mother o' God, where are you off to in your Wellingtons?" she asked.

I looked down at my feet and realized with desolation that I'd left my shoes on the bus.

There was nothing for it but to cross the road and wait for the bus on its return journey. It was an unsheltered bus stop and Baba's hairstyle got flattened. Then, to make everything worse, my shoes were not on the bus and there was a different conductor. He said that the other conductor must have handed them in to the lost property office on the way to his tea.

"Call there any time after ten in the morning," he said, and when Baba heard that, she said, "Turalu," and ran across the road back to the hotel. I followed dispiritedly.

We had trouble getting into the banquet room, even though Baba told the girl at the entrance that we were journalists. She rooted in her bag for the invitation cards and said that she must have forgotten them. She said they were pink cards edged with gold. She knew because the girl at the door held a pile of them in her hand and flicked their gold edges impatiently. Baba's hands trembled as she searched, and her cheeks looked flushed. The two spots of rouge on her cheekbones had been washed unevenly by the rain.

"What paper do you represent?" the girl asked. A small queue had gathered behind us.

"*Woman's Night,*" Baba said. It was what she planned to say. There is no such magazine.

"Go ahead," the girl said grudgingly, and we went in.

As we walked across the polished floor, my rubber boots squeaked loudly and I imagined that everyone was staring at me. It was a very rich room—chandeliers alight, dusky-blue, velvet curtains drawn across, and dance music playing softly.

Baba saw our friend Tod Mead and went toward him. He was a public-relations officer who worked for a big wool company and we had met him at a fashion show a few weeks before. He took us for coffee then and tried to get off with Baba. He affected a casual world-weary manner, but it was only put on, because he ate loads of bread and jam. We knew he was married but we hadn't met his wife.

"Tod!" Baba hobbled over to him on her high heels. He kissed her hand and introduced us to the two people with him. One was a lady journalist in a big black hat and the other a strange man with a sallow face. His name was Eugene Gaillard. He said, "Pleased to meet you," but he didn't look very pleased. He had a sad face, and Tod told us that he was a film director. Baba began to smirk and show her dimples and the gold tooth, all at once.

"He made So-and-So," Tod said, mentioning a picture I'd never heard of.

"A classic documentary, a classic," the lady journalist said.

Mr. Gaillard looked at her earnestly and said, "Yes, really splendid; shatteringly realistic poverty." His long face had an odd expression of contempt as he spoke.

"What are you doing now?" she asked.

"I've become a farmer," he told her.

"A squire," Tod corrected.

The lady journalist suggested that she go out there someday and do an article on him. She was nicely dressed and reeked of perfume, but she was over fifty.

"We might as well get some red ink," Baba told me. She was disappointed because neither of the men had offered to get it for her. I followed her across toward the long row of tables which were placed end to end along the length of the room. There were white cloths on each table and waiters stood behind, pouring half glasses of red and white wine.

"They weren't very pally," Baba said.

Their voices reached me and I heard Tod say, "That's the literary fat girl I was telling you about."

"Which one?" Eugene Gaillard asked idly.

"Long hair and rubber boots," Tod said, and I heard him laughing.

I ran and got myself a drink. There were plates of water biscuits but I couldn't reach them and I felt hungry, having had no tea.

"Literary fat girl!" It really stabbed me.

"Your fashions are original—rubber boots and a feather hat," Eugene said behind my back, and I knew his soft voice without even turning around to look at him.

"You brave coward," he said. He was tall, about the same height as my father.

"It's nothing to laugh at—I lost my shoes," I said.

"But it is so original, to come in your rubber boots. You could start a whole trend with that kind of thing. Have you heard of the men who can only make love to girls in their plastic macs?"

"I haven't heard," I said sadly, ashamed at knowing so little.

"Tell me about you," he said, and I felt suddenly at home with him, I don't know why. He wasn't like anyone I knew; his face was long and had a gray color. It reminded me of a saint's face carved out of gray stone which I saw in the church every Sunday.

"Who are you, what do you do?" he asked, but when he saw that I was shy, he began to talk himself. He said that he had come because he met Tod Mead in Grafton Street and Tod dragged him along.

"I came for the scenery—not the wine," he said, looking around at the gilt wall brackets, the plush curtains, and at a tall, intense woman with black earrings who stood alone near the window. If only I could say something interesting to him.

"What's the difference between white wine and red wine?" I asked. He wasn't drinking.

"One is red and one is white." He laughed.

But Baba came along, with the white muff and a bunch of potato crisps.

"Has Mary of the Sorrows been telling you a lot of drip about her awful childhood?" She meant me.

"Everything. From the very beginning," he said.

Baba started to frown, then quickly gave one of her big false laughs and moved her hands up and down in front of her eyes. "What's that?" she asked. She did it three times, but he could not guess it.

"Past your eyes—milk—pasteurized milk. Ha, ha, ha." She

told Eugene Gaillard that she worked on the lonely-hearts column of *Woman's Night* and had a great time reading hilarious letters.

"Only yesterday," she ran on, "I had a letter from a poor woman in Ballinasloe who said, 'Dear Madam, My husband makes love to me on Sunday nights and I find this very inconvenient as I have a big wash on Mondays and am dog-tired. What can I do without hurting my husband's feelings?'

"I told Mrs. Ballinasloe," Baba said, " 'Wash on Tuesdays.' " She threw her little hands out to emphasize the simple way she dealt with life's problems, and he laughed obligingly.

"Baba is a funny girl," he said to me, still smiling. As if I ought to rejoice! It was my joke. I read it in a magazine one day when I had to wait two hours in the dental hospital to have a tooth filled. I read it and came home and told Baba, and after that she told it to everyone. Baba had got so smart in the last year—she knew about different wines, and had taken up fencing. She said that the fencing class was full of women in trousers asking her home for cocoa.

Just then Tod Mead came up waving an empty glass.

"The drink is running out, why don't we all go somewhere?" he said to Eugene.

"Those are two nice girls you found," Eugene said, and Baba began to hum, "Nice people with nice manners that have got no money at all . . ."

"All right," Eugene said. "We'll have dinner."

On the way out, Baba ordered twelve bottles of hock to be sent COD to Joanna, our landlady. The idea was that, having tasted the wine, people would order some. I knew that Joanna would have a fit over it.

"Who is Joanna?" Eugene asked, as we moved toward the door. We waved to the lady journalist and one or two other people.

"I'll tell you about her at dinner," Baba said.

My elbows touched his, and I had that paralyzing sensation in my legs which I hadn't felt since I'd parted from Mr. Gentleman.

2

We had dinner in the hotel. Eugene left word with one of the page boys that he would be in the dining room if there should be a telephone call for him. All through dinner I felt anxious and wished that he would be called, so that he could go away and then come back to us. Needless to say, I thought it must be a woman.

We had thin soup, lamb cutlets coated in bread crumbs, and French-fried potatoes. He didn't eat much. He had a habit of pulling his sleeves down over his wrists. His wrists and hands were hairy. Black, luxuriant hairs. Baba never stopped talking. I didn't say much, I couldn't balance the pleasure of seeing him and talking at the same moment. He said that I had a face like the girl on the Irish pound note.

"I never had a pound note long enough to look at it," Baba said.

"You look at it next time," he said, and then the waiter came over and refilled our glasses with wine. I felt very happy and the food was nice.

"Mister Gay Lord, Mister Gay Lord," a page boy called. My heart jumped with pain and relief.

"You, you, you," I said to him, and Baba kicked me to stop being so excited and making a fool of myself. He excused himself and went out very slowly.

He looked nice from the back: tall and lean, with a bald patch on the very top of his head.

"He's a smasher," Baba said.

"Rich!" Tod added, and smiled peculiarly. He was jealous of something, I felt.

"He's a good catch," Baba said.

"Har, har, har," Tod said, but I knew by the look in his small blue eyes that he withheld something. It occurred to me that maybe Eugene was engaged or married.

When he came back we tried to pretend that we had not been discussing him.

"I'm very sorry," he said, "but I shall have to leave you. I have to go out to the airport and see someone off, to America. It's important, otherwise I would not do this."

My heart sank and Baba dropped her spoon full of ice cream back on the glass dish. I think she said "Oh."

Tod stood up, very worried, thinking, I suppose, that he might have to pay the bill.

"Actually I have to be getting along myself, Eugene. Little old Sally is expecting me in for tea," and he got red around the collar as he spoke. "I'll run you out to the airport, it's on my way."

I nearly died, thinking that Baba and I might have to pay for the dinner by washing up for the next ten or eleven years, but Eugene paid it all right.

He shook hands, apologized, and left us there to drink a liqueur with our coffee. The waiters looked puzzled—the men's departure and my rubber boots made them think we were very eccentric.

"Jesus, just our luck," Baba said when they had gone.

"I suppose lots of women have *died* for him," I said.

"He's classy," she said. "I'd like to get going with him."

All I wondered was, would we ever see him again.

"We could write to him," Baba said. "You could draft a letter and I'd sign it."

"Saying what?"

"I don't know." She shrugged, and read the menu. There was a notice printed at the bottom of the menu which said that clients could inspect the kitchen if they wished.

"Let's do it for gas," Baba said.

"No." I had no inclination to do anything but just sit there and sip coffee and beckon to the puzzled waiter to bring more when my cup was empty. Would we see him again, ever?

"Hold on for your life," Baba said at last, "I have a marvelous idea." She suggested that we buy tickets for a dress dance and invite him. She said that we could pretend that we got the tickets for nothing, or had won them at a raffle or something.

"We'll get you a partner, Tod or the Body or something." The Body was a friend of hers who trained greyhounds in Blanchardstown. His real name was Bertie Counihan, but we had nicknamed him the Body because he hardly ever washed. He said washing harmed the skin. He was big and broad-shouldered, with black curly hair and a happy, reddish face.

We did exactly as Baba planned. At the end of the week (when I got paid) we bought four tickets for a grocers' dance which was to be held in Cleary's ballroom in October. Then we got Eugene's address from Tod and drafted a letter to him. Neither of us paid Joanna that week.

We waited anxiously for his reply, and when it came I nearly cried. He wrote and told Baba that he hadn't danced for years and feared that he would be dull company at such a jolly outing. Very politely, he declined.

"Christ, we're done for," Baba said as she handed me the letter. His handwriting was difficult to make out.

"Oh, God!" I said, more disappointed than I had expected to be. All my hopes had hinged on that dance, on seeing him again.

"What a life," I said. We had the tickets but no men, no money, no dance dresses.

"We'll have to go, we can't bloody well let those tickets go to waste," Baba said.

"We've no fur coat," I said. Often when we went downtown at night to look at people going into dress dances, we saw that most of the women had fur coats or fur stoles over their long dresses.

"We'll rent dresses from that place in Dame Street," Baba said. "It's morbid."

"It's twice as morbid to sit in this dump with four bloody tickets going to waste on the mantelpiece."

"We've no money to rent dresses," I said, pleased at such an easy solution to the whole thing. I had no interest in going now.

"We'll sell our bodies to the College of Surgeons!" she said. "They come and collect when you're dead, and the students put you on a table, with no clothes, and take you to pieces."

I said that she couldn't be serious. She said she'd do anything for a few bob.

I thought of him out there in his large house, unaware of the misery he had caused us. I imagined a brown leather-topped desk, with numerous pens and pencils, and two colors of ink in special glass bottles.

"You can steal in that joint where you work, they're underpaying you," Baba said.

"It's a sin."

"It's not a sin. Aquinas says you can steal from an employer if he underpays you."

"Who's Aquinas?"

"I don't know, he's a big nob in the Church."

Finally we managed it. We borrowed five- and ten-shilling amounts from various people and hired long dresses and silver dance shoes. Baba's dress was white net and mine a lurid purple. It was the only one they had which fitted me.

We got quite excited on the evening of the dance. We bought half a pound of scented bath crystals and bathed in the same water. I put pancake on Baba's back to hide her spots, and she put pancake on mine and hooked my dress up. I could scarcely breathe in it, it was so tight.

"Bee-beep, bee-beep," the Body's horn hooted at nine o'clock, and we went down holding our dresses up so that the tails would not get dirty. He had come in the blue van, which he used to take greyhounds to the veterinary surgeon and such places. It smelled of that kind of life.

Then we collected Eamonn White, a chemist's apprentice, who was to be my partner for the night. He was a nice boy except that he kept saying "great gas," "great style," "great fun," "great van," "great gas," all the time.

On the way down we stopped at a pub in North Frederick Street to have a few drinks. The customers stared at Baba and me, in our long tatty dresses with tweed coats over our shoulders. Baba was miserable because she hadn't been able to borrow a fur.

"Name your poison," the Body said, clapping Eamonn on the back.

Eamonn was a Pioneer and wore a total abstinence badge, which he must have transferred from the lapel of his ordinary suit to his hired black suit. He said he'd have tomato juice and the Body was very offended by this, but Baba said *we'd* have large ones to make up for it.

I danced with Eamonn for most of the night, because he was my partner. "Great gas, great gas," he kept saying. It was his first dress dance. He marveled at the slipperiness of the floor, the pink lighting, the two bands, the paper roses hanging from the ceiling, and the tables beautifully laid for supper. My frock was strapless, and his warm, pink hands seemed to be on my bare back all night. He had blond hair and blond eyelashes, and the pinkness of his skin reminded me of young pigs at home.

The Body was different.

"You're a noble woman," he said to me later as I danced with him in my hired silver shoes and wondered if I would ever waltz with Eugene Gaillard. I was glad that he hadn't come, because he would have seen me in my foolish dusty dress, saying foolish tittery things to amuse the others.

We drank wine with our supper, and then as usual the Body took too much and got obstreperous and started to shout. He rolled the menu up and bellowed through it: "Up the Republic, Up Noel Browne, Up Castro, Up me."

Eamonn was frightened and left the table. He never returned. Being a Pioneer, he did not understand the happy madness which drink could induce in others.

At two o'clock, just when everybody was getting very merry and the band players had begun to toss paper hats around, Baba and I brought the Body home. He was too drunk to drive, so we left his blue van there and hired a taxi. We had no idea where he lived. It's funny that we should have known him for a year but did not know where he lived. Dublin is like that. We knew his local pub but not his house. We brought him home and put him on the horsehair sofa in Joanna's drawing room.

"Baba, Caithleen, I wan't tell you something, you're two noble women, two noble women, and Parnell was a proud man, as proud as trod the ground, and a proud man's a lovely man, so pass the bottle round. What about a little drink, waiter, waiter . . ." He waved a pound note in the air, still thinking he was at the dance.

"Have a sleep," Baba said, and she put out the light. His voice faded with it, and within a minute he was breathing heavily.

We knew that we would have to be up at half past six to get the Body out of the house before Joanna's alarm went off at seven.

"We've just three hours' sleep," Baba said as she unhooked my dress and helped me out of it. A new boned brassiere had made red welts on my skin.

"We'll sue," she said when she saw the welts. We went to bed without washing our faces, and when I woke the pancake makeup felt like mud on my face.

"Oh, God," I said to Baba as I heard the Body shouting downstairs: "Girls, les girls, there's no Gents, there's no bloody service here—where do I *go*?"

We both ran out to the landing to shut him up, but Joanna had got there before us.

"Jesus meets his afflicted mother," the Body said as Joanna came down the stairs toward him in her big red nightgown, with her gray hair in a plait down her back.

"Thief, thief," she shouted, and before we even knew it, she had pressed the button of the small fire extinguisher that was fixed to the wall at the end of the stairs and trained the liquid on him.

"I want police," she yelled. He was struggling to explain things to her, but he couldn't make himself heard.

"Stop that bloody thing, he's our friend," Baba said, running downstairs.

The Body was covered with white, sticky liquid which looked like hair shampoo, and his dress shirt was drenched. His wet hair fell over his face in oily curls.

"He's our friend," Baba said sadly. "God protect us from our friends."

"You call him a friend, hah?" Joanna said. He put his hand on the banister and proceeded to go upstairs. Joanna blocked the way.

"I want to see a man about a dog," he said, wiping the wet off his face with a handkerchief.

"What dog? I have no dog, I say," she shouted, but he pushed past her.

"Gustav, Gustav," she called, but I knew that cowardly Gustav would not come out.

"Jesus falls the first time," the Body chanted as he tripped on a tear in the brown linoleum.

Baba ran to him and got him up. A little later we helped him into the bathroom to wipe the stuff off his hair and face.

"Who's the cow out there, who the hell is she?" he asked as he looked into the bathroom mirror and saw his wild, bloodshot eyes and oily ringlets. He beamed when he saw himself.

"Look at that jawline, look at it, Baba, Caithleen; I should have been a film star or a boxer," he said. "Me and Jack Doyle and Movita. 'Oh, Movita, oh, Movita, you're the lady with the mystic smile . . .' Who's that cow out there? . . ."

Joanna rapped on the bathroom door. "You leave my house. I come from good Austrian family, my brathers doctors and Civil Service."

"Balls," he said.

"What ball you say?"

Baba stuffed the white towel over his mouth to shut him up, and through it he murmured, "Veronica wipes the face of Jesus . . ."

"Come on, we'll dance down the road," Baba said, and somehow she got him out of the house and up to the bus stop. By then it was half past seven.

Joanna found twelve eggs in a pot on the gas stove. The Body had apparently been boiling eggs and the water had boiled off. She flew into a fresh rage when she saw that the saucepan had got burned.

"You leave my house this day," she said to us. "My good, best saucepan. One dozen country eggs for nog for Gustav, and my fire extinguisher. I am not spending all this money on frivolous. I tell you this, if I go poor I am better dead." She almost cried as she held the pot of brown eggs for us to see.

"All right," Baba said. "We'll leave." She proceeded to go upstairs, but Joanna caught the cord of her dressing gown.

"You cannot leave me, eh? I am *gut* to you like a mother. I stitch your clothes and your ironing."

"We're leaving," Baba said.

"Oh, please." There were tears in Joanna's eyes by now.

"We'll think it over," Baba said, and then Joanna caught her winking at me, so that she knew we would not leave. She got abusive again.

All I wanted was to go back to bed, but it was morning and I had to dress myself and face the day.

3 Luckily for me, that day was Wednesday and (as usual) the shop closed in the afternoon.

I took the dance dresses and shoes back to the rental shop, and then collected photos of myself which had been taken by a street photographer the previous Wednesday. I felt tired and nervous from the short sleep and the mixture of drinks which we had had. I wished that I were rich and could drink coffee all afternoon, or buy new clothes to cheer myself up.

As usual I went to the bookshop at the bottom of Dawson Street where I had a free read every week. I read twenty-eight pages of *The Charwoman's Daughter* without being disturbed, and then came out, as I had an appointment to meet Baba in O'Connell Street.

Coming down the stone steps from the bookshop, I met him, point-blank. I saw him in that instant before he saw me, and I was so astonished that I almost ran away.

"Oh, you!" he said as he looked up in surprise. He must have forgotten my name.

"Mr. Gaillard, hello," I said, trying to conceal my excitement. In daylight his face looked different—longer and more melancholy. A shower of rain had brought us together. He came up to shelter in the porch and I stood in with him. My body became like jelly just from standing close to him, smelling his nice smell. I kept staring down at the long, absurd toe of my white shoe, which had got blackened from rain and wear.

"What have you been doing since, besides going to dances?" he said.

"Yes, we went last night, it was marvelous, a marvelous band and supper and everything." Oh, God, I thought, I am as dull as old dishwater. Why can't I say something exciting, why can't I tell him what I feel about him?

"The rain sparkles on the brown pavement," I said in a false fit of eloquence.

"Sparkles?" he said, and smiled curiously.

"Yes, it's a nice word."

"Indeed." He nodded. I felt that he was bored and I prayed that there would be a deluge and that we would have to stay there forever. I imagined the water rising inch by inch, covering the road, the pavement, the steps, our ankles, our legs, our bodies, drawing us together as in a dream, all other life cut off from us.

"It's getting worse," I said, pointing to a black cloud that hung over the darkening city of Dublin.

"It's only a shower," he said, shattering all my mad hopes. "What about a cup of tea, would you like some tea?" he asked.

"I'd love it." And in the rain we crossed the road to a tea shop.

I forget what we talked about. I remember being speechless with happiness and feeling that God, or someone, had brought us together. I ate three cakes; he pressed me to have a fourth but I didn't, in case it was vulgar. It was then he asked my name. So he *had* forgotten it.

"Tell me, what do you read?" he asked. He had a habit of smiling whenever I caught his eye, and though his eyes were sad he smiled nicely.

"Chekhov and James Joyce and James Stephens and . . ." I stopped suddenly in case he should think that I was showing off.

"I must loan you a book some time," he said.

Some time? When is some time, I thought as I looked at the tea leaves in the bottom of his cup. I poured him a second cup, through the little strainer which the waitress had belatedly brought. The tea dripped very slowly through the fine strainer.

"Oh, that fiddle-faddle," he said, so we discarded the strainer and left it on a side plate to drip.

I knew that Baba would be waiting and that I should go to her, but I could not stand up and leave him. I loved his long, sad face and his strong hands.

"I often wonder what young girls like you think. What *do* you think of?" he asked, after he had been looking steadily at me for a few seconds.

I think about you, I thought, and blushed a bit. To him, I said in a dull stupid voice, "I don't think very much really; I think about getting new clothes or going on my holidays or what we'll have for lunch."

It seems to me now that he sighed and that I tittered to hide my embarrassment and told him that some girls thought of marrying rich men, and one I knew of thought only of her hair; she washed it every night and measured how much it grew in a week, and it was halfway down her back like a golden cape. But it gave her no pleasure because she worried about it too much.

"Where do you go on holiday?" he asked, and I sighed, because I longed to stay in a hotel and have breakfast in bed. I had never had breakfast in bed, except once or twice in the convent when I was sick, and then there was a cup of hot senna, which I had to drink down first. Sister Margaret always stood there while you drank the hot senna, telling you that it was good for the soul as well as the body.

"I go home."

"Where's home?"

I told him.

My father had gone back from the gate lodge to our own house and he lived there with my aunt. I described it as best I could.

"You like your home?"

"There's a lot of trees. It's lonesome."

"I like trees," he said. "I sow them all the time—I've got thousands of trees."

"Have you?" I said. I felt that he was bluffing and I don't like bluffing.

He looked at his watch, and inevitably he had to go.

"I'm sorry, but I was to see somebody at four."

"I'm sorry for keeping you," I said as we stood up. He paid the bill and took his corduroy cap off the mahogany hatrack inside the door.

"Thank you. A pleasant encounter," he said as we stood on the stone step. I thanked him; he raised his cap and went away from me. I watched him go. I saw him as a dark-faced god turning his back on me. I put out my hand to recall him and caught only the rain. I felt that it would rain forever, noiselessly. The buses were full, as it was after five o'clock, and Baba was furious when I got there an hour late.

"Blithering eejit," she said. I did not tell her that I had met him.

We had coffee, and later, as arranged, the Body came. We had more coffee; he apologized for everything and gave us five pounds to cover the cost of the dance tickets. Then he took us by taxi to the greyhound track at Harold's Cross.

On the following Wednesday I went to Dawson Street and stood outside the bookshop for two hours, but Eugene Gaillard did not come, nor the next Wednesday nor the one following.

I waited for four Wednesdays and walked around searching for a sight of him, in his long black coat with the astrakhan collar. I imagined him sitting in Robert's café looking at dark-haired girls. He said that he liked dark hair and dark eyes and very pale skin; he said these things had a quietness which he liked. I sat in Robert's, too, and thought of him—he didn't eat potatoes and he drank water with his dinner, so I took to drinking water with my meals. Tap water in Joanna's was never cold or sparkling the way you imagine water should be, but it was nice to do something that he did.

I waited and walked around, certain that I would meet him, and the wild hope made my spirits soar. I could almost smell him, see the black hairs on his hands, his proud walk. But for a whole month I did not see him. Once, I saw his car parked in Molesworth Street and I waited for ages in the doorway of a wool shop which had closed down. Finally hunger drove me home, and the next day I wrote to him and asked him to have tea with me the following Wednesday.

The week went round and I came to the restaurant feeling mortified. He was there all right, sitting at a table inside the door, reading a paper.

"Caithleen," he said when I came in. It was the first time he ever said my name.

"Hello," I said, trembling, and wondered if I ought to apologize for having written. I sat down in my old coat with a new blue chiffon scarf around my neck.

"Take off your coat," he said, and I slipped it off and let it hang on the back of the chair.

"I always forget how pretty you are, until I see you again," he said as he looked carefully at my face. "Ah, the bloom of you, I love your North Circular Road Bicycle Riding Cheeks."

My cheeks were always pink, no matter how much powder I

used. He ordered sandwiches, cakes, scones, and biscuits. I worried, fearing that I would have to pay the bill, being as I had invited him, and I had only ten shillings in my purse. He put his elbows on the table, his fist under his chin. In repose his eyelids were lowered partly, and when he made the effort of raising them you were surprised by the tender expression in his great brown eyes. His face was hard and formidable, but his eyes were compassionate.

"Well?" he said, smiling up at me. "So here we are." There was a spot of dried blood on his jaw where he had cut himself shaving.

"I hope you didn't mind coming," I said.

"No, I didn't mind. I was very happy in fact; I thought of you on and off during the past few weeks."

"Five," I said hastily.

"Five what?"

"Five weeks. You know me five weeks." He laughed, and asked if I kept a diary, and I thought to myself, He's a sly one.

"Tell me more about your social life?" he asked as I bit into a cream slice and then licked my lips clean.

"I thought I'd see you," I said openly.

"I know, but . . ." He halted, and played with the sugar tongs. "You see, it's difficult, I'll be quite honest, I don't want to get involved. It must be my natural, puritan caution, because Baba and you are two lovely girls, and I'm a man more than old enough to know better."

Keep Baba out of this, I thought as I said to him, "What do you mean 'involved'?"—my voice choked, my heart pounding.

"You are a nice girl," he said, and he put his hand across and petted my wrist, and I asked then if we could have tea once in a while.

"We're having tea now," he said, nodding toward the silver pot. "We might even have dinner."

"Dinner!"

"Dinner!" he said, mimicking my breathless, surprised voice.

We had dinner that evening, and afterward we drove out to Clontarf and walked down by the Bull Wall, as it was a mild, misty November night. He held my hand; he did not squeeze my fingers or plait them in his, he just held my hand very naturally, the way you'd hold a child's hand or your mother's.

He talked about America, where he had lived for some years. He had lived in New York and in Hollywood.

The sea was calm, the waves breaking calmly over the boulders and a strong, unpleasant smell of ozone in the air. I could not tell whether the tide was coming in or going out. It is always hard to tell at first.

"It's going out," he said, and I believed him. I believed everything he said.

Walking down over the concrete pier we shared a cigarette. There were fog horns blowing out at sea and a chain of lights across the harbor that curved like a bright necklace, beyond the mist. Lighthouses blinked and signaled on all sides and I loved watching the rhythm of their flashes, blinking to ships in the lonely sea. They made me think of all the people in the world waiting for all the other people to come to them. For once I was not lonely, because I was with someone that I wanted to be with. We walked to the end of the pier, and looked at the rocks and the pools and the straps of seaweed on everything. He talked about another sea—the faraway Pacific.

"I used to drive out there on weekdays, when things became too much in Los Angeles. The sky is always blue in California, a piercing blue, and the pavements hot, and the tanned, predatory faces booming out their hearty nothings. I like rain and isolation . . ." He spoke very quietly, using his hands in gestures all the time. I could just see the outline of his face, greenish from moonlight and the glow of the filtered cigarette which we shared.

"And you drove out there?" I said, hoping that accidentally, or otherwise, he would tell me something of his personal life.

"I drove out there and walked over this great, white, Pacific beach, edged so delicately with tar oil on the one side and oil derricks on the other. I kicked the empty beer cans and wanted to go home."

I thought it odd that no other people occurred in his reminiscences. It was only the place he described, the white beach, the beer cans, the ripe and rotting oranges along the roadside.

"You always talk of places as if only *you* had been in them," I said.

"Yes, I was born to be a monk."

"But you're not a Catholic," I said immediately.

He laughed loudly. It was strangely disturbing to hear his laugh above the noise of the washing waves and the anxious breathing of two people who lay between the rocks, making love. He said that Catholics were the most opinionated people on earth—their self-mania, he said, frightened him.

At the end of the pier we looked down at the water as it lapped against the concrete wall, and he told me that he had won cups and medals for swimming when he was a boy. He had lived most of his life in Dublin, with his mother, and had gone to work at twelve or thirteen. His father had left them when he was a small boy, and as a child he had combed the beaches looking for scrap.

"I found shillings often," he said. "I've always been lucky, I've always found things. I've even found you with your large, lemur eyes. D'you know what a lemur is?"

"Yes," I lied, and then terrified that he might ask, I talked rapidly about something else.

Driving me home, he said, "It's a long time since I've spent an evening with such a nice girl."

"Go on," I said, looking at his fine profile and longing to know of all the other women he had been with and their perfume and what they said and how it had ended. He said that up to the age of twenty-five while he was apprenticed to various trades—cinema operator, gardener, electrician—he could only afford to look at girls, the way one looks at flowers or boats in Dún Laoghaire harbor.

"It's true," he said, turning to smile at me.

The smile was nice, and I moved nearer and touched with my cheek the cloth of his gray, hairy overcoat.

He did not kiss me that night.

4 We met three evenings a week after that. In between he wrote me postcards, and as time went on he wrote letters. He called me Kate, as he said that Caithleen was too "Kiltartan" for his liking—whatever that meant.

Each Monday, Wednesday, and Saturday he waited outside the shop for me in his car, and each time as I sat near him, I trembled with a fantastic happiness. Then one night he stayed in a hotel in Harcourt Street and planned to meet me at lunchtime the next day in order to buy me a coat. It was coming near Christmastime, and anyhow, my old green coat was shabby. He bought me a gray astrakhan with a red velvet collar and a flared skirt.

"I'm stuck with you now," he said as I walked around the shop, while he surveyed the coat from behind. I wished that he wouldn't scrutinize so much, because I have a stiff walk and become ashamed when people look at me.

"It suits you," he said, but I thought that it made me look fatter.

We bought it. I asked the assistant to wrap up my old one. She was very posh, with moonlight dye in her hair and a pale lavender shop coat which buttoned right up to her throat. Then he bought me six pairs of stockings and we were given one free pair as a bonus. He said that it was immoral to get a free pair just because we could afford six pairs, but I was delighted.

I thought of Mama and of how she would love it, and I knew that if she could she would come back from her cold grave in the Shannon lake to avail herself of such a bargain. She was drowned when I was fourteen. I felt guilty on and off, because I was so happy with him and because I had seldom seen my mother happy or laughing. Being in the posh shop reminded me of her. A few weeks before she was drowned, she and I went to Limerick for a day's shopping. She had saved up egg money for several weeks, because although we had a lot of land, we never had much ready cash; Dada drank a lot, and money was always owing—and also she sold off old hens to a man who came around buying feathers and junk. In Limerick she bought a lipstick. I remembered her trying the various shades on the back of her hand and debating for a long time before deciding on one. It was an orange-tinted lipstick in a black-and-gold case.

"My mother is dead," I said to him as we waited for our change. I wanted to say something else, something that would convey the commonplace sacrifice of her life: of her with one shoulder permanently drooping from carrying buckets of hen food, of her keeping bars of chocolate under the bolster so that I could eat them in bed if I got frightened of Dada or of the wind.

"Your poor mother," he said, "I expect she was a good woman."

We lunched in the restaurant off the shop, and I worried about being late back to work.

As he followed me through a narrow, cobbled cul-de-sac toward where the car was parked, he said, "You're like Anna Karenina in that coat."

I thought she must be some girlfriend of his, or an actress.

Driving back, I said rashly, "Would you like to come and have tea this evening, in the house where I stay?" Baba had been pestering me to invite him home to tea so that she could flirt with him.

He said he would, and promised to be there at seven.

As I hurried toward the shop, he called after me, laughing, to take care of the new coat. I blew him a kiss.

"Your old bottom's getting fat," he shouted. I nearly died. There were customers waiting around the door and they heard him.

When Mrs. Burns wasn't looking I wrote a note to Joanna to ask if we could have something special for tea. It was Friday and always on Friday we had roly-poly pudding. We had the same things on the same successive days of each week. Joanna called it her "new systematic."

Willie took the note over and returned with Joanna's reply on his blue, hungry lips. "*Mein Gott*, I am not spending any luxury for this rich man."

I bought her a cake in the bakery two doors away. It was an expensive cake topped with shredded coconut. I sent it over, along with a bag of biscuits and a sample jar of cranberry jelly. Willie came back and reported that she had put the cake in a tin, which meant that she had put it away for Christmas. All afternoon my heart was bubbling with excitement; happiness, unhappiness. Twice I gave wrong change, and Mrs. Burns asked me if it was my bad time. In the end I got so worked up that I hoped he wouldn't come at all. I could see his face all the time, and his grave eyes, and a vein in the side of his temple that stood out. Then I became terrified that once having seen where I lived, he would no longer ask me out.

Joanna's house was clean but shabby. It was a terraced, brick house, linoleumed from top to bottom. She had a strip of matting (which she got cheap) in the downstairs hall. The furniture was dark and heavy, and the front room was stuffed with china dogs and ornaments and knickknacks. There was a green rubber plant in a pot on the piano.

When I got home Baba was there, all dressed up. Joanna must have told her that he was coming. She wore her tartan slacks and a chunky cardigan back to front. The V neck and the buttons were down her back.

As I went into the room I heard Joanna say, "It is not good to the floor these girls with spiked shoes."

Our stiletto heels had marked the linoleum.

"I have no other shoes," Baba said in her brazen, go-to-hell voice.

"*Mein Gott*, upstairs is full of shoes, under the beds, the dressing table, I see nothing but shoes, shoes, shoes."

They both noticed my new coat.

"Where d'you feck it?" Baba asked.

"A new coat! Astrakhan," Joanna said. And she touched the cuff with her hand and said, "Rich, you are a rich girl. I had not a new coat since I left my own country nine years ago." She held up nine fingers as if I didn't know numbers.

"You give me your old one, hah?" she said, grinning at me.

"What's for tea?" I asked. I had cycled home so quickly that my chest hurt. He was due any minute.

"You asked me what's for tea! You know what is for tea," Joanna said.

"But look, Joanna, he's awful special and rich and everything. He knows film stars, he met Joan Crawford; oh, Joanna, please, please." I exaggerated to impress her.

"Rich!" Joanna said, rolling the r of that word, her favorite word, the only poem she knew.

"I tell you this, *I* am not rich. I am a poor woman, but I come from good home, good respectable Austrian family, and driven out of my own country."

"He's from around there, too," I said, hoping to soften her.

"Where?" she asked as if I had just insulted her.

"Bavaria or Rumania or some place," I said.

"Is he a Jew, eh?" Her eyes narrowed. "I do not like Jews, they are a little bit mean."

"I don't know what he is, but he's not mean, honest," I said, and I almost told her that he had bought the coat for me.

Baba, quick to deduce things, sang, "Where did you get that coat?" to the air of "Where did you get that hat?"

"My father sent me the money," I lied.

"Your aul fella is in the workhouse!" She had no brassiere on, and you could see the shape of her nipples through the white jumper.

"What's for tea?" I asked again.

"Roly-poly pud," Baba said. The sudden ring of the doorbell impinged on her high voice, and I ran upstairs to put some powder on. Baba let him in.

I put on a pale blue dress, because pale colors suit me. It had a silver, crystalline pattern like snow falling, and the neck was low. It was a summer dress, but I wanted to look nice for him.

Outside the dining-room door I rubbed the gooseflesh on my arms and paused to hear what they were saying to him. I could hear his low voice, and Baba using his Christian name already. Awkwardly I went in.

"Hello," he said as he stood up to shake hands with me. Baba sat next to him, her elbow resting on the curved back of his chair. He looked very tall under the low ceiling and I was ashamed of the little room. It seemed more shabby with him in it; the lace curtains were gray from smoke, and the smiling china dogs on the sideboard looked idiotic.

"You found us easily enough?" I said, pretending not to be shy. It's funny that you're more shy with people in your own house. Out on the street I could talk to him, but in the house I was ashamed of something.

Joanna carried in the roly-poly pudding—wrapped in muslin—on a dish.

"*Mein Gott, is,* is so hot," she said, as she laid the plate down on a pile of homemade table mats which Gustav had cut from a spare piece of linoleum. She unwrapped the wet muslin.

"Hot cuisine," Baba said to Eugene, and winked. The pudding looked white and greasy; it reminded me of a corpse.

"My own, homemake," Joanna said proudly. She cut the pudding into sections, and as she cut it, trickles of hot raspberry jam flowed onto the dish; then she respooned the jam back onto each portion.

"For my nice new guest," she said, giving him the first helping. He declined it, saying that he never ate pastry.

"No, no, is no pastry," Joanna said, "good Austrian recipe."

"The seeds of raspberry jam get stuck between my teeth," he said, half joking.

"Take your teeth out, eh?" she suggested.

"They're my own teeth." He laughed. "Let's just have a nice cup of tea?"

"You not eat my food." Her poor face looked hurt, and she grinned stupidly at him.

"It's my stomach," he explained. "I've got a hole in it, in there," and he put his hand over his black pullover and tapped his stomach. Earlier on he had asked Joanna's permission to take off his jacket. The black pullover suited him. It gave him a thin, religious look.

"Constipate?" Joanna asked. "I have the bag upstairs brought with me from my own country, what d'you call, enema?"

"Holy God," Baba said. "Let him have his tea first."

"It's just a pain I have," Eugene told her, "anxiety . . ."

"Anxiety—a rich man?" Joanna said. "What anxiety can a rich man have?"

"The world," he said.

"The world," she shouted. "You are a little bit mad, I think." Then, fearing that she had overstepped her place, she said, "It is so terrible for your poor stomach, you poor man," and she touched the bald patch in the center of his head and petted it as if she had known him all her life. Within a minute she fetched dill pickles, salami, black olives, smoked ham, and a dish of homemade macaroons.

"Oh, goodie," Baba said, cooing. She took a moist black olive and held it between her fingers while she kissed it.

"No, a mistake," Joanna said, taking it back, "these are special for Mr. Eugene."

"That's right, Joanna, we foreigners must stick together," he said—but when she went out to make tea he made us a ham sandwich each.

"What made me think that girls ate delicately?" he said to the jam dish, and this set Baba off on one of her laughing fits. Baba had developed a new, loud laugh.

She turned to Eugene and said, "There's nothing I like so much as a cultivated man."

He bowed from the waist and smiled at her.

Baba looked very nice that particular evening. She has a small, neat face with dark skin. Her eyes are small too, and shiny and very alert. They remind you of a bird darting from one thing to another. Her thoughts also dart, and she gives the impression of having great energy.

"I used to know a girl like you once," he said to her, and Baba just went on smiling.

"Good, best tea," Joanna said as she came in with the silver teapot and a dented tin hot-water jug.

"Nice? Good? Eh?" she asked before he brought the cup to his lips.

"Breathtaking," he said.

He inquired about her country, her family, and if she intended going back there. She answered with the long rigmarole about brothers and good family which Baba and I had heard five thousand times.

"Open the hooch," Baba said to me, nodding toward the bottle of wine which Eugene had brought.

"She'll open it soon as she gets sentimental," I said. Joanna was so busy talking that she did not hear us.

"She's at the height of her sentimental now, she's passed that

slob bit about her slob brother changing her nappie when she was two
and he was four," Baba said.

"My brothers spent me a night at the opera . . ." Joanna rambled
on; then Baba tapped her elbow and, pointing to the wine, said, "Give
the man a drink."

Joanna's face fell, she got confused, she said, "You like tea, eh?"

"Yes," he said, "I don't drink wine really."

"Wise man, I like you." She beamed at him, and Baba sighed
out loud.

"You must not marry a shop girl from Ireland," Joanna said.
"You must marry somebody from your own country, a countess."
Joanna was so stupid that she didn't think I'd mind her saying a thing
like that. I singed the hair on her bare arms with my cigarette.

"*Mein Gott*, you are burning me." She jumped up.

"Sorry."

Then Gianni, the other lodger, came in, and in the confusion of
introducing Eugene, I did not have to apologize any further.

When Joanna stood up to get his cup and saucer, she hid the
wine behind one of the china dogs.

"That's that," Baba said, and poured herself some cold tea.

"*Mi scusi*," Gianni, the lodger, was saying as he asked Baba to
pass the sugar. He was showing off, using his hands and making false,
conceited faces—I didn't like him. He had arrived at Joanna's the
day I hoped to go to Vienna with Mr. Gentleman, and at first I helped
him with his English and we went to *The Bicycle Thief* together.
Later he gave me a necklace and thought that he could make very
free with me because of that. When I wouldn't kiss him on the
landing one night, he got huffy and said the necklace cost a lot of
money. I offered to give it back, but he asked for the money instead,
and we had remained cool ever since.

"Some more dirty, foreign blood," Eugene said good-humoredly.

"I come from Milano," Gianni said, offended. He had the least
sense of humor of anyone I ever met.

"She can't inhale," Baba said when Eugene passed me another
cigarette. I took one anyhow. Holding the match for me, he whispered,
"You've polished your eyes and everything," and I thought of the

delicate moist kisses which he had placed upon my eyelids and of the things he whispered to me when we were alone.

"You know Italy well?" Gianni asked then.

Eugene turned away from me and let the match die in the glass ashtray which Gustav had pinched from Mooney's snug. GUINNESS IS GOOD FOR YOU was written in red on the gold-painted ashtray.

"I worked in Sicily once. We were making a picture there about fishermen and I lived in Palermo for a couple of months."

"Sicily is not good," Gianni said, making his boyish, contemptuous face.

He's a selfish fool, I thought as I watched him pack sausages into his mouth. He got sausages because he was a male lodger. Joanna had some idea that male lodgers should get better food. I was watching him when it happened. My cigarette fell inside my low-necked dress. I don't know how, but it did; it just slipped from between my fingers, and next thing I was burning. I yelled as I felt my chest sting and saw the smoke rising toward my chin.

"I'm on fire, I'm on fire." I jumped up. The cigarette had lodged at the base of my brassiere and the pain was awful.

"*Mein Gott*, quench her," Joanna said as she dragged my dress and tried to pull it away from me.

"Jesus," Baba said, and she roared laughing.

"Do something, hah," Joanna shouted, and Eugene turned to me and immediately began to smile.

"She did it for notice," Baba said, picking up the jug of milk and proceeding to pour it down inside my dress.

"The good, best milk," Joanna said, but it was too late, I was already soaking from half a jug of milk, and the cigarette went out naturally.

"Honestly, I thought it was some joke you were playing," Eugene said to me.

He was trying to control his laughing in case I should be offended.

"You *are* a silly girl," Joanna said to either Baba or me. I went out to change my dress.

"What'n the name of Christ were you doing, mooning like that?" Baba said out in the hall. "You're a right-looking eejit."

"I was just thinking," I said. I had been thinking of a plan to get Eugene to bring me out, away from them, so that we could kiss in the motorcar.

"Of what, may I ask?" I did not tell her. I had been thinking of the first night he kissed me. Suddenly one rainy night as we walked down by the side of the Liffey toward the Customs House to the city, he said, "Have I ever kissed you?" and he kissed me quite abruptly, just as people flocked out of a cinema. I felt faintly sick and giddy, and I have no idea whether that kiss was quick or prolonged. I loved that part of Dublin then and forever, because it was there I laid my lips to the image of him that I had created, and the pigeon's droppings on the Customs House were white flowers which splashed the dark, ancient stone of the steps and porch. Afterward in the car, I tasted his tongue and we explored each other's face in the way that dogs do when they meet, and he said, "Wanton," to me. While I had been thinking of all this, Baba looked inside my dress to see what damage the cigarette had done. It lay there, all gray and soggy, and my chest had got burned.

"Go up and change your dress," she said.

"Come up with me." I did not want her with Eugene. Already I was jealous of the way she said, "Absolutely," to everything he said, and showed her dimples.

"Not on your life," she said as she held the doorknob and patted her dark bouffant of hair before going back into the room, to sit near him. She looked silly from behind, with the cardigan on back to front and the buttons running down her back and a V of darkly flushed back.

I put on lashings of her perfume upstairs, and more powder and another dress.

When I came down, Gianni was sitting at the old piano, striking chords softly from its yellowed keys and humming something amid the talk which had risen in the room. The table was pushed back near the window, and Baba told me that we were going to have a singsong. She leaned on the corner of the sideboard and in her light, girlish, early-morning voice she began to sing:

I wish, I wish, I wish in vain,
I wish I was a child again,
But this I know it never will be,
Till apples grow on a willow tree . . .

And then before we could clap she began another song, which was incredibly sweet and sad. It was about a man who had seen a girl in the woods of his childhood and had gone out into the world haunted by her image. The refrain was "Remember me, remember me, remember for the rest of your life . . ." Toward the end Baba's voice quavered as if the words meant something very special to her, and Eugene said that she sang like a honey bird. She blushed a bit, and pushed her sleeves above her elbows, because the room was warm. Her bare arm with the fuzz of gold hair looked dainty as she rested it on the sideboard and murmured about being hot. I saw him look at her and knew that her singing would often dance across his memory.

Gustav came in, and Joanna opened the wine and served it in liqueur glasses to make it go far. On and off, Baba or Gianni sang. Baba then said that I would have to recite, being as I couldn't sing.

"I can't," I said.

"Oh, please, Kate."

"Go on," Eugene said. He had sung "Johnnie I Hardly Knew You," in a pleasant, careless voice.

I recited "The Mother" by Patrick Pearse, which was the only poem I knew. It was far too emotional for that small, hot room. As I recited:

Lord thou art hard on mothers
We suffer in their coming and their going . . .

Baba sniggered and said aloud, "What about the children's allowance?" Everyone laughed then, and I felt a fool, and though he said, "Bravo, bravo," I hated him for laughing with the others.

Baba sang several more songs, and Eugene wrote the words of some on a piece of paper, which he put into his wallet. Her cheeks were red, not with rouge, but with a flush of happiness.

"You're warm," he said to her, and stood in front of the fire to keep the heat away from her.

Greater love than this, no man hath, I thought bitterly as he stood in front of the fire and grinned at Baba, because of the duet which Gustav and Joanna had begun to sing.

For me the night was long and disappointing. When he left around eleven, he did not kiss me or say anything special.

Even in sleep I worried about losing him. First thing when I woke I remembered Baba singing "Scarlet Ribbons" and the way he smiled at her. It was cold, so I stood on my nightgown and put my clothes on. The window was white with frost and uneven icicles clung to the top part of the frame.

I went to work early as it was Saturday, our busy day, and I wanted to have the shelves well stocked with provisions.

"Oh, darling," Mrs. Burns said when I let myself in. She had come out to get sausages and rashers from the tray of meat things which was kept on the marble shelf behind the counter. I was wearing the coat which he had given me and she admired it. I told her that Eugene Gaillard had given it to me, and she stared and said, "What! Him!"

I guessed what she had to say, even before she began. He was a married man, she warned, and God only knew the number of innocent little girls whom he had started on the road to ruin.

There are no innocent girls, I thought. They're all scarlet girls like Baba, with guile in their eyes; and I asked if he was really married.

She said she had read all about it in the paper a year or two before. She remembered reading it the time she was in hospital having her veins cut, and the woman in the bed next to her commented on him and said that *she* knew him when he had holes in his shoes.

"He married some American girl. She was a painter or an actress or something," Mrs. Burns said, and I took the coat off and let it fall in a heap on the floor. I hated it then.

"A good job, I told you," she said as she went inside with black pudding, two eggs, and some back rashers.

I closed my eyes and felt my stomach sinking down and down. That explained everything—his reserve, the house in the country, those stories of deserted California beaches with beer cans and rotting oranges, his aloneness.

One sadness recalls another: I stood there beside the new, crumpled coat and remembered the night my mother was drowned and how I clung to the foolish hope that it was all a mistake and that she would walk into the room, asking people why they mourned her. I prayed that he would not be married.

"Oh, please, God, let him not be married," I begged, but I knew that my prayers were hopeless.

Automatically I filled shelves with tins of things, and I took eggs from a wooden crate and cleaned them one by one with a damp cloth. I put a pinch of bread soda on the stains which would not come out easily, and then I counted half dozens of clean eggs in sectioned boxes that were marked "Fresh country eggs."

Two eggs cracked in my hand; they were going off slightly, and that strange, sulphurous smell of rotting eggs has forever been connected in my mind with misery.

At times I felt violent and wanted to scream, but the Burnses were in the kitchen eating a fry and there was nothing I could do.

He rang me at eleven o'clock. The shop was packed and both Mr. and Mrs. Burns were serving at the counter.

He sounded very cheerful. He rang me to invite me to his house the following day. He had talked of inviting me once or twice before.

"I'd love to meet your wife. It was a wonder you didn't tell me you were married," I said.

"You never asked me," he said. He was not apologetic. His voice sounded sharp and I imagined that he was going to put the telephone down.

"Do you wish to come tomorrow?" he asked. My legs began to tremble. I knew that customers were looking at my back, listening to what I said. They used to joke me about boys.

"I don't know . . . maybe . . . will your wife be there?"

"No." Pause . . . "She's not there now."

"Oh." Suddenly I was filled with hope and vague rapture. "She isn't dead, by any chance?" I asked.

"No, she's in America."

I heard the ring of the cash register behind my back and knew that Mrs. Burns would sulk for the day if I stayed any longer on the phone.

"I have to go now, we're busy," I said, my voice high and nervous.

He said that, if I wished, he could collect me at nine the following morning.

"All right, at nine," I said.

He put the telephone down before I did.

On and off throughout the day, I cried, in the lavatory and places. I rang Tod Mead to ask all about the marriage, but he was not in his office, so I learned nothing that day.

5 I set out early on Sunday morning, as the church bells of Dublin clanged and clashed through the clear, bright air. Other people were on their way to Mass, but I was going to visit him in his own home. I did not feel sinful about missing Mass, because it was early morning and I had washed my hair. The city was white with frost and the road looked slippery in places.

I went up to the corner of the avenue to wait for him because Joanna had threatened to send Gustav with me.

"A chaperon you need," she said. She said that it was not right for me to be alone with a strange man in his home. She said that he might be a spy or a maniac. She called it a meaniac.

"I'm going alone and that's that," I said. I wanted to hear about his marriage.

"Gustav will not be in the way," she said. She was really worried about me. She polished Gustav's brown leather boots and put them beside the fire along with his clean gray socks. He always put on his shoes and socks at the fire, having warmed his feet first.

"Oh, all right, then," I said, and I got out of the house on the excuse that I was going to early Mass.

Eugene was ten minutes late. He was lined and gray as if from lack of sleep. He just looked at me and breathed on my face in welcome.

"Wow!" he said to the wide straw hat that I wore. It was a summer hat really, with a bunch of wax rosebuds on it.

"You look like a child bride—it must be that hat," he said, and grinned at it. I suppose he thought it was foolish. My long, clean, bright hair fell down over both shoulders and I had put on very white makeup. I told him about Gustav wanting to come with us. He just smiled. I thought the smile peculiar and wondered if I should have brought someone after all. I said a prayer to my Guardian Angel to protect me:

> *Oh, angel of God, my guardian dear,*
> *To whom God's love commits me here;*
> *Ever this day be at my side*
> *To light and guard, to rule and guide.*

He asked me if I had had breakfast. I said no. I had been too excited to eat. Then he reached to the back seat and got a fawn wool scarf, which he put around me. He tied a soft knot under my chin and kissed me before we set out.

We drove through the city and past suburbs and then along a wide road with ditches and trees on either side. Sometimes we came into a village—houses, a few shops, a pump, a chapel.

"I usually go to Mass," I said as we slowed down to let people come out the chapel gates and cross the road.

"I have a few prepaid indulgence forms and excommunication applications at home somewhere, which may fix you up," he said, and I laughed it off and said how nice the country looked. Branches and little dark, delicate twigs formed a fretwork of black lace against a cold silver sky. I hadn't been in the country for months, not since I was home the previous summer, and I thought of my aunt and my father settling to the Sunday papers and a long sleep after their Sunday lunch. My aunt looked after my father now, and they lived in our old house, occupying one or two of the large, damp rooms.

"Feel your ears clicking," he said as we climbed a long, rocky hill toward bleak mountain land. There were no trees on that stretch—just gorse bushes and granite rocks. Sheep moved between the marbled rocks, and I felt my ears buzzing, just as he said. We got to his house around eleven. The frost had melted by then and the laurel hedge was a dark, glossy green; the house itself was white, with french windows downstairs and trees all around it.

A big sheep dog ran to us and Anna opened the door. I had heard of her—she looked after him in a haphazard sort of way, and lived downstairs at the back of the house. She was married and had a baby.

"Well, at long last," she said, almost insolently.

"Hello, Anna." He handed her the parcels from the car and introduced me. There were chops, a sheep's head for the dog, a bottle of gin, and a new coffeepot.

"Booze," she said. She was a weedy woman with a greasy face and long, straight hair. She looked sleepy or drugged or something.

Even though it was winter, flowers were blooming on the rockery

—a mist of small blue flowers trailed over the marbled rocks. I felt that he was excited about showing me his house; he hummed as we climbed the stone steps to the door.

The front hall was clean and bright, with cream paintwork, black antique furniture, and walking sticks in a big china holder.

" 'Tis a divil to keep clean," Anna said as she led the way down to the kitchen, and just as we went in by one door, we heard her husband go out by another. She said that he was shy.

"Now, aren't you glad you came?" Eugene said to me when Anna went into the dairy for a jug of cream. He made coffee.

"Yes, it's lovely," I said, looking around the large, stone-flagged kitchen, and at the set of green house bells high on the wall, which looked as if they hadn't been in use for years. Small logs were stacked to dry at one end of the black-lead range, and a boiling kettle let out its familiar sigh. It was a nice kitchen.

He changed into an old oatmeal jacket and went out to saw some wood, as Anna said that Denis had gone off for the day to count sheep and mend a fence. I longed to follow Eugene, but she drew a chair over near the fire for me, so I sat and talked to her, while she chopped cabbage on the big kitchen table. She looked sluttish in a black cotton skirt and a shapeless gray jumper. She wore a man's hat and had stuck a duck's feather into the brown, stained band.

"Are you an actress?" she asked, as soon as we were alone.

"No."

"He knows a lot of actresses."

She poured herself some gin from the bottle he had brought and told me that she wasn't a servant really and that I mustn't think so. A caretaker, she called herself, nodding to the back stairs, where her apartments were and where her baby slept. She had a baby, nine months old. She talked about her womb, and about her husband.

"The only woman he ever warmed to was Mrs. Gaillard—Laura," she said, looking into my eyes. Her own eyes were a bright, malignant yellow.

"He has a little blue stone upstairs that he's keeping for her. He found it out on the mountain."

She talked of the great times and big parties they'd had in Laura's time, and I imagined the front rooms filled with people, candles on the mahogany tables, and lanterns in the beech trees down the avenue. I had not fully believed that Laura existed up till then, but I believed it now, because Anna said so—"Laura was great sport; she had a big fur coat and her own car and everything. The place is like a churchyard now"—she poured herself more gin and squeezed some lemon into it.

There were a lot of slugs in the cabbage and she just tipped them into the fire with the blade of the knife.

Eugene wheeled a barrow of logs in and she went off on the excuse that she had to do something upstairs.

"Is she drinking?" he asked. The bottle of gin was on the table with the cut lemon beside it. He took away the bottle and told me about a new power saw which he would like me to see. He had just cut the wood and you could see the bright knots of amber resin in it and smell its fresh resin odor.

"That would be lovely," I said, though machinery bores me. He tiptoed over and kissed me and asked if something worried me, because my face looked tense.

"Has she been telling you a whole long saga?" he asked.

I nodded.

"Don't believe a word of it, she's invented a big fairy tale. Did she say we had a Rolls-Royce and a butler?"

I nodded again, and smiled at the tuft of his hair which stuck out foolishly over one ear. He wore his cap sideways, and he looked pale in the oatmeal jacket.

"I'll tell you about it later," he said, and though I dreaded him having to tell me, I also wanted desperately to know everything, so that Anna could not surprise me with anything new.

We ate lunch off a little circular table in his study, and it was late, as Anna had got slightly merry from the gin and did not put on the vegetables until after two o'clock.

"To plow the rocks of Bawn," she hummed as she came in, carrying plates. She still kept on the man's hat, which made me wonder if she had shingles or something. The bacon was sliced on our plates, and she also carried a big napkin of steaming, floury potatoes.

"That's a nice bacon." She winked at him, and he smiled into her yellow face. She had put on some violet eye shadow, which didn't enhance her appearance, because there were black circles under her eyes anyhow. He said that she had appropriated all the cosmetics which "your woman" left behind. He rarely called Laura by name.

"Will you be my amanuensis in this shooting lodge?" he joked as I looked around the room to admire it. The walls were a faded blue, the paintwork cream. There were no curtains on the french windows (just shutters, which had been drawn back), and the light came in, in abundance, so that you could see where Anna had dragged a cloth over the pieces of brown mahogany furniture and only half dusted them. The view through the long window was magical. Beyond the paling wire was the front field, below it a forest of trees, and in the distance a valley of dreaming purple. He said that it was a valley of birch trees and that in wintertime the twigs of birch always had this odd, flushed purple color. He suggested that we drive down there after lunch, but I did not want to go and spoil the beautiful illusion.

"Tell me, what sort of food do you like?" he asked as he put butter on my cabbage and passed me a tube of mustard. At home we always mixed mustard in egg cups.

"I like everything."

"Everything?" He looked appalled.

I was sorry then that I didn't pretend to have some taste. He talked about his work; he had just finished a script for a picture on the world's starving people. He had traveled all over the world, to India, China, Sicily, Africa—gathering information for it. On his desk were photographs of tumbledown cities and slums with hungry children in doorways. It made me hungry just to look at them.

"Bengal, Honolulu, Tanganyika," I repeated after him in a dreamy voice, recounting where he had been. I had no idea where those places were.

"You make a lot of pictures?" I asked.

"No. I make odd little pictures; I made one I think you'd like, about a Maori child."

"Is your name on the screen?" I longed to be able to tell my aunt.

"It's such small print," he said, measuring its depth by holding his thumb and forefinger slightly apart, "no one ever reads it. I made *one* picture in Hollywood—a romance—and I bought this house with the earnings from it."

That would be in Laura's time, I thought, as he went on talking about one he was making on sewerage systems.

"Sewerage?"

"Yes, you know, water sewerage; it's a very exciting business."

I looked at him and saw that he was quite serious, and I knew that I could never tell my aunt about him now.

"They're charming films. I used to think of my life as a failure, purposeless . . . until I got older and became aware of things. I now know that the problem of life is not solved by success but by failure: struggle and achievement and failure . . . on and on." He said the last words almost to himself.

What he said reminded me of a film I had seen, of a turtle laying her eggs on the sands and then laboring her way back to the sea, crying with exhaustion as she went.

"I'd like to see some of your films," I said.

"You will." But he did not make any plans then. There was a bed in the room with a rug thrown over it. He said that it had been brought down from upstairs once when somebody was ill. He didn't say who.

We went for a walk so that I could see the woods before it got dark. He loaned me a raincoat that was lined with honey-colored fur and a pair of woman's Wellingtons from under the stairs. I turned them upside down before putting them on, because once I found a dead mouse in a Wellington. Some corn seeds dropped out of them.

"All right?" he asked.

"Lovely, thank you." They pinched a bit. She must have had smaller feet than me. Baba always says I probably have bigger feet than any girl in Ireland.

We went up by the wood at the back of the house to shelter from the misting rain. There were all kinds of trees and the ground was soggy with leaf mold. He said that huge red and purple mushrooms grew in the wood in summer. It was very quiet except for the rain and our feet breaking twigs. Even though it was winter, the wood was green and sheltered, because there were many big Christmas trees.

"So you heard that I'm married," he said as I stood to admire the startling red berries on a holly tree.

"Yes, the boss's wife told me."

He smiled and seemed almost flattered that anyone should know about his private life.

"And *you* think this is a very bad thing?"

"Oh no," I said, staring straight ahead at a split oak that looked like the legs of a giant.

He went on: "Yes, I married an American girl when I was over there. She was a nice girl, very personable, but after a few years she didn't care for me. I wasn't 'fun.' A privileged girl, brought up to believe that she is special, changes an unsatisfactory husband as she might change her bath salts. She believes that happiness is her right."

"That's a pity," I said. It was a stupid thing for me to say, but I was afraid that I might cry, so I had to say something.

"She was a failed painter. We lived in Hollywood in a plaster mansion-cottage—they're going cheap there in the last few years," he said aside, as if he were addressing the holly tree. "The unending blue sky nearly drove me mad, so did the people—'Hi Joe, Hi Al, Hi Art.' We came to Ireland and bought this house. I had money from the picture I made and she had an income. She had gone to school in a gold-plated Rolls. She hated everyone."

It occurred to me that he was secretly proud of this, though he may not have known it.

"She had big plans," he said, "hunting and shooting. She thought we might invite film directors here and writers. We did, but they never came. It rained, I got my rheumatism back." He moved his neck stiffly, as if there were rheumatism always waiting to be summoned. "I put on my long underpants and my long face, and she said that I had a feudal attitude to women because I let her carry in a log for the fire. She left one day when I was out mowing hay with Denis . . . There was a note on the table and . . ." He stopped and withdrew whatever it was he had intended to say.

"I'm sorry," I said. I *was* actually sorry.

"Oh . . . thank you." He smiled, and put his hand to catch the drops of rain that fell from the trees. It was the first time he had looked shy or ill at ease.

The dark, polished green of holly leaves was reflected on his pale skin so that he looked a little green and unhealthy, and I longed to take him in my arms and console him. We walked on.

At the top of the wood he climbed onto a grass bank, and pulled me up by the hand to show me the view.

"Ah," he said, breathing in the wonderful remoteness of the place. "You mustn't worry about my being married."

"I'm not worrying," I lied.

"I would have told you about it eventually," he said. "I don't talk about some things easily. Guilt and failure are painful topics, and as you get older you try and put them out of your mind."

I shivered slightly, I don't know why, and he put an arm around me, thinking that I was dizzy from standing on the height.

Underneath, sheep grazed on the rough, yellowish grass which stretched toward a low mountain. Some gorse had been burned, and in the fading light the charred, bent branches looked like skeletons of ghosts. The view depressed me.

"That was why I did not want to get involved with you in the very beginning," he said quietly.

"I know now," I said, and he turned sharply to see if I was crying or something.

Then he smiled at me. "You're wild, you must have grown up out in the open."

I thought of our front field at home with pools of muddy water lodged around the base of trees and I felt desolate.

"You have a look of mystique on your face," I said.

His pale expression fell to pieces, and he hollered with laughter and asked where I had picked up such a word. I realized that it must have been a wrong word, but I had read it in some book and liked its sound.

"Dear girl, you'll have to give up reading books." He took my hand and we ran down the slope of the bank and back into the wood. We had a quick look at a plantation of young pine trees which he had put down. A netting wire fence ran all around them to keep out rabbits and deer. He reached in and touched the tip of the trees and said that he must sow one for my coming. I wondered if he had sown trees for his wife and if he still loved her.

Anna and her husband went out after tea to play cards, and took their baby, though Eugene said it would get pneumonia.

I felt uneasy being alone with him in that large house. He lit two Tilley lamps, drew the shutters in the study, and said, "Let's have a little music."

There were records in small piles on the floor, and books everywhere, and antlers sprung at me from one wall. He said that the previous owner, who had been keen on slaughter, had left traces of himself behind—horns and heads, and dried skins on the floor. A strange music filled the room and he moved around, beating time to it and pausing to see how I liked it. It had no words.

"Well, what do you think of that? What does it remind you of?" he asked when the record had played itself out. It reminded me of birds making a brown V in the sky.

"Birds," I said.

"Birds!" He did not know what I meant, so he put on another, and this one sounded much the same.

"More birds?" he said, laughing, and I nodded. I think he was disappointed, because he did not play any more records that night.

"Let's look at the fire upstairs," he said, but I did not want to go up there. I feared that it might be a plan to lure me up to his bedroom. He had lit a fire there earlier on—because of a damp patch over the mantelpiece, he said.

"I'll sit here," I said as he went off, carrying a brass candlestick and a new, unlighted candle. I looked at his desk, to try to find out things about him. It was littered with papers, letters, air-mail envelopes, packets of flower seeds, stiffeners from a man's collar, copper nails in a jam jar, and ashtrays with funny drawings on them.

"Could you bring up the bellows, please?" he called down to me.

The fire in the bedroom had gone out. It was a large room with a double bed and dark mahogany furniture. Four pillows on the bed— two at either side—caught my eye.

"Well, sometimes I sleep on one side and sometimes I sleep on the other; it makes a change," he said, divining my thoughts.

"Stay," he said as he worked the bellows up and down, and caused ashes to rise toward the picture over the fireplace—a naked woman lying on her side.

"I'll have to be off," I said, trying to sound casual. A naked woman was no thing to have staring at him every night in his bed. A gust of smoke blew down the chimney into his face and made him cough.

"Could you open the window, please?" he asked as the coughing almost took his breath away. The window was stiff, so I had to tap it; it opened suddenly and unexpectedly, and the sudden draft quenched the candle.

"I'm afraid I have to go home now, it's eight o'clock," I said in a slightly hysterical voice as I groped my way toward the door.

"Go," he said. "But, my dear girl, I haven't seduced you yet!" He laughed and I thought of a portrait of him downstairs, which looked sinister. I groped for the doorknob (the wind had caused the door to slam) but could not turn it. My hands became powerless. He relit the candle and stood there, near the fireplace, holding it.

"Stop trembling," he said, and then he said that there was nothing to be afraid of and that he had been joking. I realized that I was being silly and I began to cry.

"There, there," he said, coming over to pet me. "You are a silly girl." He bent down and kissed my wet mouth more tenderly than he had ever kissed me before.

We went downstairs and made tea and talked, and then he said that he would take me home. I combed my hair, which had become tossed while he kissed me.

Outside, the stars were fierce with frost, the ground hardened with it, the pine trees very still and very beautiful. In the greenish moonlight I turned to him to say that I did not really want to leave so early. The place looked enchanting in the frost; inside in the study a warm fire blazed behind a guard, the lamp was lowered, and the last record lay on the green baize of the wind-up gramophone, silent.

"I hate going now," I said, but we had put on our coats and he had brought the car around to the front of the house, and anyhow, he said that we would have to drive slowly because of ice patches reported on the nine o'clock news.

"Back to the village," he said. It was a phrase he used whenever he drove me home.

6

I went most Sundays after that, and then, one Sunday night I stayed.

I slept in the guest room, where the floor and woodwork had been newly varnished. Everything was a little sticky.

In fact I didn't sleep, I kept thinking of him. I could hear him whistling downstairs and moving around until after three o'clock. He had left me a magazine to read. It contained a lot of drawings—people with peaked noses and staircases growing out of their ears—which I did not understand. I kept the light on because Anna said a woman had died in that room just before Eugene bought the house. A colonel's wife who took digitalis pills.

Toward morning I dozed, but the alarm clock went off at seven and I had to get up to go back to work.

"Did you sleep?" he asked. We met going down the stairs, and he yawned and pretended to stagger.

"No, not very well."

"Nonsense, isn't it! Two people at opposite wings of the house lying awake. Next time we'll keep each other company and put a bolster in the bed between us, won't we?" he said as he kissed me. I looked away. I had been brought up to think of it as something unmentionable, which a woman had to pretend to like, to please a husband.

He brought a rug for my knees and a flask of tea, which I drank in the car, as there was no time for breakfast.

The next Sunday I stayed, and I still went to my own room. I did not want to sleep in his bed; he put it down to scruples, but actually I was afraid. Early the next morning he tapped on my door, and as I was awake I got up, and we went out for a stroll through the woods.

There are moments in our lives we can never forget: I remember that early morning and the white limbs of young birches in the early mist, and later the sun coming up behind the mountain in crimson splendor as if it were the first day of the world. I remember the sudden brightness of everything and the effect of suffused light as the sun came through the mist, and the dew lifted, and later the green of the grass showed forth very vividly, radiating energy in the form of color.

"I wish we could be together," he said, his arm around my neck.
"Will we be?" I said.

"It seems so natural now, so inevitable, I was never one for neck-ing in backs of cars, it strikes me as being so sick," he said.

Kissing, or "necking," as he called it, suited me nicely, but I could not tell him that.

But I could only postpone it until Christmastime.

He invited Baba, Joanna, and Gustav for Christmas dinner, so that I would feel at ease, as his friends terrified me. They were mostly people from other countries who told each other obscure jokes, and I felt that they looked on me as some sort of curiosity brought in for amusement.

It was a pleasant dinner, with red candles along the table and presents for everyone on the tree; Joanna was in her element, she got an old gilt frame to bring home and some logs for the dining-room grate. Baba waltzed with Eugene after dinner to gramophone music, and everybody had plenty to drink.

At midnight the guests went home, but I stayed. It looked quite respectable really, because Eugene's mother was also staying. She was a frail, argumentative little woman, with a craggy face and a big forehead like his. She coughed a lot.

Eugene helped her upstairs to the guest room (the room I usually slept in) and brought her hot whiskey and a little mug for her teeth. Then he came down and we ate cold turkey and cream crackers.

"I hardly saw you all day, and you looked so pretty at dinner," he said as we sat on the sheepskin rug in front of the fire, eating. He read to me, poems by Lorca, which I didn't understand, but he read nicely. He wanted me to read one but I felt shy, sometimes I became very shy in his company. One side of my face got very hot, so I took off one of my red lantern earrings. Raising his eyes from the book, he saw the warm lobe blackened a little by the cheap tin of the earring clip, and he groaned.

"Your ears could go septic," he said as he examined the red ear-rings which I had bought on Christmas Eve so that I would look glamorous for him.

"Made in Hong Kong!" he said as he threw them in the fire. I tried to rescue them with the tongs but it was too late; they had sunk into the red ashes.

I sulked for a bit, but he said that he would buy me a gold pair. "If I didn't care about you I wouldn't worry about your ears," he said. I laughed at that. His compliments were so odd.

"You soft, daft, wanton thing, you've got one mad eye," he said, looking into my eyes, which he decided were green.

"Green eyes and copper hair, my mother wouldn't trust you," he said. His mother had cold blue eyes which were very piercing and shrewd. A smell of eucalyptus oil surrounded her.

I lay back on the woolly rug, and he kissed my warmed face.

After a while he said, "Will we go to bed, Miss Potts?" I was happy lying there, just kissing him; bed was too final for me, so I sat up and put my arms around my knees.

"It's too early," I said. It was about two in the morning.

"We'll wash our teeth," he said, so we went upstairs and washed our teeth. "You're not washing your teeth properly, you should brush them up and down as well as back and forth."

I think he just said that to put me at my ease. I had stopped talking and my eyes were owlish, as they always are when I am frightened. I knew that I was about to do something terrible. I believed in hell, in eternal torment by fire. But it could be postponed.

The bedroom was cold. Normally Anna lit a fire there, but in the excitement of dinner and presents she had forgotten about it.

He undressed quickly and put his clothes on a wing-backed armchair. I stood watching him, too self-conscious to move. My teeth chattered, from fear or cold.

"Hop in before you get cold," he said as he got something out of the wall press. His long back had one vivid strawberry mark. Dark tufts of hair stuck out from under his arms, and in the lamplight the smooth parts of his body were a glowing honey color.

He got into bed and propped his head on one fist while he waited for me.

"Don't look at me," I asked.

He put his hand across his eyes; the fingers were spread out so that there were slits between them. While I undressed, he recited:

Mrs. White had a fright
In the middle of the night,
Saw a ghost, eating toast
Halfway up a lamp post . . .

Then he asked me to unscrew the Tilley lamp. A trickle of paraffin flowed out from the metal cap and mingled with the toilet water which I had poured on my hands and wrists.

"You're such a nice plump girl," he said as I came toward him. The light took a few seconds to fade out completely.

I took off the coat which I had been using as a dressing gown, and he raised the covers up and gathered me in near him.

I shivered, but he thought it was with cold. He rubbed my skin briskly to warm it and said that my knees were like ice. He did everything to make me feel at ease.

"Have you fluff in your belly button?" he asked as he poked fun at it with his fingers. It was one thing I was very squeamish about, and instantly (I began to tighten with fear) my whole body stiffened.

"What's wrong?" he said as he kissed my closed lips. He noticed things very quickly. "Are you filled with remorse?"

It was not remorse. Even if I had been married I would have been afraid.

"What is it, darling, little soft skin?" If he had not been so tender I might have been brave. I cried onto his bare shoulder.

"I don't know," I said hopelessly. I felt such a fool crying in bed, especially as I laughed so much in the daytime and gave the impression of being thoughtlessly happy.

"Have you had some terrible traumatic experience?" he asked.

Traumatic? I had never heard that word before, I didn't know what to say.

"I don't know," I said. "I don't know" was the only sentence which formed itself in my crying brain.

He tried to assure me, to say that I need not worry, that there was nothing to be afraid of, that surely I was not afraid of him. He caressed me slowly and gently, and I was still afraid. Before that, on armchairs, in the motorcar, in restaurants, I touched his hands, kissed the hairs on his wrists, longed for the feel of his fingers on my soft secret flesh, but now everything had changed.

He said that I should talk about it, tell him what exactly appalled me, discuss it. But I couldn't do that. I just wanted to go to sleep and wake up, finding that it was all over, the way you wake up after an operation.

I lay in his arms crying, and he said that I must not cry and that we would do nothing but have a big, long sleep and wake up full of energy. He was a little quiet. He blamed himself for being so stupid, so unthinking, for not having known that I would be nervous and afraid.

Eventually he turned over on his other side to go to sleep. He took a sleeping pill with a glass of water.

"I'm sorry, Eugene . . . I do love you," I said.

"That's all right, sweetling," he said, patting my warm bottom with his hand. At least we had got warm.

"I won't be afraid tomorrow," I said, knowing that I would.

"I know that," he said. "You're just tired; now go to sleep and don't worry about a thing."

We joined hands. I wanted to blow my nose, as I could scarcely breathe from all that crying. I was ashamed to blow it, in case it was vulgar.

I went to sleep, mortified.

Sometime toward morning we must have come together again, because I woke up to find myself refusing his love.

Immediately afterward he got up and dressed. I apologized.

"Stop saying you're sorry," he said as he drew his braces up. "There's no need to be sorry, it's a perfectly natural thing," he said. He sat on the armchair and put on his socks.

"Are you getting up?" I asked.

"Yes, I often get up at dawn when I don't sleep very well; I go out for a walk or do some work . . ."

"It's my fault."

"Stop saying it's your fault, stop worrying," he said. I was glad that it was too dark for me to see the expression on his face; I could not have looked at him.

He left the room, and later I heard his steps outside on the gravel.

I lay on, and wept. I had never felt so ashamed in my whole life; I felt certain now that he was finished with me because I had been so childish. When daylight came, about half past eight, there were a few stars left in the heavens. They looked wan and faint as stars do in the morning.

"Go home . . . vanish," I said to the stars, or to myself, and I got up and dressed when I heard Anna poke the range downstairs. I did not know how I would face her, or Denis or his mother or him. My black, sequinned jumper, which I had thought so charming at the dinner table, seemed idiotic in the early morning. I wished that I could get out of the house and escape back to Joanna's without being seen. I looked in the mirror. My face was red, blotchy, swollen. Everyone would know!

It began to snow. It came very fast and sudden, and it fell slant-wise on the front field but did not lodge there. It melted as it touched the ground. I stuck my head out, hoping that the sleet might change my face, and then I went to the second guest room to toss the bed which I should have slept in. It seemed foolish and sad to have to do such a thing, but Anna was very observant and would have noticed. Under that divan bed I found a box of old toys and torn books.

This book belongs to Baby Elaine Gaillard, I read on the flyleaf of an animal book. I nearly died. He had never said that he had a child, but I ought to have wondered why he was so tender with Anna's baby. It made everything worse; I looked at the toys, torn and chewed, and cried over them. The sleet, my red, unslept cheeks, the silly sequinned jumper, the cold green porcelain of an unlit anthracite stove in the room, all seemed to multiply my sense of shame. I sat there, weeping, until Anna knocked on the door to say breakfast was ready.

Down in the kitchen I could not bring myself to look at him. I held my head down. He handed me a cup of tea and said, "Did you sleep well, Miss Caithleen Brady?"

Anna was there, watching.

"Yes, thank you."

He bent his head and looked sideways at my face, hung in shame. He was laughing.

"I'm very glad that you slept well," he said as he brought me over to the table and buttered some toast for me.

Later his mother came down and we had breakfast together. She complained about the porridge being lumpy. She lived with a sister in Dublin, and said that there was one thing she could not stand and that was lumpy porridge.

He drove her back around noon and I thought I should go too, but he asked me to stay a while longer, as he said he wanted to talk to me. I stayed.

"See you again, dear," his mother said as he helped her into the car. She had a shawl over her fur coat and a hot-water bottle for her knees. She looked rather happy, because he had given her whiskey and chocolates and white turkey meat wrapped in butter paper. She liked to be pampered; she was making up for all the years when she had worked as a waitress to rear her son. He was quite distant with her and she was sharp with him. But she liked it when he fussed over her.

When they had gone I went up to the woods. The sleet had stopped and now it rained mildly. I did not know whether I should risk staying another night or not. I was trying to decide—the gently falling rain made a background of vague soothing noise for my muddled thoughts. I thought of other woods, dampness, cowslips in a field of high grass, all the imaginary men I had ever talked to and into whose strong arms I had swooned in a moment of ecstatic reconciliation. But I could not decide; I had never made decisions in my life. My clothes had always been bought for me, my food decided on, even my outings were decided by Baba. I walked round and round, touching the damp trees, inhaling the wild smells of the damp wood.

When I heard the car come back I walked toward the house and then I heard him whistle as he came up to the woods to find me. He wore an old brown hat, which made him look rakish, and as he came toward me I knew that I would stay another night and risk making a fool of myself again.

"I'll stay," I said instantly, and he was pleased. He said that I looked a lot better since I came out and that rain suited me and that

I must always live in rainy country and wear my hair long, like that, and wear a dark mackintosh.

"And I won't be afraid," I said as we ran down the wooded hill toward the yard in order to make some tea. He was dying for tea. I did not feel sleepy anymore. We spotted Anna looking at us through his field glasses.

"She'll break those glasses," he said, but by the time he got in the house, she had restored them to their brown leather case, which hung on the end of the curtain pole in his study. When he complained, Anna said that he must have been seeing things. He prepared a turkey hash, while Anna and I chopped vegetables.

Before dinner he carried a white china lamp upstairs to the dressing table in his room so that I could make up my face. He stayed there, watching, while I applied pancake makeup with a damp sponge and spread it over my face evenly. It made me pale. In the mirror my face looked round and childlike.

"The old man and the girl," he said to the spotted mirror, which was wedged at the right angle by a face-cream jar—one of Laura's no doubt. He debated whether or not he should shave.

"Am I likely to be kissing anybody?" he asked the mirror as he stroked the stubble on his chin.

I laughed.

"Well, am I?" he asked again. I loved kissing him. I thought, If only people just kissed, if all love stopped at that.

He picked up my hairbrush and began to brush my hair very slowly. I liked the slow, firm strokes of the brush on my scalp, and after a while I felt exhilarated from it. He smiled a lot at me in the mirror.

"I have too much chin and you have a shade too little. We should make perfectly chinned children," he said. He expected me to laugh, but I didn't. There were some things which I was very touchy about: babies, for instance. Babies terrified me. Then I remembered the box of toys; I had never forgotten it really, just postponed thinking about it.

"There is a box of toys in my room, under the bed," I said.

"Yes, I know, they're mine. I had a child."

"Oh."

"I had a daughter, she's three now." I thought his voice changed, but I could not be certain. I imagined him giving a little girl a pickaback, and the thought stabbed me with jealous pain.

"Do you miss her?" I asked.

"I miss her very much, almost every minute of the day I think of her, or think that I'm hearing her. Once you've had a child you want to live with it and watch it grow."

He went on brushing my hair, but it was not the same after that.

I slept in his bed that night, and he loaned me a white flannel night-gown with rosebuds on it, which was exactly like one my mother kept in a trunk at home, in case she ever had to go to hospital. He set the alarm clock for seven and put it on the bedside table, and put the lamp out. I thought of Laura, because he said that he had bought the clock in New York one night when he was walking around, very late. He said you could buy things in the middle of the night there, or go to the pictures. I longed to go with him to London, where he was going in a day or two. During dinner a telegram had been delivered, asking him to go to London as soon as possible. I read it in the study after dinner, when we were eating mandarin oranges. It said: YOU OLD SOD CAN YOU COME AND DO SOMETHING TO THIS LOUSY SCRIPT ON SEWERAGE. IT STINKS. It was from somebody called Sam, and Eugene said that he would have to go there for a few days. He took a canvas travel bag from the gun bureau to remind him to pack.

" 'Tis well for you," I said, and I thought that he might bring me, but instead he asked me what I did with orange pits.

"I swallow them," I said. There were so many that it would have been a day's work to remove them.

"You swallow them," he repeated, raising his eyes to the cracked ceiling. "How am I ever going to take you into society?"

"I'll be very polite," I said, sure that he would invite me to London, but he didn't.

We went to bed early and he got me the nightgown from the hot press and set the clock for seven.

"Not so cold tonight," he said when we got into bed. There had been an oil heater on in the room for several hours and the air was fuggy.

"Not so strange, either, is it?" he asked as he rubbed my cold knees briskly and asked if I usually slept with half a dozen hot-water bottles. Baba and I had one stone bottle between us and we were always threatening to buy a second one, but it seemed such a waste of good money. We fought over it a lot and sometimes I went to bed very early to have the first of it.

"Not so strange," I lied as his hand roamed over my body and his fingers searched for the places I liked most to be caressed. I was thinking that by the next day he would be off in London, far away from me, and already I had begun to tighten with fear and nervousness. I drew my nightgown down over my knees and said that we would just talk about things.

"But I want to love you," he said. "I've been thinking all day of how I shall make love to you and make you happy." He went on caressing me, and in a halfhearted way I caressed him and wished that I could stop myself from being so afraid. But that night was a failure, too.

We were up and ready to leave for Dublin long before the alarm went off. I heard it ring when I was putting on my coat, but I was too downcast to go up and press in the button.

In the motorcar he hardly spoke. His profile looked gray and forbidding, and I thought, He has a hard, unforgiving face.

"I hope you enjoy London," I said.

"I hope so," he said, and asked if I had the two books he loaned me. He had loaned them to me the previous night, before we went up to bed. One was a novel, and the other was called *The Body and Mature Behavior*.

"I have them here," I said, kicking my bag to indicate where they were. I thought for one minute that he was going to ask me to give them back, but he didn't.

"Will you write to me from London?" I asked.

"Of course," he said, but coolly. I'll send you a card." And I thought with desolation of how different it would have been between us if I had not been afraid in bed.

I longed to do something dramatic, to scream or throw his new coat back at him, or jump out of the car while it was moving. A minute later, I longed to be in his arms, unafraid, pleasing him. More than anything I longed to please him. It seemed like weeks since he had put my hair behind my ear and whispered, "I am never going to let you go." In fact, it had only been nine or ten hours before that we had got into bed and he had kissed my frightened nipples and they had sprouted like seed potatoes—before I got the fit of shivering.

He drove me right up outside the shop. I asked him not to, in case Mrs. Burns should be looking out the bedroom window, but he ignored it, or else he did not hear me.

I got out quickly, said goodbye, and thanked him.

"Goodbye," he said. He was as offhand as if I were some stranger to whom he had given a lift. I ran to the shop door and unlocked it with the key, which I had ready in my hand. I went inside, without turning back to wave.

A moment later when I drew up the blind of the shop window, there was no sign of his car. I knew that he was gone. It was all over, Christmas, kissing, everything . . .

7

He had been gone five days now and there was no news of him. Baba said that he had probably arranged to meet his wife in London and that we would never see him again.

"You got a coat out of him," she said. "I got sweet damn all."

"It wasn't his wife," I said angrily. "I read the telegram myself, it was about his work."

"It's bound to be that bitch he married," Baba said. Baba maintained that all wives were bitches.

Anyhow, she said that we would soon know, because we were on our way to a fortune-teller in Donnybrook. At Donnybrook Church we got out of the bus, and as we had never been in that church before, we nipped in for three wishes. Two women who were filling lemonade bottles with Holy Water from a tub inside the door directed us to the fortune-teller's house.

It was a large brick house. In the cold tiled hallway, seven or eight girls waited. Three of them told us that they came regularly every week and each of the others had been to the fortune-teller at least once before.

"She's marvelous," they said. They also said that she was moody. The place reminded me of the convent—the walls tiled halfway, the group of girls with their various smells of sweat, and perfume, and soap; the absence of cigarette smoke. A homemade, inked sign said NO SMOKING. It didn't even say "please." I had only to close my eyes to smell again the convent cabbage and hear a nun admonishing Baba about the hole in her sock.

"Come into the place," Baba said to me, and together we went into the downstairs lavatory to have a smoke. A block of pearl-colored disinfectant was placed in a saucer on the ledge—it gave the place a hygienic smell.

"Jesus, this place gives me the creeps," Baba said, and we debated whether or not we should leave. But I wanted to know very badly about Eugene, so we stayed. When we came out and took our places on the stool, four more girls had arrived. To many of the girls it was a recreation; they came once a week, instead of going to the pictures or to a dance.

"Now, don't give her any clues, about any damn thing," Baba warned me, and just then a middle-aged woman came out of the fortune-teller's room, crying. We all stared at her. I supposed that she had heard something awful, such as that her husband was leaving her for another woman.

"We'll go in together," Baba whispered, and I said yes.

We had to wait an hour.

"Sit down," the fortune-teller said in a disinterested voice as we went into her room. We guessed that she must be in one of her bad moods, because the others had told us that if she didn't talk, it meant bad humor. She sat beside an electric fire, drinking tea and warming one hand around the cup. She was dressed completely in black and her pale face suggested that she never had any fresh air. The room was large and drafty, with a faded screen dividing it into two. Baba nudged me as much as to say, It's awful.

"Well," the fortune-teller said at last, picking up Baba's hand as if it were some loose object which was not joined to Baba's arm.

"Why are you wearing an engagement ring, you're not engaged."

It was her mother's engagement ring which Baba wore. She took it off and gave it to me to hold.

"There's trouble in store for you," the fortune-teller said, staring into the palm of Baba's neat hand. Poor Baba looked very frightened and sat with her shoulders tensed up.

"You'll marry a rich man," she went on, "that is, when you give up this married man."

Baba blushed. I knew that it must be Tod Mead.

"You have one brother, and your birthday is in June," she said as she dropped Baba's hand abruptly and asked us to change places. The routine was that she read hands first, then read the cards, and finally the crystal. A beautiful crystal of green glass rested on a side table.

"You'll make a journey," she said to me. She had a black scarf tied around her head so that you couldn't see her hair. Her voice was low, extraordinarily flat, and monotonous. She had no interest in the things she told me.

"It's an unpleasant journey," she noted, "and before the new year is out, you'll marry an eccentric man; you'll have to marry him, because you will be the mother of twins."

"Twins," Baba said, and fell into a fit of laughing and could not stop. So did I. It wasn't just my face that laughed, my whole body shook with it. She waited for us to stop, but it became worse, and finally she dropped my hand and asked us to leave the room.

Baba stood up, delighted, as she felt that she had heard enough about herself. I tried to apologize, but the fortune-teller would not listen.

"A refund," Baba said gaily as she retrieved the two ten-shilling notes which we had put on a plate when we came in.

"Put that money down, young lady," the fortune-teller shouted, so Baba dropped the money and we ran out of the room, laughing.

Just as we approached the hall, a man stuck his head out of a side door and said, "Excuse me, missy, how do you spell umbrelly?"

He talked through his nose, and of course this made us hysterical with laughter.

"I don't know," Baba said, talking through her nose. "Why don't you go up the river on a bicycle?"

He laughed too, he even laughed through his nose.

"Talk about the loony bin," Baba said as we ran down the avenue. Baba said that she might set mad dogs on us, so we ran the whole way to the road.

We took a bus to Grafton Street and then got out to look at the shop windows, because the sales were on.

Then we went to Davy Byrnes's cocktail bar and ordered a Pernod between us. We hadn't enough money to buy two drinks.

"Look *fast*," Baba said. We sat near the door and Baba said that some moron was bound to buy us a drink. She beamed at a man in a leather jacket who had an absurdly curling mustache.

"That drink has to last two hours, till closing time," she said as I took a swig of Pernod. It was like licorice cough-bottle mixture and it looked cloudy when she added water to it. She kept adding water all the time, to make it go far. The barboy asked if we were all right.

"We're broke," Baba said, and he went off and got us two glasses of beer.

"That's the best I can do," he said, placing the glasses on little blotting-paper mats that bore an advertisement for something.

"I won't forget you," Baba said. He was a young boy, just up from Tipperary, and we had spoken to him one night before.

"Right," he said in a falsely brave voice.

"I'll send you my garter in the post," Baba said, and he went off, blushing and grinning.

"Decent of him," I said to Baba. The beer tasted insipid after the Pernod.

"Decent! It's my charm that gets us these sorts of favors," Baba said, and then she turned to look at the man with the mustache. He stood by the counter, drinking alone. I suppose with that mustache no one could sit or stand opposite him without laughing.

"Excuse me, have you got the right time on you?" Baba leaned over and asked him.

Right time! There was a wall clock staring her in the face. It was twenty minutes past nine o'clock.

He moved away, agitated. A tremor began in his right cheek. I suppose he thought we might damage his good name, just by talking to him. I knew him well by sight, as he sold scooters in a shop in D'Olier Street. Suddenly I felt cheap and humiliated, and I wished that Eugene would come and take me to the cathedral of tall green trees behind his house.

"We'll ring the Body," Baba said. It was what she always said—ring someone, anyone—when we had nothing special to do. He drank in his local pub in Blanchardstown most nights from nine o'clock on. She got three pennies and went off to telephone.

A country-looking boy came over to me and said, "I was looking for Bovril."

"Were you?" I said, cutting him dead with my cheeky look. My hair was loose around my face and I tossed it out of one eye at regular intervals. He just stood there, looking at me, with his coat open and his jacket open, and a glaring yellow pullover inside it. Baba came back and he repeated to her that he had come in to get some Bovril.

"Have a whiskey," she said.

"I never broke my confirmation pledge," he said in a rough, humorless voice. He sat at our table.

"Where's the Body?" I asked Baba.

"He's gone to Mount Melleray to confession." Every January the Body went to the Cistercian Monastery at Mount Melleray to fast and pray. He always returned full of good resolutions, but after a week or two he was on the drink again.

The country boy told us that he was from Oranmore and that he had come to Dublin for treatment, because he had had an accident the summer before and was still lame from it.

"I'm going into the Rotunda tomorrow," he said, and Baba laughed, because the Rotunda is a maternity hospital. He rooted in his pocket for an envelope and we saw that it was addressed to the Richmond hospital. The envelope was black with fingermarks and you could see that it had been opened and restuck.

"Poor you," Baba said falsely. He bought us a whiskey each, and a pork pie, and coffee for himself.

" 'Twas an aul tractor," he said, "it rolled over me. I was nearly in pulp, only for me father—"

Baba flapped her hands behind his back and signaled to me to shut him up. He was talking loud and everyone could hear him.

At closing time we left and walked with him to his hotel. We promised to visit him in hospital, but we didn't think we would.

"We'll write t'him care of the Rotunda," Baba said as we ran up Amiens Street to catch the last bus.

At home, we heated soup.

"You're getting dull," Baba said.

"I know," I said. The night had been stupid, boring, paltry. Nothing interested me now, unless it had to do with Eugene; I thought of him and of his sudden outbursts of nervous energy, which made him dance around and conduct an imaginary orchestra or chop wood for an hour. It even gave me pleasure to think of his sheep dog, and of the old house with its dark wood always creaking and shutters rattling at night.

"It's Eugene?" Baba said.

"Yes," I said despairingly.

Then the soup began to boil and a nice smell pervaded the small kitchen. We had to open the window to let the smell out, otherwise Joanna might have come down, as the soup was part of next day's lunch.

"Did he try it on?" Baba said. The two drinks had made her outspoken.

"Sort of," I said. Shame stifled me as I remembered the soft bed, with the nice smell of clean linen and an owl crying in one of the pine trees.

"How far did he go?" Baba asked.

"Oh, don't ask me such a thing!"

I drank the soup and remembered back to the evening at dinner when the telegram asking him to go to London had been delivered. Anna, who is cursed with the curiosity of the lonely, had said, "No one dead?"

"No one dead," he had said, and gone on with his dinner. Anna had sulked. She had looked funny that night, because she'd taken her curling pins out for dinner (he would have remarked on them), and her long dark hair was neither straight nor curly but quiffed in places. I thought of every detail of my visit—even the kind of soap he used, and the color of his facecloth.

"You'll never hear from him again," Baba predicted, but she was mistaken.

Next morning I had a letter, and Baba had a card.

"How dare you read my correspondence," she said, snatching the card from me, "sly bitch."

I read my own letter upstairs.

Dear Sweetling,

How are you? We parted bad friends and don't think I didn't notice the resentment in your fat bottom as you hurried into your huckster shop.

Anyhow, I've been thinking of you and I forgive you everything. I'm working very hard on those glorious sewerages which I told you about; and I'm staying in a hotel, which is full of young American girls! Makes me nostalgic for the old days, but have no fears, none are as awkward or as pretty as you. You are a nice, kind, dear, sweet, round-faced pollop and now that I'm all mixed up in you and your mad hair, don't set fire to yourself until I come back to you.

If you have any days off, please go out and light fires in the bedrooms and open windows, as I'm sure A. won't.

Good night from your devoted

E.

It was written on hotel paper and I read it several times.

On the way to work I could see his face as clearly as if he were walking with me—his long, unyielding face with the well-defined bones and the fine skin that came away from the bone when you pinched it. I could see his body, too, his nakedness; the curious elegance with which he walked across the room. I remembered the funny hang of the pouch between his hairy thighs and how I had been afraid.

"It won't bite you," he said, and to the touch it grew miraculously like a flower between the clasp of my fingers.

I wondered if I would be afraid next time.

In the shop I wrote to him and posted it at lunchtime.

As I came in to lunch there was a smell of stew in the hall and a typed letter on the table for me. My heart leaped with pleasure, as I thought it was a second letter from him, but it had a Dublin postmark. It read:

Are you aware that this man is evil and has lived with numerous women and then walked out on them. If you cease to disregard this information I shall have to secure your parents' address and inform them.

A friend

I nearly fainted black out when I read it. I reread it, and noticed that two words had been crossed out before the word "evil." At first "treacherous" had been put down, then "bad," and finally "evil." It was a typed letter. I had no idea who could have sent it.

I could not eat any lunch. I knew that something was going to happen.

8 It happened at four o'clock, as I packed an order of groceries into a cardboard box.

It was New Year's Eve and we were busy with orders. Suddenly the shop door was pushed open with a bang, and two very small men helped my father into the shop. He had been drinking.

"Happy New Year," he said to me.

"Hello," I said. My breathing quickened and I began to shake all over. He introduced me to the two men and told them how clever I was, and that later on I would do an examination for the Civil Service.

"No future in this place, no future in it . . ." His eyes roamed around the dusty shelves and spotted the cartons of Hall's Wine along the top ledge of a glass case.

"They're empty," I said. They were empty. We just put the cartons on display and kept the bottles in a press under the counter.

"Give me a bottle," he said, his eyes red-rimmed and frantic. I got a half bottle from the press and said that we had no more in stock. He tore the paper seal and uncorked it and drank. He had a new hat. Always when he set out on a binge he bought a new brown hat. Our wardrobes were stacked with brown hats.

His friends were smaller than me—they were jockeys. They asked if they could weigh themselves, but my father was leaning against the porcelain scale and it did not register properly. Soon after, they left.

"Good friends of mine, they gave me a good tip for the Curragh Races," he said as they walked toward the door, and I knew that the minute they were out of sight he would turn on me.

"I wasn't expecting you," I said.

"I wasn't expecting this," he said, searching in his overcoat pocket. He took a letter out and said, "I want to talk to you, my lady; you living like a heathen . . ."

"What's that?" I said, snatching the letter. It was a typed letter and I read it feverishly.

Dear Mr. Brady,

It is high time you knew about your daughter and the company she keeps. For over two months now she's having to do with a married man, who is not living with his wife. He is well known in this city as a dangerous type. No one knows where he gets his money and he has no religion. He shipped his wife to America, and the house is a blind to get young girls out there and dope them. Your daughter goes there alone. I hope I am not too late in warning you, as I would not like to see a nice Catholic Irish girl ruined by a dirty foreigner.

A friend

I read it again through a mist of tears, not only because my father stood over me bursting with temper, but because someone thought of Eugene as being like that.

"Nice thing for your poor father to get in his old age." I had forgotten how tall my father stood, and how harsh his voice sounded.

"It's not true," I said. "None of it is true. I know this man"—I couldn't bring myself to say Eugene's name—"but Baba knows him, too, and my landlady, and everybody."

"Is he a divorced man?"

"He is, but . . ."

His thin face was very red. "Where is he? I'll hammer the life out of him."

"He's gone away," I said.

"He's having nothing more to do with you," my father said. "You'll never set eyes on him again."

That was too much to hear. "I'm my own boss, I'll do what I like."

"I'll have no impertinence!" he shouted.

Mrs. Burns rushed out to see what all the commotion was about. She told my father what a nice girl I was and suggested that I take him over to Joanna's for a cup of tea. She did not want him in the shop, because he was shouting and he looked wild.

Joanna did not want him either.

"Maybe throw sick on the best carpet and Gustav out," Joanna said to me in the kitchen, as we made a pot of tea. My father sat in the dining room, drinking the Hall's Wine and threatening what he would do to Eugene.

I took three pounds from his old overcoat, which was hanging on the hall stand. It had a smell of stale drink and cigarettes. There were pound notes in various pockets, so that I didn't think he'd miss the few pounds I took. He must have got the money for grazing, because although Jack Holland owned most of our land, my father had kept some fields at the far end of the boundary.

After he'd had the tea, Joanna asked me to take him away, as he was falling asleep on the chair.

I took him up the road, toward the phone booth, so as to ring for a taxi to go to the railway station.

"You're coming home with me, you know that?" he said.

I walked in front, to separate myself from him. "I can't leave my job," I said.

"Don't think you're fooling me," he said. "You're coming with me, and that's that." He pushed his new hat back on his head and scratched the top of his forehead where the hatband had made a red rim.

"Stop shouting on the road," I said. A lot of customers lived on that road and I did not want to be disgraced.

"You're coming home," he said.

I did not want to go home. Even at the best of times the house saddened me. After my mother was drowned, our place was mortgaged and Jack Holland bought it. My father moved to the gate lodge and Jack let our big house to an order of nuns. The nuns left after a year or so, because the house was too damp and too expensive. While it was idle, stories began to circulate about my mother's ghost being seen there. A bank official who was to have rented the house changed his mind when he heard about the ghost, so in desperation Jack Holland asked my father to go back for a few months, to dispel the foolish rumors about Mama. My father had been there for over a year now, and my Aunt Molly (my mother's sister) came to look after him when her own father died. She had but the wind and a few bantams to talk to, in her house in the Shannon island, so that she liked caring for my father and seeing the postman and an occasional visitor.

I rang the nearest taxi rank, and asked the driver to collect us outside the phone booth, then waited, stiffly, my face turned away.

"You haven't a lot to say to your father."

"Should I have?" I said bitterly.

I was planning something. I decided that just as he got into the taxi I would run away, on the excuse that I had left something important at Joanna's. But even as I planned it, I saw how fruitless it would be.

We waited. My toes felt cold, and I curled and uncurled them to try to keep warm.

"Here it is," I said, putting up my hand, and the taxi slowed down.

I opened the door and he got in awkwardly. He was too tall for getting in and out of motorcars.

"Oh, I forgot my bag of clothes, I'll have to run back for it," I said.

"What run? We'll drive back for it," he said, with suspicion.

"No, there's no need," I said; "anyhow, the taxi couldn't turn around in the cul-de-sac, I won't be a sec." And I closed the door on his shouting voice and ran back in the direction of Joanna's house. I knew that it would take the driver a few minutes to turn around on the main road, so I reckoned that if I got to Joanna's side road in time, I could knock at the first house and hide. I knew the woman there, as I often gave sweets to her two children.

I ran recklessly, bumped into a lame man, and didn't even wait to apologize. I was nearly at the corner of Joanna's road when I heard the car close behind me.

"Come back here," my father called. I ran faster, knowing that he was too drunk to catch up with me. But the car drove on a little, passed me by, and then he jumped out just as I turned to run the other way. He caught me by the belt of my coat.

"I tell you, you won't do this again."

"I'm not going home, I'm not going home," I screamed, hoping that some passing stranger might rescue me.

"Get in that car," he said. I held on to a railing.

"I'll tell the police," I said, and by now the taxi driver had come out of the car, and both of them hustled me toward the door, which was swinging open.

They pulled me across, and I was afraid that my new coat (Eugene's) would get torn. Children gathered across the road to look at us, and the taxi driver said I ought to have more sense and why would I not go with my father, who wanted to save me from the streets.

I sat as far away from my father as I could, and during the ride he abused me and told the taxi driver what an impossible girl I had been, and how I had driven my mother to an early grave.

"Good beating she wants," he said as I cried to myself.

At the station he bought two one-way tickets, and we passed through the ticket barrier and down the platform toward the train, which was due to leave in about twenty minutes.

"D'you want a cup of tea?" he asked as the train began to move. It was the first word we had spoken since we got in. I knew that he suggested it so that he could go to the bar; the bar and the restaurant adjoined each other on those trains.

"No, thanks," I said to spite him. I was wondering how I'd escape; whether I'd get off at the first stop or pull the emergency cord when he wasn't looking and jump off. In my mind I planned very brave things, but the moment he spoke to me I quavered.

"You go and have a cup of tea," I said, but he guessed my motives and told me to come with him. I followed him up the open corridor, between the rows of seats, in search of the bar.

He ordered a double whiskey for himself, and tea and a ham sandwich for me. The tea was served in a plastic carton which was so hot that I had to hold it with my handkerchief.

"Well, I declare to Christ if it isn't Jimmy Brady," a voice said behind my back.

"Tim," my father said, standing up to greet an old friend. They grabbed each other's coat collar and looked into each other's red, drinking face and swore about the coincidences of life.

I simply said, "Oh, God!"—knowing now that everything would be worse and that my father would drink twice as much. The man's name was Tim Healy and he had played hurley with my father at school.

They went across to the counter and Dada bought drinks for Tim Healy, and for two other friends who had been drinking with Tim before we arrived.

"That's my youngster, I'm bringing her home." Dada nodded toward me, and the three strange men clasped my hand, and one man squeezed it until the signet ring on my little finger dug a mark into the next finger. Tim Healy ordered orangeade for me, and came and sat with me.

"Move up there," he said, and I moved to a new part of the bench where it felt cold. He sat on the space I had nicely warmed.

"Well, Caithleen? Caithleen, isn't it? How are you? You're a fine girl, and so well you ought to be, you have a decent father and a lovely mother. How's your mother?"

"She's dead," I said. "She got drowned."

Sudden tragedy filled his bull-like face and he looked as if he was going to cry. He caught my elbow and said that he wouldn't have wished it for twenty thousand pounds.

"The best go first," he said, sniffling to control his tears.

"Yes." Stupid Christmas streamers were hanging from the windows and a tinseled PEACE ON EARTH TO MEN OF GOOD WILL was on the wall underneath a caption to drink more porter.

Tim Healy wanted to go over and sympathize with Dada, but I asked him not to. I knew that they would drink very much more if Dada was reminded at that moment of my mother's death.

"You know me," Tim Healy said, "I wouldn't hurt a fly."

Later on he told me that he inspected sausage factories and was on his way to Nenagh, to do a job there the next morning.

"If you saw a sausage made!" he said, opening his mouth wide and drawing his head back to indicate some unmentionable scandals in sausage factories. He bored me, but I put up with it because I saw in him a fresh chance to escape. I decided that when he and my father started reminiscing about hurling matches, and goals scored, I'd slip away, hide in a lavatory, and get off at the next stop.

My father spoke out bravely about the blackguard who had tried to ruin me. They shook their heads, saying that I was only a child and had no sense. Four glasses of orangeade were lined up for me.

"Givvus an aul song there," Tim said to my father.

"I can't," my father said, "I'm getting old—we'll all sing something," and they sang "Kevin Barry." Some were a few words ahead of others, but that did not matter. The young barboy looked uneasy, as if he should stop them, but Dada shook a friendly fist at him and asked him to sing up.

"The bloody English," Tim said when they had finished. A sigh of agreement went around the bar.

Without warning, my father started to sing, "I sigh for Jeannie with the nut-brown hair," and all the time he kept raising his chin and pulling his shirt collar away from his Adam's apple, as if it was choking him. His eyes filled with tears and I supposed that he thought of Mama, because he used to sing that song at Christmas when we had a card party and Mama gave two geese as a prize.

I looked out the window and saw the dark, formless fields slipping past me as we sped farther and farther from Dublin, toward the central plain of Ireland.

I could go now, I thought, so I stood up, ready to slip toward the exit.

"Where are you off to?" my father called.

"To the cloakroom," I said. I didn't like to say lavatory.

"Oh, a natural requirement, a natural requirement," Tim said, and then winking at my father, he said, "I'll show the lady," and he linked me up the corridor. My father must have told him to keep an eye on me.

"Don't worry," he said as we stumbled along over the jolting floor, "you'll meet a nice boy yet, one of your own kind."

I did not tell him this but I now knew that I would never marry one of my own kind.

Passing through the restaurant car, I saw with longing people eating rashers and eggs, tucking clean napkins under their chins, saying ordinary, pleasant things to one another. The calm of their lives made me furious with my own fate.

"We'll be 'bona-fide' if we walk much farther," Tim Healy said as we went through the eating car and past a row of first-class carriages where people lolled their heads against linen headrests and three priests played cards.

"I'll wait for you," he said. I did not manage to escape that time.

At Nenagh, Tim Healy and his two friends got out. There were big, maudlin farewells and large whiskies all round.

Then I was alone with my father again.

He was quite drunk now, swaying on the high stool. He took a box of squashed cigarettes from his pocket. "Here, have one, have one of mine," he said to the barboy, who linked him up the corridor, back to the enclosed carriage, where I had left my gloves and an evening paper. Some carriages were open, but ours was an enclosed one.

"I can walk on my own two feet," he kept saying.

"Of course you can," the barboy replied, but still linked him.

Dada sat in a corner seat and closed his eyes instantly.

Roscrea was the next stop, but I knew that it was not for thirty minutes or more, by which time he might have waked up. Still seated, I edged up near the window, above which was the emergency cord and the red sign saying FIVE POUND PENALTY FOR IMPROPER USE. I was going to pull it. As I prayed for courage I tried to think of the fun of it, of him being woken up suddenly by a guard and asked for five pounds. By then I would be gone, vanished into the dark fields. It looked very dark outside and I hoped that there would be a house somewhere near. Then I thought of savage dogs guarding a farmhouse gate, but I still decided to go.

I stood up quietly and took one last look to make sure he was asleep. A quenched cigarette was hanging slackly from his lower lip and he slept with his head tilted backward. I felt a little sorry for him —so weak and broken, and unlovely.

Don't be an ass, stop pitying him, that's what ruined your mother's life, I told myself as I raised my hand to the black emergency cord. I was shaking like a leaf.

"Pull it, pull it quickly," I whispered to myself.

Either my anxious whisper woke him, or else he had not been asleep at all, because suddenly he sat up and said, "Where are we, where are we?"

I took my hand down and collapsed onto the seat, almost pleased that I had been saved the ordeal of pulling the cord.

"I was just looking out to see where we were," I said, hating my-self for being so cowardly.

"You've traveled this long enough to know where you are."

He lit a cigarette, and by some manner of means stayed awake for the rest of the journey. A hackney car met us at our own, dimly lit station. I had sent my aunt a telegram earlier in the evening.

Our kitchen was as dismal as I had remembered it—old clothes of Dada's across a chair, a faded piece of palm stuck behind the picture of the Sacred Heart and before it a small red lamp burning. We put him to bed, and my aunt then lectured me, as I knew she would.

She made some tea and we ate the remains of a Christmas cake which was kept in a rusty biscuit tin. It was awful, but I ate it to please her. She rambled on and on about the good education I'd had, and the shock it was for my father to get such a letter.

Later she stole his shoes and hid them, so that he could not go out the next day and raise the wind for more drink. We said the Rosary aloud.

We could not go to bed, in case he might set fire to the blankets; so we sat there, and after a while she dozed on the card chair. It was a chair my mother got for cigarette coupons before the last war. I was four or five when the war began, and it meant nothing to me except that the cigarette people stopped putting coupons in the packages and we got no more of those folding chairs with the green canvas seats.

While she dozed, I planned what I would do—leave on the first bus the following morning, before my father woke up. I knew that it was disloyal to her, but I was determined to go back to Eugene, Eternal Damnation or not.

I counted my money, counted the hours, heard her snore slightly, and sometimes from my father's room I heard a moan or the gluggle of drink being poured. He had left the light on.

I was going away again, going away forever.

9

Toward morning my aunt sat up and rubbed her startled eyes with the back of her hand.

"What are you *doing?*" she asked. I had my coat on and I was applying makeup in front of the smoky glass of the Holy Picture. It was her makeup, as I had forgotten my own. I had found yellow powder in an old envelope and a worn puff beside her prayer book. There was lipstick, too, which looked as if it would give you disease, as it was dried up and smeared with hairs. My aunt must have found it somewhere, as she never used lipstick herself. I was applying it, when she spoke to me.

"I'm getting ready," I said as casually as possible.

"Ready for what?" she asked, running her hand through her gray hair, which was broken in many places from having been burned too often with a curling tongs.

"I'm going back," I said. "I have to go back to my job."

"You can't do that," she said, "run out and leave me," and she staggered up. "Don't go, don't leave me," she pleaded. "He'll kill me," she said. "To find you gone." There were tears in her tired eyes. A life of tears. She had had her own sorrows. Her young love had been shot one morning on the Bridge of Killaloe, during the time of the Black and Tans. She remained loyal to her murdered love and kept a picture of him in a gold locket on her neck. It was impossible to leave her; she was too nice and had made too many sacrifices.

"I'll stay," I said wearily. Her arms came around me and I felt her damp eyes on my neck.

It was New Year's Day and we should have gone to Mass, but she said that God would forgive us, as we had to stay and look after my father.

Then we heard cows lowing as they went toward the yard gate, and Maura pounded on the back door. She was a local girl who came to milk morning and evening.

"Mam, are you up?" she called as she lifted the latch and stuck her head in. She grinned from behind new steel-rimmed spectacles.

"Welcome home," she yelled to me. She always yelled, no matter how near to her you were; she spoke as if against the force of a terrible wind.

"There's a calf hanging out of the cow dead," she said to my aunt.

"Who's dead?" my aunt said, raising her eyes to the ceiling. Maura's simplemindedness appalled her.

"The calf is hanging out of the cow dead," Maura repeated, thrilled at having something important to relate. Then she said that she'd go for the vet, and before we could stop her she ran off. I wanted to go because Mr. Brennan, the vet, was Baba's father and I knew that he would help me or that his wife, Martha, would. I thought of their pretty house, with white rugs on the maple floor and a picture of Baba and me on the gray wall. I called Maura back, but she did not heed me. She ran pounding across the front field, sometimes taking great leaps off the ground and letting forth a yell of satisfaction.

We went out to see what was wrong.

In daylight the place looked more desolate. The privet hedge had yellowed from some disease and the wild-rose shrubs were trampled. Cows came in and out over the sagging paling wire.

"There's black frost," my aunt said. Two tea towels spread out to dry had frozen stiff. Walking past the empty rusted water tank, my aunt said, "Do you remember long ago?"

Hickey, our workman, used to stand there on summer evenings, admonishing the cows to drink up. The cows—which belonged to Jack Holland mostly—now drank from cement troughs, farther down.

As Maura had told us, a calf's head hung from the cow. The poor cow was moaning and lashing her tail, but there was nothing we could do for her until Mr. Brennan came. My aunt ran back to get hot oatmeal, and while she was away, the bus for Limerick passed at the front gate. I cried two solitary tears, knowing that I was doomed to stay among the dead thistles.

The cow would not take the oatmeal, and she kept trying to turn her head around, to see the dead calf.

When Mr. Brennan came, he got Maura and my aunt to drive her slowly to the yard, and he followed on in his motorcar, taking care to avoid the tree stumps and hillocks of grass on the way.

Walking back alone, I sighed at the sadness of the damp, dilapidated house, and wondered if there was, as my aunt had said, a curse which had been put upon it. Jackdaws flew in and out of the various chimneys. Dada was in the kitchen, searching for his shoes. Nervously I got them from the coal scuttle and dusted the slack off them with a new goose wing.

"They must have fallen in," I said.

"Fallen in!" He took his hat off the dresser and did not wait to hear about the sick cow. He wanted to get out for a drink.

I laid the table for breakfast. The teaspoons were tarnished and they smelled funny. In Mama's day there were boards in the cutlery drawer marking a division for knives, forks, spoons. Now everything was jumbled in there, cutlery, the old scissors, hairy twine, a tin opener, butter papers that had gone rancid, and cow horns. They kept cow horns for pouring paraffin oil or machine oil and dosing cattle.

"And how are you, hadn't time to shake hands with you," Mr. Brennan said as he came down later on to wash his hands. I poured water from the kettle into a tin basin and got a clean towel.

"Thanks," he said, looking at me sharply. He came to the point quickly; I tried to talk about Baba, but he interrupted me, "I saw that letter your father got."

"It's funny how people want to believe the worst," I said, without knowing how I said it.

"I'm very, *very* disappointed in you," he said. "I thought I could rely on you."

I felt that I had lost him as a friend, but I thought that his wife, Martha, would help me, as she professed to understand about men and love. I was glad therefore when he suggested that I go home with him, to collect penicillin for the sick cow.

Martha was arranging a bowl of roses when we got into their centrally heated hallway.

"Here she is," Mr. Brennan said, showing distaste, and left us together.

"My goodness, Caithleen, you've grown half a foot." She shook hands with me. Tim Hayes, the hackney-car owner, must have said that I came home, because she was not surprised to see me.

"Nice flowers," I said, feeling uncomfortable. Mr. Brennan had given me another lecture in the car.

"Yes, smell them." They were plastic roses which had been sprayed with some sort of perfume.

"Aren't they pretty?" she said. They were sickening.

"Baba all right?" she asked casually.

"She's fine."

In the kitchen, she made me a cup of tea. They had papered the walls with new striped paper, so I admired it. We had a cigarette.

"Tell me all the news," she said. I sat at the end of the table and told her about Eugene. I just said that we met a couple of evenings a week and had dinner, and that he was very nice and very good-looking.

"You'd like him," I said to soften her. Her expression did not change, but she blinked a lot.

"Will you help me to get away from here," I said desperately.

"Help you!" she exclaimed, and blew cigarette smoke deftly from her delicate nostrils. She laughed nervously, almost as if she were enjoying it. "But you must be mad, to think of a man like that. It's out of the question!"

"Oh, please, please, you must listen to me," I pleaded.

She said unflinchingly, "Baba's father and I agree that you should not see this man again." This was the Martha who once drank gin-and-it with commercial travelers!

I laid my head on the plastic-topped table and began to cry loudly, as I had cried when I was small and was not allowed to wear one of Mama's georgette dresses for fun.

"Sssh, ssh, the boss is coming in now, don't let him catch you crying," she said, taking out a silk handkerchief which she had tucked in the gold bracelet of her tiny wristwatch.

"I'll pray for you, honestly. If you ask God, He'll help you to bear it." She seemed to have got very religious.

Mr. Brennan had tea with us, and Martha talked of her visit to Oberammergau the previous summer.

"It would do you good to see those people," she said. "All the men leave their hair uncut for months beforehand, not knowing which one will be destined to play the part of Christ." She bowed her head as she said "Christ."

One small part of me listened for safety's sake, but the rest of my mind puzzled over how I might get away.

Mr. Brennan said something. I didn't hear it. I just saw him frown at me.

"She's upset," Martha explained.

"She'll be all right; she'll get over it in a month or two," one or the other of them said.

I was about to scream, but then I saw the expression in their eyes and I laughed instead, to confuse them.

Walking home with the penicillin, I remembered the look in their eyes—bitter, determined. Martha had said that I should stay home and I could go to the technical school with her and learn crocheting and tapestry.

I walked very quickly. Above me the clouds raced across a rainy sky and lakelike patches of blue showed between them.

Stay at home! Who was going to be the first to say that I should enter a convent? Why did everybody hate a man they'd never met? All those unhappily married people wanted to be sure that I came home and had it happen to me?

Mad Maura hid behind our wall, watching for me, and I knew with a sinking feeling that my aunt had put her there and had probably paid her sixpence to do it.

Nothing much else happened that day, except that my aunt called me aside and asked in a whisper if there was anything wrong with me. She seemed doubtful when I said no.

"But there isn't," I insisted, outraged by the indelicacy of her question. I thought of how I had failed him in the big, soft bed and I almost laughed at the irony of it.

In the late afternoon I cycled to the village for groceries. My father forgot about housekeeping money when he drank, so I had to spend some of the three pounds which I had stolen out of his pocket in Joanna's hall stand.

The sun had come out after a shower; the wet road gleamed and the hedges sparkled as if diamonds had been thrown on them.

I bought rashers, tea, chicken-and-ham paste, peaches, and then on an impulse I bought a stale iced cake that was going cheap, in the hope that it would cheer us up.

In the village I was sure people stopped to look, wanting to kill me with savage stare-you-out eyes. And schoolchildren began yelling something. Had my father been going round showing the letter to everyone?

"Divorce is worse than murder," my aunt had always said—I would never forget it; that and their staring disapproval.

I rang Mr. Gentleman's number to ask for a seat to Dublin, but his wife answered the telephone.

"Who's speaking, please?" she asked, and I dropped the phone in terror and rushed out of the booth. The postmistress, who had been listening in at the switchboard, rebuked me for doing such a thing. I never liked her. Once when I was young she asked me if Martha and Mr. Brennan slept in twin beds or not. I had not told her. She never forgave me.

I bought two letter cards so that I could write to Baba and Eugene, and then I hurried up the street to intercede for help from Jack Holland. His pub was closed, the shutters up. In the fading light I read an inked sign under the knocker which said: GONE ON ARCHAE-OLOGICAL EXPLORATION. BACK AT EIGHT.

I couldn't stay, because my aunt was waiting for the tea, so I went on home. Cycling in the dusk, with the bag of messages knocking against my knee, I thought of Eugene. Sometimes a clear and sudden image of him came to disturb me. I saw the skin of his chest, a little reddened underneath the hairs where he had scratched it. I cycled near the ditch to avoid a herd of cows straggling home to be milked.

Then a car came toward me. Its Old World shape told me that it might be Mr. Gentleman, so I got off the bicycle, threw it in the ditch, and hailed the car. It drove by, but had to slow down anyhow because of the cows. I ran after it, breathless. It was Mr. Gentleman.

"I was looking for you," I said when he wound the window down.

"Caithleen!" he said, astonished. I hadn't seen him for two years. He looked thinner, more haggard, but his face still had that strange holy-picture quality that made me think of moonlight and the chaste way he used to kiss me.

"Yes, I'm home," I said. I rested my elbows on the car window, and my face was almost on a level with his.

"And how is the world using you?" he asked casually. You'd think that we had met only the day before. I put it down to shyness, because he was always shy and slow to start a conversation.

"Not too bad," I said. I didn't want to tell him the whole story there and then, in case it might hurt his feelings. But did he know it already? Everyone seemed to. Anyhow, I knew that he'd ask me to sit in, and maybe take me for a drive.

"I didn't see you in ages," I said, recalling with shame all the letters I had written to him at his office in Dublin.

"I've been very busy, a hundred and one things, you know how it is." His voice was the same as ever, a bit foreign (he was half French) and very gentle.

"Yes. I often wondered what happened?" I said. He had persuaded me to go with him to Vienna for a few days, and on the evening that we were to go, he just did not come to collect me.

He looked at me sadly, his face made more plaintive by dusk, and he said, "It was all for the best really, we would have regretted it."

"I wouldn't have," I said truthfully.

He frowned, and I knew that he was indeed bitterly ashamed of the times we had been together, in each other's arms, kissing, and saying "I love you."

"You're young," he said. "Young people do a lot of foolish things."

"It wasn't foolish. That was the nicest time in my whole life . . ."

He sat up suddenly and took a quick breath. "You're a very— foolish—little—girl, do you know that?"

"You're ashamed of me?"

"No, no, no," he said with the same impatience as of old. I heard that "no, no, no" when I asked him to write in my autograph book, and when I wanted to keep his red setter dog for one night, so as to feel close to him.

"Home for long?"

"Not very long, I'm getting engaged," I said, wanting to hurt him then.

"Does your father know?"

I heard my voice going hysterical. "We're going to have a big wedding, caterers from Limerick coming out. . . ."

"That's great news," he said, and smiled as he looked at his wrist-watch and talked about having to go.

"Let me know what present you'd like," he said, and his small white hand groped on the dashboard for the car key. He turned the engine on.

" 'Bye," he said, with a touch of the old wounded solitude in his expression. He always gave the impression that he did not want to leave you, but that fate, or duty, or family forced him away. I don't think I said anything as he drove off.

I knew that he went to the parish priest's house on Wednesdays to play bridge. It was a custom which had arisen in the last year since Mr. Gentleman got religious again and carried a big missal to Mass, so local gossip said.

Picking up the bicycle, I walked on toward home, indifferent as to whether my aunt waited for tea or not. Night had fallen and I was guided by a full moon. I was trembling with anger and could not cycle. I thought of Mr. Gentleman with his pale face, his beautiful, loveless eyes, and I thought of how I used to think he was God. I wished I had some way of hurting him, because of his falseness.

The moon made the fields and ditches startlingly bright. Some cows lay under trees, chewing the cud, and one was wheezing. The moon threw my shadow ahead of me, and sometimes I was able to overtake it with the front wheel of my bicycle.

"What kept you?" my aunt called as she came toward me, cough-ing. She suffered from bronchitis.

"Nothing," I said. I felt sick and angry with her, and with everyone.

"We hadn't a bit of tea, I thought you wouldn't be so long," she said as I wheeled the bicycle around the house and threw it against the side wall. She said that Dada had not come in yet.

We made tea, and opened a tin of peaches, but we ate without enjoyment.

10 Three gloomy days went by. Nothing happened except that my father went out in the mornings and came home late. We suspected that he had raised some money from his uncle or brother.

On the third afternoon we buried the calf, because my aunt said that it was beginning to smell. Maura, who could do a man's work, had dug a grave earlier on, and we wheeled the calf down in an old rotted barrow. We went because my aunt said that she could not rely on Maura to do it properly. The calf was in an old sack, so that you could not discern its shape or anything about it. It was a bitterly cold day.

I thought of Eugene and wondered what he'd make of this bleak sight—us standing there watching Maura tip the barrow sideways until the sack toppled in, then reshoveling the earth over it and pressing it down with the heel of her man's boot. She wore boots and trousers, and all the people in the village called her Micky. She worked for us because she didn't cost much and was useful with milking and doing odd jobs. On the way back the barrow got bogged down in the mud and I had to lift it with Maura to get it free.

"Th'aul cow is lonesome," she said. We had put the cow in a house while the calf was being buried, otherwise she would have followed the scent. In the house she was mooing and running around kicking loose stones over the floor. The outhouses were falling down and ivy covered their tumbling walls.

"We're all lonesome," my aunt said, and Maura grinned and said that she wasn't because there were pictures that night. Traveling pictures came to the village once a week.

I had been thinking of some way of escaping, but the thought of their chasing me made me frightened.

"This vale of tears," my aunt said desolately. Burying the calf had saddened her. Death was always on her mind. Death was so important in that place. Little crosses painted white were stuck up on roadside ditches here and there to mark where someone had been killed for Ireland, and not a day seemed to pass but some old person died of flu, or old age, or a stroke. Somehow we only heard of the deaths; we rarely heard when a child was born, unless it was twins, or a blue baby, or the vet had delivered it.

"Th' evenings will be getting long soon," I said to my aunt to cheer her up, but she just sighed.

We ate dinner in the kitchen. We had salty rashers, a colander of green cabbage, and some potatoes reheated from the previous day. While we were eating in silence, a car drove up and around by the side of the house. My aunt blessed herself as she saw a stranger help my father out.

"Grand evening," my father said as he came in and handed her a brown paper parcel of meat soggy with blood. The stranger had had some drinks also but did not stagger.

"You're settling down!" he said to me. I tried to ignore him by concentrating on peeling a cold potato.

"I met Father Hagerty over in the village, he wants to have a chat with you," he said.

My heart began to race, but I did not say anything.

"You're to go and see him."

I put butter on the potato and ate it slowly.

"D'you hear me?" he said with a sudden shout.

"There, there, she'll go," my aunt said, and she linked him into the back room. The stranger hung around for a few minutes until she came out, and then asked for a pound. We had no money, but we gave him three bottles of porter which had been hidden in a press since Christmastime.

My aunt put them in a paper bag and he went off, swearing. We had no idea where he came from.

We sat by the cooker and listened for my father's call. At about nine o'clock he cried out and I ran in to him.

"I think I'm going to die," he said, as his stomach was very sick. The news cheered me up no end—I might get away—so I gave him a dose of health salts.

We went to bed early that night. I slept in the room opposite my aunt's, and when I had closed the door I sat down on the bed and wrote a long letter to Baba, for help. I wrote six or seven pages, while the candle lasted. I had already written a postcard, but had no answer.

It occurred to me that maybe they had told the postmistress to keep my letters.

A wind blew down the chimney, causing the candle flame to blow this way and that. There was electricity in the house, but we were short of bulbs. I hid the letter under the mattress and undressed. The sight of my purple brassiere made me recall with longing the Sunday morning Baba and I had dyed all our underwear purple. Baba read somewhere that it was a sexy color, and on the way home from Mass we bought five packets of dye. Sneaky old Gustav must have been peeping through the keyhole of the bathroom, because suddenly Joanna had rushed upstairs and pushed the door in.

"Poison color in the basin," she shouted as she burst in.

"You might have knocked, we could have been doing something very private," Baba said.

"Poison water," Joanna said, pointing to the weird-colored water in the basin. Our underwear turned out very nice, and some boy asked Baba if she was a cardinal's niece.

I kept a jumper on in bed. We were short of blankets. I had only an ironing blanket over me and a quilt that my aunt had made. The candle had burned right down to the saucer as I lay on my side and closed my eyes to think of Eugene. I remembered the night he asked me to do some multiplication for him. He knew all about politics, and music, and books, and the insides of cameras, but he was slow to add. I totted up the amount of money he should get for one hundred and thirty-seven trees, at the rate of thirty-seven and six per tree. He had sold some trees to a local timber merchant, because the woods needed thinning. There were blue paint marks on the "sold" trees, but he said that at night the timber merchant had sent a boy along to put paint marks on extra trees.

"Nearly three hundred and fifty pounds," I said, reckoning it roughly first, the way we were taught to at school, so that we should know it if our final answer was wildly wrong.

"And out of that he'll make a small fortune," Eugene said, detailing what would happen to the tree from the time it was felled until it became a press or a rafter. I could see planks of fine white wood with beautiful knots of deeper color, and golden heaps of sawdust on a floor, while he fumed about the profit which one man made.

I went to sleep wondering if I would ever see him again.

In the morning my aunt brought me tea and said that the priest had sent over word that he was expecting me. I dressed and left the house around eleven. My father had stayed in bed that morning and Mad Maura ran to the village for a half-bottle of whiskey, on tick.

Always when I escaped from the house I felt a rush of vitality and hope, as if there was still a chance that I might escape and live my life the way I wanted to.

It was a bright windy morning, the fields vividly green, the sky a delicate green-blue, and the hills behind the fields smoke-gray.

It's nice, nice, I thought as I breathed deeply and walked with my aunt's bicycle down the field toward the road.

I did not go to the priest's house. I was too afraid, and anyhow, I thought that no one would ever find out.

I went for a spin down by the river road with the intention of posting Baba's letter in the next village.

The fields along the road were struck into winter silence, a few were plowed and the plowed earth looked very, very dead and brown.

If only I could fly, I thought as I watched the birds flying and then perching for a second on thorn bushes and ivied piers.

I cycled slowly, not being in any great hurry. It was very quiet except for the humming of electric wires. Thick black posts carrying electric wires marched across the fields and the wires hummed a constant note of windy music.

At the bottom of Goolin Hill I got off the bicycle and pushed it slowly up; then halfway I stood to look at the ruined pink mansion on the hill. It had been a legend in my life, the pink mansion with the rhododendron trees all around it and a gray gazebo set a little away from the house. A rusted gate stood chained between two limestone piers, and the avenue had disappeared altogether. I thought of Mama. She had often told me of the big ball she went to in that mansion when she was a young girl. It had been the highlight of her whole life, coming across at night, in a rowboat, from her home in the Shannon island, changing her shoes in the avenue, hiding her old ones and her raincoat under a tree. The rhododendrons had been in bloom, dark-red rhododendrons; she remembered their color, and the names of all the boys she danced with. They had supper in a long dining room, and there were dishes of carved beef on the sideboard. Someone made up a song about Mama that night and it was engraved on her memory ever after:

Lily Neary, swanlike
She nearly broke her bones
Trying to dance the reel-set
With the joker Johnny Jones.

"Who was Johnny Jones?" I used to ask.

"A boy," she would say dolefully.

Standing in the middle of the road, thinking of all this, I almost got run over by the mail van. He had to swerve toward the ditch.

"I'm sorry," I said, shaking all over with fright. He laughed at me. He was a good-humored boy and asked if I wanted a lift. A notice gummed to the windshield said NO PASSENGERS, but two women sat in the back of the car on bags of mail. I thought ridiculously of what would happen if the mail bags contained turkey eggs from the turkey station or a gilt clock on its way as a wedding gift to someone. I asked him to post a letter for me in Limerick that evening. He drove out from Limerick every morning to deliver mail in the various villages along the way and then went back in the evening, collecting more letters.

"Right you be," he said, and I gave him the letter for Baba and two shillings for himself.

Then I got on my bicycle and cycled toward home. It was a downhill ride most of the way, so I did not have to use the pedals much. They were stiff and needed oiling. The tires hissed, the spokes hummed, and the road was a winding, tarred ribbon of blue. I was planning what I would tell my aunt, and I did not feel a bit guilty as I cycled up our own field and came home.

I nearly fell when I saw the parish priest sitting in our kitchen drinking tea from one of the good cups.

"Here she is now," my aunt said. The priest looked at me.

"Well, Caithleen! I imagined that something had detained you, so I dropped over to see how you were."

"You were gone when I called," I said hastily.

He stared at me very hard.

"If you'll excuse me, Father," my aunt said, and disappeared, so that he could talk to me alone.

Father Hagerty began at once. "Caithleen, I've heard some bad news from your father. Sit down and tell me about it."

I sat opposite him. My aunt had put a cushion between his back and the wooden rungs of the chair, and he looked as if he was settling in for a long talk.

"It's nothing very much; I met a man, that's all," I said, trying to be casual. He frowned. The frown produced four deep lines on his grayish forehead, and for no particular reason I remembered back to the time when he was collecting funds to build a new chapel and held dances in the town hall on Sundays. He served behind the mineral bar himself, and people said that he drained the dregs of bottles to make new bottles of lemonade. Hickey once handed in a pound for one ticket and got no change and, after that, always brought the exact money, which was two shillings.

"You are walking the path of moral damnation."

"Why, Father?" I said quietly, folding my hands on my lap to try to look composed. I longed to cross my legs but still held to the belief that it was disrespectful.

"This man is dangerous company. He has no faith, no moral standards. He married a woman and then divorced her—whom God hath joined together, let no man put asunder," he said.

"He seems to be a good man. He doesn't drink, or anything," I said.

"Ah, you poor child," Father Hagerty said with a frank and winning smile, which I remembered from my schooldays. He always smiled at children and gave them sweets. On the day of my confirmation he consoled me with a shilling when my white veil got torn on a spear of the chapel gate.

"More tea, Father?" I said.

"No more," he said, putting his pale hand over the top of the china cup. It was very strong tea, to which creamy milk had been added.

"Think of your eternal soul," he said, as if he were giving a sermon from the altar, "think of the harm you might do to it. We are all under sentence of death, we never know the hour or the minute . . ."

That worried me, and I held my head down and could think of nothing to say in reply. You could see yourself in the shine on his black boots.

"God is testing your love; God has allowed this man to cross your path and tempt you, so that you will reaffirm your love for Him. You have only to ask, and *He* will give you the grace to resist this great temptation."

"If God is good, He won't burn me," I said to Father Hagerty, quoting Eugene's exact phrase.

The priest sat upright and shook his head sadly from side to side. "Child, don't you realize that you are speaking heresy! You know that you cannot enter into the Kingdom of Heaven unless you obey the word of God. You're turning your back on God," he said, raising his voice. I looked into his eyes and wondered what lay behind them—pity, or just a sense of duty. He put his hand to his mouth and coughed politely. He expected me to say something, but I had nothing to say.

The side door opened and my father came in, in his shirt and long combinations. He got a shock when he saw the priest.

"Excuse me, Father, I didn't know you were here," he said, withdrawing into the hall.

"That's all right, Mr. Brady."

My father got his overcoat then, and came into the kitchen with his shoelaces slapping around and his eyes large and bloodshot. He proceeded to make himself a cup of tea. He said that he hoped Father Hagerty was giving me a real straightening out, and that I was a very stubborn girl and would listen to no one. Stubborn, that's what I'd be. They could talk and rant and talk, but I wouldn't answer; I'd just sit there, fiddling with the cuff of my cardigan, a faint smile on my face —though my father might hit me for being insolent. And that was what I did.

"She won't listen to sense," Dada said.

"She'll listen to God Almighty," Father Hagerty said.

"She hadn't even rosary beads when she came home," Dada said.

"Oh well, wait a minute," Father Hagerty said, searching in the pocket of his shabby black coat. "I brought her a little book."

It was a beautiful leather-bound volume with gilt edging—*The Imitation of Christ*.

"Thanks, Father." I took it and saw one tear of mine drop onto the brown leather cover.

"Oh, that's too good altogether, Father Hagerty," Dada said, and told me to thank the priest properly. I thanked him a second time, and he said that I should read a little of it every day and learn to model myself in the image of Christ.

Then he came to the point that I dreaded. He asked me to promise never to see the divorced man again, never to write to him, never to let my thoughts dwell on the occasions I had been with him.

"Promise me that?" he asked.

"Do what you're told," Dada said. But I couldn't.

The priest asked me again, and Dada shouted, and I just held my head down and kept silent. Dada shouted louder then, and the priest said, "Now, now, Mr. Brady," and told Dada to take his cup of tea back to bed and not to get excited.

"It's as big a sin for my father to be like that as for a man to have two wives," I said to the priest when we were alone.

"I'm surprised at you," he said, "to speak of your good father like that. Every man takes a drink. It's the climate." His eyebrows were very bushy when he frowned.

He asked again, "Will you promise me not to see that man?"

"I'll think about it," I said. It was the only way of getting rid of him.

"We'll make an Act of Perfect Contrition, the two of us, together." And he began, "O my God," and waited while I repeated the three words. Then he said, "I am heartily sorry," and paused for me, and so on, until we had finished. I felt an awful hypocrite, saying words that I did not mean.

He looked at his watch and said it was lunchtime, and when he stood up to go, I called my aunt from upstairs so that she could thank him.

"I'll see you over in the church anyhow," he said to me. "There's Women's Confraternity this Sunday, and confessions on Saturday night."

"All right, Father," I said, making no promises.

"She'll be all right now, she'll be going to dances in no time," he said, when my aunt came down. She saw him to the gate, and stayed there until his black figure was out of sight.

"Wasn't it terrible that we hadn't an offering to give him for a Mass," she said, when she came back.

We had no money. I thought it funny that two grown people living in that large house hadn't a two-shilling piece between them. A tinker wouldn't believe it if he knocked on the door.

"Well, thank God he came," my aunt said.

She seemed to think that everything was all right now, and that I was out of danger. The funny thing was that I was more determined than ever to get away.

11 Finally, my father asked us to fetch the doctor, because he felt faint, not having been able to eat for several days. The doctor gave him an injection and told us to ration the amount of alcohol he had. We sat with him in turns and gave him soda water with a small amount of whiskey in it—a smaller amount each time. I had not heard from Eugene or Baba and I was sick with worry.

"I'm sorry," my father kept saying as I sat on the bed and held the glass to his lips. His hands shook so that he could not hold a glass or a razor. He cried like a child. Always after drinking, he cried for days and was ashamed to talk to anyone. His depression was frightening.

" 'Tis nice to have you home," he said. "Why don't you get yourself a cigarette? Sure all young people smoke nowadays, I know that, I'm a fairly understanding man . . ." And I thought of Eugene's desk with packages of cigarettes strewn about, and *Cancer is painful* written in his clear, square handwriting on some of the packages.

"Go on, can't you," my father said, and I smoked a cigarette to oblige him. I wondered when he would let me back.

"I'm for your good, of course," he said. "It nearly killed me the day I got that letter, to think of you mixed up with a hooligan like that." The word "hooligan" incensed me, but I held my temper.

"I'm in the world longer than you and I know right from wrong." He spoke apologetically and wiped his crying eyes in the sheet and blew his nose.

"I'll be better when I go back. I'll be careful," I said.

"What back?" he said, rising up in the bed. "You're not going back. You'll get a little job here and help Aunt Molly and myself. I was thinking," he said—and winked knowingly at me, as if he were going to say something of the greatest secrecy and importance—"I was thinking that we might open a little business down the road, redo the gate lodge and start something going. We might pull ourselves together and buy this place back." He was quite serious.

"I'll just go back and get my clothes from Joanna's house," I said, trying not to sound too eager. I'd have said anything to get away.

His grip on my wrist tightened, and he said, "We'll go to Limerick someday, the two of us, and get you some new clothes."

"That would be waste," I said.

He asked for another drink, and as there was very little soda water in the siphon, my aunt suggested that I go over to Jack Holland's and get some, before closing time. She was in the kitchen making a soda cake in a big tin basin, the cellophane packet of brown caraway seeds on the table beside her. We all liked caraway seeds in the bread, except Maura, who picked them out, thinking that they were insects or something.

I collected the empty siphons and set off for Jack Holland's public house.

"Ah, my little auburn poem, 'Sweet Auburn! loveliest village of the plain,'" Jack recited as I went into the shop. He rushed outside the counter to kiss me, and the tip of his nose was cold and wet.

"Things cooled down at home, temperature normal?" he asked.

"Yes," I said, "we're just clearing up. We'll have a cartload of empties for you."

"And I'll have a big bill for you," he said, grinning, as he tapped my chin with his finger. "You know what your dad said when I refused him credit?"

"No." I knew it well.

"He said," Jack began. "'Isn't it as good to have it in the bloody book as in the bloody barrel.' Not funny. Not funny at all. But let me show you an example of something humorous." Jack pointed to a white cardboard sign on which he had inked a message—NO CREDIT TODAY BUT ALL FREE DRINKS HERE TOMORROW.

I gave a little laugh to make him happy.

It was Monday night and business was very slack. A tinker woman sat with her back to us, cursing into an empty porter glass. Her plaid shawl was faded. He filled her another pint and had to let it stand for a minute until the froth settled and he could add more from the barrel. It took ages. When he had placed it on the counter and taken her money, he said to me, "Yours truly is in danger of becoming imminent."

"Congratulations," I said. "What is it?"

Imminent; he'd have to do something about the shop then—a

thick dust had settled on the wine bottles, there was flypaper hanging since the previous year, and great cobwebs in the corners of the shelves. Imminent; he'd have to wipe his nose and wear different shirts. He wore a gray flannel shirt, a tweed waistcoat, and black boots.

"As a result of recent private archaeological exploration made by yours truly in the Protestant graveyard, some important objects have come to light," he whispered, so that the tinker would not hear him. Opening a drawer he pointed to several rusted things which lay on a heap of sugar—two brooches, a pewter mug, a sword, a chamber pot, and coils of raveled wire. The tinker got off the form and came across to have a look. He closed the drawer at once, and she muttered some insult to the dying turf fire.

"Jack, will you do me a favor?" I asked.

"Ah," he said, "you want to marry me now that I am likely to be imminent."

His long gray face beamed at me, and I realized as I looked into his water-gray eyes that he was the only human person in that whole neighborhood.

"Jack, will you help me?" I begged.

"A very ominous word. How about a little kiss to cheer a bachelor's dry lips?" he said, and he led me into the snug so that he could kiss me. The snug was a small compartment cut off from the shop, with frosted glass around it so that you could not see in. I kissed him quickly, to get it over with. I did not mind kissing him really, because he was sixty or seventy and I was just twenty-one and had known him all my life. He loved Mama, and later he loved me and wrote poems to us. We never saw the poems. He just hinted about them and then hid them between the yellow, fly-marked pages of Bryan Merryman's *Midnight Court*. It was one of two books which Jack kept over the kitchen fireplace, along with rock salt and horn rosary beads. The other book was *Moore's Almanac*, which gave a list of pig and cattle fairs and so enabled him to have plenty of drink in stock, and porter barrels tapped for the fair days.

At night when the men left his kitchen and walked through the dark village to their little houses, Jack sat down to read Merryman aloud. Some local boys once listened outside the window and heard him repeat lines like—"The doggedest divil that tramps the hill, With the gray in his hair and a virgin still."

Jack had found his love in that bawdy book and in my bright reddish hair and in Mama's small, shy words of gratitude whenever he pressed a bottle of sherry on her or coyly dropped apple pips inside the neck of her blouse on Sunday evenings.

"I want to go away and they won't let me," I said.

"Ah the little wanderer, faraway places with strange-sounding names are calling, calling thee," he sang as he kicked an empty cigarette carton with the toe of his dirty boot. He went away and filled me a glass of cordial, never supposing that my taste might have changed with the years. The cordial was sickly sweet.

"I love someone and they're going to lock me up and not let me see him," I said, exaggerating a bit to melt his heart. It did not offend him to hear me say that I loved someone else, because for him time stood still about fifteen years ago, and I was a child passing the shop window on my way to school, tapping to say hello, leaving a bunch of bluebells on the sill.

"I've heard the whole story, all the town is talking of it," he said.

He recited at random from "Lord Ullin's Daughter": " 'And I will give thee a silver pound to row us o'er the ferry, come back, come back, he cried in grief, 'midst waters fast relenting, the waters wild went o'er his child and he was left repenting.' "

"The walls have ears," he said, guiding me into the hall and taking a candle with him from a new package. The candlelight emphasized the pale, unhealthy color of his face. He stuck his head through the door, to make sure that the tinker was not stealing anything.

"When could you go?" he asked.

"Any time."

The door latch clicked. Another customer came into the shop, and tapped the counter with a coin. He returned to the bar to serve. Alone in the dark because he had taken the candle with him, I heard the mice behind the wainscoting. There was electricity in the shop itself, but he hadn't bothered to have the whole house wired. Too expensive.

He came back in a moment and said, "We'll make it Friday. Be here at nine o'clock and I'll have a car to take you to Nenagh."

"And can you loan me money for the train?" I hated asking. He promised to loan me five pounds on the guarantee that I would return it.

"One last thing," he added. "I help you, you help me. What about influencing your dad and Auntie Molly to go back to the cozy cot?"

The "cozy cot" was the damp gate lodge, and Jack wanted them back there so that he could let the big house. I promised to do my best, though I knew that my father had no intention of ever leaving.

Jack got me a noggin of whiskey and three siphons of soda, and he put chaff in the bottom of the bag so that the things would not get broken.

"Save the siphons and give Jack a little kiss," he said, and I touched his lips and received two or three clumsy kisses.

"Gather ye rosebuds while ye may," he said as he kissed his fingers and waved after me.

"You're an angel," I called, and meant it.

Cycling home, I considered the various excuses for being out on Friday night. The dressmaker gave me the solution. I nearly ran over her as she emptied a slop bucket over the bridge into the river. She could only empty it at night when there was no one looking. She asked for my news and I invited her over on Friday night.

At home, as I gave my father two aspirins and some tea, I said, "I'm going to the pictures in Limerick Friday night, the Brennans invited me."

When he had swallowed an aspirin he said, "Might go myself, if I'm up."

"The doctor said you can't get up until Sunday," I warned.

"Maybe your aunt would like to go?" he suggested.

"Maybe," I said, knowing that my aunt would have to stay at home and entertain the dressmaker.

I got his razor and shaving soap and a bowl of warm water. I held the mirror while he shaved.

"What picture is on?" he asked as he scraped the soaped hairs and then put them on a cracked saucer which I had left there for that purpose.

"*The Lieutenant Wore Shorts*," I said, recalling a title that I had once seen in Dublin.

"That ought to be a good picture," he said.

The next three days dragged on. In my mind I imagined myself at the moment of escape being found out and dragged back. I worked very hard and talked a lot to my father. I rubbed his rheumatism with Sloan's Liniment and brought tea to my aunt in bed each morning.

"You'll have me spoiled," she said.

Not for long, I thought as I smiled at her. I smiled a lot for those few days, fearing that if I talked I might betray myself. I smiled and worked. I cleaned the downstairs windows with a paraffin rag and scrubbed hen dirt off the yard flags. Maura offered to help me, and she scrubbed like a maniac for two minutes or so, but then lost interest and said she had to get potatoes out of the pit for my aunt. I swept the seven lonely, empty bedrooms because bat droppings dotted the floors.

"There's two bats upstairs," I said to my father, merely making conversation.

"Where?" He jumped out of bed and went upstairs in his long underpants, grabbing the sweeping brush on the way. He routed them out of their brown winter sleep and killed them.

"Bloody nuisances," he said, and my aunt swept them onto a piece of cardboard and burned them downstairs in the stove. She said that we must do something about the rooms. The walls were all damp and mildew had settled on some parts of the wallpaper. But we just closed the doors and hurried down to the kitchen, where it was warm.

On Friday evening after tea I made up my face in front of the kitchen mirror and then went in to say good night to my father.

"You'll find a ten-shilling note in my britches pocket," he said, and I rooted and found the note. It had loose tobacco flakes in its folds. A cigarette had burst in his pocket.

"See you later," I said.

"All right," he said. "You can make me a cup of tea when you come in. Wake me up if I'm asleep." I didn't shake hands or anything, in case he got suspicious.

"Well, have a nice chat," I said to my aunt. She was sitting in the kitchen waiting for the dressmaker. She had her good black dress on and her best shoes. Instead of shoelaces she used black ribbon to tie her shoes.

"Enjoy yourself," she said, smiling at me. She said it so nicely that I almost broke down and told her the truth. She looked pretty as she sat there, her face powdered, her hands fiddling with the chain and locket which she wore around her neck. There was a tray set for tea and sweet cake buttered.

"Don't wait up for me," I said as I kissed her good night and went out.

12

Once outside the house, I ran. I ran across the fields (safer than going by the road) and came out at the stone stile near the creamery. Then I ran the rest of the way to the village.

Jack had promised to leave the hall door ajar for me in case anyone should see me going into the bar. I pushed the door, and saw it fall in with a thud. It had come off its hinges the night of his mother's wake and had never been repaired since.

He must have heard the noise, because he came rushing into the hall from the shop with a candle in his hand.

"God Almighty, it reminded me of the Tans," he whispered, "the night they burst the door in."

I took the candle while he propped the door back, and then he gave me an envelope containing five pounds.

"I'll send it back," I promised.

"All set?" he whispered, and when I nodded he called to the men in the shop, "Hold on there, lads, till I come back."

He led the way down the narrow hall and through the kitchen, where two or three hens roosted over the fireplace.

In the yard the candle blew out immediately. A figure coughed and came toward us.

Jack announced, "Tom Duggan, here's your woman."

I said, "Hello," in a faint voice.

I knew Tom Duggan by name; I knew that he lived up the country and that he had one iron hand. How like Jack to find me an escort with only one hand.

"Where do you want to go?" Tom Duggan asked abruptly. He had the rough voice which most people down there have. It is a voice bred in wind and hardship, and it is accustomed to shouting at things.

"I want to go to Nenagh to catch the eleven o'clock train," I said, and wondered if Jack had told him the whole story.

"Get in," he said. I sat in the car and found that my seat sloped peculiarly. Jack wished me good luck, kissed me dolefully, and slammed the door. The gears tore, rattling the windows deafeningly, and we took three or four labored bounds forward over the cobbled yard, as he swung out recklessly onto the main street.

"Funny hour o' the night to be going somewhere," he said. I didn't answer him. Suddenly I was afraid of him, because I remembered about this queer sister he had. She was neither a man nor a woman, but a mixture of both. She was called the Freak, and he was nicknamed the Ferret, because he poisoned so many rats. Together they were known as the Freak and the Ferret, although this sister was sometimes called the Stripper, because some of the local boys said they'd love to strip her and see what she was like underneath.

"This is a nice car," I said, trying to flatter him. It was a terrible car, a black, battered old Ford that rattled in every corner.

Passing our own gateway I expected to see my father with a shotgun. I saw no one except a figure going in by the little wicker gate. It must have been the dressmaker.

Soon we were out on the quiet country road, shaving the unkempt hedges as we turned corners. He was a reckless driver and I wished that he had had his two hands.

"What are you up to?" he asked in an insolent voice. I wondered how much Jack had paid him, and if perhaps I should bribe him further.

"Don't ask me," I said, trying to convey my panic without offending him. It would be no joke if he left me on the roadside.

"Your father is a nice man. Everyone likes him, he's a decent man. I bought a heifer off him the last fair day," he said.

"He often talks about you," I said, lying.

"Does he now?" I could feel his smile as he said, "That's a fine head of hair you have, a fine head of hair to spread out on a pillow." My aunt had washed it with rainwater for me the day before.

I worried that he might twist back his arm and put his iron hand on my knee. I remembered a story I had once heard about his sister. The rate collector told how when he had gone to the Ferret's house to collect the rates, the queer sister had tumbled him in the hay. The rate collector said that rates or no rates he'd never go near that house again. Maybe it would be better after all if I got out and walked, I thought.

"What age are you?" he asked. I told him that I was twenty-one, since December.

"You'll soon be settling down," he said, and then he whistled, "If I were a blackbird I'd whistle and sing and follow the ship that my true love sails in . . ."

Later he said, "If you married me, I'd give you tea in bed in the mornings."

I pretended that it was a joke and asked him how *he* made tea. I could see Eugene scalding the little china pot, swishing the hot water around it, saying, "One of the first things I have to teach you is to make a decent cup of tea, and then we must teach you how to speak properly, softly."

"We'll have a pint," this man the Ferret said as he slowed down outside a pub in the lighted street of Invara. There were twenty or thirty bicycles thrown against the shop window, all jumbled together.

"We'll do no such thing," I said frantically as I touched his shoulder and begged him to drive on. He drove on. A little later he said, "Would you marry me?"

I remembered then having heard that no woman would marry him because of this queer sister. He had put advertisements in different papers and had even written to a marriage bureau in Dublin.

"No," I said flatly, wearily. If I hadn't been so worried I might have joked with him.

"I'm not a bad match," he said, "I've a pump in the yard, a bull, and a brother a priest. What more could a woman want?"

Did he take off his hook in bed and hang it on the bedpost along with his clothes, I wondered hysterically.

We were climbing a steep hill, and the car throbbed and puffed as if it was going to expire. I sat on the edge of the seat, my fingernails dug into my palms, praying. A luminous sign rising out of the ditch warned us that there were three miles of bends. Three miles of death, I thought, as he was a terrible driver. We passed a group of fellows who stood at a crossroads, and they yelled to us in that maniacal way which country boys have of yelling at strange cars. He hooted at them, to show that he was friendly.

"Are we nearly there?" I asked.

"Can't be far off it," he said, and he turned on a light at the dashboard and looked at the speedometer. "This bloody thing is broken," he said, and tapped it, but it did not tell him anything.

The road widened and there were cats' eyes in the center and streetlights in the distance and the dark spire of a cathedral. We were almost there.

"How is it ye asked me to do this drive; what's wrong with the two hackney cars in the town?" he asked as we drove into the railway station.

"It's a secret," I said as I got out and gave him a ten-shilling note and asked him not to tell.

I was an hour too early for the train, so I sat in the Ladies' Waiting Room eating damp chocolate from a machine, and every time a porter came by I pretended to be engrossed in a paper which I had found.

About eleven o'clock the train arrived. I had come outside to stand on the platform, and I found an empty carriage quite easily. It was a fast train which stopped at only two stations along the way. Both times I hid in the lavatory in case the police should be searching for me. There was a printed sign over the flush button—PLEASE DO NOT FLUSH WHEN TRAIN IS STANDING. Someone had written below it, in indelible pencil—*There it goes again, all down on the poor aul farmer.*

At Dublin I hid until the other passengers had gone. Then I got off the train, moved with my head down close to the wall, and went up to the last remaining taxi.

I was at Joanna's within ten minutes and found the house in total darkness. It was about three o'clock, and the baby from the house two doors away was crying for his night feed. Joanna had lids on the milk bottles as usual. Birds used to drink a little of the cream in the early morning, but Joanna soon stopped that.

Our bedroom was in the front of the house, so I threw up wet clods of clay from the flower beds and then a few pebbles and cinders from the path. I whistled and called, but Baba did not waken. Finally I had to knock. Gustav came down in his overcoat, and I looked so frightened that he brought me in without a murmur. He put the electric fire on in the dining room and went off to make cocoa. The electric fire made crackling noises, as if it was about to explode, and my body was shaking all over.

"You in trouble with Mr. Eugene?" Gustav said as he came in with the tray and found me crying.

"Is he back?"

"Oh yeh, yeh." He nodded his head. "He here with Baba. They were dining out, I am told." I could feel my stomach grow hollow with a new fear.

"You go to bed, Gustav," I said, and he went to bed and I dozed on the settee until the hands of the plate clock moved to seven. Then I went upstairs very quietly and wakened Baba.

"Well, well!" she said, yawning. She sat up and buttoned the two top buttons of her sky-blue pajamas.

"I'm back," I said.

"I can see you're back."

"Tell me about Eugene."

"He's thirty-five and he's going bald."

"Did he ask about me?"

"Yeh."

"And I suppose you told him lies. You didn't even send me the money when I wrote to you from home, they kept me locked up, I ran away last night."

"I sent you two pounds," she said. I might have known that Baba would send it, because she has a good heart.

"What about Eugene, Baba, please tell me. Do you think I could go to him?"

"You're twenty-one—it's legal for you to put your head in the gas oven even if it's against the law," she said, and she got up and gave me some more money and a travel bag to put my things in and some powder for my face. My face was gray and pulpy from worry and lack of sleep. She took her little gold watch from under the pillow and read the time.

"You'll want to hurry, your aul fella will be here with a pitchfork any minute." And she hugged me before I left.

"Good luck," she said, " 'tis well for you."

Out in the street I cried with emotion because Baba had been so nice. I caught the first bus into Dublin. There were only half a dozen people on it and they looked gray and wretched like myself.

From the General Post Office I sent two telegrams. One to Eugene, which said, ARRIVING MIDDAY BUS, and the other to my aunt, which said, GONE TO ENGLAND ALONE. DO NOT WORRY. FORGIVE ME. WRITING.

I thought that would confuse them and leave me a few days to decide what I would do.

When the nearest café opened at nine o'clock, I went and had coffee and toast. When you are frightened you are certain that everyone is an enemy. I suspected every face that morning as I drank coffee to fill in the time, and moved from one café to another to avoid being noticed.

At five to eleven I boarded the bus at the quays. I had nothing to read so I looked out the window, and when it got fogged up I wiped it with my hand and stared at nothing in particular. I knew that I should rehearse what I would say to Eugene, but I could not even do that.

It seemed a long drive, but it was in fact only about an hour. When we got there I let the others pile out first, because I was embarrassed about meeting him. I looked through the window, but his car was not there. Then I hurried out, thinking he had parked the car up the street. There was no sign of him anywhere.

"What time does this bus go back to Dublin?" I inquired of the driver, who had climbed up on the roof to hand down parcels and bicycles.

"Five o'clock," he called down.

Five hours to wait. I swallowed my pride and decided that I would go to Eugene anyhow. I knew that once he saw me he would not turn away.

I set out to walk and had gone half a mile when I saw a black-coated tall figure coming toward me.

It's a priest, I thought, or a policeman, and I ran into a gateway and climbed over in order to hide behind the ditch. A stream of water ran down the mountain field and through a pipe in the ditch.

I peeped out and saw the figure approach. It was Eugene. I climbed quickly over the rickety wooden gate and ran to him. He had his arms out to welcome me.

"Hello, hello," he said, and I fell into his arms and told him everything. I talked rapidly and mixed up the whole sequence of the story because I was so tired and frightened.

"But this is monstrous!" he said, laughing. He thought I was exaggerating.

"They'll kill me," I said.

"Nonsense, it's the twentieth century," he said, and he took my traveling bag and we turned around to go to his house. The wind blew against our faces, and he told me that the motorcar had refused to start.

"I thought I'd never see you again," I said, and he linked me and patted my wrist, above my knitted glove.

"You'll be all right," he said. "We don't let them kill you."

I wondered if he would let me stay there with him; I wanted to stay, I never wanted to leave him again.

When we came around the corner of the drive, my first thought was that his house looked so happy and peaceful. The whitewashed front sparkled in the winter sun and the downstairs windows were a pale gold.

"You see," he said, "the sun is shining, you're alive, everything is going to be all right," and we went inside.

Anna did not bid me good morning; she just took a jar of honey off the kitchen table and went up the back stairs in a sulk.

"My honey," he said out loud so that she could hear it. We heard a door bang. He said that she was in a bad humor because Denis would not give her the money to send for a rubber corset through the post. Also, she didn't like me, because I was not swanky and had no clothes to give away.

"You sit down," he said. "I'll cook you a big breakfast."

He tied a towel around him and I kissed him—just a little kiss—and felt the comfort of being near him again, smelling his skin and kissing it. He fried rashers and eggs while I laid one end of the big kitchen table. He sat at the head and I sat to one side, facing the barred window and the black cherry tree.

"They kept my letters, Baba sent me money and they kept it," I said.

"Don't talk about them while you're eating or you'll get an ulcer; just forget about everything," he said, and he leaned over and stroked my forehead lightly.

"Cheers," he said, raising a cup of tea to his lips. It tasted of hair shampoo, so did mine. Anna had put shampoo in the cups, or cheap perfume. I thought it evil of her. We washed the cups and poured a second lot of tea.

My stomach felt sick with worry, and I looked through the window all the time.

"A Jehovah's Witness was stabbed in twenty-nine places with a penknife in the village next to ours," I said, and his whole face wrinkled with pain. I knew that I had said the wrong thing, as he was very fastidious.

In a little while he said, "You look as if you've been through Purgatory."

I looked awful and my body felt cold and shivery. After breakfast I went upstairs to have a sleep.

"Get into my bed, it's warmer," he said. And upstairs I just took off my dress and shoes and got into the tossed bed.

From where I lay I could see the top of a pine tree, its branches stirring lightly, the vegetable garden wall with weeds growing on it, and more trees beyond that. I could not sleep.

The door was opened softly and he peeped in to see if I was asleep.

"Hello," I said.

"Did you not go to sleep?"

"I can't. I'm frightened."

He came over and smoothed my hair back from my face, and then he stroked my hot forehead. It was very hot. He put a damp facecloth to it and said soothing things while the damp cloth covered my forehead and eyes. It was dark and damp for those minutes, and I liked the reassurance of his voice. But then he removed the cloth and dried my eyes.

"Isn't that better?" he said. I felt anxious again.

"You can get into bed with me, if you like," I said.

"No, no." He shook his head, gave me a dry kiss. "When we make love to one another, it will be because we want to."

"But I want to," I said.

"You do, but it's for the wrong reason. You want to involve me, that's all. You know that once I've made love to you, I shall feel responsible for you." He looked into my eyes and I looked away guiltily. My eyes were hot and itchy.

"Oh, don't get cross," I begged.

"Nobody's getting cross," he said calmly. "But you must understand that relationships between people are not as crude or as simple as this. Sex is not some independent thing, it's part of what people feel for each other, and I could no more make love to you in this nerve-racked state than I could chew my old socks . . ."

I thought that he must be trying to get rid of me, so I said quickly, "Have I to go now?"

"I've been thinking," he began . . . "In fact, the wisest thing would be for you to go away."

"I have nowhere to go," I said.

"Now don't get anxious, keep calm and listen to me, I'm not abandoning you to the wolves. I'll give you the money to go to London for a week or two, and then when everyone has calmed down, you can come back again."

"I don't want to leave you," I said as I looked into his sallow face and his large dark eyes. He had a strong, hard body and I wanted him to shield me from them and from everything that I was afraid of.

"Please," I said.

He tapped his forehead with his fist and said, "Oh, God," and then he sighed for a minute, and I thought, His heart is softening and he'll let me stay here.

"Listen, listen," he was saying, and I sat up thinking that it was a car which had driven up outside. But nothing came, and he went on: "If we both stay here they'll come and perhaps force you away; if we both go to London they'll probably have the police after us. The sensible thing is for you to go away. I'll stay here and talk reasonably to your father if he should come, and then in a week or two I'll come over to London and see you."

A cold sadness came over me. He was sending me away.

"All right," I said wearily, and I put out my hand for his and we sat there in silence.

"Do you think they will come today?" he asked after a time.

"No, not so soon. I sent them a telegram this morning to say I was going to England and that I'd write, so they'll wait for a day or two."

"All right then, you can have a big rest today; and tomorrow I'll bring you into Collinstown and we'll put you on an airplane."

I had never been on an airplane and I worried about being strapped down. Baba said that they strapped you to a seat.

"You'll write to me?" I asked.

"Every day. Big, long letters." He took me in his arms and held me there for a long time while I cried and sobbed.

"I bought you a little present when I was away," he said then, and he ran downstairs to get it.

It was a portable radio, and he showed me how to work the various knobs and find the different stations.

"You can take it around with you anywhere." He turned the knob on and we heard light music. He danced with the radio in his arms for a minute, and I wondered how he could be so cheerful.

I got up and washed, and after lunch we went for a walk.

"If anyone calls, don't admit them," he shouted up to Anna.

"Are you expecting the bailiff?" she shouted down in a cheeky voice.

He frowned—and said that she was getting out of hand.

It was mild outside, the wind had died down, and it was spotting rain. Everything was very still and we could hear the men over in the forestry sawing trees. I took off my headscarf and let the rain fall on my greasy hair and on my warm face. Always with lack of sleep, my face and eyelids got warm and itchy. As we walked along he told me about a picture he had seen in London called *Golden Marie*. He told me the story of it and described the blond, sensual girl who played the part of Marie. I felt so dull and unattractive as he talked of her and moved his hands to outline the shape of her body.

We went down the narrow path that led to the lake wood. A belt of pine trees ran down on one side, like an army of green soldiers following one upon another, and a loose stone wall skirted the other side of the track. Many of the stones had fallen down.

"You'll be able to see that picture, I'll tell Ginger to take you," he said as he stooped down to pick up three white stones. Ginger was a woman whom he intended to send a telegram to, asking her to meet me. She had red hair, he said, and that was why she was called Ginger. I wondered if she loved him; I couldn't imagine any woman knowing him and not loving him.

"Is she nice?" I asked.

"She's a nice girl," he said casually. He was so casual about everything—the rain, the white stones, the pine trees swathed in a mountain mist—one thing seemed as important or as unimportant as another. I thought he was a little callous.

"You're not doleful, are you, sweetling?" he asked as he put his hand on my shoulder and told me not to brood. The rain lay on my coat in a pearl-like drizzle. The quietness of everything had an unnerving effect on me. It all looked unreal—the trees wrapped in a quiet, swirling mist so that the trunks seemed to be standing on air, and stretches of mist curtained off the lower parts of the fields.

"I hate leaving you," I said. We had come out at the edge of the wood near the lake, and loose wisps of floating mist moved in patches over the water.

"It will only be for a couple of weeks," he said cheerfully as we sat on the flat roof of the boathouse and looked across at the stony fields which ran down to the lake on the far side. The mist had not come down fully and some fields were quite clear.

"You didn't think it was as nice as this, did you?" he said, stretching his hands out to include the lake, the small sandy beach, the pebbles in the shallow water, and, across the way, a white, ivied house with a lightning rod on the chimney pot. He told me that the Miss Walkers lived there.

"It's lovely," I said, not really caring.

"It's nicer in the summer: I must teach you how to swim."

"The summer," I said, as if we would never live to see it. Then I thought of other summers and of how he must have swum in the lake with Laura, and afterward lain on the tiny beach, which was partly shaded by a very wide chestnut tree. Always when I was with him I thought of Laura, just as I always thought of my mother when I was with Dada.

"How long was Laura here altogether?" I asked.

"I don't remember rightly, she must have been here about a year."

"Could she swim?" Baba could swim and dive but I could do neither.

"Yes, she could swim," and though I expected him to say something else, he didn't.

It got dark early because of the rain, and the fields looked sad in the smudging light of evening. He helped me climb the hill by pushing me from behind, and he knew his way by tread and warned me of the various rabbit holes.

"Can I sleep in your bed tonight?" I asked as we climbed between the army of pine trees and the wall of loose stones.

"I suppose so," he said gently.

I prayed that something would happen so that I could stay. Something did.

13 At teatime a wind began to rise, and rattled the shutters. Anna rushed out to bring in napkins which she had spread on one of the thorny bushes. A galvanized bucket rolled along the cobbled yard.

I had felt afraid all day, knowing that they were bound to come—but if a mountain storm blew up, it might keep them away. By the morrow I'd be gone.

After tea we sat in the study with a map of London spread on both our knees while he marked various streets and sights for me. I was to go early the next morning, and he had sent a telegram to Ginger, so that she could meet me.

"We ought to lock the doors," I said, unnerved by the rattling of shutters.

"All right," he said, "we'll lock everything." I carried the big flashlight around while he locked the potting-shed door, the back door, and another side door. The keys had rusted in their locks and he had to tap the bolts with a block of wood to loosen them. Anna and Denis had gone backstairs to their own apartments, and we could hear dance music from their radio.

"Tell them if there's a knock, not to answer it," I suggested.

"Nonsense," he said, "they never come down once they've gone up at night. They go to bed after the nine o'clock news." He was very proud and did not wish to share his troubles with anyone.

"Now the hall door," I said. We opened it for a minute and looked out at the windy night and listened to the trees groaning.

"Go away from the window, bogey man," he said as we came in and sat on the couch in front of the study fire. The oak box was stocked with logs, and he said that we were perfectly safe and that no one could harm us.

There was a shotgun in the corner of the hall, and I thought that maybe he should get it to be on the safe side.

"Nonsense," he said. "You just want some melodrama . . ."

I could hear the wind and I imagined that I heard a car driving up to the house; I heard it all the time, but it was only in my imagination. I rubbed his hair and massaged the muscles at the back of his neck, and he said that it was very nice and very comforting.

"We get on well together, you and I," he said.

"Yes," I said, and thought how easy it would be, if he said then, I love you, or I could love, or I'm falling in love with you, but he didn't; he just said that we got on well together.

"We only know each other a couple of months," he said to the fire, as if he had sensed my disappointment. I knew that he believed in the slow, invisible processes of growth, the thing which had to take root first in the lonely, dark part of one, away from the light. He liked to plant trees and watch them grow; he liked our friendship to take its course; he was not ready for me.

"Do you believe in God?" I said abruptly. I don't know why I said it.

"Not when I'm sitting at my own fire. I may do when I'm driving eighty miles an hour. It varies." I thought it a very peculiar answer, altogether.

"What things are you afraid of?" I wished that somehow he would make some deep confession to me and engross me in his fears so that I could forget my own, or that we could play I-spy-with-my-little-eye, or something.

"Just bombs," he said, and I thought that a peculiar answer, too.

"But not hell?" I said, naming my second greatest fear.

"They'll give me a job making fires in hell, I'm good at fires." I wondered how his voice could be so calm, his face so still. Sometimes I rubbed his neck, and then again I rested my arm and sat very close to him, wondering how I could live without him in London for the while—until things blew over, he said.

"The best thing you can do about hell . . ." he began, but I never heard the end of the sentence, because just then the dog barked in the yard outside. She barked steadily for a few seconds and then let out a low, warning howl that was almost human-sounding. I jumped up.

"Sssh, ssh," he said, as I stumbled over a tray of tea things that was on the floor. He ran across and lowered the Tilley lamp; then we waited. Nothing happened, no footsteps, no car, nothing but the wind and the beating rain. Yet I knew they were coming and that in a moment they would knock on the door.

"Must have been a badger or a fox." He poured me a drink from the whiskey bottle on the gun bureau.

"You look as white as a sheet," he said, sipping the whiskey. Then the dog barked again, loudly and continuously, and I knew by her hysterical sounds that she was trying to leap the double doors in the back yard. We had not locked them. My whole body began to shake and tremble.

"It's them," I said, going cold all over. We heard boots on the gravel and men talking, and suddenly great banging and tapping on the hall door. The dog continued to bark hysterically, and above the noise of banging fists and wind blowing I heard the beating of my own heart. Knuckles rapped on the window, the shutters rattled, and at the same time the stiff knocker boomed. I clutched Eugene's sleeve and prayed.

"Oh, God," I said to him.

"Open up," a man's voice shouted.

"They'll break down the door," I said. Five or six of them seemed to be pounding on it all at once. I thought that my heart would burst.

"How dare they abuse my door like that," he said as he moved toward the hall.

"Don't, don't!" I stood in his way and told him not to be mad. "We won't answer," I said, but I had spoken too late. One of my people had gone around to the back of the house, and we heard the metallic click of the back-door latch being raised impatiently. Then the bolt was drawn and I heard Anna say, "What'n the name of God do you want at this hour of night?"

I suppose that she must have been half asleep and had tumbled down thinking that we had been locked out or that the police had come for me.

I heard the Ferret's voice speak my name. "We've come to take that girl out of here."

"I don't know anything about it. Wait outside," Anna said insolently, and then he must have walked straight past her, because she shouted, "How dare you!" and the sheep dog ran up the passage from the kitchen, yelping. The others were still knocking at the front of the house.

"This is beyond endurance," Eugene said, and as he went to open the hall door, I ran back into the study and looked around for somewhere to hide. I crawled under the spare bed, hoping that he would bring them to the sitting room, because he did not like people in the study, where he worked. I heard him say, "I can't answer you that, I'm afraid."

"Deliver her out," a voice demanded.

I had to think, to recall who it was.

"Come on now." It was Andy, my father's cousin, a cattle dealer. I recalled strange cattle—making the noises which they made in unfamiliar places—being driven into our front field on the evenings preceding a fair day. Then cousin Andy would come up to the house for tea, and sitting in the kitchen in his double-breasted brown suit he'd discuss the price of heifers with my father. Once he gave me a threepenny bit which was so old and worn that the King had been rubbed off.

"Where is my only child?" my father cried.

She's under the bed, she's suffocating, I said to myself, praying that I would be there only for a second, while Eugene picked up the lamp and brought them across to the sitting room. Could I then hide in the barn—and take the flashlight to ward off rats!

"My only child," my father cried again.

For two pins I'd come out and tell him a thing or two about his only child!

"Who are you looking for?" Eugene said. "We'll confer in the other room."

But my father had noticed the fire, and with a sinking feeling I heard them all troop into the study. Someone sat on the bed; the spring touched my back, and smelling cowdung from his boots, I guessed it was cousin Andy. I recognized two other voices—Jack Holland's and the Ferret's.

"Don't you think it is a little late in the day for social calls?" Eugene said.

"We want that poor, innocent girl," cousin Andy said—he, the famed bachelor, who had spoken only to cows and bullocks all his life, bullying them along the road to country fairs. "Hand the girl over, and by God if there's a hair astray on her, you'll pay dear for it," he shouted, and I imagined how he looked with his miser's face and his mean little mouth framed by a red mustache. He always had to carry stomach mixture with him everywhere, and had once raised his hand to my mother because she hinted about all the free grazing he took from Dada. On that occasion my father, in his one known act of chivalry, said, "If you lay a finger on my missus, I'll lay you out."

"This is outrageous," Eugene said.

Various matches were struck—they were settling in.

"Allow me," Jack Holland said, proceeding to make introductions, but he was shouted down by my father.

"A divorced man. Old enough to be her father. Carrying off my little daughter."

"To set the record straight, I did not bring her here, she came," Eugene said.

I thought, He's going to let me down, he's going to send me away with them; my mother was right: "Weep and you weep alone."

"You got her with dope. Everyone knows that," my father said.

Eugene laughed. I thought how odd, and immoral, he must look to them, in his corduroy trousers and his old checked shirt. I hoped that all his buttons were done up. My nose began to itch with the dust.

"You're her father?" Eugene said.

"Allow me," Jack Holland said again, and this time he performed the introductions. I wondered if it was he who had betrayed me.

"Yes, I'm her father," Dada said, in a doleful voice.

"Go now and get the girl," Andy shouted.

I began to tremble anew. I couldn't breathe. I would suffocate under those rusty springs. I would die while they sat there deciding my life. I would die—with Andy's dungy boots under my nose. It was ironic. My mother used to scrub the rungs of the chair after his visits to our house. I said short prayers and multiplication tables and the irregular plurals of Latin nouns—anything that I knew by heart—to distract myself. I thought of a line from *Macbeth* which I had once recited, wearing a red nightgown, at a school concert—"I see thee still and on thy blade and dudgeon gouts of blood . . ."

"Are you a Catholic?" the Ferret asked, in a policeman's voice.

"I'm not a Catholic," Eugene answered.

"D'you go to Mass?" my father asked.

"But, my dear man—" Eugene began.

"There's no 'my dear man.' Cut it out. Do you go to Mass or don't you? D'you eat meat on Fridays?"

"God help Ireland," Eugene said, and I imagined him throwing his hands up in his customary gesture of impatience.

"None of that blasphemy," cousin Andy shouted, making a noise as he struck his fist into his palm.

"What about a drink to calm us down?" Eugene suggested, and then, sniffing, he added, "Perhaps better not—you seem to have brought enough alcohol with you."

I could smell their drink from under the bed now, and I guessed that they had stopped at every pub along the way to brace themselves for the occasion. Probably my father had paid for most of it.

"Well . . . a sip of port wine all round might be conducive to negotiation," Jack Holland suggested in his soft, mannerly way.

"Could I have a drink of water—to take an aspirin?" my father said.

"Good idea. I'll join you in an aspirin," Eugene said, and I thought for a second that things were going to be all right. Water was poured. I closed my eyes to pray, dropped my forehead onto the back of my hand, and gasped. My face was damp with cold sweat.

"I would like you to realize that your daughter is escaping from you. I'm not abducting her. I'm not forcing her—she is running away from you and your way of living . . ." Eugene began.

"What the hell is he talking about?" Andy said.

"The tragic history of our fair land," Jack Holland exclaimed. "Alien power sapped our will to resist."

"They get girls with dope," the Ferret said. "Many an Irish girl ends up in the white-slave traffic in Piccadilly. Foreigners run it. All foreigners."

"Where's your wife, mister? Would you answer that?" Andy said.

"And what are you doing with my daughter?" my father asked fiercely, as if recollecting what they had come for.

"I'm not doing anything with her," Eugene said, and I thought, He has shed all responsibility for me, he does not love me.

"You're a foreigner," Andy said contemptuously.

"Not at all," Eugene said pleasantly. "Not at all as foreign as your tiny, blue, Germanic eyes, my friend."

"What are your intentions?" my father asked abruptly. And then he must have drawn the anonymous letter from his pocket, because he said, "There's a few things here would make your hair stand on end."

"He hasn't much hair, he's near bald," the Ferret said.

"I haven't any intentions; I suppose in time I would like to marry her and have children . . . Who knows?"

"Ah, the patter of little feet," said Jack Holland idiotically, and Dada told him to shut up and stop making a fool of himself.

He doesn't really want me, I thought as I took short, quick breaths and said an Act of Contrition, thinking that I was near my end. I don't know why I stayed under there, it was stifling.

"Would you turn?" my father said, and of course Eugene did not know what he meant by that.

"Turn?" he asked in a puzzled voice.

"Be a Catholic," the Ferret said. And then Eugene sighed and said, "Why don't we all have a cup of tea?" and Dada said, "Yes, yes."

It will go on all night and I'll be found dead under this bed, I thought as I wished more and more that I could scratch a place between my shoulder blades which itched terribly.

When he opened the door to fetch some tea he must have found Anna listening at the keyhole, because I heard him say to her, "Oh, Anna, you're here, can you bring us a tray of tea, please?" And then he seemed to go out of the room, because suddenly they were all talking at once.

"She could have got out the back way," my father said.

"Get tough, boy, get tough," Andy said. "Follow him out, you fool, before he makes a run for it."

"Poor Brady," the Ferret said when Dada had apparently gone out, "that's the thanks he gets for sending that little snotty-nose to a convent and giving her a fine education."

"She was never right, that one," cousin Andy said, "reading books and talking to trees. Her mother spoiled her . . ."

"Ah, her dear mother," said Jack Holland, and while he raved on about Mama being a lady, the other two passed remarks about the portrait of Eugene over the fire.

"Look at the nose of him—you know what he is? They'll be running this bloody country soon," Andy said.

"God, 'tis a bloody shame, ruining a girl like that," Andy said, and I thought how baffled they'd be if they had known that I was not seduced yet, even though I had slept in his bed for two whole nights.

I heard the rattle of cups as Eugene and my father came back.

"How much money do you earn in a year?" my father asked, and I knew how they would sneer if they heard that he made poky little films about rats and sewerage.

"I earn lots of money," Eugene lied.

"You're old enough to be her father," Dada said. "You're nearly as old as myself."

"Look," Eugene said after a minute, "where is all this ill temper going to get us? Why don't you go down to the village and stay in the hotel for the night, then come up in the morning and discuss it with Caithleen. She won't be so frightened in the morning, and I will try to get her to agree to seeing you."

"Not on your bloody life," cousin Andy said.

"We'll not go without her," my father added threateningly, and I lost heart then and knew that there was no escape. They would find me and pull me forth. We would go out in the wind and sit in the Ferret's car and drive all night, while they abused me. If only Baba were there, she'd find a way . . .

"She's over twenty-one, you can't force her," Eugene said, "not even in Ireland."

"Can't we? We won our fight for freedom. It's our country now," Andy said.

"We can have her put away. She's not all there," my father said.

"Mental," the Ferret added.

"What about that, mister?" cousin Andy shouted. "A very serious offense having to do with a mentally affected girl. You could get twenty years for that."

I gritted my teeth, my head boiled—why was I such a coward as to stay under there? They'd make a goat ashamed. Tears of rage and shame ran over the back of my hand and I wanted to scream, I disown them, they're nothing to do with me, don't connect me with them, but I said nothing—just waited.

"Go and get her," my father said. "*Now!*" And I imagined the spit that shot out of his mouth in anger.

"You heard what Mr. Brady said," cousin Andy shouted, and he must have risen from the bed, because the springs lifted. I knew how ratty he must look with his small blue eyes, his red mustache, his stomach ulcer.

"Very well, then," Eugene said, "she's in my legal care. A guest in my house. When she leaves she will do so of her own free will. Leave my house or I'll telephone for the police." I wondered if they'd notice that there was no phone.

"You heard me," Eugene said, and I thought, Oh, God, he'll get hit. Didn't he know how things ended—"Man in hospital with fifty-seven penknife wounds." I started to struggle out, to give myself up.

I heard the first smack of their fists, and then they must have knocked him over, because the Tilley lamp crashed and the globe broke into smithereens.

I screamed as I got out and staggered up. Flames from the wood fire gave enough light for me to see by. Eugene was on the floor, trying to struggle up, and Andy and the Ferret were hitting and kicking him. Jack Holland was trying to hold them back, and my father, hardly knowing what he was doing, held the back of Jack Holland's coat, saying, "Keep out of this, you fool. Now, Jack, now, Jack, God save us, now, Jack—oh Jack—"

My father saw me suddenly and must have thought that I had

risen from the grave—my hair was all tossed and there was fluff and dust on me. He opened his mouth so wide that his loose dental plate dropped onto his tongue. They were cheap teeth that he had made by a dental mechanic.

"Oh, Lil, oh, Lily," he whispered, and backed away from me clutching his teeth. Long after, I realized that he thought I was Mama risen from her grave in the Shannon lake. I must have looked like a ghost—my face daubed with tears and gray dust, my hair hanging in my eyes.

I shouted at the Ferret to stop, when the door burst open and the room lit up with a great red and yellow flash, as Anna fired the shotgun at the ceiling. The thunderclap made me stagger back against the bed with my head numb and singing. I tried to stay still, waiting to die. I thought I'd been shot, but it was only the shock of the explosion in my ears. The black smoke of gunpowder entered our throats and made me cough. Jack Holland was on his knees, praying and coughing, while Andy and the Ferret were turned to the door with their hands to their ears. My father leaned over a chair gasping, and Eugene moaned on the floor and put his hand to his bleeding nose. Shattered plaster fell down all over the carpet and the white dust mixed with gun smoke. The smell was awful.

"There's another one in it. I'll blow your brains out," Anna said. She stood at the study door, in her nightgown, holding Eugene's shotgun. Denis stood beside her with a lighted Christmas candle.

"Out you get," she said to them, holding the gun steadily up.

"By God, I'm getting out of this," the Ferret said. "These people would kill you!" I went to Eugene, who was still sitting on the floor with blood coming from his nose. I put my handkerchief to it.

"Dangerous savages," my father said, his face white, holding his teeth in one hand. "She might have killed us."

"I'll blow your feet off if you don't clear out of here," Anna said in a quivering voice.

"Get out," Eugene said to them as he stood up. His shirt was torn. "Get out. Go. Leave. Never come inside my gates again."

"Have you a drop of whiskey?" my father said shakily, putting his hand to his heart.

"No," Eugene said. "Leave my house immediately."

"A pretty night's work, a pretty night's work," Jack Holland said sadly as they left. Anna stood to one side to let them pass and Denis opened the hall door. The last thing I saw was the Ferret's hooked iron hand being shaken back at us.

Eugene slammed the door and Denis bolted it. I collapsed onto the bed, trembling.

"That's the way to handle them," Anna said as she put the gun on the table.

"You saved my life," Eugene said, and he sat on the couch and drew up the leg of his trousers. There was blood on his shin, where he had been kicked. His nose also was bleeding.

"I'm sorry, I'm sorry," I said between sobs.

"Oh, tough men, tough men," Denis said solemnly as we heard them outside arguing, and the dog barking from the back yard.

"Get some iodine," Eugene said. I went upstairs but couldn't find it, so Anna had to go and get it, along with a clean towel and a basin of water. He lay back on the armchair, and I opened his shoelaces and took off his shoes.

"Wh'ist," Denis said. We heard the car drive away.

Anna washed the cuts on Eugene's face and legs. He squirmed with pain as she swabbed on iodine.

"I shouldn't have hidden," I said, handing him a clean handkerchief from the top drawer of his desk, where he kept them. "Oh, I shouldn't have come here."

Through the handkerchief he said, "Go get yourself a drink. It will help you to stop shaking. Get me one, too."

After a while the nosebleed stopped and he raised his head and looked at me. His upper lip had swollen.

"It was terrible," I said.

"It was," he said, "ridiculous. Like this country."

"Except for me where would we be?" Anna said.

"What about a cup of tea?" he said in a sad voice, and I knew that he would never forget what had happened and that some of their conduct had rubbed off onto me.

. . .

We went to bed late. His shin ached and a cut over his eye throbbed a lot. It was an hour before he went to sleep. I lay for most of the night, looking at the moonlit wall, thinking. Near dawn I found him awake and looking at me.

"I love you," I said suddenly. I had not prepared it or anything, it just fell out of my mouth.

"Love!" he said, as if it were a meaningless word, and he moved his head on the pillow to face me. He smiled and closed his eyes, going back to sleep again. What could I do to make up? I cried a bit, and later got up to make some tea.

Anna was in the kitchen putting on her good shoes and silk stockings, preparing to go to Mass.

"I'm not over it yet," she said.

"I'll never be over it," I said, and to myself, They've ruined, and ruined, and ruined me. He'll never look at me again. I'll have to go away.

14 She came back from Mass bubbling over with news.

"They think in the village that you must be a film star," she said as she took a long hatpin out of her blue hat, removed the hat, and stuck the pin through it for the next Sunday. She said that I was the topic of conversation in the three shops. My father and his friends had stopped at the hotel for drinks on the way up.

As she put the frying pan on the range, I noticed the tracks of mice in the cold fat.

"I expect you'll be leaving today," she said.

"I expect so."

It was after ten, so I made Eugene's tea and carried it upstairs. Standing for a moment in the doorway with the tray, I felt suddenly privileged to be in his room while he slept. The hollows of his cheeks were more pronounced in sleep and his face bore a slight look of pain.

I drew back the curtains.

"You'll break the curtain rings," he said, sitting up. His startled eyes looked twice their normal size.

"Oh, hello," he said, surprised to see me, and then rubbed his lids and probably remembered everything. I put a pullover across his shoulders and knotted the two sleeves under his chin.

"Nice tea," he said as he lay there, like a Christ, sipping tea, his head resting on the mahogany headboard.

Anna tapped on the door and burst in, before he had time to cry halt.

"I handed in the telegram—it will go first thing in the morning," she said. It was to his solicitor.

She told me that my black pudding, below on the range, would be dried up if I didn't go down and eat.

"Black pudding!" he groaned.

"Your nose is a nice sight," she said to him.

"Probably broken," he said, without a smile.

"Oh—not broken!" I said.

"Lucky I don't earn my living with my nose," he said. "Or make love with it."

"Hmmmh," Anna said as she stood in the middle of the room, hands on hips, surveying the tossed bed and my nightgown in a chair.

"All right," he said to us both, "trot off," and I went, but she stayed there. I listened outside the door.

"I saved your life, didn't I?"

"You did. I am very grateful to you, Anna. Remind me to strike you a leather medal."

"Will you loan me fifty pounds?" she asked. "I want to get a sewing machine and a few things for the baba. If I had a sewing machine we could mend all your shirts."

"We could?" he said mockingly.

"Will you loan me it?"

"Why don't you say 'give me fifty pounds.' I know that word 'loan' has no meaning here."

"That's not a nice thing to say." She sounded offended.

"Anna, I'll give it to you," he said. "A reward."

"Good man. Keep it to yourself, not a word to Denis. If he knew I had fifty pounds, he'd buy a bull or something."

She came out of the room beaming, and I ran away, ashamed at having been caught listening.

"Telltale-tattle," she said as I hurried guiltily along the carpeted passage. "Come on, I'll race you down the stairs," and we ran the whole way to the kitchen.

She read the Sunday papers.

"She's the image of Laura," she said, pointing to an heiress who was reported as being in love with a barber.

"Fitter changes sex," she read aloud. "Mother of God, I don't understand people at all. Do they never look at themselves when they're taking their clothes off!"

She read our horoscopes—Denis's, the baby's, Eugene's, mine, and Laura's. She included Laura in everything, so that by the time she went out after lunch with Denis and the baby, I had the feeling that Laura was due back any minute. It was with this unsettling feeling that I made my first tour of the house. Eugene had gone down the fields to look at the ram pump.

There were five bedrooms. The mattresses were folded over and the wardrobes empty, except for wooden hangers. The furniture was old, dark, unmatching, and in lockers beside the beds there were chamber pots with pink china roses on the insides of them.

In the top drawer of a linen chest I found a silver evening bag with a diary of Laura's inside. The diary had no entries, just names and telephone numbers. There was also a purple evening glove that smelled of stale but wonderful perfume. I fitted on the glove, and for some reason my heart began to pound. There was nothing in any of the other drawers, just chalk marks stating the number of each drawer.

Near dusk, I came downstairs and raised the wick of the hanging lamp which Anna had lit for me before she went out. The rabbit was on the table, as she had left it, skinned and ready to be cooked. Denis had caught it the day before.

"The dinner," I said aloud, as I got a cookery book and looked up the index under R.

> Radishes
> Ragout of Kidneys
> Raisin Bread
> Raisin Pie
> Raisin Pudding
> Rarebit
> Raspberries

Rabbit was not mentioned. The cookery book had belonged to Laura. Her maiden name and her married name were written in strong hand-·writing on the flyleaf.

"The dinner," I said, to suppress a tear, and then I remembered how Eugene had asked, earlier in the day, "Can you cook?"

"Sort of," I had said.

It was a total lie. I had never cooked in my whole life, except the Friday Gustav and Joanna went to a solicitor's to make a will. I brought home two fish for lunch, one for Baba, one for me. Baba laid the table while I fried the fish. I knew nothing about cleaning them.

I just put the gray, podgy little mackerel on the big frying pan and lit the gas under it. Nothing happened for a few minutes and then the side of one fish burst.

"There's a hell of a stink out there," Baba called from the dining room.

"It's just the fish," I said. Both fish had burst by then.

"It's just what?" she said, rushing into the kitchen, holding her nose.

When she saw the mess she simply took hold of the pan and ran down the garden to dump it on Gustav's compost heap.

"Phew," she said, coming back into the house. "You should have been alive when they ate raw cows and bones and things. A bloody savage." And she put the pan into the sink and ran the tap on it.

We went out to lunch at Woolworth's. It was a big thrill being able to march around with a tray, helping ourselves to whatever we fancied—chips, sausages, trifle topped with custard, coffee, a little jug of cream, and lemon meringue pie.

Sitting in the big flagged kitchen, I thought of Baba and cried. I missed her. I had never been alone before in my whole life, alone and dependent on my own resources. I thought with longing of all the evenings we went out together, reeking with vanilla essence and good humor. Usually we ended up in the cinema, thrilled by the darkness and the big screen, with perhaps a choc ice to keep us going.

"Oh, God," I said, remembering Baba, my father, everyone; and I buried my face in my hands and cried, not knowing what I cried for.

Three or four times, I went around the corner of the front drive and leaned on the wet white gate to see if there was a sign of anybody coming. Nobody came, except a policeman who cycled down the by-road, stood at the gate lodge for a minute, relieved himself, and cycled off again. He was probably keeping an eye out for poachers.

By the time Eugene came back I had dried my eyes; and I wondered if perhaps he expected me to have left discreetly while he was out.

"I'm still here," I said.

"I'm glad," he said as he kissed me. It was dusk and we proceeded to light the Tilley lamps.

As we sat by the study fire he said, "Oh, you poor little lonely bud, it's not a nice honeymoon for you, is it? Think of nice things . . . sunshine, mountain rivers, fuchsia . . ."

I lay in his arms and could think only about what would happen next. He had put a record on the wind-up gramophone, and music filled the room. Outside, rain spattered against the window; water had lodged on the inner ledge of the window frame. It was very quiet except for the music and the rain. His eyes were closed as he listened to the music. Music had a strange effect on him: his face softened, his whole spirit responded to it.

"That's Mahler," he said, just when I expected him to say, "You can stay or you can go."

"I like songs that have words," I said to clarify my position. But his eyes were closed and I did not think that he heard me at all. The music still reminded me of birds, birds wheeling out of a bush and startling the mellow hush of a summer evening; crows above an old slate quarry at home, multiplied by their own shadows, screaming and cawing incessantly. I wondered about my father then, and felt that they would come again, that night.

"But this music has words," Eugene said unexpectedly. So he had heard me. "Words of a more perfect order; this music says things about people, people's lives, progress, wars, hunger, revolution . . . Music can express with as simple instruments as reeds the gray bodiless pain of living."

I thought he must be a little mad to talk like that, especially when I was worried about my father coming, and feeling very apart from him, I jumped up, on the excuse that I must look at the dinner. We had put on the rabbit.

It simmered very slowly and the white meat was falling away from the bone, gradually. I thickened the gravy with cornstarch, but it lumped a lot. Little beads of the starch floated on the surface.

'Twill have to do, I thought, as I went away to put some more powder on my face—the steam of the dinner had reddened my cheeks. When I came back to the room he was reading.

I sat opposite him and stared up at the circle of wrecked plaster—

the result of Anna's shot. I thought, When I leave here tomorrow it is this that I will remember, I will always remember it.

"I'll go tomorrow," I said suddenly. The yellow lamplight shone on his forehead and the reflection of a vase showed in the top part of his lenses. He had put on horn-rimmed glasses.

"Go?" he said, raising his eyes from the paper which rested on his knee. "Where will you go?"

"I might go to London."

"Do you want to?"

"No."

"Then why are you going?"

"What else can I do?"

"You can stay."

"That wouldn't be right," I said, pleased that it was he who suggested it and not me.

"Why not?"

"Because it would be throwing myself at you," I said. "I'll go away, and then when I'm gone you can write to me, and maybe I'll come back."

"Supposing I don't want you to go away, then what?" he asked.

"I wouldn't believe it," I said, and he raised his eyes to the ceiling in mild irritation. I kept thinking that he asked me to stay because he pitied me, or maybe he was lonely.

"Why do you want me to stay?" I asked.

"Because I like you. I've lived like a hermit for so long, I mean, sometimes I feel lonely." And he stopped himself suddenly, because he saw my eyes fill with tears.

"Caithleen," he said softly—he usually said Kate, or Katie— "Caithleen, stay," and he put out his hand for mine.

"I'll stay for a week or two," I said, and he kissed me and said how pleased he was.

We closed the shutters and had dinner. The rabbit meat and potatoes were crushed in the flour-thickened sauce, and the meal tasted very nice. He said that he would buy me a marriage ring, so that Anna and the neighbors would not bother me with questions.

"We can't actually get married, I'm not divorced and there is the child," he said as he looked away from me, toward the crooked ink on the graph paper of the barograph. I followed his gaze—the jagged ink line suggested to me the jagged lines of all our lives, and I said, to hide my disappointment, "I don't ever intend to get married, anyhow."

"We'll see," he said, and laughed, and then to cheer me up he told me all about his family.

He began—"My mother is a hypochondriac"—he seemed to have forgotten that I had met her—"and she married my father in those fortunate days when women's legs were covered in long skirts. I say fortunate because her legs are like matchsticks. They met going down Grafton Street. He was a visiting musician—tall, dark, foreign, on his way to buy a French-English dictionary—and very courteously he asked the lady if she could direct him to a bookshop. I"—he tapped his chest—"am the product of that accidental encounter."

I laughed and thought how odd that his mother should have charmed the stranger so quickly. He went on to tell me that his father had left them when he was about five. He remembered his father dimly as a man who came home from work with a fiddle and oranges; his mother had worked as a waitress to feed them both, and like nine-tenths of the human race, he had had a hard life and an unhappy childhood.

"Your turn," he said, making an elegant gesture in my direction.

Fragments of my childhood came to mind—eating bread and sugar on the stone step of the back kitchen, and drinking hot jelly which had been put aside to cool. Sometimes one word can recall a whole span of life.

I said, "Mama was in America when she was young, so she had American words for everything—'applesauce,' 'sweater,' 'greenhorn,' and 'dessert.'"

I thought of incidental things—of the tinker woman stealing Mama's good shoes from the back-kitchen window, and of Mama having to go to court to give evidence and later regretting it because the tinker woman got a month in jail; of the dog having fits; and of a hundred day-old chickens being killed once by a weasel. In talking of it I could see the place again, the fields, green and peaceful, rolling out from the solid cut-stone house; and in summertime, meadowsweet, creamy-white along the headlands, and Hickey humming, "How can you buy Killarney" as he sat like an emperor on the rusted mowing machine, swearing to me that dried cow dung was sold in the shops as tobacco. I watched the grease settle on the dinner plates, and still I sat there talking to Eugene as I had never talked before. He was a good listener. I did not tell him about Dada drinking.

We went to bed long after midnight. He limped upstairs while I followed behind with the Tilley lamp and wondered foolishly if I was likely to drop it and set fire to the turkey-red carpet.

"So we both need a father," he said. "We have a common bond."

He did not make love to me that night. We had talked too much, and anyhow, he was stiff from having been kicked.

"There's no hurry," I said.

He petted my stomach and we said warm, comforting things to lull each other to sleep.

15 On Monday afternoon Eugene's solicitor drove out from Dublin. We had a fire in the sitting room, as we were expecting him. He was an austere, red-haired man with sandy eyebrows and pale blue eyes.

"And you say these people assaulted Mr. Gaillard?" he asked.

"Yes. They did."

"Did you witness this?"

"No, I was under the bed."

"The bed?" He raised his eyebrows and looked at me with cold disapproval.

"She's getting it all garbled, she means the spare bed in my study," Eugene explained quickly. "She hid under it when they came, because she was afraid."

"Yes, a bed," I said annoyed with both of them.

"I see," the lawyer said coldly as he wrote something down.

"Are you married, Miss—ah . . . ?"

"No," I said, and caught Eugene smiling at me, as much as to say, You will be.

Then the solicitor asked me what was my father's Christian name and surname, and the names of the others and their proper addresses. I felt badly about being the cause of sending them solicitor's letters, but Eugene said that it had to be.

"It is just routine," the solicitor said. "We will warn them that they cannot come here again and molest Mr. Gaillard. You are quite certain that you are over twenty-one?"

"I am quite certain," I said, adopting his language.

Then he questioned Eugene, while I sat there looping and un-looping my hanky around my finger. Eugene had made notes of the whole scene which led up to their attacking him. He was very methodical like that.

I brought tea, and fresh scones with apple jelly and cream, but even that did not cheer the solicitor up. He talked to Eugene about trees.

He left shortly after four, and I waved to the moving motorcar, out of habit. It was getting dark and the air was full of those soft noises that come at evening—cows lowing, the trees rustling, the hens wandering around, crowing happily, availing themselves of the last few minutes before being shut up for the night.

"Well, that's that," Eugene said as we came back into the room, and he felt the teapot to see if the tea had gone cold.

"They won't trouble us again," he said, pouring a half-cup of strong tea.

"They'll trouble us always," I said. Recounting the whole incident had saddened me again.

"They'll have to accept it," he said; but two mornings later I had a wretched letter from my aunt.

> *Dear Caithleen,*
>
> *None of us has slept a wink since, nor eaten a morsel. We are out of our minds to know what's happening to you. If you have any pity in you, write to me and tell me what are you doing. I pray for you night and day! You know that you always have a welcome here, when you come back. Write by return and may God and His Blessed Mother watch over you and keep you pure and safe. Your father does nothing but cry. Write to him.*
>
> *Your Aunt Molly*

"Don't answer it," Eugene said. "Do nothing."

"But I can't leave them worrying like that."

"Look," he said, "this sentimentality will get you nowhere; once you make a decision, you must stick to it. You've got to be hard on people, you've got to be hard on yourself."

It was early morning and we had vowed never to begin an argument before lunch. In the mornings he was usually testy, and he liked to walk alone for an hour or two before talking to me.

"It's cruel," I said.

"Yes," he said. "Kicking me with hobnailed boots is cruel. If you write to them," he warned, "they will come here, and this time I leave you to deal with them." His mouth was bitter, but that did not stop me from loving him.

"All right," I said, and I went away to think about it. Out in the woods everything was damp; the trees dripped and brooded, the house brooded, the brown mountain hung above me, deep in sullen recollection. It was a lonely place.

In the end I did nothing but have a cry, and by afternoon he was in better humor.

That night he said, "We're going into town tomorrow." And taking a spare wallet from a drawer, he put notes in it and gave it to me. His initials were in gold on the beige-colored leather, and he said it had been a present from someone.

"We'll buy you a ring and one or two other things," he said; and then as he had his back to me, hefting a big log onto the fire, I peered into the wallet and counted the number of notes he had given me. There were twenty in all.

Next day, walking down Grafton Street in a bitter wind, I felt as if people were going to accuse me of my sin in public.

"Bang, bang," he said, shooting our imaginary enemies, but I was still afraid, and glad to escape into a jeweler's shop.

We bought a wide gold ring and he put it on me in the shop— "With this expensive ring, I thee bed," he said, and I gave a little shiver and laughed.

We bought groceries and wine and two paperback novels and some notepaper. I asked him in the bookshop if he was very rich.

"Not very," he said. "The money is nearly gone, but I'll get your dowry or I'll work . . ." There was some talk about his going to South America in the spring to do a documentary film on irrigation for a chemical company. And already I worried about whether he would bring me or not.

He had a haircut in a place that was attached to a hotel. He left me in the lounge, sipping a whiskey-and-soda, but the minute he was out of sight I gulped the drink down and fled to the cloakroom in case anyone should recognize me. I washed my hands a few times and put on more makeup, and each time I washed my hands the attendant rushed over with a clean towel for me. I suppose she thought that I was mad, washing my hands so often, but it passed the time. My ring shone beautifully after washing and I could see myself in it when I brought my hand close to my face.

I must stop biting my nails, I thought as I pressed the cuticles back, and remembered the time when I was young and bit my nails and thought foolishly that once I became seventeen I would grow up quite suddenly and be a lady and have long, painted nails and no problems. I gave the gray-haired attendant five shillings, and she got very flustered and asked if I wanted change.

"It's all right," I said. "I got married today." I had to say it to someone. She shook my hand and tears filled her kind eyes as she wished me a long life of happiness. I cried a bit myself, to keep her company. She was motherly; I longed to stay there and tell her the truth and have her assurances that I had done the right thing, but that would have been ridiculous, so I came away.

Fortunately, I was back in the lounge, sitting in one of the armchairs, when I saw him return. Even after such a short absence as that, I thought when I saw him, How beautiful he is with his olive skin and his prominent jawbone.

"That's done," he said as he bent down and brushed his cheek against mine. He had had a shave, too.

I had put on a lot of perfume and he said how opulent I smelled. Then, as a celebration, we crossed the hall to the empty dining room and we were the first to be served dinner that night. He ordered a half bottle of champagne, but when the waiter brought it in a tub of ice, it looked so miserable that he sent it back again and got a full bottle. I asked to be given the cork and I still have it. It is the only possession I have which I regard as mine, that cork with its round silver top.

We touched glasses and he said, "To us," and I drank, hoping that I would stay young always.

That night was pleasant. His face looked young and boyish because of the haircut, and I had a new black dress, bought with the money he gave me. In certain lights and at certain moments, most women look beautiful—that light and that moment were mine, and in the wall mirror I saw myself, fleetingly beautiful.

"I could eat you," he said, "like an ice cream," and later when we were home in bed, he resaid it, as he turned to make love to me. He twisted the wedding ring round and round my finger.

"It's a bit big for you, we'll get a clip on it," he said.

" 'Twill do," I said, being lazy and feeling mellow just then from champagne and the reassurance of his voice in my ear, as he smelled the warm scent of my hair.

"That ring has to last you a long time," he said.

"How long?"

"As long as you keep your girlish laughter."

I noticed with momentary regret that he never used dangerous words like "forever and ever."

"Knock, knock, let me in," he said, coaxing his way gently into my body.

"I am not afraid, I am not afraid," I said. For days he had told me to say this to myself, to persuade myself that I was not afraid. The first thrust pained, but the pain inspired me, and I lay there astonished with myself, as I licked his bare shoulder.

I let out a moan, but he kissed it silent and I lay quiet, caressing his buttocks with the soles of my feet. It was very strange, being part of something so odd, so comic: and then I thought of how Baba and I used to hint about this particular situation and wonder about it and be appalled by our own curiosity. I thought of Baba and Martha and my aunt and all the people who regarded me as a child, and I knew that I had now passed—inescapably—into womanhood.

I felt no pleasure, just some strange satisfaction that I had done what I was born to do. My mind dwelt on foolish, incidental things. I thought to myself, So this is it; the secret I dreaded, and longed for . . . All the perfume, and sighs, and purple brassieres, and curling pins in bed, and gin-and-it, and necklaces had all been for this. I saw it as something comic and beautiful. The growing excitement of his body enthralled me—like the rhythm of the sea. So did the love words that he whispered to me. Little moans and kisses, kisses and little cries that he put into my body, until at last he expired on me and washed me with his love.

Then it was quiet; such quietness; quietness and softness and the tender limp thing like a wet flower between my legs. And all the time the moon shining in on the old brown carpet. We had not bothered to draw the curtains.

He lay still, holding me in his arms; then tears slowly filled my

eyes and ran down my cheeks, and I moved my face sideways so that
he should not mistake the tears because he had been so happy.

"You're a ruined woman now," he said, after some time. His
voice seemed to come from a great distance, because in hearing his
half-articulated words of love I had forgotten that his speaking voice
was so crisp.

"Ruined!" I said, re-echoing his words with a queer thrill.

I felt different from Baba now and from every other girl I knew.
I wondered if Baba had experienced this, and if she had been afraid,
or if she had liked it. I thought of Mama and of how she used to blow
on hot soup before she gave it to me, and of the rubber bands she put
inside the turndown of my ankle socks, to keep them from falling.

He moved over and lay on his back and I felt lonely without the
weight of his body. He lit a candle, and from it he lit himself a
cigarette.

"Well, a new incumbent, more responsibility, more trouble."

"I'm sorry for coming like this, without being asked," I said,
thinking that "incumbent" was an insulting word; I mixed it up with
"encumbrance."

"It's all right; I wouldn't throw a nice girl like you out of my
bed," he joked, and I wondered what he really thought of me. I was
not sophisticated and I couldn't talk very well or drive a car.

"I'll try and get sophisticated," I said. I would cut my hair, buy
tight skirts and a corset.

"I don't want you sophisticated," he said, "I just want to give
you nice babies."

"Babies—" I nearly died when he said that, and I sat up and said
anxiously, "But you said that we wouldn't have babies."

"Not now," he said, shocked by the sudden change in my voice.
Babies terrified me—I remembered the day Baba first told me about
breast feeding, and I felt sick again, just as I had done that day
walking across the field eating a packet of sherbet. I got sick then and
hid it with dock leaves while Baba finished the sherbet.

"Don't worry," he said, easing me back onto the bed, "don't worry
about things like that. It will come out all right in the end. Don't
think about it, this is your honeymoon."

"The bed is all tossed," I said, in an effort to get my mind onto something simple. But we were too comfortable to get up and rearrange it. He reached to the end of the bed for his shirt and his undershirt, which was inside it. I helped him put it on and kissed the hollow between his shoulder blades, recalling their apricot color in daylight.

"Are you hungry?" I asked, when he lay down. I was wide awake and wanted to prolong the happiness of the night.

"No, just sleepy." He yawned, and lay on the side nearest to me.

"I was a good girl," I said as he put his hand on my stomach.

"You were a marvelous girl."

"It's not so terrible."

"No more chat out of you," he said, "go to sleep." I could feel my stomach rising and falling gently under the weight of his hand.

"What's your diaphragm?" I asked.

"Meet you outside Jacob's at nine tomorrow night, Miss Potbelly." He was asleep almost as he spoke, and slowly his hand slid down off my stomach.

I did not expect to sleep, but somehow I did.

When I woke the room was bright and I saw him staring at me.

"Hello," I said, blinking because of the bright sunshine.

"Kate," he said, "you look so peaceful in your sleep. I've been looking at you for the past half hour. You're like a doll."

I moved my head over onto his pillow so that our faces were close together.

"Oh," I said with happiness, and stretched my feet. Our toes stuck out at the end of the tossed bed. He said that we ought to have another little moment before we got up and washed ourselves; and he made love to me very quickly that time, and it did not seem so strange anymore.

In the bathroom we washed together. We couldn't have a bath because the range had not been lit and the water was cold. It was freezing-cold water which came from a tank up in the woods and I gasped with the cold of it, and the pleasure of it, as he dabbed a wet sponge on my body.

"Don't, don't," I begged, but he said that it was good for the circulation.

He washed that part of himself without taking off his clothes again; he just rained the rubber tube that was fixed to the end of the cold tap on it, saying that it had had a monk's life.

"Have to make up for lost time," he said as I dabbed it dry with a clean towel and asked, unwisely, if he loved me.

"Lucky you don't snore," he said, "or I'd send you back."

"Do you love me?" I asked again.

"Ask me that in ten years' time, when I know you better," he said as he linked me down to breakfast and told Anna that we had got married.

"That's great news," she said, but I knew that she knew we were lying.

16 The days took on a pattern then. We slept until ten or eleven, got up and had a light breakfast. During breakfast Eugene read letters, and sometimes he read them aloud to me. They were mostly letters about his work, and it seemed certain now that he would have to go to South America for a few weeks, to make the picture on irrigation. There did not seem much chance that he would be able to take me.

"Anyhow, it won't be until April or May," he said, "so let's enjoy this lovely day and not worry about what's to come. This is life, this now, this moment of you and me eating boiled eggs."

After breakfast we usually went for a walk. It rained a lot up there, but we did not mind the rain. He showed me oak apples and badger holes, and things I had never noticed before. He loved being out, along the hedges, among the trees, watching the river.

"Look," he sometimes said, and I would turn, expecting to find a person, but it would be an animal, often a deer, or a shaft of intense green light between the trees. The sky forever changed color—slate-black, blue-black, blue, and white-green. He clowned to amuse me, becoming an old man by hunching his shoulders and letting his gloves dangle, so that the wagging fingers looked like those of a withered man.

We did some work on the farm—put stones back on a wall, mended a fence, drove cattle from one field to the next.

"It looks as if you're going to stay, Kate," he said, one day out on the hill.

"I'll stay a few more weeks," I said. I loved being with him and being in his bed, but I missed going to the pictures with Baba.

In the afternoons he worked at his desk, while I helped Anna to prepare dinner. We had stew and potatoes baked in wood ashes, and sometimes watercress soup. On Sundays we had wine with our meal, and cashew nuts and fruit on Thursdays, the day the groceries were delivered. He liked frugality and did not eat very much.

After dinner if he still wanted to work (he was preparing a short film for the BBC on spring in Ireland), Anna and I went for a walk, after she had put her baby to bed. She came to like those walks up the drive to the road, telling me loudly the secrets of her private life. Her cherished ambition was to become a cook in a big house, but she had met Denis at a dance and they spent their first night in a hedge. Much, much later of course.

" 'Tis all right for you, Mr. Gaillard talks to you," Anna said. Denis had only a kind word for the baby and the sheep dog; I used to notice him myself not answering her for days, as if he wanted to punish her. I liked her better than at first. She gave up talking about Laura. I'd bribed her with ten-shilling notes and odd nylons. She began a dress for me on the new sewing machine and was saving porridge package tops to get me a necklace. We had porridge every morning.

But on the evenings that Eugene did not work I sat in the study with him and rubbed his hair while we listened to records on the wireless. In rubbing his fine hair I kissed his neck to smell it, and we would embrace each other and eventually go up to bed. We undressed very quickly and made love in the dark room, between cool sheets with the owl crying in his usual tree outside. Later we got up again, washed, and had supper before going out for another walk.

I cannot describe the sweetness of those nights, because I was happy and did not notice many things. There always seemed to be a moon and that fresh smell that comes after rain. I'm told now that some men are strangers with a woman after they have loved her, but he was not like that.

"Love suits you," he often said, "makes you prettier."

I felt pretty; happy. We walked under trees, and down to the bottom of the wood to see the moon on the lake and on the curving stretch of river that flowed out from the lake to the distant sea. Once, we saw a whole troop of deer, but in that split second after they had seen us, as they were already running. A dead, shot deer drifted down from the upper reaches of the lake and Denis helped him to bring it home. We gave away a lot of the meat. It reminded me of long ago when they killed a pig at home and I carried plates of fresh pork to the houses of neighbors and was given sixpence or a shilling—but there was still a lot left for eating, and by the time it was finished, the smell of it remained in my mind, no matter where I went.

At night, the bog, as he called it, had a strange quality of time-lessness, as if the scrub oak and rushes and little half-grown birches had never been trod on. He got no turf from it; it was just a sanctuary for pheasants and the gray deer. One night we came on the afterbirth of a deer and we looked at it for a long time, under the moon, as if it were something of great importance. It may have been, to him.

After about a month, Baba came unexpectedly, and brought the Body with her. They blew the horn so much as they drove up the avenue that we thought it was the police coming to take me away. It was only Baba, in the Body's battered blue van, which smelled of greyhounds. The Body opened the back door of the van to let Baba out (the side door was permanently broken), and a flock of greyhounds tumbled out with her and set off down the field to chase the cattle.

"Who is that?" Eugene said. We were in the front room having tea.

"The Body," I said, and my heart sank, knowing that the meeting between them would be awkward.

Baba climbed the steps—wearing a green jacket which I had left behind at Joanna's—and the Body came in, full of welcome for himself. He took a whiskey bottle off the sideboard and proceeded to drink from it. It was cow's urine, which Eugene was to take to the veterinary surgeon later in the day. After the first taste, the Body threw the bottle down, and went over to the fireplace to spit out what was in his mouth.

"Eugene!" Baba said, embracing him. That helped a bit, because he liked Baba.

The Body looked at me quizzically and said, "What have you done to yourself? You don't look the same anymore." He frowned, trying to puzzle out what it was about me that had changed, and I thought slyly, Being in bed and being made love to has altered my face, but in fact it was that I looked tamer because Eugene had asked me to make up more discreetly. He bought me paler powder and narrow black velvet ribbons for my hair and a pair of flat, laced shoes which I saw Baba eyeing at that very minute. He had showed me diagrams of ruined feet, but I still wore high heels when I was going out.

"I know you well," the Body said to him. "I often saw you around town and took you for a Yank."

I was afraid that Eugene might say something sharp such as "There are no Yanks nowadays," but he didn't; he offered the Body a chair, not a soft armchair, but a straight-backed chair. He had told me before that some of the armchairs were likely to come to pieces and not to encourage fat people to sit on them. Life with him carried many rules, which I resented slightly.

I got extra cups out of the sideboard and poured some tea, which was still hot.

"Well?" Baba said, looking at me for a full explanation of everything. "What happened?"

"I almost got kicked to death by a rabblement of drunken Irish farmers," Eugene said.

The Body winced, and I knew that he was saying to himself, What is Caithleen doing with a cynical bastard like that, but I could not explain to him that Eugene guarded me like a child, taught me things, gave me books to read, and gave pleasure to my body at night.

"Show us," Baba said, and Eugene pulled down his sock and showed her the scabs.

"That's a luscious scab, 'twould win a prize," she said, mocking a Dublin accent.

The Body picked at his tooth with a matchstick, and looked at me with a smile which asked, Are you happy?

The four greyhounds had come to the window, their moist black snouts pressed to the glass as they sniffed and moaned to be let in.

"Are these yours?" Eugene asked the Body.

"They're mine," the Body said proudly. And pointing to one of them he said, "She'll make a fortune one day, that little lady. Mick the Miller will only be trotting after her," but Eugene had never heard of Mick the Miller. I had grown up with a photograph of the greyhound pasted on a kitchen calendar. His childhood had not been like that: it was full of silences, and sheet music, and tripe, or sweetbreads for dinner, and his father bringing home oranges, until the time he left them.

The Body slugged the tea down, and told Eugene that he'd like to see the outhouses, and have a breath of air. With relief I saw them go, and heard the Body say, "Did you ever hear that one about the woman who took her son to Killarney and stayed in a big hotel—'Monty, Monty,' said she, 'open your mouth wide, we're paying for the air down here!'" He laughed at his own joke. I knew that his next joke would be the one about the Vice-President, and after that the incident of how he had been struck by a grandfather's clock in Limerick and had been obliged to break the clock.

"Well, Jesus, you're in a nice mess," Baba said to me.

"I'm not in any mess," I said, "I'm very happy."

"Are you fixed up yet?"

"Fixed up what?"

"Married, you eejit."

"That's my jacket you're wearing," I said, to get off the subject.

"This old rag," she said, holding a corner of it up to the light, "you could strain milk through it."

"Did you bring my clothes?" I had written to her to post me my clothes.

"What'n hell clothes are you talking about? There are no clothes of yours except a few dishcloths that Joanna gave to the rag man in exchange for the saddle of a bicycle. She said you owed a week's rent anyhow."

"Where's my bicycle?" I said. I had put it in a shed with a torn raincoat over it, to keep the mudguard from rusting.

"Old Gustav goes to work on it. You should see him! He'll break his bloody neck some morning; you'd know he was a foreigner the way he sits on that saddle, you'd know he didn't speak a decent word of English."

"It's my bicycle," I said.

"Are you preg?" she asked. "'Cos if you are, you won't be able to cycle. Your aul fella is writing to me every day to get you back."

"Is he coming?" My heart began to race again. I hadn't heard from him for over two weeks.

"You'll have to get a layette—lay it—if you're preg," she joked.

"Is my father coming?" I asked again.

"How would I know? I suppose he'll come some fine day when he's blotto and shoot the lot of you." She shot at the portrait of Eugene over the fire. "Blood and murder, and then he'll start singing—'I didn't know the gun was loaded and I'm *so* sorry, my friends; I didn't know the gun was loaded, and I'll never, never do it again.'" Baba hadn't changed a bit.

"What are you doing with yourself?" I asked in a piqued voice.

"I'm having a whale of a time," she told me. "Out every night. I was at an ice show last night. Terrif. The Body and I are going to a dinner dance tonight, and someone wanted to paint my picture last week. I met him at a party and he said I had the nicest profile he ever saw. So next day, as arranged, I went along to his den and he wanted the picture in the nude. 'Chrissake,' says I, 'what has your nude got to do with your profile?' He was in a pair of shorts whanging a dog whip about in his hand. God, you wouldn't see me running!" She looked around the room with its brown furniture and shelves of books. "How long are you staying in this bog?" she asked, and answered for me, "Till he gets tired of you, I suppose. You're a right-looking eejit in those flat shoes." She had her black high-heelers on.

"Have you a boy?" I asked. She made me restless.

"Oh, def. You can ask Joanna how many cars call now. I've got oodles of men, and John Ford is giving me a screen test this week."

"It's a lie," I said.

"Of course it's a lie," she said. "Give us another cup of tea; any grog in the house?"

There was a bottle of whiskey hidden in the gun bureau, but I did not want to open it, as it was not my house. When they came back, Eugene did not open it either, and they left soon after, disappointed, I suppose, because they weren't offered a drink. Before she left, Baba told me that she had heard from her mother that my father was coming to see me along with the bishop of the diocese. I didn't think that she was serious, but in fact she was.

Next day my father came. We were in the study, giving instructions to the local plasterer about doing the hole in the ceiling.

"My father, my father," I said as I saw the Ferret's car drive up to the hall door.

"Get back from the window," Eugene said.

"What's up?" the plasterer asked.

Then the knocker was pounded.

I ran down to tell Anna not to answer it, and we locked the back door.

The knocking resounded all over the waiting house; the dog barked and my heart beat rapidly, just as it had done the first night they came.

"Caithleen, Caithleen," my father's voice called plaintively through the letter box. I ran to the study and whispered to Eugene.

"If he's alone, maybe we should see him?" His voice calling my name had made me pity him.

Eugene had been looking through the binoculars to see who was in the car, and he whispered, "There's three others in the car, there's a bishop or something, I can see his purple dicky."

"Caithleen," my father called, and then he knocked steadily for about two minutes. It was a good thing we didn't have a doorbell or we would all have been deafened.

"I'll settle it," Eugene said, and he went out and put the chain on the hall door and then opened the door suddenly. It could only open a few inches, because of the chain.

"Anything you want to say to your daughter will have to come in writing to her."

"I want to see her," my father said.

I stood behind the study door, praying and gasping. The plasterer must have thought I was going to die. The cement was going hard on him, but he couldn't start work because Eugene had told him not to make a sound.

"Your daughter does not want to see you," Eugene said. The words sounded very cruel when put bluntly like that.

"I just want to have a chat with her. I have a friend of hers here, Bishop Jordon; he knows her since she was a child, he confirmed her. We won't lay a finger on her." I knew from the pitch of his voice that he was frightened and ashamed.

"Look, Mr. Brady," Eugene said, "I have written to you through my solicitors; I do not want you here and I do not want any

Monseigneurs meddling in my affairs. I thought that we had made that clear."

"We're not doing any harm," my father said in a desperate voice.

"You are trespassing on my property," Eugene said, and I wrung my hands in shame. "She's twenty-one years old and here of her own free will."

"You think you're very important," my father said, "but this is our country and you can't come along here and destroy people who've lived here for generations, don't think that . . ." But his voice faded, because suddenly Eugene shut the door.

Outside, my father knocked with his fists on the wood, but after a few minutes he went down the steps and then I saw the car driving off. He sat in the back and looked through the back window as they drove off.

That was Saturday afternoon, and for the rest of the evening I cried and disliked myself for having been so cruel to my father. I did not bother about my hair or my appearance, as I wanted to look awful so that Eugene would realize how wretched I felt.

"I'm in love and I'm miserable," I said aloud to myself. He overheard me and said, "Take two aspirins." I couldn't cry, or wash my hair, or talk to myself but he noticed it.

"Will you take me to Mass tomorrow?" I asked. I could feel the goodness going out of me, as I had not been to Mass for five weeks.

"Of course I'll take you to Mass," he said. He was very unpredictable like that; he would sometimes say yes when you expected him to say no.

"Of course I'll take you to Mass, you poor little pigeon," he said as he put his arm around me and patted my shoulder.

"You've got no shoulders," he said. I had sloping shoulders like Mama's, and they were very white and frail-looking.

We did not go to the local chapel because I knew that the priest would accost me on the way out, as he had written me three letters. We drove instead to a village eight or nine miles away. It was a new concrete chapel set on a treeless hill and there was a white notice board outside stating the extent of debt which the new church had entailed. Although it was a February morning, the sun shone, as it sometimes does in Ireland, to compensate for a whole week's rain. I left him in the sun, sitting on the low mossy wall opposite the chapel gate, reading the *New Statesman*. The inside of the chapel was cheerless, the brown plastered walls had not been painted, and there was scaffolding in one of the side aisles.

I had no prayer book, just the white beads that a nun gave me in the convent, so I tried hard to say a Rosary. The people distracted me— their coughing, their ill-fitting clothes, and that sour smell which comes from drying their faces with dirty towels. I could see Eugene's bright eyes mocking me, "Only egomaniacs see Christ as God come especially to save them. Christ is the emanation of goodness from all men"—and I lay my forehead on the new oak rest and thought of the time when I had a crush on a nun, and decided to be a nun, too, and another time, for a whole week, I had decided to be a saint and kept pebbles in my shoes as a penance, which is what we called "making an act."

The sermon was about Grace, and I came out from Mass wondering if I had spurned God's Grace once too often. For a minute I forgot that Eugene was waiting for me, and as he looked up from his *New Statesman* and said, "Did you have a nice Mass?" I realized with slight shock that he was waiting for me.

With the sun in my eyes, I said, "When I came out just now and saw you here, I forgot that you were waiting for me, isn't that funny?"

"No, it isn't funny," he said, and I thought with panic, I have insulted him and he'll be cold with me now for days.

"So, when you're in there, you become a convent girl again," he remarked. I thought of myself looking like a crow in black shoes and stockings and a serge gym frock which was never ironed properly, because Mama died before I went away to boarding school and I had to attend to my own uniform.

"I was never really a convent girl," I said, recalling the sky-blue Holy Picture on which Baba wrote the dirty thing that got us expelled from the convent.

"I don't know how you can do it," he said, remarking on my hypocrisy. "How can you live two lives? In there"—he nodded toward the concrete church—"you're deep in it with crucifixions and hell and bloody thorns. And here am I sitting on a wall, reading about atom bombs, and you say, 'Who am I?' For that matter"—he tapped my chin with his index finger—"who are you and what are you doing in my life?" He was laughing all the time, but I still did not like what he said. I hung my head, but he recognized the flashes of unhappiness in my face—the mouth drooping at the corners, the slight pout. He jumped over the wall, plucked a branch from a budding chestnut tree, and presented it to me with a deep bow.

"What unites men and women is not God or the *New Statesman*," he said, putting the sticky bud under my nose. Then he kissed my cheek, and we sat in and drove home.

"You won't brood for the rest of the day, will you, sweetling?" he said as we drove along between the rows of winter hedges. The sun shone, and old women and children—the ones who had been too old or too young to go to Mass—sat outside cottages and waved to us. The children were in their good clothes, and I remember the pink face and white hair of one albino girl who sat on a whitewashed pier, swinging her legs, wearing patent shoes with silver buckles on them. And I thought to myself, I'll never forget this moment because somehow it is very important to me, even though I don't know why, and I waved to the little pink girl, and said to Eugene, "No, I won't brood." But already I had begun to brood and relive the scene outside the chapel in my mind; and from afar I scented trouble and difficulties, but I could not arm myself against him, as I loved him too much.

"It's all right for you," I said helplessly, "you can think things out, but I'm different."

"We're all different," he said as he started to sing, "I wonder who's hating her now." It was a song he often sang, and I imagined that it was directed toward Laura. He sang to jolly things up, he said.

"I wouldn't get married," I said rashly, "unless I got married in a Catholic church."

"I'm glad you told me," he said, "I'll make a note of that," the merest hint of sarcasm in his rich voice. A rainbow was arched in the bottom of the sky and looped across the sunny hills. I counted its seven colors; behind it the sky was changing from blue to water-green and

I could feel my attitude to him changing, like the colors of the changing sky.

We gave a lift for part of the way to two young men who were making the journey to a youth hostel seventeen miles away. They sat in the back seat, whispering; and when I turned to speak to them, I was conscious only of their knees. They wore shorts and their thick knees were on a level with my face, because the back of the car was so small. They were about my age, and it occurred to me that I ought to be with them, walking from one village to the next, worrying about nothing more than the price of a cup of tea. But then I consoled myself with the thought that young men, with their big knees and their awkward voices, bored me.

17 When we got home Eugene's mother was there. She came to lunch most Sundays.

She had a little present for me—a hand-embroidered tray cloth. It was a wedding gift. We pretended that we were married, and anyhow, I wore a ring. We drank sherry, and then she sat in the sun until lunchtime.

During lunch a row broke out because I had put chopped onions in a sauce. She took the tray cloth back, saying that I must have put the onions in on purpose, knowing that they would make her bilious.

"I knew I could never trust a red-haired woman," she said to the water jug as we ate in silence. She had pushed her dinner plate away, and was calling the dog, "Shep, Shep."

Eugene winked at me, and I went on eating.

"Well, things have come down a lot here. Laura was an adventuress, but she knew how to entertain."

"Have some orange mousse," Eugene said, but she said that she couldn't trust that either.

"I'll have a piece of bread and butter if it's not too much trouble," she said; and ignoring the sarcasm, he got her some bread and then disappeared. He always fled from a row. I finished my dinner and got up as soon as I decently could.

He helped me to wash up. He peeped through the dining-room door and saw her eating the dinner, including the mousse, which she had so vehemently refused. No talk of poison now.

"Come here," he whispered, and I looked through the keyhole and saw her spooning the mousse from the bowl.

"I'll tell you a secret," he said when we were back in the pantry. "She'll see us all to our graves yet." And then he kissed me, and while I was in his arms the warm hum of love began again.

A car drove up as we were kissing and he slipped away to welcome two guests whom he had invited out from Dublin.

"I'll comb my hair first," I said, and I went up and put on a lot of makeup to compensate for my social inadequacies, because his friends terrified me. The man was a lecturer in history and wrote poems on Sundays, and he had a pudding of a wife who thought she knew everything. By coincidence a third guest came, another poet, Simon, an American, who had cycled over from Glencree, nearby. Eugene's mother wore an Indian shawl and sat in state on the velvet chair beside the fire, telling everyone that onions repeated on her.

Simon the poet said "Wow" when I was introduced to him, and stroked his reddish beard. I knew from Eugene that he had been a friend of Laura's, and I was frightened of him. He called all women cows—"a fat cow," "a thin cow," "a frigid cow," "a nice cow."

"Things went wrong with the food today," Eugene's mother said to the pudding wife, who sat opposite her, wearing green tweed trousers.

I went off to the kitchen to make some tea, and Simon came to help me. Standing in the middle of the flagged floor, his green close-together eyes looking on me, he said, "Well, here you are, shining quietly behind a bushel of Wicklow bran."

"You pinched that," I said to him, because I remember everything that I have read, "from James Joyce."

"Who the hell is James Joyce?" he said, and then asked how I got on with old Eugene and what we talked about and if he was good in bed.

Such impertinence, I thought, and remembered a proverb of Mama's—"By their friends you shall know them." I resented Eugene for knowing a man like this.

"Did you measure it?" the poet asked. He winked and looked at me in such a way that my stomach suddenly felt sick.

"What?"

"What! You ask me what! Wow, you need lessons. His *you*-know-what. All my women measure mine; it's great fun; you should try it."

I kept my head down so that he would not notice how I blushed, and I hated him, the way I hate people who tell me smutty stories which are not funny. He had sandy red in his beard, and a little Irish somewhere behind his American accent—though he claimed his people were blue-blooded English.

"Shall I butter these for you, Caithleen?" He pointed to the sliced currant cake.

"Do." He said my name too often and was affable and ugly alternately—as wicked people often are.

"How's old Eugene's work going? Any epics coming up? God, how he'd love to make *Moby Dick*, or something great."

"I don't think so," I said. Once, I asked Eugene if he had secret ambitions to make a famous picture, and he shook his head gravely and said, "No, not a famous one; I'd like to compile a long chronicle about the injustice and outrage done by one man to another throughout the ages, and of our perilous struggle for survival and self-protection—but who'd want to look at it?"

"You know what his big ambition is," Simon the poet scoffed. "To have a drink with someone in MGM."

"You're behind the times," I said, trembling with emotion, as I always tremble when I want to say something that is important. "He says that what matters is to have a conviction about your work; to do your duty according to your lights."

"Duty, har, har," Simon laughed, as if some laughing machine had been wound up inside him. "Laura would love that. Jesus, that's priceless; he's good on propaganda. Duty! God, Laura will love that when she comes."

"Comes?"

"Yeh. Hasn't she told you? She must be saving it up as a big surprise, because she's sailing for Cóbh next week. Now what about some lemon for my tea, Miss Caithleen Brady?"

"It's over there." I pointed to a bowl of fruit on the dresser. The lemon looked brown and wrinkled but I didn't mind; my legs were trembling because of what he'd told me.

"There'll be a hot time in the old bed when she arrives. Have you ever seen her? Wow!" And then he began to sing, "Do not forsake me, oh, my darling, on this our wedding day . . ."

I had seen a photo of her. She had short hair and a strong face. I'd looked at Eugene's pictures one day when he was out. He kept them in a locked box, but I found the key under one corner of the carpet where it was not tacked down. There were a lot of pictures of his daughter, and on the back of each one he had written details of

where the picture was taken and what the child had been doing—
"Elaine eating bread and jam in high chair," "Brown Dog sleeping in
Elaine's pram." They distressed me, and putting them away guiltily, I
wondered when the child's birthday was and if he sent her presents.

"Old Heathcliff is a bit gone on her still, you know, old hatreds
die hard," Simon the poet said, crashing in on my worried thoughts.

"The tea is made now," I said, desperate to escape from him.
Earlier on he had confided to me that he sucked birds' eggs, which gave
him a special virility. "Alone with nature and the little birds," he said
mockingly.

"The tea is made," I said again, and piled the last few things
onto the tray.

"Now, there's an efficient girl, that's what I like; an efficient girl
and cool. Wow cool! You've got a clever tear in your eye, Caithleen;
clever because it's not real. I am a poet and I know these things. After
you." And he carried the tray as I walked ahead of him, up the narrow
dark passage toward the dining room.

"You've got a nice little ass," he said, and as usual my high heel
caught in the rat hole along the wooden passage. (Once in a snowstorm
a rat had gnawed his way into the house, and Anna said that Laura
had stood on a chair and screamed, just as any woman would.)

"You brought the wrong cups," Eugene said when he saw me
unload the tray. They were kitchen cups.

"They'll do," I said, getting red.

"No, no, no. It's Sunday afternoon, we're entitled to nice cups,"
he said good-humoredly as he repiled the unmatching cups back on
the tray and carried it out.

"Well, what can you expect?" his mother said to the big log in
the fireplace. "Country girls. Fresh from the bogs."

Simon stroked his beard and looked from one to another of us.
The other couple sipped their port wine, and the woman smiled,
either sorry because of what had happened or to show her pleasure
over it.

"Sit down, dear," she said. I hate people who call me dear.

"Excuse me," I said, leaving the room. I got my coat and went
off to hide in the lady's garden.

For that hour I hated Eugene. I hated his strength, his pride, his self-assurance. I wished that he had some deep flaw in his nature which would weaken him for me; but he had no flaw (except his pride); he was a rock of strength. Then I remembered—as one does in a temper—the ugly side of his nature: of how cross he could be, of the day he shouted, "You're a mechanical idiot who can't even turn off a tap." He had been doing something with the water cistern up on the roof and he had explained that I was to turn the tap on and off when he said the words "On" and "Off." I turned it on all right, but when it came to turning it off, I got flustered and turned it on more, and then he shouted that he was being flooded, and I got quite helpless and could do nothing. His jibes and pinpricks leaped to memory— "Baba, when I have a harem you'll be in it," "I'm teaching Kate how to speak English before I take her into society," and "Run upstairs on your peasant legs." For that hour I hated him.

"I hate him," I said to the early birds who had come to make their nests. They did not so much sing as warble, and make noises to clear their throats, in preparation for their long song of beautiful courtship.

"Courtship," I said bitterly, and wondered who Baba was with, and if she still saw Tod Mead. I thought, or tried to think, of the various men I knew, all simple boys compared with Eugene. I remembered then a story he had told me of how he shared one room with another man somewhere in London and each washed his own half of the floor on Saturdays; and it seemed to me to be a cold, inhuman thing to do. I could not see myself washing half a floor without letting the cloth slide over to include the other half; but they were methodical, they had a line drawn across the center of the linoleumed floor. I thought of this and of Simon the poet saying to me, "How do you feel about breasts?" as he buttered slices of cake and took the foundations from under my life by telling me that Laura was coming back. His high-pitched laugh re-echoed in my mind, and I worried because Eugene knew such a person.

I stayed there moping and wishing that he would come for me. There were catkins on the sally tree, white as snow and hanging like tassels, and along the granite sundial there trailed a shoot of winter jasmine, its spare yellow flowers giving hope and brightness to the sad day. Eugene had said that wild thyme would grow there later on and that the garden would be filled with the bouquet of wild thyme. I wondered if I would be married by then.

"He'll never marry you," Baba had said, and I thought, It's true, because he's a dark horse. The good and the bad of him alternated in my thoughts, as I remembered first his scowling expression and his unyielding nature and then his tenderness—he brought me toast to bed once and put lanolin on a welt of mine, and got three pillows so that I could be propped up to read. For a while I welcomed the fact that one day I would be old and dried, and no man would torment my heart.

It got chilly once the sun went down. He came to look for me when the visitors had gone.

"Trying to make little of me in front of people," I said as he stood over me in the dusk, patting my hair and apologizing. The dark violet hush of evening had descended.

"I'm sorry," he said, "I didn't mean to offend you. I just thought that the cups looked awful and that Mother would complain and that we might as well get the better ones."

"Cups don't matter." I almost shouted it. "Cups are not important; you're always the one that's talking about inessentials—well, cups are inessentials."

"All right, all right," he said, patting me to keep me still.

"You shouldn't have done that to me in front of all those people." It maddened me to think that it happened in front of that wicked poet and the two women who would remember it, no doubt forever.

"You know no nice people, no sincere people," I said.

"My dear child," he replied, almost smugly, "there are no wholly nice people, there are no sincere people; I mean, a worm is probably sincere, if that's what you want."

I remembered how "sincere" had been Mama's criterion for everyone. "Lizzie is sincere," she said of some mean woman who asked us to tea and gave us sandwiches with tomato ketchup in them, and rhubarb. "They're sincere," Mama would say of mean cousins in Dublin who expected her to send them homemade butter for nothing, all during the war. It was how she judged people.

"And that Simon fellow, talking to me about intimate things . . ." I complained.

"Oh, I should have warned you—his male appendage, I gather, is rather small and some woman once laughed at him."

He looked up at the violet sky; the birds in the darkening trees singing their night songs, and the calmness in the air, seemed to give him such pleasure that he hardly heard what I was saying. He's happy, I thought, when his friends walk on me and say filthy things to me!

"He's a funny friend to have," I said.

"He's not a friend," Eugene corrected. "In this country there are so few people to talk to that one is thankful for any friendly enemy who can speak one's own language." He sighed at the dark sky as if he would like to ascend into its calm loneliness.

I broke in on this moment. "Simon says that Laura is sailing for Cóbh."

"Indeed!" he said, without any apparent surprise. "I'll be delighted to see her."

I got off the wooden seat and stared up into his calm, impassive face.

"You what?" I said.

"I'll be delighted to see her, we can discuss things; maybe I can get a divorce and marry you. We'll share the child." (He never said the little girl's name.) "Laura can come here and we'll all be good friends. You can wash her hair; she can wash yours . . ."

"You mean . . . ?" I began but did not go on. There was nothing I could say, because I was thinking, He's a prig, an indifferent, unfeeling prig. I let out some sound of despair.

"All right; I'll write to her about a divorce. I can see that not being married is injuring your immortal soul."

The words stung me. Something—everything—had struck the whole, laughing pleasure of my life.

. . .

That night while I sat by the fire reading the opening chapters of *Anna Karenina*, he typed out a letter to Laura. I longed to know if he had begun it with "Dear Laura," or "Dearest Laura," or "My darling," but I could not look over his shoulder.

We walked to the village to post the letter. The night felt warm and springlike; the fields on either side were damp with dew, and he did not link me.

Halfway along the dusty mountain road we found that they had begun to tar it, and the tar being fresh, our feet left marks on its blue-black surface.

"Cheers," he said, "we're going to have a tarred road." It was the first word he had spoken since we set out.

In a sad, doomed voice I said, "It's not fair, is it? We just can't be left alone."

My father had written three times, the local priest wrote, the head nun from the convent sent me prayers and medals, and now Laura would be coming.

"Nothing's fair, it's not a fair world," he said in a tired, dull voice.

In the village I heard piano music from the lounge of the one hotel, and it made me lonely for all the gay nights with Baba, hearing her say, "Down the hatch," to some man or other. When he had posted the letter I said, "I'd love to go into the hotel."

"You don't want to go in there." He frowned toward the yellow-sashed building with porter barrels outside, under the window.

"Just for one drink," I said, and though he sighed, he took off his cap and escorted me into the lounge bar. The place was crowded, the room thick with smoke and commotion. Someone was singing. They were mostly local people and they all stared at us. It was because we weren't married. He ordered two whiskies. The noise, which had subsided when we came in—while people nudged and whispered— began again and a fat woman continued to play the piano. They had painted the piano white, so that it looked like a washstand.

"Do you know any of these people?" I asked in a low voice. They had not saluted him. Anna had told me that they didn't like him, because he never got drunk or bought free drinks for them on fair days. Some of them drove cattle and sheep into his land at night, and in the morning Denis drove them out again. A herd of goats kept coming in, and he wrote several times to their owner, but she ignored the letters. He would not have minded if she had asked for permission, but like most people in the neighborhood, she was dour and unfriendly. Someone had cut the tops off hundreds of small trees in the new plantation shortly after I came there. It was regarded as a big disgrace for me to be there, and they used to question Anna, every Sunday, when she went to Mass.

"I know one or two of them," he said.

"So his nib's got rid of the American woman and now he has this young one," I heard one man tell another. I blushed and looked down at the glass-topped table.

"He forgot the soda," I said to Eugene as I stared at the yellow paper doilies under the cracked glass of the table. As I was not used to whiskey, it tasted awful without soda.

A drunk man came up just then and raised his cap and asked Eugene to sing.

"I can't sing," Eugene said, and the drunk man then asked if I would sing.

"We don't sing," Eugene said, and the drunk man hummed a few bars of "The Old Bog Road" and held his cap out, so that we could put money in it. I did not know what to do; I just felt the blood rising in my neck as I prayed that he would go away and leave us alone. Then suddenly he flicked my wool beret off, and it fell onto the table and overturned my drink.

"Come on," Eugene said, standing up. We went out quickly, and I heard people laugh, and the drunk calling, "Pagans, pagans."

"I'm sorry," I said when we got outside, "it was my fault; I didn't realize that it would be like that."

"Stone Age people," he said; but he wasn't angry with me, he linked me. Walking home, I said, " 'Twill be different tomorrow, I'll have cheered up again."

"It's funny," he said, "the difference between fantasy and reality. When I met you those first few times in Dublin by accident, I thought

339

to myself, Now there is a simple girl, gay as a bird, delighted when you pass her a second cake, busy all day and tired when she lies down at night. A simple, uncomplicated girl." He spoke mournfully, as if he were speaking of someone who had died.

"I'll be like that again," I said. But he shook his head sadly and I knew that he was thinking: It was all an illusion, it was the clear whites of your eyes, and your soft voice, and the chiffon scarf around your throat, which gave me the wrong impression. I'm sure he thought something like that, even though he may have put it in different words.

Simon the poet lost no time. Laura's first telegram came on Thursday. Eugene was out when it was delivered, and I opened it because he told me to always open telegrams. It said:

WELL EVERYBODY DESERVES A LITTLE FUN. ENJOY YOUR-
SELF. LAURA

I ran to look for him. Anna said that he had gone for a ramble and that maybe I'd find him on the mountain, helping Denis to bring the sheep down. The sheep were brought down to the fields near the house weeks before lambing time. I ran out of the house and through the woods to the wasteland which led to the mountain. I heard sheep long before I saw him.

"Is that you, Kate?" he called out as I hurried along a narrow track, and saw two figures, Denis's and his, herding the sheep. Denis had a lantern.

"That's me," I said in an angry voice, and when I was within a few yards of him, I told him about the telegram. Denis moved away, calling the dog and pretending not to hear me.

"So that's why you're gasping and blowing," he said, and grinned. I handed him the telegram, which I had crumpled, in my state of outrage.

"I think it's awful," I said. "The post office, everyone, has read it." Young gorse pricked my ankles and my stocking caught in a briar, but I didn't care.

"It's just a joke," he said. "You have no sense of humor. We'll have to give you one."

"Humor!" There was a narrow path between the thickets of gorse, but I kept wandering off it.

"There, there, there." He linked me, but I refused his arm. In the dusk the clumsy bodies of the sheep appeared to be tumbling down the hillside recklessly.

During dinner he read. Always during a coolness he read; he could read for days to avoid a scene.

Laura's letter came on Saturday. Her name was on the back of the pink envelope; his name, in fact—Mrs. Laura Gaillard. He did not show it to me, but in the afternoon, when he went out, I rooted among his papers and found it. I read:

Eugene my dear,

I haven't written for months. We're both fine and the weather is just marvelous. Well, of course Simon (he is an old woman) has written and told me everything, including some trivial little incident about wrong cups. I always said you had a feudal attitude to women! And since then, I've had your sweet letter in which you say, "I have met a girl; she is Irish and romantic and illogical," and I say, What is she doing with dat man of mine! Honestly I was bowled over. Don't fall off the chair or anything but you know we still have a sneaking attraction for one another which defies all the laws of gravity. Sometimes at night when I am in a perfectly empty room (Elly asleep in her bed) and I think, Gee-whiz, he's a wonderful man and he's funny and has talent and he loves me, I guess it is love. I have all your letters including the very first you wrote me after the night we met at Snope's party and it's signed "Heug." You remember how we used to play with each other's name? Heug for you, and Alura for me. Your letters are in my G file, and when I read them I realize how wise and subtle you are and how you once loved me. I'd let you see them, but you must promise to send them back.

The weather is fine—have I ever told you that the climate here is the most beautiful in the world? At night there is a sea mist (do you remember when we all swam naked that time down in Killarney, and you caught a chill?).

Elly is fine and I hate to tell you but she doesn't miss you. We play together for hours and have fun, and I envy her the lovely, secure childhood she is having. But she will know you, I'm sure, when you come.

At this point the paper began to tremble in my hand, and I read on feverishly.

When is this film scheduled for and are you going to South America first, or here first? Let me know by return, I want to have everything nice for you. I have painted the walls a powder blue and the ceiling dove gray. You'll adore it. I'm having an exhibition later on and I've just finished a darling picture which I think is it. It expresses everything I have to say about life, the soul, neuroses, love, and death . . .

Elly sleeps on her right side with her hand under her cheek, and she is a doll.

Love and kisses,

Laura

P.S. The thing that worries me is that Mom and Ricki and Jason and everyone think we were made for one another.

He did not have to ask what I had been doing when he came in. The letter was in my hand and my lips trembled.

"Oh no," he said, putting his hands to his eyes. "I'm so stupid, to leave a thing like that under your nose."

"It's terrible," I said wildly.

"You shouldn't have meddled in my affairs." He took off his cap and scratched his head in irritation.

"It's my affair."

"It has nothing to do with you," he said calmly. "I didn't intend you to read that letter and you had no right to do so."

I threw the letter down on the desk. "I'm glad I did. I now know what I've let myself in for. You going off to America to see her, and not even to tell me." If I had to bring all the bitterness and hatred of the world into my heart, I was going to make him take me; that's how I felt about it in that state of raw and ugly temper.

"So you know it all," he said. "Well, that's more than anybody else knows. Every time I look at you, you're crying about something. If it's not her"—he nodded toward the letter on the desk—"it's your father, and if it's not him, it's something else."

"Deceiving me," I said. It was all I could say.

"I beg your pardon," he said in a very cold and controlled voice, "am I to understand that my past life has deceived you?"

"No, not that," I tried to explain, "but the way you do things, you're so independent and you don't tell me anything."

"My God!" he sighed, and put his cap on. His angry eyes turned away. "So you want ownership, too, signed and sealed? One hour in bed shall be paid for by a life sentence?"

I lost my nerve and could not look at him. "It's just such a shock," I said in an appeasing voice now, because I had vowed to be good, and anyhow, I wanted him to take me with him.

"Will you take me with you?" I said, but he did not answer, so I said it again and touched his hand. He took his hand away to remove his cap, and threw it on the desk. It overturned an open bottle of ink, and in a flash I saw it flow onto the maroon carpet and heard him swear and grind his teeth.

"Will you take me with you?" I said, in a last effort to extort a promise from him.

"Oh, for Chrissake," he said, going over to soak up the ink with a sheet of blotting paper, "go away and postpone your scene until later on." It was as if he had flung me out of the room; I walked out quickly, went upstairs, and began to pack my clothes into a canvas travel bag—one of his.

I had not very many clothes, but still the bag was stuffed to capacity, and the zipper would not close. The straps of a slip and a brassiere stuck out, and my three pairs of shoes were on top. I had no money.

"Can I have a pound for my bus fare?" I said as I came downstairs and tapped lightly on the study door, which was ajar. He was on his knees, washing the ink stain out of the carpet.

"A pound for your bus fare?" He looked up and saw that I had my coat on, and then his eyes fell on the stuffed travel bag.

"I'll send you back your bag," I said, knowing that he was going to comment on it. "It's the best thing—to go away," I said, trying not to break down until I had left.

From the green cash box he took five pounds and handed them to me.

"One will do," I said, touched by this last-minute generosity.

"You'll want your bus fare back again, won't you?" he said, giving some sort of smile. Then he looked at the bag (the indecency of it, with underwear straps sticking out), and he said, "You'll give the wrong impression, you know, leaving in a disheveled state."

"I'm sorry," I said as he put his lips to mine to kiss me goodbye. I don't know why I said "I'm sorry," it's just that he had this marvelous faculty for being right and I always felt sorry, no matter whose fault it was.

"I'll drive you to the bus," he said; but of course by then he had kissed me and I was crying and we both knew that I would not leave at all. We put the bag down and we sat on the couch, while he told me in a concerned voice that I would have to grow up and learn to control my emotions. Discipline and control were the virtues he most lauded. These and frugality. In fact, the things I was most lacking in.

"We'll have a cup of tea. Did I ever tell you my daily motto?" he said, after he had talked to me about being patient.

I shook my head.

"When about to cement fourth wife under kitchen floor—pause, and make tea."

I wondered if he had told Laura that, after sitting on a chair and lecturing to her calmly about self-perfection and mind control and things like that. So often she crept into my thoughts, coming between me and what he said.

We made tea and ate fancy biscuits, and then went for a walk and saw the first snowdrop of the year. I felt very happy and elevated by all that he had said to me—I was going to be different—large and placid and strong.

That night, when he loved me and sank into me, I thought to myself, It is only with our bodies that we ever really forgive one another; the mind pretends to forgive, but it harbors and reremembers in moments of blackness. And even in loving him, I remembered our difficulties, the separated, different worlds that each came from; he controlled, full of bile and intolerance, knowing everyone, knowing everything—me swayed or frightened by every wind, light-headed, mad in one eye (as he said), bred in (as he said again) "Stone Age ignorance and religious savagery." I prayed to St. Jude, patron of hopeless cases.

18 Everything was all right for four or five weeks. He wrote to Laura about a divorce; I wrote to my aunt and said, to cheer her up, that I would be married very soon.

Buds like so many points of hope tipped the brown and black twigs—green buds, black buds, and silver-white buds that looked as if they should sing as they burst upon us, waiting. Lambs were born at all hours of day and night, and two lambs whose mothers died were brought in the house and made pets of by Anna. They were a nuisance.

Baba came one weekday morning (Sunday was her usual day for coming) just as I was picking daffodils down the avenue. I had conveyed Eugene up to the top of the road to open the various gates for him. He went to a cattle fair to buy calves, as we had extra milk now. There were a lot of daffodils in bloom on the grass verge at either side of the graveled avenue, and on the way back I gathered an armful to pass the time. Their roots were wet as if spittle had been smeared on them and they smelled slightly unpleasant, as daffodils do. Then I heard a car, looked through the trees, and seeing that it was a strange car, I ran back to the house to hide. I thought it might be my father, but in fact it was Baba.

"Baba, Baba!" I unlocked the door and ran to her. She wore a white mackintosh and a red beret.

"This is marvelous," I said, kissing her. I wished, though, that she hadn't found me without my makeup.

Her eyes were large and excited, the way they get when she has something important to tell. In the hall the two pet lambs ran up, making baa noises and pretending that they were frightened of her.

"Baa, baa," she said, chasing them, "it's like a bloody zoo!" Then she whispered, "I want to talk to you, it's urgent. Where's Chekhov?"

"He's out," I said, and we went into the study and I closed the door—Anna expected to be included in all conversations with visitors. I poured us some port into tumblers; the tumblers were dusty, but I did not want to go away and rinse them. Baba appeared to be very nervous.

"Are you cold?" I asked her. The ashes from the previous night's fire were still warm and the walls warm to the touch.

THE LONELY GIRL

"Brace yourself," she said, touching my glass with hers, "I have bad news." My heart started to thump because I thought it was a message from my father.

"I'm in trouble," she said.

"What kind?" said I, hopelessly.

"Jesus, there's only one kind."

"Oh no," I said, drawing back from her as if she had just insulted me. "How could you?"

"Listen to who's talking," she said. "What the hell are you doing?"

"But you can't," I said, in a panic. "You're not even living with anyone."

"Can't! It's the simplest bloody thing, I mean it's simpler than owning two coats or getting asked to a party."

"Oh, Baba," I said, holding her hand.

"Give me a fag," she said abruptly. She hated pity and that slop of holding her hand.

While I rooted on Eugene's desk, she filled out two more drinks. "Don't," I said, "he'll miss it."

"What? You're not in a bloody monastery." And then she put the tipped cigarette in her mouth wrongways. We sat down and tried to decide what she should do.

"Whose is it?" I asked, but she wouldn't tell. She said that he was a married man and he worried in case his wife might get to hear of it. I felt certain that it must be Tod Mead. She said that the man had taken it very casually and said goodbye to her on the upstairs of a bus the day before. "See you around" were his parting words to her.

"I can go to England or I can come here," she said. The "come here" made me speechless for a moment. I foresaw a situation where she'd be in our bed and ordering me to get up and cook breakfast. And I did not want a baby in the house. I dreaded babies.

"Can't you do something?" I said.

"Do something!" she shouted. "It's morbid. I've done every bloody thing, took glauber's salt, and dug the garden, and I did so much waxing in that dump that Joanna got rid of the charwoman on the strength of it . . ."

I almost said, "It's an ill wind . . ." as I thought of Joanna's

347

half-blind joy at finding Baba on her knees waxing. But Baba was too worried for me to say anything; her teeth chattered, and I sat there consoling her until Eugene came.

"It's morbid," she kept saying, "everything's morbid. Someone filled me up with gin in a basement in Baggot Street. 'Baba, you're a noble woman,' he said, standing there in his he-man's string vest, and I hadn't the heart to tell him that I'd rather go home. That's me," she murmured, "the loser in the end."

I advised that she go to England. She had received three hundred pounds from an insurance policy when she was twenty-one and her parents should be made to give it to her.

But when Eugene heard about it he said that if nothing fortuitous happened, Baba might have to come to us.

"We'll have a harem," he said, joking her, and she cheered up enormously and began to give me impertinence. I wasn't a bit sorry for her, as she sat there in a brown kimono dress with her legs painted tan and her ankles crossed.

"Do you still shave?" she said to me.

"I never shaved. How dare you!"

"Who are you tellin'?"—and she peered closely at my chin. Once in an emergency, when we had no tweezers, she had bitten two short black hairs off my chin with her sharp teeth.

We had lunch, and though she had complained earlier of morning sickness, she ate like a horse. Then Eugene said that as it was a historic day, he would take photos of us, so we brushed our hair and went out to the lady's garden with him, and waited for the sun to reappear. Baba stood on a stone to be as tall as me.

"This place would give me the creeps," she said, looking around the cluttered garden, with one shrub thrusting its way between two others, dew still on the grass, and the young rose leaves opening, wine-color. Only the daffodils were in bloom.

"Cheese," Baba said as he took the picture, and I still have that picture and look at it in a puzzled way, because I had no idea when he took it that my life would undergo such a sudden twist.

Driving Baba to catch the evening bus back for Dublin, Eugene assured her that she could come to us if the worst came to the worst and she was at her wits' end.

"We'll help you," I said, trying to have a share in his kindness.

"Yes," she said to me, "you were always good at bringing oranges to sick people in hospital."

He helped her into the bus with as much solicitude as if she were an old woman, and it occurred to me that if I had a baby he would probably marry me.

"Poor Baba," he said, "the poor old bitch," as we waved to the moving bus and shut our eyes because of the dust it scattered. I did not feel for her in the way that he did—women care mostly for themselves or for their children, who are extensions of themselves, or for their husbands, who fill their days and their thoughts and their bodies: as he filled mine. Though he was not my husband.

I hoped that we would be married soon, and I was saving up for a trousseau.

"Something old, something new, something borrowed, and something blue," I used to say as I put ten shillings away each week, in a box.

We went home, and in a day or two I forgot about Baba, except to worry vaguely about her coming to live with us. It was rainy, lilac, April weather—sun and squally showers, and then a wind rose to dry the rain off the hedges and blow the white apple blossoms all about, so that it appeared to be snowing flowers. There were two or three weeks of happiness—I helped him mow the lawn, and the cut grass clung to the soles of my canvas shoes and we could smell it in bed when we had the window open.

One day, as Anna sharpened knives on the stone steps and sang "How much is that doggie in the window?" we carried two basins out of doors and he washed my hair and rinsed it with rainwater. Afterward he took photos of me with my wet hair (to finish out the film), and one of Anna sharpening the knives. A heavy shower began to fall; then we went upstairs; he tied my damp hair in a knot so that he would not get entangled in it, and he made love to me, while the rain refreshed the garden. We could smell the rain, cut grass, and primroses, and I said, "What will Anna think of us?"

"She'll think we're going the pace," he said. And rivers of love flowed into me, through him, carrying long-drawn-out ripples of pleasure which made me cry back to him and, in crying, worry that Anna might burst into the room with a batch of ironing, as the door did not lock.

"All those little seeds we let go to waste," he said tenderly to me, and I made some vague reply about having a baby next year. It must have been while we lay there talking that the postman came on his pop-pop bicycle and delivered two telegrams. One was for me and one for him.

Mine was from Baba and it said:

CHEERS THE CURSE CAME. GOING TO ENGLAND SOON.

and I wished that she had worded it more discreetly, as I could not show it to him.

"It's only from Baba," I said as I looked and saw his face whiten and his thin lips pressed together in anger. Leaning over, I read his telegram:

IF YOU MARRY HER YOU WILL NEVER SEE ELAINE OR ME AGAIN. I PROMISE YOU. LAURA

(Another installment for the village to read.)

"It doesn't matter," I said as I looked at him and feared, and also knew, that something dreadful was coming to wrench us apart.

"It doesn't matter; don't worry," I kept saying, and I wanted him to come and sit in the room while I made some tea, but he said that he would go out for a while. I watched him go down to the front field with his head lowered, the dog following close behind, brushing his trouser leg with her fluffy white tail. And I thought, He's making a choice between me and them, and I wished that I could have a baby in some easy, miraculous way.

He came back later, with a bunch of red and white hawthorn in his arms, and I smelled its sickly-sweet smell and said, "Don't bring it in the house, it's unlucky."

But he scorned my remark and put it in a big vase on the hall table.

We were kind to one another for that day and the next, and I did not barge in on his thoughts or ask what he intended to do in relation to Laura.

His face looked haggard and the lines around his eyes seemed to grow deeper. Neither of us slept well. Nothing is as aggravating as lack of sleep, and by the fourth day we were edgy with each other and he complained about inessential things, like the towels in the bathroom or the worn dish mop. He worked at his desk, preparing for this picture on irrigation. He had maps and encyclopedias spread out on his desk, and I carried his meals in on a tray. Seeing him there working and looking at me guardedly, I imagined that he was planning to go to Brazil without me; and each time I had to run from the study to stop myself from saying something foolish.

In the evening he listened to music and sat very still. Obviously he was thinking that this was a problem only because I made it so. He gave me the impression that he was sad, not only because Laura had blackmailed him, but because I had allowed it to affect our relationship. Gloom spread over the house as the mountain mist spread over the fields in the wet evenings, and I felt that I had never known him. He was a stranger, a mad martyr nailed to his chair, thinking and sighing and smoking.

On Thursday I had a letter from Baba saying that she would come out on Sunday to say goodbye. She was no longer pregnant. Her prayers had been heard! But she had made up her mind to go to England anyhow.

"I'm leaving this curse of a country, so you can have a few fivers ready for me on Sunday," the note said, and I thought of the night the Body was flashing twenty-pound notes in the Gresham Hotel, and he bought the biggest bottle of brandy that I had ever seen and tied it around his neck, so that he'd be like a St. Bernard dog.

Just as I finished reading her letter, a lorry drove up which seemed to be full of telegraph poles and men in blue overalls. One of the men knocked on the door to tell me that he had come to install a telephone. Ever since the electricity had been put in, in February, we had been trying to get a telephone. I called Eugene and we decided where we would have it—in the hall.

"Won't it be marvelous," I said, carrying away the vase of hawthorn, which had shed most of its petals onto the carpet. Two men worked in the hall, and two others were outside putting a post in the front field.

"It will spoil the view," he said as we looked through the window at the men working, and at the daffodils, some of which had lodged in a yellow sea from the night's windy rain. I made tea for the men, and watched them work, and longed for the moment when the telephone would be connected and I could ring the grocer or someone.

In the afternoon, just as I sat down to read, Simon the poet drove up in an old-fashioned Austin car. There was a girl with him, a tall American girl called Mary. I brought them in to the sitting room and called Eugene.

"What a beautiful place," she said. She spoke in a quiet accent, not at all like the American cousins of Mama's who came one summer and shouted and boasted for a full four hours.

"Simon's been telling me about you," she said to Eugene. "I think it's wonderful that you should come out here and bury yourself in this haven. So many smart men go to pieces nowadays that it's nice to see someone getting away from it all."

"The Irish nearly had me in pieces," he joked, and I hated him for bringing up the subject so unnecessarily.

"The Irish nearly crucified him," Simon the poet said, sneering. "Was it hatchets or penknives?"

"Hobnailed boots," Eugene said.

"Boy, you were darned lucky they didn't cut the balls out of you," Simon said.

The tall girl shook her head at me, disclaiming all responsibility for what they said. She had long brown hair that looked as if she brushed it night and morning, and she wore black trousers with silver threads running through the black. Her body was neat and well-shaped.

"Wait until the Pope is in Galway," Simon said to her. "You know that one about the cardinal fainting?"—and she shook her brown hair and asked eagerly that he tell her.

"The last time the Virgin Mary appeared at Knock she revealed that the next Pope would be tortured. Upon hearing this Cardinal Spellman fainted. Ha. Ha." He had this funny mechanical laugh, and she joined him in it, and said, "What fun."

"Do you have a comb? I feel as if I'm wild or something," she said to me, touching the curled ends of her thick hair. I took her upstairs. I couldn't tell her age but guessed that she was about twenty-two—like me. She knew a lot more than me, though. In the bedroom she admired a Renoir print of a girl tying her shoe, and the view of pine trees through the back window, which reminded her of her own New England. She began to describe the place where she grew up, and I could have sworn that it was a description she had learned out of a book; it was all too pat, those bits about "pines thrusting into the sky."

"I'm afraid my comb isn't too clean," I said. It was a white comb, which showed up the slightest trace of dirt between the teeth.

"It's fine." She smiled at it and drew the comb through her hair and smiled at her image in the mirror. I asked some stupid questions. "Do you like Ireland? Do you like America? Do you like clothes?"

"Sure. I like Ireland and America and clothes." She grinned as she tucked the pink seersucker shirt she wore down inside her slacks. "I like sweaters best." I imagined her wardrobe full of clean shirts on hangers, and rows of different belts that matched different sweaters. She drew up one leg of her trousers to scratch a midge bite that was swelling on her calf. Her legs were hairy, but since she had trousers on, one would not see that. She wore flat shoes and I felt that everything about her was calculated to appeal to Eugene.

I was going to say to her then, "I'm a bit nervous and unsure, don't hurt me," but I saw her redo her lips carefully with a little camel's-hair brush and revive the pink of her mouth. It came to me that she was hard and clever.

"I've never used a lip brush," I said. "Is it very difficult?"

"It's simple. I'll leave you this one," she said, "you can practice." And she left the gilt case containing the brush on top of a powder bowl. Then we went down and she was smiling and pleased with everything she saw, even the "nice cobwebs" in the corners of the dark wallpaper along the landing.

"I simply adore this place—the view!" she said to Eugene in the sitting room, looking upon him with straight gray eyes.

"Come here," he said, and he crooked his finger and she followed across to the french window to look at the valley of birches in the distance, which was now a blur of lime-green instead of purple. He opened the window a little and she put out her hand in a flutterlike movement, as if she were a white bird about to fly.

She astonished him by saying that she had seen a "darling film" of his at the National Film Theatre in London. She talked animatedly for a few minutes, and then, looking around the shabby high-ceilinged room, she said, "It's got great charm, this house." I glanced about the room which he had made, and realized that I had contributed nothing to it—not even a cushion. I went off to make some tea.

When I came back he was playing records for them—that classical stuff that reminds me of birds—and she stood by the window marveling at everything and moving her body to keep time with the music. He came across the room to take the tray from me, and smiled as I had not seen him smile for several days.

"So you're getting a telephone, Caithleen," Simon the poet said to me. "You can telephone all your friends."

"Yes, I can," I said. I had only two friends: Baba and the Body, and neither of them had a telephone.

Eugene poured the tea and passed Mary the first cup. Then he came around with the sugar bowl, and standing over me he said, "Do you take sugar?"

"Sugar?" I repeated sharply as if he had just said, "Do you take arsenic?" and shook my head and glared at him, and said, "No, I don't take sugar."

At any other time I would not have minded, but that day I was more touchy than usual.

"Oh, you don't take sugar, of course, I was thinking of somebody else," he said, and grinned as he moved on to hold the sugar bowl for Simon.

"Watch it," Simon said, and winked at Mary. She asked me some polite questions, such as did I think sugar was fattening?

"How's New York?" Eugene asked tenderly, as if it were some girl he inquired after.

"New York, that awful place," she joked, "I'm never going back there. I like Europe. There's a much greater intellectual ferment here. All you painters and writers and artists are more embodied into your society. I mean, I met a bus conductor the other day who'd read James Joyce. Do you like New York?"

"In a way"—he wrinkled his face—"I suppose I do. I hate it, but I like it also; some of my soul is there. Let's say I spent a lot of money in Brooks Brothers."

They laughed, but I didn't understand the joke.

"Me too—I never carry more than twenty thousand dollars in cash," said Simon the poet.

I felt very lonely and did not want to be with them. Eugene and I were all right alone, but when anyone else came I lost him to them, even to the poultry instructress with her knitted stockings. I had nothing to talk about really, except things about my childhood, and he had heard all of that.

"Have you been to America?" Mary asked me.

"Not yet," I said, "but I hope to, next year."

"Over my dead body," Eugene said. "I like that old song about stay as sweet as you are."

Mary told him that he must let a girl travel and that he mustn't be unkind to women because there was a rumpus about it now. They had a moment of teasing each other and he ended it by saying, "Would you like to step outside, please?" as she hit him playfully with the knitted tea cozy.

She looked tall and pretty as she stood there near the window, with her back to the brown shutter. Eugene looked at her and said to Simon, "She's so like 'your woman' that I can't get over it," and Simon laughed and said that they must both have had the same vitamins.

"They got a system now to grow them like that," Simon said, and grinned, and I knew that they meant that Mary was like Laura. I felt a lump rise in my throat to choke me, and the pain which precedes tears. I got to the door, muttering something about fresh tea, and was gone before anyone really noticed.

I went to my secret seat in the lady's garden where I sometimes had a cry. So she was like Laura! Laura was like that—bright, talkative, throwing tea cozies with charm and not knocking anything over, the way I would. Every second of it came to mind, the way he smiled at her and brought her to the window to see the view, the wonder in her voice, the man's wristwatch outside her sleeve. (Hadn't Anna told me that Laura wore a man's wristwatch, too?)

I cried and felt wretched and swore at everything for being so cruel. It was such a shock to me to know that he could love me at night and yet seem to become a stranger in daytime and say to me, "Do you take sugar?"

Up to then I thought that being one with him in bed meant being one with him in life, but I knew now that I was mistaken, and that lovers are strangers in between times.

So she was like Laura—tall and long-legged. If Laura came back, it would be like that; or if he went to Brazil and dropped off on the way to see her. It would be like that, only much worse, because there was also his child, the little girl whom he had framed a picture of, the day before, and hung in the bathroom, saying, "I hope this doesn't affect you anymore."

I cried insanely and walked around, chewing a stalk of grass to calm my temper. And he brought up the whole thing about my relations again. He always did, causing me to suffer over their red faces and their blundering stubborn ways. When he ridiculed them I felt sick and doomed, knowing that one day he would leave me because of them. I foresaw it all in one of those violent flashes of self-illumination which come to us after whole years of complacency, and still crying and chewing that same stalk of tough grass, I came back and peeped in through the side of the sitting-room window. What I saw filled me with panic. They were talking, laughing. Mary had her feet curled up under her on the sofa, her shoes some distance away on the rug. To me there is something marvelously dangerous and frank about a woman who takes off her shoes in company—it's almost like taking off her clothes. I can't do it.

They were drinking whiskey and he seemed to be telling them some story, because they laughed a lot, and Mary put her hand to her side, seemingly begging him to stop telling her such funny things, because she had a stitch there. Simon sat on the rocking chair, rocking and laughing. No one missed me.

I went away and cried more and crushed a harmless flower between my fingers, and thought of Laura's letters to him and wondered how he replied to them. I could see the telegram, too, the exact wording of it—"If you marry her you will never see Elaine or me again. I promise you"—and farther down a sticker which said, "Send your reply by Western Union." I had no idea if he had replied, or not. He always did things without telling me.

It would be better for me to go in and talk to them as if nothing had happened, or else to pack my clothes and leave him, but I did neither. When I came and peeped through the window a second time, I saw that he had lit the fire and the tall shadows of flames leaped on the pink wall. The room looked enchanting, as rooms do in that twilight time, when people are eating and talking and drinking whiskey. With all my heart I wished that I could go in and say something casual or funny, something that would no longer mark me as an outsider.

Instead, I went in by a side door and up to my room to powder my face. They did not leave for another hour and a half.

"I'll just see if she's here," I heard Eugene say downstairs. He called my name. "Kate, Kate, Katie." And then he whistled. I did not answer. Finally I heard their car door bang and the engine start up. At last they were gone.

He came into the house calling me and went to the kitchen to ask Anna, "I wonder where Caithleen is?"

She must have nodded to the bedroom, because he came up at once. My heart leaped with anger and relief as I heard him climb the stairs, whistling, "I wonder who's kissing her now . . ." It was almost dark and I lay on top of the bed with a rug over me.

"Having a little rest?" he said as he came into the room. I did not answer, so he came around to my side, and bending down he said, "Are you in one of your emotional states?"

"I am," I said tersely.

"What the hell is wrong with you?" he said suddenly, in a grievous tone. It surprised me, because I had expected him to coax me for longer.

"You just make little of me and ignore me," I said.

"Make little of you because I have a pleasurable time. Am I to stop talking to people because you haven't learned to speak yet? If you can't accommodate yourself to seeing me being amused by other human beings, we'd better just both go home right now," he said rapidly.

"You should never have made me come here," I said.

"You came. I didn't make you, any more than I invited the posse of relations who came after you."

He was too articulate, too sure of his own rightness.

"I give you everything—food, clothes—" He pointed to my clothes hanging in the wardrobe. Sometimes the wardrobe door opened quite suddenly as if there were a ghost in it. It had opened just then. "I try to educate you, teach you how to speak, how to deal with people, build up your confidence, but that is not enough. You now want to own me."

"I like it when there is just us," I said, lowering my voice so that he might lower his.

"The world is not just us," he said, "the world is this girl coming, and Simon, and all the people you've met, and all the ones you will meet. Honestly"—and he sat on the bed and sighed—"I don't think I can do it, I don't think I can start from scratch again on a wholly simple level. It's too difficult, there's not enough time left in the world anymore, and hundreds of girls, ready-made." He nodded toward the door as if Mary were in the passage.

He pointed to me.

"Your inadequacies, your fears, your traumas, your father . . ." And I began to cry, knowing my inadequacies like the back of my hand.

"Young girls are like a stone," he said, "nothing really touches them. You can't have a relationship with a stone, at least I can't."

"But you like teaching me," I protested. "You said you did. Some girls wouldn't take it, but I don't mind you telling me about the Ice Age and evolution and auto-suggestion and the profit motive. Maybe she wouldn't like you telling her things like that . . ." I wanted to tell him that her legs were hairy, too, but I thought that would betray my nature completely.

"Maybe she wouldn't," he said, "but that doesn't prevent me from talking to her, from liking her . . ."

"But you like me," I said, "you like me in bed and everything."

"Please!" he said in a strained voice. He put out his hands to catch a moth which had come through the open window, then stood up.

"I suppose if Laura came back it would be the same thing," I said.

"It might," he said. "One relationship does not cancel out another, you're all"—he thought for the word—"different."

"Well, if that's the case then, I don't know what I'm doing here."

"I certainly don't know what you're doing here, acting like a barmaid," he said urbanely as he walked slowly over to the fire grate. There were papers and matches and hairs from my comb in the grate.

"I was thinking just now that I'd be better off if I'd never met you," I said.

He leaned his elbow on the mantelpiece, pushed a bowl of primroses in from the edge, and said, "You are incapable of thinking. Why don't you get up and wash your face and put some powder on? Do something. Sink your inadequacy into washing walls or mending my socks or conquering your briary nature . . ."

I watched him, strong-featured and hard, standing there, speaking to me as a stranger might.

"Are you seeing that girl again?" I asked.

"Probably. Why not?"

"She's with Simon, she's Simon's girl," I said.

"Oh, for God's sake, stop coming priestly ethics on me; nothing's irrevocable," he said. And I thought, Not even us, and I knew as I thought it that if I loved him enough I would put up with anything from him.

"If you see her again, I'll go away and I won't come back," I said. It was not just her charm and looks that I was jealous of—though there was that, too—it was the fact that she reminded him of Laura. I wanted him exclusively for myself.

"In that case you ought to start packing now, because I'm having lunch with them tomorrow."

"And me?" I said, outraged that he should not have included me.

"And you," he said wearily, "if you can be relied upon to behave with dignity and not indulge in one of your states." He moved toward the door. "Look at yourself in the glass—you're like a red, swollen washerwoman."

"Eugene, Eugene—" I got off the bed and he turned around to say "Yes?" but the bitterness on his face made me swallow whatever I had intended to say. I could not reach him.

He went downstairs and put some music on, and I sat there planning what I would do to teach him a lesson. I decided to go away and put him to the trouble of finding me. I remembered a story that Baba had told me of how Sally Mead (Tod Mead's wife) had left Tod once, and he searched the pubs and streets and hotels for three days, and finally a policeman found her, eating an ice cream, alone, in the back row of a cinema. She'd spent the days in a cinema and slept in some hostel at night; but I need not do that, because I could go to Joanna's. I could help Baba to pack, and all the time he would search for me and swear never to let me out of his sight again.

19 It was a long night. I got a suitcase from the top of the wardrobe and packed my clothes; I put my jewelry (some trinkets of Mama's and a gold chain that he had bought for me) in a box. At about two I went downstairs to heat myself some milk, and on the way I listened at the study door. He seemed to be moving around inside and a flute was being played, mournfully, on the radio. For one second, I had the temptation to knock and go inside, and beg his forgiveness, and listen to the music with him; but I went on down to the kitchen, heated the milk, and brought it up to bed. Anyhow, I could always apologize when he came up later on. But that night he slept in the guest room, and I minded that more than anything.

In the morning we did not speak, and while he shaved I put the case in the trunk of the car, and the marriage ring he had bought for me in an ashtray on his desk. I had finally decided to go away for a week, to give him plenty of time to miss me. I had a short letter in my handbag, ready to hand to him when we got to Dublin. In the letter, of course, I pretended that I was going away forever.

The new telephone was there in the hall, clean and shiny, waiting to be used. Anna looked at it, and said that she hoped it wouldn't ring while we were out. In boredom, she had bleached her black hair blond, but it was badly done and you could see the black roots clearly. I didn't tell her that I was going away, because I knew that she would implore me either to stay or to bring her with me.

Eugene and I did not speak half a dozen words as we drove down the mountain, past the brown fields, and down the long rocky hill which led to richer grass and cows grazing, and potato fields blue from a recent spray of copper sulphate.

"Where are we having lunch?" I asked.

"The Shelbourne," he said, and I looked out the window at the two crooked chalked signs on a limestone wall—UP THE IRA and SHUN CYCLING SLAVES, and memorized them, telling myself that I might never drive this way again; telling myself, yet not believing it.

As we passed a grove of Scots pine trees I said, "Now I know the names of trees," but he did not answer me. Their limbs were flushed in the sun.

When we got out at Stephen's Green, I walked a little ahead of him, toward the hotel. As we came through the revolving doors I said, "I'm just going into the cloakroom for a minute, won't be long," and he went into the lounge without answering.

In the cloakroom I took the letter out of the paper bag (I had put it in a paper bag to keep it clean), came out, gave it to a page boy along with two shillings, and asked him to hand it to Mr. Gaillard, who was in the lounge. Then I ran out of the hotel and felt more exalted than I had felt for ages. I got my case from the unlocked trunk of his car (it never locked) and took a taxi to Joanna's. In the taxi I mused over how shocked he would be when he read the note, and of how he would hurry to Joanna's looking for me. The note was short. It said simply:

> I love you, but I do not want to be a burden to you, so I am leaving. Goodbye.

In the taxi also, I powdered my face so that when I got to Joanna's I should not look too desolate.

"Jesus, look what the cat brought in," Baba said, opening the door to me and then going back into the hall to call Joanna.

"*Mein Gott*, have you fill up with baby and that man send you back to us?" Joanna asked as she saw me standing there with the stuffed suitcase, one latch of which had come open. She wore a summer dress which I had left behind, and it was funny to see her in it. She must have had it let out. Baba wore blue jeans and a sleeveless blouse. It was very hot.

"No, I just came back for a few days to help Baba pack and see her off," I said cheerfully, and they brought me in.

Joanna was making lemonade from some yellow powder stuff. The kitchen window was open and the flowered curtain ballooned gently under the raised sash. I saw my bicycle outside, and thought with sadness of all that had happened to me since I last rode it. Baba began to question me, and very quickly I broke down.

"My mother is bloody right," Baba said. "All men are pigs."

"True, is true," Joanna said, because Gustav was out, "smoking and trinking and start to shout if I go cross. I myself am nerves and I cannot say anythink."

"Let Cait talk," Baba said, shutting Joanna up. Baba looked pale from her recent misadventure, and she smoked more than ever.

"Come to England," she said to me. "We'll have a whale of a time. Striptease girls in Soho, that's what we'll be."

She was going to England the following Friday, and her parents had allowed her to take her insurance money out of the bank, having reconciled themselves to the fact that she would never pass an examination now. She had told them that she was going to take up nursing.

"Nursing!" she said to me. "Shaving people and changing sheets. I'm going to Soho, that's where I'll see life. You should come with me."

"Ah no, he'll want me back," I said, telling them about the note which I had given to the page boy. Joanna put us to tidying the front room, so that the place would look respectable when he came. It was funny dusting a rubber plant on a summer's day, when nice flowers bloomed in the garden outside. There were wallflowers out, and peony roses just opening. I did not expect him until half past three or four, as I knew that he would lunch first with Simon and Mary, behaving as if nothing had happened.

"Give her a drink," Baba said to Joanna at a quarter to four. I sat near the front window, holding the net curtain up. Sometimes I let it drop in the belief that he would come the minute I stopped looking. My hands were shaking and my stomach felt sick.

At half past four, when nothing had happened, Baba dolled herself up and went out to look for him. I made excuses and clung to stupid hopes, as one does in times of desperation. I said, "He didn't get the note," "He doesn't know where I've gone," "He always forgets Joanna's number," and with these paltry hopes and egg cupfuls of Joanna's homemade advocaat, I passed the time from the window to the door, to the hall, upstairs and then down again, until finally Joanna had one of her brainwaves and gave me a pullover to rip. I foresaw our reunion, and debated whether I should sulk for a bit when he arrived with Baba or run to him with open arms.

Meanwhile, Gustav came in for his tea and shook hands with me, and Gianni, the lodger, arrived looking as conceited as ever.

"How do you like the country?" he asked. "Have you seen much wild life?"

"Wild life!" I said, and took my cup of tea into the back room, where Joanna kept buckets of preserved eggs and apples on the window ledges.

"Baba should be back now," I said to the plaster nymph in the fireplace whose cheeks Joanna rouged from time to time because everything got mildewed in that room. The roof leaked.

Eventually I heard the door being opened and I rushed out. Only Baba was there.

"Baba, Baba," I said. Her cheeks were flushed and I knew that she'd had one or two drinks.

"Come upstairs," she said, making a face toward the dining-room door to indicate that she did not wish them to hear.

"Is he outside?" I asked as she linked me upstairs to the bedroom which I used to share with her. We closed the door.

"Where is he?" I asked.

She looked at me squarely for a second and then said, "He's gone home."

"Without me?" I was shocked. "Isn't he coming for me?"

"No," she said, sighing, "he's not coming for you."

"Is that Mary gone with him?"

"That moron! Says everything is 'cute and moving.' You telling me she was good-looking. Jesus, she's only in the halfpenny place next to us; all she has is her underwear and a necklace down to her stomach. I cut her dead," Baba said, smiling victoriously.

"Where is she? Is she gone home with him?"

"She's a right-lookin' eejit, she got the collywobbles, and that spy with the beard had to take her home. 'Wow,' he says to me. 'Bow-wow,' says I back to him. You're too soft with sharks like him!"

"But what about Eugene?" I asked.

"Sit down," she said, giving me a cigarette.

She began, "I told him that you were here, and he said, 'Naturally!' Then he ordered me a brandy, and when th'other pair went off, I told him that you were having a fit and he said that he'd made up his mind about you . . ."

I trembled all over, and clutched the bedclothes to prepare myself for the worst.

"He says you're to stay here," Baba said flatly. "He says old men and young girls are all right in books but not anywhere else. You're to stay here," she said, pointing to the two iron beds, "until maybe you've growed up a bit and he comes back from making his irrigation thing in America. Are you up the pole or anything?"

I shook my head and sobbed and gripped the satin bedspread until she thought I'd tear it. Then I lay on the bed face downward and began to moan and cry.

"Jesus, don't have a nervous breakdown," she begged as she clutched my shoulders to steady me, "or convulsions or anything. Don't go off your head."

"I'm entitled to have a nervous breakdown or go off my head," I shouted as Joanna came in and said something sympathetic and then told Baba to take the spread off the bed before I ruined it. I had my shoes on, lying there. Baba pushed me toward the edge of the bed, and I lowered myself on the floor and pounded the brown linoleum while they folded the bedspread and put it away in a drawer.

"A little bit hysteric, eh?" Joanna said, and Baba recalled how our friend Tom Higgins got put in Grangegorman for a lot less. He kissed a strange nun on O'Connell Bridge because she reminded him of his dead sister. His sister had died of tuberculosis in the bed next to Baba's in the sanatorium, and before that his brother got killed in Spain.

"I'm going to Eugene, I'm going to him," I said, getting to my knees.

"No, you're not," Baba said firmly. "He doesn't want you."

"He does want me, he does want me," I shouted, and then Gustav came in, and opened his mouth with shame and wonder when he saw me kneeling and crying on the floor, my hair wild about me.

"Miss Caithleen who is so gentle," he said, and I thought, Yes, I was so gentle and now I am a wild, debased person because of some damn man, and I lay flat on the floor and howled.

They lifted me onto the bed, gave me pills and whiskey, and more pills, so that I would calm down. I slept with Baba in the single bed, and once in near-sleep I thought that her arm around my stomach was his arm, and I woke up, relieved, only to face the truth again, and the emptiness. That was the time I missed him worst. Baba's arm was around me, but it was his body I smelled, the sweet and languid smell of his body in sleep, the dark mesh of hairs on his chest, the honey color of his skin, and the warmth which had enveloped us, night after night. I stayed awake then, my mind muddled from pills and crying.

Baba had stopped going to lectures, so at about eleven next morning we went to a phone booth and Baba put a call through to his house. The person in the exchange told her that the telephone had not been connected yet, but to try later.

At home I sat by the window and looked out at the peony roses, which were opening, and at the leaves of the birch tree blown upward by the wind. Baba brought me tea, and went out three or four times to telephone him, but could not get through.

I thought, While this peony rose is opening into a large red bloom, he is on his way to me; but I was mistaken, because when Baba finally got through, late that evening, Anna told her that Mr. Gaillard had gone away and taken a travel bag with him.

"He may be in London or somewhere for a couple of weeks," Baba said.

"Weeks?" I said. "I'll be out of my mind if I have to wait weeks."

"I'm going to England this Friday," Baba said, wagging her finger at me, "and for God's sake, don't stop me, don't ask me to stay here and nurse you. I've wanted to go for months, and I don't want anyone or anything to stop me."

"I won't stop you, Baba," I said, certain that he would come in a matter of days. "He'll come."

"Supposing he doesn't?"

"But he will."

"But supposing he doesn't," and she went on like that, and I thought she was disheartening me because she was jealous. She said again that if I wanted to I could go to England with her.

"You'll see him there," she said. "He might even be over there now." It was quite possible, because the various companies he made films for were in London. I thought, however, that most probably he had just gone away for one night to some hotel to do a bit of fishing. When he was worried about something he always went fishing; and I knew well that he was missing me.

That night I did not promise to go to England with Baba, but next day she was on about it again, and I said that I maybe would go, although I did not believe that I really would. Making plans to go gave me something to think about, and also, I thought it would prove to him how independent I was. I wrote to him, telling him that I was going away, marking the letter *Urgent* and *Personal*.

Meanwhile, Baba made plans for us to leave. She rang her mother and got her to tell my father that I had left Eugene and was going to England with Baba. My father was delighted. In a letter he praised me for being so loyal to my family, and to my religion. He sent me fifty pounds' reward—collected no doubt from cousin Andy and other rich relations. They wanted me to go home for a few days, but Baba told her mother on the phone that there was no time. Baba had already got the tickets. In the back of my mind was the nice thought that I could get a refund for my ticket or give it to some poor person when Eugene came. I felt that he had to come, because if he didn't, it made everything between us meaningless.

I wrote to him again and asked him to have a drink with us, to say goodbye. I said nothing about being hysterical because I knew that once he saw me he would love me and want to protect me again. I said to myself that people were like that with me—they forget me easily, but when they see me, they are drawn again and somehow feel protective.

No answer came to that letter, and twice I went into a telephone booth to ring him, but vanity or terror stopped me from trying to get through. Anyhow, I did not want to talk to him on the telephone; I wanted him to come and see me. But really I was afraid to find that he had gone away.

Baba and I were out a lot, saying goodbye, getting new clothes and underwear, having our hair done, drinking with Baba's friends. Sometimes in a pub it would come to me that he was outside Joanna's waiting in his sports car, and I would run from my friends and get a taxi home, only to be disappointed again.

The nights were the worst: thinking of him sitting at home in his study listening to music, and moving those ivory chessmen on the checkered board, or skimming the cream off the milk so that he would not die of thrombosis at fifty. The inside of my lips were covered with water blisters, and these aggravated the craving pain to be with him. And I thought of what he had said about young girls being like a stone and I wanted him to know that this was not true.

Four days and four nights went by. On the fifth day we were due to leave. Baba had booked a double cabin and she had the tickets in a little cellophane envelope. I packed and kept up the pretense that I was really going, but I knew that just as I got on the ship, he would be standing there, mournful, and when he tapped my shoulder and said "Kate," I would turn and go to him. In a letter I had told him the exact time we were sailing and where from, so I knew he'd come.

20 On our last day we bought labels and twine. We sent a barmbrack and twenty cigarettes to Tom Higgins, who was in a mental hospital (we were afraid to visit him), and Joanna had chicken for lunch as a celebration.

After lunch, we packed last-minute things and Joanna kept plaguing us to leave her some clothes and perfume in the ends of bottles. Baba half-filled three perfume bottles with water to keep Joanna happy.

When we had packed we hurried from one neighbor's house to the next, saying goodbye, and Baba came with me to say goodbye to Mr. and Mrs. Burns in the shop where I used to work. Mr. Burns gave me a pound and said it was God who had saved me from that awful man. No one except Baba seemed to realize that I wanted only to go back to Eugene.

"Cheer up, when we're in London you can write to him; he's bound to come over and take us out for big dinners," she said as we walked home, smelling the hawthorn scent that carried in the wind from the bushes in people's gardens. I wondered if he would come or not. Two or three times I thought of asking Baba to ring up again, but I thought that it might spoil everything and stop him from coming.

At home, in Joanna's front garden, the peony roses had opened out—into a deep, glistening red. Joanna had watered them and everything was nicely moist. He still hadn't come. Baba had arranged to meet the Body and Tod Mead in a pub.

A taxi came for us at six, and Gustav helped the driver with the cases. When they were all in, I ran back and stuck a note under the knocker—*Gone to pub opposite boat*—so that he would know where to find us. I didn't want Joanna to know I left the note, because she'd say it gave burglars a fine opportunity to break in.

It was a dark pub, decorated inside to look like a ship, and along the mantelpiece were various-sized ships in bottles, and a picture of Robert Emmet on the wall. I made circles with the toe of my shoe in the sawdust and wondered how much longer I could wait without ringing him.

"Come on, Caithleen, cheer up, love," the Body said, handing me a drink. It was rum and lemon, and I did not like it.

"If you bowl over any publishers, let me know," said Tod Mead, who had some vague idea about writing a novel and becoming famous.

"How's Sally?" I said. Although I'd never met her, I pitied her a lot, ever since Baba was pregnant that time.

"She's in great form, doing a lot of gardening," he said, and though I wanted to ask him how she really was, I didn't. His slight irritableness stopped you from asking him anything that mattered.

"I wonder how they get those ships into bottles," he said, nodding at a white ship in a long bottle. That was how he evaded things, always changing the subject to something trivial. I would remember him, blue-eyed and secretly bitter, with an old fawn Crombie coat, and a knot in the belt where the buckle should be, setting himself up as an authority on wine and American writers and ships in bottles.

Two students from Trinity College came to bid Baba farewell, and she tried to coax a college scarf from one of them, so that she could show it off in London.

All of a sudden, as I watched her and listened to Tod, I got frantic and stood up. "I'm going to ring him," I said to Baba.

"All right, ring him, there's no one stopping you," she said as she put the striped scarf over her head.

The telephone was in the hall. I had to get a single shilling and some pennies, and then wait for several minutes while the exchange connected me to his number.

Anna answered the telephone.

"No, he's not here," she said, yelling into it. You'd know that it was the first or second time in her whole life that she had used one.

Then she faded away, giving me the impression that she had turned to say something to someone.

"Anna, I'm going to England and I just want to say goodbye to him. Ask him to come and say goodbye to me."

"He's not here," she said again. "He's out the field, honest to God." She heard me sobbing and she said, "If he comes in I'll get him to rush in and see you. Where are you? How much longer will you be there?"

I had to shout into the bar to ask the name of the pub, and several people shouted the name to me.

"God, 'tis well for you going to England," Anna said. "Love, I'm in trouble, I'm up the pole again, is there any pills you could send me?"

"I'll try," I said. "Is he there?"

"He's not here, there's no one here, only me and the child. Will you send me the pills, will you?"

"And you'll send him here, before I leave?"

"If he's here at all, I'll tell him!"

"Anna, I wrote to him," I said.

"I know, there's a pile of letters here on the hall table that he hasn't opened." It was that quality about him which I admired most, that lonely strength which allowed him to postpone a pleasure or a worrying letter for days or weeks.

I asked Anna if the American girl, Mary, had been to the house.

"No one came, only the rat man, 'tis like a monastery here since you left. He was away for two nights, and since he came back he's like a monk, brooding. Will you send the pills?" she begged, and then my time was up and I said goodbye and came away feeling worse than ever. I could see his brown eyes as I had last seen them in the hotel, full of sadness, and full of knowledge that I was not the girl he had imagined me to be. A stone, he'd said. I thought of stones bursting open in the hot sun and other stones washed smooth by a river I knew well.

When we were leaving the pub I left a message that he should follow across to the ship; I still thought that he might come. It was getting late and I imagined him speeding down the mountain in his little car, hurrying to me. Anna had promised to go out and look for him, but he might be anywhere.

The Body knew the superintendent of the ship and managed to get permission for all of them to come on board. He tipped several porters as we all trooped on. Baba held her ticket between her teeth, to show it to the ticket man, as her hands were occupied with flowers and travel bags and a new red raincoat. Walking across the gangway, I thought,

I can still go back and wait for him, because he's coming. But I went ahead, propelled by the Body's hearty voice and by someone who pushed me from behind with the sharp corner of a suitcase.

Our small cabin was thick with company: Tod, the Body, Joanna, Gustav, and the various bunches of crushed flowers which they had given us. The Body passed a half bottle of Irish whiskey around and urged us to drink up.

"I not get the germs," said Joanna. She was quite merry from a few sherries, and the Body pushed her hat sideways so that everything about her looked lopsided.

"Jesus meets his afflicted mother," the Body said to her, reminding me of the night we went to the dress dance and of later when he tripped on her stairs. And for a minute we all felt sad; but the Body shouted, "Baba, Caithleen, your health; your fortune; stay as sweet as you are and don't let a thing ever change you"—he sang the last bit, and fondled Baba's bottom and lifted her into the air.

"Jesus," she said as her head hit the white porcelain lampshade.

A bell rang then and a commanding voice announced that all people aboard who were not traveling should disembark.

"Holy Moses, we'll have to swim the channel," the Body said, and Joanna said, "*Mein Gott*," and Tod pulled up the back of his coat collar and made the sign of the cross in mockery over us. They scrambled toward the door and left us with the crushed roses and the half bottle of whiskey, which had the damp of their various mouths on its neck.

"He never came," I said to Baba, and she put her arms around me and we both began to cry.

"I'll go mad, I'll go mad," I sobbed to her.

"Oh, not the loony bin," she said. "Wait till we go to England, everything is free there"—and then recollecting that we possessed so much money she said, "Our handbags; Jesus, our money," and she flung coats and cases off the bed and found both handbags under the numerous brown-paper parcels. At the last minute we had found that all our clothes did not fit in our cases, and we had to make various parcels. Baba said we'd need a wheelbarrow to cart the stuff off the boat when we docked at Liverpool.

"We'll stay awake all night," she said. "You wouldn't know who'd come in here and rape us and take our money."

"I'll never forget him," I said to her as I went across to dry my eyes in front of the mirror over the washbasin.

"There's no one asking you to," she said. "Anyhow, cheer up, we'll have a whale of a time in Soho."

There was another announcement from the ship's loudspeaker, and I listened, trembling, in case it might be him, but it wasn't.

"Would you know by looking at me that I had a past?" I asked her. I no longer had to suck my cheeks in to look thin.

She replied to the mirror, "You'd know you hadn't a decent night's sleep for about six months, that's what you'd know," and then for devilment she pressed the two bells beside the bunks, just to see what would happen. A steward came.

"Just did it for gas," she said; and he looked around at the chaos of our cabin—clothes on the floor, flowers on the floor, me crying, Baba nursing the whiskey bottle on her lap. He shook his head and backed out.

"If they're wondering how big a tip they'll get tomorrow, they'd want to watch out or they'll get nothing," Baba said loudly.

"A pity beyond all telling is hid in the heart of love," I said, light-headed as a result of the whiskey, and finding consolation in the words.

She put her hands to her ears. "No, no, Jesus, are you reciting those mortuary cards again?"

"He always washed his own socks and made metal things to put in them, to keep them from shrinking," I said, "and he boiled his corduroy pants one day and they shrank, so he had to use them on a scarecrow."

"I tell you something interesting, I think he was touched and you're better off away from him." She tapped her forehead. "He'll become a monk."

The ship began to rumble and I swayed a little and she said, "We're off, come on, let's wave to them," and she led me by the hand as we ran up on deck to see the last of Dublin. The Body and the others were still on the quay, waving hands and hats and evening papers, but there was no sign of him.

"The Body is sincere," I said to Baba, re-echoing Mama's words.

Baba waved a clean hanky, and we leaned on the rails and felt the ship move and saw the dirty water underneath being churned up.

"Like a hundred lavatories flushing," Baba said to the foamy water as the seagulls rose up from their various perches along the rails and flew slowly, with us. I could hardly believe that we were moving, that we were leaving Ireland; and through my tears I saw our friends waving us away, and cranes and anchored ships and the long, uninspiring stretch of quay which we rode past. And gradually the City of Dublin started receding in the mauve twilight of a May evening—the city where I first kissed him outside the Customs House; the city where I had two teeth out, and pawned one of Mama's rings; the city I loved. We were both crying.

"Poor Tom Higgins shut up in the loony bin," Baba said, as if it were for him she cried; but I thought, She's crying, too, for that part of herself which she squandered, and for the aloes she took, and for all the bus conductors she flirted with.

We could see Dollymount sands now, where I had been first with Mr. Gentleman and then with him—both times in love. I pictured sand dunes with grass growing out of them and swore never to set foot there again, love or no love. We felt chilly, as we had forgotten to put on our coats, and it got dark fairly soon and lights came up on all sides of the bay.

Down below us the people traveling third class carried their drinks outside, and they leaned on the rails and sang.

"We'd have a lot more gas down there," Baba said. There were mostly priests and married couples traveling first class.

The gulls flew slowly with us, their screaming unwinding the scream inside me. By degrees, the sky darkened; a mist rose from the sea; the stars lit up.

"I brought pills, in case we puke all over the damn ship," Baba said, so we went inside and took three pills and hoped that we would be all right.

I missed him then, more than at any other time; it was terrible sitting on that bed, knowing that he had chosen not to come for me.

"If I'm sick, 'twill spoil everything," Baba said as she burped, and then put a hand towel over her new dress, for safety's sake.

"Remind me to feck a few towels," she said, and I knew that if anyone was to save me from going mad, it would be Baba, with her maddening, chattering voice.

"We're on our way," she said, raising her arms exultantly to the ceiling. "We're on our way, English and American papers, please copy." And the ship named *Hibernia* moved steadily forward through the black night, toward the dawn of Liverpool.

21 I work in a delicatessen shop in Bayswater and go to London University at night to study English. Baba works in Soho, but not in a striptease club, as she had hoped. She's learning to be a receptionist in a big hotel. We share a small bed-sitting room, and my aunt sends a parcel of butter every other week. Baba says that it makes us look like a right pair of eejits, getting that mopey parcel tied with hairy twine, and I keep telling my aunt that butter is not rationed here, but still she sends it. It's all she can do to prove her love.

It is hot summer, and I miss the fields and the soft breeze, and I sometimes think of a brown mountain stream with willows and broom pods hanging over it; and I think of the day I went fishing there with him, and he wore big boots and waded upstream. At unguarded moments, in the last Tube, or drying my face by sticking my head out the window (we aren't allowed in the garden), I ask myself why I ever left him, why I didn't cling on tight, the way the barnacles cling to the rocks.

He wrote to me after I came here—a very nice letter, saying what a nice girl I was, and what a pity that he hadn't been younger (in mind) or I hadn't been older.

I answered that letter and he wrote again, but I haven't heard from him now for a couple of months and I take it that he has gone back to his wife, or that he's busy in South America, doing that picture on irrigation.

If I saw him again I would run to kiss him, but even if I don't see him I have a picture of him in my mind, walking through the woods, saying, in answer to my fear that he might leave me, that the experience of knowing love and of being destined, one day, to remember it, is the common lot of most people.

"We all leave one another. We die, we change—it's mostly change—we outgrow our best friends; but even if I do leave you, I will have passed on to you something of myself; you will be a different person because of knowing me; it's inescapable . . ." he said.

It's quite true. Even Baba notices that I'm changing, and she says if I don't give up this learning at night, I'll end up as a right drip, wearing flat shoes and glasses. What Baba doesn't know is that I'm finding my feet, and when I'm able to talk I imagine that I won't be so alone, but maybe that too is an improbable dream.

Girls in Their Married Bliss

1

Not long ago Kate Brady and I were having a few gloomy gin fizzes up London, bemoaning the fact that nothing would ever improve, that we'd die the way we were—enough to eat, married, dissatisfied.

We've always been friends—as kids in Ireland we slept together and I used to push her out of bed on purpose, hoping she'd crack her skull or something. I liked her and all that —I was as jealous as hell of course—but she was too sedate and good; you know, that useless kind of goodness, asking people how they are, and how their parents are. At National School she did my compositions for me, and in the Convent of Mercy we clung together because the other eighty girls were even drippier than she, which is saying a lot. When we vamoosed from the convent we went to a linoleum slum in Dublin, and then on to another slum here in London, where, over a period of eighteen months, we got asked out to about three good dinners apiece, which meant six meals for both of us because we had a pact that whoever got asked out would bring back food for the Cinderella. I've ruined the inside of more handbags that way . . .

We weren't here a year when she remet a crank called Eugene Gaillard, whom she'd known in Ireland. They took up their old refrain, fell in love, or thought they did, and lost no time making puke out of it. The marriage was in the sacristy of a Catholic church. Question of having to. They wouldn't do it out front because he was divorced and she was heavily pregnant. I was bridesmaid. Pink chiffon and a hat with a veil, for which they paid. I looked like the bride. She was in a big, floppy, striped maternity dress and a child's face on her. She's sly, the sort that would look like a child even if she kept her mother in a wardrobe. The priest didn't look toward her stomach once.

When we came out, Eugene drove away very quick, and that shook me, because he's the sort of fusser that issues instructions before he lets you into his motorcar. "Don't step on the running board, don't push the seat too far back, don't push the other seat too far forward." To make himself important. He tore out of the place and down the road like a sportsman. He was laughing, too, a thing he doesn't do often.

"What's up?" says I.

"Our Beloved Father is finding a little surprise," he said, and Kate said, "What?" just like a wife.

It seems the envelope which he handed to the priest, and which was supposed to contain twenty pounds for marrying them, contained one, orange-colored, Irish, ten-shilling note, wrapped in several pieces of paper to make the envelope bulky. Well, she flew into a huff and got violet in the face. He told her she was nothing but a farmer's daughter reverting to type, and she told him he was so mean he wouldn't let her buy things for the baby. A dig because he was married before and had kept pram and nappies in storage. He said she had no breeding, and if she wanted to be crude she'd better step out of the car. He said he'd give the twenty pounds to some less pernicious organization, and she said, "Well, go on, give it, stop some poor woman and give it to her," but he sat tight at the wheel and drove with a set purpose to a middling restaurant in Soho where we had a cheerless breakfast and a bottle of light, sparkling wine, which he liked so much that he took the dampened label off and put it in his wallet so that he'd remember it. For the next marriage! She sulked all through and I couldn't very well laugh.

They went to live in the country after the child came, and she wrote me a note that I kept. I don't know why I kept it. It said:

> Dear Baba,
> We are in a valley with a hill of golden, trampled bracken to look out on, and birds are nesting in the hardly budded trees. We have a gray stone house with stone slates on the roof and wooden beams inside, and whitewashed, bumpety walls and pots for flowers everywhere; the boards creak and he loves me, and there is something about having a child and being in a valley, and being loved, that is more marvelous than anything you or I ever knew about in our flittery days.
> Always,
> Kate

Always, Kate! I was miserable at the time. Never, Kate! That night I put on my best things and went to an Irish club. Fate of fates, I met my builder.

His name was Frank and he was blowing money around the place and telling jokes. I'll repeat one joke so as you'll have an idea how hard up I was: Two men with fishing tackle have an arm around an enormous woman and one says to the other, "A good catch." When people are drunk they'll laugh at anything, provided they're not arguing, or hitting each other.

Anyhow, he drove me home and offered me money—he has a compulsion to offer money to people who are going to say no—and asked if I thought he looked educated. Educated! He was a big, rough fellow with oily hair, and his eyebrows met. So I said to him, "Beware of the one whose eyebrows meet, because in his heart there lies deceit." And sweet Jesus, next time we met he'd had them plucked over his broken nose. He's so thick he didn't understand that the fact they met was the significant thing. Thick. But nice, too. Anybody that vulnerable is nice, at least that's how I feel. Another dinner. Two dinners in one week and a bunch of flowers sent to me. The first thought I had when I saw the flowers was, could I sell them at cut rates. So I offered them to the girls in the bed-sits above and below, and they all said no except one eejit who said yes. She began to fumble for her purse, and I felt so bloody avaricious that I said, "Here's half of them," so we had half each, and when he came to call for me that evening, he counted the number of flowers that I'd stuck into a paint tin, for want of a vase. And you won't believe it, but didn't he go and ring the flower shop to say they'd swindled him. There he was out on the landing phone, yelling into it about how he'd ordered three dozen Armagh roses and what crooks they were, and how they'd lost him as a customer, and there was I in the room with a fist over my mouth to smother the laughing. "You may not be educated," said I, "but you're a merchant at heart. You'll go far." It ended up with the flower shop saying they'd send more, and they did. I was driven to go out to Woolworth's and buy a two-shilling plastic vase because I knew the paint tin would topple if one more flower was put in.

He didn't propose bed for at least six dinners, and that shook me. I didn't know whether to be pleased or offended. He was blind drunk the night he said we ought to, and my garret was freezing and far from being a love nest. The roses had withered but weren't thrown out, and I had this short bed so that his feet hung out at the bottom. I lay down beside him—not in the bed, just on it—with my clothes on. He fumbled around with my zip and of course broke it, and I thought, I hope he leaves cash for the damage, and even if he does I'll have to go to a technical school to learn how to stitch on a zip, it's that complicated. I knew the bed was going to collapse. You always know a faulty bed when you put it to that sort of use. So he got the zip undone and got past my vest—it was freezing—and got a finger or two on my skin, just around my midriff, which was beginning to thicken because of all the big dinners and sauces and things. I reckoned I ought to do the same thing, and I explored a bit and got to his skin, and the surprising thing was, his skin was soft and not thick like his face. He began to delve deeper, very rapacious at first, and then he dozed off. That went on for a while—him fumbling, then dozing—until finally he said, "How do we do it?" and I knew that was why he hadn't made passes sooner. An Irishman: good at battles, sieges, and massacres. Bad in bed. But I expected that. It made him a hell of a sight nicer than most of the sharks I'd been out with, who expected you to pay for the pictures, raped you in the back seat, came home, ate your baked beans, and then wanted some new, experimental kind of sex and no worries from you about might you have a baby, because they liked it natural, without gear. I made him a cup of instant coffee, and when he went to sleep I put a quilt over him and put the light out. I sat on the chair, thinking of the eighteen months in London, and all the men I'd met, and the exhaustion of keeping my heels mended and my skin fresh for the Mr. Right that was supposed to come along.

I knew that I'd end up with him, he being rich and a slob and the sort of man who would buy you seasick tablets before you traveled. You won't believe it but I felt sort of sorry for him, the way he worried about not being educated, or being fooled by florists, or being taken for an Irish hick by waiters. Never mind that they're Italian hicks. I could tell them all to go to hell because I had a brazen, good-looking face and was afraid of none of them, not even afraid whether people liked me or not, which is what most people are afraid of, anyhow. I know that people liking you or not liking you is an accident and is to do with them and not you. That goes for love, too, only more so. Well, to cut a long story short, I married him, and we had a big wedding with names being yelled out and red carpet to walk on. Strictly speaking, it wasn't carpet but cording stuff. Not that I drew his attention to it, because he'd have had a fight right there and then with photographers at hand to verify it. We were married by an abbot from one of the monasteries that Frank's outfit built. The wedding was a big do with speeches about hurling, and happiness, and all sorts of generalized garbage. There were ninety-four telegrams. I learned afterward that he had instructed his secretary to send a host of them and put workmen's names to them. He'd die if he didn't get a bigger number of telegrams than anyone else, or make the wittiest speech. It was easy to be witty with the guests we had. He planned his own speech for weeks before. Imagine it. He had a voice trainer come in for four evenings. You'd pay not to talk like her. She was screeching all over the place, and he and her were in the room saying "A" and "O" for several hours. She was one of those fat Englishwomen that are stuffed with bread and lah-di-dah and nothing else.

Of course, everyone got drunk at the wedding and when we got to the airplane, me in a powder-blue Paris going-away suit, we couldn't be let on because of him being incapable. He got very obstreperous and said did they know who he was, and did they know his wife was wearing a Balenciaga. Anyhow, we had to turn back, and the one thing I was relieved about was that he wouldn't want to sleep with me that first night, because that was the one thing I dreaded. You see that was the one aspect of him I didn't like at all. I liked his money and his slob ways: I didn't mind holding hands at the pictures, but I had no urge to get into bed with him. Quite the opposite.

I even confided in my mother. I hardly ever talked to my mother about anything, because when I was four I had scarlet fever and she sent me away to a Gaeltacth to learn Irish. She really sent me away so that she wouldn't have to mind me—the maid was on two weeks' holiday—but she thought up this Gaeltacth stunt so that it sounded wholesome. I was only there a day when I had to be put in the infirmary. They made me dictate letters: *Darling Mummy* [I'm not your mother,

I'm Mummy you used to say], *I am getting better. I drank orange juice through a straw this morning. Love to you and Daddy, darling Mummy.*

I don't want to sound all martyrish about it, it's just that I didn't tell her things, but I did mention this physical ordeal and she said it would be all right, to just grit my teeth and suffer it. She said it was because of physical attraction that most marriages went wallop, that physical attraction was another form of dope. Dope was my mother's word for anything that people got by on. I don't hold it against her. I don't expect parents to fit you out with anything other than a birth certificate and an occasional pair of new shoes. She said what she did because she was feathering her nest, too. That's how he really hooked us—financing us all. Because of his money my mother was over here in London having the life of Riley: her corns attended to, new clothes, gin slings every evening in hotels, and then we'd all (he never stirred with less than ten or twelve people) repair to some joint where a coarse man or woman played the piano and titivated their wares. As if that was exciting. My mother had a right old time. "He's a good man, your Frank," she'd say to me across a table in one of those lurid places, and then she'd look around for him and raise her glass and say, "Frank, take care," and they'd drink to me: the bloody sacrificial lamb. Twenty years before she wouldn't have let him use the outside lavatory in our house at home. You'll think I'm bitter about my mother, but I'm not. She died soon after that. She got cancer of the stomach and died in a matter of months. I believe that for the twenty-four hours before she died she screamed and fought against it, and I missed her more than I ever thought I would. I suppose up to the time people die you think their lives will improve, or you'll get on better with them, but once they're dead you know neither thing is possible.

Well, that's how it happened. We moved into a posh house. I love the smell of rich houses, rich shops, flowers, and carpets. I'd have the whole world fitted with flowers and carpets if I could. We looked out on the river Thames—great view, storm windows, burglar alarms, double doors, the works. Some of it was a lark, hanging pictures and getting rooms done like the Vatican. Our bathroom was in a fashion magazine, with me sitting on my cane throne. We bought dozens of copies and sent them back to Ireland, to the relations. Twin beds for a while until he read that they were out. He got a king-size monstrosity with a Scandinavian headboard. That finished my tranquillity. Apart from anything else he moves in his sleep like a truffle hound, banging and sniffing and rooting all over the place.

Brady came back to London, too—nature and silence-in-the-evening didn't work out, after all. We met regularly to discuss our plight. Her life like a chapter of the inquisition. He wanted her to stay indoors all the time and nurse his hemorrhoids. One day she had a funny glint in her eye.

"What's up?" said I. I might have known. She'd met someone else, she was in love, the old, old story. She began to rave until I thought I'd puke. He turned out to be a prize. They came here in the afternoons for cups of tea, and to talk; I even went out to give them a chance, but they never got past the front room. Songs about the oppressed took over. I used to wonder when it would end, but apart from that I didn't put much consequence on it. Which goes to show how wrong I can be.

2

"Long legs, crooked thighs, small head and no eyes . . ." Her son Cash asked the riddle for the fifth time as they walked by a gloomy pond, their gloved hands joined.

"A crooked man," Kate said.

"No. Will I tell you?" the child asked, impatient to air his knowledge.

"Give me one more chance," she said, and guessed again, wrongly, "A crooked woman."

The child began to laugh aloud in a shrill and forced way. A thing he did often to try to induce a little gaiety into their lives.

"A tongs," he said, triumphant, and she bent down and pressed her damp nose against his. They ought to feed the ducks so that they could hurry in out of the cold. The pond was partly frozen, and partly not. Chunks of ice bobbed about, and the ducks swam around the borders of the ice. One duck perched on a balcony of ice but got off quickly, finding it so precarious. When they saw the bread they swarmed toward the bank and the three swans came right out of the water onto the frozen cinder path. She hated swans. Their greed. Their ugly bodies. Their webbed, slime-like feet.

"Mind your glove," she said. A swan had bitten off the child's red glove one day, a year before, and carried it to the opposite bank, where the park keeper had to rescue it with a hook on the end of a fishing rod.

"Me mind me glove," the child said.

"Stop talking like a child," she said as she stood there wondering how she was going to get away that evening and should she wear her good clothes or not.

It was now between three and four on a winter's afternoon and the light was beginning to fade. It had snowed on and off for several weeks, but because there hadn't been a recent fall, what lay on the grass was a soiled and despairing yellow.

"Are you going out tonight?" the child asked. Something momentous about the way he looked up into her face and caught the two tears she had been holding on to, like contact lenses.

"Yes."

"With Dada?"

"Without Dada."

"Don't go," he said, parodying a sad face. He affected sadness as easily as he laughed, but that did not mean he wasn't troubled. No more than that her tears were shallow.

"Look," she said, to distract him, and she held the bag upside down and sprinkled the remainder of the bread on the water. The ducks and swans converged on it.

When they got to the wastepaper basket that was nailed to the bylaw board, she threw the rolled paper bag in, and read for the child's benefit the names of the fish which according to the notice proliferated in that unlikely half acre of miserable, stagnant water.

"— —, carp, bleak, bream."

They did not sound like the names of fish at all, but like a litany of moods that any woman might feel any Monday morning after she'd hung out her washing and caught a glimpse of a ravishing man going somewhere alone in a motorcar.

No one was out but themselves. It was teatime and fire-lighting time. The first foul whiffs of smoke rose from several chimneys. She could well believe that there were gas pokers alight in all of these houses. Identical houses with identical things going on behind the brick fronts.

"Do me smell me custard powder?" Cash asked, knowing well that it wasn't. In the summertime, depending on how the wind blew, they could smell custard powder from some factory. A niceish smell in the light, airy summer days with the electric chime from the ice-cream van, and stoic men sitting on canvas stools fishing for whales in the "— —, carp, bleak, bream" pond. They crossed the road and walked toward their own house.

"That was a short walk," Eugene said, opening the hall door for them. He had the ashen look that he'd worn through autumn when the light was bronze from the trees outside, and through winter now, his chosen, destined season. Weakness, timidity, guilt overcame her. She thought, He knows, he knows. If only he'll give me this last chance, I'll change, reform, make myself so ugly that I will be out of the reach of temptation.

"The sink smells again. I told you not to strain cabbage or cauliflower down," he said.

"Maura must have done it. Where is she?" Kate said, relieved that his wrath was for the sink only.

"I don't know where she is," he said as Kate advanced toward the well of the stairs and called to the young giggly servant with as much authority as she could muster.

They had steamed fish and cauliflower. The fish had gone cold, and Maura ruined the vegetables by overcooking them.

"All right?" Kate said out of habit. They sat at their accustomed places, he at one end of the mahogany table, she at the other, Cash and Maura in between, facing each other, making daft sounds, golluping their food one minute, chewing it to distraction the next minute.

"I wouldn't say it was the best meal I've ever had," he said, lifting his face from the plate of white, insipid food to stare over her head at the greenhouse, where the branches of an old vine wormed and gnarled their way.

"Cauliflower needs only a little water," she said, giving Maura a hint. She wanted to sound practical so that after tea she could decently stand up and say, "I'm going over to see Baba for a couple of hours."

Baba, her friend since childhood and now the wedded wife of a builder. Baba owned one ranch-mink stole and intended owning several more. She'd even promised one to Kate. Baba had hazel eyes that drooped at the corners and were inclined to flashes of wickedness. An occasional blow from her husband gave to one or the other of those green eyes a permanent knowingness, as if at twenty-five she realized what life was all about. She had plans for them both to leave their husbands one day when they'd accumulated furs and diamonds, just as once she had planned that they would meet and marry rich men and live in houses with bottles of grog opened, and unopened, on silver trays.

As soon as he put the knife and fork down and pushed the plate to the side of the table, Kate would tell him that she was going out. Then she would fly upstairs, make her face up, but not overdo it, wear her second-best coat, carry her earrings and her fur hat in a paper bag, saying it contained homemade scones for Baba, and set out in a flutter. She could put them on, as always, in the ladies' room of the Underground station.

"I think it's the coldest day we've had," she said, hoping for a response.

"The wireless says there'll be more snow," Maura said.

"Oh no," Kate said, and caught a look from him that said, "We are all inconvenienced by it, not just little you."

"Goody, piles and piles of snow, we'll make a snowman." Cash was always threatening to make a snowman but never did. He hatched indoors like the rest of them. Waiting for the spring.

"You weren't out at all today?" she said to her husband. He wasn't working. He'd saved enough money from the previous project to see them through a few months. He directed documentary pictures but was always buying leisure, as if in the course of leisure he most found what he had been ordained to do.

"No," he said. They were surrounded by silence. Simply to fill in the silence she said that the oil heater in the room tended to give her a headache.

"Oh well, everything has its drawbacks," he said. Every word pierced. Tonight she would tell her friend that they must not see each other for a while. Anyhow, the joy of seeing him was diminishing, and she was more conscious of the risks than of the pleasure. She thought how it is impossible to tell in the beginning of an attraction whether it is the real thing or not.

They'd met at a party, and they were attracted to each other the way hundreds of people are, out of hunger. It would have ended there but that they met by accident a few days later, as she was coming out of a white sale.

"Are you plunging in?" she said. There was something sissyish about seeing a man shop for sheets. She had a parcel of them in her hand and a new fur hat on her head. Saved having it wrapped.   •

"Would you like some tea?" he said, apparently too ashamed to shop now. He steered her down the street to a cramped restaurant with atrocious masks on the wall, and high stools that made no allowance for the small of the back. It was March. Windy. Pieces of paper and dust blowing about, and people with a look of fortitude because they had to fight the wind. He said something about apple blossoms, how it was probably blowing about in orchards all over Kent and how he wished he was there. But then he would not have met her! Some such compliment.

He asked her to have tea the following week, and she agreed, telling herself that she was not in love with him and therefore not party to anything wicked. The love came later. Or something bordering on it. They began to meet oftener; they made furtive telephone calls, wrote ardent letters, swore they would have to do something, but did nothing. Her husband began to sense it at once, although there was no evidence that he knew. He took to wearing pajamas in bed, to going for walks alone, to commenting on her slackening midriff. At Christmas, a few weeks before, she gave him a calendar on a marble stand and he said, "You're sure this is for me?" He produced two packages, one for Cash and one for Maura.

"You forgot me," she said to him sullenly.

"I give presents when I want to," he said, "not out of duty."

"You're quite right," she said, but in the wrong tone.

"I see you're getting your persecution complex back, put a sign out," he told her, and turned to Cash to explain the principle of the steam train he had just given him. Maura received high boots and matching gloves, and she marched around wearing both, hitting her gloved hands together, saying she was well away. It was strange how a happy face automatically became a pretty one.

"You'd like tea or coffee?" Kate said, because he had pushed the half-eaten fish aside and was awaiting the next course. They had no pudding that particular evening.

"Tea."

She and Maura automatically had the same, and Cash had milk, which he drank through a straw to make it exciting. Outside, they could hear the spatter of snow falling on the greenhouse. The wind began to howl. For some reason she thought of a dog she'd once known as a child, who had taken fits and had been locked up in an outhouse. She had feared that the dog would break loose and do terrible damage to them, just as now she knew the wind was intending to do harm.

"I hope it's not too bad, I promised Baba I'd go over," Kate said as casually as her guilt would allow.

"On a night like this?" he said.

"Well, I promised," she said, carrying her own cup of tea out of the room, to the refuge of the freezing upstairs, where she adorned her face with vanishing cream and a new gold powder she'd bought.

When she came down she found that he had his coat on, and she smiled and asked if he was having a little constitutional.

"I'll come with you," he said. "Haven't seen Baba for months."

"Oh," she said, getting all solicitous, "you'd better not, Baba's in trouble. She and Frank are not hitting it off and she wants advice from me."

"In that case," he said, "I'll go somewhere else."

She almost froze to death. They each kissed the child, warned Maura about the oil heater, and went out into the bitter night.

"Which way are you going?" she said, pausing at the gateway. He did not reply but walked beside her toward a bus stop that was at the end of their road. The steady, pitiless blobs of snow beating against her face, the emptiness and darkness of the street—only two of the seven streetlights functioned—irritated her. Why could he not use his car like other men? Why did they have to live in that place? she thought, forgetting that she had coaxed him to come there. It was a long, dull street. Trees. Some shed red berries that children later stamped into the tarred road so that they were like the tracks of someone who had gone by bleeding. Deathly quiet in the daytime. Rag-and-bone men rumbling along, yelling an inexplicable cry that she would never have understood except for seeing the junk. And always funerals. Coffins garnished with flowers, one or two courtesy cars following behind. Flowers instead of friends. Death, as bleak as living. She hardly ever talked to her neighbors. No wonder. They were mostly housewives who waved their husbands goodbye in the mornings, shopped around eleven, collected plastic tulips with the packets of dust-blue detergent, and wrote to the County Council about having the trees chopped down. They believed trees caused asthma and were always petitioning her to write and say the same thing. How did they survive? Endurance! That was a thing to aim at, and maybe asthma. A disease that she could talk about, and use as a weapon to live.

"Missed it!" she said to Eugene as the bus trundled by. They had to wait ten minutes for the next one. She timed it on his watch, touching his wrist each time, to feel his regard for her. Nothing.

The bus had that flat, after-Christmas feeling. People with new gloves, handbags, headscarves were making the dutiful trip to thank whoever had sent them these dull gifts in lovely, frosted-paper wrappings.

"But take me," a girl behind was explaining. "People see me and they say, 'Hello, Judith, how's Janice?' "

"She must be a twin," Kate said, turning to Eugene. He was not listening; his eyes were centered on a beautiful Indian woman who sat quite still, and with such presence that every other woman seemed foolish or strident.

"I should have some Indian children," he said.

"Cash is all right," Kate said, pricked.

"Of course he's all right."

It was useless. He occupied most of the seat, too, and was crushing her new skirt.

"If you sat on the other seat I'd have more room," she said to Eugene. The words cut like a lancet through the fog-filled chatter. She stopped short. They looked at each other for some time. It was the last look of pity that passed between them. Each turning to the other had felt the ghost go out. A little phrase had severed them. He moved to the seat behind.

"I was only joking," she said. He did nothing but smile, a bitter, cunning, tell-you-nothing smile. Kate got out first because Baba's house was nearby. She said she'd see him later. The cunning smile ushered her away.

" 'Bye," he said.

She crossed the road and took the same number bus back to the station, fretting because she was over an hour late for the appointment with her friend.

3

Kate came into the warm, mahogany-brown pub; looked, and through one of the glass panels she saw him rise to greet her.

"I love you," he said, even before he said hello. He helped her off with her snowy gloves, so then they could plait fingers in passing.

"Do you hear me?" he asked, his jaw twitching, his top lip yellow from the froth of beer. They moved to the open fire. She caught sight of herself in the old-fashioned mantelpiece, and saw her nose, not quite purple, but a cold, unlovely blue. The gold powder was useless.

"Look," he said, as if it were their last chance of saying anything, "I thought how ghastly if you didn't come."

"Well, I did." She winked to seem funny for him. Mad. Mad.

They sat themselves on a long bench behind a stained, unsteady table, spreading out their coats and their drinks to discourage others from sitting next to them. He had a large whiskey waiting for her, and beer and whiskey for himself, which he drank from alternate glasses.

"I would never do it like that," she said, and looked away, knowing she was going to do it another way. She knew his face by heart anyhow: a pleasant, full face that was not overfull; blue, affectionate eyes; one jaw that twitched; waved graying hair; and a ring on his marriage finger. That irked.

"Tell me everything, what you've been doing and thinking," and then he said quickly, "I have so much to tell you."

Would he leave his wife, forfeit his chance in politics? Sometimes he was reckless, but only in drink. He was drunk now. They could go on exactly as they were. But no, they'd already worn it out, with talk.

"I couldn't be without you—it would be like dying," she said. A sentence that he'd nursed when she first spoke it months ago. She thought that phrases were like melodies, they went on appealing long after one had stopped listening. Then one day they fell out of favor.

"I am alive, and in some ways happy," he said. His bloodshot eyes closed on her face many times, either because they were tired or because he wanted to feast on the image of her.

"I am not," she said, without humor.

"I would bless you for that," he said.

"Why?"

"Because you are candid, honest, outright."

He ought to be Prime Minister; he had a fierce gift for words.

"Really?" she said, believing and not believing him.

"That is the truth of it," he said.

It was quiet except for the soft hiss of soda being splashed from a siphon down the side of a glass. She looked around to search the faces near her to see if there was anyone listening.

"I hate to say it," she began, "but everything at home is getting worse, bleak." It was not so much that she hated to say it as that she was inadequate. How could she give any notion of what it was like to ascend her own stairs, meet her own husband on the first landing, see him turn away, and hear him cough politely as if she were a deformed person? Anyhow, it was not for this kind of chat that her friend picked her that windy far-off day.

"Dear God," he said, beating his forehead, "I am now filled with blackness."

"Forgive me," she said.

"Of course," he said. "I knew it, anyhow. We are as one, I knew it by your face."

"I look awful," she said, seeking flattery.

"On the contrary. How very beautiful you are, your face has a new dimension."

He was overdoing it again. He ordered large drinks; they clenched hands, sat like two people in an air-raid shelter wondering why they had come down there and not met death up above.

"We are guilty," he said, "and no doubt. But who is to judge us? It happened."

"It happened," she repeated after him, as if they were on trial.

"What will we do?" she said. He beat his lined forehead again, curled and uncurled his square-tipped fingers, searched for her hand, swore at the gods, and called her "Milis," which is the Gaelic for sweet.

"The world is hard," he said at last. She did not doubt it; he had a leaden wife and school bills for five children, and a town house and a country house and a job to keep. At least she could mope around all day and dwell on her unhappiness, but he had to work: keep his minister informed of things, appease the voters, ward off complainers, dress well, and make conversation at ludicrous dinner parties engineered for reasons quite separate from friendship. He had to pretend great enthusiasm.

"So what ought we to do?" she said.

"No harm must be done, to anyone," he said.

"It has been done," she said, not knowing the full truth and consequence of her remark.

Then he said what she expected of him, and almost what she wished: that they must not meet for a while, that they must suffer it, that they must consider the feelings of other people, that they must cling to the seeds of their love and spit out the unpleasant but necessary pips. More apple images. She nodded, and shivered, and half wept, and drank, and reshivered. She thought of a girl she knew who wrote a letter to a man, and finding that it was not soulful enough, she sprinkled it with tapwater to convince him more.

"You know what I know," he said, holding both her hands in both of his, "and how I care." She returned from the trance of his strong, preaching, Welsh accent stating their respective duties, returned to the noise and fog-laden smokiness within the pub. And felt a little fortified. It was almost closing time. Meanwhile, the place had filled up and Irish barmen were going around collecting glasses and yelling at the latecomers who circled the brown, solid counter, jostling for service.

"Let's go," he said. Out in the street, because it was late and in a minute many more people would clamor for taxis, they took the one that came instantly. He kissed her a troubled good night. He was already three hours late for his dolorous wife.

"Sit on it, lock it up, be brave," he said as she vanished inside and deposited herself on the cold leather seat and heard him ask what the fare would be. He had nice ways.

She thought of asking the driver to let her out so that she could telephone Baba and make sure her lie had gone unquestioned. But it was late and she had no coins, and anyhow, since the affair had terminated, her guilt and unease seemed to lessen. They merely deluded themselves about postponing it; it was over.

It was a mean thought and she knew that, but she still wished that she had asked him to return the skeleton of the leaf. Probably he had lost it or left it between the pages of a long-winded report. She suddenly attached superstition to it, its return would preface the return of everything good. It had been a gift from her husband, this skeleton leaf, mouse-brown in color with a fine lace texture and a tail long and thin like a mouse's, too A delicate thing created by chance in the autumn when it fell and the flesh of the leaf shriveled away. They got it in Wales. She had given it to her friend the third time they met, and now she wanted it back.

She was like that, she gave too quickly. She did not have her husband's instinct to preserve. She thought of him throughout the drive. Not as he was at dinner, but as she remembered him before. Calling her out of a crowded room once, simply to kiss her, and go back in again. And she had prayed into his mauve tongue that such a miracle would last forever. Prayed one thing and done another. Tonight she was returning to him. She would communicate it in some way, linger over him, pour myrrh on his scalded soul, ask him to forget, forget and forgive, the way the song said.

"Here, just here," she said. The taxi had gone several doors past her house. Just as well. She got out and walked back, planning how she would break the ice with him. The snow was thick and vaporous in the pathway, and the tracks of his twelve-inch, crepe-soled shoes were fresh on it.

4 Kate came in quietly and found him in the study standing over Maura, who was sitting on the couch. At first it seemed as if he had his arms around the girl.

"Oh, togetherness," Kate said. "Perhaps I'm too early." He turned around, acknowledged the fact that he saw her, and returned to attend to Maura's eye. He was obviously taking out a smut, because he had a small paintbrush in one hand, and an eyeglass fixed in the socket of his left eye.

"It's all right, sir, it's all right," Maura said as she leaped up and went out of the room.

"Well, that's one way of returning," Eugene said.

"Have I done something wrong?" she said gently, undoing the last two buttons of her coat.

"No, no, just your customary kindness," he said.

"Oh," she said, and waited. She would have to withdraw the remark.

"I think if you make too free they take advantage," she heard herself say.

"Indubitably." A word he used when he had no intention of saying anything.

"She drinks milk straight from the bottle, it's rimmed with lipstick." She, who meant to dispense only kindness.

"Baba's well," she said then, in the hope of retrieving the evening. She had her coat across her arm and was intending to hang it near the fire in a moment.

"Cheers," he said. "I was breathless to hear how she was." She stood wondering, then asked if she could get him some supper, and when he declined she asked why in a grieved tone. He didn't feel like supper. He felt like tidying all his records, dusting the sleeves, putting some sort of order into them.

"I thought of making soup for us." She stood there at a loss, chagrined, sorry, moving from one foot to the other, thinking that as she counted ten he would say something to detain her. He was in one of his moods. He reminded her then of a lightning rod, tuned only to the elements, indifferent to people. His back was getting thicker, or perhaps it was the winter woollens that made him shapeless. He still held himself more erect than anyone she knew.

"Well, I suppose I'd better go to bed," she said.

"Suppose you'd better." He did not turn around and give the semblance of a kiss by making a kiss-noise, as was his habit lately.

Upstairs she lay awake and planned a new, heroic role for herself. She would expiate all by sinking into domesticity. She would buy buttons, and spools of thread other than just black and white; she would scrape marrow from the bone and mix it with savory Marmite to put on their bread; she would put her lily hand down into sewerages and save him the trouble of lifting up the ooze and hairs and gray slime that resulted from their daily lives. She listened in vain for sounds.

When she came down in the morning she looked for clues to his humor. There was the skin of an apple on a plate, and the daily sentence in block capitals for Cash to write out. Until such time as he went to school his father wrote something out for him to copy. Underneath there was a scribbled sentence, which Kate took to be a memento for herself:

> *Now and then he thought all women could not possibly*
> *be bitches, but not for long, reality was always at hand.*

She read it a few times but decided not to comment on it.

At twelve o'clock, as usual, she brought his tea on a tray, but she chose a nicer cloth, and had worried away the tea stains in his china cup by applying bread soda.

"I thought I'd do it properly," she said as he sat up and reached for the heavy, thick-knit jersey on the floor.

"Yes," he said, "it helps to make an effort." She sat on the side of the bed, holding the tray that he had balanced perfectly on his knees. He kept looking at one pane of the diamond-paned window. It was caked with snow.

"I must clean those windows," she said, trying to humor him. She both knew and did not know that what she said had come too late. Finally, when she'd made no progress, she went downstairs, calling Cash. He was with Maura, dancing to pop music from the radio. Like a little miniature man, he steered the clumsy, pink-armed girl around, and smiled lovingly up into her jolly, flushed face.

"It's time we got on with the lunch," Kate said in a pinched voice.

"Oh no," the child said, "me like dancing." His mother put her arms out and drew him from the warm kitchen into another room, where she reclaimed him with frantic kisses.

"What game will we play?" she said, humoring him.

"Put treasure in a box," he said, "and draw a map and I'll look for it."

She found a box under a sofa where Eugene stuffed things— papers, maps, books, shoe trees, carrier bags, fishing rods.

"What will we put in it?" she asked.

"Treasure."

"Sixpence?"

"No."

"What?"

"I told you. Treasure."

She heard Eugene call from upstairs, "Turn off that cat-alley moaning."

Maura still had the radio going, full blast.

"Turn off that cat-alley moaning," Kate said, passing on the blame.

She put a bead from a broken necklace in the box, drew the map, and sat there while her son crawled around the room asking if he was getting hot or cold, depending on where he was. She said what she had to say, but had no heart in it.

For weeks Eugene barely spoke. It continued to snow. Bulky icicles hung from the ledge of the coal bunker, and when they washed clothes they had to dry them indoors. The quiet, sad drip of the wet clothes and his silence were the only sounds she noted during those weeks. He put ammonia around the house in saucers to take the sulphur fumes away, and when the fog came down in the evening it, too, seemed not to move or wander the way fog does, but to stand still and be hardened by the frost. Even the clothes stiffened in the night, if the boiler went out.

He's freezing me out, she thought as she watched for him to get up, to eat his toast, to go to the lavatory, to put on his coat, to go out, and then hours later to come back in again. Sometimes, if there was a program in his pocket, she knew he'd been to a concert or to theater. Jealousy drove her to search for ticket stubs, to see if there was one or two, but he was careful not to leave anything like that around. She hardly slept, except for the first half hour after getting into bed, when she would fall asleep from total exhaustion and then waken crying, fully alert to everything. They shared the same bed, but he saw to it not to retire until it was morning and time for her to get up.

Once, she stayed on in the morning, and in his sleep he touched her and drew back suddenly, as if he were an animal who had just touched an electric fence and received an appalling shock. For the first time she looked old, really old.

5

One day after lunch Kate took several swigs of whiskey from a bottle that she kept in her handbag, and braved it.

"What are we doing, what are we doing?" she said to Eugene, thinking that by an open appeal she would break through to him.

"I haven't noticed that I struck you lately." He was putting his coat on to go out.

"We're like enemies. We're not like man and wife at all."

"I should hope not."

"But why?" she begged. "Why? Why?" After all, he had been the one to urge marriage and child on her, and he must have known that she was impetuous.

"It's not just my fault, it's yours, too, it's ours," she said, thinking guiltily of all the women's things he had done for the child, like putting a drawstring of twine through a Fair Isle jersey that did not gather in around the neck.

"I must say it took me quite a time to get to know you," he said. "I must congratulate you on your simpleton's cunning, and your simpleton's servile ways."

He, who exacted obedience!

"We all have faults," she said, moving back a bit in case he smelled the whiskey and delivered a lecture about alcohol.

"Fortunately, some of us know about honor," he said. It was strange, though consistent, how in a row he stiffened and talked the wooden language of tracts.

"Honor," she said, unable to think of her own words or resort to her own argument.

"The things you do, count, not your cheap little justifications." He had his gray-flannel scarf on and was smoothing his hair down before putting on a corduroy cap. Luckily Maura and Cash were out feeding the ducks, so they could talk without fear of being heard.

"Can't we talk," she said, "really talk?" Even if they did, what would they say? He had been a great believer in airing one's difficulties, but at this point neither of them was capable of listening.

He was giving his attention to the cap.

"Eugene," she said desperately.

He moved his face from its image in the mirror and looked at her, as though looking at the most ultimate outrage that could have befallen him. Where was the woman he had never had the good fortune to meet?

"We'll get over it, we'll get through it," she said, pitying him, pitying herself. "I'll be better."

He shook his head and looked at her grimly, the look of a gravedigger.

"You won't. It's your nature to lie, like your lying, lackeying ancestors."

"Oh, stop," she said, gripping him.

"Excuse me, I detest vulgarity," he said, picking her arm up and dropping it at her side. He put his hand on the door catch.

"Just say one nice thing," she said, trembling. If he went now it was final. Because his temperament—at least he called it temperament—was such that when people failed him he detached himself from them completely. They ceased to exist anymore for him.

"You live your life, I live mine. That's fair, isn't it?" He had opened the door and icy air rushed into the hall.

"Where will I live?"

"Plenty of cozy bed-sitting rooms around."

Was he telling her to go?

"And Cash?" she said.

"I might let you see him on humanitarian grounds, but of course your morals make you unfit to be a mother." The two words "humanitarian" and "morals" stuck out like barbs on wire. And the tears she shed now were tears of rage and self-pity.

"I didn't sleep with him," she said. It was no longer necessary to hide about Duncan. She wished she had the courage to say the word "fuck" and offend him more.

"The intention was there," he said. "In the eyes of the law that is what counts."

"You bastard," she said directly to his gray-flannel face. In his mind he had already dealt with her and meted out the punishment that a judge would have done.

"You vicious bastard," she said.

He struck her once across the cheek.

"That's right, hit me," she said. "Contradict all your noble, potty theories." He believed in the gentle art of persuasion, in change through knowledge, in the twentieth-century game of brainwashing. One cheek blazed while the other felt as cold as stone.

"I don't have to," he said, almost smiling. "There are other things I can do." And he went out.

"But what things?" she called, but the men shoveling snow off the footpath made it impossible for her to repeat it. She was in her bedroom slippers and could not very well follow him out. She ran to the window and watched him walk down the street, his gait free as a man who had just had lunch and was enjoying a little fresh air. True, what he once said to her about being born to stand outside windows and look in at the lit-up muddle of other people's lives. The scene they had just had was her scene, not theirs. He was apart from it; as he said in jest, he did not attach himself to living people. To sky, to stones, to young girls, he said. To young girls, she thought bitterly, whom he would never meet and therefore never know well enough to despise.

She went upstairs to find the handbag with the broken clasp in which she'd hidden Duncan's love letters. Better put them in the boiler before things became terrible. The bag was wrapped in a night-gown—the very one in fact that she wore when the water broke and Cash was pushing his way into the world—just as she'd left it. She pulled it open and found that the letters were gone. The inside of the bag, smeared with face powder, was treacherously empty. A small typed note fell out:

> *They are where you cannot find them, safe with my lawyer. I have no doubt but that they will come in useful.*

She trembled with shame, with anger that he should know and not have confronted her, that he should have confiscated them and not be ashamed, that he should be as small and mean and obsessional as herself.

406

She ran downstairs, opening drawers and books, wildly and without direction. She opened a ledger in which he normally kept notes about his earnings, his health, and the weather, and on the center page she found her obituary:

> So this is her, my special, hand-picked little false heart, into whose diseased stinking mind, and other parts, I have poured all that I know about living, being, and loving. To-night I had the pleasure of actually seeing her in the arms of that chinless simpleton whom we met months ago at D.'s party. At supper she patently lied to me about having to see Baba and I accompanied her, guessing that her excuses were flimsy. She could not bring me to Baba, it was too private; she got off a bus, took another, donned some idiotic clothes in a ladies' room, and went to a pub to be with him. I could have gone in and knocked out the few front teeth he has left, but it would have been contamination. I went to a pub down the street and had a whiskey and got home in plenty of time to await her. I did not tackle her. There is no need to now. In a way it is a relief to know it is over. Somehow I always knew she would destroy it.

It was dated correctly. He'd written it the night she saw Duncan last. He'd even blotted it carefully, not one smear, and commas in the right places.

For the first time she felt some intimation of the enormity of his buried hatred for her, for women, for human follies. There was no doubt about what she must do. She sought out Cash and Maura, sent the girl on a half-day, and brought Cash home, telling him they were going on a little journey. She packed some things into a suitcase and some boxes, and prayed that they would get away without being caught. She'd rung Baba and a taxi was on its way to take them from the violated lair to somewhere less awful.

6

She came here later in a taxi carrying two fiber suitcases and two cardboard boxes. Stuff that I wouldn't be seen dead with.

"Are we on our holidays?" the kid kept saying because of the luggage. Not that it looked jolly. Far from it.

"Come in," I said. Because I knew everything she was going to say before she said it.

"Oh, Baba," she said, "I think I'm going to kill myself."

"Come on, girl," I said, "facts."

"He found out about Duncan," she said. "He hit me and threatened to take Cash away, and he hates me." Millions of women getting hit every day, and I myself forced to strip once on the imprimatur of my husband because three of his pals bet I had no navel. How could I have functioned without a navel? The telephone rang.

"Don't answer it," she said, jumping up. She said he'd be on her trail soon. He was out for a walk and would come in and find her note.

"What's in the note?" I asked.

"Just that we weren't right for each other."

Imagine leaving a note like that when he was a fanatical man.

"He says I'm rotten," she said. He was full of character, of course, and she wasn't. She wasn't bad, but like any woman she'd take mission money to buy clothes, or if she met some man she liked she'd persecute him until she had loaded him with the love trophy. Knowing this about her, Eugene was so righteous he made a constant splash about his integrity. They were mad in two different ways.

"I've left," she said. "It's all over." She'd obviously done some very thorough packing because the kid was unloading the contents of the boxes into our elegantly louvered drawers: curtain rings, empty perfume bottles, old envelopes, broken belts.

"What did you bring that junk for?" I said.

"Association," she said, without a smile.

Association or not, she'd have to take them away. Frank wouldn't have her in our house with danger brewing. Frank was very careful; you know, slaughter your wife so long as you do it indoors.

"Who's that?" the child said, holding two photographs. One of Kate as kid leaning on her mother's shoulder. It was the mercy of God her mother got drowned or she'd still be going around tacked onto her mother's navel. And one of Eugene looking like an advertisement for hemlock. That, as you can imagine, started her off on a right orgy of drip. His strong face. Where had it gone wrong? A year ago she had written evidence from him that she was the genuine Kate in ten thousand Kates, because of her alarmingly beautiful face, and disposition, her tender solicitude and worth; and she'd written back to him—he was only in the other room, for God's sake—that he was her buoy, her teacher, the good god from whose emanations she gained all.

"Ring Duncan," I said. I would have said "Ring the Prime Minister" if I'd thought it would have helped. I sent her upstairs to do it in privacy while I chatted up the kid. It was really serious for me. She didn't know it, but Frank got very difficult after we were married. He stopped being a slob, if you know what I mean. I traced all back to the evening of our wedding. For a start we were refused admission on the plane because of his being drunk and he said did they know that his wife was wearing a Balenciaga while they hauled him away to cool off in some private room. Next day when we got away—to some bloody resort that an agent fixed for us—there were gangs of men smirking at me in my buff-colored suit, and he sent me upstairs to put something respectable on. I owned nothing respectable. At dinner he said the food was oily. He's the sort who, the minute he gets across the English Channel, says the food is oily. That night to add to our joys I had the curse—excitement or some bastard thing—even though I'd worked out all my dates well ahead. He wanted to call a doctor.

"What curse?" he kept saying, as if I were a witch or something.

"It must be the food," he said. He'd pushed the twin beds together and everything.

"Don't you know about women?" I said. He just looked at me with his big, stupid, wide-open mouth. He didn't know. What sort of mother had he? He said to leave his mother out of it, that she was a good woman and baked the best bread in Ireland. I said there was more to life than baking good bread. He got vicious then. And went down to the bar. The upshot was that we didn't sleep together that night, and when we did a few nights later it was pretty uneventful. For me, that is. He said what was wrong with me? I said it wasn't as simple as he thought, that for women hand manipulation, coaxing, et cetera had to come into it. He said it made us sound like a bleeding motor engine. But as I saw it he was the one who treated us as an engine. If things go wrong at the start they often stay wrong. He knew no other way and neither did I. Birds of a feather . . . As time went on, he minded that I wasn't getting preg—interceding to the Holy Spirit, we were—and he'd say to me in front of people, "Baba, you'll have to go to a doctor and have yourself seen to." And then, in a drunker state he'd look at some little man who was the father of five and say, "I'm not half the man you are." I don't know what was up with him. I could never figure out whether it was his mother, or indoctrination from one of those flogging Christian brothers, or had he been with sheep and chickens as a kid and got all his associations, as Kate would put it, mixed up. It changed him, though. He got very rough in his ways and would say "Cut it out" if I said he ought to see a doctor and discuss not being preg. He took a great interest in crime and murder and filed the really juicy ones. I could see that bullfighting would be tops on the agenda.

"I'll ask thee a riddle," said Cash, looking into my face. He says "thee" to get attention. I must have been miles away.

"Long legs, crooked thighs, small head, and no eyes?" he said. I'm supposed to be as surprised as hell. He's a pure slob really, because I taught him that riddle, and he expected me to be dope enough not to know it. I answered wrong. I suppose I liked him. I could see that his father would go mad to lose him. Anyone would. His mother came in just as he was telling me the answer.

"A tongs," he was saying, his front teeth square and very white, but one chipped at the edge.

"No one is sincere." She was wringing her hands.

"He's coming on a white horse," I said, knowing the worst. She shook her head and repeated the conversation to me, verbatim. It went more or less like this:

"Did he ring you?" she said to her Duncan.

"No, should he?"

"I've just left him; it was awful."

"That's terrible, Kate."

"He'll be ringing you, Duncan. He found your letters and everything."

"Good God, I wouldn't have wished that."

"Well, it's happened now. He's furious."

"I wouldn't wish him an hour's, nay, a second's unhappiness."

"Duncan, will you help me? I'm desperate."

"But of course. You must think first of him, after all it is between him and you. Go back, talk it over, iron it out."

That more or less concluded it. He begged her to ring him next morning, but we knew that he'd have some hatchet-voiced secretary laid on to tell Kate some boring and familiar lie, like that he was in conference.

"Time is running out," she said, looking straight at the grandfather clock. Talk about being worried. I was a wreck myself, with Frank due any minute.

"Premises," I said. "We'll have to get you some." I knew of a sanitary shop on the King's Road where they leave the baths out all night, and I said she could rip up there, sleep in a bath, and put a sign up: KEEP OUT. GONORRHEA. She'd be safe, like a titless woman. Do you think she'd laugh? Not a glimmer.

"I could book you in a hotel," I said. I hated to say, "You can't stay here."

"I'm in your way. I'm a nuisance," she said. Damn right, she was. I'm a pure phony—I heard myself say, "No, but eventually you'd like a place of your own."

"Yes," she said, "I'd like a studio with white walls and pictures, and a garden smothered in hedge."

I thought, If she goes on like that I won't have to worry, there'll be a team of doctors in here to certify her.

"But for tonight," I said, "I'll get you both a hotel."

"No," she said, clinging to me, "we can't go out; he'll take Cash. We must stay here, we must."

"Me like it here," the kid was saying, like a skilled blackmailer. He was flicking through our leather-bound encyclopedia—nothing, Frank says, like a self-educated man—having demolished a tin of cocktail snacks.

"Now don't worry. Leave it to me," I said, calming her down. Madman, I am.

The bloody phone rang again.

"Hello, Eug," I said to stop him in his tracks. Lucky it wasn't him, because of course I gave us away rightly. It was Frank to say he'd met a bunch of very interesting people, and I was to get my Dior on and come on, because he was taking us all to a new restaurant.

"Super, darling," I said. That must have shook him, because since the argument over my navel I haven't associated with his mates.

"When and where?" I said. At least 'twould keep him out of the house till late, and Brady could hide until morning. I wrote down the details and told him to take care, which was strange coming from me. Normally I'm praying he'll fall off a scaffold.

She made me go around the house with a crowbar closing all the windows. She said she didn't think she'd live the night, and even the kid was beginning to fret.

"Listen, listen," she'd say every time a board creaked or the boiler let out some sort of noise. It was like being at a suspense picture, only worse. Plenty of human interest! Was I glad to go out! We made an arrangement that I'd telephone once, put the telephone down, and then dial again immediately. Otherwise she was to answer nothing. I conducted her to a room at the top of the house where Frank kept easels and things since the time he had the urge to be a painter.

"I wouldn't wish you an hour's, nay, a second's unhappiness," I said, trying to be funny, as I put a pile of blankets, sheets, and pillows into her arms. She looked about eighty, and the kid had his face to the wall, sniffling. Had she landed us in a mess!

"I'm meeting men—I'll get you fixed up with one," I said. She put on the droopy, look-upon-me-with-pity face. But boy, did she destine our future!

I got there in my gold shoes and the Dior dress with the enormous rosette on the back. It transpired that he'd met an actor that day—nearly ran over him in the street—and they got chatting and the actor introduced him to a poet, and the poet to a drummer, and the drummer to a Jew, and they had all forgathered for grub. The locals in the pub nudged themselves when I took off my coat. Because of the place the rose was positioned.

"Meet my wife, my wife," Frank kept saying.

There were two other women in the party: a blonde with the roots badly done and a very quiet-spoken American girl. The actor had just come from work and Frank was fussing over him and buying quadruple brandies. It was the first actor he'd ever met, for God's sake.

"He's a good actor, keep him happy, keep him entertained," Frank kept saying to me.

In my experience actors have a hernia if anyone else does the entertaining. I sang dumb except to say "Chin-chin" at each round.

"I must congratulate you on your taste," he said to Frank, meaning that I was dishy. I thought it a bit of a neck, but I let it go, because I was trying to edge my way across to talk to some real men. The Jew looked interesting and sort of wronged, so did a small pale boy—you couldn't call him a man even though he was about twenty-five or -six —with a girlish face. Dead wrong for a man, of course, but still . . . His complexion was blue, as if he'd been left out nights when he was young, and his lips had no color, and his hands were about as big as a child's. I never got near him because Frank said the actor was hungry and the muses must be fed. You know that sort of faker-than-fake talk. Before leaving he stuffed pound notes into a couple of collection boxes that were on the counter.

"Poor hungry devils," he said, meaning neglected dogs or kids or whatever he was financing. Charity! He and his brother sack men on Christmas Eve and rehire them on St. Stephen's Day to escape holiday pay. He dropped about ten quid in all.

The restaurant was so new that there was no one else there except us. That sort of shook Frank, but the poet said we'd make it swing, so we began to troop around and pretend we were about two hundred people. The pale boy drummed on the tablecloth. I reckoned he was the drummer.

"Sit, lads, sit," Frank said, the old accent getting bog-thick with drink and excitement.

The place itself was very posh, with built-in sand dunes and cacti and water sprays. Like a bloody jungle, if you want to know. I could see Frank taking stock of it all. For our interior decor. We were in our rented-flower era. A firm sent a man around every Monday morning to take away a big, vulgar display of plastic flowers and replace it with another. Identical. I suppose they swapped them around from house to house. He was planning to hire a dance floor, too, since the day he saw a van go by which said HIRE YOUR OWN DANCE FLOOR AND BE SMART.

"Are they lilies?" he said, looking at some chrysanthemums.

"Quite," said the actor. An ignoramus, too.

"Give me wax roses any old time," I said. I was dead drunk, mainly from nerves.

"Do you like gardening?" the actor said to me. God Almighty, what grouping! I was beside him again.

"When I was in the convent," said I—when tight I get reminiscent—"we had to till a patch of garden—life is a garden, old chap—and I used to steal flowers from other girls' plots and stick them in my own. I didn't even plant them properly!"

Damn actor didn't wait to hear the end of the story.

"Let's have some of the old Mateus, amigo," he was saying to Frank, coming on all Continental. You know, greengrocer's son from Wakeley with his eye on a knighthood.

"What play are you in?" said I. I knew if 'twas posh we'd have heard.

"Is it Shakespeare?" said Frank. He knows about nothing else.

"Actually," said the actor, and then started up a fit of coughing and stammering and took five minutes to tell us he was in a thing called "Something, Something, Rubbish." At that minute the poet cocked his ear. "Oh," said the poet, who'd timed it beautifully, the way spiteful people do, "he is the hind legs of a good old British horse."

414

"I'm the front legs," said the actor, going all blubbery. "You are a very naughty blond Christopher." I knew by the way the one smirked, and the other sulked, that they lived together and that the American girl was wasting her bosoms raving away to the poet about iambic pentameter, when she'd be better off at home in Minnesota having dull old fun. They were ill-matched: the actor was long and thin with a sort of "hold my hand, Mammy" expression, and the poet was wiry, with a hard, hungry, jaundiced face. For some reason I thought of Kate wringing her boring hands out, and it occurred to me that they might have her as a lodger. I knew that queers like to have a woman around for status so long as they don't have to lay a finger on her, and boy, was she straight out of some chastity unit.

"What are we all having?" the actor said. He stuttered ever so nicely. I expect he went to that school where you are thought sensitive if you stutter.

"I don't know," I said. The menu was like the Magna Carta.

"We'll have soup, lads," Frank said. I tried to catch his eye to get him off the soup jazz. He thinks it's the poshest thing out. He knows it isn't, but he thinks it is, because they only had it once or twice when he was a kid. I made a face at him.

"Stop worrying how much it's going to cost," said he to me, real loud. That's what I mean about him getting treacherous.

In the end we ordered oysters and snails and swank stuff. While the food was coming someone said that someone ought to tell a joke.

"Yes, sport," said the Australian. I forgot to say there was an Australian among us, and every time he opened his mouth it was to tell some dirty story, and the actor would intervene and say, "Ladies present." Pure routine jokes about bishops and dirty postcards.

"You should see your face," said the drummer, leaning across the table to me. I knew I looked bored. He said he liked my story about the flower garden. He said it was anarchy and he liked anarchy.

"Plenty more where that came from," I said. He was giving me the eye all right. It was ages since I'd had a fling.

"Don't look so furious," he said. It was then I missed the Jew. He'd quietly left us.

"You don't know anybody who has a studio to let?" I said, leaning, too, to meet the drummer halfway across the table. We both had our elbows up, shutting out the others. I didn't go on about the white walls and privet hedge bit in case he thought I was nuts.

"I may do," he said. He had a low conniving voice. Dead sexy.

The waiter was putting down plates of snails and various consignments of cutlery, and Frank was telling everyone not to give a minute's thought to the cost, while we all decided on steak au poivre. You know how it is in a big restaurant, one person says steak and they all say steak. The blind leading the blind. The headwaiter was pressing us to have the plate of the day, but we were wise to that. No chicken gizzards for us. He looked mummified. Before that Frank had to bribe him with a fiver to admit the poet, in a boiler suit. As far as I'm concerned it's much more ridiculous to be bribing waiters than to own a presentable suit, but you know the length some people will go to, to be thought rebellious.

"A studio for yourself?" the drummer said to me, real interested. I suppose I looked rich, with my Dior and my rings and gear.

"For a friend," said I, hoping Frank wouldn't hear. I knew I should ring Kate but kept postponing it.

"We'll talk about it," said the drummer, while Frank lifted the wine out of the ice bucket and drenched the hands of the two who were next to him.

"How marvelous," said the American girl. We were getting the actor's account of how he lived on kippers for three years when he toured the provinces. I know that story backward. If it was true of even five percent of the people who tell it, there wouldn't be one kipper left in the world. The poet rounded it off with some corny verse, and Frank started to clap.

"How did you get to be a poet?" said he, real awed. "Did you enter for a competition?"

Well, of course, everyone began to laugh and Frank didn't know why.

"I would have thought it started that way," said he, making a bigger fool of himself.

"Your approach, if I may say so, is distinctly amateur," said the poet, and Frank knew there was an insult there. He got flushed the way he does before he starts a fight. God, I thought, the lilies and furniture and stuff are in for a bit of reorientation now when he wrecks the joint. I didn't care because the drummer and I were playing what the actor would call "footsie" under the table, and having a rare time. He began it. I felt this thing on my leg and I thought it was a mouse and nearly screamed, but he stopped me with a look. I have this daft thing about mice. See them out of the corner of my eye when they're not there. Pure lunacy, but I do. It was his toe. I wouldn't let him go too far, of course. I knew that tune about being hard to get, et cetera. We were both chewing away like fiends and didn't as much as look at each other. The old chairs were creaking under us, but no one heard because the actor was trying to get Frank and the poet to shake on it and be friends. Boy, was he a coward.

"Yes," the American girl was saying to my drummer, "I'm all right now, I've got the world by the short hairs." He was smiling away and she thought it was for her, but I could see the little flush in his cheeks.

"That's why I can never ignore it," the actor said to me, all of a sudden.

"What?" said I, thinking he had gauged the proceedings.

"The telephone," said he. "My dear old mother is alive, she lives on solvents now, she is likely to die any minute."

That sort of brought me back to life, that and his asking me what pudding I would like. There are people in the world and you know they are going to say pudding and tell you about their mothers living on solvents.

"No pudding," said I, sort of flat and lonesome now, because I'd dismissed the old toe before things got too runny.

"I'm altering," said the actor, and I thought, Why does he have to get confidential with me over dinner? But in fact he was telling the waiter that he'd have a choc ice instead of vanilla.

"I'm serious about this studio," I said to the drummer. He looked sort of huffed now, as if he mightn't go on with it.

The rest of the evening was uneventful, except that Frank fell asleep before the coffee came and they all nearly died of shock in case they'd have to pay. They got him awake with shaking him, and boy, did the poet hand out a lot of baloney about the best way to make friends with a good man was to have a row with him.

It worked out easy for me to give the drummer a lift in my Jag because Frank was taking the others in his. That American girl came, too. She kept calling the drummer Harvey all the time. We dropped her and then went on to his place.

"Do you want to see the studio?" he said when we got there. We'd been talking real cool in the car.

We went up some flights of stairs—me holding on to the shaky railing—and the linoleum gave out after the third flight. I thought of Brady making a big song and dance about this, saying how environment affects the mind and so forth.

"It's your studio," I said as we went in, and he switched on a lamp, showing the big room, a tossed bed, a chest of drawers with no handles, two drums, and colored pictures of nudes pinned to the wall.

"Why is it to let?" I said. "Are you leaving?" We were dead formal, like house agent and client.

"Yes," he said, "I don't fancy it. It's too bourgeois for me!" Bourgeois. There were orange boxes as chairs, for God's sake, and a floor mat over the bed.

"It's for a friend, a girl, who's left her husband," I said, in case he thought I wanted it for a love nest.

"It's not for you," he said, smiling. He had this fab smile.

"Not me. I live with my husband."

"Will he expect you home?"

"Sure."

"In that case," he said, "let's be practical. We can't tonight, so why waste time and make him suspicious. When can I come?"

Talk about alacrity. I fixed it that he come to tea the next day, and then I had a quick look around to see if Brady would find the place habitable. There wasn't a cup or a saucer, or any evidence of eating.

Just before I left he put the light out. "Open your mouth," he said, and gave me this kiss. I went down the rickety stairs singing "Careless Love" to my heart's content.

I got home in about ten minutes and walked straight into tally-hoo. Old Eugene was there acting like a madman. You know, talking about the law and civil rights and stuff. At four in the morning. It seems he was pounding on the door when Frank got there.

"Sit down," I said, "and have a cup of tea." He's a great one for tea. I was most friendly.

"Is my wife here, is my child here?" he said. My, my, my.

"They couldn't be," said I. "We were out to supper and we've just got in. Is there something wrong?" I sobered pretty smartly. Frank was walking around like a shop walker, saying he was an honest man and would let no loose woman hide in his house.

"I warn you," Eugene said. "If she's here, you're culpable by law for abducting my child." The gripes. A raving encyclopedia of the law, he was. I thought, If this is how true love ends, I'm glad I've never had the experience. He listed all her faults, you know, really intimate details that you wouldn't want known.

"By Christ," said Frank, "if she is here I'll have plenty to say to her, upsetting my night's sleep like this."

"She isn't here," I said. I had to be casual. The pair of them were stamping around all the time and I had visions of her creeping in, in a nightgown, saying, "Did somebody call?"

"Look," said I, coming the old honor, "if she gets in touch with me I give you my oath that I'll ring you." I'm amazing when I want to be. He made me repeat it, then left me a four-page letter for her, enumerating all her faults to her, and departed saying he'd use force if necessary. I saw him out, and boy, did I chain that door after him.

Of course, I had to tell Frank, I just had to. He nearly ripped the roof off. He tore up the stairs, with me after him, calling her name the way you'd call cows. She came out peppering.

"You get out of here," Frank said. She pleaded to be left until morning. It was really debasing to see her pleading. He said no. He said he didn't want to end up in the divorce courts, thank you very much, and that he had his reputation to think of. I'd have injured him if capital murder wasn't operating in this country and pig-faced ministers weren't screaming daily to bring back the birch. She looked as if she might die. I told him to go to bed and that she'd be gone before he got up. She and I spent the rest of the night figuring out where she'd go. I told her a bit—not too much—about the drummer's place and she began thanking me and slopping over me, and I hate it when people thank you beforehand, because then it means you've got to help. Anyhow, I rang hotels, but none of them would have her. They were all full up. I suppose they thought she was a jail bird. So I had to try friends. Imagine ringing people at that hour of night and saying, "I was just thinking of you. I just thought I'd ring up for a chat," because of course I couldn't decently ask at once. They all said why didn't I have her? She was crying and supplicating and saying, "Why did it have to happen to me?" Exactly my sentiments, too. Because to tell you the truth, I wasn't having all that much fun ringing people up in the middle of the night. Two lots banged the phone down on me.

"What was Eugene like, how did he look?" she kept saying. I said he looked shaken, naturally.

I said, "You know what old Scott Fitzgerald said about the three-o'clock-in-the-morning state." Giving her back one of her own tags. She's full of tags. Things that Scott said in bars, and wise saws that Ernest Hemingway gave out to whalers. As if she were their best friend and had breakfast with them on their ranches every morning.

Finally in the early morning I had to resort to blackmail. There's a crow who lives on our road and I let her keep her wheelbarrow in our treble garage, so I rang her. She wasn't one bit forthcoming. She hummed and hawed, and I gave her the tune about a friend in need is a friend indeed, so she said, "Well, maybe for a week or two." She wouldn't hear of having the child, because her dog bit kids.

"We'll have to put the kid in a kennel," said I, real sarcastic, and I fixed it that Kate would move in by eight in the morning and take her chances with the dog.

When I put the telephone down I knew what was coming. Remorse! As if I hadn't enough for one day. She pitied Eugene, she said. He was a misfit. He loved his child. She couldn't be responsible if he went mad. For whom the bell tolls. I mean, I don't have to go over the rigmarole. You've heard it millions of times before.

The upshot is, her on the telephone to him, bursting over with apology and saying she shouldn't have done it. I thought after all that trouble I'd gone to, to get that room. She was so goddamn servile I could have killed her. Telling him that he should have met a good woman, but that there was no such thing. Letting the sex down with a bang. The happy conclusion reached was that she'd bring Cash home and take the room herself, to brood over her faults for a few weeks.

"And we're still friends," she kept saying. You could just imagine her saying that to a hangman.

We dressed the kid about seven and took him home. He was dead disappointed. He thought he was out for a month at least. We told him his mother had to go to hospital. The things kids are told! When we let him out and he trotted up his own path, she looked after him and said, "Poor Cash, he doesn't know what's ahead of him," and that was the only time that I really made a fool of myself and cried. I mean, he looked so harmless in the thick blue gabardine raincoat she had on him. And he turned around and grinned at us as if we were coming back in a few minutes.

"Parents," she said.

Parents, I thought, the whole ridiculous mess beginning all over again. Hers and mine and all the blame we heaped on them, and we no better ourselves. Parents not fit to be kids. Talk of tears, we bawled and bawled, and the driver had to go around the square twice before she was ready to go into her new lodgings. I couldn't go with her, it was too hurtful.

"How will I get through the day?" she asked.

"Have a sleep," I said. You know, like, "Have fun."

"I can't."

I knew 'twas unbearable for her, but what could I do? What can anyone do for anyone else? I gave her Sweet Dreams pills and a few crisp fivers. These were the only times I found marriage at all pleasing —when I was handing out his money. Then, to liven her up, I said if she was going to do herself in, to be sure and make a will and leave me her diaries.

"I won't forget you, Baba," she said, dead serious, dead dopey. I cannot stand serious people.

7 Later in the day I set to preparing for Harvey. I got the bedroom organized, removed our sleeping attire and Durack's toothbrush. It looks prehistoric, gray hairs soft and bushy and worn right down to the butt. He'll buy a helicopter but not a toothbrush. I then carted some of the more disastrous antiques to the shed. At four o'clock the old "Home Sweet Home" doorbell chimed. God grant it's not Kate or a manure man, I thought. Once I was so bored I took pity on a manure man and bought stuff. Town manure stinks like nothing else you've ever dreamed of—what they add to it!

"All right, Mrs. Cooney, I'll get it," I said, real cool. That's our charwoman. She was halfway up the stairs, but I beat her to the door and greeted him with a plastic smile. You won't believe it but he was standing there with a big drum and drumsticks and everything. It was very flashy, with red stones around the rim.

"It's not a concert," I said. I didn't know what to say, really.

"I thought you'd like to hear me play," he said. Thought! He had a hell of a cheek bringing all that gear, not knowing whether he'd get in or not, or whether he'd have to sneak out the pantry window in an emergency.

"Charming," I said, bringing him into the room. I had a real hostess face on, and gold tights. He was in brown himself. Shirt, jacket, trousers—everything brown. I thought only someone really full of himself could wear such a boring color and get away with it.

"You match the tobacco tones of the room," I said, sarcastic.

"So?" he said, smiling. It was a grin really, a grin that said, "I can twist you around my little finger."

Not me, baby, I thought as I watched him take a swig of the brandy I'd given him—we have all our grog bottled specially with our name on it.

Then he beckoned me to come over near him and I leaped across and he put his lips to mine and gave me brandy from his mouth. I nearly passed out with the thrill. I don't want to get all eejity about nature and stuff, but it was just like the way birds chew the food and then feed it in the mouths of their young. He could twist me around some barbed wire if he wanted to.

"Now sit down," he said, "and talk to me." I went and sat on our studio couch with its patent floating comfort suspensions. "Our playground," I said, smiling. I thought he'd come and sit next to me but he didn't. He put a cushion on the floor, crossed his legs, and sat like a mystic. He was looking around the room, sizing it up.

"What's that crazy thing?" he said. It was an antique miniature coach that we carted one Sunday from Windsor.

"An antique—Queen Anne," said I. I thought of the consignment of stuff out in the shed and what he'd make of that. But I was damned if I was going to get insulted in my own house. "Being a garret man," said I, "you wouldn't probably know much about it."

"I like simple wooden furniture," said he.

"Gracious living," said I, thinking of the orange boxes. We were really hitting it off.

"I'd love some more brandy," I said then, meaning from the mouth. He got up and filled me a boring glass, and put it on the bamboo table in front of me. Durack read somewhere that bamboo was in, that Cecil Beaton had a bamboo whatnot in his studio, so he sent to Ireland to his poor old mother and got her to rake up all the bamboo in the place. Junk!

"Where are you from?" I said. I couldn't think of one witty thing.

"A nomad," he said. Anyone else saying that would look a right fool, but not him. That was the thing about him. He wouldn't look a fool ever, no matter what he did. He had it all figured. He had the world by the short hairs, too. He knew what to say, but mostly it was a question of what not to say. No one would catch him out. There are people like that, quite a lot.

He said he'd lived all over, in Australia and Mexico and places, and that he had Apache Indian blood. I thought, How the hell can you be so white if you have Indian blood, but that's not the sort of thing you can say. Indian blood is all the rage now.

"We'll have some tea," I said, and rang the bell, although I hated to, but Cooney was so moody that if I didn't let her have a look in she mightn't show up for days. At least I warned her not to say the bit about "keep your faith in God and your bowels open." She says that to total strangers, like it was a recitation.

"Did you call me, madam?" she said, hopping in, in a clean apron, with the hat on. It's an atrocious hat with veiling but she thinks it does wonders for her. The "madam" nearly killed me; she calls me by my Christian name, for God's sake, when we're alone. He started to smile, and of course that gave her leeway to come in.

"Lovely drum," she said. He said he was glad she liked it and would she like to hear him play?

"Oh, goody," she says, and sinks onto the couch with her stupid feet up in the air. Her legs are that short. He played some very earthy stuff, I mean 'twas loud and like the noise savages make with bones. We were a good audience. She was clapping like a maniac; I mean, clapping in the middle and places where she shouldn't. He was all intense and didn't pay attention to me once. That maddened me. I'd peeled off most of my underclothes and was freezing.

"Give us lavender blue," Cooney said when he looked like stopping.

"I think we'll have tea, Mrs. Cooney," I said. She'd switched off. Strap. She has this hearing aid. She can hear better than anyone, but she got it for nothing on the health scheme. She's the sort would have her own teeth taken out just to avail herself of the free ones. I gave her a nudge in the ribs.

"Very nice of you, madam," she said, and leaned over to the bamboo table and took a fistful of fags from the silver cigarette box. She put them all in her apron pockets except for the one she lit.

"Put a beggar on horseback and he'll ride to hell," I said. She just ignored me and went on looking at his drumming. You'd think he was making love to that drum, the way he brought it to life. He had his legs around it. She was clapping and humming. Finally I had to go make the tea myself. The tray was set for three but I removed one cup and saucer. When I came back into the room she noticed this straightaway. She jumped up in a huff and shook hands with him and said he was a gentleman. She shot out of the room and came back almost at once with her coat on, saying in a toff's voice, "Mrs. Durack, I want a personal word with you at once."

"I'm not at all pleased with you," she said to me out in the hall. "Discriminating like that, as if I were black or something."

"He's Albanian himself," I said, just to confuse her.

"Jumped-up Irish scum," she said to me. A hell of a neck. She smelled like a brewery.

"I think you've had too much to drink," said I. I knew that would kill her, because although she tipples all day she never admits to drinking.

"No class! Letting me wash your knicks," she said. I hoped to God he wasn't listening. It was all I needed to look alluring in his eyes. I opened the door and pushed her out.

"I know where I'm not wanted," she said.

"It takes you a hell of a long time to register it," I said. She put her head through the letter box then, and began yelling and cursing and ringing the "Home Sweet Home" bell. I came back into the room to find him halfway through the cucumber sandwiches and pouring himself another cup of tea.

"Are you all right?" I said, just to let him know that I could see he was eating rapidly.

"Did the drumming excite you?" he said when I sat down.

"Oh, very much." I was excited before ever he came.

"How?"

"Oh, you know how."

"Where?"

"In my wooden leg." Sweet Jesus, where did he think!

"Breasts or loins?" he said.

"Both." I know roughly where your loins are, but I'd hate to have to point them out on a diagram.

"Good," he said. He ripped into the cake and then a cigar from our box. Jokes—he had the least sense of humor of anyone I ever met, and boy, I know some dull people. He dropped his previous cigarette butt into the great big china jardiniere we have. It fizzled in there because there was water in the bottom since the last real flower display.

"Your husband's fetish," he said, sort of sarcastic. True enough, it did look like a great community chamber pot, but who was he to talk about fetishes.

We were getting nowhere.

"Come and sit near me," I said.

"I prefer to look at you from here," he said. "The human face is not made for closeups. There is only one time when it's bearable, that is"—he stopped as if he was going to say something revolutionary, for God's sake—"on a pillow."

"Plenty of pillows in the linen cupboard," I said, to be funny. I made a fool of myself twenty times per minute.

Then he stood up, took hold of one of the drumsticks, and came over and started drumming me, mainly on the bosoms. Playful as hell. I don't know if you go in for that sort of thing, but there's no fun in it. Merciful God. I just felt I was being pummeled.

"Turn around," he said. I got a few on the bottom.

A thought struck me about my bruises. Frank often examines me, to see what the butler saw. I could see him inquiring about this mysterious mark and me saying, "Waxed floor did it—I slipped," and him saying, "What waxed floor? We have fitted carpets," and me saying, "I took up a carpet to do it; house-proud little me, I even waxed the floor underneath." A cock-and-bull story if ever I heard one.

Ouch, he went on drumming, and boy, did it hurt.

"I've studied the art of lovemaking since I was fourteen," he said. He said he had his muscles under such control that he could make love to twenty-five women in an evening. He pointed to a little line of hair on his chin and said that it was put to use in lovemaking, too.

"My hipbones, every part of me is brought to bear," he said. Talk about the secrets of the Orient. I was raring to get upstairs.

Well, for the record, we got up there about two hours later, by which time you could have carried me on a stretcher I was so exhausted. 'Twas a ritual. I had to be drummed all over, then spin on my toes and play the damn drum with my fingers while he played it with his, and then kiss at a certain ordained moment, and not even got any pleasure out of it. 'Twas like drill at school. I had to act as if there were nothing happening. Not that there was that much going on.

"Now, one, two, three, begin," he'd say. We had to keep time, too. Talk about Pavlov's dogs. I'd have swapped with any of them.

"Will you do things for me?" he said upstairs as I clicked the Venetian blinds closed and drew the curtains. I locked the door.

"Do things!" I'd been working like a maniac for two hours.

"Have you a black brassiere?" he said. Of course I had. It's the only color you don't have to wash every day. London is so filthy you'd be out of your mind to wear any other color.

"And boots?" he said. 'Twas around the time that women were wearing high leather boots to dinner parties and everything.

"No," I said. 'Twas different for women that had legs like the back of a bus.

"You'll have to get some," he said. "And a leather coat."

"I'll get Harrods to send the lot around, straightaway," I said. And then I blew a bit about how I'd heard they sent a van to Northumberland to deliver a biro pen and a rubber. He said not to bother for then, but to put on a sou'wester rain hat if I had one.

"And plenty of soap," he said.

"Do you want basins of water, too?" I said. I'm a pure slob. I mean, I always think of soap and water together. 'Twas beginning to feel like a road accident. I got an old rain hat anyhow and left it on the pillow.

He took off his clothes and folded them real neat. I hate that. It means they're thinking more about not losing the crease in their trousers.

"Sorry about the boots and gear," I said, "but we'll have a rehearsal until such time as I get togged out."

Not a smile out of him. I got undressed real snazzy. Quicker than the instructors that train firemen. I had so little on, for God's sake. He took one look at my skin and said 'twas too white. Just think of it. Unfortunate people hanged, drawn, and quartered all over the world for being black and he had to say this. His own skin was pretty nice, smooth and sort of shiny like gold, polished wood with a line of hair down his stomach.

"Does this have a part in the mating ritual?" I said to the line of hair. Trying to get a bit of fun into it.

Well, I plugged in the old electric blanket and we plunged in.

"Have you ever had a woman?" he said.

"Plenty," said I. I didn't know for a minute what he meant. I thought of getting it straight about booking the flat for Kate, but it could wait until the high jinks were over.

"Did you ever use milk bottles?" he said, and then it struck me what he meant. So I said no, not at all, had he ever had a man?

"What makes you think that?" he said, real huffy. I didn't think it. I thought nothing, to tell you the truth, except that we were taking a long time to do what millions of people do every hour of the day before they go to their work or eat their breakfast or cut their toenails. I was beginning to have severe doubts. When he'd half smoked a cigarette he threw back the covers and began a light touch of singeing. You could smell it.

"Wait a minute," says I. I'd have enough to account with the bruise marks besides having singed hair. Like an ill-plucked chicken.

"You'll like it," he said. "It will excite you." Excite! I was about going out of my mind with excitement. I didn't like it. I knew some man that went in for that kind of frolic and giving women whiffs of ammonia, and he ended up in the clink and about ten of them ended up in their graves.

"Come on," I said, putting the sou'wester on and getting all lovey-dovey. He put the cigarette out and we got down to business.

"Is it big enough for you?" he said. Men worry about that a terrific lot.

"Enormous," I said.

"You're a bright girl," he said. Men are pure fools. Then the hipbone bit came, which I took to be a mere preliminary, and when I said he was welcome to press all, he said, "It's gone to sleep." They worry about that a terrific lot, too.

He said that he wanted to kiss my teeth. I have two teeth on a brace, for God's sake. My teeth were the last things I wanted him to kiss. We lay quite still for a while and he said our bodies were as if a painter had flung them together on canvas. Did I like that? Did I think he was clever? I said yes to everything. I asked what things in the world he liked.

"The inside of a kitten's mouth," he said. "It's like water, only it's soft."

Boy, was he making me feel wanted. I asked him then what he was afraid of. I got really frantic to make conversation.

"That I'll lose any of my teeth," he said. A born flatterer. I got the inference.

"And I'm afraid that I'm not as good a drummer as I think I am," he said, then jumped up and looked at his wristwatch, which he'd left on the bedside table. He said he'd soon have to go because he was playing that night.

"I thought we were going to make love," I said. Between you and me, I really did.

"No," he said, "not today." Then he said that I wasn't ready and that I talked too much.

"With me," he said, "it has to be pure. It has to be the most pure thing in the world, like the inside of a kitten's mouth."

"I can see how you make love to twenty-five women in one evening," I said to stab him. It worked like a dream. He got all virile then, and with the aid of me, the sou'wester, and himself, he came out of his sleep and set to, to seduce me. We were engaged about four minutes flat when I heard him say, "I came. I didn't think I would."

"You're joking," I said. By now I'd lost any notion I had that things were going to work out.

"You must promise me something," he said then.

"Anything," I said. He was that vain he didn't even notice the sarcasm.

"That you won't get pregnant," he said.

"I'll try not to," I said.

"But promise me," he said. He was an imbecile. On second thought, I was the imbecile. I suppose he thought with the tights and the elaborate bathrooms I knew all there was to know.

In about two seconds he got up and dressed himself and was all concentrated doing his tie knot in front of the mirror. I flung my clothes on, readjusted the blinds and curtains, bashed the pillows a bit, and smoothed the bottom sheet. Things weren't very tossed, anyhow. He wouldn't wait for coffee, just got me to ring for a taxi and then, real surprised, banged his pockets and found he had no money.

"Loan me a pound," he said. I gave him nineteen and eleven just to see if anything would wring a laugh out of him.

"About the studio for Kate?" I said, out on the front steps. I wanted to fix another appointment, to keep things going. Because although he bored me he didn't bore me all that much.

"Sure," he said, "I'll ring you tomorrow," and then he made his big joke by punching me in the stomach, showing me what pals we were. The taxi came and he lifted the drum down the steps and said was it all right to leave the gate open because he couldn't manage to fasten it? I closed the hall door before the taxi moved off.

I felt awful, I can't tell you how awful I felt. One thing I knew, I was going to be saddled with all this guilt and I not having a bit of enjoyment out of it, only exertion. I rang Brady to tell her the flat wouldn't be ready for a few days but she wasn't there. Out drowning herself, I imagined.

Cooney didn't come the next morning. There was an impudent note stuck under the door to say she wanted her cards and compensation.

"What does this mean?" Frank said. He opens my letters. He was in a flaming humor, trying to put on his cuff links.

"Oh, one of her moods," I said. "You know how she is."

"That's no answer," he said. He'd smelled a rat already, because when he came home the evening before I was carting the stuff in from the coal house.

"What in the hell are you doing?" he said. "That's valuable mahogany furniture, I'll have you know."

"Just french-polishing it," said I. The stuff was covered with coal dust.

Then he went to the sink and saw the two good cups, saucers, and plates.

"Who was here?" he asked.

"A poor old man," I said. I couldn't think of one person's name.

"I'll have to go and speak to Mrs. Cooney," I said, doing the second cuff link for him. We were having a dinner party that night, the brother and his wife, and some architects, and some big merchants that they were soft-soaping to get a deal out of.

"How many courses?" he said.

"About five." I hadn't a clue what we were having. I hadn't given it a thought, you can imagine why.

"Don't forget about the cranberry sauce," he said.

He got cranberry sauce in some house and he thinks it's the biggest deal he ever had.

"You can't have cranberry sauce unless you have turkey," I said.

"Well, bloody well have turkey," he said. "Have two turkeys."

"A cock and a hen?" I said. I was as briary as hell.

"None of that smut," he said, lifting a hairbrush. I skipped away in case it developed into a fracas. He shouted something going out, and I knew that he'd take revenge by yelling at bogmen that are no better than himself.

At about half past ten the brother's wife rang to know was it dress. Imagine a bunch of us tripping each other up in long frocks in our own front room.

"Wear anything you like," I said. I was looking up in the directory to see if the drummer was listed. I was going to ask him when Kate moved in. Very obvious tactics.

"What are you wearing?" she said. She thinks of nothing else. Someone could tell her a story of a woman that was raped and murdered on Waterloo Bridge and she'd say, "What was she wearing?"

"Any old thing," I said.

"That's fine," she said, "I'll do the same. I'm glad it's nothing elaborate."

"Well, I had better get a move on," I said.

"What's Lady Margaret wearing?"

"How would I know?"

Lady Margaret was the only titled person he and the brother knew. They got in with her for giving monumental subscriptions to some charity organization that she championed. Bitches like that take up charity to get their photos in the paper. Good thing he met her, because before that we had a bit of a catastrophe with a duchess. We went to the local pub when we first moved to here because it said outside DINE AND DRINK LIKE A KING and he liked that. Anyhow, there was a woman there that everyone called the Duchess. She was a gas card, all wrinkles and rouge, and one of those eejity coats with a flared skirt and a fur collar. The minute he heard one of the boys calling her Duchess he got real interested.

"We ought to offer her a drink," says he. She was knocking back gins like nobody's business. Well, he didn't dare approach her that night, but next night he said we'd go around again, and I knew what he was aiming at. We hung around that bar for hours, then she came in with a couple of midgets that were probably jockeys.

"She probably has a few good tips for the Grand National," he said.

"So have you," I said. I hated to see him that desperate to get in with anyone.

Every time a tray of drinks was brought to her table he'd look over. He was plucking up courage. Finally he sent over a round just before closing time, and she raised her glass and beckoned us to come over.

"Cheers, Duchess," he said. She lapped that up. We all got introduced, and then he said why didn't they come back with us for a drink? I was in my own kitchen making Irish coffee for them when he burst out: "Christ Almighty," he said, "it's a nickname. She's not a real duchess at all."

I burst out laughing into his face.

"Get her out of here," he said. "She might flog the silver!"

"Well, watch her," said I. *I* couldn't very well throw her out.

"Watch her! I can't face her again. I asked her what her crest was, and she said, 'Mop and pail, governor.'"

"Is the Monsignor coming?" my sister-in-law asked. I said of course. Frank won't tile a roof until he's discussed it with the Monsignor. She hates it that the Monsignor is more friendly with us than with them. I could just see him beside the fire, raving away about you can't beat an open fire, and full of well-being from the double cream sherry. Suffer the decanter to come unto me. I really was in a hell of a humor.

"Must go," I said to the sister-in-law. "See you later." The drummer wasn't listed, so I decided to give him a day, and if he hadn't rung me by then I'd drive up next day and bring Brady as a homeless orphan. I rang and told her.

"I can't sleep," she said. "I can't eat. I keep going over and over it."

"Get out," I said. "Get an interest."

"In what?" she said. I began to rack my brains. Mother of Jesus, I don't know why I was worrying about her when I had me to worry about. I was really stuck on that drummer.

One can't be tough all the time. My teacup looked ominous, too. I told Brady we were having a dinner party and if she wanted any scraps she could come around to the back door for the leavings. First she said she didn't eat, then she said she had some pride left, and thirdly she had indigestion. I hung up after I'd promised to talk to her later, to mend her life, to get old Eugene gone on her again, to fix an audience with the Pope, and some last suppers with wise, beneficent men.

"I'll make it up to you, Baba," she said. I'd been hearing that particular tune from her, in that particular tone of voice, for about twenty years now. I was tired of it.

I said, "See you later."

I had to go after Cooney and make a real servile fool of myself.

She had to get two lots of fivers as a bribe: one to keep her mouth shut about drummer boy and the other to come over and cook the dinner. I wouldn't know what side to lay a turkey on.

"Did he stay late," says she, "your pianist?" She knew well he wasn't a pianist. She was just trying to get me to contradict her so that we would have another row and I'd dole out more fivers.

"He was working," said I. "He left soon after you."

"I was thinking when I saw the curtains drawn that you'd hardly have gone to bed with him downstairs drumming."

"Hardly," I said. I was opening tins like a maniac—cranberries, blueberries, all sorts of berries. I'm a dab hand at opening tins.

"Lovely drum," she said. "Lovely instrument. I wouldn't say no to one for Christmas."

I can take a hint as well as anyone.

We worked like troopers all day, and I kept a chair near the kitchen door so that I'd hear the telephone ringing in the hall.

"You're a bundle of nerves," she said.

"For a stupid woman you have great perception," I said. Anyone could see I was a bundle of nerves. I broke three glasses, and cutlery was flying out of my hand as if I were a goddamn medium in some poltergeist play. We got things more or less right, anyhow, and she did some snazzy sauces. If only she weren't so low I'd have liked her.

At seven they started arriving. Lady Margaret first. Linked up the steps by her chauffeur, as if she were a cripple or something.

"Midnight," she said, and he tipped his hat and went off. Her boots were full of snow and she had to change, of course, and the hall was ruined with puddles. You'd think it was a little doggie or something.

"Any little Duracks on the way?" she said to me upstairs. She always said that to me when she got me upstairs, and I always said I thought there were. Just to get her off it. She took ages to do her hair, and put more stuff on her face, which was already like enamel. She said her mink had been dyed to a color that no other mink in the British Isles could approach.

"You should get one—not like mine, of course," she said.

"I will," I said. "There's tons of them at the railway lost-property offices." Honest to God, I'd seen notice boards about it. Ranch mink and wild mink and blue mink. She didn't like that; I could see by the way she hurried out of the bedroom and down the spiral stairs in a hurry.

"Maggsie," Frank said, glorying in it. It's a phony name he invented to make it seem they're old school chums. She gave him one of those non-kisses that dressed-up women give. You know, touch-me-not. I went to the door again because the little architect had arrived. She was nice enough, and took her plastic overshoes off in the hall and made no big fuss about going upstairs to view herself. The big merchant was almost on her heels and he asked me if I got the flowers before I had a chance to thank him. White chrysanthemums came. I had them on show, of course, and the room looked quite happy, with all of us apparently having a gay evening and Frank standing next to me with his arm on my shoulder. Proprietory. Married bliss. Big fire burning in the granite fireplace. Bottles of red wine stood near to warm up; white wine getting chilled. Don't think we got that information for free—I took a course along with the dreariest collection of women you could summon up.

Cooney was banging saucepans like hell down in the kitchen and Frank was coughing before getting on with the two stories he'd planned to tell. It was a month when everyone had a cough or a head cold and catarrh sounds orchestrated the hectic conversation.

"You won't believe it," he said, "but I met a man today, and he has three hundred and sixty-five shirts. One for every day of the year."

"He needs one extra for the leap year," said I to the little architect girl, who looked as if she might be realizing what a vile evening she'd let herself in for.

The thing about Frank and the brother is they hire nice people. They have boys who would sit up all night on that building site just to make sure that buckets aren't stolen. Now and then they get what Frank calls a hobo on the site. Someone with a bit of common sense that knows about unions and strikes and things. And boy, do they have *him* fall off a scaffold!

"And after he's worn his shirt once," Frank was saying, "he has it beautifully laundered by the French nuns." There's a posh laundry where nuns hand-wash and hand-iron shirts at vast expense. Must be tough on the poor nuns, never having a date with any of the men.

"And then?" the Monsignor was saying with interest. I could see he was planning to get to know this man and give religious instruction in lieu of shirts.

"Well, Monsignor," Frank said—he calls him by his name every couple of seconds—"this is where the shrewdness comes in: then he sells them to other men who are not so rich. I mean wealthy men in their own right, but not rich beyond the dreams of avarice."

"Well, it's a good thing, a wholesome thing," the Monsignor said. "After the loaves and fishes, Our Lord asked them to gather up the leavings. Waste is not a Christian ethic either." Then he made a big joke: he moved very close to Frank and looked at his thick neck and said, "Would I be right in thinking, Frank, that you're wearing one yourself?" Everyone looked then.

"Monsignor, you're a caution," Frank said. "Having me on like that."

Frank was wearing a four-pound, fifteen-shilling, striped job got in the King's Road. I could still see that impotent bastard in his brown attire, strutting around the room.

"That's how to keep one's money," Lady Margaret said. She managed to keep her own fairly intact. She had a big place in Ireland with butlers and all that, but God, had she rotten legs. Even in the evening skirt which she was wearing you'd know she had bad legs.

"Baba, what sort of hostess are you? Their glasses are empty, empty!" Frank said. He was gathering wind for his second story.

"Don't we know where it is and that we're welcome to it," the Monsignor said, helping himself. I was well oiled before the brother and his wife came. She was in a white crocheted creation. It really shook me, because I was in one of my ordinary things. I hadn't the incentive to dress, if you want to know. I knew Frank would be livid, because the competition between him and brother is desperate. The way it is between good friends.

"I know someone who wants to catch her death," I said, because her back was exposed right down to her middle.

"I simply had to show it to you," she said. "It was flown over today." I didn't even ask from where, but anyhow, she was a big hit with all and sundry. I hustled them to the dining room before nine because I had some mad idea about nipping out to find him after they'd all gone.

Cooney conducted herself very well throughout the dinner. For one thing, she didn't wear that hat or get chatting. There was one tricky second when they began to compliment me on the food. She had her revenge, though; she thrust a boiling-hot sauce boat into my hand and sailed away.

"Cranberry sauce," Frank kept saying. "More turkey, Maggsie. More ham, anybody?"

"You can't beat the Irish ham," the Monsignor said. "The succulence of it."

Succulence! It was straight from Denmark.

Then they got on to food and how poor they'd all been at one time or another. You know, vying with each other to know who had starved the oftenest. The merchant, who hadn't opened his mouth up to then, told a big rigmarole about walking around London with one and threepence in his pocket and standing outside cafés trying to decide to have a one-and-threepenny meal and no evening paper, or a shilling meal and a paper for the racing results.

"Indeed I did," he said, looking around for their reactions.

"I believe it," Frank said.

"Until the bank opened," I said, real bitchy. He got all flustered then, and Lady Margaret made some sort of disapproving sounds, as if she were spitting out pips.

"Baba has a good heart," I heard the Monsignor say. "Her only failing is that she inclines to be outspoken."

Frank butted in to tell them how good I was to the poor and how I'd given a beggar man tea from one of the good cups. That of course set me thinking about my drummer again. I could just see him dropping the cigarette into the big, vulgar china pot. And the way he had of throwing a match away. He held it between his thumb and middle finger and dismissed it like an arrow. I was miles away most of the time. I thought, One week of him and I'd be bored, but boy, would I do anything for that one week. I'd buy boots the following day and a coat like he said and one of those rain hats.

"She's not to give in to fatalism, is she, Baba?" the Monsignor was saying. Eliciting sympathy from me for the Maggsie cow.

"I don't know," said she, the arch phony that she is, "whether to drown myself in my beautiful lake or marry my butler." She had a lake in Ireland and a butler from Italy, and I'd heard that piece of timed despair before. I was about to say, "Go up the river on a bicycle," when the telephone rang. Brady, I thought. So I skipped across to one of the occasional tables and picked it up, prepared to say, "Don't get on a moaning bout." Sweet Jesus, it was him.

"Would you like to come down to the Serpentine and have a swim?" he said.

"Who's that?" I'd know his low voice in hell.

"Would you?"

"Strictly for the ducks," I said. God Almighty, the whole crew of them had their necks and ears craned. You know the way people pretend to be talking but aren't really, well, that's what they were doing. I couldn't go to one of the four extensions either, because I knew his Lordship would pick it up. I turned my back on them, not that it helped.

"So you don't want to come?" he said. Christ, was he touchy!

"Are you coming over tomorrow?" I said. It was dead difficult to say things that he'd understand and they wouldn't catch on to. Anyhow, I'm no use at it.

"It's doubtful," he said.

"Well, when?" I said. I was taking terrible risks.

"Come to the Serpentine, baby," he said. I was afraid of my life they'd hear what *he* was saying.

"Tomorrow," I said, and stopped as if I had nothing else to say.

"Well, don't forget I asked you," he said, and we hung up more or less together. I was shaking all over.

"Who's that?" Frank said.

"Just a friend," I said as cool as a breeze.

"Who is it?" he said—stubborn again. The brother, that shark with the blood pressure, was giving me the eye, too, as much as to say, "We're powerful and you can't lie to us." The vote, I thought, means nothing to women, we should be armed.

"My dentist," said I. "I missed out on an appointment." I hadn't even got one in England. I got the brace and things in Ireland.

Cooney came in with the coffee and looked at me, real interested. She knew it all and recognized his voice, of course.

"Mrs. Cooney, you've been simply marvelous," I said, to give her a bit of puff. She beamed.

"A pleas-ure," she said. We were well matched.

The thing went on for hours. They got to the Pope and Khrushchev.

"He's afraid of his life of the Pope," the brother said.

"So well he ought," said his wife. "His Holiness could wipe him out."

"Now, now, now, don't give our friend the wrong impression," the Monsignor said. Our friend the merchant was a Protestant and doing very nicely with the brandy and the sister-in-law's back to explore. He didn't give two pins about the Pope, but he felt he had to say something.

"A point I've often wanted to raise with you chaps," he said, "do priests wear trousers under their cassocks?"

Even in the state I was in, I burst out laughing. Everyone else got very red in the face and nervous, but the Monsignor replied as if he wasn't shocked at all. You know, nothing-shocks-me sort of thing.

They covered crime, too, and unmarried mothers and the morals of England. As if the morals of Ireland were any better. About twenty hours went by before their various chauffeurs and taxis came, and they were hardly out of the door before I was up the stairs to bed.

"I'm worn out," I said to Frank. I could not have endured intimacy that night. He looked very satisfied. He said he'd made two jokes, and did I notice how everyone laughed? He said the merchant looked as if he would come through. Everything looked rosy, except that I had to get to see my drummer, or die.

Next morning I ripped up there and brought Brady as an alibi.

"I hope it's a nice place," she kept saying. "Congenial." Everything had to be congenial.

"I hope we get in," I said. I knew he'd be a bit huffed about my not going to the Serpentine for an orgy, but I had a few things to cheer him up: some smoked salmon for brek and the biggest pair of boots you ever saw. I looked like a general in them.

We got through the front door because it was wide open, and we climbed as many flights as I remembered having climbed. There were no names on any of the doors. 'Twas one of these sleazy dives where people didn't want their names on doors in case they'd be found out. Hashish, pep-pills pimping, all kinds of contemporary offenses. Brady's face was a study. I got a look at it on the landing, with the foul light that came through the skylight.

We got to his door. I recognized the brass mermaid knocker.

"Smoked salmon?" I said as the door opened back. A woman faced me. An ordinary-looking crow in black.

"Is Harvey in?" I said.

"Who?" she said.

"Harvey," I said. She was a born evader.

"Oh, Harvey," she said, as if I'd been talking in double Dutch.

"Yes, him," I said, glaring at her.

"We've come about the flat," Eejit Brady said, telling our business. She always tells her business to everyone.

"I own the flat. He was living here," she said, the smug cow.

"Oh no," said Kate, as if that's what we'd really cared about.

"Can you give me Harvey's address? I want to return his piano," I said.

"I can't," she said. "He didn't leave a forwarding address."

The nomad jag had stuck in my mind. He was gone. We stood there a few more minutes and then shuffled off.

All that day we tried restaurants and clubs, because I knew he played in some dive. Sharks asked us would we like to audition for striptease, and one told me I had the makings of a lady wrestler. There wasn't a trace of him. I even rang the boring actor whose mother was on solvents, but he knew nothing. He didn't even know my name, for God's sake.

"Did you know him well?" Brady kept asking. She couldn't understand why I was so hot and bothered. He'd got my arse in an uproar and left me high and dry. I more or less knew he'd skipped. Like a fool I went to the Serpentine to see if he was there. Useless. The ducks got the smoked salmon, bag and all.

8

Kate's room turned out to be small but adequate. A single bed, a wall cupboard, and a washbasin that lurked behind a green cretonne curtain. The curtain had a smell of dust, as curtains have when they are not laundered for years. From the hot tap cold water came, and from the cold tap hottish water came, and she knew that when she left the place, as she eventually must, it was this detail she would remember—the folly of the reversed taps. In the mornings she cooked her breakfast in the kitchen—the lower shelf of the cupboard being allotted to her foodstuffs—and carried it back to her bedroom to eat it there, saluting the dog or the landlady if she met either, appeasing them both with a smile before vanishing into her cell once again. At nine she went to work. She had taken a part-time job in a cleaners, which meant she earned some money and did not have to take charity from Eugene. To be maintained by a man who did not love her was depraved. Not that he'd offered! She had afternoons free. Sometimes she walked, or saw Baba, and on three afternoons she met Cash. They would go to some park or other and she would ask him questions about what went on at home.

"Oh, boredness," he said, a word he'd made up.

"Like what?" she said, breaking all the rules of decency. He never told, he merely gathered fistfuls of snow to fling at her or, when she ducked and protested, at some uncomplaining tree stump. After a few flings he would grumble about his cold hand, and removing the wet glove, she would warm the hand finger by finger, licking each one back to life again. He liked that. He even seemed happy. But at times, looking into his overwhite face and his overliquid, dark eyes with the mauve shadows (from constipation), she would think that he knew everything that was happening, and everything that would happen in the future. They always went to a café for tea—the same one each time because she knew the prices—and he ate chips, and éclairs filled with mock cream. Sometimes he shed a few tears when they were leaving.

On one such afternoon after she had delivered him to Maura at a bus stop she found his glove in her pocket, and knowing he had only one pair, she decided to deliver it to the house later that night. When she got there it was about eight, but the curtains were not drawn—one of Eugene's many liberation schemes. The family—Maura, Cash, and Eugene—were at the dinner table. The double doors separating front and back rooms were also open, so that she could see right through to the place where she once sat, and where the girl now replaced her. There was music from the record player, Russian dance music, which he often played because he said it suggested happy, jingly, Russian people dancing about in the snow. She could see Maura's face and Cash's, and two mouths moving, and the back of his still head, and she put her nose to the window to try to catch some word of what they said. Suddenly she noticed a figure to one side of her, in front of the garage door. At first she thought it was real and was about to run, shamefaced. It was a snowman, about the height of Cash, and going to it she saw his size and his features exactly reproduced: the round face with the cheeks that hollowed ever so slightly, the big bullet head, and a little snub of a branch for his nose, as small and neat as his own nose. Eyes had been traced there, too, big eyes: a perfect likeness. Maura must have done it while he was out, as a surprise for when he got back. Kate kept looking at it for a long time, and she could see it perfectly, because the moon was full and the whiteness of gardens and hedges and gate piers gave to this figure an uncanny presence. It might not melt for days. She wanted to pick it up and carry it off, but daren't.

The glove was still her reason for coming. She thought of leaving it on the pier, where children's lost gloves are always left, but since the snow would ruin it, she stuck it through the letter box, but did not let it drop through, in case one of them might hear. Maura had remarkable hearing.

Then she ran until she was out of breath and had to stand. She had not been back to the neighborhood in weeks. Already it looked strange. The full moon and the dazzle of stars put a spell on the little houses, the powdered street, and the glassy pond where she'd long ago fed the ducks and swans. It was a dance floor now, with branches touching its surface, those laden down by their weight of snow. She stepped on the ice, first one foot, then another. She wanted to walk there, and dance there, forever, with her son or with his image, which had been reproduced by someone else. If only she could do that and lose herself, the way one reads of young girls dancing alone, with roses held between the teeth. But her thoughts kept going back to the three of them, in the warm room, beyond the iced-over window, the snow-child outside, keeping guard.

In a way it was the worst night of all.

One thing Eugene had instilled in her was the need to have a walk each day, and walk she did, no matter what the weather. It thawed and refroze all the time. Dikes of gray snow were piled in the gutters and the tires of buses sloshed this swept snow around her booted ankles. She could hear icicles cracking like girders, and women going by grumbling about the shortage of plumbers. She went to a park. Flowers were out—a few, tatty, forlorn crocuses, but they were flowers all the same and they meant something. She sat at her appointed seat and saw him come and knew then why she had come back. He was a young boy who came in the cleaners every Friday with his skin-tight, dirt-tight jeans to avail himself of the two-hour service. He sat next door—in last season's jeans—in the café, and after the two hours rivved home to change into his renewed, Romeo, silver-gray ones.

She'd met him the day before in the park and he called out "Gorgeous" after her. Gorgeous—with a body shapeless from extra clothing, and a face stricken by all that had happened. But she acknowledged it all the same.

He was with a friend now. They rode their bicycles over the snowy grass, making crazy patterns, looping around, then swerving and repatterning their tracks. And all the time shaking the handlebars at each other as matadors would wave a cape at a bull. Gradually coming closer and closer until they surrounded the bench on which she sat. She was on a bench in the middle of the park, her legs a little apart, her eyes looking beyond them at the square concrete factory with its honeycomb of square windows and a sign beginning with H commanding the horizon. The same H that she saw at night, instead of a moon. Their eyes ran up and down the length of her legs, which were covered with blue wool stockings. She did not look at them observing her, but she knew that they were. A secret flutter took possession of her, as if a bird had come between her legs and flown high up under her coat and thick tweed skirt. He made a sucking noise, the one who'd called her gorgeous. He was pale, with very drained blue eyes and spots that just missed being pimples. He wore a silver chain so tight around his neck that it could choke him. The second boy had Italian blood, and they both had long hair curling on the napes of their necks. She had not looked at them as they circled the bench, but she knew their faces from the cleaners.

"New type of kissin' come in," the pale boy said as he cast his bicycle from him and lay belly downward on the snowy grass, facing her. He had his head raised, his elbows dug into the snow, and he scratched with his thumb at the medal on the chain. His eyes ran up the length of her legs. Could he see the knickers, too? The warm, chaste, winter knickers with long legs, elastic reinforced.

If she said, "Go away," he could have said, "Belt up, I pay rates, too," so she said nothing, only stared straight ahead at the H, which would soon be a moon-bright neon. He called to his friend, "Git, there's a gorgeous bird that works in a bread shop, a real doughnut." His friend roared off, saying, "Don't tempt the girl. Can't ye see she's contemplatin'."

Kate crossed her legs and locked them at the ankles, like a lady sitting down to tea in a convent parlor where she'd once sat with abstemious nuns sitting around her, watching. He screwed up his face, frowned with his red-rimmed eyes, and rolled his half-nourished, humble little body over and over again on the dirty snow. His jeans would need longer in the vat next Friday. She felt shame because she knew she had yielded to him for an instant the week before. That was when she unfolded his trousers and asked if he wanted it "express" with something more than behind-the-counter pleasantness. A madness had passed through her limbs and shone in her eye. But now the bird between her legs died. Quicker in fact than it had taken for the blob of snow that was on her upturned collar to melt. It was trickling down her neck now, worrying her. She thought, I could easily put my hand out and let him draw me down and give him something that would briefly atone for the condemned room where he was born and the stupid parents he came out of and the accent he is doomed to. She glanced with mild pity to say this without actually saying it.

"Fabulous out of doors," he said.

"It's cold," she said stiffly, being careful to misunderstand him.

"Git your knees apart, mine aren't half warm."

"How dare you," she said, the voice of a lady brigadier, a gym mistress, a hospital matron, the voice of authority pealing down through the centuries. Where had she got it from? Her legs and knees trembled, and she stood up and raced across the field with her heart falling out of her mouth.

"How about puttin' the matter to your solicitor," he called after her, and then his friend shot back from nowhere and she heard the pale boy say, "Them dirty married bags," and the epithet cut and carried across the desolate field. She hurried to the ladies' lavatory that was behind some soot-black arbor trees shrill at that moment with starlings. Inside, the Dettol smell, the unwiped lavatory seat, the roller without a towel, and the attendant without a smell sense depressed her, not for their own sake, but because of her transgression. A week before she had led him on. As she unfolded his dirty, silver-gray jeans, she had some notion of having a vague and magic encounter, of being taken by him, and then left satiated as he tore away. Not knowing his first name or what occupation his dirt-engrained hands were put to. Not knowing anything. A voice from outside called "Paul" roughly, and with anger. "Paul, Paul."

"Somebody's calling Paul," the attendant said.

The following Friday Kate stayed away sick.

After that she went for walks only in the evening when the fog was coming down. She did not have to look people in the eye, and the river was at its best under gauze, with green lights denoting the passing of some boat. To reach the park that skirted the river, she had to pass a street of houses. Fine houses set back from the road, with ivy, with studio windows, and one with an inked sign saying BEWARE, VERY SLIPPERY PATH. Solid fortifications with beware people inside leading solid lives. Powerful smells of roast and gravy came out to trouble her. She had had mutton or beef stew, depending on the day. One-gas-ring, one-saucepan dinner! Funny that she should remember meals they had eaten more clearly than she remembered anything else. Especially ceremonial ones, like the hen pheasant that had got caught by mistake in a rabbit trap. They roasted it, and he'd stuck one of the russet feathers through her auburn hair and joked about not having to buy her a present. It was near her birthday. How could they renounce all of that? She hurried home, sat on her bed, resting the writing pad on her knee, and wrote:

My dear Eugene,
I don't know if it will make reparation but I want to say that the affair I had was foolish and trite. When I recall his letters now—the ones you have—I feel nothing but shame. Of course I did you wrong, but I did myself wrong, too. I have a screw loose, that screw which should let me know when I am on solid ground and stop me wading into a swamp. I do not know why I do bad things.

She signed it "Little Kate." A harking back to the early days.

She said nothing about the years of emotional pummeling from him, or her own compulsion to love on an octave note from one day-break to the next. She posted it but did not expect an answer, and when she got one two mornings later she trembled as she opened the brown business envelope and unfolded the sheet of foolscap. He had written:

Dear Kate,
What I have to do now is forget about little Kate (what a misnomer) and get on with those parts of my life which I have so foolishly neglected because of her.

His investment in her had been too much. She would never be free of the responsibility for the waste of his life. She read it twice and let it go into the Thames, where she was standing once again. Another evening. The tidemarks lost in the gloom. Too late. She knew the letter by heart, like a prayer. If only she had the decency to kill herself. Water was the gentlest way to suicide. It merely meant stepping off the path onto another path that was equally blurred by mist. As her mind dwelt on it, her body ran from that place and walked through the High Street, peering into the jocularity of pubs, looking at clothes she had no desire to own, at plastic chickens motionless on skewers and printed signs to testify that lambs' tongues were cheaper by four-pence. Ugly streets, ugly signs. She walked for a long time with the bouquet of frying oil in her nostrils, crossing over and back, comparing the prices in one window with those in another, longing to crash through one of those windows, as she had once seen a boy do on a drunken Saturday night. But the police would come and take her away in a big black van and things would be no better.

That night—or perhaps it was another night because all those nights were interchangeable—she had a dream: Cash was asleep, no bigger than a baby, in a cot, with a nappie bagging down around his knees. She went to Maura and asked her to kill the child by burning him with an iron. Maura did. Cash died quietly, without a whimper. It had obviously been painless. She saw a little blood on the nappie, but that image had been borrowed from real life when he was circum-cised as an infant and carried back to her from the operating theater. There had been a little rosette of blood on the nappie, and she wept because he had known pain in his unknowing, unsuspecting milk-happy euphoria. She did not waken then, screaming, as she would have expected to. The dream went on. She lived through months, years, running out of restaurants, furniture shops, hairdressers, sick with pain because she had killed the only person she was capable of loving. She eventually would have to go to Eugene and say, "I killed our child. It wasn't an accident, I killed him." She woke then, and having no thought for time or sleep, she went out to the telephone on the landing and dialed Eugene's number.

"How is Cash?" she asked.

"Are you drunk?" he asked, his voice wide awake. Was he in bed? On which side? Did he ever waken and think she was still lying next to him, pink and warm in her fleece-lined nightgown?

"Is he all right?" she asked again.

"He's asleep. He had some hot milk about two hours ago."

"I had a terrible dream about him," she said.

"Must be indigestion, take two aspirins." She did not put the phone back on the receiver, she just pushed it away from her and laid it on the ledge, where it went on emitting sounds until he realized he was talking to nothing and hung up.

Next day she said "Shit" to a bus conductor who refused her change of a pound. She knew everything that was happening but could not help herself.

Then Cash lost a front tooth. He seemed so empty, so stripped without it that when she met him she asked where his prettiness had gone. He said the tooth fell out and they had put it in an egg cup and he got sixpence. She could see the sixpence shining silver in the water and Cash putting in his finger to prize it out.

"I want Cash's tooth," she said to his father a few hours later when he was picking up the child at the railway station. So much of her life centered on that platform that she knew all the advertisements by heart and the telephone numbers of places to ring if one needed God or tranquillity or lessons in ballroom dancing. She was familiar with the various obscene messages and pencil changes done to the posters. A girl displaying a man's outsize shirt had been given a mustache, and a lipstick queen had had one eye cut away.

"The tooth is perfectly safe," Eugene said. "I've put it away for him when he grows up."

"I want it," she said.

"Now don't get all emotional, it's safe."

"I must have it," she said. It was not the tooth at all.

She got it eventually and put it in her purse, but lost it. She must have handed it between the folds of a pound note in some transaction or other. She asked in two shops but without luck. She never forgave herself.

"I lost your little hollow tooth, I'm sorry," she said to Cash when they met again. Cash didn't care. She was gloomy and squeezed him too tight and asked who he loved the most. Not like Maura. Maura played fox-and-goose and smelled like a mother and had hair between her legs, just like a mother, too. He saw her through the keyhole. She nearly split her sides laughing. Maura laughed a lot and his mother cried a lot. He'd have another loose tooth soon and get another sixpence. He tried to shift one with his finger but it would not wobble. He loved that wobble feel until it got looser and looser and was held on by one thread of gum.

"What are you doing, Cash?" his mother asked. He always had a finger in his mouth.

"Nothing," he said.

Did Maura or his father ever talk about her?

"I forget," he said.

"Try and remember."

"Dada said you're jealous of other people's belly buttons."

"What?"

He repeated it. She tried to get him to remember when, and where, and how. But he could not or would not trace it for her. He made a face and said, "Big fat sausage," so that she would chase him and tickle him the way she used to. He ran around the playground, but she remained on the wooden seat, staring at, but not seeing, the motionless swings, the squat, un-horse-like wooden horse, and the sandpit covered over with snow.

"Mama," he called. She did not rise. Other mothers had arrived, so she could not question him. And she did not hop about on the chalked squares to warm her feet either, because of formality. The mothers were supposed to sit and watch the children play. Once, when she'd got on the swings, the attendant came over and asked her was she over sixteen, and if so, to please get off.

"I got locked in this park one night," a mother was saying.

"No!" from another.

"I did, I climbed over that gate."

They were enclosed by high wire netting and by a wired gate. How had that ungainly woman mounted the gate? What breathing and puffing must have gone on. Did she disturb the leaves? Some falling leaves had never reached the ground but had got caught in the wire and were fixed there now, like decoration. Not in clusters but separate. They reminded one of something. Spring and childbirth? Autumn and rotting? So he discussed her faults. It was not enough to kill her, he had to show the sad spectacle of her corpse to others.

"I got across to the main gate," the woman was saying, "and I called a couple going by. 'I'm locked in,' says I, and they wouldn't believe me. They thought I was Candid Camera. 'Don't you heed her,' his girl said to him. 'You'll find there's a camera behind the bushes and you'll see yourself on television next week, being ridiculous.' "

"Wicked," her listless listener said.

"Mama." It was Cash again. He was walking through the maze, nodding to the wooden posts as if they were people. She went over to him.

"Did you know that some people believe the earth is flat?"

"I suppose they do." She felt bad-tempered, because she couldn't probe about what his father said.

"Yes, they belong to the earth-is-flat club. Can I have a club?"

"Do."

"A what club?"

"Ask them." She was staring at two children, one white and one colored, who were enacting the birth of a baby on the slide. The colored girl stood at the bottom and pushed a life-size doll up the slide, and the little mother at the top slid down with the doll between her parted legs, and the midwife took it from her. They had done it five times.

Cash went over, stood near, and the pause typical of children took place, while they vetted each other, and then spoke. The colored child left with Cash when the closing-time bell pealed out. Her name was Tessa.

"I have a radio of my own," Tessa was telling him. "My good mum gave it to me."

"Your what?" Kate called. Cash and Tessa were a bit ahead, linking.

"My good mum," she said. "My real mum was a rotter."

"Where is she?" Kate said, catching up with them.

"Oh, somewhere. She's a ballerina."

"And your father?"

"He comes from dark parts, as you can imagine." Tessa had a shining dark face, and curly hair, and sharp, no-fool eyes.

"A rotter, too," Tessa said. "He asked me to go to America and I said to give me time to think about it."

"Are you going to America, Tessa?" Cash said, worried.

"No, I wrote him a letter. I said, 'Dear Father, I cannot go to America with you as I have a very bad cold.' "

Without thinking, Kate reached out and embraced the strange child, not so much to comfort as to congratulate her.

"Can we have tea?" Cash said, taking advantage of his mother's gust of affection.

They crossed the road to a café.

"Just tea and one cake each, no chips," Kate said, in case they blackmailed her once they got inside. At the street corner there was a brazier alight, the red cones of anthracite beautifully glowing, and a whiff of heat shedding from it. A man sat by it, half in and half out of a hut. Cash and Tessa stood up, waited for the man to object, and when he didn't, they then threw the wrapping from the chocolate she'd given them into the fire. The silver ash from the paper lay on top of the glowing red nuts, and they looked on enthralled, their two faces rosy from the light, their gloved hands splayed out before it.

"I have another mum, too," Cash said, imitating Tessa's voice exactly. "She lives in my house with my father."

Kate drew back from the fire, stabbed by what she had heard.

9 Two days later Kate came to meet Eugene at the railway station. It was convenient for him and anywhere suited her. She arrived early and sat in the midst of the chaos, with pigeons tottering around her feet, and people on all sides apparently going or coming to something important. The trains whistled without cease. She went over what she must say to him: that he sack Maura, take Kate herself back, and move them into the country to a small white house with a vegetable garden and grazing for two cows. She would grow good, and protective, and cling to him, like the ivy he'd once planted on the gable wall of one of the many houses he'd owned. This figmented house she saw as being in a valley with one huge tree shielding it, so that the leaves got into the gutters, the way they always did. It would be their last home, their stronghold, their coffin. Her mind was made up. It was what she must do.

To ward off the cold and pass the time, she got a carton of soup from a machine. After the first sip she looked around for someone to complain to. It couldn't be her imagination, the green soup was washing-up water. Pea plates had been washed in it. She had another sip when it got cool and this verified her suspicions. The dumb blue machine witnessed her protest as she held the carton upside down so that the soup made an uneventful stream across the tarmac. It eventually settled behind the basket containing orange peel. A man had gone by with a skewer and taken up every piece of orange peel in the place. Toffee papers and cigarette cartons were not impounded, just orange peel. Must be some reason for that. Marmalade? An old, gray, stooped man with his head held down came and cursed her for having thrown the soup away. He had his eyes screwed to the ground for fags and threepenny bits. She apologized, wanted to hand him sixpence, but feared that he might curse her more.

"Oh, there you are," she said, turning. Eugene had stolen up on her. She told him about the washing-up water, intending him to laugh, which he didn't. He had leather gloves on and two wool scarves—one around his neck and the other covering the lower part of his face. He kept flapping his hands back and forth under his armpits.

"Are you perished?" she said. She herself was purposely clad in a dark-brown, hairy coat which she'd purchased at a sale. Its dull institutional look might appeal to his conscience.

"It's eight degrees below freezing," he said. Facts. Facts. Any minute now he'd tell her the strontium content of sherbet. England was screaming with facts and statistics, and not one person to supervise soup machines. She moved nearer. He shifted away.

"Well, you wanted to see me?" he said.

"I did." How to put it, and imply that she was doing it for him as well as for herself? She tried balancing the sentence and out of the corner of her eye saw more orange skin being cast away and at once being lunged at by the skewer.

"It's about Maura," she said at last.

"Yes," he said. He had that calculatedly serene voice which was observing itself say yes calmly, and with understanding.

"I think she's a bad influence on Cash."

"Oh, and how do you reach that conclusion?"

"His loyalties are at stake. He doesn't know who to love."

"His loyalties are only at stake if someone questions them."

"I never question him," she said in a self-committing burst. "I never ask if you chat to her, or take her into your study at night. He just tells me."

"God help us," he said overpiously to the roof of sooted glass panels that were backed by steel netting. Her eyes filled with tears. He avoided looking at her. No longer the fixed stare of reproach. He had renounced her in his mind, and through his body. She had always thought that people who had once loved one another kept the faintest trace of it in their being, but not him. He was free of her. Marked of course, but free in a way that she was not. She was still joined by fear, by sexual necessity, by what she knew as love. She tried again.

"It's like a volcano," she said, "you and me, it settles down and then it flares up again."

Whether he thought she was talking gibberish or whether he guessed the implications, he showed no wish to listen.

"You know," he interrupted, "the first time I began to fall out of love with you—oh, years and years ago—was the day it hit me like a bomb that you never cry for anyone but yourself."

"Does anyone?" she said. "Show me the man or woman who does," she said, and thought to remind him that he had chosen her for his own needs, too. His little dictatorship demanded a woman like her—weak, apologetic, agreeable. Self-interest was a common crime.

"Of course. Men have died for other men. Women sweat their youth away."

What had he done? Talked incessantly about wars, money, injustice, but sat at home stewing in his private pain. And yet he managed to sound superior.

She sobbed, and nodded, and sobbed.

"So that's all you wanted to see me about?"

"More or less," she said.

He had to be off, he said.

Urgent business. Snow to shovel away from his front path, tea to make, and his child to rear. It had all become his child. He slipped into the crowd and became one of the many people, apparently going or coming to something important.

A numbness took charge of her brain and she sat somewhere to puzzle things out. She'd missed her chance. It was as if he said he was setting out on a long voyage. How much more comforting if he had just said he was about to die. She knew danger as she had never known it; the danger of being out in the world alone, having lost the girlish appeal that might entice some other man to father her. It wasn't just age; she was branded in a way that other men would spot a mile away, and though still young, she had not the energy to coax, and woo, and feed, and love, and stroke, and cosset another man, beginning from the very beginning again. Everything was hazy before her eyes—around her, the heavy flights of the pigeons and porters pushing trolleys and the drone of canned music from a loudspeaker. The huge weight of terror that she had been dragging around for years had not lifted on his final exit, but had increased oppressively. Almost to test this weight she stood up to walk, and bumped into two nuns on the way. Nuns, with their serene faces, and their very white hands lost in big black sleeves. A smell of linen and starch, the black smoking wick of a candle that a nun had quenched with her fingers, the suffocating sweetness of a certain kind of lily. For an instant she remembered her life in the convent, and thought how safe, how wooden, how unscathed she was then. It had all been so long ago. She set herself the task of walking twenty times around a bookstall before she faced the certainty of the future. The icy air cut into her and her feet were damp—snow had melted between the crepe sole and the upper suede part—but she did not care about the cold. She was panting, and felt that lunatic itch under her armpits as if hordes of crawling lice nested there. A sure sign of terror, for her.

"Walk, walk, walk," she said. At some point a man went by, with a little girl who had a doll in her arms. The girl was limping.

"Come on, Emily, just a few more steps. Mummy will be pleased," she heard the father say. He had the child by the hand, but at arm's length, as if she were a dog.

"I bet you'll eat a big tea, I bet." They went toward the ticket window, and out of some compulsion Kate followed them.

"Will we get a ticket for dolly, too?" the father asked the child.

"Fuck," Kate said. Suddenly and unplanned, it escaped from her lips and directed itself to his limp, chinless, five-thousand-a-year face. He looked away into the enclosed distance as if he hadn't heard. But he had heard, because he changed his daughter to the other arm so that she would not be corrupted. Kate slung toward a giant weighing machine, and unthinkingly set about weighing herself.

"Eight stone, seven pounds," a rich Irish country accent told her. She talked back to him. There was no question of this being a metal voice.

"Where are you from?" she asked. He was probably shy, thinking she was making fun of him, as no doubt many people did. A gray cloth map on the school wall, long forgotten, rose before her eyes, a map with names that were once names and now which had the intrigue of legend—Coleraine, Ballinasloe, and Athy. Places that she'd never visited and never wanted to visit but were part of a fable summoned up by this now familiar voice.

"I bet I know," she said. Still no answer.

"Ever heard of the Silvermines? I'm from there. I didn't go home this Christmas, did you?"

She thought that maybe he had goose with soft, oozy potato stuffing, to which sweetbreads had been added. She thought of her father, and wondered why it was that he meant nothing to her at all now. It seemed barbarously unfair that someone could have had such a calamitous effect on her and still not pop up in her mind once or twice a day. Eugene sucked every thought and breath of her waking moments.

"Come on," she said to the man behind the machine, "I haven't all day to talk to you." Although, of course, she had.

She stepped off, took another penny from her purse, and weighed herself again. Again he spoke. He was still there.

"I bet you find Sundays in London lonely," she said. "I bet you miss not going out in the fields with a couple of hounds and a gun." A thing Irishmen loved to do.

"Please," she said softly, "talk." She tapped the glass, waited, to hear his breath first, then the voice saying, "Hello," or, "Where do you come from?" the way these voices greeted one in dance halls.

Possibly twenty seconds went by. Then something broke loose inside her and she started to scream and bang the glass that covered the numbered face. She hurled insults at it and poured into it all the thoughts that had been in her brain for months. She lashed out with words and with her fists and heard glass break and people run and say urgent things. She was held down by the shoeshine man until the ambulance came, and she came to, back to reality, that is, in the casualty department of a large hospital. At first she only stared at the bandages on her hands as she heard the soft-soled shoes of nurses walking by on the rubber floor. Then she remembered, first one thing, and then another: how he had come, how he had gone; she threaded their conversation together, then recalled what she had said to the man with the child, then the weighing machine, then her heart beating madly before the outburst of violence. Every detail was crammed into a capsule, so small and tight and contained that she would carry it with her forever.

A nurse asked if she was all right and if they could telephone her husband to come for her. They'd seen her marriage ring. She said no, that he was gone on a voyage, but that she had a friend that would come. They let her telephone from the almoner's office and a nurse stood over her while she did it. She got through to Baba.

"Cut out the opera-star stuff and get over here," Baba said when Kate explained the predicament.

"You're waiting in for me, oh, bless you." She had to say that, in case she would not be released. More outrage from Baba.

"I'll be there in half an hour," she said, and hung up, telling the nurse that her friend was expecting her and everything would be all right. To her there was something disastrous about losing one's grip on oneself, like a dead woman she'd seen once on the road with her clothes above her knees and one shoe a bog of blood. On her way out, she got a card to come back in a day or two for a checkup. She went into the cold street, panting because her strength had been drained away. It was a narrow escape.

 **10**

Well, curiosity killed the cat and information made her fat. That little salubrious interlude with the drummer had its results. In other words, the months went by and I did not have my regular visitor and could not eat a breakfast. I began to wonder what I could do. When did it remotely resemble a child, because what I had to do ought to be done before that. I was musing over this in my tobacco-toned room, listening to the Swedish bitch banging the vacuum cleaner all over the house, when the telephone rang. As you might expect, I had to sack Cooney the minute I got the wind up. She'd be following me into the bathroom to watch me being sick. I said we were going to Rome for a year. I didn't care what I said.

It was Brady from some hospital. She'd had a little argument with a weighing machine at Waterloo Station and took this to be the end of the world.

"Get over here," I said, "there's a real kicking problem." And I said it so furiously that she did.

First of all, I had to get rid of the Swedish bitch.

"How about takin' the afternoon off, hah? Nice shoopping and buoy friend," I said.

"Goood," she said, and dropped the Hoover without even turning off the switch. She was off in no time, wearing one of those marvelous-looking Norwegian jerseys that would make any man think she was good-looking. Kate arrived soon after with her face of woe. Guess what she talked about? Them. He didn't love her. She'd met him. His words were brutal, final, and meaningful. She did love him, but sometimes she didn't. The break came in a bus, when she was all dressed up in about nine petticoats and raging that they had to bus it. She said to him, "If you sat on the other seat I'd have more room," and he took this to be significant, and so did she, and that was how the break came.

"Shut up," I said. I couldn't take any more of that. Garbage.

"There's a real live problem facing us, get your thinking cap on," I told her.

"What?" said she.

"The old, old story," I said, sort of singing it, to make it less awful.

"Love," she said. If you say potato famine she'll say love.

"Preg," I said, remembering that I'd said it to her before when we were in Dublin and she'd said, "How?" and I'd said, "The usual way," and she'd said something else, and I'd said it was easier than owning two coats. Well, the conversation repeated itself, verbatim. At least this time we had money and we had drink, and she didn't know it, but I had a gallon tin of castor oil in the shed, if the worse really came to the worst.

"But children are nice," she said. "You're fond of Cash."

"It helps," I said, because she may have got a scholarship but in some ways she's a moron, "if they have a trace of their father's eyes, ears, nose, feet, or something. Would I be that frantic if it was orthodox?"

It dawned on her. She wanted to know who. What was he like? What was it like? Did I see him often? Was I in love? Should we go and see him? See him! He'd bolted to Greece! I was in two minds whether I should tell her or not that it was all her fault. But the thought of a big ream of apology stopped me. It was action we needed.

You won't believe it but she asked me was I hoping it would be a boy or a girl.

"Twins," I said. "Two of each."

She got all soppy then about irony, telling me a card she'd seen in a For Sale window which said UNWORN MATERNITY DRESS, FINE GRAY CHECK, SEEN ANY TIME.

"Poor creature," I said. "We'll go around now and buy it." I gave her a look that would curl her. Then I armed her with three crisp pound notes and sent her out to buy a medical book so we'd get all the dope. (I'm beginning to talk like my mother.) Anyhow, she came back hours later with a big dictionary that cost five pounds—she had to expend two of her own—and it has to be seen to be believed, this dictionary. It said things like: "Catarrh, disease of the nostrils."

"Get the preg data," I said, because she's brighter than me in educational matters. She began to read about Fallopian tubes and raised her head from the printed page to tell me she knew a woman who had two and having two meant you could have two children by two different men at the same time. I was enjoying this, I really was. I took the book out of her hand and looked up under A for Abortion. They didn't even consider that word.

"We'll have to get a doctor," she said. "Some nice understanding doctor."

I couldn't go to the shark down the road that I usually went to, because he's our family doctor and a Catholic. We got the telephone book and rang specialists. I'd have paid seventy-five quid, for God's sake. Well, they had it all so fixed that you had to have appointments made before you were pregnant—like booking for that Eton lark when the babies are conceived, before they know whether they'll be cretins or not—and you had to have a letter from your family doctor. We thought of friends. She knew someone who knew someone that had a friend who was a gynecologist. About ten phone calls ensued and the final one was me talking to this hag who was a lady gynecologist in the Knightsbridge region. She had one of those voices you hear in second-class hotels where people are pretending they don't know it's a second-class hotel.

"Fur example," she said, "aur you bleeding alort?"

"I wish I was," I said. She got very dodgy then and found that her appointment book was full for an indeterminate time.

"I hope your vowels move tomorrow," I said, and rang off.

"What now?" said Kate, fatalistic. If I hadn't been in such a mess I'd have said she was sick and ought to be in bed.

"You ought to know someone," I said, "with all your connections"; with her Madame Bovary slop, I thought she'd be adequate to it. "Or even a crook who'd do a job on a kitchen table in Bayswater," I said. She gave off a big spiff. How these crooks live a lurid life and make a fortune by telling about it in the Sunday papers. She said they had little typists living in terror.

"They can go to hell, they won't get my money," I said in a fit of sympathy for those goddamn typists, whoever they are.

We went back to the dictionary.

"There's people all over London, happy at this moment, and people getting on buses, and doing normal things," she said.

"I'll swap them this house and all this gear for it," I said. We were really low. She had a gray coat on that you could sieve vegetables through, and her skin was dry like an old cooked potato. Her eyes, which used to be her good point, were gone back in her head from crying.

"I'll buy you a coat," I said.

"Did you marry him for money?" she said. I said I didn't know.

"Do you hate him?" she said. I didn't know that, either.

"I don't hate him, I don't love him, I put up with him and he puts up with me," and then I thought of this new disaster and how it would kill his pride, and I got frantic again.

"Baba," she said, "once you have the child, it will be all right. You'll both find it is the most important thing in the world to you. A woman needs children. I'd have more myself."

"Right," said I, "we'll go on a world cruise for our nerves and come back and say 'tis yours."

Boy, did she change her tune. She wasn't ready for children, she said. Who is?

I knew then that it was up to me and I'd better do something, so I told her about the bath and castor-oil plot and asked would she stay, in case I got drowned or had a heart attack. I know she'd really like to have run, but she stayed. I'll say that for her. Not that she was much use. She nearly fainted three times, what with the steam, and the greasy look of the castor oil in the cup, and me sweating and moaning and retching. I had her play "Careless Love" on the record player. She had to go out and put the needle back on that part of the record each time it changed to another song. I thought it was kind of apt.

Suddenly I turned around in my sweating condition and she's kneeling down with her hands joined.

"Get up," I said. "Get up, you lunatic."

"I'm praying," she said. She hadn't said a prayer for years, and even I thought it a bit steep that she should be asking help of someone she'd ignored for so long.

"Nothing short of sacrilege," said I, knowing that would put the wind up her. She was on her feet like lightning, and off to change the needle and put more coal in the boiler. I could hear that boiler roaring up the chimney and I prayed it wouldn't burst or anything until this ordeal was over. He'd kill us. I had cramps and pains, and I began to shake all over. The whole place looked weird. The mirror was all fogged up, and steam all over the place, so that I couldn't see my own makeup and stuff on the various glass racks. I'd look at the hot tap running, then all around, then directly down at the water, hoping to see its color change, then back to the tap again and all around, and I don't know how long I did that.

"Kate, Kate," I said, holding on to the bath as if I was sinking.

"Kate, Kate," I yelled and roared, and she came and said I'd better get out.

"Are you out of your mind?" I said. Imagine going through all the pain and sweat and sickness that I'd gone through and then give up in the middle. I was shaking like a leaf and she held me.

"Good old Florence Nightingale, little old lady with the castor oil," I kept saying, so that she wouldn't think I'd gone too far and call a doctor or do something criminal.

"Jesus," I said suddenly, because it was as if I was stabbed in the butt of my back. I began to howl.

"I'll get brandy," she said.

"Don't leave me, don't leave me," I said. I was dead certain that if she left me I'd fade out. Anyhow, she let go of my arms and I just lolled there, and next thing I know she's giving me brandy from a spoon and saying, "I'm going to phone Frank."

Frank! That revived me. I came to for long enough to say, "If you phone Frank, I'll take twenty-four sleeping pills right now." She gave me more brandy and turned off the hot tap. I knew as she was turning it off that my chances were over, but I hadn't the energy to resist. The steam, the heat, the castor oil, and then the drink had made me feel like straw. She swears that when I passed out a few seconds later I was a hefty weight to haul out of the bath.

I came to in my own bed with two dressing gowns on me. The first thing I did was to see if anything had resulted, because I'd had a feverish dream that I was in a train and it came, and I couldn't get off the seat, and porters were standing over me yelling at me to get up. Only in the dream had it come.

"Hullo, little old lady with the castor oil," I said to her, sitting there. "T.D.L.," I said, because I was damned if I was going to get all morbid again. No man was worth it.

"Total dead loss," she repeated after me. She was more grave than me.

"We'll get our minks on and hitchhike to the Olympic Games," I said. "I'll enter for the egg-and-spoon race."

She didn't laugh. It was about four o'clock on a lousy afternoon in March, but at least the house was warm because of the way we got the boiler whizzing.

"The gardener came," she said. I could hear him shoveling the snow away. All he could do that winter was shovel snow away so that we could get our Jags in and out, and get up the front steps, drunk, without falling. Not that I'd have minded a fall at that time. It was gray and awful-looking, and I got her to put on the light and draw our sun-drenched blinds.

"Well, it's now for some crook," I said, and pitied those typists again. I was sorry for everyone and no one, the way you are when you're in a mess.

"You can't," she said.

"I go to crooks to have my hair washed," I said. "Where's the difference?"

"The difference is that one is just frivolous, and the other is violence."

Well, Christ, I roared out laughing. I mean, think of being in the state I was, and someone going on like that. Then she launched into a sermon. A whole lot of high-falutin' speech about how I was trying to destroy myself, murder part of myself. A parable, just the way it was in the Gospels. They'd all eat fish and then sit around and hear a story.

Hers was about some woman who was having a baby by a man who loved her, and she didn't want the baby. So she got rid of it. The man stopped loving her, and she fell madly in love with him and went around with a terrible loss in her, because she'd killed two good things.

"But it's not Frank's," I said. As if she didn't know.

"But the point is," she said, "that you don't know beforehand what damage you do to yourself by your actions. You only know afterward."

Well, I couldn't dispute that. I proved it every ten minutes of every day.

"You know her, too," she said.

"What is she like?" said I. There was something about that story that gripped me. I knew I'd be looking out for that woman at the hairdressers.

"We're going to tell Frank," she said, "when he comes in this evening."

"No." I didn't want to tell her the bit about him getting berserk when he got angry. If we told him, there wouldn't be a stick of stuff left in the house, and nothing of me, only bones.

"He'll wreck the joint," I said.

"We'll go to his office," she said. "He can't wreck anything there."

"No," I said.

"Look," she said. She was off again. Another sermon.

The upshot is, I'm dressing myself. She's telling me to put on white makeup and no lipstick and to look wretched. It is not difficult. She'd got me into such a state of righteousness that I was ready to be a suffragette for ten minutes. She said we wouldn't take a car, no, we'd go in all humbleness by bus or Tube. It was miles away in North London. I can tell you, I was pretty wobbly from what was behind me, and from what lay ahead. We damped the boiler, put on our coats, and set out.

Down in the Underground there was a gas advertisement. It said DO NOTHING UNTIL YOU'VE READ VOGUE. Well, in our plight, and with people starving, and having pyorrhea and all sorts of things, I thought it was very vital advice.

"We must come down in the Tube oftener," I said.

"I come every day," she said, making me feel like a rat.

Then a great big enormous pregnant woman appeared from some archway, and that was enough to make me run for the exit stairs.

"Come back, come back," Kate said, catching me by the belt of my camel coat. That minute a Tube tore into the station and she linked me into a No Smoking compartment. We changed into the next compartment at the next station and had a fag each.

"We'll have a few gins along the way," I said. Even she was beginning to lose her fervor.

We got there around four. That was the first time I'd ever been near any of the building sites. They were putting up new blocks of offices on a bomb site, and the ground was snow and yellowish muck. There was an arrow underneath a home-done sign that said INQUIRIES AT OFFICE, and we went in that direction; men booed and whistled at us. Such commotion, such noise: hammers clattering and hammering, a great bloody bulldozer churning up more yellow earth, a drill whining and men on the scaffolds yelling in Cockney at Irishmen underneath who couldn't understand a word they were saying. A din. I prayed that the brother wouldn't be with Frank.

"Don't apologize," said Kate, knowing that it was her own worst trait.

"I might funk it in the very middle," I said.

We found him alone in a small, fuggy, little corrugated-iron office with plans and papers laid out all over the table in front of him. He was on the phone.

"Christ," he said when we came in without knocking.

"No, no, Lady Constantine," he said into the phone, "it's just that somebody's capsized a bottle of ink over my notes . . ."

It was about a cesspool that he was going to install in her country cottage. We got bits of the conversation. While she was talking he put his hand over the mouthpiece and said like a savage to Kate, "I hope we haven't to get you out of another mess."

I was kind of glad that I was going to shatter him.

"Yes, it has its own waste-disposal system," he was telling Lady Con, and I knew it was about this cedar-shingled place he'd put up for her in the country. She started on about the roof then. The slates must have been cracking and spalling all over the place. He got red in the face and raised his voice.

"The roof!" he said. "That roof was perfect."

Next thing he was apologizing for his language and saying, "I'll come down there myself."

God help the roof, I thought. He could do a good thousand pounds' worth of damage in five minutes.

"At no cost to you," he said. Then he told her not to worry, and that his bark was worse than his bite. Finally, and after a typical jarvey-driver's farewell, he put the telephone down. Kate stood on my toe just to give me a bit of courage. He didn't look at us for a minute; he wrote some big important nothing into his desk diary and sat there frowning at what he'd written. I could not believe that he was my husband and that I sometimes slept near him and had seen him sick and drunk and in all sorts of conditions. He was another man in that outfit.

"We haven't come about me," said Kate, quite indignant. "We've come to tell you something."

"You'd better make it snappy," he said, "the men knock off at five and we have our conference." He called the men together every evening, and the big, brutal foreman of a brother told who was slacking during the day. Just like the countries we read about where it's supposed to be coercive.

"You tell him." Kate turned to me.

"You begin it," I said.

"It's yours, Baba," she said, very stern. In the end I had to.

"I'm going to have a baby," I said. He grinned, a terrible pathetic grin. It was like telling someone his mother was dead, and you beginning the sentence and he getting it all wrong and thinking his mother had won money. For a minute he thought it was his and that he'd proved himself. He stood up to kiss me, but I put my hand out straightaway. He went like a block of wood; he stayed quite motionless in that position, which is halfway between sitting and standing, and he didn't utter a word. The telephone rang.

"Will I answer it?" I said. He picked it up and threw it, and I ducked, knowing the throwing craze was on. He got more fluent than he'd ever been in his whole life.

"You cow," he said. "There's a way to deal with you and whores like you. I'll kick the arse off you when I get you home."

"I'll take a boat for somewhere," I said.

"You'll do no such thing. You'll bloody well stay where you are and do what you're told."

"Did you think I was going to live frustrated?" I said, just the posh way Kate would say it. I could see he didn't understand that word. There's lots of words like "frustrate" and "masturbate" that he doesn't understand.

"It's not very much for a woman living the way we live," I said. "All that huntin' and shootin' and fishin' lark is all very well in company," I said. He began to close his fist and turn his bottom lip outward, the way he does when he's furious. All this thing about women and new freedom. There isn't a man alive wouldn't kill any woman the minute she draws attention to his defects.

"Watch your language," he said. Boy, it was hot in that room with a double-bar electric heater going full blast!

"I can leave you," I said. "I don't care about a scandal."

He knew of course that it would cause a setback between him and the bishops, and be bad for his work, too, because a lot of the big contracts he got were from Catholic firms.

"I'll tell you what to do," he said.

I could hear heavy footsteps outside crushing their way along the cinder path and I knew that help was arriving. It was the brother to say the meeting was due in a couple of minutes.

"Tell your brother," I said. "He's a great one in a crisis."

The brother killed someone in Ireland once and drove on but was found. They would have jailed him except that he bought his way out.

"Get out," he said, knowing damn well what I meant.

"When I get home there won't be much of you left," he said.

"I won't be there," I said, and wrote the telephone number of Kate's dump on a piece of paper, so that he could ring me if he wanted to.

"What's up?" the brother asked. He has a murderously red face and curly hair.

"The stork," I said as brazen as hell. My knees may have been wobbling under me, but I kept a good front up.

We muddled our way through the muck and got onto the road.

"The eyes of workmen are permanently screwed up; they have to keep them like that in case mortar flies into them," she said. I thought it a boring piece of data, but it got us out of there to the dark street, to bus queues of people.

"Oh no," she said, suddenly defeated. Lucky I had money and could get a taxi to her dump.

"I'll be shacking up with you," I said. "You needn't be lonely anymore."

She looked worried. She's all unnatural about babies and birth.

He rang me about ten. He'd cooled off considerably. He said, "I've decided to let you stay on as my wife—in theory only, of course." Nothing new about that.

"That's great," I said. I suppose he expected a great slob scene from me about how generous and charitable he was. Not me. I know the minute you apologize to people they kill you. Then he wanted to know whose it was so that he could go around and kill him.

"He's a Greek," said I, "and he's gone home."

It was the only thing I could think of. Kate had her head out the bedroom door. She was as inquisitive as hell.

"Will it be white?" said he. The eejit doesn't know Greeks from blacks.

"It might," said I, "if we're lucky." He said he wanted no more cheek from now on and I had to do what I was told and nobody was ever to know the truth.

"Does Brady know?" he said.

"Of course," I said.

"Keep her away from the house. Pay her to keep her bloody mouth shut," he said. He hated her then.

"And go to confession," he said. He then told me he was having a much-deserved holiday to get over the shock, and if anything urgent in the business line arose I was to telephone the secretary.

"Have a nice time," I said, and dashed in to Brady to tell her she could live in elegance with me for a week until he got back.

"It's an ill wind," I said, and she finished the sentence, "that doesn't blow good for someone."

We laughed. A thing we hadn't done for ages.

I was in the bathroom trying to change things around—since our misadventure the very sight of it depressed me—when lo, Durack appeared. It shook me. He hadn't shaved for the three days since I last saw him, and he smelled of booze.

"You're still here, arsing about," he said.

"Where ought I be, in the Magdalene laundry?" I said, whistling like a man.

"That'll do now," he said. He stood in the doorway, he was nearly the width of it. He took a bit of a blond lady's hair out of his pocket; it was in the shape of a ringlet.

"Recommend her to your gentleman friend," he said. "Wonder worker."

"You recommend her," I said, "you're the authority." I reckoned he was telling me he'd been to some brothel and got a testimonial, and I was mighty glad.

"I find I like it," he said, "vicarious living." Well, that was a new word for certain.

"Insertion at various angles," and he looked at me, quite drunk. "You get my drift?" he said.

"It's made a new man of you," I said. I suppose he thought I ought to show jealousy or temper; I showed nothing. I was quaking.

Then he began to curse and swear in a blackguardly way. Such a volley of language. Unparliamentary. Words we never parsed at school. Then something checked the words on his tongue, as if there were another him inside the blackguardly part, and he started to cry, and I said for God's sake to hit me, assault me, kill me, do whatever he had to do, but to get it over. I took a step forward. He looked at me, big child's tears on his face.

"Isn't it a fact that I gave you everything you want?"

"It's common knowledge," I said. That worked terrific. Instantaneous. Remorse. He began to cry harder, but it was collapse and not temper that invoked the tears.

"Baba, why did you do it to me?" he said. Useless to say that I hadn't thought of him when I was doing it. Useless to say that I always thought your acquaintanceship with one person had nothing to do with another. Or to say all the things that went on in my head, the longings, for songs, cigarettes, dark bars, telegrams, cacti, combs in your hair, the circus, nights out, life. He wouldn't understand.

"I was drunk." How could he but forgive that condition?

"It was in Hyde Park," I said. A man's home is his castle. The way I said it, he could see it was no great event, and a bit of spunk came back into his voice.

"Like dogs," he said. I thought, Not even like dogs, but I sang dumb. I thought how I had this daft notion that men could make you feel it all over, and make you half faint at the same time, and it was a mystery to me where I picked it up from.

We heard Brady let herself in and heard Cash call our two names, and I for one was glad of their arrival. She brought the kid for high tea and I told him this.

"She'll blather about it," he said.

"She's demented, she'll tell no one," I said. He was glad of that.

Then he came right in and closed the door and began to talk in whispers. He said he'd give me a second chance, but on conditions. Never, never was I to do it again or he'd slay me alive.

"I'll satisfy you," he said. Ah, the land of promise. It was quite a pathetic thing to hear him say, his eyes down. I reckoned he was feeling pretty terrible. Then he caught hold of my hand and said we were never to bring it up again. We were to keep it a dark secret. Poor devil, he told no one, not even the brother. So the big biblical bond between them was all my-eye. They were allies in nothing, only making money. When it came down to fundamentals, he had no one. All by himself and that brothel he went to. There was just us, him and me. Allies, conspirators, liars together. I took the line of least resistance. In the eyes of the world it would be his and mine. I said okay. What else was there to do? Among other things, I didn't relish going out into the world to sell buns or be a shorthand typist. It would have his name.

"Give me your word," he said. I blessed myself. The visible signs of the cross. Salvage began. We shook hands and went out. Not very lighthearted of course, but then how could it be otherwise?

Our family doctor arranged for me to go and see a gynecologist, and I went one boring afternoon when lots of other people were sitting down to tea and shop buns. The nurse that let me in had very thick glasses and her eyes were teary behind them. Not that it mattered. I wasn't feeling very sympathetic. He asked me how long I'd been married and were we delighted to start a family? I had to say yes, of course. They were all Catholics. He asked me how I felt, and I told the bit about cooking Brussels sprouts in the middle of the night, and having bile in the mornings. He asked me a ream of questions about whether I'd had miscarriages, tummy aches, and other morbid ailments. I'm the kind that gets these complaints if someone reminds me of them. He wrote it all down, dead serious. God only knows how many lies I told.

Then he sent me to another room and told me to pass water. I didn't know whether I'd be able to pass water or not—it isn't a thing you can do to order. I went up there anyhow and had a look around. There was a lavatory and a washbasin with a pair of yellow rubber gloves on the side of the basin. They were sprinkled with a talcum powder that smelled of babies. I'd forgotten that smell. There was a picture that was supposed to be a joke. It was a crazy drawing and the caption said that before you have a baby you ought to measure the size of your husband's head. As I heard him coming up the stairs I mounted the black leather couch, which had stirrups at the side. I knew that they were to put my heels into for the examining bit and I was hoping to God that I wouldn't make a fool of myself.

He came in real casual. He asked if I backed horses. He began a long rigmarole about how he'd nearly brought off a tote double. All this time he was easing the rubber glove onto his hand and then smoothing it out so that there was not a crinkle in any of the fingers. He told me to grip my heels in the stirrups and I never felt so helpless or so obscene in my whole life. Just prostrate and facing a window as well.

"I would have won quite a penny," he said.

"Waterlogged?" he said. Humor!

"You're trying to be funny," I said.

"Relax," he said, sort of bullying then. Relax! I was thinking of women and all they have to put up with, not just washing nappies or not being able to be high-court judges, but all this. All this poking and probing and hurt. And not only when they go to doctors but when they go to bed as brides with the men that love them. Oh, God, who does not exist, you hate women, otherwise you'd have made them different. And Jesus, who snubbed your mother, you hate them more. Roaming around all that time with a bunch of men, fishing; and Sermons on the Mount. Abandoning women. I thought of all the women who had it, and didn't even know when the big moment was, and others saying their Rosary with the beads held over the side of the bed, and others saying, "Stop, stop, you dirty old dog," and others yelling desperately to be jacked right up to their middles, and it often leading to nothing, and them getting up out of bed and riding a poor doorknob and kissing the wooden face of a door and urging with foul language, then crying, wiping the knob, and it all adding up to nothing either.

"All right?" he said. I took deep breaths.

"I wish," said I to him, "that I'd been born a savage." So I did, where women aren't tightened up and just drop the babies out of themselves and go on cutting sugarcane or whatever the hell savage women do.

"What an extraordinary statement," he said, and I could feel his finger withdrawing. More pain, more pressure. I wondered if he ever got fresh, or if all that disinfectant and stuff put him right off. He said yes indeed, that I'd started a baby. He put it in a way that nearly made me sick.

"God has fructified your womb." That is the exact way he said it. Then he said how pleased my husband would be and he talked all sorts of technical stuff that I didn't want to hear. All about embryos.

He went down ahead of me while I retrieved my knickers from my handbag and put them back on.

Downstairs he got the runny-eyed nurse to write out for me when I was to come again, and he gave me a prescription for iron and vitamins. All I wanted was a prescription for ergot, or whatever it is wise women take. I came out and sat in the square opposite, where it said RESIDENTS ONLY, and I cried bucketfuls to the tune of "I came. I didn't think I would." If only it had been Durack's. Don't ask me to say crime does not pay because I'll say it, but I'll also say virtue does not pay, it is all pure fluke, and our lives prove it. Kids, I thought. God help them, they don't know the bastards they're born from.

11 The silence was shocking. Even the clock on his desk did not tick, though it gave the correct time. Kate looked around: the rubber plant was still there and the couch with the sheet over it. Did other patients lie down? Some of those nameless, awed people who sat outside in the waiting room, the ticking shadows, preparing to spill out their woes. He gave them pills each week—tiny white pills packed into tiny circular boxes—and fifty minutes of solace. It allowed them to keep numb, get on and off buses, walk the dog, and go to bed at night without being tempted to carry a pillow downstairs and bury their heads in the hire-purchased gas oven. It enabled them to die slowly.

It was Kate's fourth visit to the psychiatrist, and she found she had nothing to say, or had so much that it was useless to cramp it into the time allotted and then stop and retain it until the next week. Desperateness by installment. She was looking at this pale, thin-lipped man who sat like a dummy and had heard her woes as if he was hearing the weather forecast. After the Waterloo debacle, Baba's family doctor decided that Kate should see a psychiatrist because she was unstable. He'd sent her to the outpatient's department of the local hospital. On the first day she'd done nothing but weep, and on the second she'd talked about Eugene and of how she'd given him false proportions—set him up, as one sets up things that are past. Like thinking that the weather was always fine when one was young, and that the hedges were full of wild strawberries, when, in fact, there were only a few hot days and the strawberries were hearsay, found by Baba or said to have been found. Anyhow, she resented telling about her marriage. It not only violated her sense of privacy, it left her empty. Life, after all, was a secret with the self. The more one gave out, the less there remained for the center—that center which she coveted for herself and recognized instantly in others. Fruits had it, the very heart of, say, a cherry, where the true worth and flavor lay. Some of course were flawed or hollow in there. Many, in fact. Was he? This spruce Englishman in his pink shirt with the collar held down by pill-white buttons. She would have to sleep with him to know. The only way of ever really knowing a man. The thought sickened her.

Before she left Eugene, she had often thought of being with

other men—strange, distant men who would beckon to her, and as she moved they would draw back their coats on their naked bodies and have her float away on the wing of the wavering outthrust penis. Mostly dark-horse men. But one was blond and had pale-green eyes like the whey of the milk. But now that she could taste the mystery of other men she declined, and shrank back into her dream.

"What are you thinking?" the psychiatrist asked. Half the allotted time gone.

"Of a plane crash," she said, cheating beautifully. The words came out of nowhere.

"One you escaped from?"

"No, I read about it. One hundred and four people were killed outside Boston or somewhere, and when the cause of the crash was investigated afterward by millions of experts, I mean by experts, they found the engine went wrong because starlings had nested in it. That haunts me."

"Why?"

"Because I feel like the starlings."

"You feel you kill people."

"I feel I sort of destroy them, with weakness."

"How many people have you destroyed?"

"I do not know," she said, and began to sob suddenly and uncontrollably. He offered her a tissue from the box on the desk, probably kept there to accommodate the numerous cryings that went on.

"Come on now, pull yourself together." The old cliché. She sat hunched, staring down at the damp, disintegrating tissue, struggling to control herself. Why had she said such a thing? Why had it upset her? She longed for him to comfort her. She could not bear to be seen crying by someone who wouldn't for that duration enfold her, the way hills enfold a valley. Hills brought a sudden thought of her mother, and she felt the first flash of dislike she had ever experienced for that dead, overworked woman. Her mother's kindness and her mother's accidental drowning had always given her a mantle of perfection. Kate's love had been unchanged and everlasting, like the wax flowers under domes which would have been on her grave if she'd had one. Now suddenly she saw that woman in a different light. A self-appointed martyr. A blackmailer. Stitching the cord back on. Smothering her one child in loathsome, sponge-soft, pamper love. She tried to dry her eyes, only to find them releaking. She stood up, made another appointment with the psychiatrist, and went through the waiting room so distraught that she wrung the pity of people who were worse off than herself.

At the bus queue she cried more, and in the bus she kept her head fixed to the windowpane, so that when the lady conductor came she handed her sixpence, although it was only a fourpenny fare. For days she went around hating her mother, remembering her minutest fault, even to the way her mother's accent changed when they visited people, and how after going to the lavatory in some strange house or some strange hotel she would make a feeble, dishonest attempt at washing her hands, by putting one hand—the one she'd used—under the tap, when at home she just held her legs apart over the sewerage outside the back door, where they also strained potatoes and calf meal. In that fever of hate and shame she thought one day of something that lessened her rancor. They had laughed together once, and Kate put great premium now on laughter. It happened when she was eight or nine. She had gone with her mother to collect three dozen day-old chickens from a Protestant woman who lived near the graveyard. They took the upper road because it was shorter, but it was more tiring to walk on, not being tarred.

"I want to do a pooley," her mother said. "Watch for me." Her mother never took time to do a thing, hardly ever sat on the lavatory, and consequently had piles. They looked up and down, and then her mother squatted, just around the bend. Kate, the child, wandered off a few yards and began to daydream, as she always did out of doors, with birds and tall blades of sighing grass to make her fanciful. She was thinking of the day she bought a stamp and held it by its sticky side on the very tip of her thumb, and the wind which made the grass sigh swept the twopenny stamp away.

"There's a man, a man," she said suddenly, running to where her mother squatted. He was cycling downhill at a terrible speed.

"Where?" her mother said, stepping onto the middle of the road with her navy, nunnish, gusset-reinforced knickers down around her legs. The brown river she'd made was coursing over the dusty road, finding its inevitable destination to settle and be dried by sun. It was summertime. The sun was bleaching the green, ungathered swarths of hay.

"This way," the child said, because her mother was looking in the opposite direction. He came around the corner and prised through the mother's parted legs with the front tire of his bicycle. They both fell and were locked by the handlebars.

"Sweet Jesus, I'm killed," her mother screamed.

"No, but I am," he said as he tried to extract himself from the bar and from the woman.

"Where in the name of God were you going?" she said as she put her hand on the dusty road to ease herself up.

"I'm going to a funeral," he said, taking up his bicycle and shaking it fiercely to make it straight again. He wiped the saddle with the lining of his raincoat and swore under his breath. The chickens that had been left on the grass bank were screeching through their perforated box, and the child had hidden her face in an enormous dock leaf.

"You ought to look where you're going," the mother said, walking toward the chickens with as much dignity as she could muster. As she walked she tried to ease the knickers above her skirt.

"The same goes for yourself," he said as he speeded the bicycle forward, ran with it, put his leg over the bar, and cycled off, saying, "Townspeople."

"Ignorant yahoo," the mother said when he'd gone. She rested against the grass bank then, and laughed at the scratches on her hand, her grazed knee, her ripped knickers, the idiotic saddle of his bicycle stuck up in the air like a dog's nozzle.

"Going to a funeral," the mother would say, and they would laugh, and double up, and remembering some other moment of it, they would start a fresh bout of laughter.

"My good knickers, at that," the mother said. Everything was funny.

But they were never able to talk about it again, because the mother got shy once she had laughed her fill.

Ah, childhood, Kate thought; the rain, the grass, the lake of pee over the loose stones, the palm of her hand green from a sweating penny that the Protestant woman had given her. Childhood, when one was at the mercy of everything but did not know it.

She did not go back to the psychiatrist the following week. Her excuse to herself was that she had to find some place to live. Cousins, friends, in-laws, some of the nameless stock people that come to the rescue on such occasions were on their way to take her room. They were announced by the landlady the morning after Kate was caught having Cash in the house. Eugene had given permission for him to stay with her one night. She bought a chamber pot and warned Cash about not going out on the landing. Once in bed he wanted the game— the old one in which she became a ghost and frightened him.

"Go out, and come in and be a ghost," he said.

"We can't play it, you know that."

"Because of the old grump." He knew a little about the landlady with the pasted-on smile and the snarling, asthmatic dog.

"Well, go behind the curtain," he said, "and be a ghost."

She did, and no sooner had they begun the game than he begged to be tickled and frightened into insane laughter. There was a knock on the door, and the landlady, barging in, discovered the child in his pajamas, in bed. Kate said she could explain everything, but the landlady saw it as a piece of treachery. Kate took him home early the next morning.

"Tell me about the First World War, how many infantry there were," he asked. She couldn't tell him. She didn't know. "Chew your gum," she said. She'd bribed him with four gum balls from a machine because that morning when she forced his feet into his socks he'd said, "When are you coming home forever?"

"I don't know about the First World War," she said, "I wasn't born."

"Well, the Second World War," he said.

"I don't know about that either," she said. He made a wronged face and resigned himself to counting all the toy shops on his side of the street, which the bus passed by, and told her to do the same.

In the afternoon she began to look for a bed-sitting room. She knocked on doors, spoke clearly, swore that she was white, house-trained, had no pets, could dry her clothes magically in a hay box, and would keep her radio (a thing she didn't own) to a mute whisper. And to the three who thought of considering her as a lodger she suddenly excused herself on the plea that she must think about it. She ran from their terms. She ran to another address. There must be a Bowery somewhere.

In the end she found a small, single-story house in a terrace of identical houses. They looked like drawings out of a child's storybook, small and dark, with tiny turret windows and a stone cherub over each door. Inside, it was so dilapidated that Baba said it would be a cinch for entertaining the bicycle-chain, orange-box set.

They went to an auction room and bought the necessities.

"Where's my smelling salts?" the pregnant Baba said, advancing sideways up the narrow passage between the mountains of used goods. Kate felt disgust. A smell of homes that were, stained mattresses, mildewed, bed ends on which hands had laid the pickings from their noses, sofas farted into, the dregs of lives. Baba bid—a table, chairs, one armchair, a bed, a wardrobe, and an umbrella stand. On the way home they bought a tin of disinfectant and a spray gun, just to be on the safe side.

"We'll fumigate it," Baba said, trying out the empty spray gun in the hardware shop. They also bought new ash-white wooden spoons, and a fish lifter, and a kettle, and a chemical to make the sink sweet-smelling.

"You'll need this," the man in the hardware shop said, holding up a white shell.

"What is it?"

"A water softener."

"We'll have it," Kate said. There was something ridiculous about everything she did. Homes were not put together roughly, like this.

Baba blessed the house with a bottle of whiskey and they drank while they waited for the men to deliver the stuff.

"There's no doubt," Baba said, looking around at the job-lot wall-paper, "but you've got on in life, Katie. You've made a good match."

The wallpaper was purple with red veins on it, like a graph of someone's lousy bloodstream. The same pattern throughout the house.

"This will be a real salon yet," she said as they sat in front of the fireplace nursing rubber hot-water bottles.

The slight eerie noise of soot falling through the chimney and rustling onto the crepe paper, which had been laid into the grate, got on their nerves. The fire could not be lit until the chimney was cleaned, and the chimney could not be cleaned until the electricity was turned on, and the electricity could not be turned on until the wiring was repaired. Broken sockets fell away from the wainscoting, and where they had already fallen off, wires stuck out like two evil eyes of danger.

By the time Cash came, the furniture was installed and the Victorian armchair was held up partly by books and partly by castors. He sat on it. He, too, thought it was a house out of a story, where a witch might live. But he was excited.

"Good, good," he said, marching around the rooms, stamping on the boarded floor, rejoicing because everything was so empty and therefore free to wreck.

"I must go, Katie, or I'll get murdered," Baba said. The place bored her. If there was one thing she couldn't stand, it was bare boards. These particular boards were the limit altogether, because the previous owners had let their kids daub them with every color paint under the sun.

"I wish you could stay," Kate said, seeing her to the door reluctantly.

The sky was green and watery. Kate said it would rain. Not just rain, Baba said, but thunder and lightning and deluge and floods. She also said to remove the NO HAWKERS, NO CIRCULARS sign from the wooden gate because hawkers wouldn't waste their time coming near the place. The path was strewn with leaves, papers, and rainwashed notes to the milkman that had blown in from other porchways. The wall between her and her neighbor was too low. She'd put trees there so they wouldn't have to talk. Talk would only lead to questions, and then condolences and then friendship. She had no energy left for friendships.

Cash tried pulling off the sign with his nails and then with a fork, but it was firmly screwed on, and the screws had rusted into the metal sign.

"Come, we'll go around the house and plan what we'll put in all the rooms," Kate said. He'd shed a few tears when Baba went.

A Turkish carpet here, a brass fender there, a picture of soldiers for Cash to look at, geraniums, a new pink bath, a lavatory with china flowers in the bowl, occasional tables, and woolly rugs that he could snuggle into when he took off his shoes to have a pillow fight.

There were green spots of damp on the four ceilings, and older fainter stains like rivulets running from these damp spots across the center of two ceilings. A big roof job.

"Can we have bunk beds?" Cash said. He was hitting the walls and floors with the new wooden spoons, making bangs.

"Bunk beds!" she said. She was making up the secondhand bed in the front room where they would sleep together that night. She put the hot water bottles in, and lit the paraffin heater. It was brand-new, its wick white and unblemished.

"Now, what do you vote we have for tea?" she asked. It was essential to keep busy, and to keep him busy, because of the awful emptiness. Rashers and beans on toast. They ate off their laps, in the front room, close to the heater. Cash liked it better than a table because when the beans skeetered off his plate he could reach down and pick them up.

"You'll be able to bring some of your toys here and leave them here," she said, wanting him to settle in.

"Can I have new rockets?" he said. "And when will we have a telly?" She thought how pathetic that she should have to win him back with goods.

The evening stretched on interminably. It was still only six o'clock and they had finished tea, washed up, put the chemical in the sink, and gone around the house, laying a candle in a saucer in each room, with matches beside the saucer, in case they needed to go into any of these rooms urgently in the middle of the night. She'd brought one red candle as a celebration and put it in a scooped-out turnip on the mantelpiece. She was telling him about Christmas when she was a child, and how they'd always had a candle in a turnip on the window-sill in case Christ went by. He'd never seen the place where she was born. He knew nothing of the weeping, cut-stone house where all her troubles began. And he had no interest in the boring story about being afraid if her mother went upstairs to make the beds, and eventually having to follow her mother up. He wanted to draw. There were no pencils or papers. They searched the two wall cupboards and found only damp, and one shriveled football boot.

"Draw on the window," Kate said. "Be resourceful." It was thick with grime outside and dust inside. A yellow streetlight had just come on and cast light on the two dirty, encrusted windowpanes. Later in the evening, before they got into bed, she would have to hang a sheet or something, because the street gaped in at them. Later still, she would have to buy material, and measure the windows and make curtains, and hang them up and draw them in the evenings to shut out the gaping street. There would be the noise of curtain rings running back along the rods, and the fire flames leaping on the wall and people sitting down to eat. What people?

She looked across to see if he had done a house, or a pussy cat, and when she saw the enormous HELP daubed across the sooty pane, she put her hand to her mouth and gasped. It was when she ran to console him that he must have become aware of something catastrophic happening to him, because suddenly he began to cry in a way that she had never seen him cry.

"I want Dada," he said.

"We'll get him," she said.

"Now," he said.

"What's the matter?" she said. "Why are you crying?"

He wanted paper, pencils, television, toys, warmth, bunk beds, things he knew.

"Look," she said, sitting him on the bed and pushing back his fringe so that his very creamy forehead showed. She kissed its cool creamy texture and told him how forgetful she was not to have all these things, and promised she would have them the next day. He did not like the candlelight either. "It might turn into something else," he said. It was fitful and it threatened to go out when the wind blew down the chimney. She pressed him in her arms, to give him shelter, and to revive the solidity that had gone out of their lives.

"I want Dada," he said, sobbing in her embrace. He smelled of cool basins of cream in a pantry at night. When she had first carried him, his feet pressed against her stomach, and later on he bit her nipple with impatience, but at no time had she felt so close to him as now.

"I'll take you home," she said, rising. The tears which seemed to have been overflowing from him vanished as if he'd put them back in his eyes, as into a reservoir.

In the taxi he kept looking out of the window, commenting on the darkness. He could not face her, he felt too contrite.

"I'll come back if you want me to," he said, and when she did not answer he said, "Mama," but very softly, and very tentatively, as if he feared he had failed her.

"You'll come back," she said, "when the electricity is in and things are cheerful." He had reminded her more than she'd ever known of the terror of being young, of that fearful state when one knows that the strange, creepy things in the hallway are waiting to get one.

"I thought he wouldn't care for it," his father said, jubilant, as he met them at the door. Maura waited somewhere behind, and Cash went in the house calling her name.

Late that night it rained. The first, harsh, swift drops rushed through the garden tree and down the outside of the window, inside which she'd hung the patched sheet. It was one she had pinched from Eugene's cupboard one day when collecting Cash. But Maura saw her do it, so she didn't have a chance to take any more. Maura didn't like her. She knew from what Cash said. They had been passing a linen shop and Cash saw pillowcases for elevenpence.

"We'll get some for Mother," he had said.

"No, we won't, we'll get them for Father," Maura had said. It told everything.

The sudden sound of rain startled her. She'd been sitting for hours listening to sounds, and up to then she'd heard footsteps outside, passing along, and voices passing along with them, the flurry of soot falling, and the letterbox flapping as if someone or something from the outside world was coming through. But it was wind. She wanted to go to the lavatory but couldn't. Terror had gripped her. It began hours earlier as a knot in her chest, and it went down to the pit of her stomach, and now it paralyzed the tops of her legs, enveloping them in cages of iron. She could not move. Some awful thing waited outside the door for her. By morning she would be crippled. The strange thing was that the monster outside the door would only harm her if she went out. It would not come in. She jumped up and opened the door, asking it to show its face, but saw only the dark of the hall which she didn't know sufficiently to locate what recess it had stepped into. She closed the door again and came back to her seat, knowing it was fruitless to scream because nobody could come to her rescue. But terror has its own resources, and when she climbed through the front window she had no idea she was so distraught. Her neighbor, who had come out to put a tarpaulin over a scooter, turned and said, "Are you locked out, love?"

"No. Locked in," Kate said. She realized it was funny a second after saying it. The neighbor—a fat woman in an overall—straddled the low wall and came to help.

"You're at sixes and sevens," she said, looking into the front room. Nothing to her own place, which was a little palace. She'd have a whiskey, and love to. They climbed in. She told Kate to see that the mailman kept his hands to himself and not to forget that bins were collected on Tuesdays and always to knock on the wall if she wanted anything. After she'd sympathized a bit about moving in winter, she got down to her own troubles. How her man had upped and left her one day and now she was afraid of her life he'd come back because she was happier by herself. She had a boyfriend, of course, but men were different when you lived with them. She also said that for a young person Kate had a very startled face, and that the house could be improved, and that it was a dreadful night but gardens benefited, and never to underrate the pleasure of gardens, flowers, trees, and plants.

She left when Kate had calmed down. At least the terror had passed away, and she smiled when the woman said, "If you're interested in ballroom we might make up a foursome."

"I might be," Kate said, chagrined by her numerous inadequacies. At least it is true she was trying to smile, and she had not mentioned the child, not once. The woman, staggering a little from whiskey, was about to get over the wall, but on second thought decided to use the gateway and walked with ridiculous dignity.

12 Early summer days. The garden, which had been so savagely empty in winter, began to reveal things: lupins, dog daisies, and some wild kind of rambling roses that fell apart when they were touched by wind, or the clothes from the line. Although it was May there was still frost, and some mornings the clumps of thistles were a sight to see. Erect, knife-edged, covered in silver. Six months now. Spinster days and untrespassed spinster nights, except for lying awake and dreams. She often dreamed that they were back together, and in the dream she welcomed it, but not in real life; when she saw him she acted cold, wary, indifferent. Jealousy had passed away. She spotted them from a bus and Cash said, "Look, look, Dada, Dada." It was late evening and he was driving across a common in his car, which was itself the color of dusk. It would be Maura, or then again it could be somebody new, but she had no wish to know. Would that they drove to the horizon and right out of the world, leaving her and Cash to their own devices. A war was brewing. They'd stopped meeting because he wrote and said it afforded him no pleasure to gaze upon her destroyed face and her mean little dagger eyes. She thought his stares carried more hatred than her own, but knew she was not a perfect judge. They were each plotting, separately but thoroughly, both assuming total injury, both framing ugliness that would tear to shreds the last, threadbare remnant of their once "good" life. It was for Cash, they said. But what is a child between injured parents? Only a weapon.

He had found someone and so must she. But the effort!

"You could bloody well trick someone into thinking you're swinging," Baba would say, over and over again.

"I don't want to," Kate said. And didn't, until one specially lambent summer evening when her new telephone gave out a shrill and totally alarming ring. No one knew her number except Baba and Eugene. But this was a woman's voice, a total stranger asking for Kate. It turned out to be a photographer who'd once photographed Cash.

"Hiding away like a little old mole," she was saying. "Had to get your number from directory inquiries."

"How are you?" Kate said. She hardly knew the woman. They

had met in a coffee shop. The woman liked Cash's face and asked to photograph him for an exhibition she was holding. Like everyone else, she said at the end of the session that they must meet again. She said she lived with a madman who did papier-mâché figures and that Kate would love him.

"I'm ghastly. He cracked my skull and I have double vision. Oh yes, he's still here, absolutely," she was now saying.

That was the unnerving thing. Other men and other women survived their mutual slaughterings. She compared everyone's behavior with Eugene's.

"When is it?" Kate asked. The woman had rung to ask her to a party. The word "party" still had evocations, like the word "myrrh," or "Eucharist," or "rosewater," or "pearl barley."

"Now, this very evening," the voice said. "And you've got to come."

Why not. Not quite ready for a second flowering, but conscious of that all the same. A summer evening. And all her clothes beautifully clean, like clothes waiting for an outing. Since she worked in the cleaners she had everything pristine all the time. It also happened to be the night on which she did not have Cash. She and Eugene had him on alternate nights, and either one took him to school next day. He was a schoolboy now, with a life of his own, and a desk, and picture books and crayons that he had to be responsible for. One day she went to look at his homework, and in one of those copy books she had read a composition which he'd written, and for which he had been given a gold paper star. It was entitled "My Life," and it said:

> I live in a large cave with my mother and father. Each morning my father goes out hunting, if he is lucky he catches a deer. While he is out my mother dusts the cave.

"I'll come," Kate said, and took down the address. She dressed herself in blue (Mary, star of the heavens) and put on blue beads that "like a rosary" reached down to her navel.

Outside, the evening had a sort of golden afterglow that held the world in its thrall. Gold-lit houses, aslant in Thames water. Little boats going by silently, silent men pushing their way unambitiously with the help of a single oar. The tide was high, the river water clean and solid, giving the illusion that it could be trod on, as if on a silvered, swaying roadway.

She walked for a while, conscious of how gay people were, of how many bright pairs of red sweaters were abroad, and how many birds. She'd forgotten that birds sang!

The key was in the door and noise streaming down the stairs conducted her accurately to the room filled with people and many, many candles in gilt bottles. She paused for a minute at the threshold, apprehensive: meeting a roomful of people was not the same thing as thinking about them when one is on one's way and bus windows are a fiery gold. They had drawn the hand-woven curtains and shut out the evening. The music was so loud that she could not identify any face; once her hearing was impaired, she also seemed to stop seeing. Bad coordination. A man, some man, in an open-necked shirt came over and greeted her.

"You've just arrived and you look lost in that beautiful dress, and your name is what and what do you do?"

She asked if he were the papier-mâché man, and when he said no, she felt no obligation to be courteous, so she heard herself say that mainly she got through. He let out a rich, congested laugh and begged her to tell him more.

She went away from him toward the drink table, toward her hostess, who was wearing gold lamé to match the bottles that contained the candles.

"Darling, you look different. What happened?" The voice, somewhat husky, projected to her. She laughed it off and accepted a whiskey. After all, the hostess had had a cracked skull. Possibly everyone in the room had had a catastrophe, so why should hers be condolable?

"Darling, just make yourself known to everyone," the hostess said. Kate looked around. Two West Indians were arguing. Sophistication. She thought of telling them of a sign she'd seen in the Underground which said NIGS GET OFF OUR WOMEN, but they might not laugh. They might just tell her to hoof off. There was a time when she could have approached anyone. He noticed and came across, the same man who first greeted her. His name was Roger. Jokingly he began to strangle her with her own necklace.

"You're a bit fresh," she said, thankful all the same. He was very good-looking and that worried her. For months now she'd been spouting to Baba about the accident of physical attraction. She'd even decided that she would never have fallen in love with Eugene if it weren't for his sepulchral face.

"I am aloof," he said. "Except when I meet a very beautiful woman." He was so affected, he may even have been real.

He was alone obviously, because no woman's eye trailed him, as women's eyes do, in the most crowded and ill-lit rooms. He was standing much too close to her—hip to hip, you could say.

"Listen," she said, faking indifference. The woman was telling another to ring Daphne, because Daphne knew where to get antiques for nothing, and Daphne's lavatory was trad, and Daphne knew scores of handsome, potent, unattached men.

"I wouldn't think you needed Daphne," he said.

"I could do with antiques," she said, picturing her four rooms, two of which were empty except for tea chests and the folds of paper in the fireplace onto which the soot dropped. She was on the verge of telling him about it when he said, "You're married?" She still wore the plain gold that they'd bought long ago.

"Yes," she said. Then a girl came up behind him and chained his neck with thin, tanned arms and locked hands. Kate went off. She made herself promise that she would not cling to anyone, or confide in anyone, that she would skim through the party, coming and going like the soft gold moths that came in the window, fluttered about, and went out again. Except that some made straight for the candle flames!

In the kitchen there was food. Clear soup simmered in a vat. It reminded her of the soup she'd once had at Waterloo Station, but she helped herself to a mug all the same. Perhaps some sane person would come and talk to her.

"It's the greatest," a small Scotsman was telling another small

Scotsman, with witnesses standing by. They all wrote plays or sonnets or toothpaste ads; they all had something self-important to say.

"Are you an Irish nurse, or an Irish barmaid, or an Irish whore?" some kind, goat-bearded man asked her.

She acted as if she were a deaf-mute, and that, too, made them laugh.

More people came in, smelling the soup and the steam, mistaking the laughter for real, calling each other by familiar names: Do and Jill and Issa, the shortened names that were for longer names but whose use made people feel they would never be quite so alone again.

"He has the old falsies, et cetera," one joker was saying of a man who posed as a woman. The story had cachet because the poseur was a television actor.

"My hair grows an inch every day. I sit up in bed watching it grow," a starlet type said. The same one that had put her arms around Roger. She was nibbling the ends of her buff-colored hair, waiting for someone to tell her how provocative it was.

"When Clarissa is hungry she just eats her hair," Roger said dutifully. A yes-man.

"Yes," said Kate, with weary humor, turning to Clarissa but meaning it for him, "if you were in a chorus you would be almost certain to make the front row."

How bitchy she had grown! She moved away, apparently warming her hands on the mug of soup that was already going cold.

In the next room they were dancing, and she slunk in there and found a stool. She'd picked up a drink on the way and drank it with the soup. In the small dark room the carpet had been rolled back and the floor was cramped with people who shook, and wobbled, and looped their arms, and lolled their crazed and craving heads. Sometimes and for a brief moment, in the pause as one record followed upon another, the various partners came together, and the woman simpered, and the man took hold of her crotch, putting his claim on her, the way he might spit into his drink before going to the Gents in a public bar. One man asked a redhead if her hair was the same color down there.

"Come on, doll, you're not swinging." A tall man stood over Kate. She looked up and shook her head slowly from side to side, a thing she learned once, to relax her neck muscles.

"I'm drinking," she said.

"You're not swinging," he said. He had a ruddy, affectionate face and golden eyelashes. She would have liked to talk to him. She would have liked to say, "I can't dance. I drink instead of dancing, or I cry." She would have liked to say, "Teach me to dance," or, "How many of these people sleep together?" but he was exercising his shoulder and flicking his fingers to the beat of the very loud music.

"You won't," he said. "You're not a primitive?"

"Later," she said. He moved onto the floor and joined a girl who had begun to dance alone, in defiance. She was tall, and boyish-looking, and wore leather trousers.

Sitting, watching very carefully, Kate tried to do the dance mentally. She shook her arms, her legs, her hips, her shoulders, but she could not trust herself to stand up and do it.

"What do you think of it?" the papier-mâché man called over to her.

"Great, great," she said. The password. He was dancing with a girl who wore a strawberry punnet on her head to make herself taller. He winked at Kate's sandals. They were toeless and silver, with straps as thin as a mouse tail across her instep. She held his look idly for a second and then she looked around to locate another drink. She poured some from a stray glass into her own and drank it greedily. If nothing else, she'd get drunk! There were now two record players, and two opposing songs were belting out; the faces of the dancers were twisted with effort and mistrust, the sweat crying on their brows. It was hot, and unfunny, and shrill in that room. And, a little tipsy, Kate thought what the coolest thing she'd ever known had been: the exhalation of fresh brown clay, that inaudible breath when the sod is first turned over.

It was a habit of hers to escape a bad moment by remembering a better one. She thought of a day when she said to Eugene, as he walked naked across the bedroom floor, that a man's testicles had the delicacy of newly forming grapes. It must have been summer, both because he was able to wander around naked without freezing, and because the sight of hanging grapes was fresh in her mind. Far away and lost, all those moments. Part of her had died in them.

"Come on, I'm having an erection, let's go," the papier-mâché man said to the girl with the strawberry punnet, and they both shot through the door. Kate followed, stunned. She had to see if they were boasting.

They were not in the bedroom, at any rate. The large double bed was piled high with coats, and to one side of the bed, lying in its crib, was a baby looking up at the ceiling with the deepest, darkest eyes. Eyes that only babies have, that are like powdered ink when the first drops of water have been added and it is still an impenetrable blue. The baby hung a lip and thought to cry when Kate's form mooned over it, but being resourceful, Kate remembered a game from Cash's infancy. She ducked behind a bank of coats, reappeared, and went on ducking and reappearing until the baby's giggles alerted other people. Its mother came and tapped a pillow just to show she was its mother, and Roger came and stood near Kate, and said, "You must be a very real person."

"I am," she said. "I help blind men across the road," as she gave her finger, out of some buried instinct, to the child to gnaw.

"Ouch," she said, taking it away quickly, and to him, "Trust not the innocent, this child bit me." He opened his mouth and snapped quickly at nothing, as if an apple had been swinging from the ceiling on a thread. He admired her cheekbones. He asked why she hadn't danced and why she looked on with such scorn. He had been watching through the jamb of the door. She wanted to tell him the truth, to say that she felt clumsy, and tired, and considerably older than twenty-five, but she heard herself saying something quite different.

"They scream too much and they perform too much and they have no cadence," she said. She was really drunk now, using words that were affected and trying to sound superior. He asked what she'd been thinking of.

"I was thinking of clay."

She could not have said a more propitious thing: he saw her now as fundamental. Where had she come from?

"Ireland," she said. "The west of Ireland." But did not give any echo of the swamp fields, the dun treeless bogs, the dead deserted miles of country with a gray ruin on the horizon: the places from which she derived her sense of doom.

"There is a solitary stone castle," she said, as if she owned it, "on a hill, and it is intact, even down to the beautiful stone window frames, and there is always a white horse there, rooted to a cleft of the hill, and I would like to live there."

Lies. Lies. He fell for it, he said he must go, they must go there, make a pilgrimage, ride the white horses over the bogs down to the churning sea. She had filled in some details for him to be able to describe the place back to her.

"Sssh, ssh," Kate said, and put her finger to his lips. The baby's eyes were closing. She had forgotten that terrible anxiety which grips one in the instant that a baby is going to sleep, in case it won't. She remembered Cash and felt disloyal to him. Then she put a scarf on the side of the crib to shut out the glare of the table light, and looked up, smirking. She'd forgotten the pleasure of watching a man become attracted to her.

"You've made the party worthwhile," he said.

"And what about the others?" she said, meaning the soft, the bunny, the gooey, the dew-wet bitches.

"They are all lovely," he said. Rat. She'd expected some corny little lie at least.

"I must go soon," she said to her cheap wristwatch, as if it would save her. A woman who had just come to get her coat was having an argument with about twenty other coats, which she pitched onto the floor.

"Find me my bloody coat and take me home," she said to Roger. Did she know him? Maybe not. That was how people paired off now. Many met for the first time, lying down on a bed that was bound to be unfamiliar to one or the other of them. Kate shuddered, longing to be safe, in a taxi driving toward her own house.

"But I have a girl," Roger said, introducing Kate.

494

"Have two," the woman said bluntly. "You're a man, aren't you?" He repeated that Kate was his and turned to her to confirm it. Will-less now, a little drunk, trapped, she let his hand caress her stomach in a slow, circular motion.

On the way out he excused himself for a minute. To say goodbye, or make a date for later with the drunk woman, or pinch a bottle? What matter.

They drove in the opposite direction from where she lived. She wanted him to say something, to ask him where they were going and what he intended to do. Sometimes he took his hands off the wheel and flicked his fingers and wriggled his shoulders as if he were dancing to impress the wheel. He had put the radio on.

"Careful," she said. She always thought of Cash in moments of danger.

"I'm never careful, I pursue death," he said.

She kept one hand on the dashboard just in case.

They drove to a road named after a plant, where his flat was.

"I'll remember this road," she said. The mildness and the warmth of the evening still touched her with remaindered joy and she put out her hands to catch something.

She wished that they could walk. Walk and walk and delay it, or maybe avoid it. It was a luxury now to walk at night, because she had no man to escort her. No placid male friends.

"You are rare," he said, "and beautiful, and I want you."

She hadn't quite faced the sleeping question. She both expected it and didn't. She was not certain what to do. Did other people make love in the same way, or were there bed secrets that she didn't know about? To have only been with one man was quite a drawback. They climbed tall steps to the door, then climbed a staircase and another and another. His room was an attic with a door cut out of floorboards. He wound a pulley and the floor lifted up, and she climbed a few more steps and entered a room that was large and cluttered, with two enormous windows at either end, facing each other. He had clicked on the light and picked some clothes off an armchair to make a seat for her. The door came down slowly, filling the gap in the floor, and finally closing with a slight thud. It was not unlike being in prison.

Evermore, when she thought of the word "party," she would think of the willful internment that came after.

"You're cold, all of a sudden," he said. She sat on the bed very close to him and they drank vodka from tooth mugs. A white cat with a hump on its back sat surveying them.

"I want you," he said, and bit at her the way he had bitten at an imaginary apple before remarking on her cheekbones.

"Wronged eyes," he said, "big, too."

"Sometimes big, sometimes small, depends on how tired," she said, and stood up. To keep indifferent, to keep cool, to keep her heart frozen. In the mess she was in now, anyone could take advantage of her. She'd trade anything for scraps of love.

In the bathroom there were three different colors of eye shadow in small, circular boxes. Three different sets of eyes had looked in the split mirror and drunk from those Cornish tooth mugs and sat very close to him on the bed. Also a copper ring, on a twig. Things left behind by people who were certain that they were coming back. The door between the bathroom and the bedroom was missing. How was she going to use the lavatory when the need came? From the bed he waved in to her. "Hello," he said. Then when she came out he went in there and the telephone rang. She picked it up but no one answered.

"Leave it," he said. He stood at the lavatory for a few minutes, and she could see his dark form and his hand, palm downward, on the wall.

"I can't do it," he said. So he was as shy of her as she was of him. Relieved, she crossed over and held his hand, and they both waited and prayed for that pee, the way people wait in the drought for rain. She said she liked the smell of fresh pee; it was when it got stale that it got sordid. She said did he notice when he ate beetroot how red it became.

"Never ate beetroot, only rhubarb," he said. He said rhubarb backward for her. They said it together a few times, and then he did the pee, and just when they were about to sit and celebrate, the telephone rang again.

"It must be Donald," he said.

"Who is Donald?" she said, disbelieving before she even heard.
"Donald is a dear sick man whom I must go and see," he said.
"When?"
"Now. Tonight. I promised him."
"I'll come," she said.
"No, you won't. You'll wait here." He held her shoulders, said
she mustn't behave like a child, that she must get into bed and sleep,
and then wake up fresh when he got back. He lit a cigar, aimed the
red glow at one of her eyes, and put on the suede jacket which he'd
taken off when they got in. He licked his finger and placed it prayer-
wise on her pulse. A little baptism.

"Wait there," he said. She was certain he was going to another
woman. He wound the pulley up again and went down the stairs,
raising his forehead on the last step to signal up to her, and then the
door closed again and became part of the floor, and this time it was
really prison. The humped cat looked at her, the night appeared
beyond the two windows that were at opposite ends of the room.
An airplane went by, its green lights passing over on a level with her
eyes. She ought to get down the stairs before it fell on her head and
knocked her out. She ought to and she could. The cat never stirred.
She dreaded having to stay only a little less than she dreaded having
to go. And so she stayed. The beggar. There were books all around
she could read, or she could rummage and find little inklings of his
life, but she just sat there staring across the room toward the window
where she'd seen an airplane go by. "I've come to a nice end," she said
aloud, and thought, Where are convent scruples now? He hadn't
forced her, she'd come of her own accord to get a little—what? Satisfaction probably. No use ennobling it. Simple case of physical famine.
In the end she took off her shoes, her stockings, her roll-on, and put
them behind the leather sofa, where they would not catch his eye,
and after about an hour she took off her blue dress and got in between
the sheets, which were spattered with dried white paint.

When he got back she was dozing.
"I'm still here," she said, sitting up, hiding her face with her
hands, apologizing.
"Sssh, ssh, back to sleep," he said, and undressed, and slipped

in quietly beside her. Nothing happened for a few minutes. She put her hand in his and squeezed it overtightly. How dreadful if he rejected her now. How indecent. He seemed cold, temperate. Perhaps he'd gone and . . . She closed her eyes, ashamed, unable to finish the thought.

"Would you prefer to sleep first?" she said. That stung him. He moved up and lay on her, with dead weight. The pet words, the long, loving handstrokes, the incredible secret declarations that were for her the forerunners of lovemaking, all these were missing. Pure routine. The way he might turn on a fire extinguisher in a public building if someone called "Fire, fire."

"You don't really want me to make love to you," he said. His way of saying that he didn't. She watched his interest in her fade as she had watched others fade before now. The "instant love" potion proving useless once again.

She ran the soles of her feet up and down the calves of his legs, increasing the speed as she went along, coaxing herself into a fake frenzy. She remembered all the times she had longed to be with a man, and she told herself that she'd better make the most of this, it might have to see her through yet another winter.

"You want orgasm," he said cruelly. She'd heard that homosexuals, who, out of deceit or vanity, forced themselves to sleep with women, inflicted these sorts of humiliations. She simply shook her head and smiled. Vulgarity, indifference, lovelessness—these things did not surprise her anymore. She had wanted orgasm, but all she wished now was that they could extract themselves without losing face.

"Don't analyze us," she said, kissing his shoulder and coyly admiring its costly tan. Sweet Jesus, she thought, I despise him. If there was a way of making him suffer now, I would do it. If he said his wife had vanished with his babies I would swallow my last grain of pity and laugh. It was the first heartless admission she'd ever made to herself, the first time she realized that her interest in people was generated solely by her needs, and bitterly she thought of the little girl—herself—who had once cried when a workman stuck a pitchfork through his foot. It was as if her finding the pleasures in the world had made her ravenous.

"All the women I've loved still love me," he said.

"Many?" she said, to humor him.

"Many," he boasted, dwelling on the word as if they were passing through his mind in a procession; lovely vestal women.

"Any particular age group?"

"Young," he said.

And he had been the one to say to her at that crowded party, "What is absent from your life I must give to you," and she had been the one to swoon.

She stroked his back, asked where he got the tan, moved her face from left to right, smiled, frowned, made little jokes, all to let him think that she did this sort of thing often and was not a fool in a strange bed. She thought of a penciled sign she saw in a pub lavatory which said *I married Charles six days ago and I haven't been fucked yet*, and how its cruelty had shocked her, just as her own cruelty was shocking her now. With desperation she began hugging him, pressing her nails into his back, begging for kisses. She who had come home with him in heat was dry now and quite systematic! Out of decency she would have to arouse him, and feign delirium when the time came. What a cheat. Especially when one had set out to get something for oneself.

Afterward he said he should have waited longer, but she hushed that, and uttered something predictably noble about first-time hazards.

"I'm going to sleep," she said, "and I'll want tea when I wake up." She could be quite flippant, after all.

"Are you talking about tomorrow?" he said.

"I don't believe in it," she said. But earlier that night when he first flattered her, she had had some wild notion that he might fall in love, heal her, provide new thoughts, new happiness, banish the old ugly images of fresh-spattered blood, and forceps, and blunder; do away with Eugene, the guardian ghost, who shadowed her no matter what streets she crossed or what iniquitous sheets she slipped between. She honestly believed that this man, or some man, was going to do all this for her. Ah! He was going to sleep now, turning over to face the window that faced the sky where the airplane had gone by, hours and years ago. She curled up, accommodating her body to fit into the hollow of his. She thought how nice if women could become the ribs they once were, before God created Eve. How gentle, how calm, how unheated, how dignified, to be simply a rib! She pounded the pillow to get rid of some knotted flock and whispered, "Good night." Then she drew the sheet up over her face and closed her eyes.

But it did not work. She could not sleep because of the strangeness, and as the night wore on she dreaded the morning. She dreaded sitting up and having to say "Hello" and watch his thoughts curve away from her the way a river changes course when it encounters a boulder. He had already said he had to go out early. He had already hinted. She moved to the foot of the bed and got out, without even touching the hump where his feet were. She dressed carefully, studied the door mechanism, and then lifted it up, creeping away without a sound. She left no note. Another narrow escape.

Out in the street the stars, if there had been any, had vanished, and the light was deepening from dun-gray to a tenuous satin blue; blue light touching the slates of the high houses, approaching windows, behind which people slept and had made love or had dreamed of having made love or had turned over to avoid the face and breath of some hated bed companion. People were strange and unfathomable. As well as being desperate. He would be relieved to find her gone.

In the Underground station she counted her money and rubbed the tops of her bare arms. The Tube rushed like wind into the empty station, and she stepped into a No Smoking compartment along with two other girls. Had they come from illicit beds, too? They were well organized: they wore eye shadow and had cardigans and carried small travel bags. If the day got warm they would remove their cardigans and put them on again in the evening. She closed her eyes; they had already closed theirs. She closed her eyes on the thought that sleeping with a man was unimportant. A nothing, if nothing in the way of love preceded it. Or resulted from it. Did these girls know this? If the Tube was about to crash and they had seconds' warning, what was the last thing she would cry out? This newfound knowledge, or Cash's name, or an Act of Perfect Contrition? Impossible to tell. Anyhow, they were getting there safely, only three stops to go.

. . .

At work she rang him. At least he was a man. He might introduce her to someone else and that someone . . . Even in sober unslept daylight she hankered after the De Luxe Love Affair.

"You are not a one-night girl, you are for all time," he said, rambling on about how easy it would be for him to fall in love with her.

"I just want to apologize," she said, and dragged in the plea about having had too much to drink.

"I would have liked to make you happy." He was solemn now.

"But you did make me happy," she said hurriedly, rushing in with fake assurances.

"When I get back from Budapest we must meet," he said. The writing was clear on the wall.

"Have a good time there," she said. Just as well. He probably knew that any man she took up with now would only pay in pain for what had happened between her and Eugene; the brutal logic of wronged lovers taking their revenge on innocents and outsiders.

She put the telephone down and for the couple of minutes that remained until opening time she stood facing, but not looking at, the "ticker tape" sign of multicolored lettering which at that moment was still but would soon be flashing on and off, guaranteeing bargains, perfection, and total satisfaction.

The fierce arid clarity that comes from sleeplessness possessed her. She foresaw the day: four hours there, the awful smell of cleaning fluids, the stupidity of dirty, crumpled clothing, the panic on the faces of people who had lost their tickets, then relief at identifying their own garments; she would have a two-and-ninepenny lunch, her daily walk by the Thames, possibly the tide going out, abandoning old shoes—why always single shoes?—and pieces of soggy wood and men's contraceptives, pigeons gray and black and white pecking for nourishment from the relegated semen on the muddy tideless shore; and at four collecting Cash from school and taking him to a playground to swing on the swings and home to tea. Another night. But not for long. The time was coming, and she could feel it almost like music in her bones, when things would be different. It would be better once Baba's daughter could talk and walk. She would be a sister for Cash. Tracy, Baba had named her, or rather, it had been Frank's choice. In the end Frank received her like his own and made even greater consequence of being a parent than if he had actually been one. And Baba, never one to be held down by punishment, was cornered in the end by niceness, weakness, dependence. Still, she and Baba would take a holiday; for a week or two they would live as they pleased, tell fluent lies, have love affairs, dance at night, learn to ski, and slide down mountain slopes, temporarily happy with their children. She had no place in mind, but they would find a place. Baba would attend to that because Frank no longer restricted her in little things. Quite often he was too drunk to register. He merely waved an arm and said, "Powerful, powerful," to whatever was going on. There would be some very good days, weeks perhaps. And smiling at the thought, she saw the ticker tape move and heard the grunt that machines give before they start up and knew that downstairs the manager had turned on the switch that set the day in motion.

But it did not turn out like that at all. When she got to the school gate Cash was not waiting. No surprise. He was invariably last, or arrived in his school plimsols and passed her by, forgetting that it was the day to go to her house and not his father's. When he did not come she went to the cloakroom in search of him. All the metal hangers but one were free of coats, and the place looked alarmingly forlorn without either coats or children. The blue anorak hanging there belonged to a much older child. She called. She then stood outside the lavatory and called again. She remembered some drama about his being locked in the lavatory by an older boy and she called now very loudly so that he could not fail to hear her. In the end she went to the headmaster's door and knocked nervously. He received her in a small neat office, where he sat before a cold cup of tea.

"I can't find Cash," she said.

"I'm sorry, the school is sorry . . ." he said with a shake of the head, and added "Mrs. . . ." simply to acknowledge her married status. He obviously did not know how to tell her, so he asked her to sit down.

"I wasn't sure if you knew," he said then, lifting the cold cup of tea and handing it across to her. He told her how Cash's father had come and announced his decision to take the boy away. She was seized with giddiness and once again was obliged to ask herself if she was not perhaps dreaming or sleepwalking.

"When?" she asked. For a minute she believed there was some connection between her wayward night and the father's decision.

"Last Friday," the teacher said.

Five days before. So there was no connection. This seemed to give her strength. She seemed to recover her senses and drew herself up in order to rise to her feet, and then some invincible and implacable force possessed her whole body as she rushed out of the office and down the corridor and along the five streets to his father's house.

When she hit the knocker there was no answer, and she knew there would be none, and yet she repeated the move again and again and pressed the disconnected bell and peered through the windows that were coated completely with white chalk. Once, she had seen them through snow, and now through another snow she was looking and seeing nothing. It was a big moment, the one when reality caught up with nightmare, the crest and the end.

The next day there was a short letter from his solicitor enclosing a longer one from him. And both these letters told her everything she had screamed to know when she clawed the door, rapped her knuckles on the windows, and pleaded through a fastened letter box to be heard, to be answered. They had fled. Cash, Eugene, and Maura. "A flight into Fiji." She could see now how it had been carefully and beautifully worked out, as careful as a major robbery. He saw to it that she got no inkling until they had gone, and it was this that drove her to the last pitch of desperation, this mindlessness of hers. How little had she observed him. She still thought that perhaps she could catch them out, that perhaps they had broken the law.

She rang the passport office, and after frantic explanation to a telephonist and then a secretary, she was put through to the official who had in fact issued a passport for Cash. She asked why she hadn't been consulted, and the clerk said that a mother's signature was not necessary for such a thing.

THE COUNTRY GIRLS TRILOGY

"You call that just?" she said.

"What?" the man at the other end asked.

"Oh, balls," she said savagely, and hung up. The conspiracy was too enormous, the whole machinery too thorough; it was like seeing a newspaper heading that read HOLIDAY COACH CRASHES and experiencing a senseless, futile, blinding rage.

Eugene's letter was long and self-righteous. He said he had lost a daughter through a woman's heinousness and he was not going to lose a son. He outlined her faults, did it so thoroughly, so intelligently, that half the time she found herself nodding, agreeing with him, the words scratched out with care, with cruelty, indisputable, final words—"Vain, immoral, mean-minded, hardhearted, weak, self-destructive, unmaternal." She skipped and read farther down: "There is no other course open to me than to carry out my duty as his father to the bitter end. I will not allow you to destroy his future life, to turn him into one of those mother-smothered, emotionally sick people, your favorite kind. What infection—it can hardly be called thinking—makes you take for granted your well-being as of paramount importance over that of the boy's healthy future, over my work and life. It is too late. You should have planned your full-time mother career a little earlier when he was being reared by Maura and myself."

Too late! She cried out, "You are mad, mad. It is all mad, senseless." One idea after another suggested itself, and these were not very far removed from madness either. She would go there, set fire to the house, and rescue Cash; she would have the boy stolen from school; no, she would beg, appeal to his tenderness, send a telegram saying I CARRIED HIM, I BORE HIM, blackmail them, get a letter from her old friend the politician, have a delegation of politicians go out there with banners. Justice justice justice! In her thoughts she twisted and turned like a crazed woman, in the middle of a street with traffic approaching on all sides. Friends did what they could, consoled, raged, sympathized: but no one, no one in the world could remedy what had been done.

She went to see a solicitor, and as she sat there giving dates, facts, scraps of her married life, she had this certainty that what was happening was unreal and that presently someone would nudge her and laugh and say, "It is all a game, we were just testing you." But no. The interview went on. He was an old man, genial in a quiet way, and a specialist in divorce. He looked down at his notebook when the time came to ask about infidelity. He had to know.

"Well, yes," she said.

"How many times?"

"Once?"

"Would you like to tell me how it happened."

"No, I wouldn't . . ." she said as she began. She had stopped going to confession, but this was a return in memory to that ordeal and she blessed herself mentally. Telling the story aroused no contrition, just a bad taste. A night of tattiness. Absurd to have to mention it at all.

"And you say your husband did not know about this."

"No, there is no connection between the two events." Ah, no, the retribution was far more hideous, far more comprehensive than that. Retribution for what! She talked calmly, sometimes looking at his face bent over the big notebook, sometimes at his good jacket draped on a spare chair. He wore a tattered jacket with leather patching on the elbows, and had she known him better she would have made some nice comment about his prudence.

"Now, your husband, this letter is a bit extreme . . ." he said, scanning it again.

"He's like that," she said. She had no wish to say much else, no wish to list his failings or plead her case; these are things done in hope, in fury, and hope and fury had expired days before. Even sitting there seemed pointless, absurd.

"Now tell me, since you left him, did he molest you?" The very question roused them both a little.

"No," she said, shaking her head back and forth.

After he had taken all the information, he closed the notebook and looked at her.

"What did you marry a man like that for?"

"It seemed to be what I wanted."

"Marry a . . ."

"I knew less then . . ."

Although her face was to the window and light was pouring in on her, there was no trace of tears or breaking down.

"Silly girl," he muttered, but in a way that was affectionate and not reprimanding. Then abruptly he asked if he might get her a brandy, and she said no. He looked at her hand on the desk, the fist clenched, veins showing through a density of freckles, and slowly he put his own hand over hers and held it there.

"We'll do everything we can," he said in a low voice.

She made no reply.

It boiled down to a question of money. They could go there, if she could afford it; they would fight it through the proper legal channels, but it would take time, a lot of time, a lot of money. He was an honest man, he was not going to tell her otherwise.

After a little while she rose and left, and down in the street a lull occurred, as if all the traffic had been suspended, and rather boldly she crossed the road.

It took days to write, though the difficulty was not what to say but how to say it. Her mind was made up, she had withdrawn. The odds were too great, the battle already won. She did not have his wickedness. She did not have his weapons.

She wrote:

> Dear Eugene,
> I have decided to let Cash stay with you for the time being. I trust that you will do everything for his well-being, as I am sure you will. My solicitor will be in touch with you shortly.

> Dear Cash,
> My geography is not good. What is the latitude and longitude of where you are? What food do you eat? And what about your school? I expect it is all quite strange but no doubt very exciting. If you like, I will send your comics.

Nothing else, nothing too close or too tender, or too hurtful. She had not the desire to say anything else. It was as if the decision itself had washed her clean, had emptied her of purpose.

Cash sent her a map of the island. It was drawn in ink on a paper napkin, and then the napkin had been cut around the edge to the exact squat-bottle shape. Towns were marked and streams and a bread shop and a swimming pool and the sea at the bottom. There were hibiscus trees all over, and these did not look like trees at all but like triangles of black in between the other features. At the top he had written in capital letters THE HEAVENS ARE BLUE. When she looked at it, she supposed that they had been eating in a restaurant, all three of them, and one of them had said her name and Cash had decided or had been prompted to do the drawing. She studied it very carefully so that she could make comments in her next letter. Also, she had it pressed between two sheets of glass and used it as a sort of paperweight. In the next letter she told him this and enclosed the comics. It would go on like that, letters back and forth over the years, photographs at intervals, and these she dreaded, and she knew that she would have to steel herself against them.

After Christmas Kate had herself sterilized. The operation was done by a private doctor and it entailed a short confinement in an expensive clinic—money that might otherwise have been frittered on clothes or a summer holiday. On the second day Baba came to see her and found her sitting up in bed reading a newspaper article about women who for the purpose of scientific experiment had volunteered to spend a fortnight in an underground cave. Kate read: "Doctors in touch by telephone from an adjacent cave continue to be astonished at the physical resilience and lively spirits of the women, who were unknown to each other before the vigil began."

"Frank says you might as well move in with us . . ." Baba said, interrupting.

"Really?" Kate said, pleased, surprised.

"He suggested it, not me," Baba said gruffly.

"He usen't to like me," Kate said.

"He must be getting over it," Baba said, but she was glad at being able to make the offer all the same. They would have each other, chats, moments of recklessness; they could moon over plans that they'd both stopped believing in, long ago.

THE COUNTRY GIRLS TRILOGY

"Well," Baba said after some time, meaning, "What does it feel like?"

"Well," Kate said, "at least I've eliminated the risk of making the same mistake again," and for some reason the words sent a chill through Baba's heart.

"You've eliminated something," Baba said. Kate did not stir, not flinch; she was motionless as the white bedpost. What was she thinking? What words were going on in her head? For what had she prepared herself? Evidently she did not know, for at that moment she was quite content, without a qualm in the world. It was odd for Baba to see Kate like that, all the expected responses were missing, the guilt and doubt and sadnesses, she was looking at someone of whom too much had been cut away, some important region that they both knew nothing about.

Epilogue

It goes on, by Jesus, it goes on. I am at Waterloo again, the railway station where Kate gashed her wrists, thinking daftly that someone might come to her rescue, a male Florence Nightingale might kneel and bandage and swoop her off to a life of certainty and bliss. Nearly twenty years ago. Much weeping and gnashing in between. They've cleaned this place up; it's morbidly bright and neat, and even the advertisements look as if they're washed down with suds every morning. They're high up, far too high for anyone to scrawl PISS or ARSENAL or ARAB or LINDA. One features hills in Wales, rolling hills no less, with undulations. The green is unnatural; it's lurid and it's supposed to entice people to have offices in fucking Wales. I'm nervous as hell.

It's June; there's sun, masses of it coming through a bloody, girded, glass roof. I wouldn't mind a bit of rain or a thunderstorm to fit in with the circumstances. There's a letter for me, it seems. I bet it'll be elegiac . . . too fucking elegiac.

On the other side of the tomato-ketchup-colored plastic counter are a loving couple. They're both gawks, wearing glasses, and they're too goddamn pent up even to speak. He's about to depart, he's about to go ten yards to the service counter to get a doughnut or a sandwich, and what does he do but kiss her and what does she do but droop and blush like a wallflower. Bilge. A lunatic woman in a felt hat is stalking around cursing people. She has an umbrella, and with the point of the umbrella she is searching rubbish bins for some important missive. She's just the kind of cow who could guess what's happening to me and make a damn spectacle of me. Lunatics unite. Loveswain is back with a three-decker prawn and mayonnaise sandwich and is offering Miss Wallflower a loving bite. You won't believe it: it drips all over her chin and he kisses it away. I don't want to listen to what they have to say. Tautology. It's that surface fucking niceness that grates on me. Mind you, it's not happening to me a great deal of late, the tiptoe-through-the-tulip frolic, the old-high-speed sex. I should be thinking about her except that I don't want to. I am chewing a piece of bread that is so like white blotting paper it would soak up a quart of ink. The pigeons are at my feet assaulting a crust. One is lame, and I can tell you it's not getting very far in the mastication zones. They're a hell of a lot more spry than the lumps of flesh and emotion and anxiety and banality and twitch that have assembled around this horseshoe-shaped bar. Sunday papers have already been thrown away. The Queen, the baby princes, the cruise missiles, and the Sportsman of the Year are all inside someone's noddle now, bobbing around with last week's data and the week before, all accruing to no fucking avail. People have minds like sieves. Except when it comes to gain.

I wouldn't mind a large gin, followed by another, to blur the old perceptions, as Kate would say. I tore over here in a taxi, and the driver, a fairly hefty and erudite Semite, insisted on talking to me, raving to me about bikinis. Bikinis! A famous TV announcer frequenting a public bath wore a white bikini with black squares which showed off her nubile figure to advantage. This was some years ago, before she was famous, but nevertheless he saw her and had a conversation with her.

"Funny how these things happen!" he said. I wanted to say, "Nothing's funny, buster," but he wouldn't stop proclaiming, he was like a fucking gramophone, full of himself and the sagacity of his opinions.

I have availed myself of the service of two flunkies. They're from foreign parts, Pakistan or maybe even somewhere farther. They're certainly not Turks. I gave them a fiver and explained that I would need a coffin carried, when the train gets in. They seem to have grasped it. They are speaking in their mother tongue or their father tongue, or whatever the fuck tongue it is. It's unmusical. They're probably discussing the cricket match or else their tea break. They look at me from time to time as if to size me up. I think they think it's all a bit forlorn. In their country there would be wailing now, flocks of relatives beating their chests; in my country, too, and Kate's. What the hell ever happened to all the relatives we had? I can't picture her, I don't want to, I mean I don't even know if they've put a nightgown on her, or a habit or some damn thing. I bet they keep habits in that kind of place in case of emergency. They were dead matter-of-fact about it, and dead insolent. They didn't want a hearse there. A hearse would put the afflautused matrons off their kilter, as they swanned around in their pink and apricot morning gowns. She'd gone to a health farm to recoup. Recoup! She flipped. I suppose all that starvation, and time to think, brought her face to face with brass tacks, realized she was on her ownio, Good Shepherd wasn't coming. Oh, Kate, why did you let the bastards win . . . why buckle under their barbaric whims? I'm terrified that she'll appear to me some night, maybe when I'm out in the garden smelling the phlox, or she'll be plonked on my bidet in ashes and loincloth, telling me some dire thing such as repent. Repent what. People are fucking gangsters. It costs more to run into a motorcar than a person.

The most hilarious thing has happened. A fawn collie dog has broken free from its owner, has chased across, and is barking up at the Welsh come-hither hills. Now, if that isn't Mother Nature asserting herself, what is. There's a crowd cheering and the dog is so fucking carried away that it's on its hind legs doing a turn. Next to the Welsh hills there is a pack of wolves baying at a crescent of gold that is supposed to be a package of cigarettes. Underneath their midnight-blue hooves there's a government health warning about tar. Fucking absurdity. I've had to have a second carton of wish-wash tea. The waitress looks as if she came from the blackest hole on earth. There's layers of black pigment behind her skin, and you wouldn't be surprised if her blood was treacle black. She's surly, she wields the teapot way above the plastic cups—they're the color of communion wafers, for God's sake—and she veers from one cup to the next with a vengeance. She's sloshing tea all over the goddamn counter. I bet she wouldn't mind the three-minute warning. She might start a great, earth-shattering yodel, express herself as she twigged to the fact that time was running out and she'd better speak her mind and her fucking enmity. I've nothing particular against blacks, they're limberer in the buttocks, probably be all right if they were let drowse under the yamyam trees all day. I met one that I liked—you won't believe it but he was called Snowie. Earlier in the year Durack and I weren't hitting it off; I mean, there were more fisticuffs than normal, so he sent me on a holiday to one of those tropical islands—cocoa, sunsets, sugarcane, and all that. I had my own little villa and a team of girls to sweep up. They were always sweeping. I don't know what the hell they could sweep, but they were at it from six in the morning, swish-swosh, swish-swosh. They held themselves very well; chest out like coconuts, arses very comical, very imperious. They cooked me my breakfast and stood behind the table while I ate it. A third one would bring me the local paper. It was a gas —a plethora of crimes. I was following the story of one Esmeralda, who threw Lysol on her common-law man and was a wizard at the old art of evasion. A great procrastinator was Esmeralda. In the court she excelled herself: "He lashed me with broom on my back. The broom break. He jump on me and bite me on my stomach. I get serious." Every time I asked them if they knew old Esmeralda, they started to laugh. She could be their cousin, for God's sake.

The leisure began to get to me. I felt the old gurgles, minnows in the cunt, and thought, Bingo, this is it, I'm alive again, I wouldn't mind a bit of the soft anvil under the thatch. Plenty of opportunity; young fellows walking around, swaggering, their do-dahs agog and smatterings of blarney: "Enjoy you the sea. Enjoy you the scenery." I thought, Why not, no bloody discussion, no "Should we, shouldn't we, my wife, your husband, do you love me, do I love you" garbage. I decided that I would pick out some winsome fellow and invite him to my villa in the erogenous siesta hour. Only time when they weren't sweeping. There were lots of studs around selling T-shirts and neck-laces and postcards, spouting the "enjoy you" lark. I would sit on the beach and cogitate. Nothing like cogitating a harmless fuck. Big branches swaying, the sea full of sparkle, no one to nag or natter to me. I forgot Durack, I forgot the fishmongers, I forgot our pickled-pine kitchen and whether the sofa needed fucking reupholstering, I even forgot my own telephone number. I forgot our bi-weekly dinner parties, with people drinking too much and suddenly taking umbrage, tearing into one another, frothing, all their fucked-up aggression coming out over some irrelevant thing like who they were going to vote for, or who should be Prime Minister. Poor Durack, I didn't miss him at all. I even mused over getting him a present of a pair of the girls with their bracelets and their insouciance. Durack and I were man and wife again, but I wouldn't say I saw the celestial heights often, more the nadir, usually a bit too much to drink and bamboozling myself into thinking it was James Dean, or James Dean's double, or someone like

that. "Little Mother," he called me. Little mother for the one illegitimate kid that I had, a girl that had a will of her own and a mind of
her own from the second she was born. Vomited the milk I gave her,
rejected me, from day one, preferred cow's milk, solids, anything. She
left home before she was thirteen, couldn't stand us. She liked him
better than me, but that's because she could twist him around her
little finger and always did. The first pony he got her, he led it into
her bedroom Christmas morning and let it stay there. You can guess
the consequences, you can imagine what a nervous pony in a confined
space does, but she and Durack loved it, thought it was the funniest
thing, took photos of it with her new Polaroid. The pony was called
Horace. I'm not a mother like Kate, drooling and holding out the old
metaphorical breast, like a warm scone or griddle bread. She stood up
to me, my little daughter, Tracy. At five years of age she walked into
my bedroom and said, "You better love me or I'll be a mess." She
could ride a motorcycle before she was ten, and she was able to
wheedle Durack into giving her a huge insurance policy so she'd be
independent. She's pretty enough except for the clothes she wears,
either dungarees three times too large or shorts that leave nothing to
the imagination. She had glasses with pink frames that look like
lollipops. When I told her she was illegitimate she just looked at me
and said, "I've always known." No sentiment in her. She has oodles
of friends. They all flock to her pad, and they drink Southern Comfort,
eat chocolates, and discuss sex: how boring or how unboring sex is.
They're worldly as hell. I forgot her, too, as I sat envisaging the trans-
ports of the afternoon—on the floor, as I imagined it, or on one of
the sloping latticed sun chairs, with my hands bound or something
to give it a whiff of coercion. I thought, We're lonely buggers, we
need a bit of a romp so as not to feel that we're walking, talking
skeletons. Kids don't do really; at least not when they grow up, and
that was Kate's mistake, the old umbilical love. She wanted to twine
fingers with her son, Cash, throughout eternity. The rupture had to
come sometime, the second rupture, because of course the first one
came when her hemlock husband took him away and she had to fight
to get him back. At first she hadn't the spunk to fight, but then it
came to her, the old lioness tenacity—and she got geared for battle.

515

Her solicitor nearly adopted her, gave her hot lunches and a book token at Christmas. The kid was back in England with his father in a boring toad-in-the-hole suburb. Even the *au pair* girl left, saw he was a brigand or couldn't adhere to his rules; he was a great one for rules, he'd tell you how to breathe. The night before the court case the father took the kid into his study and told him, man to man, that his mother was bonkers, certifiable, and that except for him being such a ministering angel, she would never have had a child at all. You'd think he'd given birth to it. The nub of it was that he was getting the kid to write a letter to the judge to say that he wanted to be with his father. He had pen, ink, a sheaf of notepaper, and melting sealing wax with which to seal the proclamation. Instead the kid wrote "Putney"—where she lived, a dump with an attic window so that you had to get up on a chair to get a view of the old lugubrious Thames. When she got the damn custody, she and the kid went to the Savoy for lunch. He had no tie, naturally, but they loaned him one, and he ate mutton and steamed pudding and was like a little man. All in the past now, like our fucking hand-to-mouth youth and our big brazen scenarios.

I'd nearly given up when he came around the corner like a panther. Old Snowie. I had talked to him a couple of times, and given him the eye, the old Portia, fair-speechless messages. He was carrying this pile of T-shirts, all with bits of palm or a sail painted on the chest. I just smirked at him and went straight through the double doors to the bedroom, knowing he'd follow. I heard him shut the door.

"Lock it," I said. I was afraid my garrulous little attendants might be eavesdropping, or that one of them might turn out to be his sister or his wife or any damn thing, and that I would find myself in the old Esmeralda situation with broomstick over back. While I was drawing the bamboo blind he came up behind me, like a cat. He didn't whip my clothes off, he stole them off. Not that I minded. Then he put a big hand, it was as big as one of these palm leaves, over my eyes and splayed it and drew me back toward the old bed where I had lain solo for six intemperate nights. There he was, towering over me, naked, mahoganied, a chest matted with hair, eyes that looked a hell of a lot brighter because of the dark, and what did he do but take a pile of petals he had brought and strew them all over my stomach. Hibiscus and bougainvillea. Red and white trumpets, no less. Prodigious. Could be Sportsman of the Year. I thought, Give me the olden days, give me the primitive thrust, forget the guilt-ridden drips, the see-you-anon swains, the Jekyll-and-Hyde hubbies. Best few hours of my life. I felt like Jezebel, for God's sake. A long way from Tipperary. Flowers on my stomach, love bites, the works. Another thing, we didn't speak a word, nothing to break the damn spell. A blacksmith under the thatch. The old love bites. Afterward he began to walk about the room, and I thought that maybe he wanted something, that maybe he wanted money, or for me to buy a consignment of the T-shirts.

"I'll pay you whatever you want," I said, and he stopped smiling and he had a look I'll never forget. He looked angry and at the same time crushed.

" 'Pon my word," he said, and then he shook his head and laughed, but it was a sarcastic kind of laugh. He said every tourist was the same, that they only thought money, that they thought all things could be bought, even the colors of the sea. I felt stupid, I felt like a pimp. I said we were that way from getting robbed and rooked, from queueing and shoving and slandering and pretending and cutthroating in what passes for civilized society. I was damn near crying.

" 'Pon my word, you silly," he said, and he laughed, but his pique was gone. I really wanted to give him something, a keepsake, so I picked up an ashtray and handed it to him, and what did he do, only fill it with water and put it outside for the doves. They came in hordes that day and the next day and the day after, and their shit is indigo. Must be some damn fruit they eat. He came, too, and brought flowers, shells, fertility symbols, one supposed to be him and one supposed to be me. I used to think, I'll be nice to Durack when I go home, I'll be lovey-dovey, I'll be able to transport myself back to the hectic old siesta rides. We were supposed to go on a little jaunt, Snowie was going to borrow a friend's motorcar, probably a jalopy, and drive me to a part of the island that was much more rugged. Rugged! He had all the jargon of the brochures. We were going to suck sugar from the damn cane and lie in this rugged field, but it was not to be, as Kate would say. The following morning, when I lay on a mat slathered in jelly and coconut oil, trying to make myself a bit sultry, my two little maids came tripping across and I knew there was something up, because they weren't laughing, and one pushed the other ahead to deliver the message. It was a telegram. It was home. At first I thought that Durack had got wind of my iniquity through some damn ludicrous fluke. It said: FRANK SUFFERED STROKE COME HOME. DECLAN.

Thought he was drunk, they did. He drove into a stationary milk float and sent bottles and cartons skeetering all over the street. The police were called and they thought it, too. There he was at the wheel, laughing. When the policeman asked him where he lived, he mumbled that he knew where he lived but that he didn't want to go there because his wife was not at home, had done a flit. Then they took a breath test, and to their great surprise it didn't show green; which surprises me, because there must be a surplus of malt and blended whiskey in every pore of his body. When I got back the next afternoon and took one look at him in the hospital, I knew it, I knew he'd lost his marbles. A fucking vegetable. His eyes were vacant and he was like a black sheep sitting there in National Health pajamas, waiting for me. I wanted to run away, go to the airport, go straight back and work as a waitress or a beachcomber or anything. He was in a ward with about twenty people, people with shaven heads and bandaged faces, most of them nearly as gaga as him. He was trying to be friendly. He gave me a package of cigarettes and told me to go around and offer one to everyone, he even wanted me to offer one to a man in an oxygen mask. There I was in my pink cotton trouser suit, and my tan, feeling like a fucking imposter and knowing that I wouldn't be doing flits again, I'd be whiling the time attending to him, reading articles on rehabilitation, getting him to recognize a shoe from a sock. The next day when I went in, he was wiping his eyes with a big spotted handkerchief. He must have had it in his pocket when they took him in. Some young doctor, some impudent bastard, told him that he'd never come out, that he was on Death Row. I gave him the old platitudes, told him he'd be all right, told him a whole host of things that weren't true, sops for the old morale, straws really. I discharged him a few days later, brought in a suit of clothes and left a note on the bed telling them to get in touch with our doctor. On the way home he insisted that we go to the pictures.

"Pictures, pictures," he kept saying as we whizzed around Marble Arch in a beige taxi that was doing eighty miles an hour, the driver being infuriated at having to go out to Wimbledon. The crocuses were coming up; I saw them in a fucking whirl, the very same as if I were at a fun fair on the Big Wheel. We got out, paid, and went in to see *A Thousand and One Dalmatians*. I wished it was a fucking comedy we'd gone to, because he was crying most of the time, and even his crying is botched. He blurps, because he can't discharge the fucking tears through the ducts of the two eyes. It's the same with laughing. He laughs crooked, too.

When we got home he looked at the house, ran around it, began to kiss it, put spittle on his finger and daubed it like some medieval rite. Then he looked at the stump of the magnolia tree and cried. He'd had it cut down one day in a fit, had this fegary there were chaffinches in it spying.

"We'll plant another," I said. I'm a demon now for the old platitudes and the everything-is-rosy refrain. I send to nurseries for catalogues and read them to him, and plan all the herbaceous delights. Wanted to be with me all the time, nestling. He'd think that I had gone and he'd tell me that Baba had gone when I was there in the kitchen making fucking potato cakes and barley soup to remind him of his martyred mother and all that Mavourneen mush. I was full up to the gills with guilt and pity and frustration. He'd stand up in the middle of the dinner and put the soup tureen on his head, or he'd go out and piss ceremoniously from the hall doorstep, and laugh and ask me to come and see. Oh, sweet Jesus, all the rows and all the belting and all the hoodwinking and all the bitterness reduced to this, to his beseeching look, to his dependence on me, like a spaniel. He'd ask for pen and paper and write me a letter:

I love you, do you here. Answer me now.

I would nod, but he didn't want me to nod, he wanted me to write a letter so we'd be passing notes like two dummies, with him getting excited and pawing and slathering.

"An old soldier, Baba," he would say . . . "An old soldier" . . .

He went down to the shops one day, or rather, I drove him down, and then he told me to scoot, said he wanted to be alone, wanted to do something in private. I thought that he was going to buy me an eternity ring or some damn thing, but you won't believe it, he went to a shop that sells lace garters, suspenders, and various titillations, aids to the old connubial doldrums. Brought back two dirty books. One for him and one for her, so's we could cuddle. Weird, making love or half-love to a man with the most of his body banjaxed and to see his eyes struggling for performance. I realized that I didn't hate him anymore and that maybe I never hated him. There we were, like two Mohawks on our chintz sofa, perusing these things so as to work up to a steamy crescendo. My manual featured a pert maid with bobbed hair, frilly cap, and white apron tending to a hulk who had his hand on her crotch, and his had bevies of buxom Victorian ladies, in their boudoirs, with their bums jutting out and your all-time, mustached Romeo leering above a screen. All the time I was hoping the damn doorbell would ring and that one of our friends, who are rabid for the corporal works of mercy, would arrive with homemade marmalade or a novena. St. Jude, patron of hopeless causes. No such bloody luck. Paid me court. Compliments. Said my skin was the same as when we first met. It's all that fucking rainfall where we grew up, soaking into us. The same with Kate. Her skin hadn't changed a bit, but by God her nerve ends had.

He tried to shave but only shaved half his stubble, and the same with his dinner. He would only eat from one side of the plate, so I'd have to turn it around before he could eat the other. What fucking got me was the way he strove to be self-sufficient, asked for a basket so that he could keep his personal belongings near him, his comb, his wallet, his razor, his notebooks, and a compass, as if we were going safari-ing. He'd see men cuddling me and he'd start to scowl, but he didn't get the old blunderbuss and belt me, like before. He told these various Lancelots to get the hell out of his parlor, off his site, to get back to work, because common laborers they were and nothing more. It must have been the men at work in their dungarees that he envisaged. A few of them come on pay night and bring presents, records about Innisfail and Malachi's collar of gold. They call him Guv. He likes that. He damn near blushes. His kineshite Christian brother, Declan, doesn't come much. Too guilty. He and a foreman by the name of Danno held this big caucus to ratify things. Danno was one of your hill-and-dale robbers, brown ganzy like a dishcloth, always saying, "Take care" and "God bless," and jollop like that, chewing Rennies for his indigestion. They bought Durack out. It wasn't difficult, because he was up to his tonsils in debt, gone in for property development, thought building was too lumpen, like cattle jobbing, not suave enough. Bought a morgue in Hampshire that he was going to do up and flog to an American bank. Predicted he'd be one of the richest men in the British Isles. For a year we were within saluting distance of a few million, we were going to have homes all over the goddamn place. My wardrobe worried me to death, what I'd wear in the different countries and how I'd interview cooks and gardeners. I learned Spanish, for God's sake. They made him a partner. Sleeping fucking partner. Hardly any money coming in now, but of course they bamboozled us with sheets and figures that Galileo wouldn't understand.

He's dead worried that we'll have to sell out and that I won't be cared for, so he gets blokes over from Christie's and Sotheby's to value things—scornful bastards with pimples and pocket calculators. They have no time for our pictures or our commodes, and I'm not surprised, because everything we have is onyx and leatherette, stuff you'd find on any High Street from here to St. John of Groats. Tracy, my beloved daughter, got him a jigsaw puzzle—Emily Brontë on a black chair with the nape of her neck pink-colored. Emily Brontë was not someone he had a penchant for. We scattered the pieces all over the floor and put them together again. We play another slob game where you pick a theme, and he picked sport, and takes about three-quarters of an hour to say Danny Blanchflower.

I'm dreading the winter, because it's dark at five; at least now we sit outside on the old hammock playing these blasted games and knocking back the cocktails. Cooney stays on to humor him. She has a new hip, and no topic since Copernicus has engendered as much conversation. It's called Marmaduke. It doesn't like rain or cold or east winds, and I'll tell you, another thing it doesn't like is hard work. I get down on my knees and wash floors while Cooney does the flowers and tells me inanities about the hospital, the food, the other patients, mostly scum, and the way nurses waken you too early to do ablutions. She expected to be in a fucking three-star hotel. Our other regular caller is the Monsignor, who has got very ecumenical with the times, which really adds up to the fact that he approves of Pope John Paul II traveling. Now, when Pope John Paul II travels he says what Popes have been saying since *secula seculorum*—"Thou shalt not sin." He's still for keeping women in bondage, sexual bondage above all, as if they weren't fucked up enough with their own organs, and whoever said that all women in the world enjoy all the fucking they have to do—no one, certainly not me. The Pope is all for bevies of children within wedlock, more children to fill the slums and the buses and smash telephone kiosks, because of course it's usually the ones in the slums that breed so profusely, part of their routine, like a fry-up. The smarter ones know all the ropes, know how to keep in with the Pope and still swing from the old chandeliers. I don't discuss this with the Monsignor because it would be a beetroot face and a sermon, and to tell you the truth, I like him to come and sit with Durack and reminisce. I'm as crooked as everyone else, except that I don't want to be. The old Monsignor will reminisce about anything, the number of species of potatoes—there's more than Kerr's Pink and King Edward, comrade. He has dire things to say about Communism, the tortures of Pol Pot, and is fearful that priests in the Third World are forgetting the divine call. If anyone weighed up the conceited garbage that anyone else speaks in an hour, it would fill a turf bag. Often thought of asking him in jest if he thinks there is copulation in heaven, apostolic emissions from Peter, or Paul, or Simon the Tanner. I can just imagine it, me asking, his eyes and his neck swelling up like a bull's, and me having to dial 999 for an ambulance, because it would be a second brain tumor, instantato. He's in Lourdes now with Durack and I can tell you it's a jaunt I wanted to miss—all those freaks in their winding sheets getting in and out of wells, muttering prayers and ejaculations.

If I went anywhere it would be back to the island, to seesaw with old Snowie. I don't see myself going far except to the off-license and a gymnasium once a week to keep my limbs from atrophying. You should see where old Snowie lived, a shack made of wood stuck up on a few concrete blocks. Toy Town. Next to it another shack, identical. His sitting room crammed with the most ghastly things—photographs, statues, artificial flowers, and a gigantic television set. His sister was there in her curlers, looking at television in the middle of the day, with the temperature over a hundred. I called on my way to the airport to say goodbye. Pure slop. I don't know why I do things like that.

"Lady lady . . ." The flunkies are calling me. There seems to be some development. The damn train is in. They're up and off toward the barrier, dragging this big trolley. They're midgets really, Tom Thumbs. Other people are pouring out of the train, with normal things like kids and carrier bags and bunches of flowers. I dawdle. Anything to postpone it. Two native bruisers have to help them with it, they not being broad-shouldered enough, probably not having enough to eat in their far-off climes. I hand over another fiver to the natives and hope to God no one comes up and sympathizes with me.

"Where now, where now, lady?" the two steadies ask me. I point automatically to the gates, which are ceremoniously slung open, and I follow them. They're crawling. Out of respect, I suppose. A guard has given me her suitcase and a letter. The suitcase is fawn and has a label from a visit she made last Christmas to the old sod. Her son and I will have to take her ashes there and scatter them between the bogs and the bog lakes and the murmuring waters and every other fucking bit of depressingness that oozes from every hectometer and every furlong of the place and that imbued her with the old Dido desperado predilections. I hope she rises up nightly like the banshee and does battle with her progenitors.

It could only happen to hicks like us. The fucking hearse isn't here. I'm in the middle of Waterloo Station, outside a shop that's selling warm croissants, with a coffin, two Pakistanis, and not even the name of the undertakers, since they weren't booked by me.

"We'll have to hang on," I say. The lingo is too subtle for them.

"*Non arrivo*—late, like trains," I say.

"Okay, lady; okay, lady." They're dead stupid and dead affable.

. . .

The cow in the health farm was rabid about keeping it hush-hush. It was death by accident, they had a coroner in at dawn. Death is death, whether it's by accident or design. She was taking swimming lessons, had an instructor, trailed back and forth holding on to a bit of plastic, doing well, as the officious bitch said—too well, as she emphasized— because she got carried away and went in there after dark and took the plunge. Alone and covert as always, not knowing whether it was deliberate or whether she just wanted to put an end to the fucking torment she was in. Probably realized that she had missed the boat, bid adieu to the aureole of womanhood and all that. No more cotillions. Her letter to me says nothing, inanities about fasting and jogging and being on the mend. A blind really, so that no one would know, so that her son wouldn't know, self-emulation to the fucking end.

I'm guilty as hell, of course. We lost touch—different lifestyles and so forth. There was a falling out. It was really between Durack and her, her with Keats's odes, and him with the old chip on the shoulder because of not having a university education. I know people with a university education and they read comics. Instance: Tracy's beloved boyfriend, Dominic, who can only phrase two sentences— "Have you got a light?" and "Have you got the time?" It was Durack's fifty-fifth birthday, and we had half London coming, people we hardly knew, boxers, their managers, people we'd met at the races, trainers, bookies, crooks, a couple of toffs like old Lady Margaret, who by now was missing a breast but coping and having radiation, darling. Kate came early. She was to spend the night with us because she lived out of London, ran a bookshop in a theater, and had a little cottage-type house with a gate and roses and bantams and all that. I went there once, as remote as hell, down a cul-de-sac, not even a number over the door. Anyhow, she came early, with her rush bag and took out her suede shoes, her black frock, and a satin flower with a middle in it that looked like caviar. She always had something that no one else had, bought from gypsies or at the Amsterdam airport or some damn place. There were fires all over the house, big consignments of flowers in urns, with bathtubs clogged with champagne. The three of us were imbibing to get warmed up, and all of a sudden it happened, a goddamn eruption. She and Durack began to argue. It was about fuck-all. Just like people who have it in for one another, they'll argue about anything: how to pronounce a word or the population of China or why fishermen can't swim. His old stroke must have been brewing then, 'cause he'd get into tempers and you'd think his veins were going to burst, they were like tires. Working twenty hours a day, wheeler-dealing the Americans, waiting for the big coup, talking bull, about hard sell, soft sell, and push-into-shove garbage, all that trans-mangling of the English language that they do to make them feel they invented it. Invented it. Scrolls of the King James Bible should be put in their microchips to get them to utter a reasonable sentence. Anyhow, he and Kate were tearing into one another, daggers drawn. It was all about roots, values, not losing one's identity, and so forth. Had it been anyone else, he would have agreed. He was mad for roots. Even got books on genealogy, trying to prove that he went back to Brian Boru, on his mother's side. Most nights when he got splifi-cated he'd put his arms around me and say we'd go home one day, home to Innisfree. It was a prospect I dreaded. Said we'd build a house in the Burren, nightmare place, all limestone with a few gentians in the spring that people rave over. He felt inferior with her because when he was young of course he, too, dreamed, he did amateur dramatics and could spout Tom Moore and all the meeting-of-the-waters' slush.

"So you think I'm a phony?" he said.

"I haven't said that," she said.

"But you think it," he said.

"Frank," she said, trying to mollify him, but the harm was done. The thing is, he always mistrusted her because she and me were pals before he entered the arena, and somewhere I think he blamed her for my big adulterous epoch, little knowing that I'd commit adultery twice a day if I could. Anyhow, they patched it up, and kissed and all that, but it was false mollification; they even danced, for God's sake, and I prayed for gangs to arrive, which they soon did.

Hours later it re-erupted. She'd gone out of the room, she'd probably gone to the bathroom to mope, and he stood up and announced to the assembled guests, who were mostly illiterate, that he'd written a poem for his birthday, in honor of his native land. It was called "Corca Baiscinn." Off he started.

> *Oh little Corca Bascinn,*
> *The wild, the bleak, the fair!*
> *Oh little stony pastures,*
> *Whose flowers are sweet, if rare! . . .*

Kate came into the room and took up the refrain.

> *Oh rough and rude Atlantic,*
> *The thunderous, the wide . . .*

Thunderous! He picked up a bronze sphinx and threw it at her. Told her to keep her gob shut.

"What's wrong?" she said.

"Oh, fuck off," he said, and followed it with a discharge of curses that were wizard. It was clear he hadn't written the goddamn poem, and several of his pals began to boo and snigger. She ran out of the room in tears, and I would have followed, but he gave me a glare which told me in no uncertain terms to stay put. Luckily some warbler started up—"Come back, Paddy Reilly, come home, Paddy Reilly, to me . . . to Bally James Duff," and I wished to Christ that I was in Bally James Duff. Anywhere instead of my own lounge, scorching with drink and flounder. I knew that we wouldn't see her again, that there would be presents at Christmas and birthdays, that kind of stupid clinging on, for old times' sake, that cowards do. When she heard about his stroke she wrote a nice letter, and to tell you the truth, I thought that now that he was a semi-simpleton they'd hit it off great. They could discuss lost Atlantis and the Brehon Law to their hearts' content. Poor Durack. I don't think he ever had a voluptuous fuck in his life, certainly not with me, and the ones before me were no oil paintings—drips, legions of Mary-ites; one was an ex-nun, for God's sake, and the other lived with her mother. Of course, he pretended he was a rake, innuendos as heavy as concrete slabs; he'd nudge one of the lads when they saw a waitress with bosoms and give the old salacious wink that said, "I could be there, mate," or "Space rocket," or some cretinous thing.

I used the old menopause as a ploy for celibacy, gave him the oft-trotted plea about headaches and flushes. Fell for it. Men are fools in some ways and traitors in another. It's the way they can't resist a compliment even if it's from some barmaid. I suppose it gets the old elasticity going, makes them think they're taut again. Nature is a bitch. To tell you the truth, the menopause didn't make a damn difference except that I hadn't a pad affixed to me every month and didn't have to wash a sheet before old Cooney got in and accused me of a Roman orgy. I don't think old Cooney herself ever bled, couldn't part with it. Old Cooney begrudges me every bit of malarkey I've ever had, like a Reverend Mother, always eyeing you and telling you about widows and divorced women and women with cancer, wanting you to join in lugubrious confraternity.

I'd still do anything, if I found the right bloke, frontways, sideways, arseways—funny when you come to think of it, must be chemical, when there's other dopes that make you puke if you have to stand next to them in the Underground, recoiling in case they rub garments with you. They try it on, especially in summer, when they're friskier. Worse in Venice. I nearly got a statutory rape in a vaporetto with Durack only two yards away. He would have brained the gink. It was our second honeymoon, for God's sake, one of those patching-up fiascos, where you go to the same haunts and order the same dish and say how lucky you are.

I hadn't seen Kate since the imbroglio, until about a week ago she came, all thin and trembly, like a lath; she brought this little pot of violets, trembly, too. I suppose she couldn't afford anything more. We sat at the kitchen table and talked about strokes, and Frank and Lourdes, and all sorts of garbage. She kept jumping up to add water to her tea. I could see it coming. I knew there was some bloody man and that he was probably married and that she saw him once a fortnight or less, but of course saw him in street lamps, rain puddles, fire flames, and all that kind of Lord Byron lunacy. This was the real thing, it was different from all the rest, he and she were meant, Tristan and Iseult, soulmates, et cetera. Well, if they were meant, why weren't they together, is what I thought, and why was she looking like something from Ethiopia, all dugs and bone. They would be together if it weren't for his kids, his job, his principles. This was no lorry driver but a big cheese, and by the sound of things, someone with the old ambition in the ascendancy. A photo of him was produced. He had appeal, I'll say that, but he was a conceited-looking bastard, and you could tell that in his cradle days nannies had yodeled and told him he was the cat's meow.

She'd gone to witches, fortune-tellers, sages, faith healers, and God knows what. The prognostications were that he'd chuck in his dearly won status and come to her, but even as she said it she knew she was talking gibberish. Her eyes were like anthracite, only shiny. I was livid with her on two counts: first of all, why should she be having this goddamn, occasional illicit ecstasy when I had to settle for a boring life and put jelly in my privates to fake a bit of long-forgotten desire, and secondly, why couldn't she see reason, why couldn't she see that people are brigands, what made her think that there was such a thing as twin-star perpetuity, when all around her people were scraping for bits of happiness and not getting anywhere. She opened a notebook, things she had written. You'd need a brain transfusion to understand them—"The flushes of youth are nothing to the flushes of age, the one is rose leaf, the other the hemorrhage of death." Reams about him. Walking streets where he worked, with data about rain and flowering cherries and the quack-quacks in St. James's Park. Useless. He was the Holy Ghost because of his fugitive ways.

"Ring him," I said, but she shook her head; she knew it was curtains. She knew he'd gone home to wife and kiddies, put her in aspic, and wouldn't think about her till he was eighty or ninety and gaga, sans guilt, sans testicles, sans everything. He'd given her some spiel about honor, duty, how they should have met before he went up the aisle. Fucking mendicant, she was.

The worst bit was when she started accusing herself, said she was ashamed of being miserable when there was war and drought and famine and holocausts. She kept jumping from one thing to another, said she couldn't pray anymore, mumbled petitions to St. Anthony but felt a hypocrite. Then she quoted Van Gogh, said he wanted to paint infinity. I thought, Her ear will be off next. Asked me what I thought was infinity, if there was something more to life. She said it was the emptiness that was the worst, the void. Then she contradicted herself and said it was the hallucinations. At times she thought she was stitched to the sky with a safety pin or daggers, and other times her teeth were too big for her mouth, were like a sink or a cattle trough inside her mouth, crushing her. Her brain was like a whirling dervish. One minute it was her son, his globe head, his eyelashes, how when he was six she admired them and he went to tear them off to give to her; then his motorcycle, how many cylinders it had, and how she used to stay awake at night until he got safely home; then the big rupture, his leaving for America, the letter on the kitchen table saying, "I am never far from you and always at the other end of a telephone." Got a scholarship to Harvard. Full of brains. Probably knew it was best to vamoose.

I was the one that had to break it to him. I said it straight out, couldn't gloss it.

"Has she?" he said, as if he already knew it, not that she had appeared to him or anything like that, but because he knew she was prone to the old Via Dolorosa. God knows what he was feeling or if he was in bed with a girl or something. I kept holding on to the bedside table and smoking like a chimney so's I'd act normal. All of a sudden I thought of the thing she'd read to me about the flushes of youth versus the flushes of age, and thank Christ, I didn't blurt that out. I told him how apparently she had swum a few strokes and probably got carried away, and then went in alone and lost her bearings.

"Poor Nooska," he said. That was his pet name for her. It was the way he said it, so grown-up and so fucking tender that it made me bawl. I'm sure he heard me. He said he'd go to the airport straightaway because there might be crowds.

"I'll pay your fare," I said.

"Oh, don't worry about that," he said. I expect he's a stowaway or coming the cheapest way there is.

Even he was slipping from her mind. She said she couldn't

picture him anymore, that it was like a tassel or the banister of the stairs which disappeared as soon as you touched it. Everything was disappearing.

"What's happened to you, Kate?" I said. I was trying to bring a bit of normality into the situation. She was crying into the tea, slopping everything.

"I don't know," she said, "I don't know what's happened to me." She raved about some dream, some apocalyptic dream, Christians and Muslims fighting, weapons none other than pools of blood, wrapped up in pouches of human flesh and thrown up into the air like jam tarts or rosettes. She was in Battalion 3 and about to go into battle, when she saw God, who apparently told her that it was not for earthly considerations we fight, we suffer so. Earthly considerations! She was in the fucking Azores.

All of a sudden she steadied herself, began to make plans—she was going to do social work, she was going to read poems to prisoners, read Rilke.

"Who's Rilke?" I said. One line was enough—"For only solitaries shall behold the mysteries."

I could just see prisoners getting chuffed over that.

"If I get through this, I'm all right," she said.

"Through what?" I said.

"This last big breach," she said, and I went all cold, because I sensed something calamitous.

She put her hand to her heart and said she'd like to tear it out, stamp on it, squash it to death, her heart being her undoing.

"It's only a pump," I said, trying to give her a jolt, trying not to show that I was quaking. She jumped up, said she had to go. I mumbled some platitude about having put tea roses in her room. She was always a great one for roses. I followed her out, but she wouldn't listen, said she'd telephone me the next day. She was going to his office, she was going to stand outside the iron gates until he emerged complete with briefcase and ask him the one question, the question being, whether it had had meaning for him. Why the fuck are people like her always looking for meaning? The crows were cawing like mad and I should have known it would lead to this. I wanted to call someone but I didn't know who. For one split second I thought, I'll call Kate. That'll show you how mad I was. Another thing, I have this feeling that there's a second letter, a truthful one, and that it'll come to light someday. It could be in the post now, it could be saying that what she did was deliberate. I pray not. Ignorance is bliss. On the back of my letter there was a bit about nature: "Saw on my evening walk just now the young ferns, lime-green and wand-like, as if waiting to be picked and carried onstage to accompany lines of Shakespeare—oh, Shakespeare deepest and powerfulest of friends, father of us all." Father—the crux of her dilemma. I daren't think of the hours beforehand, the frenzy, trying to dodge it, trying to circumvent. I suppose it was the future she couldn't face, the thought that it would be the same forever, eons of fucking emptiness. It'll hurt Durack, it'll cut him up, remind him of such dire things as his own irreversible plight, and it'll make her son a fugitive for life. I don't blame her, I realize she was in the fucking wilderness. Born there. Hadn't the reins to haul herself out. Should have gone to night school, learned a few things, a few mottos such as "Put thy trust in no man."

I doubt that she went to his office, that she confronted him, in case he cut her or was incognito all of a sudden. I expect she ran, hither and thither, one place to another, up steps, down steps, along by the river, into a café, into a church, prostrating herself, expecting a fucking miracle, that he'd divine it, that he'd appear, that they'd walk down the aisle to the old

> Morning has broken, like the first morning
> Blackbird has spoken, like the first bird . . .

Jesus, is there no end to what people expect? Even now I expect a courier to whiz in on a scooter to say it's been a mistake; I'm crazy, I'm even thinking of the Resurrection and the stone pushed away, I want to lift her up and see the life and the blood coming back into her cheeks, I want time to be put back, I want it to be yesterday, to undo the unwanted crime that has been done. Useless. Nothing for it but fucking hymns.

We'll go through all the motions and all the protocol, the wreaths and the roses and Mozart and Van Morrison, and then the coffin off on its little rocky ride, as if to a jamboree, except that it isn't. I'm walking toward the hearse now and thinking of Durack's motto— "An old soldier, Baba, an old soldier," and I'm praying that her son won't interrogate me, because there are some things in this world you cannot ask, and oh, Agnus Dei, there are some things in this world you cannot answer.